TAYLOR CALDWELL'S TRIUMPHANT
BESTSELLER
DEAR AND GLORIOUS PHYSICIAN
The Story of St. Luke

"A portrait so moving and so eloquent I doubt it is
paralleled elsewhere in literature. Here indeed is
Taylor Caldwell's major novel!"
—*Boston Herald*

"Alive with the bustle of ancient times and places
and illuminated by flashes of genuine lyrical intensity . . . Movingly reconstructs St. Luke's search
for God."
—*The New York Times*

"Magnificent! Taylor Caldwell, who has always
had splendid powers of narration, unleashes them
all in this her finest novel! She has made St. Luke
a real and believable man and recreated on a vast
canvas the times and people of his day. You see
as large as life all the glory and decadence of Rome
and all the strife, turmoil and mysticism of Africa
. . . A glowing and passionate statement of belief!"
—*Columbus Citizen*

TAYLOR CALDWELL
DEAR AND GLORIOUS PHYSICIAN

"Our most dear physician, Luke."
ST. PAUL

BANTAM BOOKS · TORONTO · NEW YORK · LONDON

*This low-priced Bantam Book
has been completely reset in a type face
designed for easy reading, and was printed
from new plates. It contains the complete
text of the original hard-cover edition.*
NOT ONE WORD HAS BEEN OMITTED.

DEAR AND GLORIOUS PHYSICIAN
*A Bantam Book / published by arrangement with
Doubleday & Company, Inc.*

PRINTING HISTORY

*Doubleday edition published March 1959
16 printings through September 1961*

Bantam edition / March 1962

2nd printing .... March 1962	13th printing . December 1971
3rd printing ..... April 1964	14th printing ...... June 1972
4th printing .... March 1965	15th printing ...... May 1973
5th printing .. February 1966	16th printing ... January 1974
6th printing . December 1966	17th printing . December 1974
7th printing .... March 1968	18th printing .... March 1975
8th printing .... August 1969	19th printing ..... April 1976
9th printing .. February 1970	20th printing . September 1976
10th printing ...... June 1970	21st printing ...... June 1977
11th printing ...... May 1971	22nd printing ... January 1978
12th printing .... August 1971	23rd printing ...... June 1978

ISBN 0-553-11581-2

Published simultaneously in the United States and Canada

---

*Bantam Books are published by Bantam Books, Inc. Its trade-
mark, consisting of the words "Bantam Books" and the por-
trayal of a bantam, is registered in the United States Patent
Office and in other countries. Marca Registrada. Bantam
Books, Inc., 666 Fifth Avenue, New York, New York 10019.*

PRINTED IN THE UNITED STATES OF AMERICA

Dedication

For Dr. Samuel A. Vogel and Frances Vogel,
Buffalo, New York

Any resemblance between Ancient Rome and the United States of America and/or Russia is purely historical and not a coincidence.

Foreword

This book has been forty-six years in the writing. The first version was written when I was twelve years old, the second when I was twenty-two, the third when I was twenty-six, and all through those years work did not cease on this book.

The last version began five years ago. It was impossible to complete, as the other versions were impossible to complete, until my husband and I visited the Holy Land in 1956, and until my husband could give me the information for the last third of the book, and other assistance.

From my early childhood Lucanus, or Luke, the great Apostle, has obsessed my mind. He was the only Apostle who was not a Jew. He never saw Christ. All that is written in his eloquent but restrained Gospel he acquired from hearsay, from witnesses, from the Mother of Christ, from disciples, and from the Apostles. His first visit to Israel took place almost a year after the Crucifixion.

Yet he became one of the greatest of the Apostles. Like Saul of Tarsus, later to be known as Paul, the Apostle to the Gentiles, he believed that Our Lord came not only to the Jews but to the Gentiles, also. He had much in common with Paul, because Paul too had never seen the Christ. Each had had an individual revelation. These two men had difficulty with the original Apostles because the latter stubbornly believed for a considerable time that Our Lord was incarnated, and died, only for the salvation of the Jews, even after Pentecost.

Why has St. Luke always obsessed me, and why have I always loved him from childhood? I do not know. I can only quote Friedrich Nietzsche on this matter: "One hears—one does not seek; one does not ask who gives—I have never had any choice about it."

This book is only indirectly about Our Lord. No novel, no historical book, can convey the story of His life so well as the Holy Bible. So the story of Lucanus, or St. Luke, is the story of every man's pilgrimage through despair and life-darkness, through suffering and anguish, through bitterness and

1

sorrow, through doubt and cynicism, through rebellion and hopelessness to the feet and the understanding of God. This search for God and the final revelation are the only meaning in life for men. Without this search and revelation man lives only as an animal, without comfort and wisdom, and his life is futile, no matter his station or power or birth.

A priest, who helped us write this book, said of St. Luke, "He was Our Lady's first troubadour." Only to Luke did Mary reveal the Magnificat, which contains the noblest words in any literature. He loved her above all the women he had ever loved.

My husband and I have read literally over a thousand books about Luke and his times, and a bibliography is included at the end of this novel for anyone who wishes to do further reading on these matters. If the world of Luke sounds astoundingly modern to any reader, with modern implications, it is a fact.

This book may not be the best in the world, but it was written with love and devotion for our fellow men, and so it is finally given into your hands, for it concerns all mankind.

Almost all the events and background of St. Luke's earlier life, manhood, and seeking, also his family and the name of his adopted father, are authentic. It should always be remembered that St. Luke was, first of all, a great physician.

When I was twelve years old I found a large book written by a nun who then lived in Antioch, containing many of the legends about St. Luke, which will not be found in historical books about him nor in the Bible. She related the legends and some obscure traditions about him, including the many miracles, at first unknown to him, which he accomplished before he even went to the Holy Land. Some of these legends are from Egypt, some from Greece. They are included in this novel about him. He did not know at the time that he was one of the chosen of God, nor that he would attain sainthood.

The mighty and splendid Babylonian Empire (or Chaldea) is not familiar to many readers, nor its studies in medicine and its medical treatments by the priest-physicians, and its science—all of which the Egyptians and the Greeks inherited. The Babylonian scientists understood magnetic forces, and used them. These things were contained in thousands of volumes in the wonderful University of Alexandria, which was burned by the Emperor Justinian several centuries later in an excess of misguided zeal. Modern medicine and science are beginning to rediscover these things. The present age is poorer for Justinian's fervor. Had Babylonian science and medicine come down to us unbroken, our knowledge of the world and man would be vastly more advanced than it is at present. We have not as yet discovered how the Babylonians lighted their sails at night by a "cold fire, more brilliant than the moon," and how they illuminated their temples by this same cold fire. Apparently they had some way of utilizing electricity unknown to us, and not in our present clumsy manner. It is reported that they used "land vessels" without horses, lighted at night, and attaining great speed. (See the Book of Daniel.) It is also reported that they used strange "stones" or a kind of ore for the cure of cancer. They were expert in the employment of hypnotism, in psychosomatic medicine. Abraham, a resident of the city of Ur, in Babylonia, brought this treatment of psychosomatic medicine to the Jews, who used it through all the centuries. The Magi, "the Wise Men of the East," who brought gifts to the Infant Jesus, were Babylonians, though that nation long before had suffered a great decline.

Where authorities differ about some of the incidents in this book, or the background, I have used the major decisions. The Gospel of St. Luke is used exclusively here, so much that appears in the Gospels of Sts. Matthew, Mark and John is not included.

I wish, at this time, to thank Dr. George E. Slotkin of Eggertsville, N.Y., famous urologist and professor emeritus, School of Medicine, Buffalo, N.Y., for his invaluable assistance in the field of ancient as well as modern medicine.

TAYLOR CALDWELL

PART ONE

"Surely God chooses His servants at birth,
or perhaps even before birth."
—Epictetus

Chapter One

Lucanus was never sure whether he liked or disliked his father. He was only certain that he pitied him. Simple men of no pretensions could be admired. Wise men could be honored. But his father was not simple or wise, though he considered himself the latter.

Bookkeepers and record-gatherers had their important place in life, especially if they were diligent and knew that they had a value as bookkeepers and record-gatherers, and did not imply that they possessed larger gifts. It was not good when they spoke of "lesser men" in highly cultured and superficial tones. But the mother of Lucanus smiled so tenderly and so mercifully when her husband intoned his ridiculous prejudices that the light of her compassion mollified her son.

There was the matter of Aeneas bathing his hands in goat's milk each morning and night, rubbing the rich fluid into every wrinkle and crevice and joint carefully. By the time he was ten years old Lucanus understood that his father was not merely trying to soften and whiten his hands but was attempting to obliterate the scars of earlier servitude. This irritated Lucanus, for even then he knew that work of any kind was not degrading unless it became so in the mind of the worker. But when Aeneas shook his wet hands delicately to dry them in the soft Syrian air, Lucanus could see the disfigured areas on the palms, and the long ugly cicatrice on the back of the slender right hand, and his pity came to him in a flood of vague love. But his real understanding was still childish.

Aeneas was at his best when, just before the evening meal, he would pour the customary libation to the gods. Lucanus always watched him then with a veneration that was without words. His father's voice, so thin and meager and lofty, as a rule, became humble and hesitant. He had gratitude that the gods had freed him, had made possible this small and pleasant house in its gardens of palms and flowers and fruit trees, had lifted him from the dust and had granted him authority over other men. But the most solemn event, to Lucanus, was when Aeneas refilled the wine cup and, with even more reverence, poured out the red liquid slowly and carefully, and said with almost inaudible softness, "To the Unknown God."

Tears would fill the large blue eyes of ten-year-old Lucanus. The Unknown God. The libation was not only an ancient custom of the Greeks, to Lucanus. It was a mystic salutation, a universal rite. Lucanus would watch the falling ruby drops and his heart would clench with an almost unbearable emotion, as if he were witnessing the spilling of divine blood, the offering of an inscrutable Sacrifice.

Who was the nameless and Unknown God? Aeneas would answer his son: It was a custom of the Greeks to perform this ritual to Him, and it was necessary to maintain civilized Grecian custom when one lived among Roman barbarians, even barbarians who ruled the world. His scarred hands would fold themselves in an unconscious gesture of homage, and his narrow face, so insignificant and ordinary, acquired distinction and gravity. It was then that Lucanus was sure he loved his father.

Lucanus had been carefully tutored by his father about the gods, for whom he used Grecian names, and not the gross names given them by the Romans. Even so, with their poetic and lovely names, they were, for Lucanus, merely man grown gigantic and immortal, possessing all man's cruelty, rapacity, and lust and hatred and malice. But the Unknown God appeared not to possess the attributes of man, neither his vices nor his small virtues. "The philosophers have taught that He is not to be comprehended by man," Aeneas had once told his son. "But He is mighty, omniscient and omnipresent, circumambient yet in every particle that has being, whether tree or stone or mankind. So say the deathless thinkers of our people."

"The boy is too serious for his age," Aeneas once said to his wife, Iris. "However, one should remember that his grandfather, my father, was a poet, and so I must not be too censorious."

Iris knew that the poet grandfather was one of her husband's more pathetic fictions, but she nodded in agreement. "Yes, our son has the soul of a poet. Yet I see and hear him playing with great liveliness with the little Rubria; they chase the sheep together and hide from each other among the olive trees, and sometimes their childish laughter is boisterous and loud."

She watched her husband gently as he lifted his long head with importance and attempted to frown. In his poor heart he was flattered, for all his contempt for the Romans. "I trust he does not neglect his lessons," he said. "With all respect to my employer, it is hard to forget that he is a Roman barbarian, and that his daughter cannot offer my son any intellectual diversion." He added, quickly, "However, one must remember that he is but ten years old, and the little Rubria is still younger. You say, my dear one, that they play constantly together? I have not noticed it, but then I am busy from dawn to sunset in the tribune's house."

"Lucanus assists Rubria with her own lessons." Iris shook a golden lock from her forehead. "How unfortunate it is that the noble tribune, Diodorus Cyrinus, does not employ you to teach her."

Aeneas sighed, and touched his wife's white forehead with his grateful lips. "But who then would manage these Roman affairs in Antioch, and keep the records and supervise the overseers of the slaves? Ah, these greedy, sucking Romans! Rome is an abyss into which all the wealth and the labor of the world sinks without a sound, an abyss from which no music rises or has risen."

Iris considerately forbore to remind her husband of Virgil. Aeneas usually compared him disdainfully with Homer.

It offended Aeneas that his employer was only a rude tribune, and not an Augustale. True, many of the Roman tribunes were Augustales, but not Diodorus, who loathed patricians and whose hero was Cincinnatus. Diodorus had considerable education and much intellect, and was the son of a sound and virtuous family of many soldiers, but he pretended to the soldier's scorn for men who preferred the things of the mind. He hugged his old-fashioned virtues to his breast and affected ignorance of the things he knew, and spoke in the harsh and simple accents of a soldier to whom books were contemptible. In his way he possessed as many affections as Aeneas. They were both frauds, Iris would tell herself sadly, but they were also piteous frauds. Let Aeneas condescend to the soldier whose father had freed him, and let Diodorus deliberately use bad grammar and display bad manners: it did not matter.

The father of Diodorus Cyrinus, a moral man of noble qualities, had bought the young Aeneas from an acquaintance who had been noted for his extreme cruelty to his slaves, a cruelty which had become infamous even among a callous and cynical people. It was told that there was none of this man's slaves who did not bear scars, from the workers in his fields and vineyards and olive groves to the youngest females in his house. Nor, in spite of the laws, did he desist from the wanton killing, at will, of any slave who displeased him, and he had devised manners of torture and murder which gave him immense pleasure. An Augustale of proud if decadent family, and of immense wealth and power, he was also a senator, and it was said that even Ceasar feared him.

There was only one man in Rome who dared to scorn him publicly, the virtuous tribune, Priscus, father of Diodorus, who was loved by the Roman mobs, who, themselves debased and vicious as their masters, yet paid him honor for his integrity and his soldierly qualities. The mobs even admired him for his kindness and his justice to his slaves, and this was paradoxical among a people to whom a slave was less than a four-legged beast.

Aeneas, the Greek slave, had been one of the workers on the senator's land, and no one was quite certain how Priscus had acquired him, except Aeneas, and he never spoke of it. But Priscus had brought the wounded and broken youth to his house, had called his physician to treat him, had assigned him a place in his household, and had required only obedience from him. "We are all subject to obedience," Priscus had told his new slave, sternly. "I obey the gods and the laws of my fathers, and there is pride in such subjection, for it is voluntary, and demanded of all honorable men. The man without discipline is a man without a soul."

Aeneas was illiterate, but he was quick and respectful and had a shrewd and orderly mind. Priscus, who believed every man, even a slave, should be developed to his full capacity, had permitted Aeneas to sit in a corner of a room where his young son was being tutored. Within an amazingly short time Aeneas had caught up with Diodorus; his memory was astounding. It was not long until Aeneas, at the commnad of Priscus, was sitting at the foot of the table where Diodorus sat with his tutor. "Have we a Greek scholar here?" Priscus asked the tutor ironically. But the tutor replied with sagacity that Aeneas was no true scholar, but only a young man of clever mind.

By the time Aeneas was twenty-five he was managing the Roman estates of his master, Priscus, while Diodorus had taken up his proper profession as a soldier and was assisting the procurator in Jerusalem. He had also fallen in love with

another slave, the young Iris, handmaiden to the wife of
Priscus, a beautiful Greek girl, the pet of the household,
educated personally by Antonia, who regarded her with the
affection of a mother. Priscus and Antonia had presided over
the wedding of the young people, and had given them many
gifts, including the priceless one of their freedom.

Diodorus Cyrinus, returning home after the death of his
parents, had been pleased with the freedman, Aeneas, for
the Roman estates were in fine order. He remembered his
old fellow student as being a "commonplace fellow" of no
particular brilliance, but he recognized his qualities and
honesty, though he was annoyed at the petulances and small
arrogances he displayed against the slaves under his command. But, as Diodorus was extremely intelligent, and
secretly merciful, he understood that in this way Aeneas was
compensating for the years of his own slavery.

The lonely young Roman, who was now twenty-seven, five
years younger than Aeneas, soon married a young woman of
a sturdy Roman family, who had his own robust qualities
but not his intelligence. Shortly after this, Diodorus was assigned to govern Antioch, in Syria, and he took Aeneas and
Iris with him. Here Aeneas found wider scope for his talents
of meticulousness and management and bookkeeping and
precision, and for the first time he had a home of his own
on the estate in the suburbs of Antioch. In the evenings he
dreamt his dreams of the glorious men of old Greece, and
identified himself with them, and read the poems of Homer,
and declaimed them aloud to his wife and son. His learning,
intellectually, remained small and meager. He prated of
Socrates, but the dialogues were beyond his real comprehension. He knew very little of the lesser giants of Greece,
and almost nothing of the statesmen of his nation. He served
his gods as dutifully as he served Diodorus. Perhaps they
meant Greece to him; perhaps, in their loveliness and delicacy
and splendor, they reminded him that their Roman counter-
parts were gross and lascivious and brutish, beyond all sub-
tlety and grace, merely enlarged shadows of the Romans
themselves. In his gods Aeneas found refuge from his
memories of bitter slavery; in them he found pride for himself, for even Romans honored them and built temples to
them, and began to draw distinctions between them and
their own deities.

Aeneas had preferred Rome to Antioch, for though he
disdained the Roman rabble he had liked the bustle in the

crowded streets and the excitements of the city and the air
of power. Antioch, to him, was too "foreign," for it was
constantly being invaded by rough seamen from hundreds of
nameless and doubtful barbarous places. He had a conspicuous aversion for them, and would shudder at them
fastidiously. But he had a small and pleasant house of his
own, with cool stone floors and bright woolen curtains and
arches and gardens, and it was far enough away from the
larger house of Diodorus to give him the illusion that he was
a master of land in his own right. Much of this pleasure,
however, was spoiled frequently for him when he came
into contact with Diodorus and was forced to listen in
silence to the Roman's soldierly expletives and coarse
language.

Diodorus was even lonelier in Syria than he had been in
Rome. His wife, Aurelia, was a buxom young woman who devoted herself to her household and its slaves and her husband and her young daughter. She was pious and virtuous in
the manner of an old Roman matron. But she was unlearned
and only shrewd, and as naturally unpolished as her husband
was naturally if secretly polished. She chattered about the
slaves, her daughter, the newest fashions from Rome, suspected depredations in the kitchen, the climate, the health
of her family, and the dishes she herself concocted under the
eyes of the cooks. There was no doubt that she was an
estimable woman, and there was no doubt that though she was
a trifle too fat she had much prettiness of round pink face and
large brown eyes and luxurious black hair. Diodorus would
listen to her fondly, and then would retire to his library, there
to bring books out of assiduous hiding and read until midnight, long after all in the household had retired. He especially delighted in poetry and history and philosophy. He
would whisper a whole poem to himself, with a kind of
wanton abandonment to phrases and cantos.

It never occurred to him, as an anachronistically moral
Roman, to seek some sexual diversion in the teeming brothels
of Antioch, nor did he consider it proper to gather together
with some fellow Romans in the city for gaming or cock-
fighting or even simple companionship. A man's place, after
his work, was in his home, according to Diodorus, no matter
how trivial his wife's conversation. He drank very little at
the table, and believed drunkenness to be one of the major
sins, so he had no escape except in his work.

Aurelia had women friends among the Roman families in

Antioch, but they were as virtuous and ordinary as she herself. She and they would gossip about the more emancipated women of their acquaintanceship, and would deplore them with shivers. They were all completely and innocently unaware of the depravity of their nation, its corruption and its moral viciousness, its licentious manners and mores, and they criticized other women for conduct which was common in Rome, and accepted. Their lares and penates were the most important things in their lives, and their gossip was as exciting as a bowl of stewed beans. But they were happy; they had husbands and children and gardens, and they were industrious and devoted.

It was among the simpler soldiers in Antioch that Diodorus Cyrinus found some respite, and he talked with them easily of military matters, to the smothered vexation of his junior officers. The officers themselves considered that they were exiles in this country, and they longed for the delights and gaiety and vices of Rome, and they thought of their superior officer with wonder and secret derision. They never doubted his morality, but this did not inspire their respect; rather, they believed him a fool. Even his stern justice, which was never overcast by a moment's pettiness or caprice, was, to them, something inhuman. He would punish an officer as quickly as a common foot soldier, no matter his family or his standing in Rome. Aeneas sympathized with them, and when they would wink at him over some rigid order of Diodorus' he would pompously pretend to hide a smirk.

Matters had been particularly perplexing and obnoxious today. Diodorus, surrounded by his officers, had watched the fruits of Syria, honey, olives and olive oil, wool, and many other things, being loaded by slaves on a Roman ship. Though it was December, and the feast of the Saturnalia was approaching, the sun had been unseasonably hot, the air wet with humidity, the greasy waters glittering as if covered by lighted fat. The shouts of the overseers had been exceptionally irritable, and the cracking of whips had snapped unceasingly against the wall of damp air. But the slaves, sweating profusely, were sluggish. Suddenly, with an impatient curse, Diodorus had left the table on the docks where Aeneas was meticulously recording the bales and the barrels, and had himself seized a particularly large box on his shoulder as easily as if it had been a small lamb. He had strode up the plank of the ship and hurled the box with swift precision on the other boxes. Then he had stood there, smiling happily.

The officers gaped; Aeneas looked delicately aside; the soldiers stared, the overseers and the slaves were petrified. But Diodorus had flexed his muscles and breathed deeply, and had said: "Eh! But that is good for a man's soul!"

Aeneas, the Greek, shared with all Greeks a contempt and detestation of manual labor, and he was shocked to the heart. He and the others were even more shocked when Diodorus shouted to the slaves, "Are you men or sickly worms? This must all be loaded before sunset or you will work by torches in the dark. Come then, let us move like men with a purpose and have done with it!" Again he had bent and seized a barrel and rolled it up the plank, and his muscles strained in his shoulders and legs and arms. It was obvious that he was enjoying himself. The slaves, spurred by whips, hurried back to work and, inspired by Diodorus, quickened their movements. He began to sing hoarsely in a rollicking rhythm, and the slaves laughed and sang with him. Long before sunset the ship was loaded. Not a single officer had assisted, and not even a foot soldier, for Diodorus had indicated, with a contemptuous glare, that he repudiated their assistance.

Then Diodorus stood among his officers and wiped himself with a kerchief one of them offered him, and he grinned at the ship. The captain approached him with awed respect, and Diodorus shouted, "Tell the effete lady-men in Rome that Diodorus Cyrinus, son of Priscus, himself helped to load this ship! Tell them, as they perfume themselves with nard and attar of roses and listen to the lutes and dip nightingale tongues in honey, that today you have seen a Roman work as Romans once worked, and as they must work again if Rome is to survive and not die forever among vases and flowers and singing-girls and wine and elegance."

Then he had turned to his officers—who were blushing in shame for him—and had cursed loudly and had shouted again, "Where are your scars and your calluses, your muscles, and your brown shoulders, you exquisites? Do you know what war is, and labor, and the strength of bodies which live sparely and with fortitude? To Hades with you all! By Mercury, you are less men than these poor slaves!"

This was unpardonable. The slaves snickered among themselves, and the faces of the Roman officers had darkened ominously. But they dared not reply. Diodorus was quite capable of slapping an impudent face openly; he had done it often enough, even before foot soldiers and slaves.

Diodorus, unfortunately, was not done. He wrathfully

surveyed his men, and continued, "Cincinnatus left his plow to save Rome, and he did not halt even to wash his stained hands or put his sandals on his soil-dusted feet. But not one of you would leave the arms of a Syrian whore to save the life of a man, or to uphold, in your jurisdiction, a law of Rome."

He had swung away from them then, and had pounded back on the docks to his horse, and had galloped off home to the suburbs. He left his chariot behind to be brought by an officer to his stables, and Aeneas rode in it with the officer. Once at home, Aeneas had related the whole horrifying episode to Iris, who had listened in silence. He expected her to be appalled, as he was appalled, but she had said mildly, with her lovely smile, "The noble tribune was once my playmate in the house of Priscus. He was always a strenuous boy; he would sometimes carry me on his back and pretend that he was Jupiter in the guise of a bull and I Europa."

She had watched the aghast expression on Aeneas' face for a moment, and had added gently, "Ah, but we were only children then, dear one."

There were times when Aeneas could not understand Iris, and he said pompously, "I see that you do not grasp the larger implications of this incredible episode of today. Diodorus is constantly talking of discipline, yet he publicly derided his officers before their men and the slaves. Does that enhance their authority?"

Iris understood that Diodorus' wrath had not so much been expended on the men immediately about him but upon the modern mores and corruption of Rome, which he could not endure. They had been but the precipitating factor that had relieved the smoldering and chronic rage of the tribune. She sighed, and said to her husband, "I am certain he will never do that again." Aeneas replied severely, "One can never be sure with such a capricious man. I confess I never understood him."

The furious elation of Diodorus had lasted all through the evening meal. He had told Aurelia about it, and she had nodded with wifely wisdom, though the whole matter was beyond her comprehension. She let a little pause follow, and then had said with anxiety, as if her husband had told her nothing at all, "The little Rubria is again coughing blood, and is complaining of the pains in her arms and legs. The physician has ordered effusions on her throat and joints, and she is sleeping at last, though her face remains flushed. How sorrowful it is when a child suffers, a child who has never been healthy, and how much more sorrowful it is, dear husband, that I have given you only this weak little lamb and not strong sons."

Diodorus immediately forgot his anger, and took his wife in his arms and kissed her. She was not revolted by the heavy stench of his sweat, but rather comforted. She wound her arms about his neck and said, "But I am still only twenty-five, and it may be that the gods will grant us sons. I must go to Antioch soon and make a special sacrifice to Juno."

The child, Rubria, was heart of Diodorus' heart, though he believed that only he knew this. He softly climbed the white stone stairway to her apartments and noiselessly moved aside the thick draperies of crimson silk. The child lay in the cool early twilight on her bed, sleeping, her nurse by her side. The small window was a square of scarlet, and purple shadows hovered in the corners of the room. Was it only the reflection of the setting sun which was reddening the little face, or was it that sinister and unknown fever? Diodorus bent over his daughter, and his indomitable heart fluttered at her fragility. Long thick black lashes trembled uneasily on the thin and brightened cheek; the pretty childish mouth burned. So sweet and dear a creature, so full of laughter and gaiety, even when in pain, so tender a dove! The gnarled hand of Diodorus touched the black sweep of hair on the white pillow, and he pleaded desperately to Aesculapius for his help. "Pray, you Master Physician, you son of Apollo, that you send Mercury on the wings of compassion to this child, who is more precious to me than my life, and that your daughter, Hygieia, look tenderly upon her. Mercury, hasten to her, for is she not like unto you, swift as fire, quick as the wind, changeful as an opal?"

He promised to sacrifice a cock to Aesculapius, who preferred that sacrifice, and a pair of white oxen to Mercury, with golden rings in their noses. Terror seized him as he again touched Rubria's hair and saw the tremor of the small hands on the sheet. Surely he had honored the gods all his life, and they would not take from him his very heartbeat. Never have I feared a sword or a spear, nor any man, nor any thing, yet I am weakened by fear tonight, he said to himself. It is not that this illness is something new, but my soul trembles as if with premonition.

He renewed his prayers, and added one to Juno, the mother of children. To him the gods of Rome had never been depraved, not even Jupiter, for all his prospensities with regard to maidens. He wondered if he should not implore Mars, his special deity, the patron of soldiers. He decided against it; Mars would not understand a soldier who held a child more precious and important even than war. Such a prayer to him might inspire his anger. Diodorus hastily besought Mercury again, with his winged sandals and his staff of serpents.

When Diodorus joined Aurelia again he found her in the anteroom of her chamber, industriously spinning fine wool into cloth for her child's capitium. She was the very personification of a matron of old Rome as she sat there, her foot moving rhythmically on the treadle, her hand at the wheel, her black hair braided severely about her round head, her pink face serious and absorbed. Her white garments flowed about her full figure in modest folds, and sleeves half covered her voluptuous arms. To Diodorus she was a reassuring figure. Rather than wail uselessly over her child, she spun warm cloth for her. Diodorus touched her head lovingly with his hand, and then his lips. The busy foot and hand did not falter, but Aurelia smiled. "Why do you not, my beloved, walk among the gardens in the sunset? You will find comfort there, as always." Her voice was steady and calm.

Diodorus thought of his books. Today, by special messenger, he had received a roll containing the philosophies of Philo. Rumor had it that Philo was considered superior to Aristotle. This Diodorus did not believe, but he was both excited and curious. But all at once a flatness and heaviness of heart came to him, and he decided to do as his wife had advised. The book could wait; he was too restless to give it his full and thoughtful attention.

He stepped out into the courtyard. A dark crimson was drifting through the fronds of the palms; the scent of jasmine rose in clouds in the warm air. The ornamental orange and lemon trees were globed in golden and green fruit. Insects hummed with a sound of thin wires, and suddenly a nightingale sang to the purpling sky. The white stones set among the exotic flower beds were flooded with heliotrope shadows, and a dim blue light filled the arches of the colonnades which surrounded the courtyard. A fountain, in which stood a marble faun, tinkled sweetly, mingled its frail song with the song of the nightingale. The mingled purple and crimson of the sunset glimmered in the bowl of the fountain, which was alive with brilliant little fish. Now the palms clattered a little in a freshening wind from the distant sea, and through the moving fronds of one Diodorus could see the gleaming radiance of the evening star. The trunks of the trees, set along the high walls of the yard, resembled gray-white ghosts.

No sound came from the high square of the house behind Diodorus; the pillars shimmered in the half-light as if made of some unsubstantial material and not marble. Diodorus found the silence suddenly oppressive; the voice of the nightingale failed to entrance him as usual. It was a voice that had no consolation in it, but only melancholy, and the fountain murmured of non-human sorrows. Diodorus, assaulted again by his loneliness, thought of Antioch, and the celebrations begun there in honor of Saturn. They would end in a general debauch, as usual, but at least there would be the sound of men and women. He considered riding back to Antioch and summoning a few of his officers who were the least repugnant to him. But he knew he would bore them; they would want to participate in the riotous gaiety, and he would just inhibit them. If only I had a companion, thought the lonely tribune. If only there was just one with whom I could talk, in order to drown out the voice of the fear in me, one with whom to share a cup of wine and discuss those things which are of importance to me. A philosopher, perhaps, or a poet, or just a man who is wise.

He heard the slightest movement, almost the breath of a movement, and he turned towards the fountain again. The sunset sky brightened for an instant above the muttering heads of the palms, and it struck on the fair head of a child leaning against the marble bowl of the fountain in complete enchantment, unaware of the presence of Diodorus.

Moving silently, Diodorus advanced towards the child, who was sitting on the coarse green grass and staring up at Rubria's window. When he reached the opposite of the wide and shallow bowl, Diodorus thought, Why, it is the young Lucanus, son of my freedman, Aeneas. His heart bounded with a nameless longing, and he thought of Iris, his old playmate, Iris with her aureate hair, her wonderful blue eyes, soft white flesh, and round, dimpled chin, and her slender Grecian nose. He heard, as from echoing down long and clouded corridors, the sound of her child's laughter, the questioning of her call to him. Iris, for him, had not existed even as a remembered playmate since her marriage to that stilted and precise mediocrity of an Aeneas. But now he remembered that when he had been off on his campaigns, before the death of his parents, Iris had shone like a star in his mind, sweet, wise Iris, his mother's young slave, his mother's petted handmaiden who had been to her as a daughter.

He, a tribune, young and ambitious and stalwart, of unimpeachable family, had even dreamt of being married to Iris. His parents, he believed, in spite of their love for Iris, would have expired of humiliation if their son had condescended to a slave, and if she had said to him, "Where thou art, Caius, there am I, Caia." Yet when he had heard of their deaths, while still stationed in Jerusalem, his first thought, after the initial pang of sorrow, had been of Iris. He had returned, to find her not only freed but married and pregnant, and he had put her sternly out of his mind. Surely, then, his loneliness had begun, and he had thought it merely a yearning to return to his active life in the Orient.

The whole courtyard filled with soft mauve shadows, in which the leaning head of Lucanus was like a yellow harvest moon. Diodorus could see his fine profile, and he thought, It is the face of the child, Iris. He had never been interested in children, except his daughter, Rubria, and though he had wished for sons he had thought of them as young soldiers, and his heirs. Now he peered at Lucanus, his eyes straining through the colored twilight, and again his heart bounded and was filled with tenderness.

Lucanus sat in motionless silence, still gazing at the dwindling square of Rubria's window. He wore a thin white tunic; his long legs, so pale that they resembed alabaster, were folded under him. In his hands there lay a large stone of unusual form and hue, restless with dull light. The whole attitude of Lucanus was one of prayerful rapture, yet he was very still. His rosy lips were parted, and the hollows of his eyes were filled with a strange blueness. It was as if he were listening, and Diodorus, superstitious as were all Romans, watched with a kind of nervous fear, his skin prickling.

He spoke suddenly and loudly: "It is you, Lucanus."

The boy did not start. He only moved a little and turned his entranced face to Diodorus. He did not leap to his feet; he merely sat there, the stone in his hands. It was as if he did not see the tribune at all.

Diodorus was about to speak again, more roughly, when the boy smiled and appeared to notice him for the first time.

"I was praying for Rubria," he said, and his voice was the voice of the young Iris.

Diodorus moved around the circle of the fountain, hesitated, then squatted on his heels and looked earnestly at the boy, who sat in such utter relaxation and bemusement before him. The tribune had removed his heavy military clothing on returning home; he wore a loose white tunic, belted with simple leather inlaid with silver. Under the thin material his browned body was square and hard, and his thick legs bulged with muscles. He folded his strong arms on his knees and contemplated Lucanus, who smiled at him with simple serenity.

Lucanus was neither awed nor frightened by the soldier. He regarded the fierce dark face, beaked and stern, as tranquilly as he would have regarded his father. The harsh and jutting chin did not alarm him, nor the sharp and penetrating black eyes set under black and swelling brows. But Diodorus, confronted with the very image of the child he had once known, was conscious of his own hard round head covered with stiff black hair, shorn and lusterless, and the crude strength of his disciplined body.

The boy had no business in this courtyard, thought Diodorus automatically. And then he was ashamed, remembering Iris. But what had he said? "I was praying for Rubria." The two children were playmates, just as he and Iris had been playmates.

Diodorus softened his grating voice. "You are praying for Rubria, boy? Ah, she needs your prayers, the poor little one."

"Yes, Master," said Lucanus, seriously.

"To what god are you praying?" asked Diodorus. (Surely, he thought, the gods were especially touched by the prayers of innocents, and some of his pain lightened.)

Lucanus said, "To the Unknown God."

Diodorus' dark eyelids flickered in surprise. Lucanus was saying, "My father has taught me that He is everywhere, and in all things." He extended the strange stone to Diodorus simply. "I found this today. It is very beautiful. Do you think He is here, and that He hears me?"

Chapter Two

Diodorus took the stone in his hands, gravely, still squatting on his heels. He could barely see it in the twilight now, but he felt that it was warm, and when he turned it in his fingers it gave off a curious faint glow of many colors, which caught the last light.

It was warm, most probably because it had lain so long in the palms of the child's hands. But the warmth did not decrease, though the air was cooling rapidly. Rather, it increased. The superstitious Diodorus wanted to drop the stone, but that would be an embarrassing gesture before the child.

"Do you think, Master, that He is here, and that He hears me?" repeated Lucanus. He had a clear and steadfast voice, without servility, the voice of one of patrician birth.

"Eh?" said Diodorus. Again he turned the stone about in his fingers and peered at it.

"The Unknown God," said Lucanus, patiently.

Diodorus knew all about the Unknown God. Once, in a Greek temple, he had sacrificed to Him, though the Greeks had believed He did not wish sacrifices. Who was this God who had no name? What were His attributes? Of what men was He the Patron? There were no images of Him anywhere. Could He be the God of the Jews, of whom Diodorus had heard much in Jerusalem? But he had known that they, the Jews, sacrificed to Him, doves and lambs, on some festival, the Passover, in the spring of the year. The Jews called Him Lord, and they appeared to know Him very well. In his mind's eye Diodorus could see the great gold and pale marble temple hanging against the peacock sky of Jerusalem. Lucanus was a Greek, not a Jew. It was possible that the Greeks had heard of the Jewish God, and as they did not know His name they called Him the Unknown.

Diodorus shook his head. A great moon, like a bowl filled with soft fire, was rising behind the palms now. It filled the courtyard with a stream of shifting light, and the shadows of the palms fell sharply on the white stones and the white walls of the house, and crept into the colonnades, which had begun to gleam as if made of yellow marble. The scent of jasmine rose in waves about the man and the boy, and crickets shrilled in the grass and among the colorless flowers. Somewhere, out of sight, a carapaced animal scraped over the stones.

Diodorus remembered a name he heard from a Jewish princeling: Adonio. He said to Lucanus, "Is His name Adonio?"

"He has no name, Master, that men know," replied the boy. "Anyway, I seem to remember that it just means 'Lord,' " said Diodorus abstractedly. "He is the God of the Jews."

"But the Unknown God is the God of all men," said Lucanus, earnestly. "He is the God not only of the Jews, but of the Romans and the Greeks and the pagans and of slaves and Caesars, and of wild men in the forests and in lands yet unknown."

"How do you know this, child?" asked Diodorus, with a slight smile.

"I know. I know it in my heart. No one has told me," said Lucanus, with simplicity.

Diodorus was strangely moved. He remembered that the gods often preferred to give their wisdom to children, whose minds were not distorted and crippled by life.

"Someday," said Lucanus, "I shall find Him."

"Where?" asked Diodorus, trying for indulgence.

But Lucanus had lifted his face to the sky, and his profile was flooded with the golden light of the moon. "I do not know where, but I shall find Him. I shall hear His voice, and I shall know Him. He is everywhere, but I shall know Him in particular, and He shall speak to me, not only in the moon and the sun, the flowers and the stones, the birds and the winds, and the dawns and the sunsets. I shall serve Him, and give my heart and my life to Him."

There was joy in the boy's voice, and again Diodorus felt a quiver of superstition.

"And you prayed to Him for Rubria?" he said.

Lucanus turned his face to him, and smiled. "Yes, Master."

"But what do you call Him, child, when you pray?"

Lucanus hesitated. He gazed at Diodorus as if pleading with him. "I call Him Father," he said, in a low tone.

Diodorus was amazed, and taken aback. No one ever called any of the gods Father. It was ridiculous. It would affront the gods to be addressed so familiarly by insignificant man. If this boy spoke so to the Unknown God, who knew but what, in His godly anger, He might not strike furiously at the object of the prayers? Rubria!

Diodorus said sternly, "No man, not even the sons of the gods, ever dared call a god 'Father.' It is outrageous. It is true that many of the gods have sons and daughters by mortal men and women, but even so——"

"Master, you speak angrily," said Lucanus, not in the voice of fear and servility, but in the remorseful voice of one who has unwittingly offended and begs forgiveness. "The Unknown God is not inflamed when one of His children calls Him Father. He is pleased."

"But how do you know, boy?"

"I know in my heart. And so, when I call Him Father, and ask Him to cure Rubria, I know He listens gently, and will cure her, for He loves her."

A gentle god. That was absurd. The gods were not gentle. They were jealous of their honor, and they were vengeful and remote and powerful. Diodorus stared at Lucanus. His first thought was to reprove the boy, and to make a mental note to request Aeneas to punish his presumptuous son. The words of cold rebuke were already on the lips of Diodorus when the moon struck fully on the face of Lucanus, and it became supernaturally radiant.

Then he remembered what this boy had said: "He loves her." The gods did not "love" men. They demanded worship and sacrifice from them, but man, as man, was a worthless thing to the gods.

"He loves her." Could it be possible that the Unknown God had as one of His attributes the quality of loving men? Oh, the absurdity! The presumption! And what was he, Diodorus, doing here in this moonlight talking to a child, the son of a miserable freedman, as a noble man might talk with his equal?

Diodorus stood up abruptly, in one strong and lithe movement. "Come, child, it is late, and I will take you to your parents."

He was astonished at his own words. What was this child to him, this child of Aeneas? What did it matter whether he found his way home or not, or wandered in the dark until dawn? But this was the son of Iris, and all at once Diodorus longed to see his old playmate. Too, there was danger in the sweet-smelling but menacing distance between the great and lesser houses.

Lucanus rose, and in the moonlight Diodorus could see that the boy was smiling shyly. "Master, will you take that stone to Rubria and lay it on her pillow tonight, for part of the Unknown God is in it."

The stone, the sentient stone. Was it really pulsing in his, Diodorus', hand, like a slow and reflective heart full of mystery? All at once Diodorus was no longer afraid of the stone. Sheepishly, he said to himself, It is a pretty and unusual thing, and might amuse the little Rubria, who loves strangenesses. He put the stone in the pouch which hung from his leather girdle. But Lucanus was offering him a small woolen bag. Diodorus took it; from it emanated a wild and intense odor. "It is herbs," said Lucanus. "I gathered them today in the fields, as if I were told. Master, have a slave steep them in hot wine, and let Rubria drink of it, and it will ease her pain."

"Herbs!" exclaimed Diodorus. "Child, how do you know that some of them may not be deadly?"

"They are not deadly, Master. To be certain, however, I ate a quantity of them myself, hours ago, and a headache I had disappeared."

Diodorus was intrigued. He put his hand roughly under the chin of Lucanus and tilted up his face to study it, half laughing. But the boy had spoken with authority; he had said, "as if I were told." It was possible that Apollo himself, who might possess such a face, such a clear brow, had directed the boy. It could do no harm to do as Lucanus suggested, and Diodorus stuffed the little bag into his pouch. "She shall have it at midnight, when she usually awakens," he promised.

He took Lucanus' hand like a father, and together they moved through the golden half-light, keeping carefully to the earthen path for fear of snakes. Diodorus was thinking. This was no ordinary boy, but a boy of intelligence and fearlessness and thought. No doubt he was being prepared by Aeneas to follow in his steps as a bookkeeper. For some reason this annoyed Diodorus. "You are very young, boy," he said, "but surely you have often thought of yourself as a man. What are your desires?"

"To find the Unknown God, Master, and to serve Him, and in His Name to serve man," replied Lucanus. "I can best serve man as a physician, which is my dear desire. I have been to the harbor and I have seen the sick men in the ships, and the dying, and they come from every part of the world, and I have prayed that I may help them. I know the philosophers and the physicians of Greece, and I have read their books of remedies for the ills of men, both mental and physical, much of which they had taken from the Egyptians. And I have often visited the houses of the physicians in Antioch, and they have not driven me away, but humored me and explained many matters to me. And I am learning other languages, including Egyptian and Aramaic, so that I may speak to sufferers in their own tongues."

Diodorus felt a vast astonishment. He pressed Lucanus'

hand, and said, musingly, "There is a great school of medicine in Alexandria, of which I have heard much."

"There I shall go," said Lucanus, simply. "I too, Master, have heard of it, for the physicians in Antioch speak of it reverently. It will cost me much money, but God will provide it."

"So, we have a God, who not only does not possess a name, or understandable attributes, or a face or a form, and who is everywhere simultaneously, but He is also a banker!" said Diodorus with a wry smile. "Do you think He will require interest also, my child?"

"Most certainly." The boy's voice was grave and filled with surety. "My whole life, my whole devotion."

Diodorus thought that if a man had spoken so he would believe him mad. He, Diodorus, had often heard Jews speaking of the wise men in the gates, who thought of nothing and wrote of nothing but their God. But the Jews were a people no one could ever understand, least of all a Roman, though Caesar Augustus, being a tolerant man and superstitious in addition, had ordered that in Rome the Jewish God should be given some recognition, if only to persuade Him to soften the stiff necks and sullen resentment of His people against the Romans, and thus make the ruling of them less difficult. Diodorus began to laugh softly to himself. He remembered how he, as a young tribune, had offered to put a statue of the Jewish God in the Roman temple in Jerusalem, and how horrified the high priest had been, and how he had raised his hands and shook them violently in the air as if either imploring his God to strike the tribune dead or cursing him silently. Diodorus, bewildered, had gathered that he had made an unpardonable error, but how or why, he could never understand from the stifled imprecations of the priest. He had tried to reason with the holy man; how could a statue of the Jewish God in a Roman temple affront Him, and why should He despise the honor of Romans? The high priest had merely torn his beard and rent his garments, and he had looked at Diodorus with such terrible eyes that the poor young tribune had hastily taken his leave. He had been confirmed in his hesitant belief that the Jews were madmen, especially their priests.

But Lucanus was a Greek, not a Jew, though he spoke of devoting his life to the Unknown God, as the Jews spoke of so devoting their lives to their own God. Diodorus remembered how, in the streets of Jerusalem, he had seen men called

rabbis, followed by humble crowds who listened to their
words of wisdom eagerly. There were some reputed to be
miracle workers, and this had interested Diodorus, who believed fervently in godly miracles. But he did not believe in
these men, for they were often barefoot and shaggy and
desperately poor, for all their lambent eyes and strange,
incomprehensible words. Diodorus, walking with Lucanus,
shook his head. "You should visit the temple of the Jews in
Antioch," he said, with amusement.

Lucanus said serenely, "I do visit it, Master."

"So!" exclaimed Diodorus, holding aside a thorned bush for
the child, as he would have done for his daughter. "And is
their God the Unknown God?"

"Yes, Master, I am sure He is."

"But He does not love all men. He loves only the Jews."

"He loves all men," said Lucanus.

"You are wrong, boy. I offered to put a statue of Him in
the Roman temple in Jerusalem, and it was refused." Diodorus laughed. "Do the Jews object to your entering their
temples? Ah, I remember now. In Jerusalem the temple had a
place they called the Court of the Gentiles. But they could
not enter the inner sanctum of the Jews."

"I worship in the Court of the Gentiles in the synagogue in
Antioch," said Lucanus.

What a peculiar boy! But Diodorus began to think of the
school of medicine in Alexandria. He said, "I think the Unknown God has arranged a way for you to study medicine,
Lucanus," and he laughed again, ruefully. He was a just and
sometimes charitable man, but, like the "old" Romans, he
was prudent with money and believed that two pieces of gold
should return to a man accompanied by two more.

They had now reached the clearing before the gardens of
the house of Aeneas. Tall palms stretched to the moon; the
evening air was full of the scent of flowers. In the midst of
them stood the shining white house of the bookkeeper, small,
low and compact, streaked with the shadows of the palms.
A light glowed from the open door, and as Diodorus and
Lucanus approached it the doorway was filled by the shapely
form of a young woman, and the light behind her made a
cloud of gold of her loosened hair. She was clad in the simple
white robe of a woman who spent all of her time in the
home, and she called out anxiously.

"Lucanus? Is it you, dear one?"

Lucanus replied, "It is I, Mother." Iris stepped down onto

the grass, then stopped on seeing who was accompanied by her son.

"I greet you, Iris," said Diodorus, and his voice was thick and low in his throat. He thought of the words of Homer: "Daughter of the gods, divinely tall and most divinely fair."

"Greetings, noble Diodorus," replied Iris, uncertainly. He had addressed her so gently, as a man addressed the wife of one of his peers, and yet the gentleness reached out to her eagerly and with an intonation of hope. For some reason Iris' eyes stung with tears, and she remembered the playmate of her childhood. He had been so candid and courageous a boy, so truthful and kind, so honorable, so filled with affection for her. She had not seen him, except at a distance, for a long time, and since she had married Aeneas he had scarcely noticed her existence.

Aeneas appeared in the doorway, then he too stepped down. Seeing Diodorus, he bowed. "Welcome to our poor home, lord," he said, in the trembling accents of a man who is overcome.

"It is not a 'poor' home," replied Diodorus, irascibly. "It was the home of the former legate of Antioch, before my house was built for me, and he did not consider it unworthy."

He pushed Lucanus towards his father, and said in a rough voice, "I have brought your boy home to you. He was in our garden, and he might have been smitten by a snake or a scorpion after sundown."

Aeneas was all confusion and abject fear. He had offended Diodorus, and he turned with anger on his son. "It is nothing to you that your mother was disturbed, and about to go searching for you in the darkness. It is nothing that you have affronted the noble tribune——"

"He did not affront me," interrupted Diodorus. The light from the doorway slanted on Iris' beautiful and distressed face. Diodorus yearned to put his hand consolingly on her shoulder. "The little Rubria is his playmate. I found him in the gardens, praying beneath her window, for she is ill. I have reason to thank him." He watched Iris, and noticed that she had begun to smile in grateful relief. He said to the trembling Aeneas, and strove for an easy tone, "A most unusual boy, this of yours, Aeneas, and it has been a privilege to talk with him." He hesitated. "My throat is dry. May I take a cup of wine with you?"

Aeneas was again overcome. He could hardly believe his

own ears. He looked at Lucanus with respect. This was his
son of whom the tribune had spoken! And it was because
of this son that the tribune had condescended to ask for wine
in the house of his freedman. Aeneas was dazzled. He could
only mumble and stand aside until Diodorus had strode
into his house. He looked briefly and dumbly at Iris, but she
had put her arm abut her son's neck and was leading him
forward. Aeneas followed, his knees quaking. The tribune had
brought the boy home, when he needed only to order him out
of his gardens, or, if kindly disposed, might have sent a slave
with him in the darkness!

Diodorus had recovered his good humor. He sood in the
small but not in the least humble room and surveyed it
expansively. There were flowers in a bowl on the table, and
flowers in the vases on the floor, which was of marble. The
doorways leading to the kitchens and the bedrooms were
hung with gay woolen cloth, which swayed in the night air
pouring in the small windows and the door. Here and there
Diodorus recognized, among the furniture left by the former
administrator, chairs and tables from his father's house,
which had been given to Aeneas upon his marriage to Iris.
Diodorus looked at one chair in particular, and with pleasure.
It was of ebony, inlaid with ivory, and it had been one of his
father's favorites. There was even a little table of precious
lemonwood, gleaming in the lamplight, which had belonged to
Antonia. It held the silver lamp, with its tongue of bright
flame.

"The slave I assigned to you does his work well," said
Diodorus, more and more pleased. He sat down in the ebony
chair and stretched his brown and muscular legs before him
with all the unaffected movements of a soldier. As Aeneas
stood before him uncertainly, formally clad in a long white
robe he, the bookkeeper, seemed more the patrician, with his
long slender features and narrow face and head, than the
frank and unceremonious tribune in his casual short tunic.
Why, thought Diodorus, the poor creature even possesses
a toga to wear in the secret bosom of his family.

"I have no wine worthy of you, Master," said Aeneas. But
Iris slipped gracefully behind a curtain and brought out a
ewer and two silver cups, which Diodorus also recognized
from his childhood. Iris, moving like a lovely and animated
statue, placed the cups on the lemonwood table and poured
the wine. A rosy light reflected back onto her face from the
liquid, and Diodorus thought of a marble maiden struck by

the sunset. He wanted to touch her miraculous hair, which he had touched so easily in his childhood. He could feel its silken lengths again, and he was all yearning. He thought that his mother, Antonia, ought to have opposed the marriage of Iris to Aeneas with more vigor.

"I am not a connoisseur of wines, thank the gods," said Diodorus. "One vintage is the same as another to me." He stretched out his hand for a cup and Iris gave it to him with her ineffable smile, for Aeneas was still too stunned for voluntary movement. "What, are you not drinking with me?" said Diodorus, in a burly tone. Aeneas snatched a cup, and some of the wine splashed on his shaking fingers.

Lucanus, obeying a slight gesture of his mother's, bowed to Diodorus and bade him good night respectfully. Diodorus smiled gravely, and the boy left the room. Diodorus poured out a small libation to the gods, and Aeneas, still very pale, poured the libation also. The tribune watched as the Greek poured a little more wine, his lips moving reverently. "Ah, yes," said Diodorus, "the Unknown God."

"It is a Greek custom," said Aeneas, apologetically.

"An excellent one," said Diodorus, and his fierce face became almost bland. He turned his head and saw that Iris had followed her son. He was deeply disappointed, but as an "old" Roman he also approved. "Tell me, Aeneas," he said. "I am interested in that boy of yours. What are your hopes for him in the future?"

"May I sit, noble Diodorus?" asked Aeneas. He sat stiffly in a chair some distance from his guest. He pondered over Diodorus' words, and was freshly amazed and humbled by this condescension. "I have thought, Master, that he would follow me in your service."

"Keeping books and records, that boy?" asked Diodorus, scornfully. "Ah, no. Has he not confided in you that he wishes to be a physician?"

Aeneas, paling still more, could only stare. Certainly the boy had confided in him and in Iris, but Aeneas had severely frowned at the presumptous thought, and had been offended. "I see that he did." Diodorus nodded. "Well, then, my good Aeneas, he shall be a doctor." Again he hesitated ruefully. "I shall send him myself to the school of medicine in Alexandria when he is older. In the meantime he shall take lessons with the little Rubria's tutor."

Tears rushed to Aeneas' eyes. Before Diodorus could move, the bookkeeper had sprung to his feet and had prostrated

himself before Diodorus' dusty sandals. He was beyond
speech; he could only mumble distractedly in his gratitude
and incredulity.

"Come, come, man," said Diodorus, who could never endure being thanked. "I have no son of my own, and this is
the boy I ought to have had. He shall be a physician. Rise,
Aeneas. You are not a slave. And have you forgotten that you
took your lessons with me, also?"

He knew exactly what Aeneas' pretensions were, and how
he considered his master a barbarian and he an exiled philosopher from a land he had never seen, and he knew how
small, if how honest, a mind Aeneas possessed. Would
Aeneas never forget that he was no longer a slave? Diodorus
watched, scowling at the white-robed man at his feet. He
moved them, as if fearful that Aeneas would kiss them in
his extremity of wonder and gratitude, and this, from the
husband of Iris, would have been unbearable to him.

Aeneas seated himself in his chair again and dried his
tears. Diodorus considerately looked aside and his eye fell on
a roll of parchment on the table beside him. He saw that
it contained Aristotle's treatise on Democracy and Aristocracy.
Diodorus was immediately interested. He said, "There was
delivered to me today some of the books of a new philosopher,
Philo. There is much excitement about him, and I wished to
compare him with Aristotle."

For a moment hope awakened in the lonely tribune. He
knew, from past experience in talking briefly with Aeneas,
that though the freedman could quote long sections of
Plato and Aristotle exactly, and in Greek, he was incapable
of any subtle understanding. Yet, still, hope came to Diodorus.

"Philo?" murmured Aeneas, faintly. A spasm of disdain,
totally involuntary, passed over his long pale mouth. Then,
fearful that he had again offended Diodorus, he hurried on:
"Surely he must be a great philosopher."

Diodorus shrugged. "There are too many in Rome who
acclaim him. If a man is judged by the enemies he has
made, then he is also judged by the men who honor him.
Philo, at his youthful age, has already received too much
honor to be of much worth." He paused. In many ways
Caesar Augustus resembled the "old" forgotten Romans,
for it was said of him that he was a moral man in comparison with those who thronged his court. He had tried to
respect the Senate; if he could not respect the senators, it was

not to his blame. "I have heard," said Diodorus, "that Caesar himself has conversed much with Philo. Ah, well, I shall soon know whether Philo is worthy of such consideration."

He folded his short but massive arms on his chest and contemplated Aeneas. "Aristotle," he said, reflectively. "I like his Definitions. In many ways his philosophy is superior to Plato's, for Plato, though believing himself a realist, yet veiled himself in mysticisms. Even though he taught that universals have objective existence he swathed himself in poetry, for all his *Republic*, which, in my opinion, is an aery piece of work. What did Aristotle say of him? 'I love Plato, but I love truth more.' "

Aeneas, to whom Plato was the very essence of revealed truth, could only blink. He strove frantically to follow Diodorus, who he did not believe really understood the Grecian philosophers at all. He could find no words, but contented himself in nodding solemnly.

Diodorus sighed. He saw that Aeneas was not following him. But at least the poor creature was distantly acquainted with the words of the philosophers. The tribune stretched again.

"Plato, though he inherited a mania for defining terms from his master, Socrates, had really no awareness of the real connotations of terms," said the tribune, warming to the subject. "He did not know it, but all he wrote and said was subjective. Aristotle is the true father of logic. The absolute particular was the only particular which he acknowledged. He was completely objective." Diodorus mused, scowling for a moment. "Plato was a paradox; demanding precision, he finally foundered in the sea of his generalities. It is interesting to remember that Aristotle was once a soldier, and a soldier knows there are absolutes, such as discipline, honor, obedience, partiotism, and respect for authority."

"Certainly there are absolutes," murmured Aeneas complaisantly. What, in the name of gods, was an "absolute"?

Diodorus' ferocious eyes twinkled almost gently at his freedman. He yawned, drank his wine to the last drop. "It is also interesting to remember that Aristotle belonged to the medical fraternity of Asclepiads. That brings me again to Lucanus. I believe he will be a philosopher as well as a physician. Do you not deny him access to your precious manuscripts, Aeneas."

Aeneas forgot himself for a moment and said with pride, "He already has access to them. I teach him myself, Master."

"Good." Diodorus stretched and stood up, and Aeneas bounded to his feet. God preserve the boy from his father's fogged teachings, thought Diodorus. He bade Aeneas a pleasant farewell, then went on his lonely way back to his house, through the moonlight, which had turned white and sharp. He began to brood on his frustrations. His heart ached, and he remembered Iris. Even if he desired to behave like the foul swine of modern Rome, he knew it was beyond him. Iris, a former slave, the wife of a freedman, would not dare to deny him. If she still remembered him with love, he could not violate that love. Too, she was a virtuous matron. She had looked at him tonight with misted eyes, and she had smiled at him as she could not possibly smile at her husband. He thought of the handmaiden of his mother with reverent tenderness, which was something so far different from his love for Aurelia that he could not accuse himself of licentiousness even in thought. He compared Iris with Diana, the inviolate, the eternally pure.

He looked at the moon and, in his deep simplicity, he implored the goddess to protect this Greek woman whom he had loved, and whom he still loved. Some comfort came to him.

He did not remember the boy, Lucanus, until he entered his house to find Aurelia unusually anxious. The little Rubria had awakened, and was moaning in her pain, and was asking for her father.

Chapter Three

Together, hand in hand, they ascended the staircase and entered the child's room. Two lamps burned in the small spare chamber, and increased the stagnant heat. Diodorus choked, almost suffocated after the cool night air he had encountered outside. There was a strange stench here; he looked at the little window high on the white wall, on which grotesque shadows were dancing as the slave house physician, Keptah, and the nurse hovered about the bed. The silken curtains had been drawn heavily across the window, and Diodorus marched instantly to it and roughly pulled the curtains aside. "Pfui!" he exclaimed. "It is enough to smother the child! And what is that foulness I smell?"

Aurelia's ripe cheeks paled. As an obedient matron, she rarely upbraided her husband, especially not in the presence

of slaves. She only said, "Diodorus, the night air is dangerous
at this time of the year. I ordered the window closed."

But Diodorus was breathing deeply of the fresh coolness.
He took the curtains and fanned them, thus wafting a
breeze into the room. "If the child is not already smothered
this should revive her," he said. He motioned to the nurse
to continue the fanning, and she scuttled to obey him, her
eyes big with alarm.

Diodorus came to the bed. Rubria smiled up at him from
her pillows. But it was a painful smile, and she moved her
dark head restlessly, holding out her little hand to her father.
He took it strongly in both his hard brown palms, and
though his heart lurched at its heat he said sturdily, "What
is this I hear, my daughter?" His eyes scanned the small
face, noting the dwindled outlines of it, the dry hot lips.
The fever was consuming this dearest of all creatures. Under
the flushed flesh the grayness of death was creeping, like a
stealthy tide under sun-red waters. Terror wrinkled the heart
of Diodorus, squeezing all its auricles together and bringing
with it pure physical anguish.

Keptah was saying smoothly, "Master, I have rubbed an
ointment on the limbs of the child, vulture grease, mixed
with vulture gall. It is that which is so pungent. But I was
taught that it is most efficacious in the treatment of painful
joints and sinews."

Diodorus listened to the slow and torturous breaths drawing through Rubria's young lungs; he could see, by the
struggling light of the lamps, the throbbing of tortured arter-
ies in her childish throat, and in her temples. Still holding her
hand, he put his right hand on her breast. The vibration of
her heart came to him, fast and frantic. The mysterious
disease which so afflicted the tender sinews of her body
had struck at the innocent heart and was strangling it.

He bent over the child, who, young as she was, saw her
father's fear and wished only to assuage it. She whispered
faintly, "I am much better, my father. The pain is not so
bad." He smoothed the long dark hair on the pillow with
shaking fingers; it was damp with sweat. He smoothed the
fiery cheek, the delicate curve of throat. He said in himself,
Let me die, but spare my daughter. Twist my body and throw
it into the dust, but spare my daughter. On me the fire and
sword, on me all the curses of the gods, but spare my
daughter. A great and awful silence filled him.

The physician was mixing a concoction in a goblet, and

after a moment he held it to Rubria's lips. But she retched
on it, and Diodorus motioned the physician aside and took
the goblet himself. Obediently then, and controlling her
retching, the child drank, slow drop after slow drop, pausing
frequently to gasp. Aurelia had begun to massage the swollen
portions of the pretty little legs and arms, patiently, steadily,
and Diodorus watched her as he held the goblet to his
daughter's mouth. How calm his wife was; if she felt terror
she did not betray it. Rubria was sighing now, under the
ministrations of her mother, and the spasms became less
violent. The nurse continued to fan the room with the curtains,
and Keptah moved away from the bed, inscrutable and silent.

Aurelia dipped her fingers again and again into the silver
dish of ointment as she rubbed. Her short white fingers had
strength in them, and purpose. She seemed to know when to
press, when to lift gently. She was like one moving steadfastly upon an enemy, confident and unafraid. Rubria's
body relaxed, inch by inch, became less taut against
agony, less tense with suffering. "Ah, ah," said Aurelia, in a
soft and soothing voice. "We shall drive it out. Shall we
not?" The muscles of her arms, the muscles in her plump
hands, rose and fell visibly; the light of the lamps rippled
on them. She fought, but there was no sign of the fight
in her placid face, in her serenely smiling eyes. My
Aurelia may not have much imagination, but she is a
woman, and strength lies in women like the force of armies,
thought Diodorus with new humility. Rubria clung to her
father's hand, but she unconsciously turned to her mother as
a newborn babe turns. Aurelia's robe fell forward, and
Diodorus could see the rich swelling of her bosom, that
untroubled and unhurried bosom. It glistened with sweat, but
no frightened breath made it rise and fall.

Still rubbing her child, Aurelia glanced up at her husband,
and her smile was full of love. Her brown eyes said to him,
I shall save this little one for you. Do not grieve, my dearest.
There was no jealousy in her regard. It mattered only that
Diodorus must be spared an overwhelming sorrow. Aurelia's
buxom cheeks glowed with her calm exertion, and her full
lips curved. She had loosened her black hair for the night;
it poured in a dusky cataract over her rotund young shoulders.

Now the fear of Diodorus became less. He turned to
Keptah, the physician. He had much regard for his slave, and
had frequently lent him to friends who were ill. Pricus had

sent him to the great university at Alexandria, early recognizing that the boy had a genius for medicine. The father of Diodorus had liked him as a person, and had secured Diodorus' promise that when Keptah reached the age of forty-five he would receive his freedom and enough gold to assure his security. Diodorus intended to keep that promise, but though he had resepct for his slave as a physician he disliked him as a man. There was no patience in Diodorus for the subtle, the ambiguous, the secretly smiling, the darkly enigmatic, the smoothly skeptical and silent.

For Keptah, at forty, was all of these. No one had ever known his racial origin, but there was something Egyptian in the gaunt face, so remote, mysterious and swart, with its chiseled hooked nose, tilted and hidden eyes, and thin folded mouth. His hair, as short as that of Diodorus, seemed painted by a black brush over a long and fragile skull. He was tall, almost fleshless, and under his robe his bony shoulders were wide. He had brown hands which were long and supple, with bloodless nails and large joints. Diodorus believed that these joints indicated a philosopher, but Keptah, if he had philosophies, occult and mystic, which Diodorus would have enjoyed exploring, nimbly evaded all his master's tentative probings. "I do not know, Master," he would murmur in his soft and curiously accented voice. "I am only a slave."

This haughty parody of humility never failed to irritate the intellectually hungry tribune, who felt himself rebuffed as a rough and stupid soldier. Diodorus also suspected that Keptah laughed at him. There was no denying, however, that he was a wise man and a great physician.

Diodorus, looking at him now, standing aside yet not standing aside, remembered a strange event which had taken place in this house only a few months ago.

The overseer of the hall servants had been celebrating his birthday in the hall of the slaves. Diodorus, good master that he was, and appreciative of faithful servitors, had given orders that excellent food and wine from his own tables be used on that night. As his own gift he had presented the overseer with a bag of gold coins. No restraint was to be put on the celebrations, and so Diodorus, working his way slowly but surely through an obscure treatise on ethics, had put down the roll of parchment and had frowned. It was quiet and lamplit in his library, but the tumult from the slaves' quarters was an uproarious clamor in the warm air. Then

Diodorus had smiled with an effort of indulgence. Theodorus, an old man, would not have many more occasions for hilarity and festiveness. Let the pretty girls dance before him, and the young men cavort, and the wind flow, and the bones be tossed on the marble floor, and the music pound against the walls of the house.

But the noise became more and more unrestrained. The little Rubria would be disturbed, and Aurelia, who rose before her slaves. There was a limit to all things, even birthday celebrations. Diodorus did not confess to himself that the sound of joyous human life under the moon tugged at him, for was he not an austere Roman who detested frivolity? He muttered to himself that he must halt this uproar, but his step was light and quick as he made his way to the slaves' hall.

The festivities had overflowed from the hall into the scented courtyard of the slaves. Lamps had been set on tables dragged from the hall, and they flickered on palms and flowers and the humble statues in the distant corners. The moonlight and the lamplight mingled together to show a scene of unbridled and ribald festivity. The slave girls, particularly those who had delightful rosy bodies, were almost naked, their hair tossing about them as they performed astonishingly lewd dances, their faces brilliant with lasciviousness and youth and wine. Tresses of brown and black and gold fluttered like banners over nude breasts and round limbs. The young men, dressed like fauns and satyrs, leaped about the girls with shameful gestures. And the music screamed and soared, danced and laughed, incited and lured and shrilled. Lolling like the master himself on a soft couch, Theodorus watched with joy and impotent lustfulness, his white head nodding in time with the music, his twisted fingers snapping.

The fragrance of flowers, herbs, wine, sweat and hot roasted meats and bread was like a fog in the air. The lamps, as if inspired, themselves, burned brighter, and light and shadow chased themselves in drunken shafts over the courtyard. Diodorus was appalled. In this most proper and discreet and decorous household where had the girls and the young men learned these shameless dances, these licentious gestures, these songs, these obscene shouts? It was a bacchanalia! It was not to be permitted! Diodorus, in a deep shadow, felt himself blushing. He must have a talk with Aurelia in the morning. But surely Aurelia must be hearing all this noise herself. Why had she not summoned a slave, sternly, and commanded order and an end to all this?

He hesitated. Theodorus was singing in his cracked and quavering voice. He had begun to clap his hands. Now, to Diodorus' amazement, the old man was inciting the girls and the young men to wilder antics in phrases which his master had not believed he even knew. Such words, by the gods!

More accustomed now to darkness and lamplight and moonlight, Diodorus let his eyes roam. Across the courtyard he saw a dim movement, then the glimmer of a white robe. He recognized the tall and majestic figure of Keptah, the physician. Diodorus was further astonished. Keptah did not associate with the other slaves at any time. Yet, there he was, watching as Diodorus was watching. He, too, must be lonely.

Keptah suddenly came out of the shadow, revealing himself in his long white physician's robe, erect and still and incomprehensible. The lamplight shone fully on his face, and Diodorus hardly recognized it, so strange it was, so gleaming, so cryptic, and so contained. Keptah stood and watched the leaping bodies, the tangled arms and legs, the blowing hair, the welter of hot flesh, the joyous abandon of drunken and voluptuous youth. The dancing feet whirled nearer and nearer to him. Sometimes he was obscured by the maidens, and then they receded again, approached and danced away, the young men and boys following in perfect rhythm, their hands grasping and darting after the amorous breasts and arms, or tossing hair. But Keptah did not move or retreat. He had begun to smile, and, seeing that smile, Diodorus frowned. The light on Keptah's face became a glitter.

Then Keptah lifted his right hand. If he thinks to halt them he is a fool, thought Diodorus. Only a thunderbolt would be effective.

Keptah stood with his hand upraised, and Diodorus could see the flat and swarthy palm. It was not a gesture of command. The thumb curled on the palm in a curious way, and the fingers parted. Diodorus was so absorbed in watching his physician that it was some moments before he became aware that an utter silence had fallen. Even the musicians had ceased to play their wild music.

Diodorus started. He looked about him with disbelief, and then he was struck with amazement. The dancers had halted in the very motions of their dance. The lutists and the harpists and the flutists had frozen, their hands in mid-air.

Theodorus' head had fallen to his ancient breast. Now there was only the most profound silence in the courtyard, except for the hissing of the lamps, the chirp of night insects, the distant cries of birds, the far barking of a dog. Moonlight poured into the courtyard; the lamps died lower. The dancers stood, legs lifted, arms thrown out, faces white and entranced. This might be a scene from a painted mural, or a courtyard crowded with statues, the carved bacchanalia of a mad sculptor.

Diodorus could not believe it. He gaped and stared, then rubbed his eyes and stared again. The night was very warm, but all at once Diodorus was deathly cold. Something rustled; there was the softest step. He jumped in sudden fright, and turned. Keptah was standing near him, smiling darkly and respectfully, and then bowing. He murmured, "They were disturbing you, Master."

Diodorus shivered. He moved a step or two away. He whispered, "What did you do?"

The unfathomable eyes contemplated him seriously, but in their depths there was a reddish spark. "I, Master?" said the physician, raising his tilted brows as if in surprise at some childishness. "It is nothing at all. I saw you across the courtyard and it was evident that you were annoyed. So I commanded the foolish ones to cease, and they ceased."

"What did you do?" repeated Diodorus, and now for all his trembling his voice was loud and harsh.

Again Keptah studied him in that mocking surprise. "It is something I learned as a physician, Master." He turned a little and regarded the awful scene before them. Moonlight, here and there, struck a young and marble breast, the stilled motion of a marble arm, the bend of a marble knee. "It alarms you, Master?" asked Keptah, as if astonished. "It is nothing at all."

Diodorus lifted his arm in an involuntary gesture of horror and menace. "Release them at once!" he cried, and fell back from the physician, all his superstition making his flesh crawl.

"To abandon and noise, Master?" Keptah appeared puzzled. "It will shortly be dawn."

"Release them, cursed be you!" shouted Diodorus. He was terribly frightened.

"To more decorum, perhaps?" urged that insidious voice, anxiously.

Diodorus was silent. Keptah appeared to reflect on his

master in bafflement. Then he shrugged. He lifted his hand
again, and he muttered something under his breath.

The scene did not change suddenly. But moment by endless moment the arms and legs began to move, to drop listlessly. The bodies became alive, though sluggishly. As if
moving in dreams, heads turned, feet began to move, not in
dance, but in enchantment. The moonlight, cold and motionless, shone down on heavy shoulders, heavy limbs. One by
one the slaves crept out of the courtyard, not speaking, not
glancing at each other, completely unaware of each other. It
was like watching a scene of total exhaustion and animal
unconsciousness. To Diodorus it was some soundless and
awful nightmare.

And now the courtyard was empty. Only the lamps, the
littered tables, the empty chairs remained. The instruments
of the musicians lay on the stones as if thrown down in
flight. The lamps sputtered out. The moon sank slowly and
the palms clattered.

Keptah spoke, and it appeared to Diodorus that they two
had stood there for endless time: "They will forget, Master.
They will believe they went to their beds after a happy night
of revelry and rejoicing." He sighed. "How fortunate they
are to have such an indulgent lord!"

Keptah's garments fell about him in angular folds. The
moonlight lay in the deep hollows of his cheek, emphasized
the caverns about his mouth. "You have thought me evil,
Master," he said. "But I have knowledge. There is an ancient
legend that evil and knowledge are one and the same thing. It
is not good to know. It is much better to be an innocent
animal." He looked now at Diodorus, and where his eyes
were there were caves of depthless darkness. "But," he
said, "who is there among us who would prefer to be without a knowledge of good and evil? Not to know is not to be
man. Or the gods," he added, even more softly.

He moved away, and there was no sound about him.

It was as he had said. When Diodorus, in the morning,
cautiously asked Theodorus about the night's festivities the
slave replied joyously, "Thanks to you, Master, it was a glorious night! Never have your servants been happier!" He bent
his creaking knees and kissed the hands of Diodorus. The
sun was bright on his withered face. "We shall remember
it forever," he said.

Then Diodorus had summoned Keptah, who came to
him on feet which seemed to glide. "You spoke to me of good

and evil last night, and knowledge," he said. "Your language was very obscure." Diodorus paused. He gazed at Keptah, not as a master looks at a slave, but as a man looks at a man. "You have studied the words of Aristotle during your years at Alexandria. You remember that the sage spoke of absolutes. Do you not believe in absolutes?"

Keptah was not perplexed; he knew that Diodorus had given their last conversation long thought. He knew all that was to be known about the tribune.

"No, Master, I do not."

"And why not?"

"Because, Master, there are no absolutes, except in God."

"But Aristotle was a great philosopher! Are you presuming to contradict him?" Diodorus turned in his chair with affront.

Keptah smiled his subtle smile. "Did wisdom end with Aristotle?" he asked.

Diodorus scowled, but he was shaken. "Then the last word has not yet been spoken?"

"Master, not yet."

Diodorus scowled even more fiercely. "No absolutes! No last word!" He was dismayed. It was bad enough that politics were always so unstable, that life was capricious. But philosophy, surely, and philosophy such as Aristotle's, was an eternal and unchanging thing. What was a man to hold to in an unpredictable world, if not philosophy, if not the memory of his fathers, the temples of his gods, and wisdom? He glanced up at Keptah, and saw the strange deviousness of his eyes, the obscure outline of his bloodless lips.

"Tell me," said the tribune, "what was it you did to the slaves last night?"

"It was only a form of hypnotism, Master," said the physician. "A delusion, if you will."

"Whose delusion?" Diodorus was irate.

Keptah shrugged delicately. "Who knows, Master?"

Diodorus had dismissed him irritably. The thoughts raised in his mind by Keptah were too disturbing, so he suppressed them as soon as possible. He had not remembered them again until now.

And now he regarded Keptah; he was more firmly convinced than ever that the slave considered him, the mighty tribune, a very simple man. It was simplicity, then, to believe in virtue, in patriotism, in morality, in honor, in duty, and Diodorus suspected that to Keptah, the mysterious, such

simplicity was absurd. But surely a man who believed
in no absolutes was a corrupt man! Was it well for such a
man to attend the little Rubria? But who, in Antioch, or
even in Rome, had so gifted a physician as Keptah?

It was then, for a reason unknown to him, that Diodorus
suddenly remembered Lucanus.

He put his hand to his pouch surreptitiously, and felt the
stone and the little bag of herbs. He saw that Keptah was
watching him, while not appearing to watch. He said, like a
sheepish schoolboy, "I have here an amulet."

Keptah raised his winged black brows, and said, courteously,
"An amulet? Ah, amulets often possess supernatural qualities."

Diodorus frowned. Was the man mocking him again? But
Keptah was most serious, and he was waiting politely. He
almost thrust the strange stone into the physician's hand.

Keptah studied it. And then the most unreadable expression passed over his face. He turned his back to the lamps
so that he stood in shadow, and Diodorus peered over his
shoulder. In Keptah's hands, in the dimness, the stone glowed
as if burning with an internal and quenchless fire. It cast a
frail but steady light on Keptah's long dark fingers.

"What is it?" demanded Diodorus, impatiently.

Keptah contemplated his master's alarm and his suddenly
congested face with that hidden amusement of his. "It was
given to me, tonight," said Diodorus, "by my freedman's
son, the little Lucanus, for the Lady Rubria. He told me he
had found it; he declared that the gods, or God, was in it."

Keptah's face changed. He said, "Lucanus?" He pondered.
He knew the love between the young Greek and the younger
Rubria—so innocent and gentle a love. He also knew the
tremendous power of suggestion. He went to the bed, and,
imperatively, as if he were master and Aurelia but a slave
woman, he motioned her aside and she instinctively obeyed.
Rubria was sobbing quietly, but now she stared up as if in
fear at Keptah. He smiled at the child, and showed her the
stone, which was not ordinary but possessed no powers except its beauty. "This," he said to her, "is a magical stone,
found by your playmate, Lucanus. The gods must have directed him to it. It will help you, little lady, if you believe in it,
for did not Lucanus find it for you?"

Rubria looked at the stone and touched it timidly with one
frail finger. She began to smile. Keptah lifted her shift deftly;
he pressed the rounded contour of the stone against her left

side, in the region of her swollen spleen. "Here it must rest,"
he said to the parents, and the nurse, "for many days, until
the child recovers her health." He gazed at Rubria with a
compelling look, and she appeared awed, as did Diodorus
and Aurelia.

Diodorus rubbed his chin; he might be superstitious, but
he was also a man of reason and logic. He bent over his
daughter and studied the stone, and saw its fires and twin-
klings. Then, in some suspicion, he glanced up at Keptah,
who had trouble in retaining his gravity. "I do not believe in magic," grumbled the tribune. Keptah struggled with
his almost uncontrollable desire to laugh. He said, "Master,
there is much magic in the world. One has only to believe
in it to find it."

The tribune thought this ambiguous, and frowned, but
Keptah seemed very serious. Well, thought Diodorus, it is
possible I do not know everything, and I am not a physician or
a dealer in magic, like this charlatan. His attention quickly
returned to Rubria, and he shook his head. "What is all this
that ails the child?" he demanded. "You have not been definite, but rather evasive, Keptah. The blood-suffused joints
—the bruised areas of flesh—the difficulty in breathing—the
seeping gums—the lumps in the glands."

Keptah looked aside. "It is not a rare condition," he said,
mildly, "though a difficult one—to cure." It was impossible
for him to tell this father that the child had the white sickness, which was invariably fatal; there was pity in his
heart.

"But the little Rubria will live?" demanded Diodorus, and
his eyes shrank at the very thought of her death.

Keptah regarded him for a long moment before answering,
and then he said, "It is not ordained that she die now, Master,
nor any time in the immediate future." Rubria, feeling Lucanus' stone against her young flesh, felt surcease, and this
Keptah noted. The force of the spirit, he reflected, can often
keep death at bay, and faith can sometimes accomplish the
impossible.

Diodorus was not satisfied. Fear quickened his heart. "You
speak evasively. Will not the amulet cure her entirely?"

"I do not know, Master." The ambushed eyes looked upon
Diodorus with an expression that the Roman did not recognize as a remote compassion.

"Then," said Diodorus, with angry frenzy, "she will surely
die in the future?"

"Is that not our common fate, Master?"

Diodorus let his head drop on his breast, and he drew in his lips against his teeth. He then thought of the tiny bag of herbs given to him by that most unknowable boy, Lucanus, and with shaking fingers he withdrew it from his pouch and extended it with sudden stiffness to Keptah. "Lucanus gave me this, also, and said it must be mixed in hot wine and given to the Lady Rubria."

He expected new mockery from Keptah, but the physician took the bag with a light and delicate swiftness. He opened it. Immediately the hot little room was pervaded by an intense odor, bitter yet pleasing. Keptah held the bag to his nostrils and closed his eyes and inhaled. "Where, Master, did the boy find these herbs, and how did he choose them?"

"I do not know!" shouted the frantic Diodorus. "In the fields, he said. He did not tell me how he chose them! Gods! Is there no end to this mystery? What does the bag contain?"

Keptah smiled, and carefully closed the bag. "Herbs I have not been able to find myself, though I have searched long and endlessly." He drew his bony fingers across his mouth, as though to quiet them. He gave the bag to the nurse and commanded that it be mixed in hot wine immediately. He turned silently on his heels, went to the bed, and gazed down at Rubria with the expression one wears when confronted by a miracle.

Diodorus caught the arm of his physician. "The boy, Lucanus, has said he wishes to study medicine and I have promised him——" He halted, and his fierce eyes narrowed with conjecture and thought, and his frugal mind hurried.

"Yes, Master?" asked Keptah, again the haughty slave parodying humility.

"I promised him that he may study with the Lady Rubria, and that later—later—it might be possible for him to study——" Diodorus paused, and his ferocious brows drew together. "You shall teach him, Keptah, and if you believe he has the capacity to become a physician, then"—he drew a deep breath and heroically abandoned caution—"I shall send him to Alexandria."

He expected Keptah to become incredulous and amused. But Keptah bowed his head seriously. "Master, what you have said is ordained."

"Now what in the name of Hades do you mean by that?" demanded Diodorus, perplexed. "I suppose you are speaking of the Fates again. But have not Aristotle and Socrates spoken of the free choice of men and ridiculed that which is ordained?"

"Many philosophers are not wise in all things," said the irritating Keptah calmly. "If a man were to live solely by the theories of the philosophers he would not survive, nor would he retain his sanity." He smiled fully at Diodorus, as a pitying father smiles at an obstinate young son.

The nurse had brought in a silver goblet of hot wine, and Keptah dexterously mixed the herbs in it. The little girl's moans were softer now, but it was evident she was still in great pain. Keptah gave the goblet to Aurelia, and she held it to Rubria's lips with a fond smile. The child drank obediently between deep breaths of suffering. Keptah stood by the bed and watched her acutely for long moments.

The moaning came less frequently now, and the child's eyes grew large with wonder, and quiet. Her head lay upon her mother's knees, and again Diodorus held her hand. She lifted her head, as if in surprise at the diminishing of anguish, and then she drew one moving breath after another, slow and deep, like sighs.

"Ah, gods," muttered Diodorus, his eyelids watering with gratitude.

Like a red tide, the flush of fever receded from Rubria's cheeks and lips, and was replaced by a ghostly pallor. To her parents this was excellent, for they forgot that it was this very pallor which had preceded this last acute illness, and which had, weeks ago, aroused their anxiety. Keptah nodded to himself with somberness.

"The child is sleeping!" cried Aurelia, very gently. And indeed Rubria slept, white as the dead beneath her dusky lengths of hair.

"I shall sacrifice not two, but four cocks to Aesculapius!" exclaimed Diodorus, weak with relief. "And to his messenger, the glorious, lightfooted Mercury, two hecatombs!"

He swung to his physician, and forgetting he was master of this inscrutable slave, he seized his hand, blinking his eyes to keep back his tears. "Ah, Keptah, ask what you will! It shall be granted instantly for this night's work!"

Keptah paused as Diodorus wrung his hand. He reflected that only opportunistic men sought profit from what was not their own. But slaves had no other choice but expediency. He said, so softly that his lips hardly moved, "My freedom, Master."

Diodorus was taken aback. He compressed his mouth; he

glared blackly at his slave. "Ah," he said, in a threatening voice, "you would take advantage of my emotion, natural to a father?"

Keptah shrugged. "It was you who suggested it, Master, not I," he answered.

Diodorus' short hair bristled with that sudden anger of his. The nostrils of his beaked nose flared. Suspicion glittered in his eyes. "What a sleek rascal you are, Keptah! You know that it is promised to my father that you shall be given your freedom when you are forty-five years old, and enough gold for your ease. You would have me break my promise to my father?"

Keptah could not hold back a smile at this sophistry, and seeing that smile, Diodorus felt greater anger, and considerable sheepishness. He flung away Keptah's hand, pulled his shoulders heavily up to his ears, and stood obstinately, like a lowering bull. He attempted to stare his slave down, with umbrage. But Keptah stood in quiet dignity, fingering a fold of his robe.

Diodorus forgot his sleeping daughter for a moment and shouted, "Very well, then, scoundrel! So be it. In a few days you shall go with me to the praetor." He shook his thick finger in Keptah's face. "But only on this contract, that you remain with me voluntarily until I dismiss you."

"Did you think I would desert you, Master?" asked Keptah, as if marveling. "Besides, is it not ordained that I remain in this house and teach the son of Aeneas?"

But Diodorus was not appeased. He fumed, trying to intimidate the other. Keptah was not intimidated. "The praetor and you, Master, will no doubt agree on a just stipend, which I should prefer to suggest."

Diodorus was about to burst out again when he felt Aurelia's fingers on his sweating arm. She was smiling up at him; her cheeks were ripe again, and a dimple twinkled beside her mouth. She looked like a girl, seated on the edge of her child's bed, and her hair was curling moistly on her forehead and shoulders. "Never shall it be said of the noble Diodorus that he broke a promise," she murmured.

Her appearance, her love, touched Diodorus' secretly soft heart. But it was necessary not to betray such an unmilitary weakness. He flung up his hands in a gesture of rageful surrender. "I have said, so be it!" he cried. "I shall also say that I despise an exigent man, be he master or slave. Keptah, I have respected you; now I have contempt for you."

"The contempt of such as you, Master, is worth the honor of all other men," said Keptah, and Aurelia laughed aloud, as if with delight.

Keptah waited for his dismissal, and when it was given he bowed deeply to Diodorus and Aurelia, and went at once to his own locked pharmacy, where he compounded his potions and ointments, and where he kept his powdered bodies and organs of animals and insects and strange herbs and dried blossoms and inorganic substances about which no other physicians knew, except those like himself.

This pharmacy was part of his own quarters, far from the quarters of the other slaves. It was not necessary to warn them away; they were terrified of Keptah and his abstruse air and stateliness. They were even more terrified of the magic behind that locked door. They whispered that he visited the crematoria and withdrew the blood of the dead before their incineration, and used it in his remedies. Sickening odors sometimes floated about him, like an aura, and sometimes lights glimmered long after midnight through his window. Some of the slaves swore that these were not the lights of lamps, but moving sparkles like stars, and that these sparklers often hovered on the window sills like cold fireflies.

Keptah compounded some liquid, which was brown as rust and had an unearthly smell. He poured it into a small ewer, and then held the vessel in his hand. He stood in his pharmacy, with the spectral shelves and jars all above him, and he became as still as stone, his eyes suddenly fixed on the sky beyond his window. His heart jumped, hurried like a fleeing lamb, then stopped and began to labor.

"It has come," he whispered aloud. And then, with exultation, he repeated in a trembling voice, "It has come! Blessed are my eyes that they have lived to see it!"

He felt in his breast for a small object, and drew it out. It was made of gold, and was of a simple shape. He pressed it to his lips, and bowed over and over, and he said, again and again, "Holy. Holy. Holy."

He fell to his knees and his head dropped on his breast, and he hardly seemed to breathe, caught up in some enchantment beyond the knowledge of the world. The object he had withdrawn from under his robe dangled before him on a golden chain, and the lamplight struck it so vividly that it shone like the sun, and it enlarged before Keptah's dazzled eyes until it appeared to encompass the universe.

The moon was only a pale and nebulous shadow far down in the sky when Keptah let himself out of his private door into the courtyard. But the palms interfered with the sky, and he glided away into the darkness, which was mysteriously tremulous with argent shadows. He had a need for open space in which he could contemplate. He asked himself, over and over, with his heart beating heavily in his ears, Will They let me go? Will They let my eyes see? I shall soon be a freedman, there is nothing to halt my going for a while. He clasped his hands on his breast convulsively and prayed that They would consent.

He walked through the tangled gardens far beyond the house, and noted again how every leaf, every blade of grass, was quivering with gentle and unearthly silver. It was a holy reflection to him; sometimes he paused to smile and to touch a thick and glimmering leaf, and then to glance at the sky. Those astronomers, who were not Chaldeans like himself, must now be talking fearfully of comets, though no comets were expected. But his Brotherhood knew. He wished he could join them; he had prayed, in the past, that if the Star came in his lifetime, he might be among his Brotherhood at that hour. The Star had come, and it was a long distance to go on foot to Antioch, where the Brotherhood would be keeping their joyous vigil, their dark eyes full of mystery and thanksgiving. They had kept that vigil for so long that its beginning was lost in time, from the days of Ur, from the days of the flourishing of Bīt Yakīn, from the days when they had come from some far desert, when they were still a priestly people—the Kalū—before they had been called Babylonians by the Jews. "It is not given even our wisest to know the hour; only He knows," Keptah had been taught. "Not even the Holy Ones in heaven know, but only the Holiest of Holies, blessed be His Name."

Keptah reached an open place in the great gardens, and he was on the low bank of an estuary of the Orontes River. The estuary was narrow, but swift, and it was swifter now, as if hurrying breathlessly to carry the news to the river, and then to the world-lapping seas. The banks were dark, though long lances of quicksilver light flashed through them. But the narrow stream was ablaze with a light stronger than moonlight; its wrinkled surface of black and white danced and ran, whirled and scintillated. Its voice was like the mingling of flute and drum, though there was no wind.

And now Keptah, on the bank, his garments and his inscrutable face flooded with radiance, looked up at the open sky. The Star stood in the heavens, almost as brilliant as the sun, its sharp rays beaming out steadfastly in the silent blackness around it. It had been foretold that it would move, and would point the way. It was still fixed. Then, thought Keptah, They have not as yet chosen those who are to follow.

As he watched the Star, which was so huge, so coldly burning, he began to pray humbly, falling upon his knees. "Oh, Thou for Whom the world has waited so long, blessed am I that it was given to me to see Thy Sign! Blessed is the earth that has received Thee. Blessed is she who has borne Thee in a place I do not know. Blessed is man because Thou hast redeemed man. For the dark places shall now be opened, and the secret places revealed, and the gates of the House of the Lord shall stand ajar to the end of time, and death shall be no more."

A sudden sense of incredible sweetness came to him, an intense ecstasy, as if one deeply adored had smiled upon him, had recognized him, and had sent him a message of love. Tears ran down his swarthy face; he lifted his hands to the sky in a gesture of worship and rapturous humility.

He murmured aloud, "I have been cleansed. I have been saved. Whatever there was of evil or mockery or doubt in me has been destroyed. I have been bathed in the waters of life. From this hour hence I have been born. Blessed be the Name of the Lord!"

A great quiet and stillness came to him, like a benediction. A great peace enveloped him. It did not matter that he had not been chosen to see with his own eyes Who had been born on this night. For He who had been born was with all men, in every place on the earth, at this hour, and would never depart again.

The Star was too bright for too long a gaze, and Keptah's eyes dropped. He remained kneeling, in utter quietude, watching the quickening and illuminated stream that ran before him. And then his eye was caught by the smallest movement, and there was a brighter gleam not far from him, down the bank of the estuary. He directed all his attention to it, and he saw that it was a small fair head made almost incandescent by the light of the Star.*

Now he could see the delicate profile of the child who was

* This Star was seen all over the known world.

sitting on the bank of the estuary, a profile lifted to the sky. The fine long nose, the exquisite curve of cheek and chin, the falling of the golden hair were fully outlined as if with an inner light shining through alabaster. It is the boy, Lucanus, thought Keptah, with wonder.

He rose and moved silently down the bank and stood beside the unaware boy, who was watching the Star. His blue eyes reflected its radiance; he was smiling, his hands clasped on his knees. He sat very still, as if entranced, not blinking, his white throat as clear and smooth as marble.

Then Keptah spoke softly, so as not to startle the child: "Lucanus, why are you out of your home so late?"

Lucanus turned his head slowly, and smiled. "It is you, Keptah. I could not sleep, and so I crept from my bedroom, for I had seen the Star through my window. It was as if it had called me, and I could not disobey."

His voice was serene and unafraid, and he looked upon Keptah with his usual respect, though Keptah was still a slave. "Certainly you could not disobey, child," said Keptah, and sat down beside Lucanus. Together they contemplated the Star. It is not possible that he knows, Keptah told himself. He asked in himself, Shall I tell him the meaning? He waited for the answer. It came quietly and firmly: No. But there was also a command, and a knowledge, following on the word. Curiously, Keptah scrutinized the boy. He remembered how Lucanus had a way of dogging his footsteps, appearing from nowhere when he attended slaves who were ill, and how he had watched the ministrations of Keptah from a doorway, from behind a curtain, or from some shy and anxious distance. His presence had often irritated Keptah. Boys were inquisitive little animals; they liked to look on violence or pain, some primitive savagery stirring them to excitement. Keptah had considered Lucanus in this manner, until tonight.

He said, "It is a strange Star, is it not?" and intently awaited the answer.

"Yes," said Lucanus. "It is strange. And beautiful. I feel it is telling us something." His voice was that of a young man, and not a child, and Keptah, who had rarely heard him speak before, became aware of that voice for the first time.

"And what, Lucanus, do you think it is telling us?"

Lucanus was silent. His fair brows contracted. "I do not know. But this I know, that someday it shall be revealed to me."

Keptah nodded to himself. He put his dark hand on the white shoulder of the boy and pressed it. "That I know," he murmured. He turned Lucanus to him, and the boy, surprised, looked at him shyly and closely. Keptah studied the serene and beautiful face, the strong outlines under the delicacy, the ardent curve of the mouth, the passion in the blue eyes.

"I am to be your teacher," he said, and he smiled. "So it was commanded tonight by the great Diodorus."

Lucanus' face glowed with joy and amazement. "And then," continued Keptah, with gentleness, "you shall be sent by the master to Alexandria for further study."

Lucanus caught the slave's hand and kissed it vehemently. "I am your slave, noble Keptah!" he cried, and pressed the swart hand to his breast in a moving and rapturous gesture. Keptah put his other hand on the boy's head, as if in blessing.

"You have never feared me, Lucanus?"

"No." The boy's face expressed wonderment. "I have only honored you in my heart, Master."

Keptah laughed a little, sadly. "Do not call me 'Master,' Lucanus. The noble Diodorus would not approve. He has an immense sense of the proprieties."

He thought of Diodorus with regret, and not with his usual amusement. It is true, he thought, that there are greater and more eternal things than his absurd and iron "realities." But I was wrong, and cruel, the night the slaves danced so uproariously, to attempt to disillusion him. It is well that I did not succeed.

The Star shone down resplendently on the man and the boy, its rays widening, drowning out all the lesser stars and planets, sending them fleeing across the curve of the sky towards the dawn. Keptah watched it again, forgetting Lucanus, and Lucanus fixed his gaze on that duskily carved and Oriental profile. Lucanus asked, "Who are you, Keptah?"

Keptah was silent for long moments, as if asking himself questions and receiving answers. Then, without looking at Lucanus, he began to speak.

"I am a Chaldean. That I was told years ago, though I did not know at first, coming to the house of Priscus as a babe, and a slave. My father was Kalū, that is to mean a priest, but who my mother was I do not know to this day. But there was a journey when I was still in my mother's arms; my father knew mysterious things and he was on his way —to a distant country." He stared fixedly at the Star. "He

believed, wrongly, that it had been ordained for him to see
——." He halted, and moved restlessly.

"On the way to that country the caravan in which he and
my mother and I were traveling was set upon by thieves and
slavemasters. My parents were killed. I, an infant, was sold
with the remaining men and women and children into slavery,
and Priscus purchased me and brought me to his house in
Jerusalem, and then to Rome."

Lucanus waited for him to continue, but Keptah was
silent. His cryptic face was majestic with a cold and forbidding sorrow.

"Who told you of this, Keptah, if even the noble Diodorus
does not know?"

Keptah looked at the boy quickly, and laughed with tenderness. "Ah, you have been questioning the master behind my
back!" His laugh ceased abruptly. "Do not look so embarrassed, boy. I am not offended." He sighed. "Let this be
sufficient for you, Lucanus: I was told, but by whom I can
never tell you. But I can tell you of Chaldea, or Babylonia,
and my people, and it has been given to me to tell you though
for what reason it is not as yet clear to me.

"We are so ancient a people that even the Jews, who claim
to be very ancient themselves, have not even a legend concerning our origin. But we gave one Abraham to the
Jews, who now call him Father Abraham. We first came to the
land of Ur from a place unrecorded, and once we had
the most flourishing capital, more wise, urbane, and mature
than any since on the earth, and its name was Bīt Yakīn.
But one can grow so wise, if that wisdom is without God, that
one grows corrupt—— Why do you start so, boy?"

"Nothing," whispered Lucanus. But Keptah commanded
him with his hooded eyes, and the boy said, haltingly,
"I am thinking of the Unknown God of the Greeks."

"Ah, yes. He is the same," said Keptah, with abstraction.

He went on: "In the beginning, and for centuries, Bīt
Yakīn remembered God, and flourished, and was mighty,
and wise men came from all places to study there under the
Kalū, and some mysteries were cautiously imparted to them
as well as wisdom. And the wise men took back these mysteries to their countries, and Egypt was one of them, and a man
named Moses became acquainted with those mysteries through
the Kalū who had been commanded to go to Egypt and teach
the young Egyptian prince beyond what the priests of Egypt
already knew. You have heard of Moses, Lucanus?"

"Yes, the Jews have told me, in Antioch. He brought the Commandments of God to men."

Keptah sighed, and said ironically, "And men have been busy for centuries sedulously breaking them all!"

Lucanus feared that Keptah had forgotten him, for he was silent again for so long. Then he spoke.

"Because men are men, they become proud, especially when they have a reputation. Even many of the Kalū became proud, and when that happened they lost their wisdom, for they had forgotten from whence came their knowledge of mysteries. So they became charlatans instead of priests, and necromancers, for they remembered the hidden words of magic and used them for evil ends and gain. These priests, so engaged in raw magic, were no longer astronomers, physicians, scientists and priests. They were wicked men, occupied in vulgar divinations, which they passed on to their sons. And if a priesthood decays, then a people decays, and all Chaldea, betrayed by its priests, was slowly eaten by corruption. And she became as nothing, and fell to enemies. If a nation has not God that nation must fall, but if a nation has God then all the powers of evil, and all the armies, cannot shake its foundations; no, not even if the whole world is arrayed against it."

Keptah looked at the Star, and his lips moved silently for a few moments.

"So the good Kalū, and there were so few of them, left Chaldea, weeping, and they went to many countries with their secrets, and in these countries they are the wise man of the East, and physicians, astronomers, divinators to the elect, astrologers, scientists and metaphysicians. Only they know who they are; only they will ever know who they are. For they have come to suspect mankind, and for the most excellent reasons. They form an occult Brotherhood, and they choose who shall enter."

Now Keptah gave his whole attention to Lucanus, and he thought to himself, Why was it I was so blind? He said, "This is not a story which you will learn in Alexandria, and I must charge you not to repeat it to dull ears, Lucanus." His voice was harsh and commanding.

"I shall not repeat it, but I shall remember it," said Lucanus, simply.

Keptah softened. "I know, child. There is no corruption in you. But let me continue. So corrupt and proud did Chaldea, or Babylonia, become that she no longer reverenced the

Kalū, and no longer called herself the land of the wise priests, but looked ravenously at neighbors for gold and slaves and land. And she began to call herself the nation of the Kaldi-Kašdi, which is to say 'conquerors.' And so she warred, and conquered, and enslaved and oppressed, and as all those nations who war must die, so Chaldea died, for war is, above all things, the most foul, the most abominable in the sight of God, the most loathsome, for it destroys what the Holy One has created in His love, and it degrades man to the level of the unthinking ant who obeys without knowing why he obeys and fights without knowing why he fights. For, in truth, in war a man fights for nothing."

He looked at the serious and thoughtful Lucanus for a long time. Then, as if commanded, he withdrew the golden object from his breast and held it in his open palm. "Look, child, and tell me what this is."

Lucanus peered at the object in the hand of Keptah, and he shivered. "It is a cross, the sign of infamy, for so on it do Romans execute criminals of the lowest kind."

The golden cross paled in Keptah's palm, became white and brilliant in the light of the Star. It seemed to possess an incandescence of its own. "It is the Light of the World," said Keptah. "One day you will know.

"For centuries, so many centuries that men have forgotten them, and they are steeped in dust, that Sign was known by the Kalū for what it is. I cannot tell you its meaning, for it is forbidden. The Kalū wore it on their breasts before the Jews were a nation or a people, before Egypt had a Pharaoh, before Greece was born, before Romulus and Remus were nursed by a she-wolf. Some of the Egyptian wise men brought it home to Egypt from Chaldea without knowing its meaning, and it can be seen in the Pyramids to this day, an occult sign understood by no one but the chosen of Chaldea. The priests of Greece knew of it vaguely, though not understanding, but under its influence they raised the altars to the Unknown God."

Some unnamable emotion suddenly stirred in Lucanus. His eyes filled with tears. The cross seemed to expand on the palm of Keptah. Lucanus reached out and touched it with a trembling finger, and he was all at once suffused with a sense of indescribable sweetness and love.

"See!" cried Keptah, and Lucanus started. Keptah was pointing to the sky. The great and lovely Star was moving eastwards, inflexibly, as if with purpose. Lucanus watched, awe-struck. The soft pink of dawn lay below it like a lake, and it cast its beams upon it so that it sparkled. Keptah was weeping. "The chosen have been chosen," he said, under his breath. "They are on their way. And I was not chosen."

They watched until the Star fell slowly into the rosy sea of morning and was lost to them, and they were desolated.

"It is gone," mourned Lucanus.

"No," said Keptah, wiping his eyes with his sleeve, "never shall it be lost, never to the end of time." He looked at the cross in his palm and thought, And this shall be spat upon, and despised, ignored and ridiculed, derided and blasphemed, but never shall it be forgotten, never explained away, never vanishing, despite the rage of races yet unborn, despite war and death and agony and blood and the darkness and fire of the last days, and the last senseless and despairing fury of men.

He turned to Lucanus, and for a moment felt envy. Blessed are you, child, he said in himself. And then he thought, Blessed am I that I am to teach you.

The cold austerity returned to Keptah's face. The translucent dawn, the color of a poppy, stood behind the great trees and the palms clattered freshly in the morning wind. Keptah said:

"Rubria is afflicted by the white sickness and shall never see womanhood. Hark! Do not cry out in so loud a voice, and do not be so stricken. Why do you weep? Life is not so fair a thing for the multitudes of us. We are born darkly, we live darkly, and we die darkly, and at the end we depart across the same threshold by which we entered. But what I have told you must not be told to the tribune, Diodorus, lest his heart break before its season."

Lucanus covered his face with his hands, and Keptah shook his head in compassion. To the young death is impossible, death is the supreme and unbelievable horror. He looked at the pearly sky, where the Star had stood, and he sighed.

"You must tell me where you found the herbs which brought release from pain for the Lady Rubria."

"I found them in the fields, and beside the brooks, and I knew that they were good, Keptah." The boy's voice was only a whisper of fear.

"They are good. You must find more of them, to save her from her suffering, and I will powder and dry them and distill the essence from them, for they are precious."

He stood up, tall and bony and remote, and Lucanus stood

up with him. "It is morning," said Keptah. "And your mother will be seeking you. Go, boy, and do not speak of what I have told you, for if you do I shall teach you nothing more."

Chapter Four

"Well, now, you are free," said Diodorus testily, after he and Keptah had returned from visiting the praetor in Antioch. "But I am not bound to give you that large sum of gold until you are forty-five. That part of the promise to my father I shall keep."

The day had been hot, the city particularly riotous and too colorful for the moral Roman. He sat now in his white marble hall and sulkily sipped at a goblet of cold wine and surlily sucked ripe figs which he lifted from the silver dish at his side. "Bah, this resinous Greek wine!" he exclaimed. He was in a bad temper. "I still believe you took advantage of a weak moment and imposed upon me. But let it go, let it go, you sly rascal! I am injured enough at the amount you set as your stipend. You will soon be as rich as one of the Levantines in the bazaar, and no doubt will set up your own establishment and buy your own slaves, and I will have to beg you indulgence to minister to my own house."

Keptah concealed a smile. He stood before Diodorus and regarded him with dark humor. "Master," he said, "I shall forever be grateful to you, and at your call, and where you go I shall go, and my life is still yours, at your command."

"Nice words," muttered Diodorus. His irate eyes sparkled upon his freedman with wrath. But he said, "I suppose the occasion calls for a celebration. May Hades swallow you! Beyond, on that table, is another goblet. If I may command, as you say, I command you to partake of that wine with me, and you may have a fig or two."

"Master, I prefer the Roman wines, and I beg you to relieve me of the necessity to drink the Greek."

Diodorus cursed under his breath, but he was slightly mollified. He glared at the wine in his goblet. "It is indeed wretched stuff," he said. "I respect your taste. But the next ship will have good wines, and," he added sarcastically, "I trust you will permit me to send a few bottles to your quarters for your delectation."

He clattered his ironshod sandals on the snowy floor and

peered at Keptah from under his bushy eyebrows. "Have a fig," he said.

Keptah bent his long body gracefully and took one of the fruit. Morosely Diodorus stuffed another in his mouth. "By Pollux, that is a detestable city," he said. "A mound of offal washed up from every gutter in the world. If I did not have so great a sense of duty I should ask to be relieved. But who else could deal as well with that crawling mass of maggots?"

"No one but you, noble Diodorus."

Diodorus peered at him again, suspiciously. "There is such an oil in your voice. It flows and gleams, and it stings. Acid mixed with honey."

"I am sorry I do not please you, Master." Keptah smiled again.

"You could please Pluto no less," said Diodorus, still smarting.

He took another fig, and sucked his fingers. "I shall order a sesterce to be given to each slave in your honor. What an arrogant dog you are, for all your pretense of humility! There is no one so wise as you, in your own opinion."

Keptah retained his dignity for all his impulse to laugh.

"Doubtless you will give yourself even more airs than usual, but I warn you not to play such a trick as you did on those poor slaves again."

Keptah studied him. Should he tell Diodorus the truth, that he had not in truth hypnotized the slaves, but only the tribune? He decided against it. Diodorus would never forgive him. He bowed and said, "I promise you, Master, that I shall play no more tricks. And now, if you will dismiss me, I must go to the Lady Rubria."

Diodorus' face cleared. "Ah, she is much better, is she not? She can now leave her bed, and there is a faint color, not of fever but of health, in her face. When do you consider she will be cured?"

Keptah hesitated. "I think, Master, that in another few days she may leave the house for the garden, and in another fourteen days she may resume her studies. With the tutor who will also teach Lucanus, son of Aeneas. And after those lessons it is understood that he will study with me?"

"For an extra stipend?" demanded Diodorus, angry again.

"No, Master, I shall teach him all I know in gratitude to you."

Diodorus growled, and watched the elongated shadow of

his freedman flow across the marble wall as Keptah glided between it and the sun which poured through the short colonnade at the right. "I am too easy," said Diodorus, after a pull at the goblet of resinous wine. "I treat my freedmen as equals and my slaves as freedmen. No wonder they do not respect me. I must flick the whip more regularly, and bring a little military discipline into this house." But he knew in his heart that he was incapable of being brutal and unjust, just as his virtuous fathers has been so incapable, and had respected the lives and the persons of even the humblest men. Diodorus began to brood on modern Rome again, and made a face.

The armchair generals who could direct, petulantly, the compaigns of hardened commanders in distant fields, and devise tactics and strategies as if they knew anything about them! The soft pale senators in their molded togas, buying and selling in their stock exchange, after a long morning in the baths recovering from a night of debauchery, and partially restored by skilled slaves with lubricated hands who had massaged their flabby muscles! Buying and selling, the fatted dogs, what other men had given their lives to obtain for Rome, and wafting perfumed kerchiefs in their faces as they languidly bargained and bid and outsmarted each other, and in between bids related the latest obscene gossip of the city! Their whorish women, their concubines, their depraved wives who bore the noblest names in Rome and committed adultery as if it were a fashionable pastime—which it was. The parasites, the Augustales, who moved in and out of the Palatine, as aristocratic as statues, with rottenness in their bodies and harpies in their minds, and treachery and murder in their crafty souls! The golden litters, the pampered boy slaves kept for shameful purposes, the rapine and licentiousness of a once disciplined, frugal, modest and heroic society, the slow disappearance of a sound middle class, a disappearance deliberately designed! The shining city, the mistress of the world—become a sewer of corruption, treason, greed, plotting, pleasure and decay, a stench of foulness from which wafted the fevers and madness and disease which were polluting the farthest reaches of the Empire!

And the Roman mobs of many races! Even Julius Caesar had feared them, with reason, and had cowered before them, and had flattered them and placated them. The volatile, unstable, many-tongued, bloodthirsty, heartless, ravenous

Roman mobs! Where once there had lived a sober and thrifty citizenry, proud of their founding fathers, jealous of their Republic, finding their full expression of being in work and family and their gods, and in their quiet homes and the shadows of their trees, there now lived a motley and rapacious rabble, quick to acclaim, quick to murder, quick to quarrel and as senselessly quick to approve, crowded in storied cesspools of houses, loathing work and preferring to beg and everlastingly calling upon the State to support them, fawning on vile politicians who catered to them and threatening the few honest men who opposed them for the good of Rome, and even for their own good; endlessly demanding bread and circuses, seeking mean pleasures, adoring mindless gladiators and worshiping the newest racer or actor, or discus thrower as if he were the greatest of men; devouring, in their idleness, the crushing taxes imposed on worthier men for their support, when the world would have well been rid of them by starvation or pestilence—ah, the Roman mobs, the accursed mobs, fit masters and slaves of their patrons, their politicians, the gatherers of their votes!

No wonder there were now so few sound artisans, merchants, workers, and builders in Rome. The monstrous government sucked in the fruit of their labors in the form of taxes for an idle and screaming and devouring State-supported rabble. What mattered it to the slavering, bulging-eyed, openmouthed man on the street that he had destroyed the heroic splendor of Rome, had defamed its gods, and had thrown dung on the statues of the fathers? Could he not, now, by howling and by marking on walls at night, get his bowl refilled with more beans and more soup and more bread, or watch bloodier spectacles in the Circus Maximus? The masters were worthy of their slaves, and the slaves their masters.

There was the aging soldier, Caesar Augustus, in the Palatine, a stern and moral man. But what could he do, surrounded as he was by corrupt senators and statesmen elected by an even more corrupt rabble? Diodorus suddenly remembered a letter he had received a few weeks ago from one of his friends, carefully sealed and sent by trusted messenger. (How long had it been since honest men had been forced to seal their letters from the prying and vindictive eyes of spies employed by the State?) The friend had written, "I fear me that Rome is dying. I, like you, dear friend, have believed too long, and with prayer, that the old virtues still flourished somewhere in the city, like excellent and beautiful flowers in a forgotten garden, preparing seed which would grow in the waste places once more. But the garden does not exist! It has been trampled into the mud by the mobs, and by their craven masters, who live on the favor of the mobs."

Diodorus, sunken in a despondency and hopelessness he had never experienced before, thought of the gods of Rome. Once they had personified honorable labor, love, the sacredness of home and private property, freedom, grace, kindliness, the military qualities of devotion and duty, the cherishing of children, the respect between those who employed and those who were employed, patriotism, obedience to divine and immutable decrees, and the pride and dignity of the individual. But what had Rome done to these gods? She had made of them venal and unspeakable replicas of herself in all her aspects.

Diodorus flung his goblet from him, and it crashed against the marble wall. He leaped to his feet, and walked up and down the lonely white floors, his sandals hammering on them like the frantic beat of a drum.

He remembered the ending of his friend's letter: "The only hope for Rome is a return to religious values . . ."

Not a return to the befouled gods——But to what? To Whom? The "Unknown God" of the Greeks? But who was He, and where was He? He, the Incorruptible, the Father, the Loving One, the Just? Why was He silent, if He existed? Why did He not speak to mankind, and reorder the reeking world and bring peace to the peaceless, hope to the hopeless, love to the loveless, fullness to those starving for righteousness? If He lived, this was the hour when He should manifest Himself, before the world smothered in its own dunghill, or died by its own sword.

Diodorus was filled with a wild hunger and impatience. He halted between two white columns, spreading his legs sturdily apart and standing as a soldier stands, and he looked at the sunset sky above the trees and the palms. His pain was stilled for a moment. Never had he seen so glorious a sunset before, so full of rosy light and golden lances, so brilliant and pure that the boughs of the trees, the shivering fronds of the palms, the columns of the house beamed with a radiance of their own and reflected the colors of the sky. Gentleness and majesty radiated from it, as if some mighty Voice had bestowed a benediction to all the world, as if a mighty Hand had been lifted in tenderness and love. The fierce face of Diodorus softened, became almost childlike. His disciplined mind told him that this was only an unusually resplendent sunset; his soul told him that a Word had been spoken.

Then he remembered the wild rumors in Antioch that day. A particularly vivid Star, brighter than the brightest moon, had appeared in the heavens the night before, and had been seen by many, even during the most shameful hours of the Saturnalia. There had been much fright, and mobs had run blindly through the streets in their terror, their gay garments streaming about them. But Diodorus had been informed by a priest in the temple of Mercury that it was only a comet, or a meteor, and he had spoken indulgently. "But where were you that you did not see it yourself?" Diodorus had asked. The priest had replied, "I was asleep, noble Tribune."

Diodorus searched for the Star where he had been told it had stood. There was nothing there now but the evening star, twinkling mildly. But all at once he believed there had in truth been a Star. His heart lifted on a powerful wave of joy, and he was comforted, though he could not explain it.

The night-blooming jasmine awakened in a wave of fragrance, and Diodorus breathed it in as if it were incense. He felt humble and at peace, and full of strength. "I can do what I can do, live by the values and the truths I have been taught, by the virtues and the justice I know, and surely He will remember me though all the world goes mad."

He walked between the columns along the marble path towards the women's quarters. Then he encountered two of his officers in the courtyard, youths he loved for he had trained them himself, and he trusted them because of their honest faces, their candid eyes, their devotion to him and the ancient virtues. They came to attention when they saw him, and saluted smartly, and he paused, trying to frown at them, but loving them too much.

"How now, lads, why have you not returned to Antioch?" he asked, roughly. He never kept a bodyguard about his home, as other military commanders did, for he trusted in his own right arm and disliked too great a show of militarism.

"Noble Diodorus, we have heard alarming rumors in Antioch this day," one of the soldiers replied. "Some of the rabble scream that the Star they pretended to believe they saw last night indicated the fall of Rome and the anger of the gods against all Romans. It is said the Star moved eastwards, away from the Imperial City, and this indicates, they declare, that Rome is about to fall. And when an empire falls, they reason, it is time for a subjugated country to rise and smite."

"At ease, Sextus," said Diodorus, and he laid his hand on the shoulder of the young captain. "Come, come, you are not afraid for me? Is that why you both disobeyed my express orders? I tell you, if Rome falls it will be because of the failure of disciplined minds."

"Nevertheless, noble Tribune, we should prefer to remain on guard for some nights," said young Sextus, stubbornly, but his devoted eyes pleaded.

Diodorus paused. He looked from Sextus to the centurion, and he saw their obstinacy. If I command their return to Antioch, he thought, they will lurk in the gardens, out of my sight, sleepless and foodless, and that will be a hardship on them. Is that a just return for what they consider their duty? He said, moved, "Well, then, you ox-minded young fools, remain for as long as you wish. I shall order quarters for you, and food, and you shall march about the house and guard the doors to your simple content. Not that I am not displeased by you," he added, hastily, for the sake of discipline. "When I am at home I am not a soldier. I am only a peaceful householder."

He reached the women's quarters and was about to order a slave to summon the Lady Aurelia when Aurelia herself appeared, accompanied by Iris. They were laughing softly together as sisters laugh, and Aurelia's hand rested lightly on the arm of Iris, who had never appeared so beautiful to Diodorus. It was at her he looked, and as if there had been something terribly revealing in his startled eyes, for her lovely face clouded and her own blue eyes misted as if with sorrow and distress.

To the "old Roman" Aurelia the wife of a freedman was not a contemptible object, though formerly a slave. If worthy of love, she received love; if worthy of respect, she received respect. Aurelia and Iris were tender friends. But Diodorus had not known that Iris often visited his house in his absence. Aurelia was surprised and happy to see him.

"Am I late, Diodorus?" she asked, coming to him and taking his hand. "The sun is not completely set."

"It is I who am early," he replied. He wanted to kiss her red-brown cheek, to press his mouth against her full lips. She was a refuge from something which threatened him.

Aurelia began to chatter gaily, in her usual fashion. "Iris has been helping me weave the winter linens and woolens. Look at my fingers! They are calloused, almost bleeding." She spread her hands before his eyes, and laughed. Her hair, dressed informally, hung over her shoulders in two shining black braids far below her waist, and there was a gleaming moisture on her face and about her temples, and little tendrils of youthful darkness curled on her brow and cheeks.

Iris stood apart, as unapproachable as a marble nymph, her golden hair arranged in the Grecian manner, the lengths of it bound about her head with white ribbons. Such ribbons also bound her slender waist, above which rose her perfect bosom. The sunset, falling upon her, gave her flesh a translucence, and Diodorus thought, Not Diana, but the Greek Artemis. The arms and throat and cheek of Iris became like a rose, and the composure of her quiet face, the gentle dignity of her figure were those of a dreaming statue engrossed in far thoughts unconnected with humanity. This aspect made Diodorus think, for all the presence of his wife, I am like Acteon, and surely it is forbidden to look upon her!

Aurelia saw the fixity on Diodorus' face as he looked at the young freedwoman, and Aurelia sighed. It was then Iris, after a deep bow, moved away, and her tall and shapely figure was lost in the shadows of the dreaming trees. Diodorus watched her disappear. Aurelia took his arm affectionately. There was no jealousy in her heart. She loved Diodorus too much and she knew Iris' virtue too well. Too, it was permitted for a man to look upon a woman, and his wife should have too much dignity and self-respect for annoyance.

They went together to their house, Diodorus complaining of his bodyguard. But Aurelia was relieved. She had heard rumors from the slaves about the feeling in Antioch. "We must arrange for the quarters and the food for these devoted soldiers," she said, placidly. It delighted her that others loved Diodorus also. She wished to show her husband the miraculous improvement in their child, Rubria, and though Diodorus kept up his questions about the girl's condition Aurelia only smiled and nodded mysteriously. Diodorus, followed by Aurelia, clattered up the broad stone stairway and went into Rubria's room. The nurse was there, and Keptah and the boy, Lucanus, but Diodorus saw only his daughter, sitting up in her bed and laughing. There was a freshening color in her childish cheeks, and her dark eyes were dancing, and her long black hair was tied back from her face with a golden ribbon. Her small hands held a puppet made by Lucanus, brilliantly and gaily colored, and its wooden arms and legs were flexible. The girl danced the doll on her knees and made it perform grotesque figures. Lucanus was watching her with a stern and anxious smile, and Keptah mixed a potion in a cup of wine.

Seeing Diodorus, Rubria sat up straighter in her bed and cried excitedly, "See, is not this a marvel, Father! Lucanus brought it to me today!" She kissed Diodorus hastily, wishing to return to her play, and he scrutinized her lovingly. Ah, the little one had been snatched from the very edge of the Elysian fields themselves. She would live, and delight the hearts of her parents with a good marriage later, and grand-children to dandle on their knees. But we must return to Rome, thought the tribune. This is an evil climate for a child. He would take his family to his farm in the provinces near Rome, where the air was excellent and dry, and he would be a husbandman and forget that rotted city, and rejoice in his family, and there might be sons.

He looked at Lucanus. The boy caught his glance and said diffidently, but with pride, "Rubria sat in her chair for two hours today, Master." Then he laughed with the young girl at the antics of the puppet and they were children together. For the first time Diodorus thought of the fees at the University of Alexandria without a twinge in his purse. The boy would eventually replace Keptah when the latter became too old. He would remain with the family who loved him, wherever they went. As Lucanus was freeborn he would be able to marry into a sound and virtuous family, the family of a prosperous merchant, perhaps, a Roman family. Lucanus and his wife (who would be chosen by Diodorus with an eye to her dowry and morals and fitness to become a healthy mother) would have a home on the farm. The paternalistic soul of the Roman tribune expanded. In his old age there would be the laughter and voices of children about him, and the sight of fields and forests, and the pleasant lowing of cattle, and fruit trees and shade, and the rushing cries of a river.

Happier than he had been for a long time, Diodorus ordered Lucanus to remain for dinner, and he told the nurse to send a slave to the home of Aeneas informing the boy's parents that he would be home later. Lucanus blushed; he had never before been asked to eat at the table with the tribune and his lady, but he did not demur. Rubria immediately demanded that she be carried downstairs, and Keptah nodded at his master's glance of interrogation. Diodorus carried the child in his arms, and his heart was so light that he did not feel her fragility. He was conscious only that she still laughed and had nestled her head on his breast.

The dining hall was of colored tiles, and there was a Persian rug on the floor. The windows looked out upon the palms, whose tips were dyed scarlet from the last beams of the sun; jasmine and the fragrance of roses filled the warm air. It was so still and serene that the voice of the river could be heard. Keptah, in his new honors as a freedman and a valued physician, sat far at the foot of the table, but Lucanus sat next to Rubria. He is as my son, thought Diodorus, suddenly, and he loved Lucanus' face, so like the face of Iris, and he marked the nobility of his forehead. After all, he thought, in extenuation of his sudden democracy and the violation of the proprieties, we Romans have always conceded the superiorities of the Greeks, including the philosophers. This boy doubtless had patrician ancestors, probably much older than mine.

The meal to Lucanus was a surprise, for his father's table was much more lavish and the wines were better. There was a dish of cold boiled lamb, not too expertly seasoned, and too oily. There was a plate of coarse bread, and several of the less distinguished cheeses, and the vinegar and oil on the radishes and cucumbers were of the poorer variety, due to Diodorus' thrift and lack of appreciation. Lucanus saw that the tribune and Aurelia had no palate; they were, in truth, simple and hearty people, preferring simple and hearty food, which they ate with relish. Lucanus longed for his father's table; Iris could so season and spice a dish of humble beans that it became an epicurean delight.

Keptah, admitted to the tribune's table for the first time, wrinkled his dark and aquiline nose. This was food for pigs, not men. Diodorus gnawed on a small bone; there was a pungent odor of garlic. A civilized man can be distinguished from a plebe by the amount of garlic in his food, thought Keptah, confining himself to a bit of cheese, a piece of bread, and one of the less revolting wines. Nevertheless, he felt considerable affection for Diodorus.

Rubria suddenly tired, and her vivacious young voice became slower. Diodorus carried her upstairs to her chamber. The slaves were lighting lamps all over the house. Lucanus accompanied the tribune; Rubria sighed with satisfaction on her pillows. She held out her hand to Lucanus, who took it, then gently kissed her fingers. Rubria closed her eyes and smiled, and immediately fell asleep.

It was dark now, and Diodorus informed Lucanus that he, rather than a slave, would take him to his home. On the way, through the quickly gathering night, Diodorus talked learnedly of Alexandria, which he had seen. The medical college alone was vast; the library was one of the wonders of the world. Lucanus should feel properly humble at the thought of being a student there. Lucanus nodded gravely.

"It will cost a great deal of money," said Diodorus, cautiously, trying to see the face of Lucanus in the frail light of the stars and the rising moon. "I am not a rich man, Lucanus. Your fees will be paid, but you must be frugal."

Lucanus repressed a smile. "Master," he said, "I would be grateful for a pallet on the floor of a stable, and my needs will be small. In return I pray that you will permit me to serve you. Or, if not, I shall repay you from my fees as a physician."

Diodorus was pleased at this austerity. He had taken Lucanus' hand, and now he squeezed it. "Nonsense, nonsense," he said, largely. "I wish only that you will appreciate your advantages. Of course, after your graduation, you will remain with the family. Keptah will be older; too, he will have a generous stipend of his own, left to him by my father, Priscus. What a strange and elliptical man!"

Behind them, unknown even to the keen-eared soldier, a young centurion was following, keeping to the trees at a distance, his sword drawn in protection. Finally Aeneas' house came into view and Lucanus begged Diodorus to come no farther. He then ran to the house, stopping for a moment to wave shyly to his benefactor, who saluted indulgently in reply. Ah, yes, thought Diodorus, this is the son I should have had. He was sorrowful for a moment.

He lingered. Lucanus raced into the house. Now all was silence, except for the shrill cries of crickets, the mysterious rustle of palms and trees. Diodorus did not know why he lingered, and why there was a sudden desolation in his breast. The single lamp in the house of Aeneas flickered. Then the door opened and Iris emerged, alone. The moonlight gave an aspect of flowing silver to her white and simple dress. She walked like a goddess to a tree and leaned against it, unaware of the presence of Diodorus nearby. Her golden hair flowed loosely over her shoulders.

Diodorus held his breath. He could barely see the girl's profile in the argent and diffused light. But he saw that she was looking in the direction of his house, and she was as still as a statue. The hand on the tree, and the bare arm extending from it were perfect and slender, and whiter and more radiant than the moon itself.

There was a wild thundering in Diodorus' ears. Moment by moment passed, and Iris still gazed in the direction of the tribune's house. She was so still that Diodorus thought of an apparition. Then he became aware of the sound of soft weeping, and started. Iris was covering her face with her hands.

Diodorus took a single step in her direction, then stopped. He wanted to cry out and could not. He had only to go to Iris and take her in his arms, and there was a terrible craving in his flesh. He could feel her body against his, and his hands in the wonderful hair, hair which he had played with so carelessly as a boy. It would be like yellow silk, and scented with fresh flowers.

But he did not move, for all the passionate hunger that made his arms tremble and his heart pound eagerly. He dropped his head, and soundlessly, backward step after backward step, he retired into the trees and went away.

Chapter Five

The Greek teacher of Rubria and Lucanus was a small and active young man, with a mischievous dark face and antic manners. He was a slave, and a valued one, for he had much learning. He had cost Diodorus five hundred gold pieces, an extravagance that only occasionally gave the tribune a twinge. His name was Cusa, which to Diodorus was heathenish, and neither Greek nor Roman, and he had the features of a youthful satyr, and a peppery tongue of much impudence. He feared nothing and nobody, except Diodorus, and though he was playful and not above tricks and horseplay at times with the other slaves, he had a brilliant mind and a gift for poesy. Moreover, he hated illiteracy and stupidity, and attacked them in foul language which made Diodorus laugh even when he chided his slave. "By all the gods," he had said once, "I thought, as a soldier, that I knew all the words, but your inventiveness, my Cusa, has improved upon them."

Cusa resented Lucanus from the beginning. As an ugly young man he envied the boy's Apollonian beauty. As a slave he considered Lucanus, the son of former slaves, an imposition on him. But the master was a capricious man, and his orders must be obeyed. Nevertheless, Cusa provided himself with a small whip which he used on Lucanus more often than necessary when, in the opinion of Cusa, the boy was displaying adamant stupidity. He did this out of sight of Rubria and anyone else who could report him to the tribune, and Lucanus, though indignant and smarting, did not complain. But one day, he promised himself, he would take that whip and lay it about Cusa's shoulders with good effect. Cusa would see that gleam in the proud boy's blue eyes and grin. Oi, he would think, I may be small of stature, and you may be half a head taller than I, my fine ignoramus, in spite of your age, but I am master here!

The schoolroom was small, with a single table and three chairs, and a case full of rolled books. Cusa kept the door open, and sometimes, in a gracious mood and in deference to Rubria, he would bring his pupils out upon the grass and permit them to sit upon it, Rubria on a cushion to protect her from dampness. "The philosophers wandered through colonnades," he would say, "and would recline upon stones." He would direct Lucanus to perch upon a particularly uncomfortable stone, and would say, slyly, "We must learn to be a Stoic; it is excellent for the soul and a discipline for the mind." As he was not a Stoic he would spread his crimson wool mantle on the grass for his own buttocks.

Once he said to Diodorus, "Master, I pray you will not be disappointed. This boy may be handsome, but he has a head like the marble it resembles."

"Teach it to be flesh and brain then," said Diodorus, understanding Cusa. "I warn you. You are to prepare him for Alexandria, and as fast as possible."

This made Cusa dislike Lucanus more than ever. Ah, one needs only to have yellow hair and a white skin to attract a benefactor, Cusa would say to himself, maliciously. You, my good Cusa, look like a camel, or an ape, and that is your misfortune.

Nevertheless, over the long moments and hours and then weeks and months, and then two years, he came unwillingly to a respect for the quickness with which Lucanus learned, and his thoughtfulness, and his almost miraculous grasp of knowledge. The boy had a devouring mind; facts and poetry and languages were seized upon, assimilated and made his own. He apparently forgot nothing. His recitations were marvels. He had long ago left little Rubria far behind, and she would gaze at him admiringly and applaud him. As a girl she was not expected to have an unusual amount of intelligence; her father wished her to acquire only enough learning to enjoy poetry and the less taxing books. Diodorus, hearing reports from his daughter about Lucanus' progress, said, "Ah, now, that knave of a Cusa is beginning to earn the money I expended for him."

Reluctantly Cusa began to take a pleasure in teaching Lucanus. The boy kept him to his wits, and the hours of teaching no longer bored him, as they had bored him when Rubria was his only pupil. He tried to reach Lucanus' limits by assigning him intricate lessons, far in advance of his age, but Lucanus was always one step ahead, and with ease. Cusa, a true teacher, had a secret and annoyed pride in this student, though his abusive tongue and sarcasm betrayed no part of it. "You will make a fine bookkeeper," he said, often. "But what fantasy is it that persuades you you will ever be a physician? You know nothing except by rote, and I weep for your future patients." The whip was always ready.

Within two years Lucanus could discuss the major poets and philosophers with Diodorus, to the tribune's gratification. Diodorus opened his precious library to the boy, and Lucanus studied there after the hours with his tutor, and only twilight would drive him away. There were also the hours with Keptah, and these Lucanus found the most rewarding of all.

The two never spoke of Rubria's inevitable death when together. It was true that her young body was becoming rounded with the sweetness of approaching puberty, though she was two years younger than Lucanus. It was also true that her pretty dark face was fuller, and alive with the joy of being young and cherished, and that her appetite had improved, and that she could, for brief intervals, play vigorously with Lucanus. But her mortal illness, Keptah knew, was only in abeyance. For Lucanus it was enough to be with Rubria, to touch her small warm hand, to exchange amused glances at Cusa's expense, to run over the grass and to pick a huge and humid red flower to thrust over Rubria's ear. They tossed balls to each other, laughing and shouting. They imitated the calls of birds, and gazed with awe and love at the small wild things in the forest. There were moments when they were so overwhelmed with inexpressible joy that they could only stand and look into each other's eyes with beaming enjoyment and shyness. Day by day Rubria became more beautiful, more beloved of her playmate. Sometimes he thought, Surely God will not take away this treasure from me, this dear one, this sister, this heart of my heart. Without Rubria there would be no songs, no delight in the blood, no tenderness, no reason for being. He played with Rubria's hair, as Diodorus had played with the hair of Iris, and he rejoiced in its silken lengths so permeated with freshness and the poignant scent of life. Sometimes, speechlessly, they embraced each other, and the sensation of Rubria's cheek pressed to the cheek of Lucanus overcame him to a prayfulness of bliss. He would hold her in his arms and feel that he held the world, and all beauty and softness.

Seeing, Keptah no longer warned Lucanus of the inevitable desolation. He believed himself in the presence of something holy and alight with innocence. There were times when he mourned and questioned. Did God give only to take away? Did He rob for the purpose alone of turning the human heart to Him?

Cusa came upon Lucanus and Rubria one afternoon after they had been released from the schoolroom. Lucanus was weaving a garland of grass and flowers for Rubria, and she was watching with intent pleasure. A tame bird stood on her shoulder, all scarlet and jade, and it twittered in her ear, and occasionally she turned and kissed its yellow beak. The teacher, usually ready with a caustic phrase referring to a waste of time, was abruptly silent. He watched from a distance, and was overcome with melancholy. The gods jealously resented youth and beauty and joy among mortals. Here was a boy like Phoebus, god of the sun, and a maiden of shy virginity and mildness. Cusa, weighted with foreboding, turned away. A Skeptic, he nevertheless prayed that night that the gods would not be envious of this loveliness, this artless dulcitude. The next morning he said to Lucanus crossly, "If you are to be a scholar and a physician, I advise you not to cavort with young girls so carelessly. That is for the plebe and the vulgar. Attention! We take up Socrates' dialogues again this morning. You are singularly obtuse about them, boy."

This was an exquisite summer. All was serenity. Diodorus' request for a transfer to Rome and his farm had not as yet been answered, but he had hope. He sedulously cultivated the hours with his wife, and some ease came to him. He

avoided Aeneas as much as possible, and never again escorted
Lucanus back to his home. Iris lingered in his mind as the
memory of morning, but he sternly kept himself from en-
counters with her. She was a dream, to be remembered as a
dream. If a man could not strictly control his thoughts, then
he was not a man, and particularly he was not a Roman. Life
demanded discipline of both the mind and the body, and
especially of the heart. He received books from Rome, and
immersed himself in them. They had a special meaning for
him now, these philosophies of ascetic men full of wisdom
who sounded the note of patience and fortitude as men strike
solemn and sonorous bells. Drowned in eternal philosophy,
he forgot the corruption of Rome and the fetid and clamorous present. Let the whole world fall. Truth was immortal. " 'The stupid people run to Rome,' " he would quote
to himself, " 'but man finds refuge in verities.' "

Rubria achieved puberty, and Aurelia rejoiced. There
were momentous sacrifices in Aurelia's favorite temple, the
temple of Juno. She commended her daughter to the wife of
Jupiter, the guardian of hearth and family and children.
She would look into Rubria's luminous eyes, so pure and
innocent, and would dream of grandchildren. There were
still Roman families who had staunch young sons, devoted
to the gods and to their country. One could have grandsons,
if one did not have sons. She bound up Rubria's hair in ribbons and counseled her in modesty. She taught her the arts
of the household and the kitchen, and how a woman can
best please her husband. She wrote to friends in Rome, and
commented on the growing beauty and maturity of Rubria.

"You are hurrying matters," said Diodorus one evening.
"The girl is only eleven years old." He was jealous of any
youth who would take his daughter from him and enjoy her
laughter and sweetness, and cleave her to him, and make her
forget her father.

Aurelia, musing over a wax-coated tablet on which she
was writing to a beloved friend, the mother of stalwart sons,
said abstractedly, "What will be our daughter's dowry?
Diodorus, forget your banks, I pray. We must consider
Rubria's future. She will be ready for marriage in less than
three years."

Three years. I am an old man, thought Diodorus resentfully. He said, "You are hurrying matters. The chit romps
in the grass, and she is still a child." That night he cradled
Rubria in his arms and sang her to sleep, and then sat

watching the shadows her eyelashes cast on her pink cheek
and the sweet curve of her mouth. My darling, he thought,
my heart's own darling. Surely never was there a maiden
so lovely and so innocent, so warm of flesh and so dear. A
Hebe born to serve the very gods themselves. He turned
away from the thought with a sudden surge of terror. Let the
gods get themselves other servitors! They were gods, and
had multitudes, but he had only his daughter.

One afternoon Keptah came into the schoolroom and said
briefly to Lucanus, "Come."

Cusa frowned at him and said, "The boy is studying
Plato at this moment."

"Come," said Keptah to Lucanus, ignoring the tutor, who,
after all, was only a slave. And Lucanus, without a word,
rose and left the room with the physician. But, on the
threshold, he paused to bow to Cusa, understanding that
slaves and servants are very sensitive.

Diodorus had put an ass in the service of his freedman,
Keptah. "A scurvy animal," said the physician, with some
vexation. "But I have heard that asses are frequently wiser
than men and have a sense of humor." He borrowed an ass
for Lucanus. "Today we go to Antioch," he said. "Ah, here
is your animal from the stables. It is fortunate that we do not
demand horses, for we should be disappointed. For a Roman
our master is not impressed by equine flesh, and all his creatures are flea-bitten. What is money for but to enjoy? But
there are some men who enjoy the thought of their coffers
more than the thought of profiting by them."

His ill nature made Lucanus smile. The asses were plump
and well curried, and eyed the physician and the boy arro-
grantly. "They are not impressed by us, either," said Keptah,
mounting. His long and bony legs dangled almost to the
ground, and Lucanus laughed. He sprang on the ass assigned to him, and caressed the animal's neck, and the ass
closed his eyes in boredom. Now they began to trot on the
road to Antioch, and Keptah was unusually silent. He had
drawn his hood over his head less in an effort to protect
himself from the raging sun than to retire into solitude.
Sometimes Lucanus whipped his ass to a gallop, rejoicing
in the sun and the wind, which did not sear his fair skin.
His golden hair blew behind him, and he sang. He did not
know where Keptah was taking him but it was enough to be
free and in the light, and to be young, and to see the masses

of blue, crimson and scarlet wild flowers along the narrow road. He had his dreams.

Antioch, as always, was a boisterous welter of color and heat and stenches. Now fleets from the Orient and other strange lands stood at anchor in the blazing blue harbor, their white and red sails throbbing against the sky. The narrow, rising, and curving streets rang to alien voices, and every doorway, every cobbled passage and alley, showed voracious dark faces, and echoed to profane, shouting and laughing exclamations. The shops teemed. The cries of the merchants were deafening. Camels complained, chariots roared by, asses whinnied, and there was a smell of hot broiled meat and wine and sourness and spices in heated pockets along the streets. Jews, Syrians, Sicilians, Greeks, Egyptians, Thessalonians, Negroes, Gauls and assorted barbarians in strange costumes walked or bustled along each street, raising clouds of sharp white dust in the sunlight. There were contentious arguments and brawls here and there, and pale bright buildings jutted in the air. Children played in the very passage of vehicles and animals, and cursed the riders, or begged for alms, their impertinent faces brown with the sun.

Lucanus loved the glaring city, and was excited by it. He saw men and women entering small and pillared temples, doves and young kids in their arms. He saw the bright banners, and smelled the warmth of hay and the pungency of dust. He hoped that Keptah would take him to the physician's favorite wineshop, but Keptah passed it without a glance. Roman soldiers flirted with girls in bright garments; they were particularly attracted to maidens with veils. They chaffed the young females, and dark eyes flashed in the sunlight. The din was a palpable presence in the hot and spicy air, which had an overtone of dung and garlic in it. Diodorus spoke of Rome, that Imperial City, but Lucanus thought that no city could have such odors and enticement. Women stood on balconies, and from within some of the houses came the twanging of lyres, and laughter, and then the scent of orange blossoms and roses from gardens behind high walls.

Keptah trotted along on his ass, withdrawn and secret, and, to Lucanus, a depressing presence in all this color. A group of sailors in loincloths, and with great golden rings in their ears, were quarreling on a corner, their blackened faces fierce and violent, their gestures vehement. Their strange voices, speaking in a tongue Lucanus did not recognize, clamored in the heat, and a knife glittered. Keptah moved along as if he were alone. Lucanus sighed. There was more to life than philosophy. Hot bodies pressed around his donkey, and there was an acridness of sweat everywhere. Dry palms, sifting with dust, scattered themselves along the streets. Peddlers, carrying trays of sweetmeats, blown with flies, shrilled their wares and ran after the boy and man on bare brown feet, and then, discomfited, cried curses upon them. Beggars sat against walls, wailing, rattling their cups, their beards tangled and filthy. Women offered flowers in baskets, and old men with staffs walked unseeingly through the welter as if they were no longer of this world. A group of goats being driven by a boy blocked passage momentarily, and the animals whimpered and skittered and danced. As always, Lucanus was enchanted. He laughed at an insolent monkey on a man's shoulders, and wanted to inspect a shop of parrots.

The streets became quieter and dimmer, and Lucanus was conscious of few walkers and fewer vehicles. Now the buildings, old and decrepit, had an air of gloom. The noises of the city faded. The howls of dogs diminished. Lucanus, subdued, trotted beside Keptah, and asked, "Where are we going? I have never been here before."

"Quiet," said Keptah, in a faint, hoarse voice from within his hood. "I have waited for a long time for a reply to a message, and it came only today."

The air was chillier here, the cobbled stones wet and glistening as though it had rained, the walls of the houses shut and somber. The hoofs of the asses raised echoes and astringent dust. A rill of gutter water ran over the stones, dark and slimy, and it made a throaty sound, and stank. Walls of dark stone rose on each side of the closed street, and no voices ran from them. But once or twice Lucanus heard the soft howling of unseen cats, and he thought of Isis, the hoary goddess of the Egyptians, and hidden rites, and the mysteries of the East. The boy shivered; the dewy sweat turned cold on his flesh and he wished he had brought a cloak.

Then, abruptly, Keptah reined in his gray ass and made a gesture to the boy. They had halted before a tall wall of basalt, black and blank. No window pierced its strong and forbidding emptiness. No sound of life sounded from behind its height. Only a small door stood in its repellent façade. Keptah dismounted, and dismally Lucanus followed. Keptah, not speaking, knocked on the door as if signaling. The rapping echoed from walled side to side. Keptah waited; then he knocked again. This time there was a rattling of chains, and the withdrawing of bolts. The door opened with a complaint of hinges. The aperture widened and an old man in a rough gray tunic stood there, an incredibly small one with a long white beard and the brightest brown eyes Lucanus had ever seen—the eyes of a smiling and wondering child. Keys clanked at the hempen girdle, and his feet were bare.

He spoke to Keptah in an incomprehensible tongue, quick and welcoming, and he bowed deeply. And all the time his eyes darted over Lucanus with curiosity. He opened the door wide, bowed again, and stepped aside.

Lucanus blinked, dazzled. Beyond the door lay a vast garden of silken grass, date palms, shining trees, fountains, and beds of roses and lilies, and all manner of other flowers. The garden basked in sunlight as if of another world. Clumps of willows blew like green cataracts in the softest and sweetest wind. The fountains sang and the trees answered. At some distance, in this brightness and perfume, stood a square building, low and radiant, made of white marble, and beyond it stood still another building of gray granite, with arched windows shuttered against the light, and as silent as a sepulcher.

Paths of yellow stone wound through the gardens, and marble benches were scattered here and there in clear dark shade, protected from the sun. Never had Lucanus seen such beauty and tranquillity, and yet there was an air of dignity and withdrawal in the gardens and about the buildings, and the silence was unbroken by a single voice, nor was there anyone visible in the grounds or about the marble edifice or the other building. The boy was astonished. He stood in bemusement as the door closed after him and Keptah, and he was not aware of the careful thrust of bolts and the clang of chains.

"Come," said Keptah, and Lucanus followed him over the soft grass. Birds of all colors peered down at him from gilded branches. The fountains murmured. The roses moved and exhaled warm fragrance. The lilies lifted their white chalices and breathed out their holy perfume, and bees hovered over them and thrust their golden bodies deeply into the cups. And then for the first time Lucanus was conscious of a sound he had missed before; it was a sound hardly perceptible by the ear, not song, not chanting, but a faint

combination of both. It was part of the brilliant air, part of
the fountains, part of the wind, and yet a human voice.

Keptah led Lucanus, in silence, across the grass and towards the square low building of marble, which had no windows and no porticoes. A bronze door carved with strange
figures glimmered in all that whiteness, and this opened.
"Enter," said Keptah. Lucanus, even in his bemusement, was
startled. No hand had opened the door; it had moved seemingly of itself, and with no creak of hinges. Lucanus stood on
the threshold and hesitated before entering. Keptah murmured, "Speak nothing; ask no questions. I will leave you
for a while." The door closed before his face and Lucanus
was alone.

Though there were no windows, and no open door, the
bare whiteness of the large room was suffused with a swimming and pearly light, which deepened, brightened, faded,
then brightened again. It was impossible to see the source of
the light, pulsing like a peaceful heart. It was one with a
spiciness like incense, which came from everywhere and nowhere. Lucanus sensed at once that he was in a temple, but
what kind of a temple he did not know, and for some inexplicable reason he began to tremble.

Then in the center of the room was the strangest thing of
all, not an altar, but something that struck a quick fear to the
soul of the boy. On a wide central platform of three low
white steps of marble stood the great symbol of the most infamous thing in the world, the symbol of the vilest criminality
and death. It was a huge Cross, seemingly made of transparent alabaster, and it towered almost to the flat ceiling of
smooth stone. Lucanus' fear changed to awe and amazement. The Cross soared alone, and there was nothing in the
temple but its simple and dreadful majesty, and no sound
but absolute silence.

The light pulsed and waned, and the Cross waited. But
Lucanus stood for a long time looking at it, his heart beating
loudly in his ears. A few times, a very few times, he had
seen a crucified man on one of the hills near Antioch, and he
had been moved to tears and a nameless anger. And then he
had seen the golden cross in Keptah's hand on the night of
the Star, over two years ago. He had almost forgotten.

Timidly, walking slowly so as not to disturb this sanctified
silence, and not to quicken the ebbing and flowing radiance,
he approached the Cross, and stood at the foot of the glistening shallow stairs looking up at it. Its mighty arms

stretched far above him. It had a waiting and unearthly
quality, cool and expectant. Its body was fixed and powerful,
yet airy as light. It appeared less than stone now, to the
boy, but something sentient and eternal, immovable in its
vastness, carved in grandeur.

Lucanus stood and looked at it, and could not turn aside.
There was nothing in him now but an unnamable anticipation. His throat throbbed. Without his volition his knees
bent and he knelt on the first step and clasped his hands,
never looking away from the Cross. It loomed over him, and
he felt some awful prescience in it, and yet it was as if the
arms hovered over him protectingly. Now the light in the
temple quickened, like the reflection of the moon on wide
wings.

There were no thoughts in Lucanus, no awareness of
flesh, only a deep wonderment and something like joy
touched with grief. He knelt for a long time, his blue gaze
lifted high to the Cross, his hands clasped.

He did not know at what moment the Cross began to
brighten, and at what moment the Cross itself began to ripple
with pale rosy shadows. It was as if his soul became aware
of it long before his conscious mind, and so he was not
alarmed. He was also dreamily aware of an unseen Presence, which was one with the Cross, one with the light, and
one with himself. The Presence was like a shaft of deeper
luminosity, and full of enormous masculine tenderness. Lucanus said aloud through pale lips, "The Unknown God."

During the past two years his youth and the abundance
of his life, his passionate enjoyment of knowledge, his ambitions, his dearest love for Rubria, his sense of belonging
to the world and to those who loved him, his dedication to
medicine and his engrossment with Keptah, the very joyousness and buoyancy of his age, and his leaping health
and delight in all things had obscured, made dim and illusory,
what he had known or felt as a child. Even the Unknown
God had become one of the Pantheon, and the aspects, tales,
and benevolences of goddesses had intrigued his young heart
with a tremendous fantasy of beauty. His days, for over two
years, lay like a colored and vivid river behind him and before him, full of promise. Cusa was a Skeptic, and Lucanus
had come to question things humorously, even the dreams
and mysteries he had known as a child. As if he knew,
Keptah himself had spoken less and less of the Unknown
God, and had confined himself to lessons in medicine. Some-

times his morose and withdrawn face had made Lucanus feel a sense of uneasy guilt.

And now in these moments his life became as a phantom, the life of a very young child, and he was again in the presence of the grand Miracle, which did not reproach him but only welcomed him. He did not understand the meaning of the Cross with his mind; only his heart understood and it as yet had no words.

He was filled with ecstasy, as if visions had opened before him, magnificent, yet dolorous with supernatural sorrow beyond the comprehension of men.

The flickerings on the Cross became deeper in hue and more intense, so that the white walls, floor and ceiling paled like clouds, and were as tenuous. Slowly, moment by moment, the rosy and unquiet hue resembled the flowing shadows of blood, welling, falling and drifting from the arms down the whole enormous body of the Cross. The pearly luminousness that flowed through the temple moved swifter, as if ethereal presences were gathering in greater concentration. The boy was conscious of no fear, only of growing wonderment and love so profound that his body could hardly contain it. The scarlet reflections from the Cross glimmered on his face, his white tunic, his clasped hands, and in his eyes, and on his bent knees.

Slowly, drawn as if by a spell, he stood up and mounted the shallow steps and stood on the level with the Cross. It was a tree of intermingling red and white, palpitating with a force unknown to him. He dared to put out his hand and touch it; it was cool to his touch, and yet it vibrated slightly. All at once he was overcome with a passion beyond rapture; he felt himself drawn into the very heart of the Cross. His legs weakened under him and he slipped to the platform and wound his arms about the shaft and leaned his cheek against it, and without the slightest conscious knowledge his whole body trembled with adoration and the deepest peace he had ever known. He closed his eyes; he was at the core of the universe.

The bronze door opened silently, as if touched by an unseen hand, and four men stood on the threshold, one of whom was Keptah. They stood in the aperture and saw the prostrate boy, his arms embracing the foot of the Cross, his cheek against its shaft. Three of the men, much taller and broader even than Keptah, smiled tenderly and glanced at each other. They approached the platform on feet seemingly shod in velvet, and they stood without a word and contemplated the Cross for several moments. Then all four knelt, bowed their heads on their breasts, and closed their eyes. Their lips moved in prayer.

Three of the men were dressed as stately kings, for they were kings in truth. Their tunics and their robes shimmered with crimson, blue, and white and the most delicate jade. Girdles of hammered gold, inlaid with barbarous jewels, clasped their waists. Headdresses of the purest white silk were bound about their heads, sewn with gems that glimmered in the celestial light. About their necks hung huge broad necklaces of gold and silver, one reaching down to the other, and then another, and fringed with precious metals, and intricately webbed with jewels of many colors. Their bare brown arms bore broad and gemmed circlets below the shoulder and about the wrists, and their feet were shod in golden sandals. Their Eastern faces were blackened by desert suns, and their short beards were virile and glistened with scented oils. From under thick black brows their Orient eyes gleamed like full dark stars, and their noses were the noses of eagles, beaked and masterful, and more than a little wild, as were their red lips.

When he became aware of Keptah and the strangers Lucanus did not know. But it did not seem strange to him that they were there, and he gazed at them with quiet acceptance, and waited, his arms still embracing the Cross. When they rose he did not move, for it was as if they had forgotten him or did not see him. They left the temple, and he drowsed or slept again, and this was something he could not explain to himself later. He had the deepest reluctance to leave the Cross; while he lay there he sensed safety and peace and the fulfillment of all desire.

Keptah stood apart from the strangers in the garden while they communed with each other, bending their ears towards the speaker in the deepest gravity and then nodding. They spoke in a tongue even Keptah did not know, but which had familiar resonances to him, as if he were hearing echoes of his childhood.

Then, as if coming to a conclusion, they smiled at Keptah affectionately, and one of the strangers approached him, and when he knelt the stranger put his hand on his head in blessing. He spoke now so that Keptah could understand.

"You are not mistaken, my brother," he said. "You were

truly right. The boy is one of us. But he cannot be admitted to the Brotherhood, and why he cannot I dare not say. There is another way and light for him, through long and arid places, gray and desolate, and he must find them. For God has work for him to do before he reaches his ultimate journey, and a unique message to give him. Do not be disappointed; do not weep. You have done well, and God is pleased with you. Many will be called from the utmost ends of the earth, and when and how they are chosen is not in our hands, but only in God's. Teach him what you can teach him, then let him go, but be sure he will not wander in darkness, and that he will come again to the Cross."

One of them looked musingly over the garden, as if seeing a far vision. "He will come to her, and sit at her knees," he murmured. "She will speak to him of the things she pondered in her heart, and about which she will speak to no other man. She is hardly older in years than Lucanus himself, and she too must suffer her anguish, which she accepted on the night of the angelic annunciation. He will see her beauty and sweetness, and hear her tender voice. But that is in the future, and it is not ordained for now."

"I have wanted to see her, and touch her robe," said Keptah, his voice trembling. "I have dreamt of the vision of the babe in her arms."

"You will see," said one of the strangers, in a low tone. "If not here, then in heaven."

"Mysterious are the ways of God," said still another. "We can but obey."

"I have nothing to give," said Keptah.

"You are giving your life. You are faithful and full of knowledge."

Keptah rose, then bent and kissed the hems of the strangers' robes, and his eyes were blind with tears. They raised him and embraced him, and left him for the granite building in the distance. "Give me wisdom," he whispered after them.

Lucanus came through the open door, dazed and blinking, and found Keptah alone. The boy and man stared at each other, too full of thoughts to speak for a little while. Then Lucanus said, "Who were those men? They seemed like kings."

"They are kings," said Keptah, gently. "They are the Magi." *

* Matthew 2:1.

He took Lucanus' chill hand and led him away, saying, "Do not ask questions I cannot answer. It is not permitted for me to speak."

Chapter Six

"One of our great priests in Babylonia, or Chaldea, once declared that if a man deprive himself of the good things of the world, which are permitted by the world and by God, he will be called sternly to account," said Keptah. "This is something which the long-faced and ascetic moralists, and the intellectual Jewish Pharisees, would deny, and possibly this would be denied also by our good master, the tribune. Nevertheless, it is true. This philosophy is not to be challenged by the statement of Socrates that to want as little as possible is to make the nearest approach to God. It comes down, as I have always told you, my young Lucanus, to individual interpretation, and what is happiness to one man, and good and morality, is hateful to others."

Lucanus laughed. "It is no wonder, Keptah, that Diodorus is always complaining that you are a Sophist, and that you qualify one pleasing statement with one that is displeasing, both equally true."

"My Greeklet," said Keptah, with indulgence, "I have told you: I am a tolerant man, and that is why I appear complex to the simple, and devious, and not one to be trusted. To be a man of learning, one must know not only his own argument but the arguments of others. It pleases me that you can understand that a statement that is repugnant to one's beliefs can be as true as one that is pleasurable. All this, of a certainty, pertains only to the affairs of the world, which I find endlessly amusing."

They were sitting in Keptah's favorite wineshop, much patronized by the men of business, students and scholars and merchants, of the many races in Antioch. The street outside, cobbled in black stones, blazed with hurting light, its narrowness blowing with sharp white clouds of hot dust, and clamorous with the complaints of camels and donkeys, the voices of rude men, and the shuffling of multitudes of hurrying feet, and the clatter of wheels. On the opposite side the whitish-yellow buildings threw back the heat and light like palpitating mirrors, before which passed men and women in garments of red, blue, black, yellow, green, and scarlet. But in the wineshop it was cool and quiet and shadowed, filled with the odors of wine, good cheeses, and excellent small hot pastries. Wooden bowls, heaped with the briny and very small black olives of Judea, and grapes from local arbors—purple and opalescent and shining even in the dimness—and pomegranates like globes of red fire, and other fruit, and clusters of golden dates oozing their drops of honey, lay upon the scrubbed white tables. The rough walls of the wineshop had been decorated by a local artist who, though he exhibited crudeness and lack of training in composition and delicacy, compensated for these in a creation of vivid color and innocent lewdness. The red-tiled floor was gratefully cool to the hot feet of Keptah and his pupil, as were the goblets of chilled wine to their lips.

The head of Lucanus was a halo of brightness in the refreshing gloom of the wineshop, and attracted the notice of the dark men at other tables. One tall man, swarthy and turbaned in the Eastern manner, was especially enchanted. His narrow face, cunning but vital, and illuminated by a pair of extraordinary brilliant eyes and tapering to a thin short beard, finally could not turn away from the contemplation of the young Greek. His clothing, dim crimson and pale green, assured any spectator that here was a man of position, as did the many flashing rings on his fingers. His servants stood near the open door, drinking small goblets of wine, and all were armed with daggers and had a purposeful look, their strong dark legs revealed sturdily from beneath their colorful tunics.

The stranger finally leaned towards Keptah in his long robe of pale linen and spoke in Greek with an execrable accent: "I have been listening to your discourse, Master, with much interest. Permit me to introduce myself: I am Linus, the merchant, from Caesarea, in Judea, and I deal with the silks and jades and ivories of Cathay. My caravan is on the way to Rome." He spoke to Keptah, but his restless eyes were fixed in delight on Lucanus, who, becoming aware of him for the first time, unaccountably blushed under that intent and roving regard. The boy moved uneasily.

Keptah studied Linus coolly and with deliberation, marking in particular the hypnotized stare at Lucanus. He pondered. It was not too soon, he finally decided, to permit Lucanus to learn something of the darker and more pungent aspects of life. He said, with politeness, "And I am Keptah,

physician to the Tribune Diodorus, Proconsul of Syria." He
hesitated. "From Judea, you say. Are you a Jew, Master?"

Linus' face had changed momentarily when he had learned
Keptah's position. The proconsul had a reputation much
disliked among the merchants along the Great Sea, and this
Keptah was his physician. Linus composed his features into
an expression of respect, which was not entirely assumed.
Moreover, he was plesed. This boy with the hair like the sun
was most evidently the slave of the esteemed physician, and
so matters very likely could be negotiated, as he had suspected. "May I be permitted to offer you a bottle of wine,
Master Keptah?" asked Linus. "With my compliments."

"If you join us," said Keptah, gravely.

Linus rose with alacrity, and he was a man of grace and
height and swiftness. As his garments parted a little, Keptah
saw that he wore a broad necklace of intricately engraved
gold, in the Egyptian manner, but which was now being affected by some of the young fashionable bloods among the
Romans. Lucanus, still flushed and uneasy without understanding why, moved his chair a little to make place for the
merchant, and while doing so he felt a slight pinch on his
knee which he comprehended as a message from Keptah.
The physician also gave him a swift glance, which, interpreted, was a command for him to hold his tongue under
all circumstances.

It was not odd, to Linus, that a slave should sit so familiarly with his master, when this boy was evidently the darling
and beloved of that master, the pampered and coddled one,
used for certain purposes. Now that he was closer to the
boy Linus was more and more entranced. He knew just the
Roman senator who would find this lad a joy, and who would
not cavil at the price. A thousand sesterces would not be
too much. Linus smiled, and the canine whiteness of his
teeth was a blaze against the brown darkness of his crafty
and intelligent face.

"No, Master Keptah, I am not a Jew," he said. "May Baal
forbid! I am of an older race, a Babylonian, though equally
splendid races of the East have contributed to my blood."

Lucanus looked at Keptah, who again pinched him under
the table. "Most interesting," said Keptah, imperturbably.
The shopkeeper came to the table and Linus in a lordly fashion ordered the best wine, and Keptah nodded approvingly.
Keptah said, "Abraham of the Jews was a Babylonian. Perhaps you have heard of him, Master Linus?"

"Ah, yes," said Linus, carelessly. He grinned again. "When I am in Judea I am a Jew, when in Syria I am a Syrian, when in Rome I am a Roman, and when I am in Greece I am a Greek." He laughed lightly.

Keptah helped himself to a few tiny black olives, and said, "And when you are in Africa, doubtless, you are a Negro."

Linus' smile faded abruptly. His jeweled hand flashed to his dagger. Keptah serenely spat out the pits of the olives into his dusky palm, then threw them on the floor. "A clever man is a chameleon," he said, with excessive admiration. "All things to all men. I see you are a philosopher, as I am, when I am not distilling potions and attending to the family of the illustrious Diodorus." He looked up, and his enigmatic eyes fastened themselves on the merchant, whose hand was slowly withdrawing from the dagger. "I believe I mentioned that I am the physician in the house of the Proconsul of Syria, a Roman of great virtue and influence? And particularly ready with discipline, and the sword."

Linus, whose less lawful activities had brought him twice to the attention of Diodorus, smiled winningly. "I trust he pays you well," he said, with insinuation. Keptah made his face inscrutable. "Ah, yes. As well as a thrifty gentleman will permit himself, and my master is famous for his thrift. One of the 'old' Romans. I remain with him because of my attachment to the family, though I have received excellent offers from others."

Linus relaxed, leaning back in his chair with a graceful posture. He stared again at Lucanus, who had found this conversation bewildering. The shopkeeper arrived with the bottle of fine old wine, holding its dustiness reverently in his hands, and bowing. Keptah and Linus critically inspected it, nodded their acceptance, and the wine was poured into silver goblets befitting its importance and rarity. Keptah poured a small amount into Lucanus' goblet, and the boy could smell the fine and delicate fragrance. "You will not meet wine like this in the house of Diodorus, may the gods bless his penurious purse and his barbarian tongue," said Keptah.

Linus, who had smarting and memorable recollections of the proconsul, thought he detected contempt and derision in Keptah's voice, and was more at ease than ever. "Nevertheless," said Keptah, with a furtive and quelling glance at Lucanus, "he is careful of those who serve him well, especially his physician. We have a mutual respect for each other, and appreciate the value of each other. That is why he has assigned me four well-armed slaves for my protection. They await within the sound of my voice, in the street yonder, guarding my litter."

Lucanus' pink lips parted in astonishment at this falsehood, but Keptah was now sipping his wine with the air of a pleased epicure. Linus' black eyebrows flew up in surprise, but he did not doubt Keptah's word for an instant. Here, he thought, is a man of consequence, and he has an elegant and assured air, an air worn only by those much esteemed. The shopkeeper, in honor of the wine, brought a brazen bowl to the table, and a plate. "Ah," said Keptah, in appreciation, "artichoke hearts in vinegar and oil, with a discreet touch of capers and leeks. There are a few Roman dishes to which I am partial." He dipped a piece of bread into the bowl and daintily ate of what he had fished up. "It is true that the Romans are not civilized, but occasionally they have inspirations."

Linus was becoming impatient. He was a merchant, and therefore a man of decisions. He flicked a finger in the direction of Lucanus, and said, "Master Keptah, this boy is no doubt a Greek? That golden hair, that white flesh, those blue eyes, the contour of his features—they are charming and Grecian."

"Have you seen many of him in Greece?" asked Keptah, affecting surprise. "No. The Greeks are a race of small stature and of a dark complexion. They worshiped fairness, because of these things, and have immortalized them in their statues. Be certain that the ideal of men does not resemble themselves, but only their dreams. Nevertheless, this boy is a Greek, though without doubt his ancestors ranged into Greece from the cold regions of the North, or Gaul, where the men wear skins of beasts and the horns of animals, and live in the primeval forests. Is he not of considerable beauty, but of a childish manliness also?"

Lucanus could not understand his mentor and teacher, and was indignant and humiliated. He now not only feared and disliked Linus, but he detested him.

Keptah's manner of speaking, as if Lucanus were not human and could be discussed as one discussed horses or fine dogs, assured Linus that the boy was indeed a slave, and the servant of Keptah. "A beautiful boy," he said, with hushed fondness. "And what is his name, Master Keptah, and his age?"

Keptah sipped at his wine, closing his eyes in reverence. Linus waited. His jewels glistened in the blue shadows of the wineshop. "His age," said Keptah, "is thirteen, though he is large of stature, as all the heathen are large. But he is graceful, is he not?"

Linus was more pleased than ever. The boy was thirteen years old, therefore he had not reached puberty. The old senator in Rome was forgotten. There were patrician ladies, jaded with their husbands and lovers, ladies of great wealth, who would find it piquant to bring this boy to puberty and then to their beds, there to initiate his innocence into the arts of love. It was not impossible that they would pay two thousand sesterces for such a treasure to beguile their ennui. A dissolute wife of a most distinguished Augustale, for instance, now in her forties, who had a penchant for such boys! She would be fascinated with his beauty, and would not be able to resist his purchase. Linus leaned confidentially towards Keptah and said in a low voice which did not escape the ears of Lucanus:

"The noble tribune is a man notable, as you have said, for his thrift. You remain with him for virtuous reasons, such as loyalty and devotion to his family. This boy is not one of his slaves?"

"No," said Keptah. "In a way of speaking, he belongs to me. The tribune has assigned him into my hands, as a reward for what you have kindly called my virtues."

Lucanus' lips parted again with fresh indignation, then winced at Keptah's pinch. Linus was beaming. "Perhaps, Keptah, we can come to a certain agreement. I have clients in Rome who would cherish this boy."

"Truly?" said Keptah. "A senator, perhaps, or a lady who has explored many delights and is bored." He turned to Lucanus and said affectionately, "Would you like to go to Rome, Lucanus?"

"No," said Lucanus. But Linus was saying to him peremptorily, snapping his fingers, "Rise, boy! I wish to examine you further." Lucanus, incredulous at a tone never directed at him before, and outraged, clutched the side of his chair and glared at Keptah. And Keptah, elusive and unreadable as only he could be, returned the glare with dark somberness and said nothing. It was that expression which confused Lucanus completely, and made him stand up less in obedience to Linus' command than in the first movement of flight. The face of Keptah did not change; he flung one long and emaciated arm over the back of his chair, and the folds of the pale gray linen fell from that arm like cloth falling over the outlines of bone.

Linus approached Lucanus, and the other merchants, including the students and scholars in the inn, gave their frank attention and curiosity to the boy. By Venus! thought a Roman dealer in oils and perfumes, there is truly the young Adonis himself, with hair like the sun and eyes as blue as the northern winter sky! He is like a statue, with the sweet sternness of youth in his face and the delicate severity of innocence in his mouth. And what a brow that is, like massive marble, and his feet are arched like small bridges, and his height surely comes from the gods.

Linus himself was surprised at Lucanus' stature, and a little suspicious. But the boy's short white tunic was bordered with the pale purple of preadolescence, and it was evident to Linus' shrewd eyes, after a moment's scrutiny, that, in spite of the stature and the breadth of the shoulders, the boy was truly very young. Lucanus started violently when Linus stretched out his swarthy hand and lifted his tunic, and then felt of his buttocks. The blue eyes flashed in rage, yet a new pride kept him still now and as rigid as stone. "Ah," murmured Linus, thoughtfully. "I had a caliph in mind, rich as Croesus—if the buttocks were softer and more rounded. But this is evidently the fetus of a man, not a plaything for a gentleman of Persia." He handled Lucanus with the rough interest of a man inspecting a fine animal offered for sale.

Lucanus, in spite of the confusion and rage which roared in his mind, became aware, for the first time in his life, of profound and unspeakable evil and all loathsomeness. He heard Linus' murmurous words as the inspection continued, and his white flesh prickled and became cold, and he could not have moved, any more than the marble he resembled could have moved of its own volition. But his heart quivered and his spirit sickened with this horror. He perceived depths never known to him before, and abysses, and the hot black obscenities of the human spirit. These he had never encountered in the home of the virtuous tribune, nor had he dreamt of them. Nor was he fully aware of the implications, nor did he understand them completely. He was like a child who, running laughing to a green and hidden grotto, comes upon a scene of licentiousness and, while not fully comprehending, is impressed that here is something wanton and shameful, and is terrified.

The searching, pinching and pushing hands of Linus had a monstrous hypnotic effect on the young boy. He felt himself degraded, and helpless to repel the degradation; he felt his humanity insulted, his integrity assaulted. Yet, like a voiceless victim, he had no power to resist. He could only stare sightlessly at Keptah and feel nausea at this incredible betrayal, and the fire of ignominy and furious anger in his breast.

Linus, smiling whitely, flung himself back into his chair. "Five hundred gold pieces," he said to Keptah. He removed a purse from the big gold disks that formed the girdle about his narrow waist. He poured out a shining mound of coins. "Let us be brief. You will understand, Master, that I cannot escort this boy through the streets in the daylight." He coughed, and grinned at the cryptic physician. "There has been some slight trouble before with the accursed soldiers of the proconsul, and I do not wish to encounter them again. Here are one hundred sesterces. Deliver the boy to me tonight at the inn on the Road of the Maidens, and you shall receive the remaining four hundred pieces."

All of the flesh of Lucanus was stinging as though it had been seared with flame, and the pulses in his temples throbbed visibly. One of the merchants cried, "Five hundred sesterces! It is robbery, Master. I myself offer one thousand." He half rose from his chair, eagerly.

Then Keptah spoke quietly. "The boy is not for sale."

Linus colored darkly, and leaned towards him. "Not for sale?" he repeated. "This slave is not for sale—for a fortune? Are you mad?"

"One thousand sesterces!" shouted the other merchant, approaching the table.

The others in the wineshop applauded, whistled, protested, laughed. Hearing the commotion, the shopkeeper ran into the room, carrying a tray of fresh hot pastries. Keptah crooked a finger at him, and said, "My good Sura, you will please go to the next street, at once, and tell the young captain, Sextus, that Keptah, physician to the noble tribune, Diodorus, requests his presence immediately."

The shopkeeper bowed, and ran into the street. Linus sprang to his feet, swearing. He shook his fist under Keptah's immovable nose. The others fell silent, gaping. "You accursed Egyptian!" shouted Linus. "I shall have your throat cut!" He shook with fury, and his servants came to him at once, their knives in their hands.

Keptah was not disturbed. "I am not an Egyptian, my good man of many abominable and unknown bloods. Nor am I a man who desires the blood of another. Hasten, and leave at once, before the captain arrives with his men. You have not understood. This boy is the apple of the proconsul's eye, and he is as a son, and born free in the household of Diodorus."

The others rushed out of the wineshop in trepidation, not wishing to be present when the soldiers arrived, and fearful of brutality. Linus was left alone with his servants. He looked at Lucanus, and his lean hands made unconscious grasping movements, as if he would seize him and bear him away at once. His breath came harshly. Then he whirled, and his rich garments of crimson and green blew about him. He left the inn like the wind, his servants racing after him. Keptah and Lucanus were alone. The boy sat down slowly, and his white face streamed with beads of sweat, and his eyes were bitter-cold and filled his eye sockets with wrathful color.

Keptah unconcernedly picked up a bunch of dates and chewed them with appreciation. The pile of gold coins lay on the table, and twinkled in the blue gloom. Keptah's attention came to them, and he smiled. "The rascally merchant did not stay to pay his bill," he remarked. "Nevertheless, he generously left this money, and I shall pay his bill from it and keep the rest. No doubt he graciously intended it so, and I am not a man to refuse such a gift."

"How dared you!" cried Lucanus, and now he was very young again, and close to tears. "You are not only a liar, Keptah, but you are a thief and a scoundrel!" He wept, and rubbed away the tears with the backs of his hands. Keptah studied him thoughtfully. Finally he put down the bunch of dates, and his face changed sternly and his enigmatic eyes were chill and remote.

"You betrayed me!" sobbed the boy. "You shamed and degraded me! And I thought you were my friend as well as my teacher."

"Listen to me, Lucanus," said Keptah, in a hard and quiet tone, and Lucanus dropped his hands from his eyes and stared at the physician.

"You are no longer a child, for you have seen and heard and felt evil," said the Physician. "It is good that you have known it, for a knowledge of evil brings manhood, and aversion. You are now armed." He moved a few of the coins with a thin finger.

"You were born into freedom in a virtuous household, where the slaves are treated with kindness. Never have you seen them treated cruelly, but only with justice. This is most unusual; the household of Diodorus is not the normal household."

A fierce cold flash darted from under his hooded lids. "You were shamed, your humanity treated ignominiously, your dignity as a man insulted. You have seen the scars on the hands of your father, who was once a slave, and, like a child, you have accepted them serenely, as a child, and commonplace. Have you ever asked your father what it means to be a slave, to be treated as less than a man, less, even, than a valuable horse or a good dog? Have you asked him of his own young ignominy, his own shame, his own bitterness, when his humanness was debased? Do you know what it is like to be a slave?"

Lucanus was very still. A glistening tear or two remained on his pale cheeks. Then he said in a low voice, "No. No. Forgive me. I did not understand. I was a child, and I did not understand. You have taught me."

Keptah smiled sadly. "Learning comes with tears and grief and pain. That is just, for man cannot understand God when he is young and happy and ignorant. He can only know God through sorrow, his own sorrow and the agony and sorrows of others."

"No man henceforth will be a slave in my eyes, but a man of dignity, and I shall hate slavery with all my heart and soul," said Lucanus, in a trembling voice.

Keptah put his hand on the boy's shoulder gently. "I exposed you to evil so that you would no longer be defenseless. I exposed you to the vile air of slavery so that never again will you countenance it. And now here is our good Sextus, with his two good soldiers. Ah, Sextus, please wait for a moment and drink some of this excellent wine with us. We have been annoyed by a despicable person, and we are in some danger. We desire your escort. Our asses are tied up at a little distance, and are no doubt somewhat impatient, the poor beasts."

"What rascality have you blown up now?" asked the young captain, with good humor, and some cynicism. He poured himself a goblet of wine and drank it down quickly, and

Keptah's mouth twisted in reproof. "You drink that wine as if it were not distilled from the grapes of heaven itself," he said, "and as if it were only the cheap red wine from your barracks."

Sextus smacked his lips, considered, and inclined his helmeted head to one side. "It has no particularly excellent flavor," he said. "You are a mountebank, Keptah." He winked at Lucanus. Then he was concerned at the pallor of the boy. "Is the child ill?" he asked.

"Very ill," said Keptah, rising. "But he will not die of it."

He was timidly approached by the shopkeeper, and he grandly counted out his bill, and Linus', and left an extra gold piece as a gratuity. The shopkeeper was delighted. "Good Master," he said, "I am sorry that you were disturbed. It will not happen again."

"Do not make rash promises," said Keptah. "This has been a most enlightening afternoon." He filled his pouch with the remaining gold pieces. "And now, Lucanus, let us go."

Chapter Seven

Diodorus Cyrinus awoke to three dismal awarenesses: The husband of Aurelia's older sister, the Senator Carvilius Ulpian, was an unwelcome guest in the house. He had arrived last night, and was patronizingly affectionate, and he had apparently forgotten that though he was a member of a very noble and ancient family he had married Cornelia for her money. This money had not only assisted him in becoming a senator (by bribery only, Diodorus would say savagely) but had enabled him to indulge in passion for Egyptian art. He had heard of some excellent vases and small statues dating back to the Second Dynasty, and was on his way to Egypt to negotiate for them.

The second miserable fact facing Diodorus this morning was that this was the day of the month when he had to meet with Syrian magistrates in the Hall of Justice, and to hear the complaints of local nobles and landowners and chieftains, about the taxes exacted from the province, and especially from themselves, and to listen to the reports of the rascally tax collectors, whom Diodorus hated more than he hated any other breed of man. To Diodorus a tax collector, though apparently necessary in these degenerate days,

was scurvier than the dirtiest jackal, and had something of
the jackal's habits, upon which Diodorus would dwell in a
loud voice in the company of the officials, and in the lewder
phrases of the military. This invariably cheered the victims of
the tax collectors.

The third misery was that he had a headache. He knew
these headaches, which tormented him usually on this particular day, and all Keptah's arts could barely relieve them.
He had awakened with the dastardly sudden flash of light
before his eyes, then the following nausea, then the sharp
cleavage of vision and the temporary dimming of sight,
and then the accursed one-sided headache. The fact that
Keptah could learnedly tell him it was a migraine, and
that Hippocrates had written a long and exact treatise on it,
did not abate one retching, one hammer stroke on the left
side of his head, or one sensation that death was at hand
and not unwelcome. "May Hades swallow your Hippocrates!"
he would say wrathfully to Keptah. "No, no more of your
stinking effusions and your potions!" He would invariably
submit to both the effusions and the potions, and then would
triumphantly vomit before Keptah and glare at him accus-
ingly. The migraine would not forsake him until evening.
He had only to leave Antioch on the way home and it was
gone, except for a not unpleasant weakness which antici-
pated Aurelia's loving ministrations and concern. Basking
under these, he would say to Keptah, "You see, a woman's
hands are wiser than any physician, you mountebank." To
which Keptah would only smile. He had once told Diodorus
that the headaches were his protest against the magistrates
and the tax collectors, whom he detested, but Diodorus
had been so enraged at this insinuation of womanishness
that Keptah never repeated the indiscretion.

Diodorus, the virtuous Roman, believed a responsible
household rose before dawn. The senator did not rise at
dawn, and Aurelia, who had affection even for her brother-
in-law, would not permit the slaves their usual noisy and
ebullient assault on pillar and floor and wall with mops and
brooms until the senator had called for his breakfast in
bed. This, to the tribune, was heaping degradation on degradation. A dirty house and breakfast in bed! It was typical of
modern Rome, of course. The senator's retinue, pampered
slaves and secretaries (he was always writing letters even
when he was visiting Diodorus—"making certain that his
clients will not forget to keep his coffers filled during his

absence"), were invariably assigned the best rooms in the quarters of the household slaves. He usually brought two beautiful young slave women with him, which increased Diodorus' rage, and the tribune would cloister the girls grimly. "There will be no orgies in this house!" he would say to the indulgently smiling senator, who was always surprised that the pretty slave girls in this barbarous household never caught the master's eye.

Moreover, the senator used spikenard and attar of roses, and Diodorus would say loudly, "Not only a filthy house and breakfast in bed, but perfumes!" He affected to find the senator incredible, which convinced the senator that Diodorus should remain in Syria, in spite of his letters to Rome. This was a matter about which the senator had not as yet talked with his host. He felt he needed a prolonged rest first. He had been seasick all the way to Antioch. And Diodorus was a difficult man.

The headache had been extraordinarily severe this morning, and Keptah, mixing potions while his master bellowed in denial, understood that Carvilius Ulpian was adding extra torture to the affliction. He gave Diodorus the cup and said, soothingly, "A student of Hippocrates once asked the great physician, 'Would a permitted murder not assuage the pangs of the victim?' To which Hippocrates replied, 'Certainly.' "

"Are you asserting that if I could murder—let us say, anyone at random, without a qualm, that I would lose my headache?" Diodorus demanded, outraged, sitting up in bed.

Keptah nodded. Diodorus began to swear, then he smiled longingly, thinking of his brother-in-law. "Attar of roses!" he muttered. "Pfui!" He sank back on his pillows and gave himself up to a pleasant fantasy. The migraine subsided a little and this time Diodorus did not vomit up the potion. Still, he was in a bad condition and in a bad temper when he emerged from the house in the fresh and gleaming morning, without breakfast, which he could not eat when afflicted. The son of a whole line of pigs could at least have brought Cornelia, he thought, to visit my wife, instead of mere letters. But Cornelia, as simple, sturdy and unimaginative as Aurelia, would have inhibited the senator's diversions to some extent. Diodorus consoled himself that the senator's visits were very few and very far between.

Migraine, after its first dimming of the vision, always made Diodorus see too clearly, too sharply, so that seeing was in itself a pain. This heightened awareness depressed him. He heard laughter, and winced, putting his hand to his head. Who could laugh while the master of the house was dying on his feet, and fearing the rumble and swaying and rattling of the chariot which would soon arrive to take him to Antioch? Grumbling words he never used before anyone but tax collectors, he left the outer court and went into the gardens. His daughter, Rubria, and Lucanus were playing ball with two young slaves and making noise enough to wake the dead, that is, thought Diodorus, enough to wake anyone but the fragrant senator with his oils.

It was a pretty sight, that of the dark-eyed maiden in her long rosy tunic running to catch the ball Lucanus or a slave girl threw, her cheeks pink and her black hair flowing. In contrast, Lucanus was a golden, youthful god, complementing her, and the slave girls, dressed as simply as their young mistress, and as charming, were like nymphs, their white feet sparkling with dew, their red and brown tresses streaming behind them like banners. All about the young people the garden was a garden fresh from the hands of Ceres, the palms blowing and bowing in a scented wind, the statues glowing, the fountains leaping like liquid silver, and the arch of the sky most ineffably blue.

For a moment Diodorus' bad temper became milder. He watched the girls and the boy, and he thought, How wonderful it is to be innocent and beautiful. Then he was angry again. No one had a right, even a maiden and a boy, to be innocent in this foul world which was composed of perfumed senators, vile tax collectors, magistrates, and officials and Caesars who would not answer urgent letters.

The chit is fourteen; she should be betrothed now and preparing for marriage, thought Diodorus resentfully. The fact that the senator had discreetly mentioned one of his own sons, now seventeen and ready for marriage, and that this mention had made Diodorus look like a veritable Mars with a red dart in his eyes, was completely forgotten by the tribune. Rubria, though still too slender, and given to attacks of breathlessness and pallor about the lips when tired, had a round little bosom and her legs, immodestly flashing from under the blowing tunic, were definitely the legs of a woman. Diodorus was aghast both at this new aspect of his daughter and that she was not as yet betrothed. He was also furious at Lucanus for some obscure reason.

He lifted his voice to a stentorian tone. "What is this play?

Is it not time for the schoolroom? Why this wantonness?"

The slave girls looked at him with fright, and fled from him to the rear of the house like petals scattered by the wind. Rubria, still smiling, stood with the ball in her slender brown hands, and Lucanus colored.

"It is not time, Father," said the girl, and ran to him for a kiss. She wound her arms about his neck, and he could not refrain from responding to her. But he glowered at Lucanus. "Sixteen years old!" he exclaimed. "And playing with girls! Can you find no worthier playmates among your own sex?"

Rubria contentedly kissed him again in her mother's fashion, but her father scowled blackly at Lucanus over her shoulder. The youth stood in silence, his yellow head held proudly, his face cold and remote.

"And with whom shall he play?" asked Rubria, her hands smoothing her father's arms comfortingly. She was not disturbed; she had learned from her mother to treat Diodorus like a beloved but occasionally fractious child. "None of the slave boys are his age, and there are no families with sons near us." She gave Lucanus a laugh and a mischievous glance. "He is also too sober."

"Not too sober to neglect his lessons and engage in puppyish antics," said Diodorus. He did not like the youth at all this morning. "Must one wait until the hourglass has dropped an exact number of grains of sand before one studies? Is it on such an irresponsible that I must spend my money?"

Lucanus looked at him with a hard blue light in his eyes, and he opened his mouth to answer angrily, then he saw that Diodorus was a sickly yellow, and that he had not shaved. His beard was dark under his coarse skin. Lucanus remembered that this was the day for the magistrates and the tax collectors, and that Diodorus was inevitably bad-tempered on these days. The unshaven beard could be relied upon as accurately as a water clock.

So Lucanus said mildly, "You do well to reprove me, Master."

He went away, stepping high and gracefully, and Diodorus watched him go and was more depressed than ever. "Go to your mother, girl," he said with unusual roughness to his daughter. Now his chariot was coming. He could hear the infernal clang and rumble, and winced again, and groaned. Rubria kissed hm, patted his cheek, gave him a glance of loving commiseration, and ran off. Diodorus followed her

with his eyes until she was out of sight, and there was a pain
in his heart. Yesterday she was a babe at her mother's
breast; today she was a woman, and would soon leave her
parents. It was one of nature's most unbearable tricks. He
thought again of Lucanus, and now his obscure anger returned. He had seen Rubria's ardent glance at the youth,
he had seen Lucanus reply with a deep smile. Diodorus lashed
his horses, and was frightened. If he could not be relieved of
this polluted place himself he would send Rubria and Aurelia
to Rome, and even the senator's son, who was a frail, studious
youth and not to Diodorus' exacting fancy, would not be
untenable as a son-in-law. At least some of the money will
return to the family, thought the tribune, who considered
it outrageous that Carvilius Ulpian should be able to spend
one penny of it.

An old pride came back to the Roman, and his heart
hardened with affront. He was incensed now that Lucanus,
that son of a freedman, should even look upon his daughter
lovingly. He forgot, in his gathering black anger, that
Lucanus was the son of Iris, whom he had not seen for a long
time except at a far distance, and then only fleetingly.
Diodorus decided to have a very stern talk with Aurelia tonight. He, Diodorus, would keep his promise to educate the
youth—in order that he could serve the household humbly.
A slave girl of some promise, modesty and household arts
would be freed and a marriage arranged between her and
Lucanus. The Roman master had only to command, and
command he would. Let Lucanus take his wife to Alexandria
with him and let her keep a humble house for her student
husband and bake his bread, and serve him a properly inferior wine. I have been soft and weak, thought the tribune,
biting his thick underlip and lashing his horses. I have forgotten that I am a Roman in this soft, sweltering, depraved
province. I have treated slaves as equals.

He had also forgotten many other things. The face of
Aeneas rose before him—that sly, mealymouthed, weak-
spoken imitation of a man!—and his anger made his eyes
blind for a few moments and his heart beat as if he had
been unbearably humiliated. And an old anguish, without a
face, returned to him like teeth in his chest.

He was in a fine, vengeful mood when he arrived in Antioch. He had never killed a man, except in battle, but he
longed to kill now. If only he were Hercules! He would tear
this city apart with his bare hands. To his nostrils, assaulted

by the stenches of the city, urine seemed the dominant stench. A urinous city! And what was a Roman proconsul doing driving his own chariot here, like a mean merchant? Did no one respect him? Where were his officers, his soldiers? He forgot that this was all of his own choosing, and that he had often said that he was a simple soldier and not a lady-man of modern Rome, and that Cincinnatus had ridden into the Imperial City on the back of an ass, and without attendants save those poor farmers like himself. There will be changes! Diodorus promised in silent grimness.

He was met by Sextus and a troup of soldiers, helmeted, shielded and armed, as usual on the day of justice. Diodorus shouted at Sextus, his face flaming with wrath, "How now, is this the earliest you can drag yourself out of bed to meet and escort me? Am I a provincial dog of a magistrate that I deserve no honors or escort, but must drive like the meanest peasant from my own home?"

Sextus was accustomed to the tribune's bad humor on these days, but he was not accustomed to such an attack on his integrity as a soldier and a worthy and loyal officer. So he was taken aback. He did not retire into obedient and military reserve, as was his training when tongue-lashed by his superior. He blurted out, "Why, noble Diodorus, I have only obeyed your express orders. You have constantly refused to be escorted, and have ordered that no soldiers remain about your house." He looked at Diodorus with dismay, and his soldiers kept their faces blank, and stared before them, carrying the fasces and the banners.

Diodorus pulled up his horses so hard that they reared, and a hoof just missed Sextus' face. He did not step back, however. His young eyes were filled with both reproach and bewilderment.

"Now, by Zeus!" Diodorus bellowed, lashing the horses. "Where is your military discretion!" He got the horses under control, and swore at them. "You will not only accompany me to the Hall of Justice but will return to my house with me and remain there at my orders!"

He roared off, and Sextus shook his head dismally. He then sharply ordered his troops to follow him after the tribune. Diodorus' chariot was now enveloped in hot white chalky dust at the end of the cobbled street. Sextus and his soldiers began a military trot after him, and the humiliation of the young soldier was complete when passers-by jeered at them. He gritted his teeth.

Whether or not the magistrates were more tedious than usual and the tax collectors' reports more boring, or the local nobles and merchants more complaining, it seemed to Diodorus the worst day he could remember. He shouted, he thumped his fist on the table, he scattered papers, he denounced, he insulted, he ascribed shameful ancestry to magistrates, judges, nobles and tax-gatherers alike. They had heads like asses; their mothers had been engaged from puberty in unmentionable obscenities; they were totally illiterate; they were inhabitants of the most depraved and most contemptible country in the world. Their wits were like flies. Antioch was a cesspool, and they worthy inhabitants of it. He despised them all in vivid language. At some time he had unpardonably offended the gods, otherwise he would not be here. He consigned them all to Pluto, and impugned their honesty, their decisions, their records. They were thieves, liars, idiots, cripples. Though his wrist was bound with leather thongs he sprained it by his table-thumping, and his face, swollen and scarlet, seemed about to burst. He would eat nothing; when offered wine, he expressed his opinion of it and spat.

When he roared off in the afternoon, his head one cauldron of pain and his neck muscles in spasm, those he had left were, for the first time, as one. The tribune was mad, of course, and he was a beast, like all Romans. Tax-gatherer and merchant put heads together and condoled with one another. The magistrates expressed their fervent hopes, in low and whispering voices, not only that the tribune would soon descend into hell, but Rome with him.

Sextus had provided himself and three of his junior officers with horses, and they dashed after Diodorus' chariot. They could hardly keep up with him. He drives like Apollo, thought Sextus, still smarting, without the beauty of Apollo. He should enter the races in the circus. Gods, he will kill those poor beasts! But his soldierly heart was filled with consternation. The tribune was apparently ill and temporarily out of his mind. Sextus invoked Ares as he fled along the rutted road after Diodorus. The humid heat was intense, and under their armor the gloomy soldiers sweated, and their shields were too heavy. One or two wondered what punishment would be given them for what transgressions.

The senator, Carvilius Ulpian, was graciously sitting in the outdoor portico with his sister-in-law, Aurelia, sipping one of Diodorus' more expensive wines and commenting upon it to himself in expressive language. Aurelia, the good matron, was busily using her hands in sewing, a vulgar and common habit shared by her sister, Cornelia, who would never be a fashionable lady. They were startled by a thunder of hoofs and the sight of a large cloud of luminous dust in the distance. The senator started to his feet, his white robes dropping around him. "Now, by Mithras, is that the Minotaur approaching?" he cried. "Or Pluto bursting through the earth?"

"It is probably only Diodorus," said Aurelia, undisturbed. "This is always a bad day for him. But are there not other horses with him?" She put aside her sewing and stood up to see and to listen. An optimistic young woman, she never thought that anything out of the ordinary could be ominous. "Is he bringing guests for dinner?"

"If those are guests they are probably charioteers out on practice," said the senator, shielding his eyes from the late afternoon sun and craning to see. Then he began to laugh, now glimpsing Diodorus lashing his horses and standing up like a racer in his chariot, and the soldiers hurtling behind him, all enveloped in radiant clouds of dust. He clapped his hands and cheered, like one cheering the chariots in the circus. "He will make it! He will be the first at the gate!"

"Good heaven, and in this heat," murmured Aurelia. "And with his headache. Why is Sextus with him, and the others?"

"Am I his wife that I should know what Diodorus ever does?" asked the senator reasonably, and still laughing.

Diodorus thundered to the gate, sprang from the chariot and tossed the reins aside. His followers roared up, and barely managed to avoid the halted chariot; their horses danced and pranced and reared all about it, and screamed in distress. Sunlight glanced off the soldiers' armor and off their helmets, and the horses were covered with foam. Diodorus burst through the gate at a brisk trot and then into the outdoor portico. He glared at the senator and ignored his wife.

"What! Are you still here?" he demanded roughly. "Not beginning to yearn as yet for your Corybantes and bacchantes, nor pining for your favorite gladiators and actors?" He was panting, crimson of brow, and dripping with sweat.

"Beloved," Aurelia began, astonished at this rudeness and alarmed at her husband's appearance. She took a step towards him, but he waved her away. "Go to your quarters, woman," he said, not looking at her, and Aurelia gathered up her sewing and vanished through the pillars of the house, tears in her eyes. Never had Diodorus spoken to her like that before.

The senator was not disturbed. He stood there in all his tall elegance, and his face was humorous. He thought Diodorus a boor, a military imbecile whose temper, like that of all soldiers, befitted more an animal than a man. He cocked his eyebrows, smiled, and regarded the goblet in his hand quizzically. "Bacchus would disdain such wine, my good friend and brother, and so, even if I yearn, no bacchantes are hovering about me."

The soft insult made Diodorus shake. He stood before this smooth patrician, with his fine hands and expertly folded toga, like a wild, dark figure of a military barbarian, covered with dust, his eyes glaring, and his fierce and reddened face convulsed. His panting was loud in the evening stillness. He took off his helmet and dashed it onto the stones. Carvilius Ulpian took a delicate sip of the wine and shook his head deploringly. The helmet rolled and rattled.

The senator sat down again, gracefully. His sandals were of silver laced with gold. "Sit down," he suggested, like a man playing host to one of inferior station. "Have some wine. It will refresh you. Is the headache still very bad? My physician here with me has a potion which is very beneficial. Shall I call for his services?" He sat in his chair, a foreign figure majestic and at ease on the crude portico and in front of a house he thought plebeian in the extreme and fit only for an overseer of slaves.

"May Mercury curse your physician!" said Diodorus. He flung himself into his chair and began to wipe his streaming forehead with his hands. When the senator offered him his own perfumed kerchief for the task, Diodorus rejected it with an oath. The senator laughed. "It must have been an exciting day at the Hall of Justice," he remarked, helping himself to a coarse sweetmeat from the silver plate beside him on the table. He looked about for a servant. It was too much to expect that a servant would be on hand in this barbarous household, so the senator poured some wine for the tribune and handed it to him with a bow. Diodorus wanted to refuse it, but his mouth was dry and parched with dust and fever, so he snatched the goblet and emptied its contents in one long swallow. Now he began to feel embarrassed that he had insulted a guest, even if that guest was only his brother-in-law. He sat, knees aspraddle, and his strong and sinewy body bent forward, his head dropped slightly. He stared at the interior of the empty goblet and said somberly, "I am one festering sore."

Carvilius Ulpian wondered where his own servants were. The plebeian looseness and ease in this household had no doubt infected them and the rascals were probably cavorting with the other slaves. However, he relaxed. He found the air of Syria to be quite salubrious and pleasantly warm, for he was a thin-blooded man.

The senator understood that Diodorus was less apologizing to him than being sullenly resentful that he had committed a gross breach of good manners, gross even for a soldier. He settled his aristocratic features into a pleasant and comprehending expression, and his small pale eyes, of no particular color, took on the benign look he reserved for his clients, particularly large landowners who wanted favors for a respectable fee.

The tribune stood up and stripped his breastplate from him, loosened his leather girdle and his short sword, and threw them onto a chair. He stood revealed in his homespun linen tunic the color of red earth, which the industrious Aurelia had spun, woven and sewn for him. His sturdy legs and arms and chest were covered with bristling black hair, and he exuded strength, masculinity and sweat to such an extent that the senator closed his delicate eyes. Soldiers, he reflected, were inevitably violent and stupid, and Diodorus was no exception. Though Cornelia, that simple woman, protested that the books the senator was constantly compelled to send to Antioch were for Diodorus' own use, the senator did not believe it. A Vandal. He and his father and all their ancestors had a reputation of absolute integrity and honor and soldierly qualities and virtue in Rome. That, the senator considered, was the quality of them, unimaginative, boorish and unintelligent. Still, though the Augustales laughed at Diodorus, and even cold-faced Tiberius Caesar smiled at the mention of his name, he had influence among those in Rome like him, and one never underestimated the power of tribunes and the military, mindless though they were.

Diodorus filled his goblet again, some of the wine falling on his hands. The red sunlight splashed on the white walls of the house, and made rosy columns of the pillars. A warm sweet scent drifted from the gardens at the rear of the house, and palms chattered. It was quiet and peaceful, and good for the nerves of a gentleman lately from Rome, where the very air reeked with intrigue. Diodorus sat down. He repeated in a less sullen but in a harder tone, "I am one festering sore."

The senator sighed, looked at his jeweled hands pensively. It could not be escaped. But he tried. "Surely not," he said, "in all this pleasantness, and in the power you hold in the province. Caesar is much pleased with you. He said to me just before I left, 'My greetings to our good Diodorus, and tell him I know of no other province or country so well governed.'"

"He means," said Diodorus ruthlessly, "that I am not a thief or a liar, and I send him his taxes promptly, and that I deal as justly as possible so that Syria will cause him little trouble."

The senator sighed again. He had a narrow head of sleek dark hair. His mouth was slightly effeminate, and a trifle too full and red for a man. Diodorus went on, and now his voice trembled a little. "I remember my old comrade in arms, Gaius Octavius, whom you delicates called Augustus. When you wrote me he had died at Nola, his father's old home, in the arms of his wife, my heart broke. I do not recognize his successor as my Caesar, not in my heart, even though you speak of him as a divinity. Divinity!"

The senator looked about him quickly. He hoped there was no one spying, one who could repeat such treasonable statements. He coughed, and murmured, "A man should be discreet. Do not look so irate, my Diodorus. If I remember rightly, you complained in letters to me that your 'old comrade in arms' had finally destroyed the Republic and extinguished political liberty. I burned your letters, of course, as they were dangerous."

"Nonsense," said Diodorus, with ire, and full of umbrage. "I wrote him a letter to that effect myself. Old friends, old soldiers, are honest with each other. I was like a son to him. We quarreled about the honors he had accepted, and my father quarreled with him on the same account. Yes, the Republic died with him, and it was not entirely his fault, but he was a good soldier, better, in my opinion, than Julius Caesar himself. One forgives a good soldier many things, though not, of course, usurpation of power, and so I chided him frequently, and he said to me, when he was an old wise man, 'Corrupt citizens breed corrupt rulers, and it is the mob who finally decides when virtue shall die.'"

In spite of himself the senator was surprised, and he felt his first respect for Diodorus, who could scold Caesar with impunity and receive an apologetic reply.

"This rascal, now crowned with oak leaves, and a cold-blooded person, may technically be my Emperor, and I serve him as a soldier, as my father served Gaius Octavius, but I do not have to pretend to adore him and regard him as one of the gods." Diodorus shifted in his chair wrathfully. "And I want to go to my farm near Rome and forget your accursed mobs, and all your politics and depravity, and be with my family under my fruitful trees."

"And also forget that you are a soldier, my fiery Mars?"

Diodorus hesitated. "If Rome needs me as a soldier, then I must respond. I am not needed in Syria. Send one of your scoundrels here instead; he will be more fitting in this damn-able place than I." He heaved a tremendous sigh. "At least my Caesar was virtuous, and his wife was his beloved until his death, for a whole fifty years. Tell me: Is Tiberius such a man?"

The senator rubbed his chin and his eyes darted about the portico and through the open door. He said tactfully, "I am a man who is not quarrelsome, and my business is politics, and though I see Caesar often we discuss nothing contro-versial!"

"In other words, Tiberius has ignored my letters, and you have not discussed them with him." Diodorus' vehement eyes sparkled.

"Patience, patience," murmured the senator, and wondered when dinner would be served. He was beginning to get a head-ache himself.

He said, hopefully, "There will be guests for dinner?" Guests would possibly have a quieting effect on this ram-bunctious soldier.

"Guests!" exclaimed Diodorus. "No. Do I invite inferiors to my house? You do not know Antioch. I tell you, I fester here! If I did not visit the procurator in Judea once a year or so I should expire of boredom and rage. Did you expect a banqueting such as you are accustomed to in Rome with Tiberius?"

Oh, gods, thought the senator in dismay. He said reason-ably, "Why do you so resent Tiberius? After all, he is a mag-nificent soldier, has lightened taxation when he could, in the name of economy, is a comparatively honest and honorable gentleman, is just in his dealings with the provinces, and has consolidated the Empire. As for banquets, as a soldier Tiberius does not enjoy them. Did you think him a Bacchus?"

"I was with him on one campaign," said Diodorus, gloomily, and rubbing his aching forehead. "He could not compare with Gaius Octavius," he added defensively. "But he is a silent, cold-spirited man. He defers too much to you senators —he permits too many loose tongues to wag, and that is not the way of an emperor. No discipline——"

"Nevertheless, unlike your beloved Octavius, he is a Roman of your own kidney. When he mounted the throne there were less than one hundred million sesterces in the Treasury. Now the amount grows month by month. He is frugal."

"Nevertheless, he uses vicious spies and informers, as no soldier should do," said Diodorus. "When a man is afraid of his compatriots and fears assassination, one should examine the man." Again he regarded the senator with ire. "Why does he not answer my letters?"

"Because you are administering this province to his approval. If you were not, he would recall you abruptly. I tell you, Tiberius and you are of the same kidney."

"That does not flatter me," said Diodorus. He stood up. "If I were Caesar I would put you senators in your places."

"In other words, you would be a tyrant," said the senator, smiling.

"I would have discipline," said Diodorus, pulling up his tunic belt. "I would encourage the 'new' men, the middle class, in Rome, the country squires, the merchants, the shopkeepers, the traders, the lawyers, the physicians, the builders. I understand that they are not patricians, but neither am I! Many of them are of ancient Etrurian families." His eye kindled. "So far as I am concerned, we can give Italy back to the Etruscans, and let them, and the Roman 'new men,' deal with the Roman rabble, not cater to them as you senators do for their filthy favors. Nor would I fill my chambers with gladiators and scoundrels and freedmen and call them my clients. Rabble!"

The senator was slightly amused again. "Tiberius is no Catiline, and, so far as I know, the 'new men' have not as yet produced another Cicero."

Diodorus began to stamp away, grunting in disdain. Then he stopped. "You will remember, my good Carvilius, that we dine when the gong sounds. In the meanwhile I will wash some of the stinking dust of Antioch from my hands and face."

The senator was left alone in the swift and purpling twilight, and he leaned back in his chair and sighed contentedly. A few days more would relieve his nervousness. This house, though barbarous, and containing little furniture of any luxury and distinction, and practically no ivory, no murrhine glass, few excellent statues even of the gods, and no Corinthian bronze candelabra, and no paintings of any merit, and though the bedrooms were mere holes fashioned only for plain animal sleep and not pleasure, it had a certain simple repose. Best of all, no one expected favors from him, and there was no need for him to be on guard. The barbarians, he reflected, could be admired at times. He also reflected that it did him no harm in Rome to be allied by marriage to the respected "old Roman" family of Diodorus. Even Tiberius would smile on Carvilius Ulpian more often than he smiled at his colleagues, and if that smile was invariably thin and acid at least it was a smile. And he would often inquire of Diodorus.

The fountains in the garden behind the house sounded clear and musical in the silent dusk, and the birds chorused the music. Stretching in pleasure, the senator stood up and paced towards the gardens. He had an estate of his own, outside the gates of Rome, but he could not recall that it was as peaceful as this, nor did the fountains murmur and splash with such harmony to the golden curve of a rising moon. The west had become a series of small lakes of fire surrounded by a pellucid and haunting green, like celestial verdure. The white columns of the house, simple and Ionian, and the unfretted colonnades, rsembled carved snow, dappled, here and there, with the last deep crimson of the sun.

The senator reached the gardens. The whole enclosure drifted with heliotrope light, hushed and secret, but the water in the fountains gleamed like silver. The scent of jasmine blew on the wings of a soft evening wind, and the palms fluttered their fans against a darkening sky the color of amethysts. He looked about him with pleasure, rejoicing again in the silence broken only by the sound of water and the languorous voices of birds. Then he started.

He had never noticed that beautiful, life-sized statue of a woman before, standing near the center fountain, one snowy arm extended so that the fingers might touch the faintly sparkling waters in the marble bowl. Where had Diodorus, who never appreciated works of art, ever obtained such a marvelous creation? The senator seethed with envy. From Sicily, perhaps. The Sicilians colored their statues, and sometimes with delicacy. The statue had golden hair, dressed in the Grecian fashion, and the lovely, brooding profile was so expertly touched with rose that one would swear it was living flesh. The alabaster chiton draped a most perfect and divinely beautiful bosom, which almost seemed to breathe in that drifting and mysterious light, and the folds of the chiton, simple and noble, fell from a waist as slender as a wand, and molded itself over the gleaming thighs. Never had the senator seen anything so adorable. Praxiteles had never fashioned so glorious a form and of such exquisite perfection.

Then, to the terror of the superstitious Augustale, who did not believe in the gods but only feared them, the statue swayed a little and moved. He retreated a step, moistening his lips. It would not have surprised him if the moving statue had lifted an argent bow and had turned to him, aiming an arrow at his heart for presuming to look upon Artemis in her virginity. It was then that he saw Diodorus, standing in an arch of the colonnades, unaware of his guest in that deepening purple shadow. Diodorus was looking at the stately girl, who, head bent low, was slowly gliding away to the garden gate.

The tribune's absolute stillness caught the senator's quick attention. He saw the face of Diodorus, and its dark intensity could be seen even in that dusk. He saw his profile, contorted with some heavy pain and desperate longing. The girl, not noticing the presence of the two men, reached the gate, opened it, and disappeared as into mist.

Now, by Jove, thought the senator, intrigued by the attitude and the expression of his host. He is not so invulnerable after all. That is not the expression of a virtuous husband and oblivious soldier. He is a man in love, nor do I blame him. That slave would excite Jupiter himself to ecstasies.

He heard Diodorus sigh, and it was a short and somewhat terrible sound in the dusk, and the tribune's hairy hands knotted at his sides. More intrigued than ever, the senator coughed, then approached the tribune. Diodorus started, and looked at his guest blankly, the pain only slowly washing away from his fierce eyes. He did not seem to see the senator for a moment or two.

"Now," said Carvilius Ulpian, with genial congratulation,

"that is the most beautiful slave I have ever seen. I thought for a moment that she was a statue, and that I would purchase her from you. In truth, my offer stands."

Diodorus said nothing; in fact, it seemed that he was temporarily incapable of speech. He could only stare with that strange blankness at the senator, as though he had been profoundly shocked. Carvilius Ulpian tapped him affectionately on the shoulder.

"Aphrodite was never clothed in such beauty," he said. "What merchant sold you such merchandise, and where is this paragon? Does he have similar delights? Has he a stable of such Eurydices, of such bewitching forms and Olympian faces?" He delicately smacked his lips. He was suffused with desire and envy. The senator continued, "Though it is possible she has lost her virginity," and he coughed, "I am prepared, my Diodorus, to make you a splendid offer for her."

He was aghast at the face Diodorus turned on him, a face of such wild rage and suffering and affront that the senator stepped back precipitously and wondered if he was confronting a madman. But when Diodorus spoke, it was in a low hoarse voice, as though stifling.

"You are mistaken. That woman is not a slave. She is my freedwoman."

"You freed so glorious a creature?" asked the senator, his trepidation overcome by his astonishment.

"She was to my mother as a daughter," said Diodorus, his voice still muffled. "She is not a girl. She is a woman almost thirty, and the wife of my accounts keeper, Aeneas, a freedman." He breathed heavily. "Moreover, she is the mother of my protégé, Lucanus, whom I am educating as a physician."

The senator, disappointed and chagrined, shook his head. "I would swear she was a young virgin. It is a calamity that she is free. She would bring a fortune to her master." He tapped his chin artlessly with a polished fingernail. "Was she waiting for you by any chance, my Diodorus, and did I disturb you?"

Diodorus said, almost in a whisper, "No. She did not know I was here. It is evident that she was delayed."

His eyes took on the dull shine of grief, and he turned away and vanished into the house. At that moment the gong rang, and the senator, trying heroically to swallow his annoyance at the rudeness of his host in preceding him without a word, followed him in his quiet elegance.

Chapter Eight

There was actually some Cephalonian wine for dinner. But this could not divert the dainty palate of Carvilius Ulpian. Apicius, whose cookbook was used in the very kitchens of Tiberius, had written of seventy-five ways to prepare beans, each delectable. But Aurelia and her cooks apparently knew only one, and that the grossest, fit only for galley slaves. The patrician senator looked at the dish of beans, well flavored with garlic, in which had been stewed some doubtful meat, either goat flesh or the less desirable sections of pork. The bread was coarse, the vegetables flaccid, and the only dish which did not revolt the fastidiousness of Carvilius Ulpian was the little salt black olives from Judea. He had forgotten how revolting the meals were in this house. Diodorus watched him ironically in the feeble light of the smoking lamps, which were of pewter, not silver. The tribune touched the base of one of them and said, "You seem distressed, my brother. I am sorry that these lamps are not of Alexandrian glass. If they were, you could see your dinner more distinctly."

"You say those very words each time I visit you," said the senator, patiently. What was that smear upon the bread? It was oily, and rancid, and the senator, who was a brave man, smiled and put a small piece in his mouth. He was also a polite man, and would have murmured something complimentary about the dinner if the bread had not suddenly nauseated him. "By Hecate, Diodorus!" he exclaimed in agitation. "Is it necessary to live like this? You are as rich as Croesus! You could cover your table with murrhine vases and fill your lamps with oil that does not make a man retch. You could have goblets glittering with gold and jewels, and the sound of lutes in the evening. You could also have a cook of some talent."

Diodorus, whose dark face was livid from some past emotion, scowled at the senator. "I could also have couches on which to recline at my meals, and Cyprian girls to dance abominable dances and anoint your feet with balsam. I, however, am not an Urb. I am a simple soldier, and I live as a soldier."

"What loathsome affectations," said the senator. "Julius

Caesar was also a soldier, and so was your beloved Gaius Octavius. They lived austerely in the field. When in Rome, they lived as Romans, not like base pugilists."

Diodorus began to smile. He ate the bread with relish, and there was a black twinkle under his thick black brows. "Perhaps," he said, "I prefer to save my money"—he ate a huge mouthful of beans—"for a dowry for my daughter, who is almost ready for marriage."

The senator, who had no aversion for gold, and who had four sons, lost his unusual temper. "Ah," he said, "that is a subject which interests me. The little Rubria is of a delicate constitution, yet she appears to have gained considerable health in this pleasant climate. Too, she has a beauty which is almost Oriental in its vividness."

"Yes," said Diodorus, thoughtfully. "I am considering sending Aurelia and the girl to Rome in the near future. There is no one of noble Roman family in Antioch who has a son worthy of her, nor of the proper age."

"In that event," said the senator, "it is possible that Tiberius, who is just though he has ice water in his veins, will recall you."

"Yes," said Diodorus. The two men sat alone in the dining hall, and as the tribune did not like the hovering presence of slaves he had a brass bell at hand with which to summon a slave when necessary. He rubbed his finger over the tracery of the bell, which was a cheap one. "I have been thinking much today." He shot the senator a sharp glance. "I also have a headache," he added, with what the senator thought was irrelevance.

Carvilius Ulpian was still curious about Iris, who was, he thought, beautiful enough to stir the cold Tiberius himself, and to create havoc in Rome. She was a freedwoman, yet there was no Augustale, no patrician, who would not be eager to bring her to his bed and shower upon her all the gold in his coffers. The senator daintily touched the corner of his lip with his tongue. "You will, naturally, bring all your household with you if you are recalled."

Diodorus did not answer. His headache had not been relieved. He cursed Keptah to himself. The senator, impelled by desire and the memory of Iris, went on: "Also your bookkeeper and his family; he must be invaluable to you. Did you not mention at one time that he was the slave of your father, Priscus, and that your father was pleased with him?"

"Yes," said Diodorus, in a dull voice. "However, Aeneas is as frugal as I, and he has saved his money. He has also bought a small olive grove not far from Antioch, which he deigns to have cultivated by two of my slaves. He has learned how to brine the olives as the Jews do, and they are fairly palatable. Moreover, he has a respectable herd of sheep, the flesh of which he sells to me and the Antioch markets. I doubt that he will be willing to return to Rome with me."

Conversation languished. When the senator remarked that Aeneas would doubtless be loyal to his master and regard his wishes as one regards the wishes of the gods, Diodorus shook his head. "I shall not impose on his loyalty, if he has any," he replied. "Besides, loyalty is a word with which the Greeks are not familiar."

He would never see Iris again. He regarded her now as a terror. When he had seen her in the garden, so close, so near, as he had not seen her for years, his heart had leaped. He had had to control himself to keep from running to her and seizing her and pushing his face into her golden hair. There had been a cry in him like the cry of utter joy and anguish, mingled together. Desolation overwhelmed him.

The senator watched the open passions and despairs racing across the tribune's vital and unsubtle features, and he smiled to himself. There had been a brooding sorrow in the young Grecian woman's face, he recalled. Venus never had such reluctant devotees! Diodorus was a fool. Why did he not castrate himself and have done with it? The tribune glanced up involuntarily and saw the senator's faint smile and worldly eyes, and he colored. He filled his plain goblet again and drank of the wine deeply. Then he said, "It may surprise you to know, Carvilius, that I am a virtuous husband."

"Unfortunately, it is no surprise," said the senator. He was a little astonished that Diodorus was so perceptive. He yawned, and this astonished him more. It was not a time to retire. And then he remembered that everyone in this barbarous household went to bed early. He reflected wretchedly that he would not be comforted in his hard bed by one of his pretty slave girls. Why had he thought that he could spend several days in this place? He would leave as soon as possible, after he had come to some agreement with Diodorus about Rubria.

Before going to bed Diodorus tramped into his wife's quarters. Aurelia, whose red-brown cheeks showed the traces of recent tears, and whose kind eyes were pink along the edges, was permitting a pert slave girl to brush her long dark hair. She sat at a table in her night shift of white linen, and under the cloth her voluptuous figure was unmistakably matronly. When she saw Diodorus her ripe lips quivered, her eyes lighted. She restrained herself instantly, and made her face cold.

Diodorus gave a rough gesture to the slave girl, but Aurelia, for the first time since she had been married, said with uncommon sharpness, "Do not leave me, Calliope. You have not finished braiding my hair, and there are other matters."

"Yes, Lady," said Calliope. She had a rude, unpleasant voice that grated on the ear, a large voice for so small and shapely a girl.

Diodorus was always very vague about his household servants, and rarely noticed them. But, as he had something on his mind now, he looked closely at Calliope and said, with his usual lack of tact, "Calliope! And with that voice!"

The girl smiled and bowed her head. "Yes, Master."

Diodorus studied her. She was evidently about seventeen or eighteen, with an impertinent and lively face, not pretty, but so animated as to give her a certain charm. She had a brisk and competent air, and her body had considerable comeliness, and her long, light brown tresses fell to her hips. Diodorus caught a bright if pale glimmer of brown under her eyelashes. He looked at her hands. She was accustomed to hard work, under the direction of her mistress. She was eminently fit for what the tribune had in mind.

"Would you like to be married?" he asked her abruptly.

"Oh, yes, Master." She peered at him impudently from under her drooping eyelids.

"Good. I have an excellent husband for you," he said, thus apparently concluding the matter. Again he waved her away, and this time the staring Aurelia did not countermand his order. When the girl had gone, pulling the heavy blue wool drapery over the door, Aurelia said in vexation, "I believe it is the prerogative of the mistress to arrange marriages for her slave girls and women."

"Yes, yes," said Diodorus, impatiently. "But this is a special occasion."

Aurelia lifted her silver mirror and affected to be concerned over her complexion. Diodorus finally became aware that his wife was displeased with him. He said, "What have

I done now?" Aurelia studied her complexion, and sighed. "It must be very bad," Diodorus added. "But this is no time for matronly exasperations."

Aurelia was outraged. She slapped the mirror on her table, and the lamp fluttered. Its feeble light shone on an austere bed of no bronze decorations, and no carvings. It was of unornamented wood, and the rugs that lay on the sheet were only brown wool. "Am I given to capriciousness?" she demanded. "Do I have tantrums? When have I disturbed you, Diodorus? When did I merit the insult you gave me tonight before my sister's husband?"

"Oh," said Diodorus, frowning. He sat down and stared at his bare knees. "I did not know I had insulted you. I ask your pardon, Aurelia. I have had hell's own headache today." He waited for Aurelia's usual words of concern, but she only sniffed, and the coldness on her face became even colder.

"It must be very bad," Diodorus repeated.

Aurelia began to braid her hair, and Diodorus tried to restrain his impatience. He was hurt that his wife did not commiserate with him, that she did not open her box of unguents to rub on his forehead, that she did not invite him to her bed so that she could hold him in her arms, as usual, and croon to him until he forgot his pain, or it was gone.

"I mean," said the tribune, irascibly, "that it is bad that a wife shows no solicitude for her husband." Aurelia sniffed again. The shining black lengths of her hair flowed over her fingers. "Besides," said Diodorus, in a louder voice, "I swear by all the gods that I do not know how I offended you before that elegant in his toga. Why does he wear a toga in a simple household?"

"He is a gentleman," Aurelia informed him, pointedly. Diodorus glared at her, and she glared in return. Thus was so unlike the amiable Aurelia, who had a large and diffused affection for everyone, that Diodorus was taken aback. "So, I am not a gentleman," he observed.

"You never were." In spite of herself a dimple appeared in her brown cheek. Then it faded. "What is this about a marriage for Calliope? And to whom?"

"Lucanus," said Diodorus, and slapped his knee as if it were all settled.

Aurelia's eyes rounded in astonishment. Her plump hands dropped from her hair and fell on her lap. "Lucanus!" she exclaimed. "The son of Iris?"

"Who else?" asked Diodorus, irritably.

"He has asked for this girl?" said Aurelia, disbelieving.

"No, no! I did not say so. I have decided this myself. Before he marries her, I will free her, and she will be my gift to him. Who is he to protest my orders?"

Aurelia's mouth opened incredulously. "Have you forgotten that you cannot give him orders to marry a girl you have chosen for him, even if you are a proconsul and a tribune? He is freeborn!" She was more and more incredulous. She had an affection for Lucanus, who was the son of her friend, Iris, and a handsome youth, and Rubria's fellow student and playmate. But she had thought that Diodorus was a little too enthusiastic about the boy.

"I can give him orders!" shouted Diodorus in a rage. "Who is he, but the son of a weak dog of a former slave, that Aeneas!"

Aurelia paused. Then, watching him closely, she said, "He is also the son of Iris."

Diodorus started to speak, then was silent. Aurelia went on, "Do not bellow at me. It may surprise you, but I sometimes have headaches of my own, though you seem unaware of headaches which concern others. Let me continue. Lucanus was born free. He is proud. You cannot command that he marry a slave. Nor can you have him flogged or imprisoned for no cause if he disobeys you. I believe you mentioned approvingly that Tiberius himself has issued edicts restraining violence and unlawful commands."

"Tiberius!" said Diodorus, in a tone which consigned the Emperor to the gutter. "Listen to me: I shall talk with Aeneas and tell him my will. He, at least, will not dare to disobey me. I have said it. I have done."

He stood up with an air of finality. But Aurelia was not impressed. "Have you considered Iris, whom you are about to offend deeply? I cannot permit this outrage."

The face of Diodorus swelled with fury at this. "Outrage!" he shouted. "I give the boy a slave to tend him while I pay his huge bills in Alexandria, robbing my own daughter of her dowry——"

Aurelia put her hands over her ears. When Diodorus stopped, seething, she removed her hands and spoke quietly. "No doubt you are impelled by the highest motives. However, give Lucanus Calliope when he leaves for Alexandria, if you will."

"I shall," said Diodorus.

Now curiosity beset Aurelia. "But why?" she asked.

"I have said it. Is that not enough?"

"No," said Aurelia. She began to braid her hair again. Then she shook her head. "I do not know what is in your mind. Did you know that you are occasionally sinister?"

Diodorus was about to burst out into angry shouts again, when the word caught his attention. Sinister. He had never considered himself so. For some reason the thought intrigued him. He rubbed his forehead sheepishly, and said, in a milder tone, "I have spoken it many times: I am only a simple soldier. My motives are always as pure as a cow's milk."

Aurelia looked very knowing, and this pleased Diodorus more. She said, "Even if Calliope were a pearl from Cos, endowed by the very Graces themselves, Lucanus would not have her. Iris told me today, with much concern, that he has taken a sacred vow to the gods that he will never marry."

"Never marry!" exclaimed Diodorus. "What folly! What impelled him to such foolishness? Do not the girls attract him?"

Aurelia shrugged. "I do not regard Lucanus as a son, as you often do," she said, significantly. She let that barb throb in Diodorus for a moment. "I am not in his confidence; he is too silent and reserved for so young a man. However, a man does not make a sacred vow to refrain from marriage if he is not attracted to young women."

This seemed reasonable. Diodorus wrinkled his fierce brows. He was no longer angry. He muttered, "Nonsense." Aurelia shrugged again. "You have something on your mind," she said. "And I am very curious."

Enormous relief flooded Diodorus. He smiled. "If he has taken that vow, then he will not violate it. So. It is ended."

"I am still curious," said Aurelia.

Diodorus knew that his wife was not intellectual, and not subtle. But she was shrewd. He also had a great respect for Aurelia. "I am not a man to satisfy a woman's curiosity," he said, chaffingly, his headache having miraculously disappeared. "I had thought to do Lucanus a benefit, and that is all."

"Oh," said Aurelia, unconvinced. She yawned. She lost interest in the conversation, and she forgot her injured feelings. She glanced at her bed, then smiled at her husband innocently. "You have been overwrought more than usual today, Diodorus. Were the magistrates and tax-gatherers and the nobles and the chieftains exceptionally obnoxious?"

"They were pigs," said Diodorus, expanding. He had caught his wife's glance at the bed. His hands began to unfasten his girdle. Aurelia rose, shook down her braids, then bent to blow out the lamp.

When they were in bed, and embracing, Diodorus said, "I have arranged a marriage between our Rubria and your favorite nephew, Piso." And he laid his head on his wife's breast, and it was a warmth to his heart and a coolness to his forehead. He enveloped himself almost desperately in her strength and gave himself to the gentle ministrations of her hands. He closed his eyes and willed himself to forget Iris, who had retreated like the moon behind a cloud.

Chapter Nine

In the morning Diodorus awoke in an expansive mood, touched with some regret. Lucanus was only the son of a freedman; nevertheless, Diodorus, who truly loved him as a son, was ashamed of himself. It was that cursed migraine, of course, which had the same effect on a man's reason as Medusa had on the flesh. What had made him forget that no modest Roman maiden could marry without her father's consent? It was her young heart that I was probably considering, thought the tribune. I did not want it crushed. As he had loved Iris, so was it possible that the gentle little Rubria would love Lucanus. This made Diodorus more determined than ever to send her and her mother to Rome. In the meantime he concluded the arrangements for Rubria's betrothal at breakfast with Carvilius Ulpian. They haggled over the dowry. The cautious tribune wished to be certain that if Piso ever divorced Rubria, or she decided to leave his house, her dowry would be returned to her. The senator was in good humor, though he had decided to leave this impossibly simple place the next morning.

Keptah, this rosy dawn, was in Rubria's room for his usual morning examination. He was deeply distressed. The girl had had a recession in her mortal disease which had lasted longer than any case ever recorded by Hippocrates or his disciples. But the signs of its returning were here. The soft mucous membranes of her mouth and throat showed the deadly lumps of the white sickness. One of her knees was swollen and hot, and, overnight, she had lost the color in her cheeks and her face was ghostly again. She was languid and feverish, but there was one good sign: her spirits were still merry. There could be another recession if internal bleeding did not occur. The physician examined her urine, and made certain inquiries of the nurse. So far all bodily secretions were free of blood. He advised that she remain in bed for a few days.

He met Diodorus on the stairway. The tribune had an expression of high satisfaction and contentment on his ferocious face. "Why is the maiden not with her mother?" he asked.

"She is a little weary," said the physician, in a low voice.

Diodorus stopped on the stairway. "Is she ill?" he demanded, and his heart plunged.

The physician hesitated. How long should he keep the tribune unaware that his daughter must die? Diodorus was watching his face keenly. Keptah smiled. "I think she has been romping too vigorously," he said. "She has sprained her knee. She must remain in bed until the swelling departs." He added, "I have given her a potion to make her sleep, to rest the injured part."

The tight compression around Diodorus' throat relaxed. He shook his head. "It is unseemly for a maiden of fourteen to behave as a capering child of four. I was looking for you, my Keptah. Before the spring rains begin the Lady Aurelia, and my daughter, and you, will leave for Rome. I have just arranged a marriage for her with my nephew, Piso, son of Carvilius Ulpian."

Keptah was appalled. He folded his thin and dusky hands in his white robe so that Diodorus could not see their clenching and trembling. "Master," he said, "it is not time. Rubria has made much progress in this warm and gentle climate. She has been well for a number of years. However, she is still of a delicate constitution, and to expose her to the dampness and the raw winters of Rome, as yet, will be dangerous."

"Nonsense," said Diodorus, but he was alarmed. "I have seen the sickliest girls become buxom and sturdy after marriage, and particularly after the birth of children. Rubria has been pampered too much."

Keptah moistened his lips, and kept down his eyes so that the tribune would not see the fear in them. The girl had less than a year to live; she might die within the next day or two. To take her from her father, from her beloved playmate, from the warmth and scents of Syria, would hasten her death, deprive her of tranquillity.

"A year, six months," pleaded Keptah. "She is only fourteen."

"No," said Diodorus, slapping his hand emphatically on the white wall of the stairway. "Within a month."

Keptah, forgetting his position, lifted his voice and cried, "In the name of God, Diodorus, do not send the child away from you! She is heart of your heart; she loves you more dearly than anyone else in the world."

"That I know," said Diodorus, in a softer tone. "Do you think it will be easy for me to relinquish her? But if she and her mother go to Rome, that ice-blooded Caesar may recall me. Carvilius Ulpian will do all he can. Tiberius always listens to the senators, and Carvilius has many friends among them. I wish peace. I wish to retire to my farm."

Keptah thought of the love between Rubria and Lucanus. He had watched the growing innocent passion between the maiden and the son of Aeneas. He had not warned Lucanus lately that the girl must die. They must have their young dream of love, the fairest and the sweetest dream of all, until the inevitable moment. It was a pure love; sadly, it was developing into the love of a woman for a man each day that passed. Were not Rubria dying, Keptah would have suggested to the tribune himself that he remove his daughter from a situation that would inevitably produce anguish for her.

Keptah was in a quandary. He could not bring himself to tell this father that his child would inevitably expire within a few months at the most. Yet he knew that she could not go to Rome, to die in tears for Lucanus and her father. There was only one thing to do. Bowing in silence to the tribune, he left for the women's quarters and asked a slave to beg Aurelia to grant him a moment's consultation. Aurelia, who was spinning industriously among her slaves, called him to her, not pausing in her work. Keptah studied her. She was a woman of sense and fortitude, never hysterical, never capricious, never sullen or irrational. Her cheeks were pinker than usual this morning, and her large brown eyes softer, as if she were dreaming of some past pleasure and love.

"May I speak to you in private, Lady?" asked Keptah. Aurelia immediately sent her slaves away, but her hands moved busily. "How is our Rubria this morning?" she asked.

Keptah said, "There is something I must tell you, Lady, that I dare not tell the noble tribune."

Aurelia held the distaff still in her hand, and her foot paused on the treadle. She paled a little, but her eyes did not darken, nor did they enlarge with alarm. She said, quietly, "Rubria is ill again?"

"Yes, Lady. And she cannot live. She will die before the autumn."

Aurelia became white under the brownness of her skin. She put the distaff down without a single tremor of her hands. "Tell me," she said, in a hushed voice.

Keptah had never admired her as much as he admired her now. The strength in her was as the strength of an oak, tormented by a gale but not overthrown by it. Like Ceres, who had lost her daughter Proserpine to the god of death, Pluto, so she would lose her daughter to him. Unlike Ceres, she would not curse the earth, nor go up and down it, wailing. Her roots were deep and sinewy.

"The little Rubria has the white sickness," said Keptah, and he could not keep the tears from his enigmatic eyes. Aurelia saw them, and she was touched. She said, "The white sickness. There is no cure for that, that I know. You are certain, Keptah?"

"Yes, Lady. She has had a recession for a number of years, far beyond my expectations. But now the disease has returned. God granted a miracle once for His own mysterious purposes. He will grant no other miracle this time."

Aurelia folded her sturdy hands on her knees and looked down at them. "I have not told the tribune that I am with child. I wished to be sure. Shall I tell him this in order to lighten the blow of Rubria's coming death?"

"Lady, you may tell him of the coming child in another two weeks. Then we can be sure. But do not tell him of Rubria. His heart is in her hands."

Aurelia nodded. She was silent for a long time, while Keptah stood before her in that bare and shining room. She began to weep, but in silence. She accepted even death with fortitude.

"Let him have peace. Let him be joyful in both his daughter and the child to be born," said Keptah, honoring her. "I have told you the truth, Lady, because I need your help. Rubria cannot go to Rome. As she must die, inevitably, it is well that she die here with her father beside her."

"I see," said Aurelia. Mechanically, she made as if to lift
the distaff, then withdrew her hands. "I will tell Diodorus
that I prefer to remain here until the autumn, and that the
summer in Antioch will further improve Rubria's health.
We were to leave in fourteen days."

She looked at Keptah again, and her full bosom trembled. "Thank you," she said, with deep gratefulness. And
she took up the distaff again.

Keptah intercepted Lucanus as the youth was about to
enter the schoolroom where Cusa was already laying out
the lessons. "Come with me," said Keptah, and took the
boy's arm and led him into the sweet wild blue wind of the
early spring morning. They stood in the center of the garden,
where no one could hear them. Keptah looked into the eyes
of the young man and said quietly and seriously, "I have
evil news to tell you, my Lucanus. The white sickness has
returned to Rubria, and she will die before the leaves fall."

Lucanus stiffened. His cheeks became like marble. During
the past two or three years he had come to believe that
Rubria would live. Moreover, it seemed to him that his very
spirit was entangled in hers, like the two trees of the souls
of the husband and wife who had received mercy from the
gods because of their great love. He had not talked with
Keptah of Rubria; he had been too afraid. Each day that she
blossomed he rejoiced; each hour with her was as gold,
newly mined and pristine. Her laughter was clearer and
stronger, the color in her cheeks brighter, her limbs lighter
and swifter in movement. God had wrought a miracle, and
though Keptah had warned him at first that this was only a
recession Lucanus had mutinously come to believe that the
miracle was permanent.

"I do not believe it," said Lucanus, in a strangled voice,
and tried to pull his arm from Keptah's grasp. Now his eyes
became vivid with pain and terror, and he looked at Keptah
as at a deadly enemy. Keptah tightened his hand. "I do not
lie," he said. "The girl is dying."

"God cannot allow this terrible thing to happen," said
Lucanus, and with a note of hatred in his tones. He looked
at the pellucid dome of heaven. "He cannot take Rubria,
who has harmed no one, whose heart is pure, who brings
delight and love in her very shadow."

Keptah sighed, "If God took only the wicked, then this
world would be paradise, indeed. It is said that they whom
the gods love die young. God loves this child. She will be

taken to Him, to rest in peace and light forever, waiting for you."

But the young heart of Lucanus rebelled violently. His mind was full of darkness and despair. The soft wind on his flesh made him shudder. He hated God, who could deprive the world of Rubria and tear his spirit to tatters. All that he had known of God, all the love he had given Him humbly and with joy and exultation, died down into bitter ash blowing in a deathly wind. Often he had prayed, "Not Rubria, Father, but me. Spare Rubria." And he had believed that God had heard him and would grant his prayer.

He said to himself, distractedly, I do not believe! I do not believe any longer! If God takes Rubria, then He is evil, and there is nothing but evil in the world. There is no God.

Had Rubria died when she had once been dying, Lucanus would have accepted with the simplicity and sadness of an innocent child, and would have prayed for Rubria's soul. He loved her now as a man, with power and intensity and his whole soul's longing and dedication. As a man he suddenly believed that she would die completely and be lost to him forever.

Keptah, watching him, saw the fierce hatred and agony in the youth's eyes, the bitter rebellion, the refusal. He said, with alarm, "Have you, then, forgotten all you knew, my Lucanus? Have you forgotten the Star, the love, the understanding? Have you lost your devotion to God, and your knowledge of Him?"

Lucanus said through dry lips, "I have forgotten. I dreamt as a child. I am now in a man's world."

"Then, as a man, you must accept. Revolt is for children, who have no knowledge." Keptah sighed again. He put his hand on Lucanus' rigid shoulder. He remembered that the Magi had told him that Lucanus must travel a dark and lonely path to God. Yet he wished the youth not to travel alone.

"Do you think that only you have known grief?" asked Keptah. "The heart recoils at grief, for that is natural. But you have known more than grief. You have known God. Is He so easy to forget?"

Lucanus was silent.

"Not to reject pain instantly is not to be human," said Keptah, urgently. "Be happy that all these years have been yours, that no sadness has touched you, that you have the love of your parents, and Diodorus, that your life has been serene and joyous, that you have loved Rubria. God has been tender and loving with you. Yet, at the very moment when He demands that you understand, that you have faith, that in despair and storm you accept Him as simply as you accepted Him in sunshine and beauty and laughter, you turn from Him in hate and cry in your soul, There is no God!"

Lucanus drew a deep breath. "Let Him perform another miracle."

Keptah shook his head. "Are you to lay down the rules of what He shall do?" He added, "I have been your teacher. You have gone with me through this large household. You have seen pain and suffering and death. You have knelt beside the pallet of dying slaves and have comforted them with words of peace and love and faith, and have directed their thoughts to God. But—God must not touch you, He must not wring your own heart! Are you, then, so sacrosanct that you must be spared the common fate of all other men? Oh, you egotist! Oh, you of little faith!"

Lucanus did not reply. His eyes were like blue stone. Keptah continued. "A woman is stronger and wiser than a man. I have given the news to Aurelia, and she accepted it with bravery and submission." He added, "I have not told Diodorus. He, like you, has no fortitude."

Lucanus cried, "How can there be fortitude when there is no answer to grief and suffering?"

Keptah looked at the earth meditatively. "There was a man called Job who asked that question. And God said to him, 'Where wast thou when I laid the foundations of the world?' And Job was silenced."

"That is a Sophist's answer," said Lucanus.

"Nevertheless, it is an answer more comforting than any other."

Lucanus pressed his hands over his eyes, and Keptah regarded him with compassion. Then Keptah said, "Rejoice in small mercies. It was the will of Diodorus that Rubria leave you in two weeks for Rome. Now the heroic Lady Aurelia will dissuade him, for she knows. She will not have her daughter die so far from her father. And from you. Can you not be as noble as a woman?"

Cusa emerged into the garden. "Ah, there you are, you rascally Greek!" said the Grecian tutor. "You will avoid your lessons, will you? Make haste, you vagabond!"

Lucanus looked at him with wrath. But Keptah smiled and touched his arm. "My good Cusa, your pupil is ready.

I have just completed a lesson." He turned to Lucanus. "Have I completed the lesson?"

But Lucanus looked at him somberly. And he left Keptah, who gazed after him in sadness.

Chapter Ten

"You would prefer, no doubt, to be following Keptah about among the fever-infested pallets of slaves, and be learnedly examining their pots," said Cusa, sarcastically. "Nevertheless, if you are to arrive at Alexandria with more than a smattering of learning I advise you to apply yourself to your lessons. Not," he added gloomily, "that it will do much good for one of your limited intelligence."

It was his way of spurring Lucanus to extra efforts. Lucanus would usually answer with one of his calm and austere smiles. He seldom could be aroused to anger, but when he was he became as resistive as stone, and there would be a bitter blue flash in his eye sockets.

Lucanus sat today in silence, his hand idle over the stylus, the books rolled, his head bent. But when Cusa taunted him, he glanced up and the icy fire in his eyes warned the antic tutor. However, Cusa said, "Do not look at me, you son of a former slave, as though you were my master and I had unpardonably insulted you. It is only fortune that made you free. In a more sensible house you would be swilling water over the stones and emptying the chamber pots, and not sitting at a marble table like a patrician."

"Give me peace," said Lucanus in a muffled tone.

Then Cusa saw that the youth was in some awful distress, and that further taunts would incite him to violence. The teacher had long ceased to whip him at lessons. In his heart he now loved his pupil and had almost stopped envying him for his beauty and the favors Diodorus showered on him.

"Well," said Cusa, thoughtfully, and fingered his satyr's chin. He studied Lucanus. His mind leaped about like a goat. He looked at Rubria's empty chair. The maiden had been more breathless than usual lately, and once or twice she had closed her eyes as if about to faint, her lips and cheeks turning a peculiar ghostly gray. Cusa, whose curiosity was bottomless, had spent many years studying Keptah's books on medicine, and something flickered in his agile mind. It was something deadly. He reflected that Lucanus would not be in such obvious anguish if Rubria's illness were trivial. Cusa saw that the youth was also staring at Rubria's empty chair, and that his mouth twitched rigidly. As Cusa feared, the gods, waiting in their lightning-lit silences, had struck at the maiden in some mortal and peculiar fashion, and Lucanus knew it. The teacher cleared his throat.

"Rubria is absent today," he said, watching Lucanus narrowly. "Ah, what weariness it is to be a woman! She will be present tomorrow."

But Lucanus, not hearing him, only gazed at Rubria's chair, and his throat became as stiff as marble. Cusa felt unfamiliar pity.

"Attention!" said he, unrolling a manuscript. It crackled in the silence. "Diodorus is expending much time and effort, and eventually money, on you. Let us be men, not children."

Lucanus did not answer; his fingers twisted the stylus as if he were tortured. Cusa pondered. Then he said, "Let us consider Anachrusius for a moment, in passing. Observe his philosophy. 'It is the critical moment that shows the man. So when the crisis is upon you, remember that God, like a trainer of wrestlers, has matched you with a rough and stalwart antagonist. To what end? you ask. That you may prove the victor at the Great Games.' "

A sardonic and mournful smile ran over Lucanus' lips. He looked up at his teacher. "You have always declared that God was an allegory, Cusa. A figment of poesy."

Cusa shook his head reprovingly. "So He is. But lately I have become mindful that He is something more. The vital element of the universe, as Aristotle has said."

"You will soon be sacrificing in some temple," said Lucanus, with cold disdain.

Cusa shrugged. "It has been declared that sacrifices do no harm. If the gods exist, the sacrifice will please them, and that is excellent. If they do not exist, your neighbors will comment on your piety, and that is even more excellent." He was hurt that his attempt to lighten Lucanus' somber mood had not succeeded. "Attention. Anaxagoras declared that man became intelligent because he learned to use his hands. He lacked observation; the monkeys use their hands, and their intelligence is not notable. The rabbits of the field lift carrots in their front paws and devour them as men would devour them, but rabbits are only a little less stupid than some human students I could name. Aristotle maintained that men learned to manipulate their hands because they had become intelligent. He also maintained that the brain is only an organ to cool the blood. The Eastern philosophers declare that the brain is the seat of the soul, the ego, the mind, and not the heart. Aristotle has his moments of stupidity, and I prefer the Eastern philosophers in this matter. That is not the point of discussion, however. What philosopher seems to you the most valid in this instance: Anaxagoras or Aristotle? And why?"

The stylus of Lucanus moved sluggishly, and then with greater speed as his mind lifted the problem in its invisible hands and turned it about, studying and weighing it. He wrote neatly and concisely, in small letters. Cusa admired him furtively. Some hideous knowledge had stricken the young man; nevertheless, he could let an idea engage his thoughts. Only a peasant could be overwhelmed by his emotions. However, Cusa reflected with some melancholy, the peasant enjoys considerable peace of mind, peace unknown to the cultivated man. Was the price of intelligence always pain?

Cusa suddenly yawned, as Lucanus, still very white and rigid, applied himself to his lessons. The day had become very warm, very silent, breathless. The sun shone too brilliantly. The birds were still. All at once, in spite of the sun, there came a sudden thunderous and cavernous sound, shaking the house, momentarily stirring the trees beyond the open door. The silence which followed it took on a kind of ominousness. Cusa went to the door and looked out upon the garden. The grass, the flowers, the very fountains, seemed caught up and imprisoned in absolute light, at once terrifying and strange. Each color was intensified, and vaguely enhanced by a quality of terror. Cusa found himself gasping; it was as if the lid of a cauldron had been lifted. He looked at the sky. Here the light was curiously brazen, obscuring the blue. Aha, thought Cusa. We are about to have weather. He knew these swift semi-tropical storms, violent and destructive. They passed quickly, however. But never had he seen light so brassy. In a moment the earth became citron-colored. The very palms were bathed in an ocherous light; the leaves of the deciduous trees yellowed. The blades of grass were topaz. The white lilies turned tawny. A restlessness, a foreboding, struck the air. And the heat increased unbearably as the sun appeared to enlarge, to become the golden shield of Zeus himself turned to the world, not in clouds, but in saffron immensity.

I do not like this, thought Cusa. As if replying in godlike derision, the skies exploded in amber flame. Fury seized the trees and the palms and the very grass. They writhed uncontrollably. Books blew from the marble table in the schoolroom. There was an unbearable screeching in the air, like millions of parrots going mad. All color disappeared from the gardens into one icteritious glare. The whole world has turned jaundiced! thought the frightened Cusa. He struggled with the door, for the gale had become savage blows on his body. He called to Lucanus to help him, and his voice was swept away. But the young Greek was beside him. It took their combined strength to shut the door, and then they stood, panting, staring at each other. There was no opportunity for speech. The thunder, continuous and deafening, enveloped them, accompanied by terrible and continuous lemon-colored lightning. The floor rumbled steadily under their feet. They held their mouths open, struggling for breath, for the heat was a blast from many furnaces. Once or twice they heard a wild sound, as of waters in torment.

Then the rain came, not dropping steadily, but in sidewise sheets of pure and crushing water, the color of yellow crocuses. Cusa and Lucanus went to the marble table, which trembled under their sweating palms. The lips of Cusa moved in frenzied prayer. Lucanus watched him, and his mouth curved unpleasantly. Cusa, pausing for a moment in his prayers, was startled by the expression of the young man. Cusa continued with his prayers hastily as the thunder roared like mighty chariot wheels over the earth, but he pondered. The inflamed lightning flickered again and again on Lucanus' face in the icteritious dusk, and it seemed as if it were striking the face of a tragic statue. Again and again the earth shuddered.

The gale beat against the bronze door with iron fists. The curtain at the window spread out straight, like a sail, billowing. Blinded by the lightning, and shivering to his very heart, Cusa covered his eyes. He did not see the water beginning to seep under the door. First it came in tendrils, quivering. Then it ran in broad and snakelike streams, glittering in the lightning. Then it was sheets, rising and flowing and wrinkling. It covered the tessellated floor. When it reached the sandals of Cusa, he jumped and opened his eyes. But Lucanus did not move. His head was bent. It seemed that he meditated.

Surely it will be over soon, thought the panic-stricken

teacher. But the storm increased in intensity. It appeared about to devour the earth in fire. An odd sound underlined the bellowing of the thunder, a rushing, indescribable sound. Cusa lost track of time. If the pillars of the house had come down, if the colonnades had been shattered, he would not have been surprised. No one approached the schoolroom from the inner door. The whole house was cowering. Occasionally the steady crashing of the thunder was punctuated by a splintering sound, an extra flash of flame, as a tree was stricken. The white walls of the room palpitated in waves of brilliance, fading momentarily to dimness, then igniting again.

Never had Cusa experienced such a storm. He longed for human consolation and courage. Lucanus had none to give him. He was apparently unaware of the assaults on the earth from the screaming and shouting heavens. He had rested his elbow on the table, and was supporting his chin with the thumb and index finger of his left hand. He might have been a student considering a theorem.

Then, as suddenly as it had begun, it was over. The lightning ceased to dart its flaming sword over the earth; the thunder stopped as abruptly as a crashing voice. The beating flames on the walls of the room subsided. The curtain fell limply over the window. Cusa's ears, however, rang for minutes afterwards. It was some time before he could control the trembling of his legs, and rise, and splash through the limpid water on the floor. He pulled open the door and fresh water gushed in.

A clear and innocent sun, newborn and wide-eyed, looked down on the earth. Shattered trees and palms were strewn over the ground like kindling. The fountains overflowed in cascades of silver luminescence. But the flowers had been struck to the earth like frail and colored corpses. All at once the sweetest odor rose from the ground and from the broken roses and the tossed jasmine. Birds took up a timid song of thanksgiving for preservation. The voice of the river, too close, conversed loudly and in agitation to the sky. Quicksilver ran everywhere, through beaten grass and fallen trees, and from trunks and leaves.

Slaves began to pour from the dripping house. They surveyed the destruction, and began to lament. Cusa shouted to them, "Eheu! Where have you been hiding, you cowards! Bring bread and cheese and wine at once. Are we to starve in the midst of books?"

For the first time Lucanus looked up, and he smiled slightly. But it was no longer the smile of youth; it was the smile of a weary man. A slave, still quaking, brought a tray of coarse bread, cheap local wine and a thick slice of hard yellow cheese, and some cucumbers in sour milk. He chattered, "Oh, there is much damage done! Four of the best cherry trees are down, six of the apple, and all the pomegranates are destroyed! As for the olive groves, one shudders to think of them. Many of the cattle were blasted in the fields yonder, and the sheep have disappeared."

Cusa swaggered to the table, thrust a finger into the bowl of cucumbers and sour cream, and licked it. "It is not curdled enough," he commented critically. He glared at the slave. "Are you a child to be afraid of the storm? While it was going on—was there a storm?—we were considering the 'Phaedo.' Begone."

The water was flowing through the door. Lucanus said, "I wonder who it was who was huddled near me voicing imprecations and prayers simultaneously?"

"Attention!" said Cusa. "We shall consider the Categories of Aristotle."

The hot sun dried the water, and the floor steamed. Now the whole garden, and all the earth, was enveloped in radiant mist. Still the river clamored, and Cusa uneasily wondered if it would invade the land. Everything dripped; a thousand tiny musical voices tinkled everywhere. Statues in the garden ran in watery light. The scent of the jasmine was as the odor of the white lilies along the banks of Lethe, overwhelming and drugging the senses. The voices of the slaves outside came into the schoolroom, full of ejaculations and awe at the destructiveness of the storm.

Cusa ate with relish, but Lucanus drank only a little of the wine. He appeared absorbed in his books. An hour passed, and another, and then another. The spring sun sloped to the west. Cusa could not read Lucanus' quiet face, which had a quality of massiveness about it. The stylus scratched.

The inner door opened and Diodorus entered the schoolroom, and Cusa and Lucanus rose. The tribune's face was ghastly and tight. He walked to the marble table and looked Lucanus fully in the eyes, tried to speak, and then could not. Lucanus cried out and seized the muscled arm. "Rubria! Rubria?"

"Come with me," said the tribune, and he stretched out

his arm and put it around the shoulders of the young man, like a father.

Iris was august in her sorrow. Aurelia wept beside her, but Iris did not weep. Lucanus could not approach his mother, for there was about her a majesty that repelled gestures of consolation. She stood in the center of the hall of her house, clothed in silence, her face blind and withheld, her hands pressed together before her. She seemed to hear only Diodorus, who was telling her of the death of her husband, Aeneas.

"While others fled like chickens, he stayed with his accounts in the little shelter near the river," said Diodorus, in a low voice. "There are times when bravery is folly, but who shall question loyalty and courage? He could not carry all the books with him, so he remained. But the river surged over the land, over the docks, over the shelter, and took Aeneas with it when it retreated."

He was full of wonder and reverence that his freedman had tried to preserve his records even to his death. He did not know that to Aeneas the records themselves, the mere writings of his hand, were more valuable in the moments of disaster than his very life. They had symbolized, for Aeneas, the reason for his existence; in them was recorded the evidence that he had been of importance, and in their neatness was a refutation of his former slavery. Triumphantly, at the last, he had seen Diodorus leave for higher ground, unable to move him from his tablets, his table, his stylus.

Only Lucanus, by some inner perception, understood, and he was stricken. Over these past years he and his father had grown apart, and the stature of Aeneas had dwindled in his son's youthful eyes. He had not listened too dutifully when Aeneas, in the evening, had expounded on the Greek philosophers pompously. Lucanus knew more about them, and more truly, and with profound depth. Often it had irritated him to observe his father's superficiality. Only the presence of Iris had prevented Lucanus from expressions of impatience. Sometimes he had found his father unbearable. He had angered Lucanus by derisive comments on Diodorus' lack of culture. He had hinted that in the tribune's interest in Lucanus was an acknowledgment of his inferiority as a trampling Roman. "It is a tribute that coarseness too infrequently pays to refinement," he would say. Lucanus would open his mouth impulsively, only to catch his mother's tender and warning blue glance, and then he would subside, fuming.

To Lucanus his father's death was a tragedy beyond his mere death. He could not weep. He could only sit and gaze at his mother. He wanted to fall at her feet, groveling, begging her forgiveness.

I have lived only in the house of Diodorus, thought Lucanus. I have lived only for Rubria, and Keptah, and my books. A man wishes to stand as a god in the eyes of his son. I let my father see that he was a pygmy of a man; he saw himself shrink in my regard. Oh, I could not let him believe he was important, though I tried to speak dutifully and in the false accents of respect! To such degradation did I fall.

"When the river yields up his body, he shall have a hero's funeral," said Diodorus, looking at the beautiful Iris, who stared at him with blue blindness. "I shall light the pyre myself. There will be banners and trumpets, and the presence of soldiers in full regalia. And incense, and the sound of drums, and a garment of mingled crimson and white."

Aurelia, weeping, thought how it would be for her if Diodorus had been stupid enough to try to rescue those foolish books and records.

"I shall begin sacrifices, tomorrow, in the temple of Hercules, the god of all heroes," said Diodorus. If Aurelia had not been present, and Lucanus, and Keptah, he would have knelt and kissed the hem of Iris' robe. He wanted to do her honor, in behalf of her dead husband. His detestation of Aeneas has been devoured in admiration, and in his love for Iris. Her still and wonderful face touched his heart. He wanted to cry to her, "Iris, my playmate, my beloved, my life is yours for the asking!"

Keptah had disappeared behind a curtain leading to the kitchen. He emerged with a potion in a goblet and, bowing as to a goddess, he put the goblet in the hand of Iris. She drank it, but she still looked at Diodorus with those drowning and unseeing eyes.

"I shall strike a statue for him," said Diodorus, helplessly. "It shall have an honored niche near the altar of Hercules. In the name of Aeneas a certain sum will be paid to you each year—Iris. It is the least I can do."

Aurelia wept again with a fresh rush of tears. The books, after all, had been swept away with Aeneas. His gesture of tragic heroism had been wasted. Oh, the touching folly of men, who thought a gesture was more important to their families than their lives! Men were heroes; but women were sensible. Aurelia was very sorry for Iris, who had a hero for a husband.

"I did not love him as my husband, but only as a mother loves a child," said Iris, speaking for the first time. Aurelia understood, and even while she sobbed she nodded. She was not astonished at honesty.

"He was to me as my child, worthy of my tenderness, my protection," said Iris, in a faint and dreaming voice. "He was tragic."

"Yes, yes," said Diodorus, not comprehending in the least. "But tragedy is the fate of heroes." He was very tired. He was covered with mud. He had worked for hours rescuing what could be rescued. Three ships loaded with the best produce of Syria had foundered. He had swum, with his officers, looking for the body of Aeneas, in vain. When he had seen Aeneas swept away he had plunged, breastplate, sandals, sword and all, into the raging yellow waters. He had thought only of Iris.

"I think," said Keptah, in a gentle voice, "that it would be best for the Lady Aurelia to conduct Iris to her bedroom. The potion is taking effect." And, indeed, Iris had begun to sway perceptibly. Aurelia rose and put her arms about her friend and led her through the curtain into the bedroom. She said, over her shoulder to her husband, "I will remain with her for a while. When you return, Diodorus, send my special slave, Maia, here to guard and watch over Iris for the night."

The three men were left alone. Diodorus looked at Lucanus, who, in his grief, was sitting in the presence of the tribune. Diodorus put his hand on the youth's shoulder. "Let the nobility and dutifulness of your father be an everlasting lesson to you," he said, in measured accents. Keptah folded his hands in his robe and dropped his eyes.

"I have not been a good son," said Lucanus.

Diodorus patted his shoulder. "We reproach ourselves when those we love are taken," he said. "But, if we meditate we can see how they can inspire our lives, make our years more significant by their lessons."

"I crave your pardon, Master, but you do not understand," said Lucanus, crushed with his sorrow.

"I never understand; that is what everyone tells me," said Diodorus with some irritability. His exhaustion made him weak. He patted Lucanus' shoulder again. "Remain with your mother. Comfort her. Exalt her spirit, for she has a hero for a husband."

Lucanus rose and went into his mother's bedroom. She lay like a white statue, fallen, on her bed, her eyes closed. He knelt beside her while Aurelia arranged the rugs over her snowy feet. He kissed a limp hand. Iris opened her eyes and looked at him, and her lips moved. For the first time she wept, and Lucanus lifted her aureate head against his shoulder and held her in mute and aching arms.

His heart was like a huge stone. He wished to pray for the soul of his father, which was now wandering in some ghostly Elysian field, faintly clamoring and lonely. But he could think, even then, only of Rubria, the bright, the young, the tender and the adorable, who would soon travel that grievous path into the depths of death and be lost to him forever.

Chapter Eleven

Rubria recovered a little, enough to be carried out under a tree in the warm spring sunlight. The ghostly aspect of her face lightened into a faint color. Keptah had told Diodorus that young maidens frequently had these relapses into partial invalidism. The devoted father did not know that the long sleeves the girl wore, and the woolen garments in spite of the heat, were to hide from his eyes the dolorous bleeding under her thin skin, and to warm her failing body. It had been arranged between him and Aurelia that she and Rubria would not leave for Rome until the autumn. In the meantime heated letters passed between him and the senator in the matter of the dowry.

Cusa, as much as possible, and when Lucanus pleased him particularly, would permit Lucanus to bring his lessons into the garden near Rubria in order that the youth could be with the maiden. Rubria no longer studied; her waning strength, her languor, her sudden fallings into slumber prohibited all strain. But she would smile with infinite sweetness when Lucanus recited. She would laugh gently at some of Cusa's sallies. He had always believed he was a wit; for the benefit of the girl Cusa often lay awake at night, inventing witticisms or gay stories. The heart of the crafty Greek had become like butter in the presence of Rubria. Believing only that all men were evil, that they were incapable of truly disinterested motives, that they were wolfish by nature and dissolute in all their thoughts, he marveled at himself. Before this girl one could be inspired only by love.

There were slave girls in this household more beautiful than this maiden. In comparison with Iris, old enough to be her mother, she was as a mortal compared with a shining goddess. Yet Cusa began to believe that never had there been born so perfectly lovely a creature. As her face thinned in its slender brownness, her dark eyes became enormous, shining, filled with a supernatural light, moist with dreams and love. Her mouth, Cusa would say to himself, was like a flower. Her long black hair seemed spun of glass, falling in a cascade over her young shoulders and girlish breast. She would lie back in her chair, her legs and feet covered with wool rugs even on the hottest day, and the outlines of her body took on an impalpable look, like the outlines of a spirit. When she slept she seemed not to breathe. She would awaken as suddenly as she had fallen into a doze, and would look about her with ardent shyness and affection. A Roman maiden, of a noble family, she treated slaves with the courtesy one extended to equals. She embraced life with dearness and reverence. As her mortal life declined her soul took on dimensions beyond the understanding of men.

When with her, one was convinced that all existence was good and full of meaning and poetry. Her favorite birds would light on her shoulder to eat of the bread or fruit she held in her lips for them. They would perch on her delicate finger and lean towards her eagerly, as if to learn from her some ineffable secret. Even the sun appeared to be brighter when she was present, and to shine more warmly upon her. If she were in pain, none knew it but Keptah. Tranquillity and serenity surrounded her like an aura; she was without fear. During the past months, since her sickness had seized her again, she had become a woman, and, in Cusa's humble belief, a divinity.

He knew that she was dying; all knew it, except the passionately devoted father. Cusa suspected that Rubria knew also. Her sublime patience, her tenderness, her way of looking all about the garden and at every face with quiet intensity and delight assured him that she understood that she would leave here before the winter came. Yet she never complained; she only smiled as if possessed of some divine secret.

And daily Lucanus became sterner and colder, except when with Rubria. The austerity of his face seemed worn down to the bone. He grieved for his father, and this Rubria knew. She had rarely seen Aeneas, but she suffered for Iris and Lucanus. She did not speak of the dead man, but sometimes she would sigh, looking at her old playmate. It was at her specific request that Lucanus ate often with her and her parents, when she had the strength to appear in the dining hall. To spare her father anxiety, she would come, walking slowly and weakly, to her place at the table. When there, all her attention was for Diodorus, and he would look at her lovingly. He believed she was improving. Keptah evaded his sharpest questions in a soothing tone.

Diodorus, happy that Carvilius Ulpian had finally agreed to his terms of the dowry, was elated in his belief that his daughter was improving slowly and steadily. He was also elated that Aurelia would bear him a son. "Naturally," he would say with fondness to his wife, "it will be a boy. Have I not sacrificed enough to the gods? Only yesterday I sacrificed a hecatomb, and the prices these Syrians charge, the thieves! I have dedicated the boy to Mars. He must be born in Rome, of course, not in this scurvy land."

Aurelia would smile at him. When sometimes he found her in tears, she would say to him hastily, "You must remember that women have these vagaries during the time they are with child. Put your hand upon my belly, dearest; feel your son leap like a lamb. Ah, he is strong! He is almost worthy of his father."

One day in late summer Rubria and Lucanus were alone together under the shade of a great green and glittering tree. Lucanus was sitting beside her as she drowsed, doing his lessons and unrolling his books for reference. Then all at once a fearful weariness came over him, and a sensation of overpowering despair. He put aside his tablets and his stylus. He looked at Rubria, at the long black lashes lying like shadows on her pale cheeks, at her folded hands, which were as transparent as alabaster. She had an aspect of death, of utter surrender, her breast hardly stirring. Then he knew, with absolute finality, in spite of his rebellion, in spite of his crying and sometimes blasphemous prayers, in spite of the pitting of his will against that of God, that she would die, and very soon. Her cheekbones were like ivory under her diminished flesh; her throat was a stalk. Lucanus let his head drop slowly against her knee, and he closed his eyes and gave himself up to sorrow.

When she dies, I will go away, he thought. I will become a vagabond on the face of the earth. I will leave in the night and go to the farthest corners of the world, and no one shall know my name. There is nothing without my heart's darling, without all that I have truly loved.

The birds sang and chattered, and he did not hear them. The sun danced on every leaf and flower, and there was only darkness before his eyes. He was young and warm; he felt old and cold as death. All desire for all that lived had left him. When the darkness of the grave or the funeral pyre had devoured this girl it would devour him also. A weak numbness ran over his flesh, and he felt deathly ill, as if about to die himself. A faint groan escaped him.

A hand, as light as a leaf, touched the top of his golden head and he started and looked up. Rubria was smiling down at him with the tender wisdom of a woman. All love shone in her eyes, all understanding. He caught her hand and kissed it with despairing strength. He could feel its fragility, its chill, its almost spiritual tenuousness.

Then she spoke. "You must not grieve, dear Lucanus," she said, and her voice was low and infinitely gentle.

The heart of Lucanus shook. Then the girl knew; it was possible that she had known a long time. He could not endure it, that one so young and beautiful had known the truth and had accepted it, without natural fear, without regret, and only with sublime courage. He cursed God inwardly, and thought, When she dies, then I will go with her, for there is nothing without her. A great stillness came to him then, and a quietude.

"Do not grieve," she repeated, and her voice was even softer. "I am very happy. I will not be parted long from you and my father. The gods are good; they do not hate love between mortals."

But God is evil, thought Lucanus. He put his head again at the knee of Rubria, and the beautiful garden about him became ghostly in his eyes, filled with the shapes of agony.

Rubria spoke again, and faintly. "I feel in my heart what you are thinking, dear one. You must not think so. God has a great destiny for you. He is our Father, and we are His children. Do you think He would inflict sorrow and pain on us for no purpose? He would have us come to Him."

"No," said Lucanus. "If He is as you say, Rubria, let Him raise you from that chair and put blood into your face and strength into your limbs." His throat closed on a spasm of anguish.

The maiden sighed. "Surely He knows what is best. Surely the peace I feel is His mercy and His goodness. Today I have no pain. Last night I slept as an infant, and my dreams were lovely beyond imagining. I was full of joy, and the joy is with me today. The world is beautiful, but where I go it is more beautiful, and there will be no parting any longer."

She lifted her head from her pillow and looked down at Lucanus, at his graven face, his still and rigid mouth, the bitter blue of his eyes. "Ah, you have forgotten," she said. "When we were younger it was you who told me of all this."

But it is a lie! thought Lucanus. He could not speak; he could not deprive this young girl of her last consolation, even if it were false.

Rubria watched him gravely. "It is true," she said. "All that you told me when we were children is true. My soul tells me so, and there is no lie on the edge of the grave. I go to God." She fumbled at her breast and brought out the golden cross which Keptah had given her, and she laid it in Lucanus' palm. She then gazed at the sky.

"Keptah is a strange man, full of wisdom, Lucanus. He has told me that the One who will die on the Cross is living in the world with us now, hardly more than a Child. But where He is living no one knows, and who He is no one knows but His Mother. His birth was prophesied by the priests of Babylonia thousands of years ago, and He has come. He will lead us into life everlasting, and there will be no more death, but only rejoicing."

Lucanus suddenly thought of the great white Cross he had seen in the hidden temple of the Chaldeans in Antioch. And he was overwhelmed with rage, self-ridicule, hatred, and disgust. Priests were notorious mountebanks, with their oracles, their prophecies, their conjuring, their delusions, their mysterious jargon. They laughed in secret at the naïveté of those who believed them. They fattened on sacrifices. They committed abominations. They filled their coffers with the gold of the fatuous. In the face of the ultimate death their sly faces faded, their voices were silenced.

The golden cross glittered in Lucanus' hand. He wanted to hurl it passionately from him, and to curse it for the bauble it was. But Rubria, leaning from her chair, gently closed his fingers around it.

"It is my gift to you."

The sunset stood in the western sky, a sea of scarlet and gold filled with the green sails of drifting little clouds. The gentle breeze sank; the odor of flowers and fertile earth rose like incense. Rubria slept, and Lucanus sat beside her, his head on her knee, her hand on his golden hair. He did not know how long they had remained like this. The edges of the cross cut into his hand and he did not feel it.

Then at last he lifted his head, and the hand of the maiden fell from it heavily. There was a smile upon her face, as if she had awakened to joy, serene and complete. Her cheeks and her lips had paled to absolute whiteness, and her brow glimmered. Her lashes lay upon her cheeks like the softest shadow.

Lucanus rose slowly to his feet, and the weight of age was upon him. He bent over Rubria and he uttered one single loud and terrible cry.

Chapter Twelve

"The cypress trees still stand at the door of the house of Diodorus, and at this door," said Iris to her son. "A desperate father weeps for his child, a brokenhearted mother is inconsolable. And I—I am but your mother—remember your father.

"But only you suffer! You hear no cry of bereavement but your own. When you were a child you lived as a child. But you are now a man, and should put aside childish things. Did you think the world all one dream of sweetness and happiness? That is the dream of fools, of those who would be children forever, of those who cower before the night, and would have nightingales, like Aedon, singing eternally so that they should never hear the voice of tragedy. Happiness! Those who say it exists, that it should exist, that men are entitled to it because they have merely been born, are like idiot children whose bumbling lips are smeared with honey.

"You have shut your door to that poor slave, your tutor, Cusa, and to the physician, Keptah. You have shut your door in my face. You will revenge yourself on the world because one you love has left you. You will revenge yourself on Diodorus, who loves you and cherishes you as a son. You will revenge yourself on the gods. You will wander away, and all then will be desolate, you believe. But I tell you that Diodorus will be comforted when his child is born, and he will forget you, or think of you with contempt. Your tutor will have another pupil. Only I will remember you, I, your mother, whom you have not seen as a woman without a husband and without a son."

She trembled in her anger. Beyond the doors and the windows the autumnal rains and winds mourned. Iris had entered her son's bedroom; the sad twilight showed him at his table, his head in his hands. But for the first time in a long while he was listening. Finally he lifted his head and looked at his mother and saw her. His haggard face became contorted with speechless pain.

"Oh, you who have been so blessed!" cried Iris. "You have been surrounded by love. You are not a slave. You are a free man, born free. What do you know of the world's terrible sorrow and agony? You are young, you have been nurtured. But you will not lift up your pain and carry it like a man. Like Orpheus, you must weep forever."

"I have seen suffering and death many times," said Lucanus in the hoarse voice of one who has been silent too long. "I am not unfamiliar with them." Now his sunken eyes glittered in the dusk, and he clenched his fists on the table. "Do you know what my thoughts have been these weeks? That God is a torturer, that the world is a circus where men and beasts are done to death savagely, without reason, without consolation."

Iris rejoiced in herself that her son had finally shown some emotion. But she said, sternly, "It is an evil thing to blaspheme the gods."

But Lucanus' words poured from him like some released stream. "Why is a man born? He is born only to writhe in torment, and then to die as ignominiously as he has lived, and as darkly. He cries to God, and there is no answer. He appeals to God. He appeals to an Executioner. His days are short, and never free from trouble or pain. His mouth is extinguished with dust, and he goes down into the grave, and the awful enigma of his being remains. Who has returned from the grave with a message of comfort? What God has ever said, 'Arise, and I will lighten your burden and lead you to life?' No, there has been no such God, nor will there ever be such a God. He is our Enemy."

He looked at his fists, then opened them, then turned them over to contemplate his palms and his fingers. His face became harsh and stern with wrath. "I shall learn to defeat Him," he muttered. "I shall snatch His victims from Him. I shall take away His pain from the helpless. When He stretches forth His hand for a child, I shall strike that hand down. Where He decrees death, I shall decree life. That will be my vengeance upon Him."

He stood up. He was weak from little nourishment. He swayed and caught the edge of the table. He stood and looked at his beautiful mother, and he saw the tears in her eyes. He cried out and fell on his knees before her and wound his arms about her waist and laid his head against her body. She put her hands on his head and silently blessed him, then bent and kissed his forehead.

"Hippocrates has said that this vile thing is sometimes healed spontaneously," said Keptah. "Once he remarked it was a visitation from the gods, who certainly in this event are no better than men. He recommends effusions and distillations of certain herbs to relieve the exquisite torment, and advises tampons soaked in wine and potions for the alleviation of women afflicted by the disease, which devours them in their secret places. For men he advises cauterizations and castrations. He thinks of it as only a disease of the private parts, though he is troubled in some of his assertions. Is it a single disease or many? A pupil of his thought it akin to leprosy, when it attacks the skin. Is it the same thing when a mole enlarges and blackens, and kills quickly? Is it the white sickness also? The sickness that destroys the blood, and makes it sticky to the touch, like syrup? Is it that which decays the kidneys, the lungs, the spleen, the bowels? Hippocrates is not sure. But I am sure. It is the same evil, with different manifestations. And the worst of all evils, for it comes like a thief in the night and only at the last does the victim cry out and beg for death when the knife turns and turns in his parts."

He and Lucanus were in the small hospital set aside for the slaves. Five beds were occupied by groaning and tossing men and women. Three slaves followed them with brazen bowls, oils and strips of white linen. Another slave carried a tray of small vessels filled with liquid. The physician and Lucanus had paused beside the bed of a man who was gasping in the purest agony. The left side of his face was eaten away as by a monstrous maggot, the flesh raw and mangled, the lip swollen and oozing with blood. The slave looked up at the phys-

ician who contemplated him in sorrow. And Lucanus stood
and gazed at him with bitter despair.

He murmured to Keptah, "Surely it would be merciful to
give him a potion to bring him peace and death."

Keptah shook his head slowly. "Hippocrates has declared
that is forbidden. Who knows at what instant the soul shall
recognize God? Shall we kill the sufferer tonight when in
the morning the recognition would come? Besides, man
cannot give life. Therefore it is not for him to give death.
These are reserved only for Him, who is unknowable to our
natures, and who moves in mysteries."

"Kill me!" cried the slave, lashing on his bed. He seized the
physician's arm in a skeletonized hand. "Give me death!"
His voice gurgled in a rush of blood.

Keptah turned to Lucanus, who was looking with horror
at the sufferer. He touched his arm, and Lucanus moved his
head and stared at him with obdurate severity and pleading.
"Would you have deprived Rubria of one hour of her life?
And I tell you she suffered as much as this, and even more."

He soaked a pad of linen in a portion of a white liquid
which he poured from a vessel. Lucanus clenched his teeth
with hatred. What had this poor slave, a gardener, done
against the gods to deserve this? He had been a gentle and innocent soul, delighting in the flowers, proud of his borders,
loving his lilies, soothing as a father to his roses. There were
millions less worthy of peace and life than he. The world
was filled with monsters who ate and drank and laughed,
and whose children danced in the pleasant gardens of their
homes and knew no blight.

Keptah, with great gentleness, took the slave's darting hand
and held it firmly. "Listen to me," he said, "for you are a
good man and will understand. There are those who have
this disease but of the spirit, and I tell you they endure more
than you. Where your mouth gushes blood, their souls
gush violence and venom. Where your flesh is torn, there their
hearts are torn. Niger, I swear to you that you are luckier
than they."

The slave began to whimper, and his eyes became full
and still. He whispered through his blood, "Yes, Master."

Wild scorn was like an acid in Lucanus. He watched Keptah lay the soaked linen on the awful and disfigured face. The
slave panted. The other slaves, less afflicted, watched from
their beds. Then, at last, into the slave's eyes there came a
moist relief, a tremulous surcease. A tear ran from the corner

of his eyelid. Keptah took a goblet and put his arm under the slave's head and lifted it as tenderly as a mother lifts a child, and he put the goblet to the twisted lip, and slowly Niger drank with touching obedience. When Keptah replaced his head on the pillow, Niger had already fallen into a sleep, moaning softly. Keptah contemplated him enigmatically for long moments. His dusky face with its hooded eyes was unreadable.

"It has already invaded the larynx," he murmured. "He will not live long." He turned to one of the slaves. "Give him this potion whenever he cannot bear it any longer, but never more than every three hours, according to the water clock."

"And that is all you can do!" exclaimed Lucanus.

"No. Had he come to me when the first small, hard white sore had appeared on his inner cheek, I could have burned it out with a hot iron. He did not come to me until it was very difficult for him to swallow and the inner parts of his mouth were already bleeding and corroded and sloughing away. Remember that whether it is an illness of the spirit or of the flesh, it is best to seek counsel and help at the very beginning. Later all is lost."

They moved to the bed of a young female slave who was hardly less tormented than Niger. Her bed was foul with drainings from her vagina. Keptah swung on a slave and exclaimed, "Have I not told you to keep the linen dry and pure? This is poison which is leaving her. I shall report you to the overseer, so prepare yourself for a flogging."

"Master, I have other duties," whined the slave.

"There is no greater duty than to heal or alleviate suffering. Truly medicine is the divine art. Enough. Do your work better and I shall forget the flogging."

The slave girl, in spite of her dishevelment and fever, was pretty and appealing. Keptah touched her forehead, feeling its heat. He said to Lucanus, "She attempted an abortion on herself with a filthy and primitive instrument which the savages use. This is the result."

"I could not have a child born into slavery!" wept the girl.

Keptah said somberly, "The thought was virtuous; the deed was not. You should have clung to the virtue. Have you a bad master? Had you asked him for a husband he would have given you one. This is a virtuous household. But you dallied, out of wantonness and lust. You had no excuse. You were taught to read and write, to spin and to sew, to cook and to render other valuable services. You were not as the slaves in Rome, summoned to the bed of the master at his will. Ah, well. Let us look at you."

But first he washed his hands with water and then rubbed them with pungent oil. Then he examined the weeping girl, and touched her inflamed and pus-streaming parts. "Will I die, Master?" cried Julia in terror.

Keptah did not reply. He twisted a piece of linen into a thin cone of whiteness. He dipped it into fluid from one of his vessels. The girl blanched. But Keptah firmly separated her legs and thrust the cone into her body. She screamed. The air was filled with an aromatic odor. "Let the tampon remain until night," Keptah directed his slave assistant. "Then remove it and destroy it. It is contaminated and dangerous. Afterwards wash the parts with flowing clear water, make another tampon, and let the girl herself insert it. By then it will be less painful."

He patted the girl's wet hands, gave her something to drink. He said to her, "You will not die, I pray. You will live to sin some more, I am afraid."

He looked at Lucanus. "Visit her at nightfall. Enforce my orders."

"Why do you reproach this poor child?" asked Lucanus, resentfully. "Is she greater than her nature, with which your God endowed her? He gave her her normal instincts."

"Where normal instincts can be dangerous, then one controls them," said Keptah. "And what is normal? The world? One must have discipline to defeat the urgings of the world, or man is no more than a beast."

The girl, somewhat relieved, smiled at Lucanus coquettishly. He turned away, sad but revolted.

The windows were open to the cool wintry air, and breezes filled the room. "Air and light are enemies of disease," said Keptah, against all the advice of other physicians. "Cleanliness is also an enemy. Not to mention self-respect and esteem for the flesh in which the spirit is clothed."

They stopped at the bed of a young and comely woman with a huge belly. Beside her crouched her equally young and handsome husband, whose face was stained with tears. He rose eagerly and looked at Keptah with bright and urgent eyes. "Ah, Master!" he said. "Surely she is with child, and it is about to be born?"

Keptah sighed. "I have told you, Glaucus. This is no child but a great tumor. She must be relieved of it or she will die.

I have left it in your hands, though I could have operated before. You have waited, and so diminished the chances for her life. It cannot wait any longer. Make your choice now."

"Master, I am only a slave. You have only to command," said Glaucus, tearfully.

Keptah shook his head. "No man is a slave, no matter how bound and chained, until he admits he is a slave. You are a man. Shall I save your wife now, or will you wait and let her die? She will surely die without the operation; she may live if I perform it."

He turned to Lucanus. "Palpate the belly," he said. Lucanus was full of pity for this stoic young woman who did not cry but only smiled bravely. He lifted her shift. The belly was as smooth and veined as marble, and glimmered with stretched tension. He felt it carefully, closing his eyes so as to concentrate through his gentle fingers. It was like feeling stone over her right side, but there was a gurgling of liquid, and a sponginess as he moved his fingers to the umbilicum. "I am certain it is not carcinoma," he said to Keptah, who nodded in a pleased way. "It is a lipoid and serum tumor," said the physician. "Very common. It should have been removed many months ago, but this is a couple who longed for a child and believed the tumor was one, after three years of marriage. It is fastened to the right ovary, which will have to be removed also."

"Then she will have no child!" wept Glaucus. "Or only a girl!"

"Do not be foolish," reproved Keptah. "Aristotle dismissed the ancient theory that one ovary produces a girl, or a boy, or one teste produces only one sex. Your wife will have her left ovary, and it is the mysterious choice of God whether she will later have a son or a daughter."

He ground some fresh and acrid leaves in a pestle, added a little wine, and gave the result to Hebra, who took it obediently. Keptah said to one of the slaves, "Stay with her and give her a large goblet of wine, and then another. When she sleeps call me." Hebra's eyes were beginning to close, while her husband watched her fearfully. She languidly raised her kind hand and touched his cheek in consolation. "Women, you observe, are less afraid of death and life than are men," Keptah said to Lucanus as they moved to another bed. "Is it faith? Or, as women are realists, do they accept reality with better spirit?"

Lucanus glanced at him sullenly. Perhaps, he thought,

all these remarks which have been directed to him this first morning of his return to the house of Diodorus and his lessons were subtle barbs for his sensibilities, and reproofs. He was angered and ashamed.

The man in the next bed was grossly fat and as white and flaccid as dough. He regarded Keptah in resentful silence. Keptah looked at the little table beside him, on which stood a pitcher of water and a goblet. "You have drunk all this water today, my friend?" The man muttered something in his throat. An odor of apples, or hay, floated in his heavy breath.

"I warned you months ago to limit your love for pastries and breads and honeys," said Keptah, sternly. "I told you you had the sweet sickness, and that if you did not take care your very muscles and bones would run from you in a river of urine. But I see that you have not confined yourself to lean meats and vegetables, both of which are plentiful in this household, which believes in sufficient food for its slaves. If you do not control your pig's appetite then you will die very soon in convulsions. Yours is the choice. Take it."

He turned to Lucanus and gave him a brief talk on the subject of the sickness. "Always, a man is his own disease," he said. "He who is afflicted with the sweet sickness, where the very urine is saccharine, is often found to be of a self-indulgent temperament which arises from a selfish refusal to cherish others, but only himself. Thus others do not love him; to satisfy his natural human craving for love, he eats of the sweets of the earth rather than of the sweets of the spirit. There are other manifestations of this disease, especially in children, who invariably die of it. It would be interesting to talk with these children, who, even in their tender years, are possibly of a greedy disposition, caring only for self. We can do nothing but prescribe the leanest of meat, the starchless vegetables and fruits, and restrict or omit the sweets and the starches. Little, however, will be accomplished except painful deprivation and prolonging of a restricted life, unless the patient has an awakening of the spirit and thus is enabled to love beyond himself."

He looked at the sulky slave, who had been watching him with rapidly blinking eyes. "Look on your wife with love," he admonished. "Say not, 'She belongs to me, and she will serve me!' Say in your heart, rather, 'This is my beloved wife, and what can I do to make her the happiest of women, so that she will say she is married to the kindest and noblest of men?'"

As they moved away, Lucanus said, "Then this is not an organic disease?"

Keptah stopped and pondered. He finally said, "There is no separating the flesh from the spirit, for it is through the flesh that the spirit manifests itself. You are wondering how it is that some people contract illnesses in epidemics and others do not. Hippocrates talked of natural immunity in those who escape. One of his pupils believed that those who escape manufacture some essence in themselves which repels the disease. But why? Could it be that certain temperaments resist infection whereas others do not? Immunity? If so, then it is the immunity of the spirit, though other physicians do not believe this. I am not speaking of good and evil. I am speaking only of temperament."

They came to the last bed. Here lay a youth in high fever, his right leg contracted so that the muscles stood out on it like ridges. He had a sharp dark face with unusually intelligent, bold eyes, and an angry expression. Keptah looked at one of the attendant slaves. "I have said that this leg must be wrapped constantly in hot woolen compresses, day and night, as hot as he can endure it. Give me no excuses!" Vexed, he lifted his hand and struck the slave on the cheek. "Have we nothing here but men and women who seek only their own pleasures and satisfactions? Go to!"

He looked down at the young man on the bed. He said to Lucanus, "Here is a youth of a haughty, proud and inconsiderate nature, overweening in self-esteem, and arrogant. He despises ignorance and dullness. He has a mind like the thin blade of a very sharp knife. He loathes his fellow man, who rarely has his intelligence. He has no patience, no kindliness. I have taught him to read and write; he has access to my own library; he comes and goes at will. He never thinks with his heart, but only with his brain. You will discover that such as he are very susceptible to this crippling disease. You will also discover that the more stupid, the more bovine, rarely contract it, even among children."

Diomed was smiling with mingled pride and ill-humor. "Thank you, Master, for your words about my intellect," he said. He was evidently in great pain, but his pride would permit no expression of it.

"I am not flattering you," said Keptah. "It was almost inevitable that you have this miserable illness, which, I am afraid, is going to leave you with a limping leg."

"I care little for my body if I may nourish my mind," said Diomed.

Keptah looked at Lucanus. "You will observe this trait in people afflicted like this. Why should a man despise his flesh, and the flesh of others, when it is a marvelous invention of God's and can be more beautiful than any other living thing? It is through his flesh that he communicates with others. Men like Diomed wish no communication. They crave only obeisance and flattery for their truly fine minds. I say to parents with children like these, 'Teach your child to love, and to give, and train him in reverence for God.'"

Lucanus' lip curled, but he said nothing. Keptah said to Diomed, "I shall have some books sent to you this afternoon. I see you have finished those I have previously sent. In the meantime there is that maiden, Leda, who often writes the letters for the Lady Aurelia. She is a pretty child, intelligent and loving, and she adores you. Take her love, but return it with your whole heart. I know such a thing will be hard for you, but you can will yourself to love if you wish. Nothing is impossible with a seeking and determined and intellectual mind. The Lady Aurelia is so attached to this girl that she has told me that when she wishes to marry she will receive her freedom. Will you withhold that gift from her?"

Diomed began to sneer. Then his face softened, and he suddenly turned it to his pillow. His thin shoulders heaved. Keptah said softly, "There have been more souls saved through humble tears than all the potions in the world."

Lucanus said defiantly in himself, He simplifies too much. But he was moved by the sobbing of Diomed, who could not control himself though all his muscles were contracted in the effort. Keptah said, "Hasten and get well, Diomed. I shall need you as my assistant when you can feel pity and love for others."

Diomed reared his tear-wet face from the pillow, and joy shone in his eyes. He caught Keptah's hand. "You will let me attend you, Master?" he cried, incredulously. Keptah smiled. "You will make an excellent helper, Diomed. When you love and have mercy, and feel another's pain in your own body."

They returned to the bed of Hebra, who was as one asleep, gently breathing. Keptah ordered screens, which were placed about the bed. He drove Glaucus from the enclosure. He placed a tray on the small table, and on it were needles and sutures and a large and two small scalpels. He said to Lucanus, "It is time for you to see your first operation. If you vomit, kindly use this bucket, but say nothing. If you faint, I shall let you lie. There is a life to save. I will need your help. Take up that pad of linen and dip it in this pungent oil. There is infection in the very air."

Lucanus began to tremble. But he obeyed orders silently. He looked down at the drugged girl, who was sweet in her slumber. He was filled with a passionate commiseration. Why should any god so afflict a child who wanted only children and the love of her husband, and a tranquil life? Oh, You who do this evil to men, I despise You! he thought. Would not even the basest of men be more compassionate?

Keptah exposed Hebra's gleaming, taut belly. He palpated it with care. Then with sure strokes of his scalpel, as one drawing a careful diagram, he drew the knife over the white flesh. Its path was followed by a red streak, which widened, opened, like a hungry mouth. Lucanus sickened, but he watched. Now the shining red muscles were exposed, sinewy, threaded with pulsing veins. Keptah pushed them aside deftly and gently, and said, "Now we will use the Egyptian hooks to ligature all blood vessels, to keep the field of operation as free as possible and to prevent bleeding to death. Observe these vessels, and the pulses of the heart which throb them! Is it not all perfect? Who can look on this and not reverence God in his heart? He has designed a man as wonderfully as He has designed the suns and their planets. Ah, be careful; use those small pads of linen to keep the wound open. Do not let your fingers touch any part of the wound, for there is poison on your fingers and in the air. The Egyptians knew that many hundreds of years ago, but the Greeks and Romans deride it, asking, 'Where is the poison? We do not see it.' There are millions of things in the universe that men cannot see; nevertheless, they are there."

Hebra began to groan, to talk incoherently. "It is her assaulted flesh which speaks," said Keptah. "The spirit is also protesting the ignominy of its passiveness under the drug. There are those who say drugs subdue the spirit; it is not so. Does she feel the pain? Surely. But when she awakens she will not remember that she suffered. She will say, 'I was as one who slept through a storm.'"

Lucanus, filled with pity for the girl, said deep in his soul to her, "Rest, endure, be of courage. We will save you, dear child." He directed the full force of his mind to her, to reassure her. Perhaps it was only the drugs she had taken, and the stupefying wine, but all at once she sighed, and relaxed. The tight muscles became soft, no longer tensed.

The gray-pink and glistening intestines were exposed now. Here they were, in their convolutions, slipping mass after mass. They palpitated, writhing a little, and Lucanus spoke to them kindly in his mind, and they too became flaccid. With the most exquisite care Keptah pushed them aside, and, like a burgeoning evil, a huge opalescent bladder ascended from beneath them, pushing them aside ruthlessly, a cloudy and glimmering bladder seething with corruption and shifting patterns of blood. It bobbed restlessly over the intestines. It was attached from below by a rope deeper in color than itself.

"This is the vital moment," said Keptah, working with sure hands. "We will now look very carefully at the ovary. The slightest carelessness will explode this bladder and fill her whole belly with death." He exposed the yellow-white ovary. "Aha!" said Keptah. "It is in good health. We shall save it after all. You are too preoccupied. Use more pads, hold the flesh aside firmly."

All at once the whole scene dimmed and flickered before Lucanus' eyes. The smell of blood almost overpowered him. His legs trembled violently, and there was a huge dry retching in his stomach. He said to himself, If I fail this girl, if I faint, who will help? He looked at the wicked, restless bladder, forced calm upon his natural human revulsion. He tried to observe the layers of fat over the peritoneum, yellowish and wet as sheep's fat. He pressed the pads harder against the yawning mouth of the wound, and his muscles tensed, and he sweated. Keptah was neatly tying the lengths of the cord of the bladder in several places, pulling the linen thread tightly. The opalescent corruption dimmed to a milkiness; the patterns of blood darkened. Then, with a slow motion of the scalpel, Keptah cut the cord. The bladder lay quiet on the intestines.

With the utmost care and slowness Keptah lifted it from its position and dropped it on the tray. Lucanus' eyes were swimming, and drops of water dripped from his face. "Watch how I sew these layers now, as neatly as a seamstress," said the physician. "Not an error must be made in the sutures." He employed a crisscross pattern, using a clear thread, which he explained was catgut. "The body will absorb these in time, and the joinings will be firmer than before. Some physicians use linen thread, which the body does not absorb, and which later causes difficulties."

The evil bladder was as large as a curled, newborn child on the tray. Taking infinite pains, the physician brought each layer of the belly together, sewed it firmly. "The fat is difficult; it sometimes separates from the thread, or tears apart. There. We have it now. And now for the skin, which is very tough. Here we use linen thread, which we will cut away in a week."

The belly had become miraculously flat. The girl groaned over and over, catching her breath with desperate sobs. "She is awakening," said Keptah. He tied the last expert knot. He dipped a cloth in hot water and wrung it out and put it over the girl's heart, then he dipped another cloth and wrapped it over her feet, and another over her wrists. He bent his head and pressed it against the girl's breast. "Rapid, but strong. She will not have shock, which is much to be feared. Use the bucket close to her mouth, and hold her head."

He wrapped large white strips of cloth over the body as though they were grave wrappings. He stood back and regarded the girl contentedly. He was very calm. He glanced at Lucanus, and saw that the youth's tunic was wet and dripping. He laughed gently. "You have endured it very well. I congratulate you. Drink this wine as fast as possible. I may even say I am proud of you."

The girl opened dull eyes. Keptah bent over her. "It is all over now, my child. You are well." The girl moaned, began to cry. Keptah crushed more acrid leaves and pressed the potion into her mouth, gave her water. She swallowed feebly. She was as white as death. "Sleep," he said. "Sleep cures more illnesses than any doctor's art."

He nodded at Lucanus. "I noticed, with pleasure, that you have kept count of the restraining pads. Now you will clean up this mess, and you will visit her in a few hours."

"Glaucus," whispered the girl. Keptah moved aside the screen and summoned the husband, who came in like the wind. He knelt beside his wife and laid his cheek to hers, sobbing. "It is much more rigorous on the husband," observed Keptah, wryly.

He left Lucanus to the filthy and repulsive job of removing all evidences of the operation. Lucanus' hands moved weakly and with wincing. He washed the scalpels and replaced them on the tray. The smell of the blood was sickening, and all the effluvia of the violated body. Why could not a slave have done this labor? He was irritated. When he emerged from the screens he found Keptah genially conversing with the other patients and giving orders. Keptah said to him, "You will not always have an assistant. Too often a surgeon must stand alone and do everything himself." He looked at Lucanus, and hastily caught up a bucket, and Lucanus vomited violently into it until it seemed that his very entrails and stomach and liver would leave his gaping mouth. Keptah was patient. "Again I congratulate you, my Lucanus. It is better to indulge one's self after the emergency than during it. Go and lie down until you are ready for Cusa."

Lucanus wiped his sour mouth. "I prefer to go home."

"No," said Keptah. "You would dwell too much on what has happened. Gird yourself; continue with your work."

The autumnal winds mourned like the voices of a multitude of doves when Lucanus left the schoolroom. The gray rains drifted against the palms and the trees and through the colonnades of the house of Diodorus, and now, suddenly, the sea-voiced gale whitened every leaf, every branch and trunk, blanched the grass. A muted howling rose from the earth, a most dolorous sound. Lucanus pulled the hood of his mantle over his head and gazed somberly at the bleached and writhing garden. The fountains complained in distress; the statues ran with gray water; the flowers bent their heads in docile suffering. Lucanus was young; he forgot that tomorrow all would again be smiling and warm, the palms glittering, the birds singing to an azure sky. As it was now, to him, so it would always be, torn with ragged anguish, replying feebly to the wind that roared in from the sea, bending endlessly and helplessly like the grasses of the ghostly Elysian fields.

All is dead, said Lucanus to himself. All is beaten, all is gray, all is inundated. All is withered and drowned and lost. What I have loved is gone. Lucanus wiped his wet face with a corner of his mantle and felt a most frightful desolation in himself, a hollowness unfilled by a single dream or hope. His young flesh was weighty on his bones, as if that flesh were old and drenched and sodden with earth. He looked at the vaporous sky, as colorless as death itself, and he wanted to weep, but there were no tears in him, only an aridness where nothing grew and nothing stirred.

He longed to go home, yet he shrank from the thought. Iris, his mother, would be there, her beautiful face white with silent grief; she would gaze at him questioningly, and he had no answers for her. She was old; she was thirty-one.

The elderly possessed no wisdom, only queries. Only youth had the replies, and it could reply only when it was happy. In truth, said Lucanus in his heart, there is no answer to nothingness. And nothingness is all that there is. And then he was filled with a wild and tumultuous rage, and he lifted clenched fists against the sky. "I shall defeat You!" he exclaimed. "I shall deprive You of Your sacrifices!"

The sea-voiced gale blew against his face and body, and he felt it as a mocking and challenge. He began to walk through the gardens, trembling with fury, and came to the open portico before the house. The carved bronze doors were shut. He stood and stared at them, and felt them obdurate. He strode to them without thinking and struck them with a fist. When they opened he said to the slave, "I wish to talk with your master, Diodorus."

The chief of the hall regarded him impudently. "The master is in his library. He has not spoken for many days. Do you wish to intrude upon him, Lucanus? He will not see you; he has refused his Roman friends. Will he see the son of a freedman?"

Lucanus thrust open the door and hurled the slave aside. The spectral and watery light from the sky fell onto the black and white marble of the hall, and Lucanus went over it, his sandals echoing, his white mantle flowing about him in ghostly folds. The cool dank air of the house was like the air from a tomb, musty and unliving. No voice or movement broke the silence except the slapping of Lucanus' feet. The archway of the library was shrouded in thick brown cloth, and this Lucanus pushed away. Only when he stepped into the library did he suddenly wonder why he had come and what he was doing here.

Diodorus was sitting at a pale marble table, many books rolled about him, his head in his hands. He was as still as a statue carved in dark bronze, for even his tunic was of a deep color. When he heard the rustling of the curtain he dropped his hands heavily and lifted a lightless face and stared at Lucanus blankly, Lucanus, whom he had not seen since the death of Rubria.

Lucanus was stunned by his patron's appearance, at the ashen color of his cheeks, at the dryness of his mouth, at the hollows in which his dull eyes lurked without sparkle or interest. The very flesh of the tribune seemed to have withered; his shoulders sagged listlessly, and when he moved a little it was with an effort. Lucanus suddenly felt his own youth, the strength of his body, the flexibility of his limbs, the vitality of his blood in spite of his sorrow and his bottomless anger. Here, as his mother had said, was absolute despair, beyond the reach of consolation.

"What?" murmured Diodorus, as though he did not recognize the young man. He watched Lucanus approach him, and with complete uninterest he watched while Lucanus knelt beside him, his head bent on his chest. A muffled sound came from Diodorus, a weary and fathomless sound. Then he dropped his head in his hands again and forgot his visitor.

Words involuntarily came to Lucanus' lips. "Master, there is an old story which my father told me. An old man lost his only son, and his friends came to him and said, 'Why do you weep? Nothing can bring back your son.' And the old man said, 'That is why I weep.' "

The one high window in the library admitted wandering and crepuscular light, shadowy and vague. Silence filled the room. The youth knelt by the man and both were motionless. Then Diodorus slowly and falteringly put his hand on Lucanus' shoulder. He said, in that rusty voice, "You too loved her. But you are not her father."

"I lost my father," said Lucanus, and turned his cheek so that it rested on the hand of Diodorus. His words came in a fierce rush. "Look upon me, noble Tribune. I am a son who came not to hate his father, but to despise him lightly as a man of little learning and of many pretensions. I became arrogant and impatient, and condescending. I forgot all he had suffered, all he had known. I no longer found his bombast touching; I found it risible. I did not lose my father in those years, but my father lost a son. And now the son has lost his father, and I cannot reach him and ask his forgiveness for cruelty and impatience and the pride of youth."

Diodorus' hand lay still on Lucanus' shoulder, and for the first time life returned to the tribune's eyes, and sympathy. He could not see the face of Lucanus, hidden as it was in the shadow of the hood. He said, very gently, "Surely the gods do not reject contrition, and surely the shades in the regions of death are aware of repentance."

But Lucanus shook his head, unable to speak.

"I honored my father," said Diodorus, compassionately. "I am not a man without understanding. I can imagine what it must be to remember that one despised his father." He paused. "Aeneas was a good man, and honorable, and I trusted him without reservation. If he strove for wisdom the striving was not despicable. It is only when a man does not strive that he is less than an excellent dog. Let us honor those who know in their hearts that they are not great, for they respect and reverence greatness."

"Yes," said Lucanus. "But that does not absolve me."

Diodorus did not speak for a few moments. Then he said, as if thinking aloud, "It is good so to live that when a loved one dies one has no regrets. But who does not have regrets? Who has not been rude and harsh and unfeeling at times? Who has not been human, with all faults? Why, then, should we punish ourselves and cry aloud, 'If only I had known! If only I had watched! Then, perhaps, I could have held back death with my bare hands, before it was too late!' "

Wonder ran like frail light over his tortured face, and his shoulders lifted. He said, "I have often said to myself that I was remiss, that I did not guard my child more closely, that if I had been more careful she might not have died. But now I see that the gods have their hours of choosing, and we can do nothing but pray for the souls who have left us, that they will have peace and that they will know we have loved them and will continue to love them."

But the dryness became dustier in Lucanus, and what Diodorus had said was only an echo with no meaning.

"Yes, yes!" cried Diodorus. "Why have I drawn away from life? Why have I been less than a brute, who mourns, and then resumes his living? What the gods have willed, so be it. They need not answer us, for their nature is beyond our understanding." He shook his head vehemently. His hand clenched on Lucanus' shoulder. "I have left my poor wife to cry alone in her bed, and she the mother of my daughter, and heavy with child. I have abandoned her, and when she came to console me I turned from her. Did she suffer? Did she wander into an empty room? Did she miss a maiden's voice, and that maiden her very flesh? What was that to me, the hating, the embittered, who wished to revenge himself for the loss of his daughter? Lucanus, surely the merciful gods sent you to me today! Had I brooded much more I should have fallen on my own sword!"

"I will revenge her," Lucanus whispered to himself. "I will revenge her all my life."

Diodorus looked down at the kneeling youth, whose hard white face was hidden in the hood, and it seemed to the tribune that here was a messenger from Olympus itself. He put his knotted soldier's arms about the young man's shoulders as a father embraces a son.

"We have no longer to pray to be absolved of our crimes against the dead, but of our crimes against the living," said Diodorus. "Let us, then, rise like men and go about the business of life. The living await us."

Then, like Odysseus and his son, they wept together, and the tears of Diodorus were healing, but the tears of Lucanus were like scalding acid.

Lucanus went through the dripping forest to his home, and he said, numbly and incredulously, "What was it that I said to him? What message did I bring him? In truth, I said nothing at all. I talked about my father, for whom I do not truly grieve, but for whom I feel only regret. When I spoke, my thoughts were with Rubria, and not with Aeneas, my father. And she I will avenge against whatever gods there be."

Diodorus went into his wife's chamber, where she was lying in sadness on her bed. She started up when her husband entered, and when she saw his face she knelt on her bed with a sobbing cry and held out her arms to him, and he held her to him while she cried on his shoulder.

"Forgive me, beloved," he said to her, and his tears mingled with hers.

Iris, standing in the gloomy and foggy dusk of the evening at her door, saw her son approach, and she waited for him, not hailing him or greeting him. He came into the house and threw off his cloak, and she saw the pallor of his lips, the blue and stony hardness of his eyes. She said, "You have seen Diodorus. I prayed that you would go to him, for you have remembered that he is as a father to you. Tell me. Is he still broken with sorrow?"

Lucanus' eyes flickered. "There is something which I do not understand, and which I may have understood when I was a thoughtless child. I spoke with Diodorus. I spoke with him not of Rubria, but of my father. And he stood up and he was like a man reborn. Do not ask me what I said for I do not remember."

Iris had lit a lamp. She turned and faced her son, and never had she seemed so beautiful to him, so clothed in golden light, so like a statue carved by Phidias. She went to Lucanus and put her hand gently against his cheek.

"They to whom the gods give a message do not always understand that message," she said, and for the first time since Aeneas had died she smiled. "Others hear, and their hearts answer."

Never had Lucanus spoken roughly to his mother, but now he did so. "You talk foolishly," he said. "You talk as a woman, and women babble of nothing. Ah," and his voice changed, "I am sorry. Do not cry, Mother. You have the tenderest heart. But I feel nothing except hatred and a desire for revenge. And that revenge I shall have!"

He went into his room, not aimlessly, but with purpose. He took rolls of books from his shelves, lit a lamp, and began to study.

Chapter Thirteen

Cusa thought, Archimedes asserted that with the proper lever he could move the world. But O goddess of Cyprus, mightiest of all the immortals, you can move not only the world, but worlds, and the gods themselves; can lift life from the very arms of Pluto and give man such stature that he can defy Olympus with a single oath which will be heard by the farthest star!

He looked with concealed commiseration at Lucanus, who no longer seemed to sleep but devoured lessons as though he had all the eyes of Hydra. Once he said to Lucanus with a smile, but also with alarm, "Virgil has said that the prerogative of gods and men is laughter. You never laugh now. Is it that you hate? Remember that hatred has only Pyrrhic victories." But Lucanus gave him a short glance and unrolled another book and bent his golden head over it as if Cusa had uttered the most asinine of comments.

Cusa said with some irritability, "Virgil also remarked that humanity aroused the laughter of the gods. Is it because men are too serious, especially when they are young? By Athene, you will soon run me out of material to teach you!"

On another occasion he said, "There is more in the world than medicine. Wait until you arrive at Alexandria!" He shook his head ominously. "Claudius Vesalius, there, a mincing little person, will put you through your paces in mathematics, about which you know as much as a monkey."

Walking alone through the forests, or beside the river, or

in the gardens, or lying on his bed, or eating and drinking
sparely, or working at his lessons, or assisting Keptah, Lucanus had only one enormous question: Where is Rubria? All
the color and the light and the marvelous shapes of trees and
flowers and blades of grass, of birds and animals and insects,
of butterflies and bees and stars had gone from Lucanus'
sight. All his work was only a means to a vengeful end, and
beauty had left the measurement and awareness of his eyes.
He responded to nothing but a cry of pain; when a slave
died he was inconsolable for days. No hand was gentler or
more compassionate than his, and no glance more bitter when
Keptah was impotent to help a sufferer. "If this is all you can
do, then you can do nothing," he would say. Keptah would
reply mildly, but with some sternness, "Are men immortal?"

Comfortless, Lucanus would ask himself, If we are not
immortal, then why were we born? If only I could believe
there is no God! But I believe in Him, and from Him I will
have His victims, if not His answer! He haunts me. He
haunts all men for the satisfaction of His hatred.

Once the aspect of the world seemed lighted by some deep
radiance that did not come from the sun or the moon or the
stars, but from some emanation that lay beneath and yet
around its physical appearance, and within it. Now the
world was illuminated by a fierce glare to his sight, hurtful
to the eye, carrying with it an incandescence from hell. As
the days passed, his wrath and anguish did not decrease. He
was like a fire that is endlessly fed; each night when he slept
he was burned to ashes; in the morning he rose from those
ashes like a phoenix, winged with agony. Keptah, watching
him surreptitiously, would think, He is like Jacob, wrestling
with the angel, but my poor pupil wrestles in hatred and
torment. He does not have a vision of the ladder on which
the angels climbed to God; his ladder has steps of flame,
leading down into the infernal regions. Like the King of
Nemi, he walks his groves of wrath with a drawn sword,
waiting for the destroyer. And Keptah would pray, "Oh,
You Most Holy, Most Merciful, Most Divine, Most Compassionate, Who walks this earth today in a place I do not know,
in the guise of a child, look with compassion on one who is
only a little older in the flesh than You! As Job cried to You,
so he cries in his heart, and he has not yet heard Your voice.
Be merciful, Lord, be merciful!"

When Lucanus had been a child he had asked the simplest
and most innocent of things, "Are You here? Or there?" But

now when he noticed his surroundings at all he asked, "Where is Rubria?" The only mitigation of his pain was when he was ministering to some sufferer. The slaves would watch him approach, and Keptah would marvel at the sudden bright eagerness on their faces, and how their moans would stop when Lucanus would gently question them, and how they would answer humbly and with hope. He had only to put his hand on a feverish forehead to banish that fever, and to give the poor slave sleep. His blue eyes had a deep and penetrating quality now, and a passionate tenderness. He helped Keptah deliver children, and he would hold the little ones in his arms like a father, close to his breast, as if protecting them. The slaves forgot that he was the son of a former slave; they forgot, the older ones, that once they had ridiculed him for his pretensions, and had railed at him when he had been a child, and had scolded him and envied him, and had even slapped him. In a few short weeks he had become a deliverer, someone holy who could ease them, whose eyes could cause their own to close in rest, whose hands had a strange quality of comfort, whose voice could drive away terror or guilt. "Apollo has touched him," they whispered to each other. They regarded him with superstitious awe, with fear and reverence. When a husband or a wife or a child died, relatives caught Lucanus' hand and begged him, the uncomforted, for comfort. He had only tears to give them, but they saw those tears and thought of them as one thinks of the merciful tears of the gods, and were consoled. Keptah was not surprised at these manifestations and the magic power of healing that Lucanus possessed. His only trouble was with Lucanus himself. When he was away from the little hospital the soft brightness of the youth's face would disappear; it would become almost harsh, most austere and withdrawn.

One day Keptah called Lucanus to him in his own quarters. The physician sat at his table with many books unrolled about him, and his face was grave and somber. "You are aware, of course, my Lucanus, that you have the gift of healing. You are surprised? Do not be so. Enough, I cannot discuss it now. We are in deep trouble." He held up a vial of murky urine. "Tell me, what is it you see here?"

Lucanus took the vial, smelled of its contents, let those contents slide along the clear crystal. Then he said, "This man is very ill; the urine is full of poisons, condensed, bad and dark of color. I think I see the presence of blood. His kidneys are dangerously involved." The youthful face quickened. "We must order large quantities of water, and prohibit salt, and command steam baths immediately for profuse sweat."

Keptah said, "This is no man. This urine comes from a woman who will soon give birth. She is edematous about the belly and face, and about the ankles."

"Then we must withdraw the fluid," said Lucanus, questioningly. He examined the vial again. "She may die."

"Yes," said Keptah. He sighed heavily. "It is at least six weeks until the child will be ready to be delivered. Yet I must induce birth at once. The child will most probably die of prematurity. This is a terrible choice I must make. The only opportunity to save the mother now, who is being poisoned by her own fetus, is quick delivery. In truth, there is no choice at all! The situation is desperate."

"And the child cannot live?"

"A very small chance." Keptah put his head in his hands, and his sigh was almost a groan.

Lucanus was sorry for him, and for the poor woman, and sorrier for the child inevitably condemned to death whether delivery was induced at once or not. Then he said to himself, Still, is it good to live? He said to Keptah, "The woman will bear other children and can afford to lose this one. Has she borne a previous child?"

Keptah looked at him strangely. "Yes. One. And that child died. The woman is not young; she has waited for this child for many years, and now she will be inconsolable when it dies, too. And the husband will be as much grieved, or even more, for he has long wanted an heir."

Lucanus sat down suddenly, and his face turned white. Then his hands clenched on the table. "Aurelia," he whispered.

Keptah said, "All was fairly well until five days ago. It is the toxemia of pregnancy, and a lethal thing. I was afraid of it when the Lady Aurelia developed headaches lately, and some fever. You have observed her urine. You know now what all this means. I need your help. I am sending a slave for your mother. It is fortunate that the noble tribune has not gone to Antioch today."

He stood up and regarded Lucanus sternly. "Aurelia has had two convulsions this morning. I have given her a sedative, and her nurses are with her, not to leave her for a moment. I will bleed her very shortly, and I will need your assistance." He paused and his gaze became more fixed on the young man. "How is this? You sit like one stricken to death." He lifted his hand forbiddingly. "There is serious work to be done, and if you fail me in this then I shall advise Diodorus that he is wasting his time, and will waste his money, in your education. Come!"

Keptah led the way from his quarters through the house and to the library, where Diodorus was awaiting him impatiently. His fierce eyes were stark with fear. "Well!" he exclaimed. "Is it not time, by the gods? You sent me a message to remain at home this morning, in connection with the Lady Aurelia! What is it, what is it!"

Lucanus stared at him with pity and dread. He had not exactly loved Diodorus, for his naturally austere and reserved temperament was antipathetic to strong violence and strongly expressed emotion, and it was rare that he displayed temper or fury. To him Diodorus was too rapid in all his reactions, too ferocious, too contentious, and often alarming in his tumultuous changes of mood. He suspected Diodorus of instability, though he honored him for his learning and his love for the beauty of the written poem or high prose, and his vast and sometimes, to Lucanus, his incredible learning. Lucanus knew that the proconsul loved him, not as a son but perhaps as a favorite nephew, and he was grateful in his calm way, and tried, at all times, to return that fondness with respect and sympathy. Nevertheless, to his regret, he did not, and could not, return the full measure of Diodorus' affection.

He had been stricken less at the thought of Aurelia's impending travail and possible death than at the sudden resurgence of his grief for Rubria in a house which had known death only a short time ago. It was not Aurelia in herself who was in such jeopardy to Lucanus, but the mother of Rubria.

But now as he looked in silence at Diodorus his heart squeezed and he felt the love of a son for a father in him, and he longed to fall on his knees, like a son, before the proconsul and lay his cheek against the other's hand and cover it with tears. He knew instantly that the fierce-eyed, beak-nosed Roman was about to endure the agony of sorrow again, if not for a wife, then again for a child, and he would have given his own life in that instant to spare Diodorus that unspeakable torture.

Keptah said, "Master, I have sad news for you. I must go

to the Lady Aurelia immediately, but still I must prepare you. I must deliver the child at once, if your wife is to live at all." He stopped, and his dusky face became livid with emotion.

Diodorus fell heavily into a chair. He tried to moisten his big lips. Then he went into a paroxysm of dry coughing, as if choking. He could not look at the physician who stood beside him like a gaunt statue of grief in his gray linen robe.

Keptah continued rapidly, "We have no choice, Master. I cannot say to you, 'Shall I save the lady or shall I save the child?' Unless she is delivered she will die, and will not then carry the child to term, and the child will expire in her body. I wished to prepare you for the fact that the babe will be premature when born and will most probably die at once. Now I must go."

Diodorus caught a fold of Keptah's robe and clutched it tightly, and there was the most abject despair on his face. "Save Aurelia!" he pleaded, in a stifled voice. He looked wildly, almost blindly, at the physician, and he pulled himself to the edge of his chair, and his strong body trembled violently. "What is a child to me if my wife dies? What are a dozen children?" The veins in his temples turned purple and knotted, and huge pulses throbbed in his brown throat. "You will save her? You must save her!" There was a prayer in his broken voice, and a mounting anguish.

Lucanus went to him quickly and put his hand on that broad shoulder. He said in a clear, strong voice, "You have been as a father to me, Master, and as a son let me console you. I give my strength to you! I would give my life for you!"

Keptah, in the very act of moving, looked over his shoulder at Lucanus and smiled faintly and strangely. But Diodorus had only let the robe of the physician slip from his enfeebled hand, and though he turned his haggard face to Lucanus it was most evident that he did not see him or even understand him. "Come," said Keptah, "I will need your help, and we cannot delay another instant."

"I cannot stay with him?"

"No. Do you think him a woman? He is a man." Keptah swept from the room, his robe billowing, his sandaled feet gliding swiftly over the marble floor. Lucanus hesitated. Drops of sweat, like great wet stones, slipped weightily from Diodorus' forehead, and then lay intact on the breast of his tunic, or rolled down it. Lucanus ran to the table and poured a goblet of wine and held it to Diodorus' parched lips. Like one in stupefaction, and stunned out of human resistance, the tribune obediently swallowed, one slow sip after another.

If I could only pray! thought Lucanus, and there was a cold terror in him, and he realized fully, for the first time, what estrangement from God meant to a man in his supreme hours, and he realized his own awful loneliness. But one did not pray to a God of affliction, Who cared nothing for human travail but rather ordained it.

Diodorus whispered harshly, "If she dies, then surely I cannot live, for I have been unfaithful to her in my heart, and she the most loving and tender of wives, the most sacrificial, the most dear."

Lucanus knew that the stricken man was hardly aware of him as more than a ministering shadow. He could not endure that dry rustle of a whisper. He said:

"Master, permit me: you have been the best of husbands, and the—the gods—will not desert you. Surely she will live!"

The eyes of Diodorus were tearless; all that he could shed he shed from his dripping forehead. But Lucanus wept, bending his head over the head of the older man so that his cheek lay on the rough and bristling hair. Diodorus listened to that lamenting sound, and he moved vaguely and restlessly, then saw Lucanus for the first time.

"Ah, it is you," he muttered. "You comforted me before. You comfort me now, Lucanus."

Lucanus set down the emptied goblet, and pulled the brazier of burning charcoal closer to the shivering tribune, and caught up a woolen robe from a chair and wrapped it about those arched shoulders, for it was a chill day with pale sunshine without color. Diodorus permitted these small services of love, and a faint astonishment flitted across his face, and then was replaced by a vacant staring.

"I must go to help Keptah," said Lucanus, and he felt the dreadful loneliness in himself again. Without looking back, he ran from the room, the tears still on his cheeks.

Keptah had found Aurelia dulled from the drug he had administered to her. But she panted on her bed, and there was a terrible blueness on her puffed face. She had drawn up her legs under the rugs, and one hand was pressed against her belly in pain. Her muscles twitched all over her body as though possessing a life of their own apart from her. Her swollen tongue half protruded from her bloated lips, and there was a bloody foam in the corners. Her stertorous breathing filled the chamber. Her eyes fixed themselves on Keptah, and they were glazed and staring. The nurses gave the physician the news that until a few moments ago the poor lady had been quiet, and apparently asleep.

Keptah felt her pulse; he bent his ear against her breast and listened to her heart. It was very rapid and bounding. He lifted his head and Aurelia began to thresh against the heaped cushions tucked about her, which had been placed there to prevent her from throwing herself out of bed during a convulsion. Yet she became more and more conscious as her suffering body writhed. She said to Keptah, "You must save the child. I am very ill. I will possibly die. That does not matter. Save the child for my dear husband." She half raised herself on her bed and caught his lean arm, and her wet dark tresses fell in tangled lengths over her shoulders and breast.

Keptah reached to a tray held for him by a nurse, and he poured a golden liquid, viscous and gleaming, into a small goblet. The gasping Aurelia regarded it dubiously, and with the quickened apprehension of the almost moribund. "It will save the child?" she begged, piteously.

The physician held her in too much honor to lie to her. He said, "Lady, suppose it is the wish of Diodorus that you survive and the child die?"

Her puffed and blood-streaked lips smiled sadly. "The child will comfort him. And he will have another consolation, and I bless that consolation, and if it is permitted me when I cross the Styx I shall pray for his happiness. For he has been more to me than father and mother, brother and sister and child."

Keptah bowed to her with the reverence one gives to a goddess, and held the goblet to her lips, and she drank the contents in one painful swallow, for her throat was constricted. Then over Keptah's shoulder she saw someone, and her glazed eyes immediately became intent, yet deeply loving and pleading. Keptah followed her long glance and saw that Iris had come into the room, wrapped in white wool against the chill, her golden braids flowing almost to her knees.

The Grecian woman came at once to Aurelia, and smoothed the wet dark hair with gentle solicitude, her blue eyes studying the cyanotic and bloated face of the sufferer. Aurelia forgot everyone else in the room but her friend. She lifted her shaking hand and took Iris' hand, and between the two women passed an eloquent if unheard exchange.

Then Aurelia fell back on her cushions and looked straightly at Keptah. "It is said that Julius Caesar was cut from his mother's dying womb in order to save his life. Can you not do this to me? What is my life compared with my husband's happiness?"

"What I have given you will induce almost immediate labor, Lady," said Keptah, avoiding her eyes. "The result is with God only."

"But the child is far from term," groaned the unhappy lady.

"Not too far, hardly less than seven weeks," said the physician. "I have seen younger survive."

Lucanus came into the chamber and stood beside the physician, his face streaked with the evidence of his tears. He and his mother filled the room with beauty and stateliness and stature, and even the tall and patrician Keptah was diminished. The cool late winter wind blew out the curtain at the window. Covered brass bowls of hot embers were wrapped in wool and placed about Aurelia's convulsed body. Her mind brightened as death approached. Iris knelt beside her, for Aurelia would not release her hand. She said to the freedwoman, in a feeble voice, "All that I have I deliver to you. Do not weep. You have been my friend, and friends are more than birth, more than money, more than station, more even than Rome itself. I beg of you what you will give in any event: devotion and love, and all your heart."

Lucanus, standing beside the waiting Keptah, was confusedly amazed. What was this that Aurelia was telling his mother? What meant this strange and cryptic conversation, and why did his mother only cry silently and not question? Then he forgot all this in his passionate concern for Aurelia, for a change had come over her face, a starkness as though she were listening to something only she could hear with her soul. Her swollen body grew instantly rigid, and she threw out her arms, arched her back in a sudden convulsion. Her neck stretched, her shoulders raised themselves, and a vast subterranean groan came less from her throat than somewhere deep in her flesh. Her eyes protruded; her tongue lashed at her purpling lips.

"Watch," said Keptah in a low voice to Lucanus. He threw aside the rugs on the bed and turned back Aurelia's shift.

The mounded bluish belly, veined like marble, was palpitating strongly; muscular waves ran over it. Then from her birth canal there issued a swift gush of mingled blood and water, and the chamber was filled with the smell of it. Keptah thrust his long lean fingers into the poor lady's body, and she groaned again, and Iris took both the writhing hands and held them tightly. One of the nurses began to whimper, and the other two fell on their knees and helplessly prayed. Now Aurelia gave herself up to a steady groaning until the sound seemed part of the chamber itself, and part of the equinoctial wind.

Lucanus knew what to do. He pressed both his hands at the top of the mound and rhythmically assisted the rippling muscles in their attempts to thrust the child from its mother's flesh. But the muscles were strictured by Aurelia's convulsions; they were like resisting iron under Lucanus' hands. He closed his eyes and let his sensitive hands and fingers do their office, and when a muscular wave weakened he gave it his strength.

The convulsions of Aurelia's disease were preventing the child's delivery, but still Keptah hesitated before the awful thing he now knew he must do. He had a most terrible decision to make. The child would most probably die upon delivery, or be born dead. Still, there was a chance it would be a viable birth, and a slighter chance that the child would survive. In order that this could happen, however, the convulsed cervix would have to be enlarged by the knife and the child forcibly delivered. Aurelia, then, would die of hemorrhage, her parts severed. The child's head could not be reached by forceps in this present condition, for it had not as yet descended to the mouth of the womb because of its prematurity, and also the convulsions of Aurelia's body. Worse still, Keptah now believed, on a fresh examination, that the child was presenting itself improperly in a breech position. "Oh, my God!" he moaned aloud.

On a signal from Keptah, Lucanus put his ear to Aurelia's heaving breast. He looked with alarm at the physician, for the lady's heart was perceptibly weaker, even though it bounded like a terrorized thing. Moreover, Aurelia's agony was becoming more than she could bear. When Lucanus saw Keptah's dusky and trembling hand reaching for a short sharp knife he bit his lip strongly, and he was filled with a wild and impotent rage.

He bent over Aurelia then, and took her icily wet face in his hands. By force of his will he brought her glaring eyes to his, and he began to murmur hypnotically. "You have no pain," he repeated, over and over. "The pain has gone. You are very sleepy and tired. The pain has gone—you are very sleepy—you are relaxing—the pain has gone—you will sleep now. . . ."

Aurelia saw his eyes and heard his voice. His eyes were like brilliant blue moons to her, swimming in darkness. They filled all the universe, brightening instant by instant. And everything rocked gently to his voice; she could feel that she was floating on a lightless but infinitely comforting sea, without pain. A blissful sensation encompassed her, a lightness, a delivery from anguish. All was explained, all was understood, all was joy and peace. She did not feel the slashing of the knife in her vitals, nor the cataract of her blood. She was without body. She smiled, and the smile seemed to be returned from some far depth that was rising to meet her, a depth pervaded by love and tenderness and compassion. "Mama," she said faintly, and with contentment, and then she was still.

Lucanus lifted his head and looked at Keptah, and he was filled with the very corroding gall of bitterness. "She has gone," he said.

But Keptah was drawing the legs of the infant from the mother's body, thin, grotesquely bent legs, small to doll-likeness, and bluish. Now its minute belly appeared with increasing speed, then its tiny chest, and then its blood-wet head, hardly larger than an apple. Its face was a wax face, streaked with blood, as was all of its body, and the puppet eyes were closed, its mouth breathless.

Then the child lay between its mother's dead legs, as motionless as she and in a pool of her blood. Iris put her head beside Aurelia's still cheek and her wails filled the room in which the groaning had ceased, and it was like a continuation of the lamentable sound.

It was over; none of the lives had been saved. Keptah covered his face with his hands as he knelt at the foot of the bed. Lucanus straightened up rigidly. His very body seemed to burst with cold fury and detestation and outrage. Two had died meaninglessly, and for no good purpose. Two, again, had been done to death by the savage hand of God. "No!" cried Lucanus, vehemently. "No!"

He ran to the foot of the bed and lifted the unbreathing child in his arms. For an instant its lightness appalled him. It weighed less than the puppet he had given Rubria years ago. Its flesh was cold and pallid, its face blue, its head rolling. Lucanus forced open the infantile lips and thrust his finger into the throat. He drew out a coil of blood and mucus. No one heeded him as he caught up a warmed rug and wrapped the child in it. He opened the incredibly small mouth again, held the child to his face and forced deep breaths into its throat and lungs. He concentrated all his attention, all his will, on the babe. Iris continued to wail, and Keptah to kneel and pray for the two souls which had left their bodies, and the nurses lamented, their heads pressed to the floor.

"Live!" Lucanus commanded the child, and great drops of sweat poured from his flesh and drenched his garments. And his strong breath went in and out of the throat of the infant, like life itself, grim and purposeful, not to be denied. His fingers gently but firmly circled the child's chest, compressing then quickly relieving as he held the little one against his heart with his left hand and arm and breathed steadily into its throat.

Iris drew a coverlet over Aurelia's dead and quiet face, and her wailing died away as she saw the faint and peaceful smile on her mistress' lips. The patch of gray sky darkened with a coming storm; there was the distant sound of thunder, and then a flash of lightning. The slave nurses continued to sob and groan and pray for the dead. Keptah sat back on his heels, his head fallen. The wind and thunder mingled their voices.

Then Keptah started and leaped to his feet. For there was a new sound in the room, frail and thin as the cry of a young fledgling. It died away, then rose stronger. Keptah ran to Lucanus and exclaimed with awe, "The boy lives! He is not dead!"

But Lucanus did not see or hear him. His fingers moved steadfastly; he poured his breath and his will and his life into the infinitesimal body. The child stirred against his heart, fragilely, like a struggling bird. Its bloodstained face lost its pallor, flushed deeply. One hand, unbelievably minute, thrust against the woolen rug.

"It lives!" cried Keptah, overcome with joy. "It breathes! It is a miracle from God!"

No one but Iris saw Diodorus enter the room, staggering like a drunken man. She went to him and fell on her knees before him and wound her arms about his own knees, and wept aloud.

Chapter Fourteen

Lucanus was reading the seventh book of Herodotus, in which he had written of Xerxes, who had wept at a victory. Then the uncle of Xerxes, Artabanus, had come to him in consolation, and said, "Sire, first you congratulate yourself and then you weep," to which Xerxes replied, "I was struck with pity at the thought of the brevity of all human life, when I realized that, out of these multitudes, not a single individual will still be alive a hundred years from now."

Artabanus had replied, "In life we have other experiences more pitiable than that. Our lifetime is indeed as brief as you say, and yet there is not a single individual, either in this army or in the world, so constitutionally happy that in this span, brief as it is, he will not find himself wishing, not once but many times over, that he were dead and not alive."

"Yes." Lucanus put aside the book and leaned his head on his hand and stared blankly at a hot yellow beam of summer sunshine falling on his sandaled foot. He studied much at home now, fleeing from the schoolroom the moment lessons were over to escape the slaves, who persisted on bowing to him, or touching his garments, or falling on their knees before him, imploring for his intercession with the gods. It horrified and repelled him that he, who was so hopelessly estranged from God, should be begged to be the intermediary between the suffering and Him. He shrank from adoring eyes and lifted hands. He wanted to shout, "I tell you, He hates us! He gives us life so that we may die in darkness; He gives us eyes so we may see the ugliness of death; He gives us love so that He may destroy us! Better to worship Charon than Him!"

But he could not speak this, though it seethed desperately in his heart. Since he had saved the life of little Priscus the slaves devoutly believed that he had been touched divinely. He could go no longer to the hospital, nor would he visit a sick slave in the company of Keptah. This had gone on for six months. He would soon leave for Alexandria, where he would be only one of many anonymous and browbeaten students, the son of a former slave, the protégé of a kind-hearted Roman. In the meantime he kept his door shut against those who came humbly to it; he would put his hands over his ears that he might not hear their importunities spoken to his mother and her sad and pitying replies. He studied dead drawings of anatomy with Keptah, but he would not listen to the living. When Keptah had once reproached him he had cried out frantically, "Shall I tell them what I believe, that God is their Enemy? Surely I will say that if you press me to talk with them! And what will it avail them then? I am no liar."

"You are like a Parthian archer, who, retreating, hurls poisoned darts over his shoulder," said Keptah. "I tell you, He pursues you and you shall not escape Him. Your darts wound Him, but still He pursues in His love, not His hatred." Nevertheless, the physician understood with the deepest pity.

A bee hummed through the uncurtained window and lighted on the rolled book near Lucanus' slack hand. Its golden wings trembled; it daintily explored the scroll. Its delicate legs wandered nervously. All at once it lifted itself and lighted on the back of Lucanus' fingers. He saw its huge and brilliant eyes, and he sighed. He rose gently and slowly and went to the window and let the little creature fly from him, and he watched its shining flight until it disappeared. There was a great aching in him, and a parchness in his eyes. Oh, the innocent who lived only that they might die! Lucanus rested his forehead on the window sill and felt in himself a tremendous compassion and love for all that lived, was tortured, withered, and fell into dust, from a bee to a man, from a leaf to a child, from a tree to an ox, from a star to a spider. He wanted to encompass life in his arms, to console it, to murmur love and comfort to it, and, holding it thus, to challenge its Destroyer.

He became acutely aware of the house sounds, and a child's laughter. The child was very young, the daughter of a slave woman who was nursing little Priscus. Iris was the guardian now of the son of Diodorus; she had carried him to this house a few hours after his birth, bringing with her the wet nurse and another slave. It was Iris who fondled Priscus and tended him, never leaving him a moment during the first precarious month of his life. It was Iris who saw his first toothless smile and heard his first affectionate murmur. She dandled him on her knee; she slept beside his little bed. His faintest sound brought her running. She wove his garments and sewed them. She rocked his cradle when he was fretful; she hovered over him, crooning. She washed his tiny body. She was never apart from him.

Lucanus heard his mother's voice now, and the gurgling answer of the infant boy. Her aureate head passed outside Lucanus' window; she was carrying Priscus in her arms, tight against her breast. The child's face looked over her shoulder and his eyes met the eyes of Lucanus. The youth winced, for the small face was the face of Rubria, and he could not endure it. Priscus grinned joyously, for he was a merry soul with affability towards all. In spite of himself Lucanus smiled in answer. The baby threw back his head and screeched joyously, and nuzzled Iris' ear. She was taking him into the cool of the small garden at the rear of the house. There she would sit under a great tree, murmuring and singing until the boy slept. The sun rode towards the west, and the air was wide, diffused with gold, humming with secret life. The scent of earth, of flowers, of grass mingled with the tawny light, and somewhere a slave woman hummed as she went about her duties. Palms clapped and swayed, and birds arrowed from tree to tree, the sunlight on their wings like gilt.

Lucanus went out into the garden. Iris had picked a white flower, and Priscus, on her knee, was busily examining it. He was still small for his age, but he was plump and restless and eager, his dark eyes brimming with delight in being and seeing. He was naked except for a white napkin; his little breast was broad and brown. Black tendrils curled about his ears and neck and forehead. Small though he was, he had strength that was almost incredible in one so young, and in one born prematurely. He looked like a minute warrior, but his smile was Rubria's smile, winning and sweet, with a hint of mischief, and the expression in his eyes, melting and seeking, was Rubria's. For this reason Lucanus usually avoided the child. Priscus saw him before Iris did, and he screeched happily again and waved the flower as if in greeting.

Iris smiled at her son, hiding her constant anxiety for him. "See," she said, "is this not an archer, or a wrestler, or a charioteer? His muscles are veritable breastplates." The child's mouth was still milky from his recent nursing, and he bounced on Iris' knee so that she laughed as she restrained him. Lucanus held out a finger and Priscus seized it, examined it keenly, then put it into his mouth. Lucanus smiled. He felt towards the child as a father. Then he frowned. "It is strange that Diodorus remains in Rome so long. One would consider he would give thought to his son."

He exclaimed, "Eheu! He has teeth!"

"Four," said Iris, proudly. "Is it not marvelous?" Her face was as purely colored and as young as a girl's. After a moment she said abstractedly, "Diodorus? Yes, it is almost six months. This time he will not return until he has permission to leave Antioch. So he has written to me. I imagine," she added, with a faint smile, "that he is brow-beating Carvilius Ulpian without mercy, and haunting the Palatine. He can bear Syria no longer, and is determined to retire to his estates. I believe he has now worn Caesar to a shadow, for he is an obstinate man and has considerable influence."

She smoothed the baby's agile head. Diodorus had carried the ashes of his daughter and his wife to Rome for entombment in his family's cemetery. Iris knew that this had been a dolorous journey, and one without comfort. Diodorus, after Aurelia's death, had become speechless, and then had left for Rome, and it was many weeks before he had written briefly to tell of his plans and to inquire after his son. There had been indifference in the inquiry; he had seen Priscus only a few times and had betrayed no emotion of any kind. But his last letter had quickened. He was convinced that Syria was malefic with regard to his family. When he returned, it would be only to gather up his household and to brief his successor, and then he would leave this "malignant" land forever. His child would be brought up in the land of his fathers, in the sight of the Seven Hills, under the protection of his gods.

He had written only one line pertinent to Iris: "I trust that you, my old playmate, my sister in spirit, will consent to return with me, to continue to mother my son."

Iris sighed. She hoped for much more than that! But her own son would be far in Alexandria, her son so driven, so haunted, so unremittingly grief-stricken, so somber and desolate. Ah, she thought, but he is young, and there is much study and much to be learned. She realized that Lucanus was very like herself in nature as well as in appearance: patient, dedicated, deeply if calmly loving, reserved in speech and in action, living a hidden if vital life, disciplined and somewhat rigid in temperament. He had not yet acquired her present flexibility, her gentle resignation, her profound faith that God was good and not malevolent.

They had always communicated less in speech than in eloquent glance, a slight smile, the smallest gesture, the least inclination of head. There had always been the most profound understanding between them, until Rubria had died. Then Lucanus had withdrawn even from his mother and had stood coldly and repudiatingly at a distance. He had refused to be interested in the child he had saved until today, though Iris tenderly guessed that this was less coldness than a fear of becoming involved once more in personal love for anything, for in love, he believed, there was an ever-present danger and threat of disaster.

She was intensely moved when Lucanus suddenly squatted on his heels in order to bring his face on a level with the baby's. Priscus was delighted. He reached out and seized Lucanus' nose. "He has a hand like a gladiator!" exclaimed the young man. "And talons like an eagle!"

Priscus screamed with joy. He released Lucanus' nose and grasped the young man's curling forelock and pulled. Lucanus marveled at his strength. Here was a child who only six months ago had lain in his arms like a limp puppet, breathless and blue, limp as melting wax. All at once Lucanus was filled with pride and affection. He held out his arms for the boy, and Priscus promptly threw himself into them. The warmth of his small and sturdy body pierced to Lucanus' very heart; he kissed the bare brown shoulders, the dimpled knees and elbows. He kissed the eyes so like Rubria's, and then, very tenderly, the mouth that was a small replica of hers. His eyelids prickled and his throat tightened. Oh, let me not love again! he prayed to some faceless deity.

He put the protesting infant into Iris' arms, rose abruptly and went away. Iris followed him with a long and mournful glance, yet she was consoled.

The morning after the evening of Diodorus' return to Antioch the tribune commanded that Keptah attend him. The physician entered his master's library and his hooded eyes instantly appraised his mental and physical condition. Diodorus' face was worn and paler, and years seemed to have been added to his features, yet there was a grim quietness about him and his beaked face had acquired a harder maturity. He was more the Roman than ever, and less simple than he had ever been.

"I am in good health," he said abruptly, before Keptah could even greet him. "It is not necessary for your medical eyes to scan me. Enough. Within four weeks I shall leave for Rome, with all my household. You are no longer a slave. I understand you have been buying vineyards and olive groves in this vicinity, and that you have some investments in Rome itself. I have no time to waste. I cannot command you as a freedman, I can only ask you. Will you return with me to Rome?"

"Is it necessary to ask me that, Master?"

Diodorus said nothing for a moment. Then he said with that new quietness of his, "I have learned one thing in all those seven months in Rome: a man can never trust another man. If he does, it is at his own peril, and he who denies this is either a liar or a fool. Who was the philosopher who said, 'Be friendly with all, be intimate with none'? It is not only, as some have said to me in Rome, that man is intrinsically evil, it is that he is never the same man from hour to hour, from day to day. My question was not an insult to you. I was merely inquiring."

Keptah did not answer. He was full of compassion for this thinner and less vehement man, whose fierce eyes were still dimmed and fixed with grief. A certain buoyancy had gone from the tribune, and his vitality was in abeyance. Yet there was a ferocity and gloom about him.

Diodorus went on, "I thought that when I went to Rome I would foregather with my old comrades, and that they would remember me affectionately. You see what a fool I was. It is true that they greeted me with an affectation of much pleasure. That is because they recalled that I have much influence even with that Tiberius who at least remembers that I am an excellent soldier if not a human being. I thought I would find some surcease in Rome——" He paused, and a shadow ran over his face. He stood up and poured a goblet of wine, then motioned to Keptah to help himself.

"In short, Master," said Keptah, after he had respectfully sipped his wine, "you discovered that men are no different in Rome than they are in Syria, or in Britain or in Gaul or in Judea or Egypt or in Greece."

Diodorus put down his goblet slowly, and not with his usual thump. There was a lack of his former emphasis in his manner and his voice. He said, "That is quite true. But then I had been away from Rome a long time and I had forgotten. I will speak to you about that later." He began to walk up and down the library with a heavy and sluggish tread. "Why are intelligence and intellect so rare? Why does one have to seek them as one seeks gold?"

"The gods," said Keptah, wryly, "are still jealous of their wisdom. It is Promethean fire, and when it burns in any man the gods punish him, but his fellows punish him more. It has also been said that you cannot teach a man anything; you can only assist him in finding it within himself. If he has no mind, then all your exhortations, all your lessons, all you attempt to do to improve his environment, all your sacrifices and your ideals will not stir him from his beasthood. For your presumption that he has a mind because he has the shape of a man he will turn and rend you. And I find that a just retribution."

Diodorus gave him a sharp glance. He poured another goblet of wine and drank deeply of it. Then he looked at the bottom of the goblet and seemed to address it and not Keptah. "I need a mother for my son."

Keptah's face changed in alarm. "You have found such a lady in Rome, Master?" He thought of Iris with consternation. But Diodorus was a Roman!

"I have done a vile thing," said Diodorus, as if Keptah had not spoken. Now he looked at his physician and his face was stern. "Why do I trust you, you a man who may betray me tomorrow? Shall I bribe you to keep your peace and not bruit it about in Rome? Can I depend on it that you will not whisper it into some trollop's ear when in your cups—if you are ever in your cups? Will you guarantee that you will not become my enemy this year or next? I think it better for you not to return with me to Rome after all."

"As you will, Master," said Keptah, and there was some anger in his voice.

Now Diodorus cast the goblet down with some of his old fire. "After all," he said, "who would take the word of a former slave against the word of Diodorus?"

Keptah folded his robed arms across his breast. "That is true," he said. "Therefore you need not confide in me, Master. I have asked for no confidence. For your own peace of mind I prefer that you do not give it."

"Still, I would feel safer with you in Rome as my physician. I have heard tales! They may not be true, but it is said that Tiberius has rid himself of some intransigent men, including two senators, by bribing their physicians. It is most likely a lie; Tiberius may be coldhearted, but poison is not a soldier's way of dealing with enemies, even if he does employ informers. However, I have it on excellent authority that many rich and depraved rascals in high places in Rome have bribed the physicians of men whose wives they have coveted, or estates, or some political advantage." He gave Keptah an odd smile. "When the scandal leaked out, it was not the bribers who were punished. The physicians were usually found in the Tiber a short time later."

Keptah could not prevent himself from smiling broadly. "The Tiber does not attract me as a burial place, Master."

Diodorus laughed shortly, without merriment. "May the Furies take you! You have not yet understood. I need a friend. And I must go to a freedman for one! Is that not ironical?"

"And you found no friend among your comrades in arms, and in your own rank, Master?" asked Keptah.

"No." Diodorus sat down and regarded the marble floor between his legs. "I see you have answered my question. However, to insure your presence with my household in Rome, and to keep you faithful, I will triple your stipened and give you a house of your own on my estates."

"No," said Keptah. "I am not for sale, Master." His voice rose to hard coldness. "Rome has been unfortunate for you, I observe. I beg you to remember that you trusted me implicitly before you returned there, that your father trusted me and was deeply attached to me, that the Lady Aurelia took me into her confidence, and that I have never deceived you, not once in your life, except when I thought, in all mercy, that the truth would hurt you. May I leave, Master?"

"No," said Diodorus. He still stared at the floor. It was not proper for a Roman to apologize to one lesser than he, but he said, "I am sorry."

Keptah was astonished and moved. He lifted one of Diodorus' hands and kissed it. He said, "Master, you know how deeply I honor God. If it will help you to confide in me, though I prefer that you do not for your own sake, I swear by His Most Holy Name that I will never betray you, that on the instant of the confidence I shall forget it."

Diodorus studied him gloomily. "Then I must tell you the vile thing I have done, the lying thing, in Rome, not only because you are my friend but because I am confused, and because——" He paused. He drew a deep breath. "There is a senator who is a friend of Carvilius Ulpian, and only his wealth and his mercilessness and reputation for cruel vengeance keep his secret unknown to all save Carvilius. I discussed a certain matter with my brother-in-law, and he then imparted that senator's secret to me. I suspect, by the way, that the senator has some hold over Carvilius that would ruin him if he does not keep silent. You see how suspicious I have become!"

Keptah waited. Diodorus slowly flushed. "I did what the senator did. He loved a slave in his household, on one of his estates in Sicily. He freed her. His wife was barren, and he divorced his wife. Then he applied to a genealogist who invented a fine lineage for his freedwoman, and he married her with honor, and she is a great favorite in Rome, and a worthy matron."

Keptah frowned. "I see, Master. You have applied yourself to that same genealogist and have invented a distinguished Grecian lineage for Iris." He was enormously relieved.

"Yes," said Diodorus, sullenly.

Keptah felt the first joy he had felt in many months. Then his face darkened. "You forget, Master, that your whole household knows that Iris was once a slave. How can you assure yourself that so many will not babble?"

"In that lineage," said Diodorus, ignoring the remark, "I have had it written that Iris was stolen from her distinguished family in Cos by slave dealers who were attracted by her childish beauty, and that only lately was it discovered who she really was. Her parents died of grief; it was found that they had bequeathed their fortune to their kidnaped child, a very respectable fortune."

Keptah pondered on this quizzically. "Good, Master," he said at last. "Then you need not have confessed to me that the lineage was invented. Why did you do so?"

Diodorus shook his head slowly from side to side. "There had to be one man to whom I could not lie, or would not lie. Strange that it had to be you! I preferred, from some perversity, that you knew the truth."

"And so, while wanting to confide in me, you still threatened me."

Diodorus looked up at him with some of his former irascibleness. "For a wise man you are very obtuse!" He stood up and again paced up and down. "Carvilius Ulpian knows the truth also. But he will not speak of it, not even to Cornelia, sister to my dead wife. For many reasons."

Diodorus stopped his pacing. He spoke with his back to the physician, and his voice was very low. "I have loved Iris since we were children together. She can still bear sons. I can conceive of marrying no other woman, not even a woman from any of the grandest families in Rome. You do not know the Roman women! They have lost all womanliness. They engage in business! They have become fraudulent and dissolute men. They move about Rome in their gilded litters, unaccompanied, and can quote you the latest stock prices with the facility of bankers! Many prefer not to marry, but they have many lovers. To such degeneracy has Rome fallen. I will not filthy my mouth with the list of their abominable practices."

He clenched his hands together. "I have had many strange dreams in which the Lady Aurelia has come to me smiling, not as a shade as we are taught, but in full and youthful bloom, with love in her eyes and comfort in her hands. She has urged me to marry Iris, whom she called her 'sister.' " He swung upon Keptah and challenged him with his beetling eyes. "You think me superstitious? Would you, in your occult way, declare, as you have often done, that dreams are only the fulfillment of secret wishes?"

Keptah said seriously, "I believe, in this case, that you are not superstitious, that you are not trying to rationalize a deep desire for which you torment yourself guiltily. Before the Lady Aurelia died Iris came to her." And he told Diodorus what Aurelia had said to the freedwoman with such urgency and such hope.

While Keptah was speaking, Diodorus' face changed and paled. He fell into his chair. Then he bowed his head in his hands and groaned. Keptah was alarmed. He had expected relief and joy, but Diodorus appeared stricken almost to death.

"So," he said in that groaning voice, "I did not deceive my poor wife at all! She always knew that I was unfaithful to her in my heart! But she did not know how I struggled against it; she did not know how much I loved her. What she must have endured, and what loneliness and sadness! It was not enough that her daughter had died. It was not enough that she expired giving me a son. I must take from her what is most dear to a woman. And she suffered all that in silence, and with devotion and tenderness."

"You are wrong, Master!" exclaimed Keptah, coming closer to him. "The Lady Aurelia may not have been a learned woman, or a sophisticated one. But she understood all that there was to be understood. She was a good woman."

He wished, with some wildness and pity, that Diodorus were a less complicated, less intelligent and less difficult man, and given less to a morbid habit of critically inspecting himself. He would invent guilt for himself even if there were no guilt at all!

Diodorus dropped his hands wearily from his face. His features were streaked with redness from the pressure of his fingers, and though he had not wept his eyes were congested.

He said, very quietly, "It is all very well. But now I see I can never marry Iris. My conscience will not permit it. Nor will I take her to Rome with me. It is done. Life is over."

Chapter Fifteen

Diodorus summoned Iris to him that afternoon.

On her way, accompanied by a slave, with the infant, she addressed Aurelia in the very depths of her soul. "He has called me to him, Lady. You know how we have loved each other, and how we were never unfaithful to you, for we loved you also. I can go to him now and say to him, 'Where thou art, Caius, there am I, Caia.' Dearest friend, we will remember you with love and the most precious of memories. If we are blessed with children, we shall name the first girl for you, kindest of friends."

Her joy was so bursting that her beautiful face shone with light. She had bound her golden hair with white ribbons, and her stola was carefully draped, the fluted edges rippling over her high and snowy arches. She was as radiant as a young goddess, and her throat was rosy with her rapidly pulsating blood. She had much to do to keep from running in her rapture.

She entered the library alone, and the blue ecstasy of her eyes was like a flash of sky. Diodorus, standing at his table, felt an overwhelming agony of despair and passion and love at the sight of her, and he thought that Aphrodite, rising from the waves, had never presented such an aspect of radiance and perfect beauty to a stunned world. He had not fully remembered the marvel of her hair, the whiteness of her flesh, the molded snow of her arms, the iridescence of her flesh. But it was not only her beauty which stupefied him; she had an emanation, to him, of some divinity clothed in light, untouched by human pollution. She wore her wonderful loveliness as simply and innocently as a lily, and as purely.

He stood by his table clothed in his short military tunic and armor, his short broadsword buckled at his belt. His helmet lay on the table beside him, and it was evident that he was about to go to Antioch. There was an air of haste and abruptness about him, a cold militarism, a remoteness. And it was this air that made Iris stop suddenly on the threshold and held her against falling on her knees before him and kissing his hand. A sharp sense of calamity came to her, and the light passed from her face. This worn and leaner man, this haughty and formidable man, was not the Diodorus she knew. He was a stranger.

"Greetings, noble Master," she murmured, and the sense of calamity deepened in her. "I trust you had a pleasant journey home."

"Come in, Iris," he said, and turned his eagle face in profile to her, and she saw its iron restraint. "I shall not keep you long. I have been told of the tender and maternal care you have given my son, for which mere gold will not suffice. But it is all I have to offer."

Iris looked at him with a heartbroken smile. "You owe me nothing, Master," she said, faintly. "It was a joy to mother your son, who is like a young Mars, and full of merriment." She stopped. Her throat and breast ached painfully.

Searching his face hopelessly, she felt a deeper pang and a thrust of anxiety, forgetting herself. Was he ill? Why that expression of pent anguish, that pale harshness of lip, that bitter wrinkling of the forehead? She exclaimed with fear, "Master, all is not well with you! Were you ill of the fever of Rome?" She came to him then, her heart shaking with love and fright, and her blue eyes fastened themselves intently and searchingly on his profile. He would not look at her. His hand was on his helmet, the tendons rising in it. Diodorus! she cried inwardly. My soul's beloved! Do you not know that I would joyously give my life for you? Tell me what troubles you.

Diodorus still would not look at her. He dared not. He caught the fragrance of her flesh, warm and youthful and sweet as a flower. His hand clenched on the helmet in a spasm of acute agony.

He spoke as if she had not spoken. "In my last letter to you, Iris, I asked if you would return to Rome with me when I go from this malignant place forever, in order to care for my son." He paused. The grayish-brown flesh about his averted eyes tightened. "But now I cannot ask it of you. Your son leaves in three weeks for Alexandria. You will wish to be near him. As a gift, and a sign of my esteem for you, I am giving you Cusa, who will help to tutor Lucanus in Alexandria, and Calliope, who is now his wife, for a handmaiden to you. Moreover, I will deposit five thousand gold sesterces for you in order that you may live in comfort in some small house near the university, and each December the same amount will be delivered to you. I comprehend, of course, that all this is but a poor return for what you and your son have done for me, but it is all I have."

Terror, loss and dismay seized Iris. She stared at Diodorus disbelievingly.

"You are sending me away from you, Master—forever!" she cried, and pressed her hands against her breast. "Forever, Diodorus? I am so hateful in your eyes?" Tears began to flow down her white cheeks.

"I am trying only to be just," said Diodorus, in a stifled voice. "I thought that you would prefer to be near your son. I understand that it will be hard to part from Priscus, to whom you have been as a mother, as my own mother was to you. But life is all parting." He had heard the torment in her voice, her incredulous torment and disbelief. "You must not think me ungrateful."

Then he turned his face swiftly to her, and it changed. "Do you think this easy for me?" he asked, roughly. "Nevertheless, this is my will, for there is no other way."

"Then, in some unpardonable fashion, I have most terribly displeased you," faltered Iris. He no longer loves me, she thought, with abysmal and overwhelming despair and bereavement. He has found a lady in Rome to marry; I am now an inconvenience and embarrassment to him. He would forget I ever lived.

She was weak with her suffering; she wanted to lie down on the floor and pass into merciful insensibility, or die. An aridity like the dust in the mouth of a moribund man dried her lips, her tongue, and her heart throbbed with a crushing pain. Let me go as the humblest slave in your household, she implored him silently. Let me not even enter your sight. But do not send me from you, in the name of all the gods! It will be enough just to lie under the same roof with you, to glimpse you from afar, to hear the echo of your voice. How can I live otherwise?

"Iris," he said, then stopped. He could not change his mind. He dared never see the young woman again. He thought of Aurelia, and it seemed to him that she regarded him sternly, demanding this awful sacrifice to assuage his guilt.

He put his helmet on his head. He could not look at Iris again, for his arms felt powerless and empty, and he knew that he must flee from this room if he was to save himself. "You will want to prepare for your journey with your son," he said, looking blindly at the floor. "Iris. We shall not see each other again. I have ordered my son returned to this house tomorrow morning, with his nurse." He paused. "Iris, I wish you all the blessings of the gods, and all happiness."

She groped for a chair and sat down, her head on her breast, her arms fallen. Then she began to speak in a low voice, but very clear. "Master, I can take nothing from you. What I have done, if it is of any importance at all, was for love—for love—of Aurelia and the child. To take the smallest gift would be an insult to them. And to me."

Diodorus began to walk towards the door. Then he was overpowered with his mighty desolation and sorrow and longing. He stopped, his back to her. "Nevertheless," he said, dimly, "I am a Roman, and must express my gratitude some way."

Iris lifted her head and she looked at him as at an equal who had unforgivably offended her. He felt her force, and he involuntarily turned on his heel and faced her. She was like a noble statue sitting there, her white stola falling over her breast and her perfect thighs and lying on the high arches of her feet. And she was as colorless as marble. Dignity and pride encompassed her, and her pale lips curved with scorn.

"Diodorus," she said, and her voice was strong and angry. "There is something I must tell you. I am not a mere handmaiden to be dismissed and turned away. I have held a secret for a long time, because it was the wish of your mother, the Lady Antonia, for she thought it would offend you deeply—as a Roman! However, she gave me permission to tell you this secret when I thought it necessary, and I find it necessary now. After your father died, she legally adopted me, but in secret, as her daughter. The praetor so recorded it, in Rome, before you returned from Jerusalem. And in Rome there is much money waiting for me, which I have not yet used. My husband knew nothing of it. You stare at me as if I were lying! You have only to visit the praetor in Rome."

She rose slowly and gracefully, and she was like the statue of a goddess carved by Scopas. She filled the library with light and a stately power.

"Do not think," she said, bitterly, "that I will ever divulge this to anyone, to your humiliation! I will not intrude upon you in Rome, or elsewhere, demanding your acknowledgement as your sister. Never shall I say, 'The noble tribune, Diodorus, is my adopted brother,' for I know your terrible pride! Your mother loved me, as dear as a daughter. Though you do not know it, she did not wish me to marry my poor Aeneas. But I knew you, Diodorus! I knew that you loved me then, and had always loved me, and that you as a Roman, however, would never consider marrying me, a former slave. To end forever your yearning, your internal struggles, I married Aeneas. I would have consented, before that adoption, to be your mistress, to be the lowliest, to carry wood for your bath. But I was now your mother's daughter, and I could not offend her memory."

Diodorus stumbled back to the table, removed his helmet, then stood staring down at it. He was weak with shame. He moistened his lips, tried to speak, then was silent. He coughed dryly, and passed a hand over his forehead. "Let me speak," he said, almost inaudibly. "And then let us part." He continued to stare at the helmet. "Do you know what I suffer? Do you know how I love you, and have always loved you? Do you know that only your memory sustained me when I carried the ashes of my wife and my daughter to Rome? Do you know that the darkest nights were brightened by the vision of your face?" He paused, and coughed again. "But I have learned that Aurelia knew of my passion for you. I remember what she must have suffered because of that. I am guilty before her. I must do penance."

"Oh!" cried Iris, and she was weeping again, and her face was like the sun behind rain. "Oh, you Roman fool, you dear, beloved fool! Certainly Aurelia knew. She knew the very moment she entered your house. We loved you together, and she was content, for she was a lady of sense, and not a dolt-headed man! Not once was she disturbed. You were her husband, and you were an honorable man. Is your soul so small that you dare to insult the large and kindly soul of Aurelia, my friend? While she was bearing your son she had premonitions of death, and confided in me. And before she died she asked me to remain with you forever, and comfort you, and give you happiness. Yet you now insult her!"

She was angered again. She took a step or two towards the door.

Diodorus said, "Wait—my love. I have worse to tell you. While in Rome, I invented a false lineage for you, so that I could marry you with honor."

She stopped and regarded him with wide eyes, and then with tenderness, and then with a smile, and then with sudden sweet mirth. She ran to the door and called to the wet nurse who was waiting outside. "Bring in the child!" she exclaimed, and when the child was delivered to her she held him in her arms, and he crowed and nuzzled her.

"Your son," she said to Diodorus. "The son you neglected and would hardly see, because you believed he had caused his mother's death. The darling boy, who is like both you and Aurelia. Look at him! He does not know you, you fierce Roman."

Then she thrust the child into his father's arms and threw back her head and laughed like a girl. Priscus screeched happily, and tugged at Diodorus' hair. The tribune looked at Iris and all his delivered soul was in his eyes, and all his love.

"No," said Iris, and her rosy face dimpled. "You must kiss him first!"

PART TWO

"If a man looks with loving compassion on his suffering fellow men, and out of his bitterness inquires of the gods, 'Why do you afflict my brothers?' then surely he is gazed upon more tenderly by God than a man who congratulates Him on being merciful so that he flourishes happily, and has only words of adoration to offer. For the first prays out of love and pity, divine attributes, and so close to the heart of God, and the other speaks out of selfish complacency, a beastly attribute, which does not approach the circumambient light of the spirit of God."

—Horace

Chapter Sixteen

Iris wrote to her son, Lucanus:

"It is nearly four years since we last met, my dear and beloved son, and you have steadfastly invented excuses not to come to Rome, which I confess is not so beautiful as Syria. Nevertheless, we live quietly on our estates and enjoy the peace of the evening and the bright crystal of the morning. It is enough for me. Your sister, Aurelia, will soon be three years old, and she is the light of our souls, with her golden hair and eyes as brown and soft as the heart of a daisy. There is nothing she can demand, in her infant insistence, from Diodorus, her father, that he will not grant immediately, in spite of my protests. Your brother, Priscus, is Aurelia's fondest playmate, and his tyrant, a state of affairs which he endures with the most affable merriment. Your new brother, Gaius Octavius, named for your father's old comrade in arms, is almost a year old, and a very serious boy, with my blue eyes and his father's sober expression. He laughs seldom, and prefers to crawl over the grass and inspect each blade intently. He is certainly a philosopher. If only my son, Lucanus, were with us, we should be the happiest of mortals. You shall not escape us! In three months you will be bereft of excuses, for you will have left Alexandria, a physician.

"In the past year Diodorus has become restless. He is a man of action as well as a man of thought. For a long time he was content with his library, his olive and palm groves, his garden, his fields, and his family. Philo visited us, the Jewish philosopher, who is much admired and esteemed in Rome, and the two talked to the dawn incessantly. Since then Diodorus has begun to brood, and to visit Rome at least every seven days, and returns in a most irascible temper, and with a fresh sense of outrage. It is not possible, I say to him, for a single man to save the world or set it aright, and this serves only to make him the more irritable. I often hear him cursing in his library, and once he hurled a quantity of books against the walls and stamped heavily up and

183

down for hours. But he is as gentle as a dove to me, his wife, and to our children. Perhaps when you visit us—and I pray that you will remain with us—you will be able to lighten his gloomy expression and solace him."

Her letter glowed with her gentle love and contentment, and her solicitude for her family. Lucanus could feel these things, and he moved restlessly in the great garden near the main marble colonnade. The floor of the colonnade was of dark yellow marble, but the double row of Ionic columns gleamed like fluted snow as they rose from the floor to the white roof. Two men paced up and down in the sunset, one a respectful tall student and the other the short and harpy-faced master of mathematics, Claudius Vesalius. The golden light brightened them as they paced between the columns. Sometimes Claudius Vesalius paused to gesticulate vehemently, and his shrill womanish voice disturbed the peaceful birds, and most especially disturbed Lucanus. The teacher liked none of his students; in particular he did not like Lucanus because the young man was the best mathematician in the university and yet obdurately insisted upon becoming a physician. Lucanus smiled slightly, thinking of this. Every teacher believed his own art to be the most important of all, and all others of minor significance, with the exception of Joseph ben Gamliel, who believed God the only Importance, and all art and science and knowledge, like the roads of omnipresent Rome, leading only to a greater understanding of God and to the City of God. But then Joseph ben Gamliel was a Jew.

The university covered eight acres of land, an agora roughly square-shaped around immense tropical gardens, and all four sides were of colonnades such as the one now facing Lucanus. Each school had its particular doorway, entered from the gardens and the colonnades, and here were the schools of democracy, philosophy, medicine, mathematics, art, architecture, drama, science, epic, didactic and elegiac poetry, grammar, languages and philology, law, history and astronomy and literature. There was also a school of government for young Romans who aspired to public service, a museum guarded by vigilant Egyptian teachers, the world's most famous library, an odeum or music hall, and beyond the agora itself a theater for hopeful young dramatists, and a pantheon. Each teacher believed his own stoa to house the most profound learning—and the most stupid of students, unworthy to be taught by such a master. Only Joseph ben

Gamliel possessed humility, and his stoa of Oriental religion was the only peaceful place, unmarred by hectoring voices and imprecations against ass-headed students regularly consigned to Hades and advised to study brickmaking, or even lesser trades. It was nothing for the teachers to say, violently, "My idiot students and I resemble the Laocoön, and who will deliver me from the serpents!" But Joseph ben Gamliel would say gently, "Let us contemplate God together and try to discover His Most Holy designs."

Again, thinking of this teacher, Lucanus moved restlessly on his marble bench in the center of the gardens. He, alone, found no peace in the stoa of Joseph ben Gamliel. He often wondered, somberly, why the teacher frequently sought him out to talk with him in the gardens.

The buildings of the school, behind the colonnades, hid the sea, but Lucanus could hear its eternally unquiet voice speaking to the golden light and to the skies. Why did not Claudius Vesalius, whose shrill voice whined continuously at the silent student, go away so that the gardens could bring Lucanus the only quietude he ever knew? The great gardens lay about him, musical with fountains, brilliant with flower beds, rattling sweetly with palms, murmurous with the sea wind, harmoniously alive with the calls, songs and sleepy chatter of birds. The dark-faced slaves who came to the fountains for water, carrying their terra-cotta jugs on their shoulders, or the slaves reaching for golden clusters of dates from the palms to put in their baskets, or the slaves raking up the red-earthed paths among the flower beds did not disturb Lucanus. They were part of the natural flora and fauna. Their dusky skins contrasted beautifully with the many tall statues of gods, goddesses and scholars and philosophers which rose with white and powerful grace from bowers and looked upon the gardens with dignity and majesty. The perfume of roses, lilies and jasmine, and more pungent scents, lifted like unseen webs of fragrance in the early evening air. A parrot suddenly squawked fussily, and a slave laughed and held out a date to the bird, which flashed from a grove of trees to light in a flutter of scarlet and green and yellow on the slave's shoulder. He ate daintily of the date, and with an air of tolerant politeness. "Rascal," said the slave, in Egyptian. The bird cocked a wise and humorous eye at him, and that eye was alert, cynical and bright in the golden air. Lucanus felt an impulse to laugh. As if the parrot felt that amusement, he uttered a single harsh sound that resembled an oath. He turned his head and glared at the young man on his marble bench, then soared off to practice his swearing on the branch of a tree.

The slave laughed softly, then meekly and covertly gazed at Lucanus with his letters on his knees. All the teachers, students and slaves were aware of the beauty and stately demeanor of the young Greek, and secretly marveled at it. His fair face, which not even the fierce sun could darken, possessed smooth hard planes, as if carved from white stone. His blue eyes, so perfectly cerulean, were like jewels, and as cold. His yellow hair flowed back from his snowy brow in shining waves, and curled behind his ears. His throat was a column, his shoulders perfection under his pale tunic. He excelled in the races, at discus throwing, at wrestling, at boxing, at jumping, at throwing the spear, at swimming and diving and assorted sports required of the students. "A sound mind cannot exist except in a sound body, and a sound body cannot exist without a sound mind," said the master of the school.

Lucanus took up the letter from Diodorus, which had arrived that morning from Rome. He liked the tribune's letters; they might be fiery and salty and filled with angry oaths, but they possessed vitality and a healthy anger and some eloquence. He poured out his wrath to his stepson, understanding that here was a receptive ear.

"Greetings to my son, Lucanus," the letter began formally. Then it continued:

"All is well at home. Your mother basks among her children like Niobe, and it is beauteous to see. Unlike Niobe, she is infinitely wise, and a constant consolation to my heart, which is frequently inflamed after visits to the City. Each year finds her lovelier, as if Venus herself had touched her with the gift of immortal youth and beauty. What have I done to deserve such a wife, and such adorable children? I feel that I must strive to be worthy of such happiness. Therefore my frequent visits to Rome and my enraged arguments with the red-sandaled senators who complacently watch our world quickly descending into hell. Because of my connections, and through the offices of Carvilius Ulpian, who grows fatter daily in the body and thinner in the face, I am sometimes allowed to address the Senate. They listen without boredom, I assure you!

"They prefer serenity to thought, long, windy dissertations on their particular interests to serious reflection on the state of our country. Most of them are armchair generals, liking to sit on their terraces of an evening, with a goblet of wine in their hands, and discussing with their friends some general's campaigns, and learnedly and disapprovingly remarking on them. They prepare diagrams of campaigns. What do they know of tenting in the wilderness, of long hot marches, of struggles with the barbarians? They are lawmakers, they say. Let them confine themselves to their law and leave soldiers alone! But let there be a rumbling among the populace and the senators are the first ones who speak of Praetorians and the legions, and in pusillanimous voices. The prefects and the city police are not enough for these knaves. They would have the military protect them! Rome sometimes resembles an armed camp.

"In the meantime, while they are not addressing their fellow senators on the subject of more public baths and more circuses and more free housing for the motley mobs of Rome, and more free food for the mobs who dislike work, they furtively oversee businesses such as the making of uniforms and arms for the military, clothing and blanket factories, or help to subsidize relatives who are in those businesses or throw government contracts in their direction. I have not yet seen a senator whose hand is not sticky with bribes, or who does not extort bribes. The Senate has become a closed organization of scoundrels who loot the Treasury in the name of the general welfare, and who have a rabble-following of hungry bellies and avaricious thieves they call their clients, and about whom they express the most touching solicitude. The fate of Rome, the fate of the desperate taxpayers, is nothing to such as these. Let the public debt mount! Let the middle class be crushed to death under taxes, extortions and exploitation! Why did the gods create the middle class if not to serve as oxen drawing the chariots of senators followed by multitudes of ravenous beggars? An honest man, a man who works and honors Rome and the Constitution of the Republic, is not only a fool. He is suspect. Send the tax collector to him for fresh robberies! He is probably not paying his 'just' share of the taxes.

"The military is constantly clamoring for new appropriations for the 'defense' of Rome, and against 'the enemy.' To question these appropriations is to bring the cry of denunciation. Am I a traitor? Am I indifferent to the strength of Rome? Would I have Rome weak in the face of encompassing barbarians? Do I not understand that we must keep our allies strong with gifts from the Treasury, and arms, and the presence of our legions? Not to mention the advice of our military and political experts, whose long and expensive journeys in their advisory capacities are financed by the Treasury? It is odd that Carvilius Ulpian, who is an Egyptologist, and a lover of Egyptian art, managed to convince the Senate that it was absolutely necessary that he be financed to 'study the present defenses of Egypt,' and that his presence was needed for that 'study' in Cairo. He went, of course, accompanied by Praetorians and a whole retinue of handsome ladies and slaves and actors and gladiators, all paid for out of the funds in the Treasury. He came back and addressed the Senate, giving them the reassuring news that Egypt was loyal to the Pax Romana, though the proconsul in Cairo could have sent that news on request at the cost of a single messenger on a regular ship."

Lucanus involuntarily smiled, but the smile had a touch with dreary melancholy in it. The letter in his hands seemed to vibrate with the angry passion of the tribune. Lucanus continued to read.

"But ten days ago I was present, as a guest, in the Senate. One senator declaimed sadly, but nobly! that world leadership had been thrust upon the strong shoulders of Rome. 'It was not our choice,' said this lying hypocrite, mouthing his words heroically, 'but the choice of fate, or the gods, or the mysterious forces of history,' he giving the impression that history in some mystical way exists above and apart from mankind which makes history! 'Shall we again refuse this yoke?' demanded the vomitous liar. 'Shall we again refuse to take upon us what has been decreed because we possess the genius for government, the genius for invention, the genius for productive work? No! By Jupiter, no! Onerous though the burden is, we accept it for the sake of humanity!'

"I could not contain myself. I rose from my guest's seat beside Carvilius Ulpian and stood there with my thumbs in my belt, letting them see my armor and my sword. How these ladylike men love the show of militarism! They immediately took on serious expressions, though they have seen me often enough, Mars knows! 'Let the tribune speak!' some of them shouted, as if they could have stopped the son of Priscus!

"I lifted my fist and shook it in their mendacious faces. 'And who,' I demanded, 'has declared that Rome has been given the leadership of the world? The civilized Greeks who detest us and laugh at us and our bloody pretensions? The Egyptians, who were an old dynasty when Remus and Romulus were suckled by the she-wolf? The Jews, who had their wise code of laws when Rome had no law but the short sword? The barbarians in Britain, who tear down our fortifications as fast as we raise them? The Gauls, the Goths, the ancient Etruscans, the Germani, the millions of those as yet unblessed by Roman militarism? The millions who do not know our name, or, if knowing, spit at hearing it? Who gave us leadership but ourselves, out of our force, our craft and threats, our urge to despoil and steal, our lust for power? We are like a young, uncouth but corrupt bully swaggering among old men, or among babes growing large for the future on their mothers' milk.' "

Lucanus' fair brows knitted with sudden anxiousness. His heart beat with a vague fear. He honored Diodorus for those brave and honest words, those words flung into the faces of liars, politicians and other rascals swollen with ambition. Nevertheless, he was frightened. He tried to console himself with the thought that Tiberius Caesar was also a soldier, and that he respected Diodorus and was, in his own way, an honorable man.

"I expected to be shouted down," Diodorus' letter continued. "But those nearest me merely sat in silence and looked at me with knitted brows. One or two, younger than the others, blushed and stared at their hands. Carvilius Ulpian avoided my eyes and twitched on his seat. It is possible that he has an irritable rectum, so I forgave him. I waited, but no one answered me.

"Rome is not my Rome, the Rome of my ancestors. The Founding Fathers are forgotten, or mentioned only when some politician wishes to commit more infamy. The days of fortitude, faith and character are gone forever, and the days of courage and discipline. Why then do I struggle? Because it is in the nature of a free man to struggle against slavery and lies. If he falls, then he has fallen in a good fight, if hopeless.

"But enough of this gloom. You will return to your family in the near future. We shall receive our dear son with rejoicing and affection. May God bless you, my son."

Lucanus' eyes smarted dryly as he rolled up the letter. It was always dangerous to speak the truth. In a corrupt world such as this it was fatal. If God cared for the world of men at all, thought Lucanus, bitterly, He would create many Diodoruses, or He would protect them when they spoke in their loud clear voices.

Let me forget my family, Lucanus abjured himself with sternness. I must not love—though I love!—because if I am involved too deeply the consequences will, as usual, be tragic, and I have had enough of tragedy. If I could pray, however I should pray that the senators would hastily close and bolt their chamber against Diodorus, for his own dear and vociferous sake, and the sake of my mother and my brothers and sister.

He reminded himself that he had lately come, at a considerable price, into possession of a translated scroll from Cathay, containing wise words written centuries ago by one K'ung Fu'tze, or Confucius, as Joseph ben Gamliel had called him. The Jewish teacher had been reluctant to part with it, but Diodorus, reflected Lucanus, might be soothed by those lofty words, so calm, so resigned, so mannered, so contemplative. He would also nod vigorously at reading, "Remember this, my children, that oppressive government is fiercer and more feared than a tiger."

The harpy-faced little Claudius Vesalius had come to a pause with his wretched student very near to Lucanus, and he raised his voice. "Mathematics is indeed the Apollonian art!" he shrilled. "He who dislikes it, or avoids it, or regards it as a lesser science is a brass-assed monkey!"

He means me, thought Lucanus with some amusement, and pretended to be engrossed with a letter. The little mincing Greek was incensed. He continued to address his student but in reality Lucanus.

"I consider Pythagoras superior to any Aristotle or Hippocrates or Julius Caesar!" he declaimed. "Or any Phidias or any artist, or what not. All science and art are based on definite mathematical principles. Induction! It is all mathematics! Let us say that we wish to prove that the sum of the first N odd numbers is $N-2$, that is, one plus three plus five plus—plus 2N—one equals $N-2$. Is it not true that N equals 2? Yes! For one plus three equals four equals 2^2. It is also true that N equals K. In that case we should have——"

Lucanus elaborately yawned, and seeing this, Claudius Vesalius seethed. The young Greek rose easily and wandered to the far-off gate at the other end of the garden. The teeth of Claudius Vesalius gritted. Here was one gifted with the Apollonian art, and he preferred to dabble his hands in corpses and bloody his clothing and smell vile stenches in carnal houses or infirmaries! Argh! He hated Lucanus for all that waste. To Hades with him. Let him deliver brats who should never be born and cut for the stone in those who could not resist their lusts at the tables! Worthy calling for a worthy sniveler! Nor did this precious pretender haunt the brothels of Alexandria as normal young men did, nor was he overly respectful to his teachers. His attitudes were preposterous. Did he grace wineshops or taverns or circuses or theaters with his presence? No indeed. He was too valuable for all that. He was always careful to protect those delicate hands of his during the rougher sports for fear of stiffening a finger that could hold a scalpel.

"He is a young Hermes," said the harassed student admiringly, following Lucanus with his eyes. Claudius Vesalius squealed like a pig and slapped his face in rage.

Lucanus left the gardens and the university. Beyond lay vast green lawns over which palms and cypresses and myrtles and willows cast an emerald shade in that bright golden air. A sweet stillness lay over the earth. The sea in its unfathomable mystery stretched away to infinitude. Lucanus was alone. All was silence except for the unresting voice of the waters flowing to the west.

Suddenly the twilight descended, and the earth and sea changed. Overhead the sky became a dim and hollow arch of a greenish blue. The sea darkened to a swift and quiet purple, its far distance restless with crimson as the sun poised on the waves. The illimitable west burned with an orange and scarlet light against which drifted black clouds in the form of Roman galleons, moving on their unknown journey, their sails bellied in an unfelt and unearthly wind. The immensity of heaven and sea dwarfed the earth, towered over it, rolled about it, speaking of awe, yet doomful and foreboding to Lucanus.

Involuntarily he remembered Joseph ben Gamliel speaking on one such a twilight, and in that soft yet sonorous voice of his: "The Heavens declare His glory!"

Lucanus sat down on the grass. He felt again that terrible estrangement between himself and God. Ah, but one must never permit God to enter his heart! For with Him He brought anguish and duty and commands and exhortations and fear and tragedy. Once possessed of a man's soul, He became King, and there was none else beside Him.

"But with His commands and His laws He also brings love

and spiritual delight and bread for the soul, and a light in the darkness," Joseph ben Gamliel had said to Lucanus one twilight. "Without Him one has only the world and delusion and hunger and dust and pain, and an emptiness that cannot be filled by man. One has death, without the Most Holy One, blessed be His Name. One has only tears, which cannot be comforted. All the gold in the world cannot buy His peace, which is beyond understanding. I have taught you of the Psalms of David, the king. 'The Lord is gracious and full of compassion, slow to anger and of great mercy. The Lord is righteous in all His ways, and holy in all His works. . . . He will not always chide: neither will He keep His anger forever. . . . For as the heaven is high above the earth, so great is His mercy toward them that fear Him.'

"My Lucanus, I feel Him near you. I feel Him as close as breathing. His Hand is upon you. Fear not, my child. Turn to Him in your sorrow and dread, for I know these devour you."

"He afflicts us," Lucanus had replied bitterly. "I want none of Him. What explanation do you have, Rabbi, for what I daily see in the public infirmaries and in the carnal houses? Why should a child suffer, and a man be afflicted with leprosy? How have they offended God that He should punish them? The world is one great groan of agony."

Joseph had turned large and luminous eyes on his pupil, and they beamed with compassion. "Job was an afflicted man, and wept for himself and his fellow men, and reproached God for what appeared to him the senseless misery of the earth. And God answered him, reprovingly, 'Hast thou commanded the morning since thy days; and caused the dayspring to know his place . . . Hast thou entered the springs of the sea? . . . hast thou seen the doors of the shadow of death? Canst thou bring forth Mazzaroth in his season? or canst thou guide Arcturus with his sons? Knowest thou the ordinances of heaven? canst thou set the dominion thereof in the earth? . . . Canst thou send lightnings, that they may go, and say unto thee, Here we are? . . . Who provideth for the raven his food? when his young ones cry unto God . . . ? . . . Shall he who contendeth with the Almighty instruct Him? he that reproveth God, let him answer it.' "

Joseph ben Gamliel had stood with him on this very spot, tall and majestic and thin to transparency, clad in dark robes of brown and crimson, his high head bound with a cloth of red cotton. His bearded face, with its pearly skin, delicately aquiline nose and tender mouth, had shone in the twilight like alabaster. Lucanus loved and honored him more than any other of his teachers, yet he constantly exacerbated the young man's very heart. Still, he sought out Joseph and did not know why, except that he threw coldly furious questions at him and commented cynically on the loving answers.

On that twilight Lucanus had flung words like stones into that reverend and gentle face. "If you had ever suffered, my teacher, if you had ever endured the loss of one dearer to you than life, if you had watched that dear one die in affliction and without hope, and her vitality leaving her body like an unseen trickle of water, and she the sweetest of women! then you would not speak so. You would, like Job, pour ashes upon your head and cry out in reproof against your God! Would you, then, speak of His mercy?"

Joseph's face had changed, or perhaps it was only because the twilight had deepened. Surely it was only the twilight which had cast an aspect of tragedy and weariness on the teacher's face. Joseph never spoke except with tranquillity, like one who had dined well or who lived comfortably, without question or trouble.

Yes, it was only the twilight which had suddenly darkened and contorted his face for a single instant. Then he had smiled at Lucanus and had gone his quiet way, his garments flowing about him. It was easy for those who had no wounds to find the wounds of others insignificant, and to wonder at the complaints made about them!

Now as Lucanus stood in this present twilight and looked at the darkening sea and the far glimmer of the orange-scarlet sunset, he felt his awful loneliness again, his abandonment, and his endless, unremitting grief, not only for Rubria, who was lost to him forever, but for all that suffered and cried aloud without solace. His soul stiffened in him with resistance. Never again would God speak to him, for he had shut his ears! The unanswerable had received no answer, or consolation.

A chill wind, salty and immense, swept over his flesh. He turned away, desolate as always, to return to his small house where he lived with Cusa and the latter's wife, Calliope. He returned to a lighted lamp, a frugal dinner, and his studies. He was a soldier on bivouac, preparing for the near day when he would be armed adequately to meet the God of pain and vanquish Him.

"Bah!" said Cusa to his wife, Calliope, who stood before

him with her plump infant girl resting on her hip. "You are only a woman, and it is notorious that women possess no intelligence."

"I knew enough to get you as a husband, though veritably you are not the handsomest man alive," replied Calliope, her pert and pretty face smiling impudently. "It was I who asked Aurelia for you, and it was I who suggested to that poor and noble lady that we wished to be free. She communicated my desire to Diodorus, and so, here we are, free if not free-born."

"You are wrong," said Cusa, ill-naturedly, but smiling at his little girl, who cooed at him, "Did Aurelia free us, or the tribune, that ferocious descendant of the Quinites? No. When we were offered by him to Lucanus it was our blue-eyed Greek who said he would not accept us unless we were first freed, and as the Roman loves him as a son, and has adopted him as a son, the request was granted in order that Lucanus would not be alone in Alexandria. Did the tribune think that without our chaperonage Lucanus would become a sybarite? Or a haunter of brothels? Or a gamester? Hah! I only wish he had some appreciation of such things! He is a male Vestal Virgin. Has he no blood, no parts, no fires, no passions except for learning his accursed medicine?"

"You will observe," said Calliope, sitting down and beginning to nurse her child, "that you are full of doubts yourself, in spite of your remarks about my intelligence. Why does Lucanus refrain from all the delights of young men? Why is he so abstemious? Less charitable people would consider him either a devotee of Narcissus or one engaged in unspeakable practices with other young men. But he is neither. Something eats at the vitals of his spirit, like the Spartan fox. He is short of patience with everyone; his words are cold or somber. He sits for hours in silence on the terrace, either with his books or with his hands fallen upon them. He is curt and hard of speech at times, if he is disturbed. Have you seen him smile often? Only our little Mara can amuse him. At times I find him tiresome. I think there is a spell upon him. Yesterday I visited the temple of Serapis to pray for him. It is not that I love him; it is impossible to love such a remote young man who resembles a statue more than flesh. But I was thinking of ourselves."

"You forget that it was he who insisted upon our freedom."

Calliope shrugged. "Freedom is good for the soul. So you often say, and who am I to disagree with you? Nevertheless, it was gay in the slaves' quarters of the house of Diodorus. Doubtless, it is now gayer in Rome, or on the estates of the tribune. Who comes to this house but hectoring philosophers and tutors, and not even then at Lucanus' invitation. Has Lucanus friends among the students? Is there laughter here, and spirited talk of girls and festivities? No! We are not old, but it is like the house of old men."

Cusa frowned at her formidably, but she tossed her long, light brown tresses and said, "Humph."

"When we return to Rome in another four weeks, Calliope, you will see your friends again, and you will have your gossips and your gaieties. Diodorus has already secured a position for Lucanus as a medical officer in Rome, with an excellent salary. He will also care for a number of rich private patients, and he will be busy in the sanitoria also. We can then have our own small banquets among our friends. It is not the fault of Lucanus that we see no one here; we are strangers."

Calliope smirked at him. "With the generous stipend the tribune sends you, and your thrift, we can well buy our own small grove and farm near Rome. Is it necessary for you to become part of the household of Diodorus and tutor his children?"

"You have never heard of gratitude," said Cusa, severely. He slapped his thigh. "No, if Diodorus does not want us, we must remain with Lucanus in Rome to conduct his household. I am certain he will take a wife there."

"Hah," said Calliope, with significance. "I tell you he will never marry. Has he accepted invitations from the families of the students here in Alexandria? No. He lives alone, in that terrible marble silence of his. He thinks only of Rubria; he has never forgotten her. She is a divinity to him. In her name he strips himself of money, and that is unnatural for a Greek, to give what he can to every beggar he sees. Does he not visit the prisons to cure and comfort criminals and slaves? He is a scandal. I am a woman of intuition. He has said nothing yet about that position as medical officer in Rome, and is silent when you mention it. I fear he will refuse——"

"Do not be a fool!" roared Cusa in wrath. "Lucanus may not be natural or warm, but he is not an imbecile. For what has he been studying?"

"For some fearful reason of his own," said Calliope.

Satisfied that she had now made Cusa anxious, she retired with her child for the afternoon's sleep. But Cusa was too disturbed for rest. He walked out on the high terrace, mumbling to himself.

The house was neither large nor small, and was built of white stone, with a pleasant outdoor portico overlooking the sea through simple white columns. Behind the house lay the hot and vehement city of Alexandria, more polyglot even than Antioch, larger and more glaring, and much more corrupt. It seethed, rumbled, shouted and screamed with innumerable tongues; it was a restless stream of black, dusky and white faces, and outlandish garbs. The smothering and twisted streets boiled with caravans and camels and horses and chariots and donkeys. The jackals howled all night from the outskirts of the city. The prefect of the city could not be certain how many of his men would return at night to their stations; murder was very frequent. Even the Roman legions here could not always maintain order. Tax-gatherers disappeared when not accompanied by soldiers; their bodies were frequently found in the river or when the tides returned to the vast and brilliant-colored harbor. This was, to Cusa, the one agreeable aspect of the city, which burned as if with internal fires day and night, morning and evening. Prostitutes of all races and colors frequented the narrow and fiery streets at all hours. Every household of any consequence had its own armed guards at the gates, yet robbery was so common that few commented on it. Hot yellow dust surged over the city in such clouds that it made the smoldering skies red at night under the moon and above the torches set in sockets along the walls. Mobs assaulted each other at midnight; there were always bands of young Jews and Egyptians in conflict, cursing and beating each other with clubs, and using glittering knives. The alleys were full of corpses each dawn, evidence of other conflicts between other races also. Though the Romans had established a very adequate sanitary system of sewers emptying into the harbor, the people used the streets as latrines at night, contemptuous of the public booths within a few feet. As a consequence Alexandria stank, even during the brightest and driest of days. In comparison, Antioch was a clean sanitorium. Garlic seemed to be the popular perfume; the cobbled streets were strewn with the offal of both animals and men, despite the armies of slaves who were driven to the task of daily cleaning. It was a dangerous and flaming city, a sweltering and violent city, always clamoring with the sounds of pursuit and fleeing. Epidemics raged through the households; the prisons were always full. Chariots thundered without cessation; one was never far from the rattling and pounding of them.

But the house of Lucanus was in a more or less isolated spot, not far from the university. It was surrounded by steep gardens and a comforting high wall surmounted by sharp iron spikes. Cusa had carefully established in the city the rumor that Lucanus possessed no money, and that the house was Spartan, containing no silver or gold or anything else worth stealing. In consequence, there had been only a dozen attempts at robbery in these past four years.

Cusa cursed the city and his uneasiness as he stood on the colonnade high above the harbor. The sea was the most royal of blues, almost an imperial purple as it simmered under the white-hot sky. Hundreds of ships, small and large, crowded the harbor. Sails, blue and red and white and scarlet and yellow, hung limp from the masts, for there was no wind in that brilliant stillness of noon. No ship moved; it was the hour for sleeping during the intolerable heat. The city was comparatively quiet, for Alexandria, and only the faintest of rumbles came to the ear of Cusa. He wiped the sweat from his forehead with his bare arm and panted. That almost imperceptible breeze coming from the glittering sea was damp; Alexandria was tolerable only when a dry hot wind came from the deserts. The ships now swayed sluggishly on the slow and incandescent tide.

The palms in the garden were overlaid by sparkling yellow dusts, as were the parched grass and the languishing trees. It was impossible to combat the heat of Africa with any water, and the fountains were sluggish. Cusa could hear their feeble complaint between him and the sea. The flowers hurt the eye with their too intense colors, and the eye was further hurt by the light from the sky and the purple blaze of the harbor. Nevertheless, Cusa sat down and gave himself up to his troubled thoughts.

Lucanus had never been a merry soul, even when young, except when in the company of the little Rubria or riding madly on the small ass into Antioch with Keptah. He had always been too reserved, too quiet, too contemplative as a child, and his angers, infrequent though they were, had been as cold as ice, and as glacial. Any sunniness, warmth and love which had been part of his character had been expended on the daughter of Diodorus. He had laughed rarely, and then almost always in her presence.

If Lucanus had been difficult enough in Antioch after

Rubria's death he was sometimes unbearable to Cusa in these past four years. He would fix Cusa with a sardonic eye when the tutor disagreed with him over the tasks brought home from the university. (Cusa felt that he was the equal of any of the teachers there, and it offended him when Lucanus preferred their interpretations to Cusa's.) He would lead Cusa on, teasing him not with lightness, but with a sort of bitter goading. "You are no Socrates," Cusa would say to him, secretly wounded, "and I resent these interminable dialogues which lead to nothing, except to make me appear foolish. Is that your intention?" Lucanus would apologize, with genuine regret, but his face would remain gloomy. He is like a man who constantly bites on an abscessed tooth, Cusa would think. When, in the name of all the gods, will he forget that maiden?

Cusa sat and thought about Lucanus, on the colonnade. He shook his head over and over. Despite Calliope's complaints he had decided not to leave Lucanus unless the young Greek sent him away.

Chapter Seventeen

"It is unfortunate, my good Lucanus," said the master of arts, Rustrumjee, "that you are firmly decided upon being a physician, for you are an artist of formidable merit." Rustrumjee was a learned man from Indi; he was also curator of the art museum at the university of Alexandria, and his tastes were universal, exquisite, and perceptive. A small, graceful, and sinuous man, curiously giving an appearance of deformity, he had a dark face and strangely pale eyes and a subtle smile. To Rustrumjee a man who possessed no art, or no appreciation of art, was scarcely a man at all. Like most Indus, art to him was not apart from religion; he had also taught Lucanus Sanskrit. "As a Brahman, I belong to the exclusive caste of priests, and it is our vow to preserve our ancient language." He looked at Lucanus with dignity for a moment, then picked up two small rectangles of wood on which Lucanus had painted portraits. He delicately frowned.

Lucanus had been asked by his teacher to remain after the other students had left. The young man said, "Master, I am a physician, from my birth. I can conceive of nothing else for me but medicine."

Rustrumjee nodded, and sighed. "What has been ordained

during Karma must be fulfilled. It is probable that this is another aspect of your Karma, the transmigration of your soul, needed to complete the needs of your spirit. I often like to speculate on what sins you committed against your fellow men, during a previous Karma, which now you must expiate in saving them from pain or death."

Lucanus involuntarily smiled, the austere planes of his face breaking up from their usual rigidity into youthfulness. Then he was somber again. He never argued with Rustrumjee about religion, or engaged in discussion with him about it. He reserved that for Joseph ben Gamliel, who taught religion, who was compassionate, unlike the Indu, who had no real compassion because he believed that man's earthly fate was ordained before endless rebirth and should not be protested. Yet Rustrumjee would never kill the most obnoxious fly or other insect, for fear of interfering with its own ordained Karma. Man, mosquito or rat: they were one and the same to the Indu, moving up slowly through painful rebornings into being, and thence into Nirvana, and on the way demanding and receiving no human pity, for what they were they had so formed themselves, without the help or condemnation of the gods, through eons of time, through eons of existences. Lucanus found the vast interlockings of the Brahman's religion in some way fascinating. It seemed to explain much of the agony of life, its mysterious calamities, its seeming anarchy. What if the diseased wretches in the prisons and in the medical infirmary, suffering from apparently undeserved tortures, were merely expiating former crimes and spiritual malformations? And, in expiating them, were rising to higher conditions of life?

He had discussed this with Joseph ben Gamliel. Then the Jew had said, "No. One has only to consider the illimitable harmony of nature, which is a reflection of God, its precise laws which never deviate, its exactness. God is the Law, and the Law is perfect and immutable. Consider the Ten Commandments, the Law. The fact that when a man breaks the Law he suffers intensely either physically or spiritually, and sometimes both ways, and that in obeying the Law he has peace and love and justice, and that if he has mortal pain he has spiritual sustenance proves without doubt that perfection is not beyond him and is within his reach. Why then continual rebirth? No. The expiation is in a spiritual form, a realm of abeyance where the soul can cleanse and purify itself."

Lucanus believed Joseph ben Gamliel no more than he believed Rustrumjee, for the simple reason that though he could not reject God as existing he did not believe in the immortality of man. Convinced of both mortal and spiritual death, he was never without the deepest and most terrible anger against God.

Rustrumjee said now, "These portraits. They are the faces of men you have painted in the infirmary or in prison, dying faces. What extraordinarily passionate colors! Almost too vivid, almost too affrighting; they start from the wood. Some would say such coloring is not true reality, but only expressed emotion which comes from your own soul. There is a quality of distortion in the features, too, which does not arise from actuality, but again from your personal emotion. That agony! That huge distress! That phantasmagoria of torment! Those twisted lineaments that stand out so that one feels one can touch them and find them raised, like a boss! The sweat on the foreheads and on the cheeks seems livingly wet, and one expects the beads to roll. The dilated eyes of suffering pulse with blood; it would not surprise me if they should turn upon me in despair and pleading, begging for surcease. The other masters are horrified by your paintings, but I am not. Ah, Lucanus, you belong in Indi, and I feel that in several of your Karmas you have lived there, for only the Indus paint so, and so are an affront to the moderate Greeks, who prefer Olympian beauty and harmony to reality, and prefer to carve statues of their gods and to color them beyond the natural color of men. Yet Zeuxis painted a bunch of grapes so realistic, it is said, that a number of birds darted into the exhibition room to devour them!"

He looked at Lucanus wistfully. "You are certain you feel no urge to be an artist rather than a physician?"

"No, Master. I am a physician."

Lucanus went to the infirmary, though, as he had spent two hours there that early morning, he was not compelled to go again today. There, too, was an Indu physician, but he was a Buddhist striving to alleviate torture so that the soul could attend to peaceful contemplation. There was also a Jewish physician, who had the gentlest of hands and the deepest of pity for all that suffered. There was also a Greek and an Egyptian, and even a Roman interested in epidemiology, which was his subject. Lucanus had long observed that in Alexandria the teachers possessed no arrogance about their individual races or creeds or family backgrounds. Not even the Roman ever declared proudly, "I am a Roman!" The humility, the fraternity, the eager exchange of knowledge among the teachers, the acceptance of each other and their reverence for each other were at first a revelation to the young Greek. They were a brotherhood dedicated to truth and enlightenment. Truth was all, and the imparting of that truth.

They saw Lucanus entering, and greeted him with affectionate smiles, knowing that to him medicine was the divine art, above all other arts, and knowing him dedicated. But only the Jew could understand his fierce personal preoccupation with pain and death. To the others he seemed a student like themselves, academically interested in the aspects of disease and entranced with research for the sake of research alone. To them death was only one of their failures, the final failure, and they would become disinterestedly agog over it and discuss it endlessly. They experimented for the sake of experimentation.

The clean white infirmary held ten beds. Here were brought the hopelessly sick from the prisons or poor quarters of Alexandria, the chronically ill, the desperately afflicted. As all the patients were either slaves or destitute, experimentation upon them was sometimes merciless and quite often the experiments had no relation to the immediate disease at all. This Lucanus found intolerable and hateful, and again only the Jewish teacher understood. The others kindly laughed at Lucanus. "Is it not justifiable that one man die so that others, multitudes, may live?" they would ask him. To which he would reply, while the Jewish teacher listened in searching silence, "No. One man is as important as a mass, and perhaps even more so."

This queer attitude did not diminish the affection and respect of the physicians. But when Lucanus would lament over a mortal illness and work until he sweated to relieve its pain and to save the patient, all but the Jew were puzzled. Truth, knowledge, was the object of medicine. Death was the fate of all men, and pain also. "Yes, men must die," Lucanus would say, bitterly. "But is it not our duty to be most greatly concerned with pain? Even the pain of a slave?"

He would not experiment for the sake of experimentation alone. He treated the disease, for to him as to Keptah the disease was the man. Beyond the infirmary was the mortuary, where bodies of slaves and the abandoned who died in the infirmary or in prisons were dissected. The laws of Egypt, unlike the laws of Greece and Rome, permitted such dissection, for slaves and the poor were regarded as soulless, and Egypt was not particularly obsessed by flesh except when it was royal or aristocratic.

The Indu doctor, and assistants, had taught Lucanus the art of vaccination against smallpox. He permitted himself to be vaccinated over and over, and would vaccinate the patients. "You are inconsistent," one of his teachers would jeer at him fondly. "No experimentation for you!" "He is not inconsistent," said the Jew. "He only wishes to help the patient, who may recover from his present disease, to avoid smallpox in the future. But he would never operate on our—victim's—eye, for instance, when that eye is not diseased, nor would he inject a patient with another disease, medicine or poison merely to observe the result because the patient cannot resist. He will relieve pain, and give all treatment that he believes will relieve pain or that particular disease, but he will not inflict pain or disease in the name of research."

The Egyptian master and his assistants were specialists. They treated the eye, the heart, and various organs as apart from the whole body, and Lucanus resisted the idea of specialism. "If the liver be ill," he would protest, "then the whole man is ill, for its toxins reach the blood, the eye, the heart, the stomach, the intestines, the skin. And so with ulcers, degeneracies, and all other diseases. It is not only the peritoneum which is inflamed; the whole body is inflamed in sympathy. Cancer is a disease of the whole man, not merely that part which is attacked. If a man has arthritis he does not have it solely in the shoulder, the knee or the ankle or the toes or hands. He has it universally."

The Egyptian doctors would be amused, except for the Jew, who agreed. And the Jew told Lucanus privately, "The disease is not only the whole man, but also his soul. A sick spirit creates a sick body, or a sick body creates a sick soul. Not only must the flesh and its disease be treated, but the mind also. It is very possible, though not proved, that all diseases, even those epidemic, originate in some secret chamber of the soul."

The patients were not slaves or the destitute or the criminal to Lucanus. They were man, who must be helped to defeat the inexorable hatred of God for man. Their sufferings tormented him personally; treating a man with heart disease, he would feel thrills of pain in his own heart. The arthritis which twisted and crippled the joints of a sufferer very frequently twinged his own joints. He would actually feel the devouring of cancer in his own sound flesh when treating a cancerous patient. A tumor of the brain in a slave would give him pounding headaches. It was as if a disease sent out invisible filaments from the patient, entangling him in its symptoms and agonies.

The Egyptian teacher and his assistants often used magic in the treatment of their patients in the infirmary. This gave rise to comradely hilarity among the learned Greek and Roman teachers, who had long lost their national beliefs in the worth of amulets or incantations or rites. But the Jewish teacher had told Lucanus, "As the soul is also sick as well as the body, it can be cured quite often with mysteries, and, as the disease of the body may well originate in the mind, that mind can be convinced by thaumaturgy that it is cured, and therefore the body frequently cures itself."

He added, "These Egyptians are not so wrong as the others believe. You will notice that when you lay your hands tenderly and with a kind of fierce resistance on a patient the Egyptians become exceedingly interested, though the others chaff you. For the Egyptians have discovered, from observation, that you have a mysterious healing power. The others are rationalists, believing solely in potions and surgery. The Greeks, however, you have observed, are not of the Cnidos school, which treated only the diseased organ. They also believe, with us, that the sick man is part of his setting."

Just now Lucanus was particularly interested in a man who suffered from a baffling disease of the brain. Some of the surgeons suggested a tumor; it was not often that they were given the opportunity of studying a living brain. Lucanus suspected that they did not truly believe the man had a tumor. Now that he had completed his studies and was a physician he could make protests which would not have been permitted in a student. Moreover, the patient was the Jew's, and after he had listened to Lucanus he would not let his colleagues interfere with their eager saws and burrs and trephines.

The man was a slave, and his master had sent him to prison for a petty theft. Under the law he could have had him executed, and actually he had been condemned to death. The master had been persuaded to send him to prison. Within the last few days the Jewish teacher had purchased the poor creature, and had given him to Lucanus as a patient. "If you cure him, Lucanus, he is yours." "If I cure him," Lucanus had replied, "then I will purchase him from you and set him free." "I then give him to you as a gift, and you shall make him free yourself. For I remember we Jews were slaves in Egypt."

Lucanus went to the man's bed at once, and the Egyptian doctors gathered around to watch. The slave's name was Odilus, and he was of obscure racial origin, like many of the slaves in Egypt. He had a thin aquiline face, deep and flaming dark eyes, a sensitive and eloquent mouth, and a tall emaciated body with restless fine hands and long delicate feet. He was about twenty-two years old. He looked at Lucanus imploringly, and in silence, but his hands lifted a little as if in prayer.

Lucanus pulled a stool to the bedside and regarded the slave with anxious pity. He unrolled a papyrus and again scanned the symptoms of the man. No steady pressing pain, as in tumor. No signs of paralysis—yet. No muddying or darkening of the irises. No failing of any faculties or senses. But the man was in agony. He had great control over himself, but often he screamed in anguish, pressing his hands to his head. His blood pressure was erratic; sometimes his heart would bound and leap, though there was nothing organically wrong with it. Sometimes his whole body would go into spasms. Upon his being given a sedative the spasms would quickly subside, and a look of profound relief would settle on the drowsing face, a look most moving and touching to Lucanus. There were no physical signs of disease in any of his organs; his skin, though frequently livid or blotched and quivering, was healthy. But the pains in his head, he had told Lucanus piteously, were either crushing, bursting, darting, piercing, or burning. They varied in intensity and in form, but they were always there in one aspect or another.

The other teacher-physicians strolled to the bed and watched Lucanus make another of his meticulous examinations. They watched him hold a candle to the man's eyes and again search the irises. They watched him as he commanded Odilus to lift his hands, his legs, his feet, his head. Lucanus searched for exaggerated or lost reflexes. All was practically normal, but the man twitched on the bed and moaned. He was intelligent, and he could read and write three languages, and had been his master's secretary.

Lucanus folded his bare arms on his breast and considered the man for some long moments. "What is the pain today?" he asked, absently. Near his shoulder the Jewish teacher hovered, watching closely.

"Oh, Master," groaned the slave, "today my skull is too tight for my brain! It is about to burst from its cage."

"Tumor, obviously," said the Greek master, avidly.

Lucanus shook his head, not looking away from the slave. "He has been here for over a month, and shows no loss of any faculty or sense, no epilepsy, nor is there the slightest sign of even the most minute paralysis or blindness or deafness. Reflexes are only a little exaggerated today. No, it is not a tumor, which is relentlessly progressive in its damage. He has said he has had this condition for a number of years, though in less acuteness. He has no tumor, therefore, either benign or malignant."

His handsome face bent over the moaning slave, and it was filled with commiseration and tenderness and sympathy. He took one of the slave's hands, and immediately the moaning ceased and Odilus searched his face pleadingly. Lucanus said, "I will give him essence of opium, not enough to stupefy him but to ease his pain. Then I will question him. There is something stirring in my mind——" He paused. "Today his blood pressure is dangerously high."

"Impending stroke," suggested one of the young assistants.

"It is possible he will have a stroke," assented Lucanus. "But not from any tumor and possibly not from any disease of the brain. Or any disease of any other member of his body. Could it be possible that strokes may result, at times, from causes other than organic?" he mused.

The slave was given a tincture of opium, which he swallowed ravenously, knowing the relief that would come to him. Lucanus waited. Minute by minute the moans became fewer, the twitching of the muscles diminished visibly, and the carved lines of agony subsided on the thin and mobile face. Odilus smiled a feeble smile of gratitude and did not look away from the merciful Lucanus. His eyes began to close. "I will sleep," he murmured.

But Lucanus pressed his hand strongly. "Bear with me, Odilus, so that you may be healed," he said.

Odilus said, with a sob, "Master, I do not want to be healed, for then I shall be returned to my master for execution."

Lucanus opened his mouth to say something in consolation, and to tell him that his master no longer owned him. But he held back. The stirring in his mind quickened.

"Before you were condemned, Odilus, and when your master trusted you, and you had not yet stolen, you still had these awful pains. Please open your eyes and answer me! Is it not so?"

The drooping eyes opened protestingly. "It is so, Master. Ah, let me sleep! If only," he murmured, "I had had the courage to kill myself when I was younger!"

"Ah," said Lucanus, in excitement. "Tell me, Odilus, how long you have been a slave."

"I do not know, Master. My earliest memory is of being a very young child, and of being conveyed to Egypt by a Persian slavemaster for sale here. I do not know if I was born free or slave. My present master has owned me since I was three or four, and I do not remember my parents or who they were."

"Why did you steal, Odilus? Your master was not unduly harsh to you, and he trusted you."

The slave's dimming eyes quickened into dark fire. "I dipped into his coffers—for he was a very rich man and did not always know the full amount in the coffers—so that I could run far away. I intended to take a bag of gold. But he had sent the money that morning to the stronghold in Alexandria and there was only one small bag of silver left. I did not want it, yet I took it. Once in the coffers, I could not resist."

"Why? Such a small amount!"

"Yes, Master." The slave was silent for a few moments, and his expressive eyes welled largely with some deep and aching thought. "Still," he continued, "it was a first step to freedom."

Now he burst into sobs and tears with such intensity that his shuddering body made the cot shake.

"Even if I had been able to steal gold it would not have saved me!" he cried. "I should have been found!" He grasped Lucanus' hand with sweating fingers. "You cannot understand, Master, you who are a free man, what it is to be a slave! Many there were in that household to whom I talked of freedom, and they gave me strange and wondering smiles. Were we not sheltered, fed, clothed adequately, and were we not on holy days, and when we particularly pleased the master, given recreation or even a piece of silver? We were better than the free poor of the city, who slept in gutters or under arches, and begged for bread, or starved. Why, then, an onerous freedom to die like dogs?"

"Yes," said Lucanus. "Ah, yes."

The slave looked at him pleadingly, and saw the moistness of his blue eyes. He raised himself on his elbow, forgetting the others present.

"Master, I know now that I wished to steal because I knew I would be caught and killed! And I preferred death to slavery! Can you understand this?"

"Yes," said Lucanus. "Yes, yes."

The slave fell back on his bed, and groaned again. "Do not heal me, Master. Let me die here. Then I shall be free forever."

He held his hands to his head and his eyes sank in their sockets in a renewal of torment. "Opium, Master. Enough opium to kill me at once. Then I shall fall into a deep sleep and never awaken, and shall be one of the countless company who are forever free."

Lucanus raised his voice loudly in order to reach the man's dulling ear. He looked at the other physicians, who were watching intently. "Is there need in this university for a man skilled in bookkeeping and accounts, who can be trusted?" he demanded.

The slave opened his eyes, staring in utter confoundedness. The other physicians frowned, trying to understand.

"He is a slave, Lucanus," said an Egyptian, "and he does not belong to us, but to his master."

Lucanus laughed softly, and shook his head. He put his hand on the slave's cheek, like a brother.

"No. He belonged to my teacher, Jacob, here, who purchased him from his former master, but now he belongs to me, and tomorrow I shall visit the praetor and free him."

The slave started up in the bed, and uttered a smothered scream of dazed joy. He flung his arms around Lucanus' neck. He withdrew the arms, caught up Lucanus' hands, and covered them with kisses. He sobbed and moaned; he was beside himself. His whole face was ablaze. He panted, threw himself on the floor. And then he lay, embracing Lucanus' feet and alternately pressing his brow to them.

Lucanus lifted him with the utmost gentleness and placed him on the cot again, but the man seized his hand and would not let it go. He looked at Lucanus with adoration.

"My dear colleagues," said Lucanus, "I repeat my offer, and the offer of Odilus to you. Do you need him?"

"I can use him immediately as my own clerk," said Jacob, whose eyes had filled with tears.

Lucanus pretended to doubt, and shook his head. "Ah, how very sorrowful this is," he murmured. "Poor Odilus is free, but he is ill, and who knows if he will recover?"

The sick man started up again, and the blaze was brighter on his face. "Master! I am no longer ill! The pain has left my head; it is clear and cool and soothed! Let me serve here, I pray you!"

"As you will be free in the morning, and are tacitly free now and able to plan your own future, you must not say, 'Let me,' " said Lucanus, with mock severity.

Odilus, whose eyes were on fire, looked at him as one looks at an angel. Then he smiled radiantly and said, "Master, if the physician, Jacob, wishes my services, it will be my delight to serve him, as a free man."

"And at a stipend which we shall discuss," said the youthful and bearded Jew.

"Now, sleep," said Lucanus, rising. "When you awaken, Odilus, you will be without pain, and the pain will never recur."

The physicians laughed a little and moved away, with Lucanus among them.

A Greek said, with amusement, "Now we are deprived of a living brain to study."

"But you have seen the dying brought back to life," said Jacob. "Look at him sleeping there, with the smile of a joyful child on his face. For freedom is more than life to such as he, and may his name be legion. May God grant that soon all men shall be free, so that they do not think of death as the only escape."

"Odilus suffered from no illness of the body or brain," Lucanus said respectfully to the pragmatic Greeks. "He suffered from an illness of the soul, and he is now cured. In your rationality you had forgotten Hippocrates."

Chapter Eighteen

The lilac twilight suffused the air of Alexandria when Lucanus, exhausted, left the infirmary and mortuary. Here and there a streak of dead blood splashed his tunic, and his head throbbed. He encountered Joseph ben Gamliel, who had apparently been waiting for him.

Joseph said, "Greetings, Lucanus. I wish a favor of you. I have a dear friend who has been living in Alexandria for two months, not out of choice but because he is very ill and is close to death. His name is Elazar ben Solomon, a rich trader who travels all over the world. An exceedingly rich trader, and a good man. Will you see him?"

Lucanus said curtly, "I am sorry, Joseph, but I have no wish to treat any rich man, anywhere. I have made up my mind to travel to every port, on any ship, to treat the destitute and slaves in every city, and the galley slaves, for there are no sanitoria anywhere for them, except in Rome, which, therefore, does not need me."

"We say in our Scriptures that wisdom with an inheritance is very good," said Joseph, smiling. "Do not color so, my Lucanus. I am merely congratulating you on having a wealthy adopted father. Otherwise how would you live on your journeys to the ports? I have not heard," added Joseph, "that rich men suffer less in their diseases than do the poor, nor that God has granted them any immunities. A cancer is as agonizing in a Caesar as it is in his lowliest slave."

"Nevertheless, I do not wish to treat any rich man," repeated Lucanus, coldly. Then he was curious. "I am a tyro as yet. Has not your friend consulted any of the competent physicians in Alexandria, those avid for fat fees? I could name you a dozen!"

Joseph gazed at him reflectively. "Lucanus, I believe you could help Elazar ben Solomon, and you alone. He is dying; it is probable you cannot save his life. He is also stricken in his soul, and you could comfort him."

"I!" exclaimed Lucanus, and he smiled wearily, "I, the comfortless, give comfort?"

"You do so all the time," said Joseph, with gravity. "Will you come as this favor to me, for I love Elazar ben Solomon. We were children together in Jerusalem, before I came to Alexandria." His face changed, became subtly desolate. "My litter is waiting outside the garden."

Lucanus hesitated. There was something mysterious in Joseph's manner, he thought, and in spite of the young Greek's repugnance to treating the rich and privileged his physician's heart could not be denied. He said, "It is possible he may have a disease in which I am interested, so I will come."

Joseph smiled in his beard. They approached the gates, which were opened for them by armed slaves. Joseph had no slaves himself, nor had his family; they employed only freedmen, whom they had bought as slaves and then freed. His litter bearers were strong young men who bowed affectionately to their master. The evening was very hot, and the sky was a burning amethyst now. Joseph and Lucanus seated themselves side by side in the litter, pushing aside the woolen curtains to catch any vagrant breeze. Suddenly, in this tropical land, the canopy of night fell over Alexandria, and the moon leaped in her place.

The city, as usual, was a welter of color, lamps, clamoring voices, animals, and men and women, for it was only in the evening that Alexandria became fully alive. The scarlet torches hissed in their sockets; beggars squeaked and pleaded every few feet. Chariots roared down the torturous streets. Men shouted, women laughed; music rose from behind white walls pouring with red and magenta and white flowers. Quickly the moonlight came, striking down on low white roofs, as flat as the earth. It was as pale water on those roofs, on which householders were gathering for coolness. Their dark forms and featureless faces moved about; they talked and laughed and clapped hands for slaves to bring their wine, and voices called in many strange tongues. Sometimes an arched door opened in a wall and one could see illuminated gardens, sweet-smelling and full of fountains and statues on which the moonlight drifted like silver rain.

Joseph did not speak on the short journey. He seemed sunken in some melancholy of his own, and Lucanus did not disturb it. He was angry with himself; he wondered why it was always difficult for him to deny Joseph ben Gamliel anything. The voice and the scent of the sea were becoming more imminent, so Lucanus understood that the house to which they were going was near the water and, therefore, very desirable. The huge white moon stared down implacably on the hot and teeming city and brought no coolness to it. Now they reached a smooth, high white wall, and alighted, and a freedman knocked on an arched door. It opened, and beyond it slept the quiet moon-struck garden, full of flowers and trees and grass and fountains, but with no statues. A perfume of fig blossoms and jasmine wafted out into the street. The house at a little distance was large and white, with a wide colonnade and, at the side, balconies in the Eastern manner.

But even here in this warm freshness the fetid and aromatic odor of the East was insistent. The odor was not unpleasant; it even had a hint of spice in it, and incense, and extraordinarily fecund earth.

"It is pleasant here," said Lucanus, grudgingly, thinking of the infirmary at the university. "This man does not spare his money!"

"Why should he?" asked Joseph, in a reasonable voice. "Shall money be hoarded?"

"It could be used to good advantage in helping the helpless, in building sanitoria for the poor, in sheltering the homeless," said Lucanus.

Joseph sighed. "Elazar ben Solomon is known for his many charities, and his kindness, for he has the greatest heart. He redeems every Jewish slave he finds; you will discover no slaves in this house, or in any of his many houses in many cities. The more he gives, the more God gives to him."

The curtains of the windows were pulled aside, so any coolness could enter. It was very still here in the gardens as the two men approached the house. Nightingales sang to the moon, and the songs were both piercing and poignant. Crickets chattered. Somewhere parrots squawked. But there were no human voices. The big bronze doors stood apart, and the hall beyond was of snowy marble filled with high columns, and lighted by many silver lamps on tall standards. Flowers were everywhere in Grecian and Egyptian vases standing on the floor.

The most beautiful girl Lucanus had ever seen in his life hastened towards Joseph, her hands outstretched in loving greeting. She was more beautiful than Iris, the mother of Lucanus, whom the young man had considered unsurpassed even by the loveliest of statues. The girl appeared to be less than twenty, and probably closer to sixteen, and she was so slight, yet so shapely in her blue dress, that her height was not immediately apparent. She was like a queen, and she moved in a queenly fashion, gliding over the white marble. Her small and regal head floated with unbound dark tresses like billowing silk, and so fine was her hair that it appeared to be a blowing vapor. Her oval face was the color of a pearl, translucent and glowing as if with an inner light, and her lips were a bright soft red, her nose delicate and finely shaped, her eyes of a deep and shining violet. She wore a necklace, earrings and bracelet of glittering blue stones set in elaborately fashioned gold. A delightful scent, as of roses, seemed to exude from her snowy flesh rather than from her garments or hair. Her blue garment was sweetly rounded over her maiden breasts, and her slender waist was encircled by a golden girdle also set with darker blue stones. The silk flowed over her smooth young hips, rustled about her exquisite ankles. Her sandals were of gold-brushed leather.

She was joyous at the sight of Joseph, and her luminous white throat palpitated as if she were also restraining herself from bursting into tears of relief and gratitude at Joseph's presence. Joseph took her extended hands and held them warmly and looked into her eyes with the love of a father. "My dear Sara," he said, gently. "I trust your father is better tonight?"

Sara took no immediate notice of Lucanus, hovering in the background and enchanted by the sight of this virginal beauty which had a springlike quality of pureness and adorable tints. Her smile left her face; her lips covered teeth like porcelain. "No, he is not better, Joseph," she said, and her voice was as mournful and soft as a dove's call. "But he will be so happy to see you." She, like Joseph, spoke in Aramaic. Her long black lashes quivered, and her black brows, silken and shining, were like arrows against her white forehead. She had no need for artifice, for paint pots or kohl for her eyes or dye to tint the ends of her fingers rosy. Nature had endowed her with the most entrancing colors, alive as a flower.

Joseph turned to Lucanus. "Sara," he said, "here is my favorite pupil, Lucanus, of whom I have spoken often to you. He is a mighty physician; I have persuaded him to see your father."

Lucanus was so dazzled and bewitched and stunned by the sight of such young and supernal beauty that it was a moment or two before he could bow formally. His Greek blood leaped in adoration of this loveliness; he thought of a statue of the very young Hebe he had once seen in a temple in Alexandria, for Sara was born to serve in love and devotion. This was evident in her air of tenderness and solicitude and gentle humility.

"Before you see my father, Joseph," she said, her eyes suddenly fixed with fascination on Lucanus, "you must both dine and drink some wine."

"Wine we will drink," said Joseph, following the girl into a room beyond the hall which was furnished richly yet simply, and full of many-colored flowers. Here again there were no statues. The walls were of brilliantly hued mosaic depicting blossoms, twining leaves and stylized Oriental forms. The columns were of yellow marble, the lamps of Corinthian bronze, the floor of white and black marble squares, on which were scattered Persian rugs like woven jewels. "But we must return to our homes to dine. Otherwise our families will be concerned about us."

"Ah, yes, it is so," said Sara, unable to take her eyes from Lucanus, who stood uneasily in the center of the large cool room, as tall and handsome as a god. After a moment Sara started, and blushed, and cast down her eyes. Her pretty breast rose quickly, then fell. She clapped her hands, and a servant entered carrying a silver tray on which goblets rested, studded with many different gems. Sara herself poured the excellent wine, which smelled of warm vineyards in the sun. As if bemused, she gave Lucanus a goblet first rather than the older Joseph. He took it; their fingers touched, and Lucanus, in spite of himself, felt an electric thrill. Accustomed as he was to the retiring ways of Aurelia and Iris and "old" Roman women, he wondered a little at the freedom and artless ease of this young girl.

He drank the wine, which had an alluring aroma and taste, and he was annoyed with himself that he enjoyed it. Joseph, drinking also, questioned the maiden about her father in a low voice, and she answered with notes of distress. Lucanus delighted in the sound of the girl's tones, so dulcet, so varied, so eloquent. From time to time, as she spoke, she glanced shyly at Lucanus, and when his eyes met hers she colored deeply.

Finally the two men followed the girl through an open colonnade whose columns were argent and gleaming in the moonlight. She pushed aside a curtain of heavy Oriental lace and they entered a large bedchamber, shining softly with silver lamps and filled with the scent of blossoms and spice. On a large carved bed of ivory, silver, and gilt lay a man of middle age, raised high on silken cushions and with a light colorful rug over his feet. Before Lucanus saw his face he could hear the man's desperate changeful breathing, and his physician's spirit forgot everything but its dedication.

"Greetings, my dear Elazar," said Joseph, approaching the bed, and followed by Lucanus. Joseph took his friend's hands and bent over him, smiling with tender concern, and Sara stood at the foot of the bed anxiously smiling at her father.

Elazar tried to speak, but his voice, between his loud breaths, was hurried and faint. He coughed repeatedly.

"Rest," said Joseph. "I have brought the young physician, Lucanus." And he raised himself and looked at the Greek, beckoning him with his eyes. Lucanus approached, all his alertness fixed on the sick man. Immediately, without speaking, he saw that Elazar was in extremis. The Jewish trader and merchant was an emaciated dark man, leaden of complexion, and possessing large and mournful eyes still glowing with life in spite of his moribund condition. His features reminded Lucanus of Diodorus, for Elazar had that eagle contour and sharpness of face and expression, and Lucanus thought again of the strange resemblance between Jews and Romans.

Elazar tried to smile politely at Lucanus, but he was extremely restless despite his prostration. His lips and ear lobes and the tips of his fingers were cyanotic. A look of profound melancholy lay on his face. His mouth stood open as he attempted to gulp air, and the râles in his lungs made his breath rasping and wheezing. Lucanus, without speaking, lifted the man's tunic from his chest, and bent his head and applied his ear to the region of the heart. Yes, there were the extrasystoles and auricular fibrillation; the heart sounds were muffled, short and weak, interspersed with an erratic and bounding rhythm. The displaced apex beat was there, the small rapid pulse, the feeble but well-defined first sound with muffled second sound. The patient was in severe heart failure. Lifting his head, Lucanus silently studied the face again, and the mortal color of the flesh, and listened to the cough and saw the tinge of blood in the corners of the dying lips and the enlarged toxic swelling of the gland in the throat. Then the young physician lifted a vial from the golden marble table at the head of the bed and sniffed and examined the contents. He frowned; the heart stimulant here was much too strong. Nevertheless, little could be done for this sufferer now, and immediately the soul of Lucanus was moved and he forgot that Elazar ben Solomon was a rich man. He was only a man who was tormented.

Lucanus said to him gently, in Aramaic, "You have had the best physicians? Do not try to speak; merely indicate the answers with your head. I judge you were stricken a few weeks ago. You have had indigestion, vomiting, nausea and diarrhea." He paused, and said with more gentleness, "You understand your condition?"

Elazar lay on his pillows and studied the face of Lucanus intently, the carved and full but ascetic lips, the long and chiseled Grecian nose, the sloping brow, the eloquent blue eyes now filled with pity and sympathy and kindness. An eagerness came over the dying man's face, a striving for a last strength. His fixed regard penetrated into Lucanus' soul with the peculiar intensity of the dying, and he smiled. He whispered harshly, and with difficulty, "Yes, that I understand, and there is no regret in me, except for the child I must leave." He gave Sara a deeply loving glance and she burst into tears. She knelt beside the bed and placed her head against her father's shoulder.

"As a physician I can do nothing for you," said Lucanus, for he understood that here was a heroic man who should not be insulted by soothing lies. "You are beyond human help, Elazar."

"But not beyond God's help, blessed be His Name," said Elazar.

"Blessed be His Name," said Joseph, with great emotion.

Lucanus' face became cold and remote again. He turned to Joseph and said, "I do not know why I was called. Was it only to repeat what other, and better, physicians have already told Elazar ben Solomon?"

"No," said Joseph. "It was to hear his story, and to give your promise to help him. Why I believed you could extend this help I do not know. We Jews frequently have mysterious spiritual intuitions, beyond rational reason, beyond explaining." His eyes dwelt on Lucanus gravely, and he touched his beard.

"Raise me," pleaded the sick man, and Sara and Joseph lifted him on his pillows. During this he did not remove his pleading gaze from Lucanus; it was as if he knew that his last hope was there. Lucanus said, "He should rest. He should not be permitted to speak." He was greatly vexed with Joseph for his cryptic words, his logical Greek mind rejecting the sonorous mysticism of the Jews. "Nevertheless, if I can help Elazar I shall do it, though how I can help is unknown to me."

"Perhaps it is not unknown to God," said Joseph, and Lucanus ignored this remark. He mixed a little of the elixir in the vial with some wine and held it to Elazar's lips, and the merchant swallowed painfully. The huge gland in his throat seemed about to burst his tight and leaden skin. Lucanus could feel the pain in his own throat, and the difficulty of swallowing, and his head suddenly ached.

Elazar said, "I must speak, for I have little time, and I have listened to Joseph ben Gamliel and have never known him to make a foolish remark. And there is something in me also which assures me, young Master, that you can help me. Harken unto me." He paused to struggle for breath again, and Lucanus' face tightened with distress at the piteous sound.

"Two years ago," said Elazar, panting, "my beloved wife, Rebecca, gave birth to our first and only son, in this very house. She died in childbed." His eyes filled with tears like blood. "I gave the name of Arieh, the lion, to the child, and he comforted me, for indeed he resembled a young lion and was strong and beautiful. He was my heart's joy, for never in all Israel was there so lovely a child, and I gave him to God."

He pressed his thin and livid palms together in a convulsive gesture of agonized sorrow. "My time grows short," he gasped. "Sara, do not weep. I must speak. Young Master, I have no slaves, only freedmen and -women who are devoted to me and my family. One day two nurse girls played with Arieh, my son, in this enclosed courtyard and garden, and from my library I heard his child's laughter. Then I became aware of no more voices, and no more mirth. I left the library to discover the reason why. The girls lay among the flowers, their heads crushed and bleeding, and my son was gone."

He stopped and closed his eyes, and the torture of that memory leaped out over his face in large beads of sweat. He made a feeble gesture and opened his eyes again. "The prefect of the city took charge. Had I enemies? Who knows what enemies a man has among his loving friends? I have tried to be a just man, honorable in all my dealings, and I have become very rich. Did that inspire friends with envy and rage? It is possible. A man can guard against his enemies, but never his friends, for they are within his walls. The prefect, against my protests, arrested some of my good poor people and even tortured them. How, he asked, was it possible for two murders to have been committed within guarded walls and gardens, and a child abducted without the knowledge of other servants? But the overseer of the hall had seen no stranger. The guardians of the gates had admitted no one. Had bribery taken place? That was very possible. My people were freed at my insistence. They swore to me that they were not implicated."

Lucanus was filled with rage, forgetting that Elazar was a rich man, and feeling his anguish in himself.

"That was two months ago," said Elazar. "My son, Arieh, is only two years old. What have they done to my child? Is he dead, lying in some lonely place in the desert, or has he been drowned? I do not feel it in my heart. I know he is alive, and that his abduction was a deliberate malice inspired by hatred. Who is the friend who bribed a servant to kill, and steal a little one? Does he sometimes stand beside my bed, murmuring his commiserations, and drinking my wine, and consoling my daughter, Sara, and swearing vengeance on my enemies? It is very possible. My eyes have grown blind with searching every face. Who is the friend? He is cloaked in evil and therefore invisible."

Elazar lifted his left hand and showed it to Lucanus. The little finger was oddly malformed, bent sharply at the second joint so that the finger overlapped the next to it. "That finger is the mark of the males of my family," he said. "My son, Arieh, has it. It will identify him."

He ceased to speak, but his mournful eyes never left Lucanus' face.

"You will find my son," he said, and he smiled feebly. "My heart tells me this. Perhaps it will not be tomorrow, or a year, or ten or twenty years. But you will find him. I have posted a huge reward in all the capitals of the world, but still there is no answer though a thousand thousand informers and thieves and soldiers and sailors and slaves and seamen are searching in their eager greed. The hands of little boys, multitudes of little boys everywhere, are being furtively examined, in hundreds of villages and towns and cities, in alleys, in streets, in slums, in the homes of the powerful and the poor. I have freedmen all over the world investigating rumors and running down every report. But there is still no sign of my son."

"He is, then, most probably dead," said Lucanus, sadly.

"No," said Elazar. He put his hand to his chest. "My heart tells me he is alive, perhaps hidden, but certainly alive. I should know it if he were dead. And so you will find him, and you will bring him to Jerusalem to inherit what I will leave him, my son with his crooked finger, my son who resembles a young lion."

Lucanus was silent, both with compassion and anger against God. He understood now that Elazar was dying of his agony and grief.

"You will find my son," said Elazar, and a smile of trembling joy broke out on his face. "You will return him to his people and his sister and to the gates of Jerusalem."

Lucanus thought this preposterous. He opened his mouth to protest, then was silent, and he did not know why. Finally he said, as Elazar watched him, "I am a physician, and I will be among the poor always, who have no friends and no comforters and cannot pay a fee. And I will search for your son. It is all I can promise."

"It is enough," said Elazar, and he held out his tremulous hand to Lucanus, who took it, feeling its cold wetness. Elazar's face, at the touch of Lucanus' fingers, underwent an extraordinary change. A look of marvelous peace settled on it, a surcease of pain. His eyes closed, and his erratic breathing slowed, as Lucanus held his hand, and became even slower, moment by moment. And then it was gone and only the faintly smiling face, stark and ghastly, remained.

Sara rose to her feet with a heartbroken sob and stood beside the bed. Tears ran down her pale cheeks. She clasped her hands and shivered.

Joseph ben Gamliel said in a loud and reverent voice, "The Lord gives and the Lord God takes away. Blessed be the Name of the Lord!"

"Blessed be the Name of the Lord," Sara repeated through her tears.

Lucanus put down the dead hand with gentle love, but in his heart there was a rage of pain that sickened him. He glanced at Joseph ben Gamliel with fiercely sparkling eyes. How was it possible for a wise and learned man to praise the Name of the deadly Enemy of all men? He thought the words of Joseph craven and weak, the words of a servile slave under the lash. He was disgusted; his head whirled with his furious pain and loathing. He turned on his heel and left the room, walked quickly through the colonnade and left the house.

Chapter Nineteen

It was dangerous to be alone on the streets of Alexandria at night, and Lucanus eased the blade of his dagger at his belt. He was not afraid; he was an athlete, and he was tall and strong, and he was not far from home. He kept his hand on the hilt of his dagger, and he walked rapidly, filled with his seething anger and pity, the hood of his white mantle pulled over his head, his garments swinging about him. He walked down the center of winding streets, avoiding offal, seeing no one passing him, his nostrils filled with the stench, the spice and the aromatic odors of the city, his heart and mind consumed with his thoughts. Torches thrust into iron sockets on walls splattered his figure with leaping and dying red light. The great burning white moon ran over him in sheets of silver fire, and so formidable and powerful was his aspect that furtive faces peering out at him from arches and doorways winced back as if at the sight of a striding apparition.

Lucanus was not aware of distant cries and shouts, or of music or laughter, or of all the tumultuous breathings and sounds of the torrid city. He was aware only of his turbulent thoughts, his grief for Elazar and the beautiful young Sara, and his wrath against God, who endlessly betrayed and haunted in His sleepless vindictiveness against man. He thought of the child, Arieh, who he was convinced was dead, murdered in malice and hatred, and now, for the first time, Lucanus revolted against the evil in men, against their cruelty and mercilessness, against their greed and envy, against their bloodthirstiness and boundless hardness of heart and their crimes against their fellows. Here was another enemy beside God: man himself. In those frightful moments Lucanus hated both God and man, and he was sickened with his own living, his own presence in the world of humanity. The universe was evil to its very core; the very stars were tainted with the stain of life. Everything enlarged, tilted and became distorted to the young Greek's hot eyes. He was drunk with his wrath. When a passing man jostled him his hand tightened on his dagger and for the first time in his existence he uttered a violent oath, and the man ran from him in terror, catching sight of an unsheathed dagger and feeling, rather than seeing, a rage that was larger than human, aware of a blaze of eyes, even in the shelter of the hood, that surpassed the rage of men.

Lucanus' sandaled feet rang on stone like the march of a god. Without thinking consciously, except that he was looking for a shorter way through an alley towards his house, he turned down a narrow dark street, lighted only by the glimmer of a single torch at the entrance and the glitter of moonlight. Tall dark walls enclosed the street, and suddenly it was very quiet here, with a sinister quiet. The only close sound was the rippling of filthy water in the gutter, and the stench was overpowering. Lucanus continued down the street, then halted. He had come face to face with a high wall. The street had no exit. He looked about him, at the forbidding walls that had trapped him. He was alone here; he could see nothing but the dark bulks of lightless top stories of houses beyond the walls. No one spoke or cried: it was a dead place.

Fuming, he saw that he was momentarily lost. He would have to retrace his steps to the end of the street and look about him. Again he uttered that low and violent oath. Perhaps there was a door in the wall facing him which would permit him entry into a courtyard, and thence to another and less dangerous street. With the aid of the moonlight, and his sensitive fingers, he explored the wall, and encountered only rough and grimy stone. He continued to explore, and then at the juncture of the end wall and the wall of the street his hand fell on a latch. He lifted it and a door opened, small and narrow, and he looked into a cobbled courtyard surrounded by the looming tenements which housed the very poor of the city. But the windows were all lightless and closed, the doors barred. In the center of the courtyard there was a round common well built of dusky stone. No flowers bloomed here; there was no perfume of rose or jasmine or lily, but only a sour foul odor of poverty and fear and death. By the moonlight Lucanus could see that the squalid houses circled the courtyard and there was no egress to another alley or street. He closed the door and dropped the latch and began to walk back up to the end of the imprisoned alley. He became aware of the stinking water, the silence, the threatening walls, and kept his hand tightly on the dagger. The distant torch flickered crimson, and feebly, at the end.

He was near the corner when he heard the rapid pounding of as yet unseen feet approaching him. He stopped abruptly. The sound of flight aroused all his wary instincts. He considered that the fleeing people might be thieves running from pursuit. Then a man and woman turned the corner and raced towards him, their feet impelled by a palpable terror, their heads looking back over their shoulders. Lucanus could hear their gasping breaths in the intense silence, and the stumbling of the woman on the stones.

They were almost on Lucanus before they saw him, and
they halted in mid-flight and stared at him, their eyeballs
glistening like the eyes of terrified animals in the moonlight. If he had sprung up from the ground to confront them
they could not have been more affrighted. The hood of his
mantle had fallen on his shoulders and the moon struck
golden fire from his head, and the hard flat planes of his
face were like the planes on the face of a statue. The man
and the woman fell back, for there was something in the
tall aspect of Lucanus that stifled the very breath in their
throats, and they strained their gaze upon him.

He saw that they were young, and he immediately knew
that here were no criminals, though the man was dressed in
fluttering rags and his feet were bare and he wore no mantle and no arms. The woman's dress was good, modest and
respectable, and of a dim purple color, and her girdle was of
silver and there were silver rings, sparkling with simple jewels, in her ears, and her arms tinkled with silver bangles
and her feet were shod.

"What is it?" asked Lucanus quickly, in Greek. They
did not answer, so he repeated the question in Egyptian.
The woman burst into wild sobs, then she flung herself
on her knees before Lucanus and clutched his garment. "Help
us, Master!" she cried, and began to wail feebly. The young
man stood apart and could not take his eyes from Lucanus.
But he shrank back and tried to cover his body with his rags.

Then Lucanus heard the running steps of many pursuers
approaching the street and saw the red shadow of carried
torches. The young woman moaned and instinctively pressed
her forehead against Lucanus, and she again pleaded with
him for help. But the young man said in a curiously hoarse
voice, "Asah, go with this man, and he will help you escape,
and leave me. Asah, return to our children!"

The girl only moaned again. "No, I will remain with you
forever," she sobbed. "I will die with you."

The approaching sound of the pursuers aroused Lucanus.
He pulled the girl to her feet and said to the man,
"Come with me. Quickly!" He caught the girl's hand and
ran with her towards the rear wall, and the man followed. He
found the door, opened it, and thrust the two within, and
said quietly, "Remain there. I will divert them."

Trembling, they stood for a moment and looked at him,
and again they were strangely struck at what they saw. Then
the door closed and they were alone. "He is like Osiris!"

the girl whispered, and struck her hands together, and fell on the edge of the well. The man did not approach her but shrank up against the side of a circling house and shut his eyes. "You saw his face!" the girl went on, and bowed her head. "Hush, beloved," said the man, and kept himself far from her.

Lucanus went rapidly up the street, then as a crowd of men and soldiers appeared at the entrance and hesitated, lifting torches high and cursing, he slowed his step and approached them calmly. They started down the alley. They saw him approach and stopped. He walked with dignity and assurance, as a nobleman walked, his dagger in his hand. He looked at the sweating and armored soldiers, and spoke in the authoritative language of Rome.

"For whom are you searching?" he demanded, speaking only to the centurion. "I am Lucanus, son of Diodorus Cyrinus of Rome, and a physician."

The torchlight fell on the dark faces of the mob surrounding the soldiers, and Lucanus could see the wild eyes and the slavering mouths and the upraised clubs dancing in that red glare. A sharp silence fell on the pursuers, then the centurion stepped forward, raised his hand respectfully and spoke, his eyes wondering.

"Master, we are searching for a man and a woman, a man and his wife. They ran before us. Have you seen them?"

Lucanus paused. Lies were foreign to him. He said, "You see that I am alone, and there is no one with me. Moreover, this is a street without exit. Observe that rear wall. I am returning to my home and I am lost. I will be most thankful for the escort of one of the soldiers, for this is a dangerous city."

His one thought was to turn the soldiers and the mob away from this street so that the man and the woman could later escape. The centurion saluted him. "Master, one of my men will accompany you. In the meantime we must search for those people until we find them."

"Are they theives?" asked Lucanus. He drew in his nostrils against the pervading odor of sweat and violence that enclosed the pursuers.

"No, Master. The man is a leper."

"A leper!" Lucanus stood and looked at them.

"Yes, Master, one Sira. He was driven from the city into the desert a few months ago. You know it is mandatory death for a leper to return once he has been exiled to live in the caves. Yet tonight some of his neighbors caught him peering through a window of his house some streets from here, staring in at his wife and children. The woman, Asah, lives with her parents, and her father is a shopkeeper of some substance. The neighbors aroused the watch. As a physician, Master, you understand that a returned leper is not only a menace, but must die, for he has broken the law and could infect others."

"Yes, I understand." Lucanus stood in wild thought. He shuddered. Yet all at once his heart was again filled with warm compassion and sadness, and he considered the plight of Sira, who wanted only to glimpse his wife and children again before eternal exile and death.

He said, "How could the woman know of the presence of her husband at the window?"

The centurion replied patiently, "She heard the cries of the neighbors and their shouts for the watch, and she ran from her house, and, seeing her husband beginning to flee, she ran with him, knowing that he must die at once." The centurion shook his head. "There is no intelligence in women, Master."

No, only love, thought Lucanus.

He sheathed his dagger. He did not know what to do, but do something he must. He reflected that Sira had only wished to see his family. It was evident that he had had no intention of remaining in the city, or even permitting his wife to know of his presence. That meant that if the neighbors had not seen him he would have departed as silently and as voicelessly as he had returned, back to his living death and suffering in the desert. He must be given that opportunity, though death was better than life as a leper. Moreover, there was his wife to consider. She must be spared witnessing that vile mob falling upon her husband and destroying him before her eyes. Lucanus could smell the blood lust in the men, the eagerness to do death, to crush, to destroy, to trample, and it was that lust which decided him.

He said, "The situation is very serious, my good centurion. And so I will not deprive you of a single man in this search. As a physician I understand the gravity of the matter. I live not very far from here. In the meantime that wretch is escaping. Go at once on your pursuit."

The centurion hesitated. The son of Diodorus Cyrinus was an important and honored man, and a physician. He should be guarded. But Lucanus loomed over him, tall and young and strong, and he was armed. The centurion smiled and saluted, and soldiers and men rushed back up the street in the crimson banners of their torches and were gone, roaring like an avalanche.

Lucanus waited until the street was silent again. Not a single light had appeared in the dark windows high above the walls, not a single stranger had emerged, not a hidden door had opened, in spite of the noise. This was a black and sinister place, and the inhabitants had discreetly kept their peace within their houses and their walls. Lucanus returned to the door cautiously, glanced up and down the street, then lifted the latch and let himself quickly into the circular courtyard.

Asah was sitting on the low wall of the well, weeping and mourning. Sira stood at a distance, shrinking from the moonlight, and beseeching his wife, in a muted voice, to halt her tears. Neither of them was aware of the presence of Lucanus, who stood in the sharp black shadows near the closed door.

"Ah, my dearest," wept the young woman, "if only you, as a physician, had not attempted to cure the lepers! But you, so merciful, so tender, so kind, must attend them, and must sacrifice for them in the temples. You must hide them from the authorities in your hopeless compassion. 'Are they not human, and blood of my blood, my brothers, the beat of my heart?' That is what you said, my dearest one. But gods and men are cruel and without justice, and the frightful disease came to you from the afflicted. Did you consider your wife and your little children? No. You told me that the physician is dedicated to One greater than we, that he has sworn the holy oath to cherish mankind and alleviate its sufferings. And in revenge the gods afflicted you yourself with this monstrous horror and drove you from your wife's arms and from the kisses of your children!"

Sira groaned. "I did not betray my oath. If the gods have betrayed me, then that is their own crime."

The young woman lifted her pale smooth face to the moon and her dark hair drifted in disorder on her shoulders and her tears turned to quicksilver. "Ah, yes," she murmured. "It is true that men are sometimes better than their gods. Would I have turned you from the afflicted? I do not believe so now. What else can a man do but his duty?"

She rose and moved to her husband, her arms extended

to him pitifully. But he cried out, "Unclean, unclean!"

"Not to me, not to me, Sira. I am your wife. Where you go, there shall I go. Where you live, there shall I live. What are children and parents to a wife who loves her husband? They are as nothing; they are not even phantoms when she hears her husband's voice. Will you dwell in a cave? There shall I dwell also. Will you eat the bread of charity? That shall I eat also. If you sleep with the foxes and the wild vultures, there also shall I sleep, and your bed shall be my bed. For there is nothing in the world for me but you, and no sea, no death, no bloody hand of man, no hatred of the gods shall divide us."

Sira held out his palms desperately to keep her away. "I implore you, my love, do not approach me! In the name of the gods, keep far from me. No, you shall not go with me to die as a leper, to ring a bell to warn off the warmness of others, to rot and bleed and become numb and blind and filled with sores. I have cherished your sweetness and your beauty. Shall I die remembering what I have done to you?"

"Shall I die, Sira, remembering that I have deserted you, I who swore never to leave your side?" Her hands reached for him, but he cringed against the wall and, like a reptile, scuttled along it, making a rasping sound.

"Shall you torture me, Asah, with the sight of your beloved and leprous face? Go, I beg you. Go and forget me. I am one with the dead. I have died. The rotting thing you see is not your husband. You are young. Marry again and bear other children, and weep for me, but do not remember me long."

"In my heart, forever, there will be remembrance. Do not drive me from you, Sira. Let me embrace you. Let me once again kiss your lips." Asah wept, and the faint sound of her mourning filled the courtyard with the most heartbreaking of echoes. She followed him slowly, a pursuer quivering with love and devotion.

"No!" cried Lucanus, and came from the shadows. "Your husband is right, and you must not touch him!"

Sira and Asah started at the sound of his voice, and stood mutely looking at him. His head rose from his broad shoulders like the head of a god, beautiful and most terrible in its beauty. Asah put her hand to her lips and stood motionless, the night wind lifting her hair like a banner. Sira stared at him from the shadows, his eyes burning. Lu-

canus came to him, took him by the shoulder and pulled
him into the moonlight and examined him closely and
sharply.

"I am a physician," said Sira, in a broken voice. "I have
leprosy."

There was no doubt of it. The leonine appearance of the
disease had already thickened Sira's features. Bluish-red
and yellowish-brown erythematous patches scarred his face;
here and there, on his brow and on his throat, were ul-
cerous lesions exuding serum and pus. His hoarse voice betrayed an invasion of his larynx. Even his hands revealed
the loathsomeness of the disease, and two or three of his
fingers were already gangrenous.

"How unmerciful are the gods," said Asah, her arms
trembling for her husband. "My Sira is the most gentle
of men, the most dedicated. Yet now he must die if he
cannot escape from the city unseen. But if he must die,
then shall I die with him, good Master."

"Master, take her from me," implored Sira. "Conduct her
to our home. For surely she is lost if she remains longer."

Lucanus was seized with a very ecstasy of rage and despair and pity. He grasped Sira's shoulders in his strong
hands and closed his eyes and addressed God silently but
with fury.

"Oh, You who have so tormented this man who wished
only to save Your victims from Your hatred! Must You
forever strike down those who help the afflicted, who are
innocent, who are without malice and evil? Must always
Your smile be reserved for the vile and their children, and
Your blessings be poured out on the unrighteous? Why do
You not destroy us and let us have our peace forever in
a dayless grave, covered by the merciful night, far from
Your vengeful eyes? What have we done to merit Your hate,
You who have not the eyes and the limbs and the blood of
men, and not their flesh? Do You bleed as a man bleeds?
Does Your heart tremble as the heart of a man trembles?
Have You suffered pain, O You who afflict pain? Have You
loved as a man loves? Have You begotten a son, so that You
might mourn for him?"

Sira and his wife stood like motionless stone, their ears
straining. They heard no voice but dimly they were aware
that something most awesome was sounding in this moon-
struck place, this silent and fetid place. They saw Lucanus'

contorted face, his closed eyes, his parted lips, between which the teeth gleamed like marble.

Again he addressed God in the wild bitterness and anguish of his heart.

"Oh, if You were merciful, in Your illimitable might, You would cure this wretched man and return him to his wife and his children! If You possessed only one quiver of human pity You would take from him his disease and make him whole. Am I greater than You, more merciful than You? I swear to You by all that I hold dear that if I could I would take upon me the lesions of this horror instead and flee forever to the desert, remembering that I have saved a man, his wife and his children."

Sira felt the hands of Lucanus on his thin shoulders, and it seemed to him that a strange and awful force emanated from Lucanus' fingers, like a cold and surging fire. The force pervaded him, shattered along his bones, rippled over his flesh, made his back arch and his hair rise on his head. It was as if lightning had struck him. He could not breathe or move; he leaned against Lucanus' hands and his heart crashed into sound against his ears like the sound of unearthly drums. He thought, I am dying! And the moonlight faded from his sight and became a blackness before his eyes.

"I am not God!" Lucanus cried from his heart. "I am only a man. Therefore I pity. Oh, be You merciful! Be You merciful!"

He caught Sira to his breast and held him tightly, and his tears dropped over his cheeks and fell on the other man's forehead. And Asah, understanding vaguely that something had happened beyond human comprehension, sank to Lucanus' feet and rested her head against them.

Then Lucanus felt some tremendous virtue leave him like flowing blood, and a mysterious weakness made his body shake. Gently, with trembling hands, he put Sira from him, sighing.

"Take my mantle with its hood," he said. "Hide your face in it. Here are my sandals," and he bent and removed his sandals and placed them near the leper's feet. "Here is my purse, and my dagger. No one will recognize or find you. Go from the city and do not return. And if there is a God, go in His peace."

He threw the mantle over Sira's shoulders, and pressed the purse and the dagger in his hands, and he stood before husband and wife in his bare feet and clad only in his yellow tunic. And they looked at him and could not speak for bewilderment and gratitude, and it seemed to them that this young man was the son of Isis herself.

He turned and opened the door and stepped out into the stinking street and the stone cut into his feet and he did not feel the pain. Blinded with tears, he staggered away, sunk in grief and sorrow.

For a long time Sira and Asah did not move or speak. They stood in the moonlight like carved statues of themselves, stricken dumb. Then Asah approached her husband again with outstretched arms, and he held her off. "Unclean," he murmured, and let her see his face and arms clearly in the light.

Asah uttered a loud and piercing shriek, then dropped senseless to the stones like one felled by a blow. And Sira stared at his arms and saw that they were whole and clean and without blemish. Dazed, he turned them about and examined them, and there was no spot upon them. He put his hands to his cheeks and his brow and they were as smooth as an infant's flesh, and warm and full of sensation.

He looked at the closed door through which Lucanus had vanished. He dropped to his knees beside his fainting wife and lifted his hands in prayer.

"Oh, most blessed," he murmured. "Oh, that you visited us!"

Chapter Twenty

Cusa looked with consternation at Lucanus. "It is not possible, Master!" he exclaimed, holding his head in his hands. His impish satyr's face with its plump cheeks and thin little beard, humorous eyes and impudent nose had blanched with horror.

"I am sorry," said Lucanus, patiently. "I have tried to explain it. There is no need of another public medical officer in Rome, which is filled with modern sanitoria. Yes, I understand that the Public Assembly has graciously appointed me, at the behest of Diodorus, and at a considerable stipend. But shall a physician not go where he is most needed? Hippocrates has said this, and I have taken his oath. My work will be among the poor and oppressed and the abandoned, the

dying and the desperately ill for whom there is no provision
in the cities along the Great Sea. I shall minister to slaves and
to those hopeless in poverty, and I shall ask no fee except
from a rich master of slaves. I shall go among the prisons and
in the galleys, in the mines and in the slums, in the ports
and in the infirmaries for the indigent. There is my work and
I cannot turn away from it."

"But why?" cried Cusa, incredulously.

Lucanus sat on his bed in the stark white bedroom where
he slept and studied and looked at his long pale hands. "I
have told you," he said. "I must go where I am needed."

Cusa rocked his head in his hands. Was Lucanus mad? Had
the red Furies disordered his mind? Had Hecate secretly visited
him in the night? By all the gods, this was not to be understood or to be endured! Cusa spoke reasonably, and quietly,
as one speaks to a man afflicted with insanity.

"Master, your family needs you. Your adopted father is
proud of you, and he the proudest of Romans. Your mother
has not seen you for years; your brother and your sister have
never looked upon you. What will it be said of Diodorus that
his adopted son is a wanderer, ministering to the scum of the
earth in hot barbarian cities and highways and byways? That
is good enough for a slave physician, but not for the son of
Diodorus Cyrinus. What will you say to Diodorus, and your
mother? They will be shamed before the face of Rome."

Lucanus shook his head. "I have no words to reach you,
Cusa, or blow away the fog of your bewilderment. Enough.
You and your family will leave with me tomorrow for Rome
and my father's estates. There you will be happy." He
smiled affectionately at his old teacher.

"My lack of understanding is mild to the lack of understanding Diodorus will display, Master."

"I know." Lucanus frowned, then smiled, remembering the
bellicose Roman. "But I must do as I must."

"You do not know what poverty is, Master! When you are
a beggarly physician drifting from port to port—for certainly
Diodorus will not sustain you with his careful money under
the circumstances—you will discover what it is to be hungry
and filthy and homeless and in rags. You will not delight in
it, Lucanus, you whose flesh has been carefully nurtured
and tended and clothed in fine linen and wool. Lucanus,
enlighten me. What is this madness? What is a slave or a
poor man or a criminal? They are less than human. It were
better for you to treat the dogs and other animals of the

rich and patrician in Rome! It would bring less shame and grief to Diodorus."

Lucanus reflected. How could he say to Cusa, "I must deliver the tormented from their Enemy"? Cusa would then be completely assured that he was mad.

Cusa watched him narrowly. Then he burst out, "It is that accursed Joseph ben Gamliel! I have overheard him speaking with you in the gardens. Master, the Jews are incomprehensible, with their merciful God and His Commandments and His ridiculous laws for the temperate dealing of man with man. It is all superstition, and deplorable, and adds gloom to life. Have you seen a Jew with a happy face? Have you heard the laughter of Roman feasts and Roman abandonment and dancing in a Jew's house? No, that is only for a barbarian Roman! Not," added Cusa, "that I consider a Roman much more than a barbarian. But at least he is a man of sinew and blood and has a proper respect for the arts of Greece, though he is a wolf cub. The Roman is a realist. The Jews deal with transcendent superstitions. They speak of freedom, which is absurd. They expect the impossible from their God, and one of sense understands that the gods never deal in the impossible and expects no great virtue from them."

Lucanus said with anger, "I do not believe that God is merciful and good! I do not believe what Joseph ben Gamliel tells me of Him! Spare your breath, Cusa. I must leave you for a last farewell to my teachers."

Cusa, smarting, wounded and quite confounded, understood that he had been dismissed and he went to find his wife. Calliope listened as she nursed her child, and she puckered her lips thoughtfully. Then she shrugged. "I have always believed that Lucanus was extraordinary," she said.

Lucanus had no regret for leaving Alexandria. Since Rubria had died he had felt no attachment for any single spot in the world, no desire to visit it, or to travel as a rich young man. The world to him was a carnal house, full of groaning, and no beauty of architecture, no music had power to lighten his endless sorrow. But last night he had dreamed of Sara bas Elazar, Sara whose father had been buried yesterday. It had been a most confused dream. She had come running to him through a field of flowers, laughing sweetly, and when she reached him her face was the face of Rubria, sparkling as if under spring sunshine. Her dark hair had fallen back from her white brow and Lucanus had experienced the rapture of complete bliss and joy. And then he had seen the violet of her eyes and pain had come to him. In his dream, he did not know why, he had said to her questioningly, "Rubria?" And she had answered in her dulcet voice, "Love." He had shaken his head. "There is no room in my life for love. I shall not take love again, for love is a serpent in the heart, filled with poison and agony." She had retreated from him then, looking mournfully to the last at his face, as if searching and sad, and the flowers had risen up and hidden her from him. Then he had known his old grief again and had cried out, and had awakened.

He remembered his dream as he packed his large leather physician's pouch with his precious surgical instruments: forceps, scalpels, amputation saws, probes, syringes, trephines. Each instrument, of the most carefully wrought iron, and perfect, had to be wrapped in a woolen cloth impregnated with olive oil to guard against rust. There were older instruments, too, of copper and bronze, clumsier. These were also gently laid in the pouch in their own wrappings. To these he added his precious medical books, a number of ligatures in a silken case, and some special vials of Eastern medicines. Cusa would care for his personal effects, of which he had few. Lucanus examined them to see what he could give away to the poor and penniless in the infirmary at the medical school. A small bag dropped to the floor from some garment, with a heavy sound, and he picked it up and opened it. The golden cross Keptah had given Rubria lay in his hand, its golden chain twinkling.

Lucanus felt a sudden boiling and despair in him, and he wanted to hurl the cross from his sight. But Rubria had pressed it in his hand at the moment of dying. He could not remember bringing it here. He had forgotten it. Now he breathed on the gold and rubbed it with his sleeve until it brightened, and, remembering Rubria with a fresh access of pain, he kissed the symbol of infamy and replaced it in its bag and dropped it in his medical pouch. And he thought of Sara again, the beautiful young Sara with her graceful figure just burgeoning into womanhood, and her white neck and lovely, artless eyes. He left the room hurriedly, as if fleeing, and went to the university.

His teachers greeted him with affection, and all gave him amulets, even the cynical Greek physicians, and all expressed their regret at his departure and all blessed him. "Remember, my dear Lucanus," said one of the Greeks, "that medicine has always been associated with the priesthood, for there is more to medicine than the body and a physician must also treat the souls of his patients, and, at the last, he must depend for a cure on the Divine Physician." Lucanus was surprised at this statement from this most lucid-minded Greek, but the man regarded him seriously, then kissed him on both cheeks. "I do not fear for you," he added.

There was only one of his teachers whom Lucanus wished to avoid. But he found Joseph ben Gamliel waiting for him, and the teacher drew him into his library in his stoa. The library was small and cool and austere, the furniture simple. "We shall not meet again," said the Jewish teacher, sadly, looking at Lucanus with his large and luminous eyes. "Never again shall we meet. This is farewell for us."

"You do not know," said Lucanus.

"Ah, but I know." Joseph ben Gamliel was silent for a moment. He turned his bearded head in profile to Lucanus and the hot white light glaring through the small window struck that profile, giving it a mysterious radiance, sharpening it and changing it. "I must tell you a story," said Joseph.

Lucanus smiled impatiently. "I have discovered that the Jews always have a story," he said. "Everything is in poetry or metaphor, or hypothetical or obscure, or delivered in the form of an involved question. Life is short. Why is it that Jewish scholars treat time as if it did not exist and there was an eternity for discussion?"

"For the reason," said Joseph, "that time does not exist and there is an eternity for discussion. Do you still believe, my poor Lucanus, that man's spirit is bound by time or events?" He turned to Lucanus then, and again his face changed and it was very strange and infinitely mournful, and Lucanus thought of the old prophets of whom he had been taught by the Jews in Antioch and by Joseph in Alexandria.

"You will remember the hope of the Jews in a coming Messias, of which I have told you," said Joseph. "He will deliver His people, Israel, according to the promise of God. It was Abraham, the father of the Jews, a Babylonian from the ancient city of Ur, who brought those good tidings to us. You have read the prophecies of Isaias concerning Him. He will be called the Prince of Sorrows, according to that prophet, and His Mother shall crush the serpent's head with her heel, and man shall be delivered from evil and suffering, and death shall be no more. By His wounds shall we be saved."

"Yes," said Lucanus, with growing impatience. Joseph gazed at him. "I know the Jewish Scriptures," said Lucanus. "I know the prophecies concerning your Messias. But of what concern is that to me? All people have their myths and their gods, and what is a Jewish God to others?"

"There is only one God," said Joseph. "He is the Father of all men. Did you think the Messias will come only to the Jews? They are a people of prophecy, so it is comprehensible why the prophecy was given to them. The Law was delivered into their hands by Moses. By that Law man lives or dies. This the Gentiles must learn, through the rise of their empires and their bloody decline and the vast and moldering dust of the centuries.

"Lucanus, you will remember that the prophecy of the Messias has seeped into all the religions of the world, and not only in the Scriptures of the Jews. God endowed every man everywhere with the dim knowledge of His coming among men. The soul has its knowledge beyond the sterile reasoning of the mind. It has its instincts as the body has its instincts."

Lucanus did not answer. His impatience was growing wild. He fumbled at the gold chain at his throat, and then remembered that he had removed Keptah's cross from the bag at the last moment and had hung it about his neck. Now the cross dropped over his tunic and Joseph saw it and a great emotion flashed across his face. But he continued to speak quietly.

"Thirteen years ago, Lucanus, I was a teacher of holy law in Jerusalem. My wife gave birth to a son one cold winter night. It was a very strange night, for a great Star had suddenly appeared in the heavens, stood steadfast for a few hours, then moved to the east. Our astronomers were much excited. They called it a Nova, and prophesied that its appearance portended tremendous events. I remember that night well. Herod was our king, and an evil man. A rumor spread through the city that in the little town of Bethlehem had been born the King of the Jews. It was brought to Jerusalem by humble and simple men, among them shepherds who had a most awesome tale to tell. They spoke of the Heavenly Host appearing to them as they tended their sheep on the hills, and giving them tidings of great joy. As kings are suspicious, they have a thousand ears, and so this story reached Herod's ears, the story of illiterate and nameless shepherds. He immediately, in his fear for his power, ordered that all boy children who had been recently born be killed by the sword."

Joseph paused. Lucanus listened with unwilling fascination. Then all at once he remembered that great Star he had seen as a child in Antioch and his heart beat with dread.

Joseph said simply, "My son was among those murdered by Herod, and my wife's heart broke, and she died."

Lucanus was immediately filled with compassion and he was ashamed of his impatience, and more ashamed of the vehement and angry remarks he had addressed to Joseph in the past. Joseph had known death and sorrow and bitter pain, and he, Lucanus, had accused him of not knowing. He regarded Joseph with pity. He said, "How much you must have hated not only Herod, but God, for those senseless deaths!"

Joseph shook his head and smiled faintly. "No. How can an understanding man hate God? That is for children's passions."

He was silent for so long a time that Lucanus felt he had forgotten him. Then Joseph, gazing into the distance beyond the window, continued even more quietly.

"At the last Passover I visited my old home in Jerusalem. The city was teeming with pilgrims from Galilee, Samaria, Judea. In an inner court I was conversing with my learned friends and commentators. It was a day of most lovely spring, filled with the scent of blossoms and the rich odors of spice and incense. The sky was a gleaming pearl and the city was flooded with light and the sounds of song and rejoicing. Never have I seen so beautiful and calm a day, and the people's hearts were glad in them, and they forgot Caesar and Herod, for God had delivered them again out of the Land of Egypt. The sounds of cymbals and trumpets were everywhere. The city was bright with colored banners, and the Temple hung against the sky like a golden jewel. Though I was a widower with only one child, a daughter married in Alexandria, I felt my first joy in thirteen years, and my heart rose on a wave as of expectation."

He paused. His quiet hands linked themselves together and his face lifted and he smiled dreamily.

"Roman soldiers filled the streets. They too had felt the unusual delight in the spring. They had only one way to express it, for they were aliens in a strange land which hated them. The poor boys. They wished to be part of the general rejoicing, but the Jews ignored them on their holiday.

The soldiers became drunk and went through the streets singing. It is a sad thing when any man is rejected by his brothers, and I was compassionate for the Romans.

"We have Temple guards which protect the inner courts from intrusion. Where was the guard of this room that day? I do not know. But all at once the curtains parted and a young boy entered the court, a tall young boy of much handsomeness, clad in the rough drab robe of the common people. His feet were brown from the sun and bare. His fair skin was browned also by the sun, and his light locks were bleached by it, and fell on his shoulders. His eyes were as blue as summer skies, and he had a stately and majestic air. He smiled at us, not as a boy who has just reached the age of Bar Mitzvah, and therefore still shy in an adult world. His smile was the smile of a man, and he was at ease, like a man among his peers, like a scholar and a wise man among scholars and wise men.

"We were much astonished. Some of us frowned. What was this boy doing in our secluded court, dedicated only to wisdom and discussion? Where was the guard? The boy was obviously a peasant. Later they wondered why they had not immediately bidden the boy to depart. But I, seeing him, thought of my son, who, if he had not been murdered, would have been this boy's age. I said to him, 'Child, what are you doing here, and where are your parents?' And he replied to me, with his serious smile, and in the gross accents of the poor and unlearned in Galilee, 'I have come to question you, and to answer you, Master.' "

Lucanus' face and scalp prickled. Then all at once he wished to leave and he sprang to his feet. But Joseph appeared not to see this and continued in his far and dreamlike voice.

"He was as regal as a king, this young peasant of Galilee with his work-worn hands and his bare feet and his lifted head. I think it was this aspect of him that prevented the doctors and scholars from dismissing him angrily. We do not regard the people of Galilee with much respect. They are shepherds and workmen, and their speech is unlettered, and they are humble people. But this boy was as a king.

"He sat among us, and he talked with us, and soon we were amazed at his questions and at his replies, for, in spite of his Galilean accent, he spoke as one with authority and one of profound learning. We became engrossed with him. We asked the most difficult and obscure of questions, and he

answered them simply. It was like a light dawning in a dark
room crowded with learned books full of involvement. And
he had barely emerged from childhood, this young countryman from the stark hot hills of Galilee, where there are
no doctors and no wise men.

"And I said to him, 'Child, who is your teacher?' And he
smiled at me with a smile like the sun and did not answer.
It was then that the curtain parted in agitation and a rough
bearded man and a beautiful young woman, dressed in peasants' garb, burst into the court."

Again Joseph paused. He smiled, and his smile was in-
finitely sweet and remote. Lucanus slowly seated himself.
He said inwardly, I must not listen! This is obscure nonsense.
But he listened, and waited for Joseph to continue.

"I shall never forget that young woman, Lucanus, for her
face was the face of an angel, radiant beyond describing.
I remember that I was instantly astonished at that face,
rising from neck and shoulders clad in cheap dull garments.
A blue cloth floated from her head, and I saw her shining
hair and her pure brow. How can I describe her? There are
no words in any language. She must have been about twenty-
seven years old, not a great age even for a woman. She
gave the impression at one and the same time of being as
old as Eve and as young as the spring. History and the
future were blended in one; she was without time and without
years. I knew she was the boy's mother at once, for she had
a queenly aspect.

"The bearded peasant said nothing, though it was apparent
that he was distressed. He stayed near the curtain but the
woman advanced to the boy and he turned his head and
looked at her. And she said to him, 'My son, why did you
leave us, so that we missed you on our way home, and no
one had seen you? We have sought you in great anxiety.'

"The boy did not answer for a moment, and then he said,
very gently, 'Why did you search for me? Do you not know
that I must be about my Father's business?' And his eyes
beamed with tender love at her."

Joseph fell into silence and Lucanus waited. But Joseph
did not speak again and Lucanus said impatiently, "Is that
all?"

"That is all."

Lucanus bit his lip. "You have explained nothing, Joseph
ben Gamliel. Who was that boy?"

Joseph rose and Lucanus rose with him. Joseph put his

hand on his shoulder and regarded him with deeply penetrating eyes. "That you must discover for yourself, Lucanus."

He smiled at Lucanus with sudden sadness. "It is said in our Scriptures that God will not always strive against the spirits of men." He hesitated. "When God strives against the spirit of a man it is for a most holy and mysterious purpose, and that purpose sometimes remains hidden from the man to the day of his death. In your case, Lucanus, I do not believe it will always remain hidden from you." He lifted his hands in blessing. "Go in peace, my pupil, you dear and most beloved physician."

Chapter Twenty-one

It was only when he stood on the deck of the ship in the harbor of Alexandria and looked at the gaudy and vociferous city crowded against the ardent blue sky that Lucanus was startled to feel a pang of nostalgia. He let his eyes rove over the city and all at once he wondered where the years had gone and why he had never felt any fondness before for his companions and his teachers, and why time had been as a dark dream to him. He had presented excellent gifts to his teachers at his farewells but he knew now that they had been given without feeling, and he was ashamed of himself. It was too late to go to the masters and say what he felt in his heart, "I loved you and reverenced you, for teachers are the noblest of men and labor for little and only from the fullness of their unselfish souls. In your name, and in my memory of you, I will do the best I can, and remember you always."

The big galleon heaved sluggishly at anchor. Smaller craft with sails of red and blue and white and yellow and scarlet darted as if in mischief around its greater bulk like dragonflies, hurling their reflections vividly on the still and purple water. They were filled with half-naked fishermen, their brown bodies glistening in the hot white sun, their red mouths open to emit curses, jeers, laughter and song. As they fled by the Roman galleon they looked far up at Lucanus and greeted him or joked obscenely in their hoarse voices, or called up for alms. Smiling as he had not smiled in many years, he opened his purse and tossed the coins to them, and the coins seized the sun and glittered in gold or silver.

The men caught them deftly, and as they were gay rascals they kissed the coins, bowed ironically, and made lewd comments, then darted off again. The water lapped placidly at the ship. It was still being loaded from the pier; black Nubian or Scythian slaves rolled heavy barrels of oil and honey and wine up the ramp or carried bales of cloth or kegs of olives or baskets of coconuts. Others brought up bags and wooden boxes loaded with spices and other produce of the East. Then a sound of wailing rose from the crowded pier and a number of chained slaves, men and women, black from the desert, were whipped up the ramp, and Lucanus, watching them, no longer smiled. He turned and gazed at the desperate and weeping faces, and something rose up in him in a passionate anger. Some of the women carried infants; here and there a little child ran beside a father or mother, crying. The slaves were herded below, where the lamentations were more subdued and yet more insistent.

Two Roman centurions who had been assigned to guard him during the journey appeared at his elbow, and he looked at their sunburned and youthful faces with aversion. "Master," one of them said, "we are at your service." They were delighted to be returning home, even though in attendance on a Greek, which they thought demeaning. Therefore they were grateful to Lucanus. "I need nothing," he said, curtly. One of them took off his helmet and said "Whew!" and wiped his sweating face. "A scurvy city," he said, nodding towards Alexandria. "I broil under my armor like meat under flame."

"Why do you not remove it then?" asked Lucanus. The two young soldiers were shocked at this impropriety, and withdrew to a distance. Lucanus smiled faintly. It was not the fault of these boys that the slaves had been driven to the ship, and he had been illogical in displaying his dislike. He glanced at the soldiers who stood and watched the docks and the loading of wares, their thumbs in their leather belts and their backs even straighter than usual, as if rebuking him. He looked about for Cusa, who was fussily supervising the purple awning over a section of the rear of the ship, a section which was to be reserved for Lucanus. He called Cusa, "Attention!"

Cusa looked at him irritably, then issuing renewed warnings and threats to the perspiring seamen who were struggling with ropes and fabric, he swaggered importantly to Lucanus,

clad in a very rich tunic of Egyptian cotton, bright red with
an intricately embroidered border of yellow silk. His thin
beard had been anointed with perfumed oil, and his hair
also, and he carried a slim Alexandrian dagger in a silver
sheath at his belt. "You smell," said Lucanus, "like a harlot."

"Hah!" replied Cusa, with a lascivious grin. "How would
you know that?"

"Never mind," said Lucanus. He indicated the offended
young soldiers with a nod of his head. "Bring up a jug of
our best wine. If we have a best wine."

"For them?" asked Cusa, incredulously.

"For them."

"But, Master, the wine of the country is good enough.
Is that not of which the Romans brag, that, as cosmopolitans,
what the country produces is palatable to them no matter
what it is?"

"I said," remarked Lucanus sternly, but with a twinkle in
his eyes that had never appeared there since he had been
very young, "the best wine we have."

Cusa considered. Then he regarded Lucanus with an
open candor that did not deceive the young man. "Master,
you know we never have any best wine. Without disrespect
to you, I must admit that you have no palate."

"Thief," said Lucanus. "You always take care that the best
is on your own table. Did I not catch a glimpse only a short
time ago of several crusted and webbed bottles being tenderly carried aboard by you, cradled in your arms like a cherished infant? Bring one to me, and three goblets. I myself am
curious to taste such nectar."

Cusa bridled. "Master Lucanus, I bought those bottles out of
my own purse, from the generous stipend paid to me by
Diodorus Cyrinus."

"Very well," said Lucanus. "I will buy a bottle from you."

Cusa bowed elaborately. "Permit me, O Baal, to present a
bottle to you with my compliments." He spoke with sarcasm. Then he hesitated and stared at Lucanus imploringly.
"It is a crime against the gods to permit those Roman barbarians to wash out their leather mouths with such a wine!
Now, I have a good sturdy Alexandrian wine more to their
taste."

"The best wine," said Lucanus. "And do not deceive me. I
shall examine the sealings carefully."

"I suppose," said Cusa, "that it would not be permitted if

I should bring up a fourth goblet and stand meekly at a far distance from those Roman patricians and sip a little of my own, my very own, wine?"

"You may have a little, a very little, of the wine I am purchasing from you," said Lucanus gravely.

"I am presenting it to you," said Cusa, with loftiness, and went below.

While waiting, Lucanus watched the city again. The violent colors made him blink. The sun glittered fiercely on the purple water, and evoked smells of hot wood and oil and tar from the ship, the stench of dead fish and the sting of salt and sweat. Its fervid light danced on the smaller craft scurrying below; their sails seemed to burn. The soldiers' armor blazed. The loading slaves began to sing mournfully and the overseers rasped at them and cracked whips. More and more wagons loaded with goods lumbered to the wharf.

Cusa, with great dignity, appeared with a silver tray on which stood four goblets, one of silver encrusted with turquoises for Lucanus. He put the tray on a coil of oily rope nearby with a gesture that indicated he was more accustomed to marble tables. The centurions turned their heads and watched with interest, and as they saw the rosy wine they licked their lips furtively. They were astonished when Lucanus called to them, "Will you give me the pleasure of joining me in a drink of this excellent wine, which my teacher assures me is the best in the world?"

They came to him with smiling alacrity, forgiving him at once. Lucanus, waving Cusa aside, poured the wine for them. The sun reflected on it and it was like a distillation of pale rubies. Lucanus gave them a goblet each, and poured one for himself. He tipped a few drops in libation and they followed suit. He sipped a little and said, "Excellent. Excellent! My teacher has the most impeccable palate in three worlds."

"And how would you know that?" muttered Cusa, unappeased. He poured a goblet full like a priest attending an altar, slowly and reverently. At least one of four would appreciate this delight. He stood aloof from the group composed of Lucanus and the soldiers and sipped his wine. This was a wonderful vintage, of the best of all possible years. The sun was in it, and warm sweet fire; it lay in the mouth, perfumed and delicious and intoxicating. Cusa, glancing at Lucanus and the soldiers, was depressed. The soldiers, it was evident, were only aware of the fact that the wine was heady, and as for Lucanus, it was impossible to conceive that he even tasted the exquisiteness. He was conversing, to Cusa's surprise, with more animation than he had ever displayed before, and with more kindly interest. Now what, thought Cusa, has struck him? I can almost believe he has pulsing flesh and is not rigid marble after all. By Bacchus, was that actually a joke he made? And not one of the utmost delicacy! He must have acquired it unconsciously from one of those ribald students. I wonder if he knows what it really means? Ha, ha, it was very good, very good, and beautifully naughty. Cusa was much cheered. If Lucanus maintained this mood the journey would not be as dull as expected. The teacher, beginning to feel gently exhilarated, did not even wince when Lucanus poured more wine for the soldiers and himself. If he should get drunk, thought Cusa, I would rejoice exceedingly.

The captain of the ship approached Lucanus, but before he could speak Lucanus cried, "My good Gallo, join us! Cusa, bring another goblet!"

Cursing the captain, whom he suspected of having a nose for a bottle, Cusa obeyed and brought up another goblet. The middle-aged captain, a burly man with a coarse but intelligent face, began to relate very indelicate stories, at which the centurions hooted in mirth and Lucanus smiled. Sourly Cusa said to himself that at least these bawdy tales were beyond Lucanus' comprehension, for a wandering look had come over the young Greek's face, an indication that he now found the conversation either boring or distasteful. It was evident that Gallo had acquired the jokes in a number of the less exclusive brothels, and even Cusa found them a trifle too ripe for his taste.

Expansively, Gallo said, "It is an honor to have you aboard, Lucanus. You are our only passenger of any consequence. This, as you know, is a cargo ship, but it is fast, and does not dally like ships of pleasure. Even though we make a number of ports of call we shall arrive speedily in Italy."

"I am anxious to be home," said Lucanus.

"At one of the ports of call there will doubtless be letters for you." The captain squinted up at the huge white sails beginning to be unfurled like the wings of giant birds against the sky, and he shouted some admonitions to the sailors who were scampering about on the masts. Lucanus poured more wine, but not for himself. "We have a fair wind," said the captain, dropping his voice to a normal level. "And when the tide goes out we shall sail. That will be in less than an hour."

Lucanus looked at the city, and for some reason he did not examine he was suddenly assailed by a powerful longing and sadness. His heart ached in a nameless desire, and he felt lonely and lost. An almost irresistible urging came to him to leave the ship. He forgot the captain and the soldiers. He struggled with his emotions, to which he would assign no face and no voice.

"What is it?" Gallo was asking of a junior officer who came up to him, saluting. The officer murmured in his ear; the captain glanced swiftly at Lucanus and his smoky agate eyes, so jovial yet shrewd, lighted up, and his sun-darkened face burst into sprays of smiling wrinkles. He turned to Lucanus and clapped him heartily on the shoulder and winked.

"A litter borne by well-clad Bithynian slaves has just arrived on the wharf, Lucanus!" he exclaimed, and winked at the centurions also. "I am no Delphic oracle, but I will wager you three sesterces that it is a noble lady! Ah, what it is to be young! Did I mention that the slaves indicated the lady wishes a word with you before you sail?"

Lucanus started. He looked at the wharf, and saw indeed that a litter waited there, closely curtained and borne by six swarthy Bithynians, whose strong arms were bound by broad silver circlets. The blood rose high in Lucanus' face, and he began to tremble. "I know no one," he murmured. "Are you certain it is a lady?" He peered at the shrouded litter.

"I will wager you!" cried the captain. Cusa, hearing this commotion, came closer and also peered at the distant litter, screwing up his eyes the better to see. A woman? That was impossible in the case of this male Vestal Virgin. Cusa shook his head doubtfully. But Lucanus went down the ramp slowly, his head shining in the sun, and the gleeful soldiers and the captain and Cusa leaned on the ship's railing and gave the litter all their attention.

When Lucanus stood beside the litter he said, "Who wishes to speak with me?" The curtains of the litter parted and he saw the pale and grieving face of Sara bas Elazar looking up at him. She was clad in deep black, and Lucanus saw that her garment was slashed here and there in the Jewish manner of bereavement, and that her beautiful violet eyes were smudged with sorrow.

"Sara," said Lucanus, and there was a huge swelling in his throat. She held out her small white hand to him and he took it. "I should not have come, Lucanus," she murmured, "for I am in mourning for my father." Her black hair bore the traces of ashes. She tried to smile, but only sobbed without tears.

Her hand was cold in his. All about them was the bustling of the wharf, the running of slaves, the shouts and cries, but Lucanus saw no one but this very young girl, and he thought, Surely she is like Rubria!

"Sara," he said again, and now his longing and urging had a face and a voice.

"Joseph ben Gamliel told me that you were departing today," she said, her voice faintly hoarse from past weeping. "I had to come to you, though it is wrong and scandalous, to thank you, dear Lucanus, for the surcease you brought my father and the promise you made to him."

"It was a promise made in the knowledge that it will probably be impossible to fulfill," said Lucanus, absently. He thought that the spring morning stood in the girl's eyes; a fragrance like frankincense rose from her garments. Even in her grief she was lovelier than any woman he had ever seen, her brow purer and whiter, her virginal body sweeter and softer. The sun glinted in on her face through the parted curtains, and her cheeks showed the traces of tears.

"You will find my brother, Lucanus," she said in her dulcet voice. "And I will be waiting, in Alexandria or in Jerusalem. Or," she added in a lower and shaking tone, "anywhere. You can always find me, Lucanus."

They were silent then, looking at each other. Lucanus' face was as pale as her own. Then he said, "Sara. Where I go, no one else can go, no brother, no sister, no mother. No wife. There is much that I must do, and I shall be homeless and a wanderer. There is no room in my life for a personal love, for love to me means loss."

He suddenly remembered Asah in the courtyard, and her words to her husband, and he shook his head in desperate denial. But he did not release Sara's hand.

She said, "I can always find you, Lucanus," and her eyes filled with yearning. Again he shook his head. But he lifted her hand to his lips and kissed it and turned away abruptly and went up the ramp again. Even when she called after him, "Farewell! God go with you!" he did not look back.

Lucanus did not use the purple-awninged space reserved for him on the deck, so Cusa took advantage of this and sprawled on the cushions like a king and meditated. Now why, he asked himself, did that incomprehensible fool of a Lucanus stay below all these fine autumn days, coming above-ship only at twilight? He would sit below all day with his books. But at twilight he would come on the rocking wooden deck indicating that he wished no conversation. He would lean on the railing and gaze at the violent sunset skies and the dark fire-slashed sea, unaware of the sailors, the cen-turions, the captain, and the few other passengers. His face had a closed still expression like stone; his eyes were haggard. He was lost in some tormenting dream from which nothing could arouse him.

At this hour the sea's voice, quiet and rippling all day, began to clamor fitfully. The white wake, and the white sails tilting against the sky, took on the shadow of blood from the wild sunset, so silent yet so menacing. Once the skies ex-ploded in a short but turbulent storm, black clouds with lightning-bright crests fleeing close to the high and rocking masts, thunder echoing in a giant voice across the mountain-ous and glaring waters. But Lucanus seemed unaware of this and leaned heavily against the railing, not feeling the drench of warm and smothering rain. He looked towards the east as if trying to cross the lengthening miles with his eyes. He was sick with his enormous emptiness and yearning. Above and below the thunder and the tumultuous gale he heard Sara's voice.

The ship halted at various brilliantly colored ports during the day, but Lucanus did not come up to see them. It was as if life had become a terrible hurting thing to him again, as if all his wounds had begun to fester with new infection. His struggles with himself had reached the unbearable state. I cannot love again! he would cry in himself. Love is fetters and chains; love is death. Love is a binding to a hearth, and the fire in the hearth destroys a man's peace.

Greece did not lure him; he sat below in his hot little room, empty-eyed and with his hands clasped between his knees. "At least, you should glimpse the home of our people," Cusa urged him, with mingled impatience and concern. But Lucanus only shook his head. "If you would tell me what tears your soul . . ." Cusa began. And Lucanus only shook his head again. "You do not eat," said Cusa. "I have brought

my own wine, my precious wine, and you barely sip it."
Lucanus was silent.

One day the sea and air were so calm that the sails dropped
and drooped and the sun was a fury. The ship went on more
slowly, as the galley slaves were now the only means of
propulsion. At twilight the ship was like a wandering moth
on the flat and heliotrope floor of the ocean, and the wake
hissed with a barely audible sound. Then Lucanus, on the
deck, heard the deep and dolorous chanting of the slaves, and
it seemed to him that it was an extension of the misery in
himself. They must sing so all the time, he thought. I have
not heard it before! I have been thinking selfishly of my own
pain. As he thought this, and turned about, he saw some men
climbing up the ladder from the lower deck, weightily carrying a naked black man. They pushed the body over the rail
and it sank with a faint splash into the sea.

The slaves watched it disappear, then they lifted amulets
hung about their necks to their lips and scurried below. Death
came to ships as well as to towns, thought Lucanus. He remembered that he had vaguely heard that ominous sound of
a body being consigned to the sea on other twilights. He
frowned. Then he went in search of the captain, who was
sitting in his own room below with some of his junior officers. He looked up at Lucanus as the latter entered, and
Lucanus saw that the broad face was anxious and angry. But
the captain rose and smiled.

He said, heartily, "I thought I had offended you, Lucanus.
You have not spoken twice to me since we sailed from Alexandria. Will you dine with me?"

"Thank you. But I have dined, Gallo." Lucanus hesitated,
searching the man's face. "I have just seen a body thrown into
the sea. Am I wrong in believing I have heard burials several
times lately?"

The captain paused. He glanced at his officers with dark
furtiveness, then smiled wider. "Ah, there are always a few
deaths on a long journey such as this," he said. "Bring wine,"
he said imperatively to his officers. "Not such excellent wine
as yours, Lucanus," he added to the young Greek. "But adequate, I trust."

He beamed at Lucanus and offered him the broad seat
near the porthole. The captain's room was hot and stifling;
the walls were hung with maps. On a wooden table stood his
sextant and a diagram of the stars. Lucanus sat down. There

was a curious dry smell in this closed air, and he suddenly
recognized it as spice and incense and medicinal herbs. He
then noticed that these were burning in a small lamp on the
table. A large lantern swayed smokily from the ceiling.

An officer brought in a jug of wine and some goblets, and
the captain and his officers and Lucanus drank slowly. For
some reason there was an odd taut silence in the cabin, and
Lucanus' physician's soul began to stir. He studied the faces
of Gallo and the others; they were definitely shut and se-
cretive. The ship barely rocked; it seemed to be moving in
thick oil. The chanting of the slaves was closer and shriller.

Then Lucanus said quietly, "Tell me, Gallo."

The captain looked at him in pleasant surprise. "And what
shall I tell you, Lucanus?"

Lucanus gazed at him steadily for a few moments. "You
have forgotten, Gallo. I am a physician." He looked then at
the fuming lamp significantly, but he did not miss the quick
interchange of glances between the captain and his officers.

"Ah, so you are," said Gallo, brightly. "And I have not forgotten." He nodded to the officers and they left the cabin. But
when they had gone Gallo was in no haste to speak. He stared
into his goblet, then refilled it, closed his eyes, and pretended
to be absorbed in the wine's bouquet and taste, which were
inferior.

Then he said, "I am glad you stay apart, Lucanus, and
that you have not mingled with the other passengers. After
all, you are our most important cargo."

"It comes to me, Gallo, that I have seen nothing of the
other passengers, though I confess that I have not been seeking their company."

"They stay below at my suggestion." Gallo put down his
goblet and bent over the diagram on the table.

"Plague?" said Lucanus, softly.

It was as if he had not spoken for a minute or two. Then
Gallo pushed aside his diagram and leaned his chin in his
palm. "You may have noticed that we have missed a few
ports of call," he said. Then he slapped his hand on the table
and he was no longer smiling. "I should have told you before
for your own protection, but then you were never among
others. Yes, it is the plague. We are flying a yellow flag now,
which you have probably not noticed. The ports will not let
us put in when they see that flag. But there have been only
a few cases, and those among the galley slaves." He sighed.
"The cursed East! All the troubles of Rome have come from

there. When we reach home we will not be permitted to land until we have been free from the plague for at least a week. That is the law."

"I am a physician," repeated Lucanus.

"We carry a ship's doctor," said Gallo, annoyed. "You are a passenger. You are not at my service. You are the son of Diodorus Cyrinus. What would happen to me if I exposed you to danger, or if you caught the plague and died?" His hazel eyes sparkled with umbrage. "I have told you: only the slaves are afflicted, and we keep them locked up far below decks. Last night we did not have a death. It is unfortunate that you saw the burial in the sea tonight. Lucanus, they are only slaves and dogs and criminals," he added reasonably.

Lucanus thought of the faceless wretches in the hold, chained together, sweltering and sick and dying. He said, abruptly, "Summon your physician."

The physician was a tired and middle-aged man, a Gaul with darting dark eyes, and a slave himself. "This is my own physician, Priam, Lucanus," said Gallo.

Priam looked at Lucanus and bowed.

"It is plague on board?" said Lucanus.

"It is only the galley slaves," said Gallo, impatiently. "But now that you know, Lucanus—and I feared to let you know— I shall order one of these fumigating lamps sent to your own cabin. Your Cusa already knows; he keeps himself and his wife and babe locked up now in his own cabin, except when he serves you. I ordered him, as captain and the absolute authority on this ship, not to divulge the plague on board in an effort to spare you disquietude."

"The slaves are men," said Lucanus, in a hard voice.

Gallo stared at him in amazement. Priam's face became strange, and he too stared at Lucanus.

"What is a slave?" Gallo was aghast. He could not believe his ears. He knew that Lucanus was peculiar and unlike other young men, but this was beyond belief. "Lucanus, these creatures are felons, murderers and thieves, condemned to the galley for years or life."

"Nevertheless, they are men," said Lucanus. His white face now bore spots of furious red on the wide cheekbones, and his blue eyes raged below his fair brows. Gallo was convinced he was mad. A galley slave a man! Gallo was alarmed. He said, with solicitude, "Your appearance is unwell, Lucanus. The climate in Alexandria is arduous, I know. If you will permit Priam to prescribe a light sedative for you——"

"You do not understand me," said Lucanus, trying to keep his voice quiet. "To me, as a physician, a slave is a man, a human being, capable of suffering as fiercely as a Caesar. A criminal, a felon, a murderer are also men. They are not apart from us in their humanity."

Gallo's eyes tightened. He would have Lucanus' wine drugged. Gods, he thought, I am not responsible for his derangement! But what shall I tell the authorities when we arrive home? That the adopted son of Diodorus Cyrinus had been confined as a madman? The thought made him shudder. He said, in a brotherly tone, trying to soothe Lucanus, "Yes, yes. Certainly. Priam will conduct you to your quarters. He will stay with you for a while, Lucanus. He was graduated from Tarsus, and no doubt you will find much medical knowledge to discuss together." He half rose from his chair. But Lucanus leaned forward and said in a repressed tone, "You still do not understand. You are a Roman, and you feel and think as a Roman, Gallo. A slave to you is less than a jackal. To me he is a brother."

Gallo was in despair. He had troubles enough, and a madman was on his own precious ship with him! He glanced at Priam, who was gazing at Lucanus as one hypnotized, and a tear lay at the corner of his eyelid. Gallo stared at his physician. Was the rascal drunk? He said angrily, "Priam, conduct the noble Lucanus to his quarters and prepare a draught for him at once! He is obviously ill."

But Lucanus turned to Priam and said, "My Indu teachers have taught me that rats and their fleas spread that disease. Have you heard?"

Priam was unable to speak. He shook his head dumbly.

"It is true," said Lucanus, as one physician to another. He pointed at Priam's thin dark legs. "You should wear wrappings of linen on them to protect yourself from the fleas when you go among the slaves to minister to them."

Gallo lost control of himself, and shouted, "Do you think I would permit my physician, for whom I paid a thousand gold sesterces—a thousand gold sesterces!—to go into the galleys? He is here to protect my passengers, not slaves, and none of the passengers has been stricken. The moment he reported to me that the plague had struck the galley slaves I forbade him even to approach their locked door. I am the captain! My orders are of life and death on this ship, and I seek no pardon from even you, Lucanus, when I remind you of this!"

Lucanus answered calmly, "I suggest that every rat on this ship that can be found be exterminated at once, that every room be fumigated against the fleas, that every inch of wood on this ship be washed with lye."

Gallo had regained his control. Lucanus was speaking rationally, but madmen also had their rational moments. He said, "I will give these orders at once. And now——"

Lucanus rose. "And now I will go into the galleys and see what I can do, after I wrap my own legs and arms in linen against the fleas."

Gallo got to his feet. He said, in a deadly tone, "I must remind you again that I am captain, and that even if Caesar were my passenger he would have to obey the maritime laws. While we are on this ship, my ship, I am the supreme authority. You will return to your quarters, Lucanus, and my physician will go with you to calm you."

"No," said Lucanus. "Unless you drag me there. I am a physician, and I too have my duties, and my laws."

He will have to be confined closely, thought the unfortunate captain. At any moment he may become violent, and the gods only know what will happen. How was it possible even for a madman to reach such heights of madness? "I shall go into the galleys——" Gallo hesitated. He would summon his officers and have a light chain attached to Lucanus' legs and wrists. The dismal prospect opened before him of delivering the adopted son of Diodorus Cyrinus, the descendant of the Quinites, the former Proconsul of Syria, chained like a criminal, at the home port. Diodorus' tempers and rages were notorious. The captain himself would have to answer for this serious offense against the person of Lucanus, even though he was only too obviously mad. Gallo debated. The dilemma was hideous. But still he had the law with him, and it was for Lucanus' protection that he must act.

"Have you no pity, Gallo?" asked Lucanus, hopelessly. "I know that a slave, particularly a galley slave, is less than an animal to you. Galley slaves can be slaughtered with impunity. But consider. Let your heart listen and be moved for a moment. The slaves bleed as you bleed; they die as you die. And where your spirit goes, there go their souls also. Are you concerned with my own health and safety? Yes. If I should sicken, or die, then you would fear Diodorus, my adopted father. I understand." His voice softened. "You have only to leave the galley door unlocked. I have my medicines, and I swear to you that I will do all to protect myself, and I absolve you of blame in my behalf. No one need know but us that I am ministering to the slaves. I will come and go unseen except by them."

"I am weary, Lucanus," said the captain. "Leave for your quarters at once or I must—I must—have you taken there by force."

"Unless I halt the disease, Gallo, it will spread to the passengers. We may float into port a ship filled only with dead men."

Gallo turned away. "Go to your quarters," he repeated. "In the meantime I will give orders to do as you have suggested."

Chapter Twenty-two

"I must get into those galleys," said Lucanus, after he had summoned Cusa at midnight. He had listened for hours to slaves and seamen hunting and destroying rats and washing down the ship with lye.

Cusa said, "You are insane, of course. I will heat some wine for you and spice it."

Lucanus considered him. "You are a clever man, my Cusa. How fast could you pick the lock to the galleys?"

Cusa refused to take him seriously, or rather refused to show that he took Lucanus seriously.

"I pick a lock, Lucanus?" He laughed merrily. Then he gave a mighty yawn. "Why did you wake me at this hour? Was it to exchange pleasantries?"

"You wily Greek," said Lucanus. "Certainly you are an expert lock-picker. There was not a coffer or a chest or a closet safe from your prying in Antioch. You call Calliope a gossip; you are the worst gossip of all! I used to watch you admiringly, I confess, from a distance, when I was a child. I remember your talents well. Do not look so wounded." He listened a moment. The squealing of the pursued rats was gone; the ship creaked and groaned and swung listlessly. Only the call of the watch could be heard here and there.

Lucanus began to muse aloud. "The ship sleeps, except for the galley slaves and the watch and the officers on deck. From past observation, Cusa, I should judge that a few moments would suffice for you to unlock that door in the bowels of the ship and let me in with my medicines."

Now Cusa was greatly alarmed. "Master! Consider if you become infected yourself. Ah, yes, you have already said you have considered it. Am I to deliver a dead body to Diodorus? Your face is set like iron. Let us then consider more practical aspects of the situation. Gallo has refused you admission to the galleys, and I apologize to him because I had considered him a gross person to whom to offer good wine is a blasphemy. He has supreme command over this ship. Should the watch discover me tampering with the lock, the captain would throw me in irons, and that is only what I should deserve. You and he, then, would maintain an icy silence while I languished, waiting for the day when we landed so I could be dragged off to prison. Yes, yes," and he lifted a delicate palm, "I understand that you would take the blame. But Gallo would not put Lucanus, son of Diodorus, in irons. He might confine you to quarters, which he ought to have done the moment we sailed. I have a wife and child; the prospect of prison for violating maritime law does not invite me. Consider the wife and child, Lucanus."

Lucanus became impatient. "I have considered everything," he said. "I will go with you to the door, and if we are caught I shall tell the captain that you did what I asked under the most ferocious of threats, and you can then ask the captain to protect you against my madness. If irons are still the result, Diodorus will have you freed in a twinkling."

"I doubt it!" cried Cusa. "You know what a stickler for law he is!"

Lucanus' face brightened, and he snapped his fingers. "Bring me Scipio, the younger of the centurions!"

"At this hour?"

"At this hour. Hasten, Cusa. Your arguments bore me."

Shaking his head dolefully, Cusa left the smoky cabin and soon returned with Scipio, who, though red-faced with sleep and swollen of bleary eye, had first put on his armor and his helmet and his sword, as befits a soldier. He lifted his right arm in salute to Lucanus, and Lucanus returned the salute. "Sit beside me, my excellent Scipio," he said. "I wish to talk with you."

Cusa stood by the door and listened, scratching himself under his night tunic and full of anxiety. Lucanus said, "Scipio, as a soldier you have no high opinion of seamen, have you?"

"Master, as a soldier I despise them. They are fit only to maneuver warships into good positions so that soldiers may attack." Scipio's black eyes began to shine with interest, but as a military man he did not question why he had been called at midnight. Lucanus, to him, was proxy for that powerful soldier, Diodorus, whose name was reverenced by all soldiers.

"Seamen are so arrogant," said Lucanus, sighing. "Do you know that Gallo threatened me tonight, threatened to bolt me in my quarters because I differed in opinion with him? He shouted at me that he was king on this ship."

Scipio was outraged. "He spoke like that to you, Master, you, the son of Diodorus Cyrinus?" He could not believe this monstrous thing.

Lucanus sighed again. "He did. In the presence of his slave."

"In the presence of his slave!" Scipio's young face blackened, and he put his hand on the hilt of his sword and started to rise.

"Now," groaned Cusa, throwing up his hands, "who is the wily Greek now?"

Lucanus ignored him. "I am a physician, Scipio, and surely a physician is more intelligent than a mere captain of a cargo ship, and certainly more valuable. There is plague aboard."

At this, Scipio paled, and slowly sat down again. "Unless I can check it in the galleys the whole ship will become infected, and perhaps we all shall die. Have you seen cases of the plague, Scipio? Ah, it is most frightful. Your glands distend, become suffused with pus; your body rots; you vomit blood; you cough blood. You hurl yourself, in delirium, into the most dangerous situations. That is what confronts all of us. Death. There is little chance for survival when one acquires the plague. But that puppethead of a captain refuses to permit me to treat and stop the disease! Is that not incomprehensible?"

The simple young soldier was incredulous. "But what can one expect of a miserable sailor, Master?" He was becoming excited.

"May I speak?" asked Cusa.

"You may not," replied Lucanus, hastily, and Scipio scowled at Cusa.

"Naturally, as a physician, and a man of nobility and family, you wish to ignore the orders of that swinehead of a captain," said Scipio, boiling with wrath.

"Scipio, you are a young man of the most astute understanding," said Lucanus, with admiration.

"Eheu," groaned Cusa. "I have been accused of having a serpentine nature, but here is one who puts to shame the very serpents of Isis!"

Lucanus continued to ignore him. Scipio said in a trembling voice of rage, "How dare he presume to give orders to the son of Diodorus Cyrinus?"

Lucanus nodded mournfully. "He shouted his authority at me; he beat his fist on the table. He threatened me with—what did you call it, Cusa? Ah, yes, irons."

Scipio sprang to his feet. "Someone shall pay for this!" he exclaimed.

"And all I wished was to protect all of us from the plague. We fly the yellow flag, Scipio. We may not even be allowed to land in Italy. We may even be returned to Alexandria, or left to float at sea until we are all dead. You know how rigorous those doctors of Rome are. How long has it been since you have seen your sweetheart, Scipio, and your parents, and Rome, where Romans are Romans and not guardians of a whole ungrateful world?"

Tears filled Scipio's eyes. He could have murdered Gallo at once.

Cusa gaped at Lucanus with astonished admiration. The valorous idiot was as subtle as an Oriental!

"I need your help, Scipio. There may be a watch at the locked door leading to the galleys. Or the patrolling watch may make his rounds before my wonderful Cusa here picks the lock."

Picking locks was reprehensible. For a moment Scipio's face showed doubt. Then it cleared. What was lock-picking to a Greek?

"So," said Lucanus, with a wave of his hand, "all that is necessary is for you, Scipio, to be sleepless or commanded by me to guard me tonight because I am a very nervous man at times and subject to nightmares. So you wander suspiciously over the ship. You come to the door of the galleys; you discover for me if the door is guarded. If so, you will have no trouble in luring away the guard. Then you will divert the patrolling watch while Cusa picks the lock. I need but an hour or two. Cusa will tell you when I emerge from the galleys. Naturally, as he is a pusillanimous man, he would not venture in there."

"Being pusillanimous has nothing to do with it!" cried Cusa. "It is a matter of law!"

Lucanus regarded him more in sorrow than umbrage.

"Cusa, you have forgotten what it means to be a soldier of Rome, who is executor of the supreme law."

"We are the law," said Scipio, giving Cusa a curdling glare. "Do you think a sailor's order is more important than we?" But Cusa only looked at him with pity for being the victim of a scheme he thought not only dangerous but nefarious.

"I command you to be silent, Cusa," said Lucanus.

"Be silent!" said Scipio. "You have heard your master speak."

"Eheu, yes. But he has not told you——"

Lucanus interrupted. "It is very quiet now, Scipio. Take my thanks and go. Do we not wish to arrive home well, and soon?"

"And in irons," said Cusa, desperately.

"Go also, Cusa, and bring that little black leather bag of yours, with those fine lock-picking tools you probably bought from a thief," said Lucanus, smiling. "And, Cusa, I charge you not to attempt to whimper your cowardly fears in the ear of a soldier of Rome when you are out of my sight."

"Master," said the young centurion, proudly, "a Roman is deaf to the conversation of a freedman."

Cusa returned alone with his black bag. Lucanus was busily examining the contents of his physician's pouch. "Naturally," said Cusa, with bitterness, "you will send some of my fine wine to Scipio, to console him, when the captain throws him in irons. And you will neglect to send the same wine to me."

"You worry too much," said Lucanus. He was as alert and brisk as if he had newly arisen. His cheeks were rosy; his eyes flashed with satisfaction.

"I never thought that my pupil would condescend to the degradation of lies," said Cusa.

Lucanus checked his scalpels. "I never uttered a single lie," he said.

"No, no, of course not. You are a Sophist. You reek with virtue. That makes you a Stoic, too. You are a man of many parts, Lucanus, and I confess that I have underestimated the streak of villainy in you. And so, as your teacher, I admit I was full of illusion, which was very foolish of me."

"Very foolish," agreed Lucanus, with a youthful grin.

Scipio returned, glowing with satisfaction. "The galley door is not guarded, Master. Evidently it was not thought necessary. As for the patrol, I discovered that he is a pleasant acquaintance of mine, whom I have been instructing in military procedures. I think," added Scipio, with the shine of a conspirator, "that a small jug of wine, drunk in my company, on the upper deck, will sharpen his interest in military campaigns."

"A jug of wine," said Lucanus to Cusa, who, groaning like one in extreme pain, went to fetch it. Scipio agreeably discovered that it was a full jug, and went off on his work of luring away the patrol and keeping him quiet. "The captain will hang the patrol from the mast or the yardarm or whatever the heathen thing is," said Cusa. "That, naturally, will not disturb you. You've forgotten the officer on watch on the upper deck."

"Scipio is an intelligent young officer," said Lucanus, dismissing this. "He, like you, loves gossip, and knows all the officers on board, and so there will be happy conversation among all of them. How lonely it must be to be on watch in such a becalmed sea. Come, let us go. Within three hours it will be dawn. Ah, wait a moment. I need two buckets for water. Do not move like an old man, Cusa. You are not about to be executed."

"That, I doubt," said Cusa, miserably.

They took the lantern in the cabin and carried it into the narrow corridor outside. Lucanus was sorry both for Cusa's fear and the teacher's belief in absolute authority, and his unquestioning acceptance of it. While the captain had the right of death and life over those on his ship, for the sake of others themselves in the face of an unpredictable and capricious element where danger was always present there was, even more important, a moral law which no man had the right to abridge. The captain had his laws; they became not laws but oppressions when he denied to these poor slaves any succor or alleviation or the right to life.

Lucanus remembered the many authentic stories of ships such as this, when galley slaves became ill of a violent and fatal disease and so were locked below without help. Those of passengers and other slaves who had not become infected were permitted to disembark after examination by public health officers, and then the ship was towed out to sea with its burden of imprisoned, dying, and hopelessly stricken galley slaves and set afire. He shuddered at the remembrance. This was the fate in store for the poor wretches in the hold.

The young Greek had covered his legs with tight strips

of linen, and his arms and hands also. He was enveloped in
his mantle, with the hood pulled over his head. Cusa held
the smoking lantern high. The narrow wooden passageways
were absolutely silent and dark as the two men crept down
them. Scipio had done his work well; they encountered no
watch. As they slipped past shut doors, holding their breath
and walking as lightly as possible, they could hear the far
and rhythmic plying of oars deep in the ship, the creak and
moaning of timbers, and distant snores. The whole ship reeked
of lye and tar and assorted stenches of cargo and humanity
and oil and the past day's heat and salt. The floor of the
passageways, as they moved like ghosts down the ladders
deeper into the vessel, were almost as still as earth. The ship
slid over the face of the ocean with barely a perceptible
movement.

Deeper and deeper they descended, and the rank stenches
became almost overpowering. Now was added another stink:
the odor of death and disease. The roof of the last passageway became so low that Lucanus had to bend his tall head.
He saw that bilge was seeping here in little black rills,
infinitely nauseating to the nostrils. In an effort to halt the
creeping infection herbs and spices and noxious substances
had been burned down here, adding to the smokiness, the
choking heat and the foulness of the air. The lantern threw
shadows behind the two men which crawled over the polluted
floor and rotting wooden walls and dripping ceiling.

Lucanus became conscious of a sound like a ceaseless
wind, wild yet muted, sonorous and melancholy. It was the
voice of the slaves in the galleys, the hopeless voice, less
than human and yet filled with the agony of all humanity.
Cusa stopped, affrighted. "It is only the slaves," whispered
Lucanus, comfortingly. But Cusa was trembling. Lucanus
pushed him on gently; the lantern swayed in Cusa's hand.
Cusa whispered, "How can we keep this from the ears of the
captain? There are many slaves, and an overseer, down there.
It will leak out."

"Probably," answered Lucanus. "But a fact accomplished
is a fact accomplished, and I, only, will be seen. However,
if I succeed, and I feel I will succeed, the captain will be
the first man to be congratulated by the authorities, and
be assured he will not mention my part in it!"

The corridor was so narrow that they had to file behind
each other, and it was very short. At the end stood a thick

wooden door, bolted and locked. Lucanus motioned to Cusa, who crept towards it, opening his bag of clever little tools. "Do not kneel," whispered Lucanus. "There is infection in the water." Cusa bent over the lock and began to work on it, his wet and agile hands shaking, the sweat running into his eyes. Lucanus held the lantern close, and kept glancing over his shoulder. The lamentations of the slaves beyond the door seemed to be part of the very air, and the walls and floor and ceiling vibrated in them. Other slaves were confined in an adjoining corridor, for theirs was the duty of bringing food to the galley slaves, and water, and they were held to replace those who died. Most of them were those Lucanus had seen being brought aboard the day of sailing. They had been condemned to death, without fault, by the captain, and they knew it. Lucanus could hear the muffled sobs of their women and the cries of their children through the walls.

As Cusa worked, Lucanus emptied packets of disinfectants into the two pails of water which they had brought down with such difficulty. One was for the drinking of the sick and dying slaves; the other was for his own use. He would keep his hands wet while ministering. The odor of the disinfectant added to the other intolerable odors, and Cusa sneezed wretchedly, wiping his nose on his sleeve as his hands worked. Then there was a sharp click and the lock was undone. "Go at once," whispered Lucanus. "I will not open the door until you are far from here. Remain in my cabin; if anyone comes, tell him I am asleep."

But for a long moment the small teacher stood and looked at Lucanus strangely by the light of the high lantern, and his active eyes were oddly still and fixed. He was thinking, If I had had a less just and good master than Diodorus, I too might be in such a galley, dying, without help and without hope. If it had not been for Lucanus, I would still be a slave.

He whispered, "Master, I shall not leave you." Lucanus frowned at him, and he repeated, "Where you go, there shall I go also."

Lucanus smiled, and it seemed to Cusa that his face was ringed in a sudden brief light. "Come with me," said the young Greek. A few rats which had survived the general slaughter this night ran past them, squealing and scuttling, and Cusa believed that they kept to the walls of the corridor as if something seen only to them, and unearthly, had given them an unheard command. At this, Cusa took courage. He felt a sudden surge of exaltation. Nothing could ever injure Lucanus, nor those who served him.

It took the strength of both of them to swing open the door, and then only with tremendous effort. They had placed the lantern and buckets and pouch on the floor, on the driest spot, and so the lantern's light fell only on the floor of the galley. The rest was absolute blackness. But such an overwhelming noxiousness and heat rushed out from the galleys that Cusa felt them as powerful blows on his body and face, and he staggered back, covering his countenance with his sleeve. The groanings and lamentations of the slaves filled the whole corridor with echoing sound.

"Quickly!" whispered Lucanus. He picked up the lantern and his pouch, and Cusa, recovering himself, but retching, lifted the buckets of disinfected water. Lucanus cast the feeble light of the lantern into the galleys, and Cusa followed. The door swung closed, sluggishly, behind them as the sea heavily rolled for an instant.

Lucanus had been prepared for a scene of dreadfulness. This was beyond his imagining as he slowly threw the lantern's light in the galley. Only high small portholes, uncovered, admitted any light at all, and this light came only from the starred but moonless sky and the phosphorescent sea. It was hardly a light; it was only the shadows of light, like the reflection from the wings of moths. And in this vagrant illumination, assisted by the coated pale luminescence on the oars protruding through the portholes and by the dancing beams of the lantern, Lucanus could see the naked and bearded men on their benches, the chained and shackled men, white, black, yellow and brown, their heads bowed, their eyes shut against their pain, their breasts heaving, their ribs and bones visible under the stretched skin. Their arms moved in mechanical rhythm, their voices mourned in one vast groan, and the clanking and clangor of chains and shackles added a low iron chorus to their lament. Along the walls near the door lay the dead and dying, heaped together, those who still lived, those who had newly died, those dead for hours, their faces like taut skulls in the uncertain light. The overseer, himself a slave and a criminal, walked up and down between the rows of laborers, his whip cracking, his eyes staring with terror. He stopped when he saw Lucanus and Cusa, and he stood mutely, wetting his lips.

Lucanus thought that this was a scene from hell, filled

with tortured specters, pervaded with stenches only a carnal pit could expel. Deep bilge, black as crawling serpents, swung back and forth on the floor in the movement of the ship. Blood had been vomited; bloody feces had been expelled on the floor, and tainted urine.

The overseer recovered from his astonishment at seeing these two intruders. He thought that they were ghosts in their white garments. Then he came towards them fearfully. Lucanus said at once, calmly, "I am a physician, and I need your help, and this is my assistant. We are nameless. We must work quickly." The man stood there, staring, as naked as the other slaves. Lucanus motioned to him impatiently. "We must work," he repeated. "Or all will die. Quickly! Take this bucket and give each man a mouthful."

His voice cracked with authority, and the overseer reached for the bucket, recovering from his amazement. But first he gulped from the bucket himself. Lucanus and Cusa, in the meantime, splashed the contents of the other bucket over their faces and hands, and Cusa wet his legs also. While the overseer obeyed him, Lucanus examined the ill lying beside the dead. Those who appeared not to be in extremis he pulled apart from the dying to the opposite wall, propping them up against it. Those who were beyond help he let remain with their expired fellows.

It was certainly the deathly plague. The spleens of the sick men were enormously swollen, their tongues thick with white fur, their skins fiery. Buboes bulged, tumescent with pus and blood, in inguinal regions, palpitating. The sick men's legs trickled with blood from the rectum; blood trickled from the mouths of others. Some of the buboes had already ruptured; their contents dripped from the men's bodies.

The heart of Lucanus rose in his throat, throbbing with pity. No treatment was effective for these sufferers already stricken, only some alleviation of their suffering. He quickly opened his pouch and brought forth small bags containing heavy sedations in vials. Into each gasping mouth he poured a little of the liquid. The men looked up at him, as mute as tormented animals. Lucanus smiled at them gently; the lantern drew sparks of golden fire from his half-exposed hair; his blue eyes beamed down on them with the deepest and tenderest compassion. The swollen lips of the men moved silently; one or two reached out, without volition, to touch his garments, for they felt his pain for them and his love. The overseer returned with the empty bucket and looked at Lucanus with queer, distended eyes. Cusa refilled the bucket from a barrel nearby, and at Lucanus' gesture he poured fresh medicine into it.

Lucanus said to the overseer, "Each hour that passes, give the men another sip from the bucket. Tomorrow similar buckets, for those not afflicted, will be placed at the outer door. Command the slave who opens the door to bring them in. And there will also be buckets of water containing disinfectant, marked with a red mark. The well must dash the water over their bodies at frequent intervals. And search out any rats and kill them at once and throw the bodies through the portholes."

"Yes, Master," whispered the overseer. He regarded Lucanus with awe. He smiled tremulously. "Master, it is as if a god has entered here. I have drunk of your medicine, and new life has come into me, and into the galley slaves."

It was Cusa who became aware that the men were no longer lamenting. In the light of the lantern he could see scores of eyes directed at the ministering Lucanus, and they were the eyes of men who suddenly had acquired hope in this stench-filled and rotting hole. Some of them cried out in a nameless song, and after a moment the others joined them. It was a chant of thanksgiving and gratitude, mingling with the swish and creak of the oars. Even the dying and ill heard it, and moved their heads and ceased their moaning. Cusa's antic face held a lighted expression as he assisted Lucanus. Here were no slaves in this watery pit; they were men.

"Good," said Lucanus, absently. He stood among the wrack of the ill, the dying and the dead, and to Cusa he did indeed have the aspect of a conquering god. He had hung the lantern on a hook in the oozing ceiling. His garments were stained with blood and corruption. But his face was a radiance. He said to the overseer, "On the deck, two above, there are wide enough holes or windows. Take two or three of the oarsmen and have them remove the dead from among you, and drop them quietly into the sea. This cannot wait until tomorrow. The dead are your danger."

The overseer shrank. "Master, it is forbidden for me and the oarsmen ever to leave these galleys!"

"If this is not done, and now, you will all die," said Lucanus, sternly. "Move as lightly as possible. You will not be heard. This must be done! It is my command."

The overseer hesitated, then he saw the authoritative blaze

in Lucanus' eyes and he could no more have hesitated further than if commanded by a god. He called to three of the strongest men and unloosed their shackles. They rose stiffly and weakly from their rough benches and staggered forward. They began to lift the dead on their shoulders, their own bodies drenched with mingled sweat and disinfectant. One or two, recognizing the faces of friends, sobbed aloud.

The door swung open, creaking, and the slaves with their piteous burdens crept out. One by one, as Lucanus continued to administer to the ill, the dead were removed silently. The ship swayed and murmured in all her timbers. When the panting overseer stood at his elbow again, Lucanus said, "You must also dampen the walls and the ceiling with this disinfectant. Remember my orders! It is your only chance for life."

The overseer said in a hushed voice, "Master, I have been thinking. Those whom we consigned to the sea are more fortunate than we."

"Yes," said Lucanus, and his fair brows wrinkled. "Nevertheless, some of you will be eventually freed, after you have served your sentences. As for the others, while they live they can hope."

He said, passionately, "Do you think me more fortunate than you? I tell you, all that lives is condemned!"

The sick and dying slept suddenly, huddled together. In the faces of some of the ill there was a great alleviation of pain, and a peace on their filthy and bearded faces. Cusa stood and gazed at them with fear. "There is no hope for them," said Lucanus, sadly. "We have no effective method of treatment. Even under the best of circumstances the plague is almost always fatal." His shadow was high on the walls, and seemed winged.

He gave the overseer the rest of his unopened vials. "Be merciful, for you are a man," he said. "Let each of the sick and the dying have sips of these every three hours, so they may die in peace and without pain."

He paused. And then he said involuntarily, "God go with you." And it was not he who really spoke but Sara through him; he repeated her words mechanically, seeing her face before him again. He drew his breath on a harsh sound and motioned to Cusa and took down the lantern and lifted up his pouch. He had work to do. He must distill more of his disinfectants and medicine, alone in his cabin, so that the slaves would have supplies. Scipio and Cusa, in some way, would leave the buckets at the door in the mornings.

He and Cusa pushed open the door. The voices of the slaves rose behind them in an ecstatic wave of tremulous rejoicing, and it was on that wave that they shut the door and relocked it. It was then that Cusa bent and lifted up the hem of Lucanus' tunic and kissed it speechlessly.

Three days later the captain summoned Lucanus to his cabin, and Lucanus obeyed after a calming word to the affrighted Cusa. "Mine is the blame. None was with me," he said, soothingly.

Gallo's face was broad with smiles. "Sit down, honorable Lucanus!" he exclaimed, to the young Greek's astonishment, for he had been prepared for any calamitous happening. "Wine? Yes, wine! I am a happy man this day, my dear friend! A very happy man!"

Lucanus sipped at the wine the captain gave him with a bow of delighted ceremony, and he looked at the captain's good-natured face, in which the eyes were dancing with triumph. The captain sat down opposite him, his big hands on his spraddled knees, and he regarded Lucanus with mockery. He shook his finger like an affectionate but admonishing father at the young physician.

"All your gloomy prophecies!" he exclaimed. "Ah, if you were not the son of Diodorus Cyrinus I would laugh at you! But you are young and inexperienced, misfortunes time will cure!"

He was exuberant, and Lucanus was bewildered. "You have had good news?" he ventured. "From the port we touched briefly last night?"

"We did not touch the port," said the captain. "A small craft rowed out to us, bringing letters. One is for you. It is here on this table. We were not allowed to touch port, carrying a yellow flag. But the flag is being furled today!" He shouted with joy, and slapped his thigh and grinned tauntingly at Lucanus.

He shook his head tolerantly. "You physicians! Even my Priam was mistaken. There was no plague aboard! You know that all die who are afflicted. But even those galley slaves who were stricken recovered, and for three days we have had no illness among them. Do you hear me, young Master? Even the stricken have recovered, and that is impossible with the plague! From one hour to the other they rose from the floor of the galley and took their places at the oars." He struck his thigh again and bellowed happily in his relief. "And not a single death in three days! It was no plague at all!"

Lucanus was incredulous. "It is not possible!" he exclaimed. He almost betrayed himself, then added, "Your Priam is an excellent physician. He could not have been mistaken. He has seen plague before."

He was greatly shaken in his self-confidence. Was it possible that both he and Priam had made an error? He brought up the faces of the dead and dying before him; he again saw the buboes; he smelled the red vomit; he felt the scorching fire of the fever. He shook his head in absolute bewilderment. The sick and dying had been beyond hope. Yet they had lived, they had recovered quickly, they had been restored to health! Something impossible had happened.

Nor had it been the medicines he had left for those beyond hope. They had contained only standard opiates to relieve the agony of the moribund. The disinfectant had had its share in preventing fresh infections of the plague, but even this was often ineffective in the face of such virulence. But the sick and dying had lived! Lucanus shook his head again, numbly, and he thought, What sort of a physician am I? The only explanation is that I was mistaken. But the buboes, the hemorrhages from rectum and lung! Could it be that some other as yet unknown disease simulates the plague?

"From one hour to the next the apparently sick and dying rose from the floor and lived and were well!" said the captain, jubilantly. He reached out his hand and clapped the shoulder of Lucanus. He chuckled over and over. "I have talked with the overseer, and you know how superstitious these animals are. He swore to me that Apollo and one of his attendants, shining like light, entered through the locked door—the locked door!—and ministered to the dying, and they recovered!" The captain wagged his head amusedly. "Ah, well, let the poor wretches have their dreams. It is all they have."

"Yes," said Lucanus, rising. "It is all we all have."

He took his letter from the captain's table, and followed by the captain's laughter, he left the cabin and went to his own cabin with a heavy step and a musing mind. Let this be a warning to you, he told himself with severity. Make no hasty judgments. He found Cusa in his cabin, Cusa, who was shivering in the expectation of being seized and thrown into irons. Lucanus smiled at him feebly. "Do not be afraid," he said. "All is well." And he told Cusa of his conversation with the captain.

Cusa listened, and his lively face became grave and still. He gazed at Lucanus with the strangest of expressions. "It is as I suspected," he murmured, and before Lucanus could stop him he fell on his knees and laid his head on Lucanus' feet, to the young man's amazement. "No, no," he said, "I did not cure them, my good Cusa! It was not the plague after all." But Cusa kissed his feet and said nothing.

Lucanus raised him, trying to laugh. "Let us be sensible," he said, and took up his letter from Rome, to read it. Iris had written him.

Then Lucanus uttered a great cry of sorrow and despair, and when Cusa came to him, he threw himself into his teacher's arms and wept uncontrollably.

Chapter Twenty-three

Two weeks before Lucanus had left Alexandria he had written to Keptah, and now this morning, five weeks later, Keptah unrolled that letter, it having arrived that morning through the agency of both a fast sailing ship and special couriers. The physician read the letter, then looked thoughtfully and with melancholy over the garden in which he sat. Beyond the open portico the trees sang in the soft autumn wind, and the earth exhaled such a sweetness and freshness that it was a poignancy to the heart. The bright sun glittered on rough fountains and on large crude statues, for Diodorus preferred forms and movements that resembled the earth in their strong outlines and motion and simplicity. Hence the bright colors of the tiles which formed the floor of the portico, the sturdy unpretentiousness of the columns surrounding it, the vital hues of the flowers, the powerful and sinewy trees.

Far beyond the garden rose the low mosaic-colored hills of ripening grapes, vineyards belonging to the estate. Their perfume blew on the wind like a rich promise. The olive and fruit groves climbed other hills, and between the house and these hills the pasturage was still emerald green and populated with the placid forms of cattle and sheep and horses. The little stream that moved through the meadows was a brighter green, but very calm, forgetting the turbulence of spring. An air of peace, almost palpable, hovered over the land, tinged with the mellowness of wide warm gold.

Keptah had grown scarcely older these past four years. There was the agelessness of the East about him, and its secret wisdom. But the hooded eyes were disquieted this morning. Keptah thought of Diodorus. Should he tell his master of the decision Lucanus had reached about his future? Or, considering the tribune's physical condition, was it best left to Lucanus himself? Keptah reread the letter, and especially the latter part:

"I have some dark and dreadful premonition about my father, Diodorus. He has written me, and my mother also, of his frequent appearances in the Senate as the guest of Carvilius Ulpian. I do not know this senator, who is my father's kinsman, but a stir of uneasiness comes to me when thinking of him. Who could know Diodorus and not honor and love and respect him? Surely only evil men.

"I understand why Diodorus, who is a man of action as well as a man of thought, and patriotically loving his country, should feel that he must do what he can to save Rome. But I have come to the conclusion that Rome is not worth the saving, so base has she become these past hundred years, so corrupt and monstrous. Why then should my father strive so desperately? Moreover, man's fate is in hands of God, and God is not notable, according to my observations, for showing mercy or loving His prophets. Only yesterday a teacher of mine rebuked me for my conviction. He said to me, 'You are too absorbed in man. Suffering and death are the common fate of all men, so why are you in such bitter rebellion? What would you have, that all men be immortal and never feel pain again?' I saw he misunderstood me. But I said, 'When God made the world and man, why did He make them so imperfect, so full of agony and torment and evil?' And he replied, 'You are young. But I have told you of our prophets and heroes, and our ancient religion and legends. God gave man free will, otherwise man would be as the innocent animals of the fields. As man is an immortal soul, as well as a physical body, the honor of choosing his own fate was bestowed upon him, for the spirit is not one with trees and beasts.

If man choose evil, and its attendant pain and suffering and death, man alone is to blame, and not God.'

"It would seem then that Rome has chosen pain and suffering and death through her bloodthirstiness, crimes against humanity, and libertinism and oppression. Shall my father strive against these unavailingly? There are also my mother and my brothers and sister to consider. If you still believe in the power of prayer to a God who loves not man, pray that my father return to the peace of his estates, of which he spoke constantly in Antioch. For I fear for him."

And I also, thought Keptah. The overseer of the hall came to him then, winding his quick way across the graveled paths of the garden. "My lord wishes to see you, Master. He has one of his headaches."

Frowning, Keptah rose and took his majestic way into the large yet simple house, and went to Diodorus' chamber. Diodorus was lying on his bed, writhing and cursing, holding his temples fiercely between his palms. Seeing Keptah, he sat up and glared wrathfully at him. "I have another migraine!" he exclaimed in accusation. "But this one is the worst of all, and I am to be the guest of Carvilius Ulpian in the Senate today, and I shall address the scoundrels in one last effort to stir their vulture souls. You physicians! You cannot cure even a simple headache or snuffles in the nose or phlegm in the throat, while you speak learnedly of obscure diseases and their treatments! Bah!"

He groaned and fell back on his bed, and cursed blasphemously. It was obvious that he was very ill. His low forehead was flushed a bright crimson; there was a grayness under the brown of his broad cheeks, and the lobes of his ears and his lips were pallidly blue. His eyes squinted with agony beneath the black and ferocious brows, and trickles of sweat ran from his temples. Pulses beat ominously and visibly in his sturdy throat, and he appeared to be having some difficulty with breathing.

Keptah sat down quietly beside the bed. He spoke. "Master, I have told you this past year that what afflicts you is not your ordinary migraines. Your blood pressure is exceedingly high; I have had to bleed you on numerous occasions. Your heart has alarming sounds at times. I have begged you to struggle for calmness and tranquillity; a man is not the victim of his emotions unless he permits himself to be. I implore you to wait for that root from Indi, as I understand that the physicians there have been using it with marvelous effect for over a thousand years, in the treatment of high blood pressure, distressed minds, and insanity. Lucanus' Indu teacher has promised to send me this root, and it should be here now within four weeks."

Diodorus sat up suddenly, enraged, caught his temples again, groaned, then regarded Keptah furiously. " 'Insanity!' " he roared, swearing. "You infernal slave!"

Keptah replied with an affectionate smile. "I am no slave, Master, thanks to you. And as a physician, and free, under the laws of Julius Caesar I am also a citizen of Rome. No, Master, I do not consider you mad. I consider you a noble spirit of complete rectitude and filled with the passion of justice and truth. We owe our poets and our heroes to your turn of mind and soul, our artists, our teachers, our scholars, our patriots, and all those who, like Pygmalion, try to turn obdurate stone into glowing flesh. And who knows? Perhaps thousands upon thousands of years from now their words of exhortation and beauty and strength, their godly reproaches, will echo with overwhelming power in the hearts of men, and there shall be no more evil."

Diodorus listened irately, lying there holding his head. Then he bellowed, "All very fine words! But shall no voice but mine be lifted in behalf of Rome? And if there is only my voice, shall I withhold it? I am not interested in nations yet unborn. I am interested in my country! How can I live with myself otherwise?"

Keptah sighed, and did not speak. Diodorus sat up painfully, and now his voice was quieter, almost pleading. "You are a wise man, my good Keptah, but you are a philosopher, waiting for the dust of wildernesses to become governments in the far future. Suppose we all took the words of philosophers seriously and let present evil have its way, supinely? Then evil would become universal and there would be not only no rejuvenated present but no future either!

"Keptah, I am in this world now, and in this present. The future belongs to my children. Shall I not strive for a world of law and order and justice for them when I am ashes with my fathers? Or shall I mumble, like you, of future great generations and let my children immediately inherit degeneracy, lawlessness and crime?

"Listen to me, Keptah! A man's first duty is his duty to God and his country. Nations are God's expression of spiritual realms. When those nations become abandoned and debased, given up to bloody pride and debauchery, to war and tyranny, then they have defaced the kingdoms of the earth, and the penalty is death. Rome will inevitably die unless many like me shall speak, and where are the voices raised in her behalf? Who shall cry out to Romans, 'You have destroyed what God has built and you must return to freedom and purity and virtue at once, lest you die'?"

He lifted his hand to prevent the physician from speaking. His brow was almost as red as blood, and purple veins writhed at his temples, and he panted.

"Let me finish. God and country. They are the Law. You would speak of my family, as you have done before, warning me uneasily of deadly danger. But my first responsibility is to my God and my country, and the memory of my fathers, who died for both. If I die, then I leave the fate of my family in the hands of God. Should they die also, because of me, then they will not have to endure the horror of living in a world that has become depraved, without mercy or goodness. I should prefer them to die, for who, being a man, would choose life and slavery?"

He lifted his clenched fist solemnly. "Better to die than to live in the world as it is now. And it is my desperate duty to try to change that world, even if I fail."

Keptah rose and bowed to him profoundly. "Yes, Master, I understand. Forgive me for placing my love for you before the mighty and just passion that fills you. I will now prepare for you a potion which will temporarily relieve your suffering and permit you to go to Rome this morning."

He started from the chamber, when Diodorus, in a voice strangely gentle, called him back. The tribune reached out shyly and took the physician's hand. "My good Keptah, loved both by my father and me, and by my household, you obscurantist wretch! I know you will never leave my family."

Keptah could not speak for emotion. He could only raise Diodorus' hand to his lips.

"Let the noble tribune speak" shouted the senators, and here and there the chorus was derisive

Diodorus stood up, a dark and eagle figure in his military tunic and plumed helmet and armor, with the broad short sword at his belt. He lifted his mailed hand, and the senators, some contemptuous, some grim, some smiling, some old, some young, some patrician, some despicable freedmen of no honor, fell silent and stared at the tribune. The sunlight slipped on their white-robed shoulders, and here and there a noble face was carved in somber light, or a lip was illuminated, or an eye sparkled or turned to fire, or a mean profile was revealed in its craven outline like the crude drawing of a young child. The marble floor and walls shimmered, the columns gleamed, and soldiers with drawn swords stood at the open bronze doors.

Diodorus looked at them all and a strange and formidable foreboding came to him. It only enhanced the growing power of wrath in his heart, his detestation, his sensation that the weldings of his body strained against the bursting passion of his soul. He strode to the podium, and in the silence the echo of his ironshod sandals sounded from wall to wall, from pillar to pillar, and the sunlight glanced on his helmet and armor in a sudden blaze. He was Mars, buckled and warlike, armed with lightning, and there was a quality of high grandeur about him.

He rested his hands on the lectern and looked at the senators, and he smiled, not pleasantly, but with rage.

"You, Romans, friends and countrymen, have heard me before. I speak today in the name of Rome for the last time. Then I shall be silent."

He drew a deep breath, and his breast swelled with passion and strength.

"I come not to honor Rome but to bury her."

A voice shouted, "Treason!"

Diodorus smiled again, and bent his head. "It is always treason to speak the truth." He lifted his head and fixed the senators with the mighty flash of his eyes.

"In this very Senate, not many years ago, a senator was done to death because he spoke the truth. Not by knife or sword or spear was he murdered, and not by honest stones. No honorable hand struck him down, for there was no honorable hand here. He spoke of Rome. He cried out that Rome was no longer a republic, and that she had become a bloodthirsty empire, ruled not by men of wisdom and not by law, but by Caesar and his legions, and his generals and his rapacious freedmen and his palace politicians. The senator stood on this very podium and he wept for the Republic. He wept that emperors were not elected by the people, but by infamous legions and the idle and ravenous mobs who wished only to devour the fruits of the granaries and the treasuries, and to be amused by charlatans and mountebanks and actors and singers and gladiators and pugilists—at public expense.

"That senator was a young man with a bright eye and a heart like a sacred bull, fired by his love for his country. A brutal young man, who used no polished phrases and had no elegances. He had only love for his country. A passionate young man who believed that truth was invulnerable, and that lies were as fragile as a spider's web! But, you see, he only loved his country, and only fools love their country."

The senators fell into a hard but intent silence, but some of the older men bent their heads, remembering their shame, and were enraged against the tribune who recalled their shame to them. The soldiers paced slowly at the door and listened, and turned their faces to Diodorus, and some were young and patriotic and their hearts beat faster.

The tribune struck his mailed hand on the lectern and it was like a crack of thunder in the shining marble silence.

"For greed, that young senator cried to you, the mobs in this city supported evil Caesars, who lusted only for power, because those Caesars promised them loot from the public treasuries. Venal senators supported those Caesars, for profit and power. The lying Caesars spoke to the mobs and told them that our country could not defend itself against barbarians without allies, who must endlessly be bought and cajoled and flattered. And the traitorous Caesars plotted against their nation, mad with the lust to be gilded like gods by the whole world, and to be acclaimed by millions of thieves and beggars and wrestlers and freedmen and the pusillanimous, who never felt a pulse of patriotism in their vultures' hearts!"

"Treason!" several voices cried, aghast, and faces turned to each other in fury and alarm.

Diodorus stood behind the lectern and put his thumbs in his belt and looked at them with hatred and scorn.

"Those are not my words, though I have said them before to you. They are the words of the senator you did to death in this very chamber."

He rent the tunic on his breast, and the armor clanged on the floor. "Look at my scars, the evidences of my wounds! You senators, you scoundrels, you perfumed liars, look at my wounds! You sleek rascals who bed in silk to the strumming of lyres and the murmurs of prostitutes and dissolute women and bought concubines—look at my wounds! Are they on your smooth flesh? Are similar wounds in your hearts, you who betray Rome with every breath and lead her to hell with every law?"

He turned his scarred and naked breast slowly, so that all could see. It was a terrible sight, and a few older senators covered their eyes with their hands.

The voice of Diodorus rose, but was deeper in gravity and strength.

"Such wounds were on the flesh of the senator you did to death here on such a day. Not with an honest sword, not with a blunt thrust. But with lies and condemnations, with ostracism and with silence. Because he dared to love his country, and dared to try to save her from traitors and murderers and the ambitious, and from liars! His heart broke, and there was none to comfort him.

"Could you have comforted him, you who have betrayed your country and have upheld your treasonous Caesars? Dared you have comforted him, you whose tongues poisoned his very blood and did him to death? He, who only loved his country and innocently believed that you also loved your country?"

Diodorus struck the lectern again, and now it seemed to some of the older senators that Mars himself had struck that sound against their ears.

"Let me move your hearts!" he cried. "It is not yet too late! The course of empire leads only to death. Senators, look at me! Listen with your hearts, and not with your evil minds. Turn back to liberty, to frugality, to morality, to peace, to Rome. Think no longer of those who appoint you, those whose bellies demand to be satisfied by the very blood of Rome, the very flesh of Rome, the hard-earned gold of Rome. Bow no longer to false Caesars, who, defying our very Constitution, issue mandates against the welfare of Rome and place themselves above the law which our fathers formulated, and for which they pledged their lives, their fortunes, and their sacred honor.

"Rome was conceived in faith and in justice, and in the worship of God, and in the name of the manhood of man. Return our country to the rule of law and strike down the rule by men. Restore the treasuries. Withdraw our legions from foreign lands which hate us, and will destroy us at a moment's notice when it serves their interests. Repeal the taxes which crush those who work hard and industriously.

Tell your multitudes that they must work or they shall starve. Drive from the Palatine itself the masses of toadies and self-seekers and thieves! Drive from the Palatine the puny freedmen who say 'Yes, yes!' to Caesar, and bow before him as though he were a god and not human flesh! Cleanse this chamber of rascals and mountebanks and demagogues who declaim in rounded phrases that the welfare of the people is close to their hearts but who really mean that they will do the will of the mob in exchange for vile plaudits and power, and bribery!"

He lifted his hands to them in an attitude of importunity, and his fierce eyes filled with tears as he surveyed the motionless senators.

"Romans! In the name of God, in the name of Cincinnatus, the Father of his Country, in the name of heroism and peace and manliness and freedom and justice, I beg of you to restore yourselves as the guardians of Rome, to cast out the usurper of the powers which rightfully belong to you, to impeach and to punish those who seized those powers in order to pervert the laws of our fathers! Let your Roman hearts speak and your Roman spirits cry out against the expedient and the corrupt, against the vainglorious and the traitors, against Caesars who anoint themselves as gods and hold court for the depraved and the ambitious and those who would dissipate the strength of our people, our Constitution, and our traditions! If you turn from your country, then she will die, and a thousand thousand legions shall not save her, and a thousand bloody Caesars will vainly shout to the winds."

His eyes roamed their faces in despair. Then his head dropped to his chest and he stepped from the podium and walked slowly, in that cowardly silence, to the doors, not looking back. The young soldiers there gazed at him with shining faces and stood at attention and saluted, and he turned his blind and tearful eyes upon them and smiled like a brokenhearted father.

Then he straightened, and like a wounded general expiring for his country, he returned their salutes.

Carvilius Ulpian was rushed to the Palatine in his litter. His overseer whipped the Nubian slaves to a furious speed, and his trumpeter ran before the litter blasting his horn and shouting, "Make way for the noble senator, Carvilius Ulpian!" The seething mobs parted on the Appian Way, scuttling, but some stopped to jeer and spit in the direction of the curtained litter.

Alighting at the Palatine, Carvilius bounded up the long marble steps like a young man, holding up his senatorial toga about his thin legs, which contrasted with his swollen belly. His set face expressed terror and abject apprehension. The lackeys and soldiers fell away before his frantic passage. The overseers of the halls were impressed by his agitation and promised to inform Tiberius Caesar that the senator wished to see him at once, and on the most urgent necessity.

He was admitted to the library of Caesar. Tiberius was languidly reading military dispatches. He lifted his cold pale face when Carvilius Ulpian appeared, and his pallid lip curled. He said, "Greetings, Carvilius. I congratulate you on arriving so fast on the heels of my informers. You must have flown from the Senate Chamber. Did Mercury lend you his wings?"

He lifted a goblet of wine to his lips and sipped it, and over the golden and jeweled brim his eyes were a black frost full of malicious amusement.

Carvilius was taken aback. He fell on trembling knees before Tiberius and kissed the indifferent pale hand held out to him. "Lord," he said, in a shaking voice, "you have already been informed, so it is not necessary to tell you of the wanton treason of my kinsman, Diodorus Cyrinus. I swear to you, Divine Caesar, that had I known he would speak so I should never have taken him. In his previous visits to the Chamber, as my guest, he served only to amuse the senators, and I thought this would be the case today. Little did I know that my ears and the ears of my colleagues would be seared by treasonous utterances against your godlike person, and that he would shout out against you and all your decrees!"

He clasped his hands before him in an imploring gesture, and his face sweated in his fear. "He is my kinsman, but I denounce him."

"You are a discreet man, and again I congratulate you," said Tiberius, dryly. He did not urge the senator to rise from his knees, and did not offer him wine. The Praetorians at the great golden doors stared at Carvilius Ulpian, and their faces seemed carved of bronze, and as emotionless.

Tiberius contemplated his goblet. He sat in his carved ivory chair in his white toga bordered with imperial purple, a tall lean man with a cold, intent face and an inscrutable expression. Then he spoke in a hard and melancholy voice, as if to himself:

"I am a soldier. I am surrounded by sycophants and liars, and in that Diodorus speaks truth. What is lavish and uncomprehending praise given out of self-seeking and fear? What is flattery if lips that speak it only fawn, and in that fawning profit? The dull ear is servant to a duller tongue. As a soldier I prefer men of simple truth and without complexities who speak in honor and patriotism. I also prefer the condemnation of intelligence to the plaudits of the rabble. But where are men today in Rome?"

Carvilius Ulpian listened to this incredulously, moistening lips that had suddenly become parched. He was affrighted.

"Divine Caesar," stammered Carvilius Ulpian, "I do not understand."

"No," said Tiberius. "You could not understand." He contemplated his goblet again.

"As a soldier I can honor Diodorus Cyrinus. I know him well. He is not a liar, and never have I heard him utter a lie. He loves his country." The Emperor laughed a short and bitter laugh. "For that alone he deserves death! Who loves Rome now? You, Carvilius Ulpian? I, Caesar?"

The senator squatted on his heels and shivered.

"Let me tell you this," said Tiberius, quietly. "Venal Caesars, power-mad Caesars, never seize power, never destroy law and their country. The power is forced on them by an evil and despicable people, a greedy people, a stupid and craven people, a selfish and pusillanimous people. Where are the guardians of the people's liberty then? You are silent, you are slaves in spirit, you are thieves and cowards. But a people deserve their lawmakers."

He raised his hand and pointed ruthlessly at Carvilius Ulpian. "They deserve you," he said.

Gods, help me! thought the senator, his mind whirling. He bit his lip; he trembled; his whole body shuddered. Tiberius smiled darkly.

"What I have said to you now will not be repeated by you, my dear Senator, my dear and devoted friend."

"Divine Caesar," said the senator, through shaking lips, "I have not heard!"

"Good. It is very sad that even Caesars must sometimes long to tell the truth. I thank you for my happiness, Carvilius."

He struck the goblet down on the gold marble of the table

beside him, and as he was not a violent man the gesture was more terrible than the gestures of one more vehement.

"Rome!" he said. "Do I recognize this Rome of polyglot slaves, of Scythians, Britons, Gauls, barbarians, Greeks, Assyrians, Egyptians, and the scum of a whole world? Where are the Romans? They have lost their identity. They have lost their tongues, their minds, their souls, their virility. What have I to do with such a Rome? I am not an honorable man! I am what my people have made me. I am their captive, not their Emperor. There is no escaping the evil of a debased people."

His hands clenched on the arms of his chair. "I am here only to do the filthy will of a nation obstinately determined to commit suicide. If I break the law and the Constitution in their greedy behalf, they applaud me. If I have given up my hope of restoring the Treasury, they praise me for having their welfare at heart. Their welfare! Dogs and jackals!"

He stared at the astounded senator, who cringed before him. There was an utter and ringing silence in the great library. The soldiers stood at attention, like blind statues.

Then Tiberius spoke again. "Nevertheless, it is too late for truth, and those who speak the truth no longer have a right to live in Rome. Therefore Diodorus Cyrinus must die. How dare he speak truth in such a nation!"

He motioned to the Captain of the Guard, who came to him at once, saluting.

"You will go at once, Captain, to the estate of the tribune, Diodorus Cyrinus, and you will tell him that his Emperor, his General, has no further use for his services, and that in this event he will obey."

In spite of himself and his treachery Carvilius Ulpian winced. He knew what this order meant. Diodorus was being commanded to fall on his sword.

The captain saluted, swung on his heel, motioned two soldiers to accompany him, and left the library. Carvilius remained on his knees, his head sunken. Tiberius smiled at him evilly.

"It is done," he said. "And again, congratulations to you, Carvilius Ulpian. My informers were inferior men, skulking in the Senate, and I, as the god you have made, could hardly take their word. Diodorus needed to be condemned by one of his peers, and you have given me that service."

The senator lifted his head, and Tiberius nodded.

"Yes, I understand," said the Emperor. "It is customary to

confiscate the estates of those who denounce Caesar and speak treasonably. But I am moved to mercy. I shall decree that the wealth of Diodorus remain with his widow and his three children. Applaud me for my compassion, Carvilius Ulpian!"

The senator was overwhelmed with dismay. His eyes were caught by the glacially cold eyes of Tiberius, and Tiberius nodded again.

"You thought, did you not, that as my devoted friend and adorer, as the exposer of a traitor and a speaker against me, that I would reward you with the estates of Diodorus Cyrinus. Ah, now, Carvilius, you are a very rich man, and I shall reward you in my own time and in my own way. But not with the wealth of Diodorus, and not in such measure."

The senator was sick with despair and disappointment. And also with a sense of degradation. He was not an entirely wicked man. He would have preferred it if he could have lived a life of peace and pleasant luxury. He had not for an instant believed that Diodorus, who was excellent enough at attacking senators, would have overstepped safety. After all, Diodorus was esteemed by Tiberius, personally, and the senator had enjoyed listening to him attack the other senators, of many of whom he did not cherish a good opinion. He had even flaunted Diodorus in their crafty faces, knowing that they also knew that the Emperor admired him. But when Diodorus had spoken against "false Caesars" in such a tone, and when he had implored the Senate to restore to itself its ancient laws and prerogatives, Carvilius knew himself to be in deadly danger, also.

But on his way he had considered that Tiberius would reward him with the estates of Diodorus. He had not forgotten Iris, and each time that he had seen her since the family had returned to Rome his lust for her had become a desperate hunger in him.

He bowed his head before Tiberius. Then he faltered, "It is indeed most compassionate of Divine Caesar not to beggar the children of Diodorus, who is noble and a tribune. But the wife of Diodorus is a freedwoman; she was once the slave of his parents, the widow of a former slave, who was also freed."

Tiberius frowned. "Is this so?"

Carvilius looked at him eagerly, and a speck of saliva spotted a corner of his lascivious lips. "Yes, Caesar. Diodorus invented a false genealogy for her, so as not to offend his friends in Rome, and you."

Tiberius' frown became formidable. He tapped his fingers on the table and considered. Then involuntarily his eyes fixed themselves on the senator, who was squirming on the floor in his excitement and eagerness.

"Ah," said the Emperor, "she is a beautiful woman, this freedwoman?"

"Most beautiful, Sire!"

Tiberius smiled. "And you would be the guardian of the children of Diodorus, and particularly of their coffers. And you would have me revoke the freedom of the beauteous wife of Diodorus and give her to you in my gratitude?"

"I have desired her for years, Sire, since I first saw her in Antioch. She is Aphrodite herself!"

Tiberius scrutinized him impassively. Then he said, "I shall issue a decree tomorrow that the wife of Diodorus be the guardian of her children, and their father's wealth, and that her name, and her false genealogy, be inscribed in the public books of Rome."

Carvilius gaped at him, his eyes starting, his arms slack at his sides. He was filled with terror, and shame.

Then Tiberius lifted his goblet from the table and threw the contents into the face of the senator.

"There," he said, "is your just reward, my noble Senator."

Chapter Twenty-four

Keptah sat, overwhelmed with exhaustion and sorrow, in the garden, and it was sunset. His hands lay weakly on his knees, and his tired eyes drooped. He saw the reddening sky over the hills, and shivered, and though the air was still warm he was cold. The myrtle, oak, pine and willow trees basked in a rosy light, and the zenith of the heavens glowed with many delicate colors, like an opal. A cowbell sounded sweetly, as the cattle slowly wended their way to the barns, and a goat lifted his voice. The hiss of geese protested against the driving of the herdsman, and sheep lay down peacefully under the olive trees and on the slopes of the nearer hills. Now a little new crescent moon trembled in the crimson western sky. There was no tranquillity in Keptah, and his dusky face was pale and drained.

As in the morning, the overseer of the hall came to him excitedly, but the man's face now was contorted with fright. "Master!" he exclaimed. "There are three Praetorians who have just arrived, one a high officer! They demand to see the tribune at once. I have told them——"

Keptah paled. He stood up. "I will see them immediately. Have you offered them wine?"

"Yes, Master. But they refused."

Keptah halted in the very motion of walking, and he closed his eyes spasmodically. Then he entered the house and went to the great hall, with its rough mosaic floor in blue, yellow, red and white, and its squat columns and simple furniture. The crimson beams of the sun flowed into the hall and in their ominous light the physician saw the Praetorians, their armor as red as blood, their helmeted heads high and grim.

As Keptah approached, searching their faces with quiet desperation, he saw that the superior officer's eyes were rimmed with dry scarlet and that his young face expressed complete misery under its layer of dust.

"I am a physician, a citizen of Rome, and I care for this household," Keptah said to the officer, bowing. "I understand you wish to see the noble tribune, Diodorus."

The officer looked at him for a moment, then he said, "Yes. I come directly from the Divine Augustus, with a message of great moment."

Keptah studied him and saw more keenly the scorched rims of the young soldier's eyes, and he considered. "Is it possible that you know Diodorus?" he asked.

The officer's head lifted and he shifted his fierce Roman eyes away from Keptah. He said truculently, "He was my general when I was very young and new in the field, and he was my father's friend. My name is Plotius Lysanias. The tribune knows me well. He was sponsor for my little son, born a year ago, and I gave that son the name of Diodorus, in honor." His throat was suddenly convulsed, then he raised his head still higher. "I must see the tribune at once."

Keptah said, very gently, "It will grieve you to the heart to know that Diodorus is dying. He returned from Rome today and collapsed in this very hall, in my arms. He has been dying for two years. Now he has been stricken with the last mortality, and he will expire before the moon fully rises. His wife and his children are with him now."

The officer stared at him disbelievingly for a few moments, then suddenly his youthful eyes were filled with tears. He looked at his soldiers, and said, "Leave me alone with this physician."

When they were alone, Keptah said to him, "And what will your message be, noble sir, to a heroic Roman who is dying as a soldier dies, full of wounds?"

Plotius was silent. Then he sheathed his drawn sword and looked at Keptah proudly. "As the tribune's junior officer I know how to address my general." He hesitated. "My uncle was the brave young senator, Plotius, for whom I was named, who was done to death in the Senate some years ago, and not by a soldier's sword and not protected by a soldier's shield. He died ignominiously by the poison of men's minds."

"He did not die ignominiously," said Keptah, with sadness. "No hero truly dies so. He lives in the hearts of his countrymen forever, and in the shining core of history."

He led the way to Diodorus' chamber. The tribune was lying on his bed in the deep crimson sunset, and he was very still. But he was conscious, surrounded by his wife and young children. Plotius, overcome though he was, saw that Diodorus' wife was as beautiful and as regal as Venus as she sat by the bed holding her husband's hand, and that her demeanor held in it love and devotion and a spiritual fortitude. The children stood by their father's bed, weeping pitifully, and the tribune was trying to soothe them.

"Ah, my Priscus," he was saying to the oldest child in a loving but feeble voice, "you must not grieve. You are my son, and you will be a soldier, and soldiers do not weep. You must care for your mother, and your brother and sister, and must always remember that death is preferable to dishonor."

He suddenly panted and gasped. Iris bent over him and kissed his pallid forehead, which was running with the death sweat, and then his lips. Her golden hair fell over him like a veil. He lifted a weak and trembling hand and stroked that hair. Iris laid her head on his heaving breast, and was very still.

"My dearest, my most beloved wife," he murmured. "The mother of my children. I go, but I do not go forever. I will wait outside these portals for you, and when your day comes I will be there, to take your hand again in eternal peace and brightness."

Keptah and Plotius approached the bed, and Diodorus became aware of them. His dying eyes were vivid and alive.

"Ah, Plotius," he said, in faint wonder, "you have heard that I have had a summons to the halls of Pluto. Thank you for coming, for you were as a son to me."

The arrogant Praetorian knelt on the other side of the bed and looked at the tribune, and his soldier's eyes ran with a soldier's tears. He said, "Noble Diodorus, I have a message for you from Caesar, which I am to deliver to you personally."

Diodorus' gray face changed. He tried to lift his head. He looked at Iris after a moment, then at his children, and his face dwindled and the last agony he was to suffer ran like a livid tide over his features.

The soldier lifted his voice and said clearly, "Caesar will weep this night. For the message I have brought to you, my general, is a summons to his presence in order to discuss a certain unsatisfactory general's replacement in the field. He wishes you to make that replacement in your own person."

A great wave of joy engulfed Diodorus' face. He regarded his wife with rapture. "Have you heard that, my beloved? I spoke against Tiberius today, implying he was a false and corrupt and bloodthirsty Caesar, yet at the last he remembered that he was a soldier and that I am a soldier, and he wishes to give me a soldier's honor! Ah, then I know that he is not as venal as I thought, and that there is now hope for Rome, my dear country!"

His wavering hand sought the hand of Plotius, and the young officer bowed his head and kissed that hand, feeling its deadly coldness against his lips.

Diodorus spoke in a louder voice. "Tell Caesar that Diodorus Cyrinus cannot answer his call, for I have been summoned by One greater than he, into Whose hands I must commend my spirit."

He tried to raise Plotius, but Plotius only knelt and wept.

Then Iris uttered a broken cry and fell across her husband's body like a white birch tree struck down by the lightning.

Keptah and Plotius returned to the hall, and heard the sound of wailing raised from every quarter. Plotius stood in silence, his head bent, his stern lips quivering. Finally he looked at the physician and said:

"It was Carvilius Ulpian who went to Caesar, but in any event the result would have been the same." He paused. "Do not be anxious for the wife and children of the tribune.

With my own ears I heard Tiberius give the word that they would not be injured, and that the wife of Diodorus would be appointed the guardian of the children and their wealth, and her genealogy would be inscribed in the public books of Rome, testifying to her patrician ancestry."

"God is merciful," said Keptah. "Even out of evil He can evoke good, blessed be His Name."

The Senate, hearing of Diodorus' sudden death, decided furtively among themselves that they would not dare to attend his funeral for fear of Caesar's wrath. They were stunned with bewildered astonishment when Caesar commanded them all to be present, with full honors and in their senatorial togas. They could not believe it when they also learned that Tiberius' own Praetorian Guard would escort the body to the pyre in complete military regalia, and that a detachment of old soldiers, members of Diodorus' former legion, were to carry the body draped in the banners of the Empire. The last stupefying report was that Tiberius himself would deliver the funeral oration, dressed in his military garb and standing in his own military chariot. Ten trumpeters were also to be there, and ten drummers.

Before the body was consigned to the pyre Tiberius said, "Here was a soldier of Rome, simple in his speech, tender in his heart, quick to righteous wrath and quick to mercy. Here IS a soldier of Rome, who helped to forge the Empire with his courageous sword, who was never known to lie, to deceive, to betray either his country or his fellow man. We, standing here, cannot do him honor, for honor was given to him at birth, stood beside him on the battlefield, and lay down with him when he died! It is not we who deliver him to the ashes of his fathers and into the hands of his gods. He never deserted them."

A few days later Carvilius Ulpian was mysteriously poisoned. When Keptah was told of this he said, "Let him have peace, as Diodorus has peace."

Chapter Twenty-five

It had been the most miserable of winters. The Seven Hills shouldered up like mounded graves, still as death, crusted with snow for long and bitter days. The Campagna alter-

nately crackled with ice, then blackened with spongy marsh-
iness. Snow blew into the faces of the people; the roads
glittered like mirrors, steamed coldly at noonday, glittered
again under a steely moon. The white palaces stood like
upended slabs and bones against the whiteness that surrounded them, and their columns dripped with deathly water
and their cornices shivered with icicles. The Tiber stilled
sluggishly, and sometimes its current ran between the snow
like the dark current of the Styx, reflecting a pale sky and
a pale sun. Smoke rose from the centers of temples and from
the homes of the wealthy, but in the Trans-Tiber there was
a quietness like the plague, and the people, poor, desolate
and hungry, huddled together closely in tiny and fetid rooms
for warmth. At times the wintry gale bellowed through the
great clustered city in godlike wrath, and the people declared
that it was filled with savage and unearthly voices. Few
went abroad, not even the ladies in their rich fur coats and
their warmed litters. They preferred to sit in the smallest
and warmest rooms in their homes, drawn close to braziers
red with embers. Sometimes multitudes gathered in the Pantheon, in the center of which, and on the very marble floor
protected by a sheet of iron, had been built a great fire.
The statues of the gods and goddesses, in their gilded
niches, seemed alive and moving in the flickering crimson
shadows. The smoke of burning wood and incense revealed
then hid them, then revealed them again, as if through
clouds. The mighty hole in the ceiling belched out the smoke,
then when the wind capriciously changed the hole was
choked and the smoke driven back into the temple, where
it almost smothered the shivering inhabitants. The statues
slowly took on a griminess and the white feet darkened.

The old graybeards said pompously to their youth, "This
is not the worst winter. I remember when the Tiber lay in
frozen arms for weeks and the bridges resembled icy marble and glittered so blindingly in the sun that passengers
going across were dazzled. You youngsters are weak and
soft!"

The pigeons gathered in hordes under eaves; some froze
and their bodies dropped on the pavement. Their voices were
silent.

His Majesty, Augustus Tiberius, his court, all the Senate,
all the knights and the Augustales and their households and
favorite slaves and freedmen and concubines and wives and
children and gladiators and singers and dancers and wrest-

lers and pugilists and charioteers left Rome in a vast exodus
to the warm islands in the Bay of Naples, or to Pompei
or Herculaneum. There, in the warm green and gold of a
gentler clime, they sunned themselves and sailed on brilliant blue waters and gave and attended banquets. Couriers
on fast horses raced between the city and Naples and its
islands with the latest gossip and news and market quota-
tions and reports on the weather. The granaries were reported to be ominously emptying, the people despairing and
vindictive. But the court and its entourage shrugged. It was
pleasant to see the plum-colored sea at sunset, drifting with
red reflections from the burning sky, to dine on terraces and
in enclosed gardens filled with the sound of restless birds
and fountains, to visit Tiberius and to gamble and drink,
and to laugh and be amused by the motley entertainers who
had followed them like scavengers. Tiberius had built great
baths on the island of Capreae, and colorful boats ran to
them regularly, filled with laughter and the tinted faces of
ladies.

Then almost between one day and one night the south
wind softly roared over the northern blasted land, filled with
the scent of life and the fragrance of far fields of flowers
and the promise of summer. In Rome everything began to
drip and tinkle in the sudden thaw; columns blazed with
light; cornices ran like cataracts; the Seven Hills and their
crowded palaces and fora shone with lively sun. The streets
overflowed with water of a bad odor, but the people were
happy. The shops opened and the markets rampaged again
with life, the movement of animals and humans, the color
of merchandise. The wineshops filled; a perfume of pastries
and roasting meat fluttered in the warm wind. Streams of
travelers appeared eagerly on the roads leading into the city.
The fields blew with sheets of little red poppies, like living blood. The Campagna, as usual, stank, and clouds of
mosquitoes appeared. Even these did not annoy the people
too much; they were all heralds of spring again. The winter
and its iron miseries were forgotten. The Tiber ran greenly
under the sun and the bridges swarmed. And Tiberius and
his court returned to the city.

"It is too bad the Senate is returning, too," said some
skeptics, sourly. "At least in the winter we did not have to
endure them and their corruption. Eheu!"

Tiberius was not popular; his cold nature and fixed pallid
face did not endear him to the volatile Roman populace,

who preferred a certain vividness and histrionics in their Caesars. Gaius Octavius, a simple soldier, had not suited their temperament, and Tiberius suited them even less. Some of the old men talked of Julius Caesar and the liveliness of his friends. They only shook their heads when their sons and grandsons reminded them that Julius had been a potential dictator and a despiser of the Senate, and that Gaius Octavius and Tiberius deferred to the Senate in accordance with law. "Do you call these laws?" demanded the old men, with superb contempt. "The Senate may have the show of power but Tiberius is the power. They abdicated to him in order that they have more power themselves! It is not a paradox at all."

The multitudes flocked to the Ostian Gate to watch the return of Tiberius and his retinue even before the sun rose in golden splendor over the most eastern houses and palaces and hills. Caesar had first stopped in Antium to visit his villa and to entertain in his parsimonious way, and to sacrifice to Ceres and Proserpine now that the latter had returned to her mother from the crepuscular halls of death. Even his own still and colorless face seemed to take on a glow of returning life, and his tone was less nasty than usual with the senators. When he saw the vast mobs awaiting him at the Ostian Gate, surrounded as he was by his Praetorians carrying the eagles of Rome, he even smiled in his wintry fashion. Contemptuous of the teeming rabble, he was yet human enough to be warmed by the thunderous ovation they gave him. He stood in his golden chariot like a racer and held up his right arm stiffly in a soldierly salute. Yellow dust, illuminated by the sun, glittered about him, and this too, after the wet and icy winter, delighted the people. Though they whistled at the ladies, shouted laughing imprecations at the senators, and even commented sardonically on Tiberius himself, and mocked the Augustales and the patricians, they were happy.

The grim dark winter, lashed with snow like biting sand, had been forgotten, too, on the estates of the dead tribune, Diodorus. Almost overnight, it seemed, the hills burst with green, the olive groves glimmered with fresh silver, the stream glistened with the most heavenly blue, the sky softened to delicate azure, the fields danced with poppies, the black pointed cypresses, leaning against the skies, lost their rigidity. Buds swelled and unfurled on the trees, the pastures velveted and turned emerald, the new lambs capered

behind their mothers, the horses took up their eternal lewd
jesting with the mules, the cattle ambled forth and stood in
their reflections in the small blue eddies of the narrow river,
tiny leaves appeared on the rose bushes in the gardens and
the released fountains sparkled and chattered again. Doves
with purple breasts murmured among the porticoes and
arches and colonnades; birds cried vehemently as they prepared to build new nests. And at sunset the air beamed with
wide warm gold and the evening star was newborn, and the
copper moon hovered low on the horizon in a haze of last
scarlet. Sweetest of all, and the most exciting, was the passionate and all-pervading scent of the earth, at once holy
and carnal, at once peaceful and perturbing.

Lucanus had never seen a Roman spring before. The turbulent red East had merely taken on a more tumultuous
form at this time of year. Now this green and springing
softness, this murmuring sweet clamor, this gentle contrast
of hues enchanted him for all his grief and his chronic uneasiness of spirit. Even in the small sanitorium for the
slaves he could not refrain from lifting his head in the very
midst of grave examinations and listening to the voices of
the earth and smelling the divine and insistent perfumes and
feeling the warmth of the soft wind against his cheek.
Sometimes then he would actually smile, and was young
again.

"Even the most hardened wretch must feel a promise in
the spring," said Keptah to Cusa one blessed evening as they
sat in an outdoor portico and looked at the sky. "It is the
deep promise of God, and no man can resist it though his
heart be as empty as a broken vessel."

"Lucanus resists it with more or less success," said Cusa.

"He thinks of Diodorus too much," said Keptah, sadly.
"Once he upbraided me for permitting the tribune to go to
the city on that last fatal day. I should have drugged him,
he cried at me. That the tribune's fate was inevitable as a
man of character and integrity and honor, did nothing to
ease this young man's anger against me. Like all youth, he
is inconsistent. He is determined to pursue his way along
the Great Sea, on the noisome ships and in the stinking
ports and towns and cities, for that, he believes, is his duty.
I tell him that Diodorus was concerned with his own duty
as savagely as he is concerned."

"And what does he say of that?" asked Cusa, avidly.

"He said that Rome was already lost, but that man is not

lost, a sophistry I did not refrain from pointing out to him.
Man is his own executioner; he hangs himself on his own
cross; he is his own disease, his own fate, his own death.
His civilizations are an expression of him. But our young
physician has no concern for civilizations. He thinks only
of the oppressed and the despised and the rejected, who are
so because their nation is rotten and because they have made
it so. Nevertheless, he is as fixed in his narrow idea as a fly
in amber. Men suffer from men I tell him, but he replies
that something amorphous like society is the torturer of man.
Only God, thinks he, and the powerful He has created, are
the oppressors."

Keptah turned to Cusa, who was reflecting on this. As
he had asked many times before, he asked now, "You are
certain it was plague on that ship?"

"Master Keptah, of a certainty it was. I have described the
symptoms over and over to you, and the look of the dead,
and the buboes and the bloody vomit."

Keptah nodded. "Even though I know much I cannot tell
you, my good Cusa, I am still amazed at what you have
told me."

Cusa peered at Keptah curiously in the warm gold and
scarlet sunset. "You are very mysterious. I myself believe
him touched with divinity. He is a protégé of Chiron;
there is no doubt of that. I try to remember it when he most
exasperates me."

Keptah was silent a little, then he said, "There is something else which devours and saddens him besides his sorrow over Diodorus."

Cusa brightened, for he was as bad a gossip as his wife,
Calliope. For the first time he told Keptah of the hidden
lady in the litter who had come to say farewell to Lucanus
on the docks of Alexandria. "I saw her white hand," he said,
with relish, "though not her face. But the hand was remarkably small and beautiful, and I have never seen an ugly
woman with a hand like that, nor a truly lovely woman who
had an ugly hand. And Lucanus came back to the ship with
a dead still face, and his eyes were sunken with grief and
despair. Incidentally, he had kissed that hand."

Keptah sat up and stroked his chin; there was a look of
excitement in his expression. "A lady! Ladies do not come
down to docks crowded with slaves and rabble to say farewell unless they love and are loved. Ah, it is all of a piece!
He has renounced the lady, and all ladies, because of his

obsession. Nevertheless, I rejoice. Let us continue to hope. If the lady has a litter and slaves, then she has money, and a woman in love and with money is as relentless and audacious and unshakable as a tiger. He will see her again!"

"She will have to be very ruthless indeed," said Cusa, wryly. "But again, it is possible you are right. He spent many nights wandering around the ship like a shade, unspeaking, I also heard him cry out in his sleep, mournfully, as one cries for the lost."

Lucanus sat with his mother and brothers and sister in the evening. He was even more quiet than usual. He looked at the shadowed green valleys and the sunset-lit hills; the air was iridescent, as if filled with powdered jewels, and in the darker hollows of the gardens the fireflies began to sparkle silently.

The flesh of Iris had lost its rosy glow and had become palely translucent, like mother-of-pearl, and the blue of her eyes had intensified with the silent serenity of resigned sorrow. Lucanus was filled with pride and pity; he saw her not only as his mother but as a wife and a woman, and he often wondered what her thoughts were, and her desires. Sometimes he was shy with her. Sometimes she amazed him by her acceptance of events and the death of her beloved husband. He would have preferred rebellion and anger against fate. Once she had said to him, "I know that Diodorus lives, and that someday I will join him in gladness and joy, for God is good, and He will not disappoint His children." There were times when she had an impenetrable mystery for Lucanus.

She loved her own children by Diodorus, little Aurelia and Gaius Octavius, but she seemed to love the son of Diodorus and Aurelia even more. The merry Priscus was affectionate and devoted, and adored his stepmother, and for all his affable nature he had a deep sense of responsibility, though he was hardly five years old. He was as a father towards his little sister, whose hair resembled her mother's and whose soft brown eyes glimmered with sweetness, and towards his little brother, not yet two, who toddled gravely about on the grass and inspected flowers like a philosopher. Little Gaius recalled his father astonishingly, and sometimes this amused Lucanus. But Priscus stirred his heart with pain, for his face was the face of his dead sister, Rubria, and he had Rubria's vivacity and gaiety.

Gaius wished to inspect the fireflies, but Iris caught him

just as he stumbled and held him on her knee, kissing him. Her golden hair was illuminated briefly by a last lance of sunlight before it expired behind the darkening hills with their gilded crests. Gaius inspected his mother's face seriously, then leaned his dark round head against her bosom, and she bent over him. "Though he barely speaks as yet," said Iris, "he has the most profound thoughts and asks the most profound questions of the world." She glanced at Lucanus. "Like his dear and beloved brother," she added, softly.

Lucanus said nothing; he had tried, all these months, to hold himself apart from his family for terror of loving them too much. He was filled with a wild restlessness and anxiety. He must leave as soon as possible or these children and their mother would seize his heart and break it with grief in their hands. He watched the burnished moon quivering over one hill. To him the moon was like an old skull, weathered with sorrow and tragedy. Its beauty, therefore, did not move him, for it was the beauty of death, just as in love there is always that threatening beauty.

Iris was watching him from under her lashes. She saw the white gloom of his face, the rigidity of his expression, and his withheld eyes. She sighed. Then she said, "I was never a woman of so ardent a temper that I could tell my emotions freely. But you must understand, my dear son, what it means to me to have my family with me, and you home at last after all those years. Is it not wonderful that you have been appointed, through the graciousness of Caesar, to be the Chief Medical Officer in Rome? You will be in the city three days a week only, and then will return here, where the household needs you. And your mother most of all," she added, in a lower tone.

Lucanus' lips parted, then he was silent again. He looked at the beautiful ring Diodorus had had made for him; the tribune had intended to present this ring to his adopted son on his return. It had been most cunningly and exquisitely made, a broad and intricately carved band of gold in which was set a large green emerald. On this emerald there had been imposed the golden caduceus, the sign of the physician, the staff entwined by two serpents and surmounted by the wings of Mercury inset with rubies. To Priscus had been left the knightly ring of his father, yet it was not so marvelous and rich as this, and, to Lucanus, it was not half so significant. Diodorus had not forgotten Lucanus in the matter of money. He had made him the beneficiary of a very large sum and had appointed him, in the event of the death of their mother, the guardian of his children. But, Lucanus told himself, though his mother was old, almost thirty-eight, she was in good health and could be expected to live a number of years yet.

He saw that he must speak now, though he had avoided this for over six months, fearing to disturb his mother and heighten her grief. He said, as gently as possible, "I must tell you, Mother. I cannot accept the appointment of Tiberius. I cannot remain here."

Iris waited. Lucanus gazed at her, expecting tears and protests and disbelief. But Iris waited calmly. Then she said, "Tell me, my son."

And so he told her, and she listened, her head bent, her hands absently fondling little Gaius, who was falling asleep. Priscus and Aurelia busily pursued the fireflies, and their young chatter and laughter mingled with the evening songs of the birds, and the moon rose higher and the pungent scent of earth and the cypresses and the newly flowering trees became insistent. All at once the tips of the cypresses silvered.

Iris was so silent after Lucanus had finished speaking that he said at last, "You do not understand."

"Yes," said Iris, "I understand. You are very like Diodorus, my dear son, and this makes me happy. You have the same sternness and discipline of character, the same dedicated duty, rare things in this debauched world. You are aware, of course, that the path you have laid out for yourself is a sorrowful and lonely one, and filled with sharp stones, and lighted by no sun?"

"Yes," he said. "But that does not matter. I have long known that the world holds no promise of joy for me, or happiness."

"I had prayed," said Iris, "that you would marry and bring your wife to this house, and that there would be grandchildren to rejoice me."

Lucanus shook his head.

"You have not forgotten Rubria," Iris said, and sighed again.

"I shall never forget her." Lucanus hesitated, then spoke abruptly. "Mother, I love a woman who seems to me Rubria reborn. It is in her nature that I have found the resemblance, the same gentleness and soft gaiety, the same pureness of character, the same womanly strength. Her name is Sara bas Elazar. That is all I can tell you. To me she mingles in my mind with Rubria so that they are one and the same. Yet as Rubria vanished, so she must vanish from my life."

This, to Iris, was a great calamity. Tears stood in her eyes. "The love between a man and a woman is a holy thing, my son, and is blessed."

"It is not for me," said Lucanus, with firmness, and his mother saw his face. After a while he said, "I have written today to Caesar, thanking him for his offer, but refusing it. Rome has no need of me, as I have told you. The city is full of excellent sanitoria and excellent physicians. There is even a good sanitorium on an island in the Tiber for the most abandoned of slaves and criminals. But in the cities and towns and lost places along the Great Sea there are few places for the sick and the poor."

Though she understood, Iris was a little baffled. So handsome and gifted a young man, and of such wealth, and with a loving family, and looked upon by Caesar himself with graciousness! Yet he would abandon all these for the faceless multitudes in cities without a name for her.

"I wish to be free," said Lucanus. "The more wants a man has, the less freedom. I want nothing for myself." His hands lay still on his knees, and they were like carved stone in the rising moon, and the marvelous ring on his finger faintly glittered. He wore a simple cheap tunic. His wardrobe was as poor and limited as a humble freedman's. Yet, thought his mother, he has a majesty beyond that of Caesar's and a nobility like the gods'. Her heart suddenly lightened and she was mysteriously comforted, and she looked at the darkening sky as if she had heard a voice from it.

The nurses came from the pleasant house behind them for the children, and Iris rose. When the nurses bore the children away she followed them with her blue eyes, which were tenderly misted. Then she put her hand on her son's shoulder. "God be with you always, my dear Lucanus," she said, and left him.

Keptah found Lucanus alone in the mellow moonlight under the glossy myrtle trees. The cypresses leaned blackly against the moon, and a great stillness enveloped the gardens. Keptah sat down in Iris' chair and stared at his old pupil. "You have told your mother," he stated.

Lucanus moved restlessly. "I have told her. She understands."

"You have the most amazing view of life," said Keptah. "As I do not have that view, though honoring yours, I can only be astonished. Yet, of course, it was ordained."

"By whom?" asked Lucanus, contemptuously. "I have ordained my life."

Keptah shook his head. "No." He paused a moment. "You are also in error about a number of things, and this error must be corrected or you will not truly find your way. To you nature is chaotic, swept with the winds of anarchy, senseless, inspired only by violence, and clamorous but essentially purposeless life. Civilization, to you, is man's pathetic attempt to bring order to nature, to regulate it into some form of meaning, to guide its pointlessness into some semblance of significance. To you nature in its seeding, its growth, its death is a sum without an equation, a circle encompassing nothingness, a tree that flowers and bears fruit and dies in a grim desert. Such thoughts are lethal; they are freighted with death."

"What else?" said Lucanus, impatiently. He thought that Keptah was becoming as tedious as Joseph ben Gamliel.

Again Keptah shook his head. "You are wrong. Nature is absolute order, ruled by absolute and immutable laws laid down at the beginning of the universe by God. Civilizations, so long as they agree with nature and its laws, such as creation, freedom of growth, the dignity of all that lives, and beauty of form, and reverence for the being of God and their own being, survive. Once they turn to rigidity and anonymousness under the State, and regulation of large and small forms to one flowerless level, the degradation of the best to the fruitless masses of men, the rejection of freedom for all—then nature must destroy them, through wars or pestilences or quick decay. You are in the midst, in these days, of the workings of the Law."

"We are only continuing the endless conversations on the same matter which we have had all these months," said Lucanus, wearily.

"I will not discuss it again," said Keptah. "I only wish to remind you that you are wrong. Man is not the poor, voiceless, and suffering creature you think he is. He is a Fury, born of Hecate, and only One can save him from his self-determined fate."

He waited for the stubborn Lucanus to speak, but he did

not. Then Keptah said, "Are you of flesh and blood, and not stone? Your concern for men is impersonal, though compassionate. I fear it is even vengeful. You are still young. The world is full of kind and loving women. You should have a wife."

Lucanus flushed and turned to him angrily. "Who are you to speak so? You have never married."

Keptah looked at him strangely. "Aeneas and Diodorus were not the only men who loved your mother. I have known Iris since she was a child. You think me presumptuous, I who was once a slave?"

"I think of no man as a slave," said Lucanus. He stared at Keptah, and his hard young face softened for a moment.

"But all men are slaves. They have willed it so. Only God can free them, He who gave them freedom at their birth, though they have renounced it and always will renounce it." Keptah stood up. Then, without speaking again, he left Lucanus.

Lucanus looked at the sky, which was now exploding with blazing stars. He suddenly thought of the Star he had seen as a child. The Egyptian astronomers had told him of that Star. It was only a Nova. At first they had believed it a meteor, but it had moved too slowly, had been too brilliant, too steadfast in its passage. It had vanished by the next night. Lucanus remembered the deep stirring of his heart when he had seen that Star, the passionate and nameless assurance which had come to him, the intense joy. Now he was suddenly overwhelmed by a sensation of profound loss and sorrow, and he covered his face with his hands.

Chapter Twenty-six

The next day, Plotius, the captain of Caesar's own Praetorians, arrived at the house of Diodorus in his official chariot, surrounded by a picked detachment of the guards. As he had visited this house often since Diodorus' death and had become very fond of Keptah, whom he honored as a wise man, his visit aroused no consternation. Keptah invited him to have refreshments, but Plotius said, "I have not come today for a fruitful gossip with you, my good Keptah. I have come on orders of Caesar. He wishes to see the son of Diodorus, Lucanus, at once."

When Keptah showed some alarm, Plotius smiled. "You will remember that Caesar delivered the funeral oration. He has repeatedly mentioned, in my presence, his deep regard for Diodorus, and his determination to honor his memory. I believe that Lucanus sent him a message yesterday, and he wishes to discuss the contents of that message with him."

"I think I know what it is," said Keptah. "Lucanus has refused the appointment of Chief Medical Officer in Rome."

"Is the physician mad?" said Plotius, marveling and nodding.

"In a manner of speaking," said Keptah.

Plotius, in his armor and clothed with the strongest laws of Rome, accompanied Keptah into the bright gardens where Lucanus was playing, like a child, with his brothers and sister. Little Aurelia was riding on his back; he was pretending to be an untamed horse, to the delight of the children, and he was making ferocious noises and tossing his yellow head. Plotius thought it a most beautiful scene. He was also amazed at Lucanus' handsomeness. But when the young physician saw his visitors he removed Aurelia from his back and waved away the disappointed children, who ran off to play at the far end of the gardens. Priscus returned after a moment, fascinated as always by the armored soldier who often brought him sweetmeats and declared him to be the young Diodorus himself.

"You want me?" asked Lucanus, who had never seen Plotius before though he had heard of him from Keptah's letters.

"Greetings," said Plotius, raising his right arm in the stiff soldierly salute. "You are Lucanus, son of Diodorus Cyrinus? I am Plotius, Captain of the Praetorians in Caesar's household. You are to come with me for an audience with Caesar."

Lucanus glanced at Keptah. Keptah said, "When Caesar commands, Caesar must be obeyed."

"Very well," said Lucanus. He brushed blades of grass from his tunic. He hesitated. "I have no grand apparel. I must come as I am."

"You shall not insult Caesar by appearing before him like a crude shepherd," said Keptah, with a smile for Plotius. "Here, my good friend, is a young man of considerable wealth. Yet he affects to be a poor countryman. Come, Lucanus, I have a fine toga, which I had made for myself, and for the arranging of the folds of which I have trained a very intelligent girl."

He took Lucanus' reluctant arm. The young man had colored with annoyance at the raillery in Keptah's tone. Plotius watched them go into the house. Priscus, as usual, was wistfully fingering the hilt of the short broadsword.

"Ah," said Plotius, "you will make a soldier as fine as your father." He unsheathed the sword and gave it to the boy, who grasped it with his strong and brown little hand. His tanned cheeks glowed, and his eyes lighted. "Now," said Plotius, "thrust like this, turning the wrist so."

"I will serve Caesar," said the child, thrusting and feinting at Plotius. "I will be a great soldier." The other children returned to watch, and Priscus proudly ignored them, though watching them out of the corner of his eye. Aurelia clapped her hands and screamed in admiration as Priscus stamped like a fencer and mightily handled the heavy sword. The little girl's hair was like a golden moon about her pretty face.

Keptah returned with Lucanus, who was clothed in a most regal toga now. A stableboy was bringing one of the household's finest horses to the gate, an Idumaean stallion. When Lucanus mounted it and controlled it with expert mastery, Plotius thought of Phoebus, for the horse and the horseman stood against the passionately blue sky like statues suddenly embued with life.

Lucanus rode silently beside Plotius' chariot into the city, the other Praetorians mounted behind them. He is very strange, thought the captain. He said to Lucanus after a while, "Rome is in a very festive mood today. The people are honoring Cybele, and her temple overflows."

"I know nothing of Rome," said Lucanus, curtly. "I passed only outside its walls on the way home." Plotius shrugged and the conversation died. But Plotius continued to admire Lucanus' horsemanship and the way he sat on the stallion. He was certainly godlike. The ladies of Rome would go mad over him.

Long before they entered the city through the Asinara Gate, Lucanus could see Rome, white and bronze and golden on its Seven Hills, crowding against the cerulean sky. There she was, enormous, swollen not only with Romans but with men of many nations and many tongues, a city fierce and depraved, the mistress of all law, the mistress of the world, glorious in potency and color, the hub of her tremendous roads, fed by her great aqueducts which brought fresh clean water countless miles from distant streams and rivers, and by her ships from every corner of the earth. Here was Rome, the devourer, the destroyer, more terrible than her eagles, before whose fasces uncounted millions of Germans, Arabs, Gauls, Britons, Egyptians, Armenians, Jews, Spaniards, Sicambrians, Indus, Greeks and Nubians, and myriad other peoples, bowed in terror. The sun blazed on distant walls and gleaming columns; it gilded far temples in blinding gold. All the wealth of the world was here, all its power, perversions and evils, all its strange appetites and stranger gods, all its depravities and tongues and customs and lustings, all its beauties and arts and philosophies, all its intrigues and plottings. No wonder, thought Lucanus, that Diodorus had at once loved and hated his city.

The stone road, the pride of Rome, thronged with horses, chariots, wagons and carts, loaded with merchandise and produce. An aqueduct ran alongside, its high waters gurgling in the warm spring sunlight. Fields of poppies and yellow buttercups blew on the borders; the air was filled with the ferment of the earth and with the sweat and effluvium of the caravans. Plotius ordered some of his lictors to surround him and Lucanus and to clear a passage. Lucanus, in spite of himself, was caught up in curiosity and fascination. He looked down at the teeming dark faces of his fellow travelers; he smelled the odor of spices and garlic; the air thundered with pounding feet and hoofs and the rattling and creaking of unnumbered vehicles. His eyes hurt with the shifting and vigorous color and the vivacious sun. "The traffic," said Plotius, with disgust, "becomes worse every day. Every other road leading to Rome is as badly overcrowded. Yet Rome is never surfeited; she is like a vast mouth eternally open and eternally gulping. She is like Cronos, who devoured his children."

Clouds of noisy cheeping swallows sailed over their heads and added to the furious din of men and vehicles and horses which seemed to shake the road. The cultivated fields on each side glistened with the almost unbelievable green of young crops set out in rows on the red and fecund earth. Infrequent copses of myrtle, oak and cypress trees cast an occasional shade on the burning stones, and here and there, beside a blue and shallow stream, stood clusters of great willows drooping their frail jade hair downwards to their pale and mottled trunks and the shining water. The tumultuous road

wound past white villas set in gardens, and pastures full of
mild cattle, and groups of chained slaves raising new walls
or repairing them.

Now the yellow dust thickened and became a bright haze
over the travelers, and a powdering like gold appeared in
the folds of Keptah's precious toga which was so artistically
draped over Lucanus' light blue tunic. Lucanus attempted to
brush it off but it clung to the fine linen. His stallion sneezed
and snorted. Plotius thought it ridiculous for a man in a
toga to ride a horse. He had offered to return Lucanus to
his home in his chariot, but this had been coldly refused by
the young man.

As they approached closer and closer to the city Lucanus'
sense of excitement grew, and a very human curiosity. Rome
was seven hundred years old, and old, now, with ancient sin.
It was fitting that she had been founded on a fratricide.
However, her decline had begun with the decline of the Republic into an absolute empire. Her world-flung banners rode
with the whirlwind; her might was maintained by a hundred
legions, and spies and informers and murderers by the multitude. Intrigue suffocated the once honest air of the Republic. But that inevitably was the course of empire, the
course of power and "world leadership." Lucretius' poem,
De Rerum Natura, which Lucanus had read, had a double
meaning, one for the latrines of Rome and one for the latrines of the Roman spirit. In the physical latrines mothers
frequently abandoned unwanted newborn children; in the
spiritual latrines men had abandoned their faith and their
character.

What did it matter that Gaius Octavius, Augustus Caesar,
had boasted that he had found a city of brick and had con-
verted it to a city of marble, which gleamed and glittered in
the sun? Better, thought Lucanus, a humble city with justice
than a marble sepulcher for the transcendent virtues. But still
he was excited. The cavalcade stopped at the gate and the in-
comers were scrutinized by the soldiers on guard, with their
drawn swords. The top of the gate snapped with the banners
of Rome, and the terrible stone eagles stared furiously down
at the road and the restless crowds of men and animals and
vehicles. Plotius and his entourage were admitted with salutes
and rode through the gate, leaving behind them a deafening
uproar of impatience. And now they were in the enormous
city, enveloped and devoured by it.

If Lucanus had been dazed by sound and noise on the

road, he was completely dazed now by the city. The rest period occurring after the noonday meal was over, and as they proceeded along the Via Asinara they were slowed to less than a trot by the multitudinous shopkeepers, clerks and bankers on the way back to work. Though Gaius Octavius had declared that all Roman citizens should wear the toga, the majority of hurrying men wore the short tunic of many colors, blue, scarlet, yellow, white, brown, crimson and green, and shades of all these hues. Most were afoot; a few of the more affluent were carried in litters. Chariots and horsemen tried to force passage over the flat or cobbled stones. The traffic was made more congested when groups of ebullient citizens insisted on halting in the very middle of the street to discuss business or exchange gossip. When forced to break up by the force of the traffic itself, they took refuge in the doorways of shops and taverns, there to shout and gesture and swear and laugh, or to conclude a bargain. The road was hemmed in by the tall houses, sometimes of as high as eight stories, where women leaned on window sills to scream at children who had escaped the courts in the rear and were adding their uproar to the general din. Here most of the buildings were built of the flat long red brick of an earlier era. Men pushed carts on which smoky braziers stood, and on the top of these braziers sausages and small pastries sizzled. Other carts, propelled by their owners, were filled with cheap merchandise for the consideration of the women who stretched from their windows and shrilled down at the vendors and insulted their wares, or nodded at a held-up length of wool or linen or cotton of violent tint, and at other sundry offerings. To Lucanus the city reeked worse than Antioch and Alexandria, in spite of the endless sanitary laws, but it was a more gigantic reek, and almost awesome in consequence. His nostrils were stricken by foul odors, by the hot odoriferousness of cooking victuals, by oil and animal offal, by the pervading miasma of millions of latrines, by astringent dust and the smell of sun-heated stone and brick. Here the cool spring of the country had been lost in an immense and choking heat, as of midsummer. Eddies of hot air flowed from other streets as from ovens. And everywhere clamor, running, shouting, expostulating, and the pound of wheels and hoofs, and billowing clouds of pigeons and swallows. When the lictors of the Praetorians broke up a particularly large mob of merchants who were vociferously disagreeing with each other in the very center of the street, Lucanus was aware

of scores of indignant black eyes turned upon him and his
escort, and, because of the noise, he could only see writhing
mouths emitting curses. The Urbs feared no one, not even
Caesar.

What most impressed Lucanus, and dizzied him, was the
height of the city, the tall buildings, the looming apartments,
crowded together and thrusting against each other, contrasting in their colors of red and yellow tufa and grayish
green peperino, their arches filled with eddying groups swirling like water. The city, contained by its walls and gates, had
only one way to grow, and that was upwards. As a consequence all the streets boiled like impetuous rapids and the
citizens, forced to push shoulder or elbow into a neighbor
for passage, were understandably irritable and were often
given to blows or open quarrels because of blocked movement. As Lucanus was now approaching a wealthier quarter,
this confusion and noise was compounded by walls, higher
buildings, circuses, theaters, private homes and government
establishments, covered with marble of many colors, not
only white, but golden and brown and red and occasionally
a slab of dazzling black. Rome had absorbed all the gods of
her conquered nations into one seething pantheon of religions,
and temples jutted everywhere, through whose bronze doors
poured endless conclaves of worshipers, those going carrying
sacrifices and those emerging emanating the scent of incense.
Many, awaiting friends, stood in porticoes, gesticulating, spitting, arguing. Now tall and fluted columns appeared, on which
soared bronze or iron or white marble statues of gods and
goddesses and mounted heroes, prickling up like giant pikes
from the seething crowds and jostling buildings and temples,
sometimes perched on each side of wide stairways leading to
public buildings and places of worship, and sometimes leaping from a broadening of the road and in the center, surrounded by small circles of earth filled with brilliantly colored
flowers in the midst of fountains, or gleaming with mosaics.
And over it all—all the stunning clamor of millions of voices,
hordes of vehicles and horses, all the power of Imperial
Rome and her marbled hills—arched the hot blue sky like a
domed and suffocating cover over a steaming and colossal
pot.

Lucanus' horse stumbled more than once in the chariot
ruts of the road. He was sweating vigorously. As it was useless to try to make one's self heard, Plotius lifted his hand
and mutely pointed to the Palatine, on which stood the palace

of the Caesars, built by Gaius Octavius. It and its surroundings appeared small and far from this distance, but Lucanus, in spite of the haze of yellow dust which hung palpably and with burning brightness in the air, could see the Imperial Palace surrounded by a grove of white columns, mounting up story by story in diminishing levels of smaller columns and ascending arches. Temples, green hanging gardens and terraces, and beautiful villas flowed down from the palace on the regal hill, surrounded by a profusion of arches, porticoes, fora, theaters and huge and crowded monuments. He thought that in that great palace lived Zeus himself, with his children in lesser palaces descending about him, cool and apart in the midst of trees and flowered courts and perfumed fountains. It all stood against the sun, shining as if with white fire, this crowded separate little city of royal might and beauty.

For the first time Lucanus, who had been absorbed by all that he had seen this day, gave thought to his coming interview with Tiberius Caesar. He tried to recall all that Diodorus had said of this man, his cold caprice, his distrust of all Romans so that he stationed garrisons of soldiers outside the Roman walls, soldiers accountable only to him. Once he had been a more joyous and happier man, when married to his beloved Vipsania, but he had yielded to the demands of his mother and his Emperor and had divorced his charming wife for a woman who later betrayed him. Since then he had become a gloomy and quietly vindictive man, for all his declarations that every Roman should enjoy free speech and thought, including the Senate, to which he outwardly deferred and which he inwardly despised. But at least he had genius for delegating power, and his magistrates and proconsuls and procurators had freedom of action and judgment. If he was now showing some ominous signs of becoming tyrannical and intolerant, and if he was usurping more and more power belonging to the Senate and the people and the courts and displaying symptoms of desiring absolute despotism, no one opposed him. This, Diodorus had written reluctantly to Lucanus, was more the fault of the Senate and the courts and the people than it was the fault of Tiberius. Nevertheless, he was, at this time, still an able administrator, and just, and still a soldier at heart, even if he was frequently the target of the coarse wit of the Roman rabble, who scrawled obscene comments about him and his faithless wife, Julia, on the walls of Rome. Sometimes, in bolder hands there

appeared, in red letters: "Where is our Republic? Long live
the free men [ingenui]. Down with the tyrant!"

But the Republic had died, and no Caesar had put it to
death.

The city, as Plotius had said, was festive today. But
Romans were always festive, and always honoring either
native or foreign gods. Anything was an excuse for a holiday,
for sacrifices, for celebrations in the circuses or the theaters
or in the countless public baths. Three circuses alone were
advertising chariot races and combats between gladiators, and
slaves poured through the populace shouting the news, including the information that some of the best and most ribald
Greek plays were about to be performed in certain theaters.
Hordes insistently struggled in the direction of these public
spectacles, cursing at idlers who blocked them and shouting
imprecations in many languages.

The young physician and his escort now began to ascend
the Palatine, and, as they mounted, the air became cooler.
Lucanus was delighted by the beauty around him, and momentarily forgot Tiberius. It was less crowded here, and those
who were borne in litters and in chariots and cars were men
and women of consequence, going either to the temples and
theaters surrounding the palace or to their villas, and
some to seek an audience with the Emperor. Lucanus looked
into the eagle faces of the men, and at the painted faces of
the lovely women, who smiled at him suddenly and with
pleasure. In spite of their prettiness they appeared ravaged
and strange to him, and somehow depraved. He saw gates of
villas opening to admit those returning to their homes, and
flashes of scintillating gardens beyond and the silvery restlessness of fountains, and white arches and porticoes crowned
with mounted gods and heroes. Never in all the world was
deity so beautifully and blatantly displayed, and never in the
world, thought the young man, was there so little faith. Gods
adorned the Imperial City; they did not rule it.

Now on a high level Lucanus looked down at the tremendous and predatory city filled with its rushing and colored
rivers of humanity, at its bristling monuments and choked
buildings, all finally disappearing into great golden distances.
Again he was stunned by the very weight and potency of
Rome, by its incredible vastness, its dynamic force, its millions of charged, grim and excitable people, its fierce if
prodigious and vulgar grandeur, its milling mobs, its furious
uproar, its storm of banners, and, from this height, its

rabid and incandescent beauty. He saw the green and sluggish Tiber and its carved bridges, and the buildings that
rushed to its edges, and the white and rosy roofs fiery in
the sun. Here and there a gilded dome blazed among pointed
cornices, like a lesser luminary. His eyes smarted; his spirit
was almost overpowered. And now he was vaguely frightened
again. Small beads of sweat burst along his fair hairline.

The gates of the palace, manned by stern Praetorians,
swung open for him and his escort. What if he should offend
Tiberius? Would the Emperor, whom Diodorus had disdained in rough language, visit that offense on Iris and the
children?

The Prefect of the Praetorians met them in the huge vestibule of the palace, a large and formidable man glaring suspiciously from under his helmet. He shone like a statue of
bronze and brown marble under the great plate glass ceiling
that topped the vestibule and admitted the sun, and his step
was measured and heavy. Plotius lifted his right arm in salute
and introduced Lucanus, who did not know how to greet this
imposing man who scrutinized him curiously. "Greetings," he
said with briefness. So this was the Greek adopted son of
Diodorus Cyrinus, a physician. "Greetings," responded Lucanus with some stiffness, disliking the scrutiny. The Prefect
smiled; he had sharp white canine teeth. "Caesar has summoned you," he remarked, conveying by the tone of his
voice that Caesar was an unpredictable person, and one given
to the most extraordinary whims.

Lucanus flushed. He said, coldly, "That I understand. Did
you think I should be here otherwise?"

Plotius hastily concealed a smile, for the Prefect was both
astonished and displeased at Lucanus' address. Yet, after a
moment, he was impressed by the young physician's proud
manner and the rigorous set of his jaw and his obvious lack
of obsequious fear. Like many brutal and military men, he
had a secret passion for boys and young men. He decided
that he liked the handsome Lucanus, and he put his hand
on the young man's unyielding shoulder.

He was more at ease in speaking the vulgate, but now he
spoke in Greek to appease Lucanus, who was obviously not
liking him. "You are greatly honored," he said, and he noted
with pleasure the young man's broad shoulders and pillar-
like neck and finely carved facial planes and large blue eyes.

Lucanus did not move. He suddenly remembered the slave
trader, Linus, and a hot sickness came to him. Nevertheless,

he did not move, quelling his sudden hatred. He said, in the vulgate, "Caesar is very kind." He looked at Plotius, who was watching intently and frowning a little. He spoke to the young captain, disdaining to move from under the gripping brown hand on his shoulder.

"How shall I greet Caesar?"

Plotius had another struggle with a smile, because Lucanus had spoken to him in Greek, the language of the patricians and the educated. He said, gravely, "You enter his august presence, and when he notices you, which may not be immediately, and when he speaks, you drop upon your knees and touch your forehead to the floor."

Lucanus said, "But that posture is to honor gods only. The Jews prostrate themselves to Jehovah, but not to any man."

The Prefect pressed his fingers deeper into Lucanus' shoulder, in a fatherly manner. "My dear boy," he said, "have you not heard? Caesar is a god, and you give him the honors of a divinity."

Lucanus saw that Plotius was shaking his head at him anxiously. So, he said nothing. The Prefect, smiling at him fondly, said, "I myself shall conduct you to the Divine Augustus." He dismissed Plotius with a curt movement of his head, and Plotius, filled with misgivings, saluted and went away. Upon an affectionate gesture from the Prefect, Lucanus followed him.

The young physician had never seen a place like this, and had never even imagined such splendor and immensity. He even forgot the Prefect in his wonder and his attempt to see everything. They passed from huge hall to huge room and to endless other halls and other rooms, and the floors of each were of polychrome or snowy marble inlaid with shining red or blue stone or mosaics, each reflecting light as if from some inner radiance. Forests of fluted columns opened everywhere, of onyx, white marble, gilded metal or alabaster. Statues of gods and goddesses stood in arches, and busts of Caesar and his predecessors rested on small columns. The walls glimmered with mosaics depicting victories and episodes in the lives of the gods, and so cunningly were they wrought that they appeared as the most delicate and heroic paintings. Divans and chairs lined the walls, of ivory, teak and ebony, decorated with gold and upholstered in cushions of red and blue and white and yellow silks. Exquisite tables of marble and lemonwood were scattered near them holding gold and silver lamps not yet lighted, and little Alexandrian crystal vases filled with flowers, and silver and gold trays laden with brilliantly colored pomegranates and grapes and figs and white and black olives. Enormous ceilings seemed to float on the columns, either of glass or marble, but some were painted white and embossed in delicate designs in gold leaf. And everywhere, in every corner, stood tall vases filled with branching flowers, vases imported from Cathay, Persia and Indi, and shining with many subtle hues. Perfumed fountains scented the air.

There was not a hall or a room which was not filled and bustling with slaves and couriers and Praetorians and high military officers, and senators seeking an audience, and patricians and Augustales here for the same purpose. Some of the latter were seated, engaged in jokes or banter or gossip, and negligently helping themselves to the dainties on the tables. When they saw the Prefect they smiled at him charmingly, knowing his power, and exchanged some words with him. But they looked wonderingly at the young man he conducted with so solicitous an air. Seeing his appearance, the gentlemen winked at each other, put their fingers alongside their noses, and whispered ribald comments.

The Prefect and his charge passed through open colonnades, then into another profusion of rooms, until Lucanus felt dizzy. Sometimes he glimpsed the gardens through a window or guarded doorway, and the green of trees and grass and strongly tinted flowers contrasted with the cool whiteness within. Sometimes he thought he was seeing vast pictures set in walls, so vivid and unexpected did the gardens appear to him on their broad terraces. His ears were assailed by voices and by distant music and laughter, and, from outside, the songs of birds and the rush of giant fountains. Occasionally a lady of the palace passed him and his escort, her beautiful face covered with cosmetics, her black or copper or yellow hair caught in jeweled and golden nets, her dress of white or fragile color flowing about her. Invariably every lady stared frankly at Lucanus and smiled at him. Jewels flashed on white necks and bosoms and arms and wrists and fingers.

They reached bronze doors of such lofty proportions that Lucanus was amazed. Praetorians guarded it. At a gesture four of them swung open the doors and Lucanus saw before him a large but sparsely furnished library. Seated at a table, frowning and reading, was an unprepossessing man in a purple tunic and white toga, who slowly raised dark and resentful eyes.

"Hail, Divine Caesar," said the Prefect, saluting. "I have brought——"

"So I see," interrupted Tiberius in an acid voice. "You may leave, my good Prefect, and take your Praetorians with you, and close the door, and wait without."

This was incredible! Only the highest potentates had private audiences with Caesar, and then on only the rarest occasions. The Prefect stared. "Go," said Tiberius, and now his tone was coldly vitriolic. The Prefect, confounded, saluted again, gestured to his Praetorians, went out and the door was shut behind them.

Tiberius leaned back in his chair and gazed at Lucanus without speaking, and Lucanus gazed at him in return and with a candid curiosity. Here was Caesar, the very heart of the center of Roman might and power, and he was just an ordinary man, tall and lean, with a bald head, bitter features in a pallid face, and patches of eczema on his cheeks, which gleamed with an oily ointment.

Lucanus was not afraid of this most fearful man. He was only curious. Also, his physician's mind automatically commented on the fact that this skin rash had been wrongly treated. Moreover, his mind continued, Tiberius evidently suffered from some obscure form of anemia for which liver had been highly recommended by the Egyptian priest-physicians.

Tiberius, in that long silence, became aware of Lucanus' acute study, and he smiled. To Lucanus it was a disagreeable smile; if others had seen it they would have been astonished as its unusual benignity.

"Greetings, Lucanus, son of Diodorus Cyrinus," said Caesar.

Lucanus hesitated, and now he remembered what Plotius had told him. But he could not kneel to any man! So, in his youthfully sonorous voice, he replied:

"Greetings, Caesar."

Tiberius' smile widened in amusement; his lips were thin and taut, and showed small and yellowed teeth. He motioned to a chair near the table.

"Sit down, if you please," he said. Those waiting to see him, and who had been waiting for hours, would have gasped with amazement, for no one sat in the presence of

Caesar, except when dining. But Lucanus apparently did not know that, and so he simply bowed his head politely and seated himself, and waited.

"A pleasant day," said Tiberius.

"Yes," said Lucanus, and waited again.

Chapter Twenty-seven

Lucanus could not know that he had been given a great honor in being permitted to see Caesar alone with no one present, not even a guard. He could not know that the astute Tiberius had seen at once that here was a young man who could be absolutely trusted. Lucanus himself was quickly judging Tiberius. A ruthless and resentful man: what was it he resented? His faithless wife, his friends, his burdens, Rome? Lucanus felt a quick compassion.

Somewhere in the gardens beyond the library peacocks screeched, and there was the distant sound of higher music. But in the library the two men, one the mighty Caesar and the other only a physician, looked at each other frankly. Lucanus sniffed; a faint but disagreeable odor from the unguents on Tiberius' pimpled face came to him. He wished to speak, but he remembered that Caesar must always speak first. Tiberius, in his turn, saw that Lucanus did not fear him in the slightest. He wondered, for a moment, if the young man were a fool. Nevertheless, he was impressed by Lucanus' appearance.

Tiberius said, watching Lucanus closely, "May I commiserate with you, my good Lucanus, over the death of your father? A just and simple and heroic man. The last of the great Romans."

His voice, though grating and reluctant, carried sincerity with it. Lucanus smiled in gratitude. It was probably no secret to Tiberius that Diodorus had disdained his military qualities, yet Caesar could speak most kindly of him, and Lucanus, though his sorrow was renewed, thought that Tiberius was, himself, a just man. Tiberius leaned back in his chair and stared at the open window, which was ablaze with the sun.

"I have commanded that a statue of him be struck for the Senate portico," he said. He idly scratched at an irritable spot on his face. Lucanus smiled at this irony. The senators would have the doubtful pleasure of always seeing the statue of the one who had denounced them on their very threshold, armed with his marble sword. "Sire, you are very subtle," he said. Tiberius raised his black eyebrows. The young man was not a fool, then.

He said, "If I had ten thousand men like Diodorus Cyrinus in Rome then I should sleep well at night. But enough. I am concerned, Lucanus, with doing all in my power to alleviate the grief of the family, and to do honor to the memory of the tribune. I do not understand your letter. I have appointed you Chief Medical Officer in Rome, to the growling of the older physicians, and you have asked me to withdraw the appointment. I am curious to know why."

Lucanus colored. He was not aware that it was not only incredible, but dangerous, to refuse what Caesar offered. It was as if a moth had defied an eagle. He said, gravely, "Rome does not need me. That is what I wrote you, Sire. But the poor and the enslaved have need of my services in the provinces."

Tiberius was silent. His eyes narrowed and fixed themselves intently on the young man's handsome face. He plunged into thought. He was confronting something he could not understand, and which seemed mad to him. He thought of the old philosophers who had commanded that men treat his fellows kindly. Too, the priests in the temples of Rome exhorted the people to be gentlehearted and, in the names of the gods, to be just, honest and merciful. However, that was all mouthings. No man of sanity believed in it, considering the world as it was and had always been. Tiberius' mouth quirked in a smile.

"You are a physician, a citizen of Rome, the adopted son of a great and honorable man, the possessor of wealth," he said. "The doors of patricians and Augustales are open to you. What I have offered you is only the threshold. Yet you would give it all up for the purpose of ministering to the worthless poor and beggars and slaves!"

Did Lucanus belong to some strange obscure sect of Stoics, or was he dedicated to a peculiar and foreign god? Lucanus said, "Yes, for all else is as nothing to me."

"Why?"

Lucanus colored again. "Because otherwise my life would have no meaning."

Tiberius frowned. What meaning was there to life except

power and wealth and position? He reflected on his own
life, and his narrow features revealed an involuntary pain.
What meaning was there to his own life? he asked himself
in stark revelation. He had done what he could; he was
a careful administrator; he had tried to arouse pride in
the obdurate Senate and had wished to return its power
to it. Tacitus disliked him, but agreed that he was a man
of sound judgment. He, a soldier, wished for peace along
all the borders and the frontiers. He had added no extra
taxes, in spite of the voracious demands of the Roman
rabble for new benefits. When courtiers complained of personal injustices he coldly advised them to take the matter
to the courts and would not interfere himself.

He was trying, at this time, to save Rome, to restore some
of the qualities which had made her great. But a depraved
people would not accept their liberty and their former discipline and their character. He could feel a terrible premonition that their pollution would eventually pollute him,
and that, in anger, he would strike back at those who insisted on corrupting him. He thought of his wife; he thought
of those who hungered for his throne. He thought of his
only son, Drusus, a young man of violent passions but
limited mind, at present clumsily setting the Germanic
tribes against each other in Illyricum, believing, in his
simple way, that the gate of peace could be attained only
through blood.

Tiberius could feel the inexorable forces about him,
which would destroy him as a just man, which would degrade him to the level of a Roman dog, out of their greed,
their cheap politics, their exigencies, their lusts, and their
own urge to power. They had, he thought with awful clarity,
made of his life a nothingness, all of them, his wife, his
son, his generals, and the Senate. But more than all else,
the contemptible mobs of Rome, the insatiable, polyglot
mobs who looked on their Caesar as a deity equipped with
a cornucopia of endless benefits to reward the lazy, the
weak, the worthless, the irresponsible, the bottomless bellies
who would feed at the expense of industrious neighbors.
Soulless beasts! Suddenly Tiberius hated Rome.

He stared at Lucanus, who had spoken to him like a
schoolboy of meaning to life! "Must life have a meaning?"
he asked. "Even the gods have not given man a meaning
for his existence."

"Yes, Sire, that is true." Lucanus' face tightened. "But

we can assign some meaning to our lives ourselves. The meaning I have given myself is to alleviate pain and suffering, to save the dying, to prevent the encroachment of death."

"For what purpose?" asked Tiberius. "Death is the common lot. And pain, also, whether of the body or the mind. Too, of what worth are the poor and the slaves?"

"They are men," said Lucanus. "It is true that pain and death are inevitable. But often pain can be avoided, death made more comfortable, or delayed. Who can look upon the world of men without pity, and without desire to comfort it?"

Tiberius thought of Rome, and smiled darkly. Here was certainly a schoolboy prattler, a fresh-bearded amateur philosopher. He knew all about Lucanus, who had lived such a sheltered life, had never been part of a military campaign, and who had spent his years in a virtuous and peaceful household and in schools. He pitied the young man. He spoke of the stinking rabble as "men." He spoke of slaves as "men." No doubt he would even consider a venal senator a "man"! The nostrils of Tiberius contracted.

"Are you dedicated to some obscure god who has not as yet made his debut in Rome?" he asked Lucanus, with a faint and mocking smile.

He was surprised when Lucanus answered with extraordinary vehemence, "I am dedicated to no god!"

"You do not believe in the gods?" asked Tiberius.

Lucanus sat in silence for a moment, looking down at the vast marble table before him. Then he said, "I believe in God. He is our Enemy. He afflicts us without reason. Even an executioner reads out to his victim the crimes of which he has been accused, and for which he must die. He has not told us why we must suffer. He sentences us to death for being what we are, He who made us what we are."

"So you would console those who have been deprived of a consoler," said Tiberius. He was much amused. He again thought that Lucanus was more than simple-minded. He said, "You have studied in Alexandria. No doubt you encountered Jewish teachers there. When I was in Jerusalem I heard the people talk of a Messias, that is, a Comforter, a Redeemer, one who will deliver the Jews from Rome and set them high on thrones to govern the world. Is it not a foolish thought? But you will see that all men are alike, wishing power."

He unrolled Lucanus' letter and scanned it musingly. Then he said, not looking at the young man, "When I was younger, and on one of my campaigns, we were astonished to see a great star in the sky one night. It was at the time of the Saturnalia. It moved eastwards and then disappeared. My astronomers tell me that the star was seen everywhere, and was a Nova, and the astrologers spoke of a great doom to come upon the world. But I have heard from the East that the star led to the birthplace of a god. That was fourteen or more years ago. If a god had been born then, surely we should have known it by this time. You will see how superstitious men are."

Lucanus was seized by some great emotion. He remembered Joseph ben Gamliel and his story of the peasant boy who had disputed with the learned doctors and scholars in the Temple. He shook his head in denial.

Tiberius put down Lucanus' letter. Then he reached out for a large flat object wrapped in yellow silk. He carefully removed the silk and displayed the object. It was made of heavy gold in the form of a shield. Lucanus leaned forward to see it more closely. He saw the face, in profile, of Diodorus embossed on the golden shield, and below it a hand grasping a drawn short sword. Under it was a quotation from Homer in Greek:

> Without a sign, his sword the brave man draws,
> And asks no omen but his country's laws.

Below it was a line from Horace, in Latin:

> *Non omnis moriar* [I shall not wholly die].

Lucanus' eyes filled with tears. Tiberius said, with grim satisfaction, "This I have ordered made to be hung behind the lectern in the Senate."

Their eyes met with complete understanding.

Tiberius smoothed his hand gently over the shield. He said, "Have you considered what Diodorus would have wished you to do? He would have desired for you to serve Rome, as he served it."

"He was a great man, who believed in the freedom of

the individual," said Lucanus. "Though he would have disagreed with me, I know, he would still have desired me to
do what I felt was right."

"Nevertheless," said Tiberius, "you should honor his memory enough to spend some time in Rome, serving the people. You have said in your letter that you wish to leave
Rome at once. In justice to Diodorus I cannot grant this.
I command you to remain here for six months. If, at
the end of that period, you are still convinced that your
duty lies elsewhere, I shall relieve you."

The stubborn Lucanus was about to protest when he felt
the force of the imperial eyes upon him, and he realized
fully, for the first time, that this was Caesar, and that he
was helpless before his decrees. For Tiberius was not smiling now. After a long moment Lucanus bowed his head.

"So be it," he murmured. "In the name of Diodorus."

"I wish you attached to this household during that period," said Tiberius. He smiled tightly. "I may even consult
you, personally, on a few matters."

The thought of being virtually imprisoned in this immense palace appalled Lucanus, but he understood now that
he could not protest.

"The public medical officers are becoming indolent," said
Caesar. "I should like you to inspect their work and to
suggest improvements. Moreover, my household here is filled
with slaves and freedmen and Praetorians. Your services
to them will be appreciated. I am not entirely satisfied with
my own physicians."

Lucanus took a little heart. "If you will permit me, Sire,
may I suggest that the treatment for your eczema is
wrong?"

Tiberius' eyebrows flew up. "Indeed? What would you
suggest?" He was amused again.

"Oily unguents only increase the natural and infected
oils contained in pimples," said Lucanus, and he was a
physician again. "I prefer a paste of water and flour of
sulphur, applied after a strenuous washing with strong soap
twice a day. This has a drying and disinfecting influence."
He hesitated. "I also believe that Caesar has some affliction of the blood. If you would permit me——"

Intrigued, Tiberius nodded, and Lucanus rose and went
to him. He forgot again that this man was the formidable
and resistless power of a great and terrible empire. To Lucanus, he was only a man who was not in good health.

With firm and gentle fingers he pulled down Tiberius' eyelids, then opened his mouth and examined the pale membranes. Without permission he sat down again. "Are you conscious of a constant weariness, Sire? A lassitude? Does work tire you unduly? Does your breath become fast on the slightest exertion, and do you often feel faint and giddy?"

As the discussion of one's health delights even a Caesar, Tiberius nodded. "You have explained it exactly, my good Lucanus."

"Then you have anemia," said the young physician. "Not a very serious variety as yet, though it can become serious. What is your diet?"

"I live sparely," said Tiberius. "I am a soldier. I am no attender of orgies or banquets. I eat as a soldier, very frugally, some cheese, some goat's milk, some bread, a plain red wine, fruit and vegetables and, very occasionally, some meat or the leg of a fowl."

"The diet is wrong for a man in his sixth decade," said Lucanus, reprovingly. "I suggest fresh meat of bullocks three times a day, and a rich and heavy wine, and few vegetables and fruit only once a day. Fish is not very good for anemia, nor fowl. Best of all, I prescribe a large serving of the liver of a bullock at least once a day."

Tiberius made a wry face. "My cooks make a delicacy of the fatted liver of female pigs which have been fed quantities of ripe figs. I detest it. Nevertheless, as you are now my physician I shall eat bullock's liver for my evening meal."

He leaned his hard chin on the heel of his right hand and stared at Lucanus. "You are young," he said, "and you are possessed of extraordinary handsomeness. You are also wealthy and esteemed and a physician. Yet you are unhappy. If I were your age and endowed with your gifts, and were not Caesar, I should be the happiest of men. I see your distress. Why is this?"

Lucanus could not speak for a moment. Then he replied in a low tone, "One of life's sorrows is the impermanence of all joy."

Tiberius shrugged. "Even a schoolboy understands that. Shall we then deprive ourselves of pleasure, and joy, today because they are fleeting?"

Lucanus looked at him directly then, and knew, instantly, that here was a man deeply troubled, cynical and despairing. And he was filled with an answering despair because he had no words to comfort this mighty man, and no hope to give him. As he himself had lost Rubria, so had Tiberius lost his love, and they shared a common desolation. Tiberius looked into his eyes and saw the welling misery and the desire to help, and the young man's impotence to help him, and he was moved and was astonished that any creature could again move him.

He answered his own question quickly. "What the gods have given us is not to be refused, whether of good or evil, for what choice do we have? Even I cannot even drink myself into the temporary belief that the world is tolerable to a thinking man!"

He struck a bell on his table and the bronze doors swung massively open and Plotius and four Praetorians entered at once. Plotius glanced with concern at Lucanus, even as he saluted the Emperor, and he was astounded to see that the young man was leaning back in his ivory chair like an accepted equal.

"My good Plotius," said Tiberius, "you will conduct Lucanus to the best of quarters, where he will remain for some time as my honored guest. And you will send a message to his mother that her son is with me."

After Lucanus had left with Plotius, the Emperor remained alone for some time, his head in his palms. There were senators and Augustales and patricians waiting to see him, and magistrates, yet he did not call them. He thought of Lucanus' lack of affectation, his noble simplicity, and that iron quality in him which could not be shifted, and his manifest virtues. He could not decide whether Lucanus was a fool or a very wise man for all his youth. Then he laughed harshly to himself. Lucanus was in the Imperial Palace now. The word would soon spread that he was here as the guest of Caesar, and corruption would seep slowly and insidiously towards him like oily black water. Would he be engulfed in it? Surely he would, for men tended towards viciousness naturally and pollution was their natural element.

"We shall see!" said Tiberius, aloud, and laughed again, bitterly.

Chapter Twenty-eight

As Plotius led Lucanus away through other forests of white pillars and crowding statues, he said to him, "It is only my curiosity, but what did you say to Caesar?"

"What did I say?" Lucanus glanced at him in surprise. "Why, we had a conversation about various matters, and he was very understanding. I also prescribed for him." Plotius shook his head, amazed. Tiberius was known to be capricious. "You insisted on your refusal?" asked the young Praetorian.

"Certainly," said Lucanus, with some irritation. "I have said Caesar is very understanding. However, we agreed that I should remain in Rome, and in this household, for about six months, to honor the memory of Diodorus. After that time I shall depart."

Plotius thought he had not heard right, and he turned his head to stare blankly at the physician. A man, and a Greek, had refused Caesar, and had not only left his presence a free man but had been graciously treated as a person of the utmost importance. They went on together in silence, Lucanus interested in all about him and Plotius in a state of confusion. If the statues had suddenly attained life he could not have been more astonished and incredulous.

They entered a wide and private corridor guarded by two Praetorians who saluted and stared at Lucanus curiously. Lucanus saw that the white walls were exquisitely painted with scenes of the utmost licentiousness and depravity, depicting centaurs and satyrs, nymphs and gods, men and women disporting themselves in shameful ways. But the soft debauchery did not sicken or revolt Lucanus, who was a physician and found nothing obscene in the intricate and marvelous beauty and functions of the human body. To him these pictures were the imaginations only of perverted and impudent children, who found pleasure in beastlike diversions. He had seen much worse painted crudely on the walls and inns in Alexandria and Antioch; these, at least, had been executed by a supreme artist. One scene was so bewitchingly amusing that he stopped for a moment to smile at it. He said to Plotius, "This man had an excellent training in anatomy, and a sense of humor." The two young men studied this work of art then glanced at each other and laughed.

The Praetorians were everywhere, stiff and saluting, even in the hall leading to a most wonderful apartment with large open doors and windows looking out upon a wide and flowery and grassy terrace. Never had Lucanus seen such luxury, and never had he even imagined it. The vast and spacious room was walled in four different colors of marble, contrasting slabs of white, shining black, golden and pink, and the gleaming multicolored floor mirrored back the light of the sky and the hues of the garden. In the center of the room stood a large bed of gilded wood in the shape of a dolphin, inlaid with glittering jewels, mother-of-pearl, ivory and silver; upon it had been thrown a coverlet of intricately patterned silk like a profuse flower bed. Slender black or white marble pedestals, scattered over the room, held bronze and graceful statuettes of naked women holding aloft silver and golden lamps or objects of the most priceless art. Lemonwood and ebony and marble tables were covered with murrhine glass vases filled with flowers, so that the nimble spring breezes drifting through the doors and windows blew with fragrance. Voluptuous divans were disposed near the tables, clothed in bright silk, and near the walls waited many chairs, elaborately carved and gilded, with legs of ivory. A marvelous chest of hammered brass, studded with red gems, stood between the windows, which rippled with delicate lace curtains. A polished silver mirror hung over the chest. Beyond this restful and luxurious room was another, entirely of rosy marble; the sunken bath was at least twelve feet long and six feet wide, filled with warm and perfumed water, the bottom revealing a lascivious scene in the brightest of mosaics.

"This is a woman's apartment," said Lucanus, accustomed to the austerity of the homes of Diodorus. Two naked slaves entered, bowing before him, and he stared at them with admiration. They were a young man and a woman, tall and slender, and of such an incredible and dazzling blackness that they resembled polished marble rather than flesh. The valleys and undulations of their bodies had a pale sheen, as if dusted with silver, and their fine features, delicately carved and patrician, seemed created by the most gifted artist. The girl's black hair flowed in soft rippling waves down her smooth back, and her breasts were high

and pointed and glimmered with a glossy light. Neither she
nor the young man wore anything except heavy golden necklaces around their necks and hoops of gold in their ears,
which cast reflections on their mirroring skins.

"These are your servants," said Plotius. It seemed ridiculous to Lucanus that he should be in this apartment
with slaves to serve him alone. He wanted to protest, but
Plotius, with a wink, saluted and left him. He looked at
the boy and girl and did not know what to say, and they
gazed back at him with their full dark eyes and wide white
smiles. They waited for him to speak, so he said, awkwardly, "What are your names?"

The boy replied, bowing again, "My name is Nemo,
Master, and this is my twin sister, Nema. Command us.
We are at your service."

The girl walked gracefully to a table and poured a
gemmed goblet full of wine for Lucanus. He took it from her
delicate hand, entranced by her incredible beauty and the
perfection of her face and body. He put the goblet to his
lips and drank a little. He had never drunk such wine,
rosy and scented and sweetened with honey. The boy
brought him a tray of ripe figs rolled in chopped nuts, and
other sweetmeats. Lucanus ate one or two. He frowned.
"I do not need servants," he said. The boy and girl smiled
at him emptily, but they stood there like statues, unmoving,
as if what he had said was in a strange language. If he
was amazed by them, they were equally amazed by him,
for never had they seen such fairness of complexion, such
golden hair, and such handsomeness. The three young people stood and admired each other artlessly.

Another servant entered, bowing deeply, and informed
Lucanus that the Augusta, Julia, had commanded his appearance at her banquet to be given that evening at the
eighth hour. He retreated, leaving the three alone again to
their mutual contemplation. Then Lucanus said, like a youth,
"I suppose I cannot refuse. But I have nothing to wear
but what I stand in." He looked at Keptah's treasured toga,
which was travel-stained, and at his dusty, plain leather
sandals. Nemo went to the brass chest, opened it and brought
out a tunic of fine linen, with an embroidered border of
gold, and a toga as white as snow, also bordered in gold,
and a pair of golden sandals and a girdle of intricately
wrought gold inlaid with gems, and arm bracelets to match.

Like a merchant reverently displaying godlike wares, he draped the garments over one arm and held up the girdle and bracelets with the other hand.

"Well," said Lucanus. He considered the wardrobe effeminate; nevertheless, he put out his hand to smooth the fabric and examine the jewelry. "I shall feel like an actor," he remarked. Nemo indicated that the bath awaited him, and that he and his sister would wash him and anoint him with perfumed oils, and massage his body. But Lucanus revolted at this. The two slaves regarded him with astonishment, and looked mutely at each other.

"I have bathed alone since I was three," Lucanus explained. The slaves merely stared at him in disbelief. He lifted his voice. "I wish to be alone," he said. Puzzled, they bowed and left him, closing the doors behind them. They took up their stations outside and played soft music, to beguile him, with a flute and a lyre. Above the sound of the frail harmony Lucanus could hear the steady iron patrol of the Praetorian who was to guard him. He shook his head. He tested a divan, and was alarmed to feel himself almost swallowed in the capacious softness. He rose and went from one work of art to another. Never had he seen such artistry. The tiny statuettes were so beautifully executed that they revealed the most minute veins in their hands and throats and feet. He ran his fingers over them, and it seemed to him that they lived.

He was aroused by the sound of young masculine voices on the terrace outside his opened doors, and he went to them. Two young men, his age or younger, and completely naked, were wrestling on the grass. Their amber-colored bodies rippled with disciplined muscles, and after a few strenuous moments their flesh dripped with bright water. They were evidently accomplished athletes, practicing rather than playing, and their handsome faces were trained and intent and unsmiling. They grunted, expostulated and shouted, unaware of Lucanus watching them with deep interest. Sometimes they cursed foully. The young physician wondered if they were slaves. He observed their falls and their grips, their straining muscles, their dexterity and strength. Then he walked through the doors. They saw him and sprang apart and frowned.

"Greetings," said Lucanus, suddenly aware of unfriendliness and hostility.

They stared at him, insolently, and deliberately examined

his travel-stained clothing, his plain sandals. As if they had spoken, he felt their sneering comment on his lack of jewelry, and their opinion that he was no one of consequence, and their wonder that such as he was even present in the palace at all. They believed him an intruding freedman, a man who had in some way wandered into this apartment so near the apartments of the Augusta. But he did not know that he had also aroused their enmity because of his appearance, for though they were handsome youths they could not compare with him. Then one scowled darkly with suspicion. Was this stranger to be the new favorite of the capricious and insatiable Julia?

"Greetings," said one, surlily, and winked with ostentatious ridicule at his companion, who coughed loudly.

"I am Lucanus, a physician, and the son of Diodorus Cyrinus," said Lucanus, and felt heat in his cheeks.

"Oh," said one of the wrestlers in a heavy tone, indicating that he was not impressed. A physician. No doubt he was a former slave. Neither of the young men had ever heard of Diodorus. The other wrestler said, "You are here to attend us?"

"I am here as Caesar's guest," said Lucanus, coldly. Then his blue eyes flashed at the obvious insults which had been extended to him. He said, while they were dubiously recovering from his casual reference to Caesar, "You are good wrestlers, but clumsy. Your trainers lacked art. You could not compete for more than a moment with an accomplished athlete. You are amateurs. Doubtless, however, better training will transform you into mediocre wrestlers, if you work hard enough."

They were silent, breathing quickly. They still could not believe that Lucanus, dressed like a countryman, was actually the guest of Tiberius Caesar. And they hated him for his criticism. "No doubt," said one, "you are a much better wrestler."

"So I am," said Lucanus, leaning against the side of the door. He ate the sweetmeat in his hand, and pretended to be engrossed in enjoying it. Then he added, while their eyes blazed at him, "I was much superior even before I was trained in Alexandria."

He went on, while they remained silent, "I could wrestle better than you when I was ten years old." And he smiled at them sunnily.

One of them stepped forward, his eyes sparkling with rage.

"My name is Hyacinth," he said. "And I have ten sesterces which say that I can throw you in three seconds."

The other echoed him. "My name is Oris," he said, "and I have twelve sesterces which tell me I can throw you in two seconds."

Lucanus lounged easily against the side of the door and licked his sticky fingers. Then he felt of the purse at his belt, and said, "And I have fourteen sesterces which have just whispered to me that I can take each of you in turn and throw you in one second."

He wondered, justly, for a moment, if he should inform them that he had been instructed in a peculiar form of combat which had been imparted to him in Alexandria by a teacher from Cathay. No, he decided. They were too insolent, too insulting, too self-assured, and he disliked them. He suddenly straightened, threw aside Keptah's toga, and then stripped the coarse blue tunic from his body. He stood before them like a column of white marble, and they stepped back, uneasily. But his body, after a moment, seemed too smooth and elegant to them. They laughed, and one of them half crouched and came towards him on arched legs. This was Hyacinth.

Lucanus waited calmly. He merely raised his right arm and extended it. The gesture was languid, almost limp, and he did not bend his body. Oris barked a single laugh. Hyacinth's teeth glittered between taut lips. Then, like a corded snake, his arm lashed out towards Lucanus and his curved hand caught Lucanus' shoulder. Oris blinked, for something had blurred before him. Dumfounded, he saw Hyacinth lying on his back in the grass, his eyes protruding and fixed dazedly. Lucanus yawned. "Well?" he said to Oris, ignoring the other young man. "That was one second. And you?"

Oris moistened his lips. Hyacinth groaned from the grass, lying there like a fallen statue. Then Oris, who possessed much courage, leaped at Lucanus. It was as if a pliant thunderbolt had touched him. He felt himself hurtling into space and he joined Hyacinth neatly on the grass, shuddering all over.

Lucanus pulled on his tunic, smiling. "You owe me twenty-two sesterces," he said. "Remember to pay them."

The two young men lifted themselves to a sitting position, carefully examining themselves. They shook their heads to clear their bemused minds. "You are not hurt, not even bruised," said Lucanus, shaking out Keptah's toga. "Of course, if you have brains, which I doubt, they are slightly addled just now. They will clear, however."

"What did you do?" cried Hyacinth, tenderly rising to his feet. "I did not see you move! I felt nothing! Yet a second later I was flying through the air. It is magic!"

"Yes. Magic," echoed Oris. "Who can resist magic?"

Rubbing themselves, they glared at Lucanus, who lifted his golden eyebrows at them. "Magic, nonsense," he replied. "You are just amateurs. Did I not tell you?"

"I won a purse of gold at the Great Games!" shouted Hyacinth, coloring violently.

"And I won the second purse!" echoed Oris, grinding his teeth.

Lucanus laughed in their faces. "Then I should win two purses," he said. "Come, what else can you do?" He was exhilarated, his strong young body eager for more exercise. "Discus throwing? Spear casting? Ninepins? Boxing? Running? Broad standing jumps? Fencing? Surely you can do more than this childish tugging at each other."

He stepped back two paces, jumped forward, bent his legs and launched himself into the air. Incredulously two pairs of starting eyes followed him. His feet rose cleanly high above their lifted heads. He dropped back to the earth like a white cat.

"Match that," he said, without a hurried breath, "and you will owe me nothing."

There was the sound of enthusiastic clapping at the door, and they turned and saw Plotius there, laughing. Then Hyacinth and Oris were frightened. They knew Plotius well, and the high esteem in which Tiberius held him for his courage and his discretion and military qualities. Plotius sauntered out onto the grass and put his hand on Lucanus' shoulder. "What an exhibition!" he exclaimed. "My dear Lucanus, you could compete in all roles at the circus and have Rome at your feet! For my instruction, I beg you to engage me in fencing tomorrow." He looked at the two young wrestlers. "Who are these children?" he asked.

But Hyacinth and Oris dropped their heads and slunk away towards the end of the terrace. Plotius said, "They needed a lesson, those pampered darlings of the Divine Augusta. Take care they do not try to poison you at the banquet the Augusta is giving tonight in honor of Cybele; she is devoted to the widowed goddess. Doubtless she would like to be a widow, too. By the way, I could not follow your movements when you wrestled those boys. You did nothing but extend your arm, then, as they seized your shoulder you bent backwards and they were flying! Like Icarus, with the same result."

"I took advantage of them," said Lucanus, grinning happily. They went back into the room together, where Plotius inquired why the slaves were absent and playing music in the corridor outside. "They wanted to wash and smear me with perfumed oils," said Lucanus. He took off his tunic and jumped into the bath, where he swam a few feet, tossing back his wet and golden hair and raising a sparkling spray of water. Plotius squatted on the brim of the bath and watched him with intense admiration. "Never have I seen such a body," he said. Lucanus slipped through the water like white alabaster, and as smoothly. "Ah, but the ladies will love you!" Plotius added, shaking his helmeted head.

None of the young men had seen a lady at the distant end of the terrace who had emerged from her apartments at the sound of contentious voices. She had stood there, watching, her beautiful face expressionless in the sun. When Plotius appeared, she retreated back into her apartments, smiling. She went to her mirror and studied herself intently, and hummed a song under her breath.

Chapter Twenty-nine

Nemo assured Lucanus that he was as "radiant as a god" after the bath and anointing, from which Nema was banished, and the garbing in the white and gold garments. Lucanus had dismissed the accolade, though not after a surreptitious glance in the mirror. He was obsessed with a curious excitement. He never admitted it to himself, but the world of men and strange new experiences now invariably stirred him, as though he were newborn. He was about to be initiated into an atmosphere of which Diodorus had spoken with raging contempt. What Lucanus had seen so far had reluctantly moved him to admiration, for his Grecian eye was not insensible to beauty, and his soul was not so stern as to be displeased by the sight of loveliness and grandeur.

Now Lucanus stood alone in the sunset, looking down at the Imperial City from his height in the gardens outside his chambers. The city fell down before him like a dream, purple, gold and violet and white, swimming in a rosy mist through which occasionally ascended a winged statue on its high pillar, an incandescent dome, a snowy wall struck into light by the last beams of the sun, a carved and powerful arch, or the enormous stone fan of a rise of Olympian stairs. All that was unsightly in the city was hidden in that roseate mist which was beginning to flow not only in the skies but over the whole face of the city, so that it was like a diffusion of millions of roses melting into one vast drift through which emerged the shapes of visions. The winding Tiber curved in a vein of polished scarlet fire, pulsing through the soft pink fog, its bridges fragile, seemingly composed of silver and ivory. Even the distant hills flushed faintly and had no substance. And now the columns of the palace about Lucanus lifted in smooth and soaring pearl, their western sides blushing. The sound of near fountains muted to frail music; the birds' voices murmured in pure reverie. A scent of blossoms and jasmine and lilies suffused itself in the sweet and colored and ethereal air. The leaves of the myrtles gleamed like metal; the grass became an amethystine glisten.

Beguiled, and caught up in the tinted mirage which was the colossal city, Lucanus leaned against a column and listened and gazed. Then he became aware of the voice of Rome, below and yet above the voices of the birds near him. It was like the turning of a giant wheel, a muffled, Titanic thunder, constant and unremitting. Slowly Lucanus became impressed by a very odd perception. Pervading though the voice of the city was, it lacked a certain strenuousness, a certain ardor, a certain intensity, a certain masculinity. Lucanus then remembered what Diodorus had once told him: "It is an angerless city now, a city without manliness or heroism."

Diodorus, that most angry, heroic and manly man, had spoken well. The hushed roar of Rome was a surfeited roar. Its imperial splendor and might was a fatness. Monstrous and cruel it might be in its many aspects. But it was the monstrousness and cruelty of an aging man who had gorged himself too well and had forgotten the strength of limbs and the eagerness of the heart. It lay in the center of the world like a bloated if still potent satyr, reclining on a couch of crimson silk and gold, his hand grasping a sword, his other hand wearily lifting another goblet of wine to his mouth, the garland slipping on his head, his heavy chins resting on a bosom swelling like a woman's.

Angerless. Unmanly. That could be the epitaphium of
Rome. It had fallen in no battles. It had won them all. It
was the same. Triumph became death no less than defeat.
If a man died valiantly in armor on some battlefield of
principle or patriotism or in the protection of what he held
most dear, then he had not lived in vain. But those who
won battles for power and baubles lived ingloriously and
died as ingloriously, the object of later satires or a warning
to the ages. It was strange that empires never learned that
lesson, thought Lucanus. It was strange that men never
learned anything at all. All at once, gazing down at the rose-
drifting city, Lucanus was filled with a tremendous uneasiness, an ominous surety. He felt that he stood on the abyss
of something which he could not yet discern; it was as if
something had changed, quickened, from the immense eternities.

The rosy mist over the city diminished. A lilac dusk, like
a vast eddy, glided over Rome, flowed into the gardens
where Lucanus stood. The moon lifted slowly into the hollow
sky. The birds were silenced, the fountains clearer. Nemo
touched Lucanus' arm, and the young Greek started and
turned to the slave. "It is the eighth hour, Master," said
Nemo. Lucanus glanced once more down at the city. He murmured, "No. It is the eleventh hour." A flare of red torches
licked up from the violet dusk below, thousands upon thousands of torches like quick and restless tongues. To Lucanus
it resembled the beginning of a conflagration.

A few moments later he was part of a white-robed throng
of men and women moving through the halls and the vast
rooms, which were now lighted with hundreds of lamps. The
women walked with hard assurance among their men, for
Rome, as Diodorus had bitterly remarked, was now a woman's
city, with arrogant women directing their men in shrill and
insolent voices. It was a covert matriarchy, corrupt, selfish,
brazen-breasted, insistent and greedy. It was for Roman
women that Roman legions fought; it was for Roman women
and their idle bodies that galleons streamed from every port
with their burdens of luxuries and foods and silks and jewels.
It was for Roman women that the banners burst over cities
and towns and the trumpets blazed. They could not invade
the Senate, but they were there in the persons of their husbands or sons or lovers. The marts and the markets, feverish with the exchange of gold and the fury of investments,

might be sounding with the voices of men, but the strident echo was the echo of women. They owned the wealth of Rome. Their soft brutality sounded in the clangor of the chains of millions of slaves.

As Lucanus walked among the throng towards Julia's court he was aware that those hastening to the festivities were becoming more numerous. It was as if the statues of gods and goddesses in togas and stolas were leaving their porticoes and niches and joining the men and women, and as if the few who remained in their places looked down with contempt or celestial indifference at the deserters. I have heard only of the world by hearsay, Lucanus marveled to himself. He looked at the beautiful, depraved faces of the women, over-laid with cosmetics; he saw their jewels, their black, brown, gold or bronze hair held in jeweled nets or bound in ribbons, in the Grecian manner. A mist of perfume floated from their bodies and their garments. Their white or honey-colored necks shimmered with gems, and their glossy arms were circled with gold and their fingers glittered. Among them were famous courtesans and former slaves freed by besotted mas-ters, and notorious women. It was impossible to tell them apart from the ladies of great houses and of great names. The married women could be recognized only by their stolas from the unmarried, whose dress had a false simplicity, and whose faces were as worldly and as disillusioned as the matrons' and the infamous women's. There was not a shy eye, a wondering young smile or a tender glance among them, only boldness and greed and a looking about to see if they were admired. A high hum of incoherent conversation hovered over them.

The men were no less ambiguous. The senators could be recognized by their red sandals, but Augustale was not dis-tinguishable from gladiator, or freedmen from patrician, merchant from men of brilliant name. Lucanus wondered if those who wore the haughtiest airs were not the basest, and if those who were the daintiest might not have risen through fortune from some gutter. Diodorus had often said that Augustus, Gaius Octavius, would never have permitted the lowborn into his palace, no matter his present wealth or position. But his degraded daughter, Julia, wife of Tiberius, frequently declaimed her democracy. To her, she had de-clared, a gladiator of fame was as welcome as a senator. She asked only that her women guests be amusing, and hinted that among concubines and courtesans she had frequently discovered more wit than among the wives and daughters of noble houses.

Her own father once exiled her for her strumpet behavior. Why he had forced her upon Tiberius remained an enigma, for Augustus had had some affection and admiration for the present Caesar. It was possible that Augustus had believed that Tiberius, cold, just, and noted for his lack of susceptibility to women, and his private virtue, might have a quieting effect on Julia.

The sound of hurrying rose above the strains of distant music. Lucanus caught glimpses of feet shod in silver or gold slippers or jeweled and brocaded material. The men laughed and murmured, staring about them insolently. The white river flowed up a low wide staircase and through long courts. Some of the ladies, in particular, looked at Lucanus curiously through lashes heavily coated with kohl, or smiled at him invitingly. Once he saw a pair of violet eyes startlingly like those of Sara bas Elazar's, and he was suddenly shocked. Once a profile reminded him of Rubria, and he was shocked again. It angered him that any of these women could resemble the girls he had loved, and whom he still loved. He bent his head so that he could no longer see them. The men darted suspicious glances at him and asked each other who he was. The lamps poured down their shifting light on the throng, and the jewels danced in it, and the predatory eyes.

Lucanus thought: Cicero had lamented that though the forms of the Republic were still celebrated the Republic no longer existed. Among these men and women there was no love for their country, no celebration of freedom, no honor for the mighty dead who had founded their nation and their institutions. Their mouths exhaled perfume from the lozenges they had sucked. To Lucanus they exhaled corruption. All at once he was profoundly depressed. He thought of his home longingly. He had the impression that he was naked in the throng, that every part of him was vulnerable.

A sweet wind blew in his face, and he looked up to see that he was being borne along a vast open portico, where, because the weather was so mild and fresh, the banquet had been laid. The portico looked out on a great garden, decorated with a tangle of shining lights which reflected themselves in the dew on the dark grass. The very statues had been illuminated in various hues so that they stood in colored

waters like figures of pale fire. Flowers had been strewn upon
the earth, or stood in tall vases, so that the warm air palpitated with their scent. The portico, also illuminated, shone
like carved snow against the black sky, and about it had
been erected artificial grottoes of mosses and flowers, in
which stood the most exquisite statues, slyly beckoning, and
glimmering in the moonlight. Musicians played unseen, with
flute and harp and lute. The tables set in the portico were
covered with crimson cloths, banded with gold and elaborately embroidered with brilliant threads, and the divans
about them were similarly decorated, and waiting. Far below
lay the vociferous city, trembling with lamps, the red torches
licking, and from it came a distant growling sound like a
forest of beasts.

The guests began to seat themselves with much anticipatory
laughter, and Lucanus stood, uncertain, near a glowing pillar.
He looked at the trees encircling the gardens as if waiting
for someone; the branches swung with lamps of strange and
fantastic shapes, and the light poured through tinted glass.
Slaves, male and female, beautiful as young gods and sirens,
and naked as statues, stood waiting for the guests to take
their places, the women in chairs of ivory and ebony inlaid
with precious metal, and the men on the divans. Lucanus
did not know what to do, for all seemed to know their
places. The voices of the guests became vehement with excitement, so that the garden and the portico echoed as if with
parrots, or lustful monkeys. The music was obliterated; only
occasionally, like a harmonious mendicant, was it heard,
when the clamor momentarily dropped. The faces of the
slaves were impassive and lovely. A bevy of little girls
now appeared, to anoint the feet of the guests with balm,
and there was an innocence about their nakedness. Stewards
appeared, bearing large silver bowls full of snow in which
had been inserted bottles of wine, and they poured this into
jeweled goblets wreathed with green ivy. The scent of the
gold or ruby liquid mingled with the scent of the flowers
and the grass. The guests tipped a little wine in libation,
and Lucanus remembered the offering to the Unknown God,
and it seemed to him that his whole body winced with bereavement and loneliness. He still stood by the pillar. Though
the stewards served wine, there was nothing as yet on the
silken tables but flowers and goblets. The guests were waiting. They talked of the latest divorces, the latest investments,
of the races and the games, and looked to the robed gladiators

for comments. Their vivacious chatter, so trivial, so malicious, was as alien to Lucanus' ears as the chattering of a multitude of raucous birds. He heard famous and ancient names mingled with scandal of the most debauched kind. A great lady, it was asserted with much laughter, had just taken her tenth lover, but this one was a female slave. A girl vehemently asserted that Cupid had visited her one night, and she described the visit with lascivious details. A senator began to quarrel with another senator about his investments in the Land of Israel; he declared that his men had discovered the mines of Solomon. The second senator assured him that he had been defrauded, and that he should bring back his discoverers in chains. A gladiator, gulping his fine wine, declared that he could strangle a lion with his bare hands. Bets were immediately made for the next games.

The air became oppressive; the gardens had a secret and lecherous appearance in the light of the moon. The guests drank more and more, and became restless, and their voices stretched for higher volume. A few ladies nearby eyed Lucanus with sudden interest. All the women had now discarded the classic stola; they sat revealed in the thinnest and finest of colored silks and linens and gemmed brocades, which, though they covered their breasts, revealed every detail of curve and nipple. Their smooth shoulders glistened in the lamplight; their foreheads were damp, their lips becoming more full and lustrous and red. Some leaned from their chairs and reclined their bodies against the men, inviting kisses on throat and shoulder and mouth. Slaves had placed garlands of roses on all heads, and now the perfume of garden and grass and flowers and balsams flowed through the portico. The shimmer of jewels hurt Lucanus' eyes; the lamps seemed to take on a greater blaze and intensity of hue. He was hungry, and embarrassed in his isolation near the pillar. The music mingled with the fragrant clatter of the fountains, when it could be heard over the voices. He noticed that at the head of the U-shaped table stood a large divan covered with imperial purple and filled with Syrian cushions. So the guests were waiting for the Augusta, Julia. He did not know that it was her custom to permit her guests to become quite drunk before making her appearance, so that the fact that she was no longer young would be lost in a haze. The Alexandrian vases which held the table flowers began to sparkle with too much color to Lucanus. He was very bored. Diodorus had spoken of orgies and "debauchery." It seemed excessively dull to the young Greek. The hoarsening voices of the men annoyed him; the shrill and insistent tones of the women were like the scratching of a fingernail on his eardrums.

A deferential hand touched his arm. One of the hall over- seers, who had been scanning the stewards for any delin- quency, stood beside him.

"Master, you have not found your place?" he murmured.

"No," said Lucanus, shortly. "I do not know if I have a place." He hesitated. "I am Lucanus, the son of Diodorus Cyrinus, and I have not been here before."

The overseer stared at him with horror. He bowed so deeply that his head fell to the level of Lucanus' knees. Then he said in a trembling voice, "But, Master! You are to seat yourself on the divan of the Augusta!" His voice became terrible, and he cast his eyes on the other overseers, who came hurrying. He said, "Here is the honored guest, and none has escorted him to his place! There will be lashings tomorrow!"

The nearby guests stopped their conversation to stare. Luca- nus, flushing, moved backwards, and his feet were engulfed in one of the Persian rugs which covered the white marble floor of the portico. "No," he said, "it is my fault, no other's."

"You were not escorted here, Master?" asked the first over- seer, as the others gathered about Lucanus, to his greater embarrassment. Then Lucanus remembered. Plotius had men- tioned that he would bring him here himself, but Lucanus had forgotten to wait. He added, hastily, "I had an escort, Plotius of the Praetorians, but I did not wait for him."

The overseer groaned. His fellows echoed him. They bowed in a body. More and more guests became interested. The overseers surrounded Lucanus like a bodyguard and cere- moniously conducted him to the purple divan. A deep silence fell on the guests as Lucanus seated himself, and every eye fastened itself on him. A garland was placed on his head; a child removed his sandals and anointed his feet. Wine was poured for him. His face was very red, and he sweated. He did not know where to look, but finally glanced at the end of the portico. Plotius was there, trying to frown but succeeding only in looking highly amused. Lucanus took a deep draught of the wine. The silence in the portico, the craning to see him, was unnerving. Now the music rose exuberantly, accompanied by many sweet voices, and the fountains sang to the moon.

The buttocks of Lucanus were swallowed in the softness of the divan. He could not bring himself to recline as the other men were reclining. He did lean an elbow on a cushion, and inwardly cursed Plotius, the guests, himself, Julia, and then Tiberius. He saw himself as a pleb in this gathering, a yokel fresh from the fields. And he was newly angered.

Then a twittering ripple ran along the guests, uttering his name. It was as if a turbulent wind were agitating rows of flowers, for gaudy jewels and rich tints and dark and alabaster complexions and gay tunics and vibrant eyes and lustrous hair mingled in ranks of confused exuberance and excitement under the swaying and prismatic lamps. The men raised themselves on their couches; the women preened, their white teeth sparkling through their red lips as they smiled boldly at Lucanus. His hands tightened about the gem-crusted goblet, and he drank another draught.

"Lucanus!" ran the murmurs and exclamations. "Lucanus, son of Diodorus!"

Then all burst into friendly laughter, and goblets were lifted to him, and the men inclined their heads, and the hands of the women fluttered about their carefully arranged hair in which jewels flashed like raindrops. "Welcome! Greetings!" the guests cried. "Welcome, noble Lucanus!" The young man tried to smile; he was most acutely uncomfortable. Plotius, he saw, was ironically bowing to him also, and then, involuntarily, he laughed. A steward was at his elbow again, filling his goblet. The wine was sweetened, and heady. The moon gleamed down through the clear air and the stars twinkled above the garden and the garish lamps swung, and the illuminated fountains threw up light on the statues within them.

Suddenly a trumpet blazed, a single trumpet, and the guests rose with one quick rustle, waiting. Lucanus had some difficulty rising, for the divan was too soft and deep, and he was beginning to feel the wine. Julia, accompanied by Hyacinth and Oris, the athletes, had appeared in the portico.

She was, Lucanus saw with considerable disgust, dressed in the old Cretan style. She was not tall, nor was she short, and her figure was voluptuous, and her flesh very white. Her tight dress, copied after those of the Cretan women, had been woven of gold, and it covered all of her body, including

the arms, with the exception of her naked breasts, whose
nipples had been tinted scarlet, and the dress flared from her
hips downward in pleats embroidered with jewels and painted
with the plumes of peacocks. She was proud of her bosom,
so flagrantly displayed, for it was snowy, and had a polished
sheen, and was faultlessly curved and lifted. Her hair, of a
russet color like old wine, had been high and elaborately
dressed, and, to carry out her Cretan theme, she had pinned
a tiny little hat like a colorful moth blazing with gems on
the very top of her rippling curls. The gold cloth of her
dress, molded to the hip as if plastered upon her, the radiance
of her jewelry, the coruscation of her hat blended together
to dazzle the eye, to stun it with magnificence. All the movements were sensual, and calculated, and, to Lucanus at least,
vulgar and carnal, and the metallic dress accentuated them.

The guests applauded wildly at this vision of scintillating
light. She paused at a little distance to acknowledge the accolade, and Lucanus saw her face, first in profile then full.
The profile, he saw, had a certain cool aloofness, reminding
him of a statue of Pallas Athene, but when she turned her
countenance it was broad, imperious and hardened, and more
than a trifle coarse. Her skin was excellent, and its fine
wrinkles had been skillfully hidden under layers of rosy
powder and paint; her strange eyes were like lapis lazuli between stiff black lashes sprinkled with gold dust; her mouth,
with its full and pouting lower lip, gleamed with red ointment. She had a short, somewhat wide nose, with haughtily
distended nostrils. She gave an impression at once cruel and
sentimental, proud and tawdry, arrogant yet too familiar. To
Lucanus she had a kind of barbaric fierceness, and he thought
of the cold and prudish Tiberius who was her husband, and
of the old soldier, Augustus Caesar, Gaius Octavius, who had
been her father. He tried not to look at the wanton display of
her breasts, which embarrassed him.

Hyacinth and Oris, familiarly touching her elbows, conducted her towards her imperial divan, and for the first time
she looked at Lucanus. Her lips parted in a seductive smile,
arch and welcoming, and it was a charming smile, like a
girl's. He bowed to her, and kept his head bowed as she
gracefully seated herself with a metallic whisper, and he was
almost overpowered by her musky perfume. Then he was
frightened, seeing that it was her will that Hyacinth and Oris,
who had scowled at recognizing him, had been seated together at her right hand and Lucanus was to sit at her left.

"Greetings, noble Lucanus," she said to the young man. She had the husky masculine voice of the low-bred woman, for all she was of a great family.

"Greetings, Augusta," he murmured in reply, and helplessly allowed himself to be swallowed by the divan again. The guests seated themselves with the sound of a small wind, and the music became higher and wilder and the singers sang a song of adulation to a goddess. Julia was in a pleasant mood. She was often dangerously bored and discontented, but tonight she was exhilarated. Hyacinth and Oris, in rosy tunics fastened with golden belts, sulked, and glared at Lucanus, which amused the Empress. The guests, believing the young Greek to be the new favorite, as he, unknown to himself, truly was, smiled at him winningly and with eagerness. But Julia, as yet, save for her welcome, ignored him. Instead, she tormented Hyacinth and Oris with special smiles, special light caresses on cheek and neck with her jeweled hand, special murmurings.

Now a horde of servants entered the portico, bearing steaming dishes and trays filled with grapes and figs and olives and other delicacies. Golden plates were placed before the guests, the goblets refilled. At each plate the servants laid golden knives, spoons of varied shapes, and toothpicks, and little bowls of warm scented water, and embroidered napkins. Curiosity overcame Lucanus' uneasiness. He studied the first course, momentarily deaf to the rise of clamorous voices and the music and Julia. A huge silver tray with indentations was filled with tiny dormice, broiled in oil and honey and dusted with poppy seeds. Other trays held spiced eggs, kidneys simmered in oil, little smoked fish, goose liver over which had been poured a pungent sauce, and boiled heads of calves. The servants milled about the guests, offering fresh napkins after fingers had been dipped into the bowls to cleanse them of oil and sauces, and refilling goblets with honeyed wine, and proffering bread in curious shapes, and very hot.

Never had Lucanus seen such a profusion of food. Naïvely, he thought this the whole feast. He shuddered at the dormice, ate a little of the liver, and a piece of cheese. The wine was beginning to give him a distorted view of the table, too brilliant, too colorful, too intense with light. His discomfort at being so close to Julia, whose breast was becoming intrusive, increased. His ears rang with voices, laughter and music, and his head throbbed. To cool his fevered mouth he ate a pomegranate, a few dates, a handful of grapes. They did not abate his fever, and he found himself gulping the snow-chilled wine again.

There came a pause in the feasting. Servants removed soiled dishes and tableware, and replaced napkins again. No one, as yet, had spoken to Lucanus. The guests were waiting for Julia to speak to him first, and they would catch, in her voice, an intonation as to the status of the favorite and how he should be addressed and treated. But Julia was half reclining now against the body of Hyacinth. The other women, too, had abandoned their chairs, which had been deftly removed by servants, and reclined on the couches nearest them, their bodies wantonly pressed to the flesh of the men. Faces flushed; garlands slipped on heads; the laughter rose to a raucous pitch. Here and there men had snatched the tunics from the shoulders and the breasts of a few young women and were kissing them ardently. Lucanus, though a physician, was freshly uncomfortable and embarrassed. So this was what the emancipation of Roman women had led to, this vulgar and unabashed wantonness, this witless shrieking, this half-drunken quarreling, this contentious chatter of business, gossip and politics, this effrontery, this noisy insistence! He thought of Aurelia and his mother, Iris, skilled in household duties, gentleness, the care of children, the cherishing of husbands. They might have known little of Virgil or Homer, nor could they have discussed military campaigns or legal suits of prominence in the public courts, as these women had done earlier, but they could bring peace and joy to a home, and honor, and their children and their husbands revered them, and divorce and adultery were unknown. Lucanus mused. Did a nation decline and decay when women won dominance and when no doors of law, business or politics were closed to them, or did the dominance of women merely indicate that a nation was decaying?

Lucanus thought of the sweet young Rubria, and the shy and lovely Sara bas Elazar. It suddenly seemed incredible to him that they had existed in this age at all. All at once he longed for Sara with a desperate passion, and he forgot his vows. His hands clenched on his knees as he listened to the women at the table. Though the portico was open and the lighted gardens merged with it, the air within the columns was polluted with scents and hot sweat. Suddenly Julia's sibilant thigh moved against his stealthily, though she affected to be engrossed in conversation with others.

Lucanus became rigid with a new access of intense disgust,

loathing and shame. This woman was the Augusta, Julia, Empress of the world, wife of Tiberius, and her voice, her gestures, her provocative motions under the narrow golden dress were the characteristics of a harlot, a dissolute woman of the streets. The thigh pressed his more insistently, and he could not move. She was lying half in profile to him; her voluptuous breasts bulged, the scarlet nipples pointing, the metallic fabric of the dress outlining every flaunting curve and indentation of her body, including the umbilicus. The musky scent of her had a carrion overtone to the young man.

The clash of cymbals announced another course in the feast, and the slaves entered triumphantly bearing aloft a huge silver platter on which lay a great living fish, iridescent of scales, and flopping desperately in its last agonies. Lucanus, horrified, could see its starting eyes, now filming, and the lash of its rainbow tail. Ceremoniously the fish was carried about among the applauding guests, who examined the poor creature with drunken exclamations. In the meantime other servants set up a copper cauldron steaming with aromatic water in the center of the U tables, and the chief cook appeared with a small serving table covered with embroidered white muslin. The fish bearers brought the frantically struggling fish to him, and he caught it in his vast hands and thrust it into the pot. Immediately the water swirled and the odor of spices and herbs mixed with volumes of steam.

The cook, with the help of two servants who acted in a ceremonious manner, finally withdrew the fish and laid it on a waiting wooden block, where it was prepared for the table. The fragrance of it now mingled with all the other odors; the flesh was pink and juicy. It was served in a little pool of piquant sauce of mingled wine and cloves and garlic and the juice of lemons. Lucanus looked at his portion and could not eat it. All at once he was nauseated. He ate another piece of cheese, some lettuce and carrots and leeks, a few olives and grapes, a piece of bread, and he drank another goblet of wine.

Julia, in order to enjoy the fish, raised herself on her elbow and inclined her body crosswise on the couch. This removed her thigh. For the first time she spoke to Lucanus in conversation, and with another of her charming smiles. "You do not like the fish, Lucanus?" she asked, and now, for some peculiar reason, her voice was not so objectionable to the young Greek, whose head was swimming curiously.

Her breast was against his shoulder now, and his eye could

not help straying to it, and he thought, Though she is not young, she has considerable beauty, if no shame. He murmured, "I come from an austere family, and luxuries are unknown to me."

She smiled, and a deep pink dimple appeared at the corner of her red mouth. She lifted her plucked and gold-dusted eyebrows quizzically. "We must remedy the austerity," she said. She touched his cheek lightly with the back of her soft hand, then pinched it. The word ran quickly, even among the drunken diners. Julia had made her favors known. From this time on this handsome young Greek would be a formidable power in the palace, and some of the senators, less drunk than the others, meditated briefly. Hyacinth and Oris flushed, exchanged glances, then gave Lucanus a look of the deepest hatred, which he ignored. The two athletes fell to brooding.

Perhaps the musicians and the singers had moved closer, in the background, to the tables, for Lucanus could hear them with a strong and sudden clarity. A woman with a rich and eloquent voice began to sing.

> *"Thou dost ask me why I weep, my maid.*
> *Now hark, while I tell thee why.*
> *I weep for a corpse that is barely laid,*
> *And the light in a vanished eye.*
> *For lips I loved and no longer love:*
> *For these do I groan and sigh.*
>
> *"Better it is to love in vain*
> *And yearn for an unknown bliss,*
> *And to be enthralled in an endless pain*
> *For a joy I must ever miss,*
> *Than it is to yawn in fulfilled desire*
> *And flee from an offered kiss!"*

Julia's lips were against Lucanus' ear, and he kept himself from shrinking, partly from a warning instinct and partly because he could not insult even this debauched woman. She whispered, " 'And yearn for an unknown bliss!' "

Now Lucanus understood what she intended for him, as he looked into her strange, dilated eyes and saw the wetness of her lips and the swelling of her breast. He was appalled, and his disgust was a strong nausea in his throat. Julia's blandishments had not been the mere flirtatiousness of a

shameful woman, bestowed on any man. They had been invitations and commands. A sudden anger seized him, and a
feeling of personal degradation. Julia was holding her own
goblet to his lips, and he was forced to drink the wine.
Though he was filled with stormy emotions, he was also dizzy.
The tables and their occupants swayed gently before his eyes,
as if they floated on a vessel. Lucanus said to himself, unable
to move from the hand that now lay against his neck, ca-
ressingly, I am not only disgusted and frightened and repelled;
I am drunk and hot. Julia's fingers were lightly and delicately
exploring his neck, and so expert were her touches, so knowing, that he felt an answering heat. Urges and thrills suddenly
ran over his flesh; his sense of shame only heightened them.
He gulped wine.

Julia laughed softly and understandingly. She removed her
hand, for the servants were bearing in another even huger
platter on which lay a wheel of young suckling pigs wallowing
brownly and juicily in a pungent sauce and roasted oranges
and hearts of artichokes. This was accompanied by other
platters containing roasted veal and assorted delicacies. The
servants again wiped the fingers of the guests and gave fresh
napkins.

The noise in the portico took on formidable proportions.
Shrieks of wild laughter burst from the women, and hoarse
shouts from the men. The smack of kisses, the smack of
palms against soft flesh, resounded against the music. Imita-
ting Julia, the women had stripped to the waist, and white,
pink and amber breasts gleamed in the lamplight. Lucanus
stared avidly; he was no longer the objective physician; he
did not think of this turbulence of naked bosoms as a display
of mere mammalian organs. The writhing thighs of the
women fascinated him, and stirred him. He forgot to abstain
from the wine, and as his goblet was refilled he drank of it
thirstily. The whole bacchanalian scene merged into one great
surge of glittering color, nudity, sensual odors and blazing
many-hued lights. It seemed to him that the columns of the
portico had a moonlike glimmer of their own, and were illuminated from within, and that the statues in the entrances
to the grottoes were alive and beckoning solely to him with
obscene and libertine gestures.

He started. Julia's lips were against his throat, and her
hand wandered. A powerful urge filled him. She seemed to
him the most beautiful and desirable of women. He shuddered
with a shameful ecstasy. Her eyes, smoldering, laughed up at

him, and she nodded as if satisfied, and lifted herself away from him, wetting her pulsing mouth. Then she capriciously and mockingly devoted herself to her former favorites, who had been meditating Lucanus' death. But the traces her fingers had left on Lucanus burned like fire.

Time became endless for Lucanus, but also hotly imminent, dazzling, seething with clangorous desires, confusion, momentary darknesses and silences filled with shifting rainbows and stupendous clamorings. He kept blinking his eyes to clear them of mists of rose and silver and blue and scarlet; his ears thundered with voices and music. Once he asked himself, believing the question the most serious and important in the world: Who am I? There were delightful tastes on his tongue; the wine was maddening. He lurched against the table; he clung to the edge of the couch for fear of falling off, for it swung under him. He was certain that his thoughts contained the wisdom of the ages, that he had come on tremendous secrets gushing in to him from the eternities. Julia's left hand, on his thigh, seemed a delicious pressure. I have missed so much, he thought solemnly, and his eyes filled with tears of self-pity. This company was delightful, and all the guests perfect as gods and goddesses, charming, wonderful in their friendship, sophisticated and loving. The moon was the shield of Artemis; he studied it, expecting that the radiant virgin goddess would emerge from behind it, argent in her beauty. The statues danced in the grottoes frenziedly. The wreath of rosebuds slipped on Lucanus' head, and he meticulously, and with slow and careful gestures, replaced it in the proper position. For some reason this appeared absolutely necessary. I am certainly not drunk, he said to himself, severely. It is just that never before have I known what it is to live. Again his eyes wet with tears, and he sobbed for his former deprived self. His hands and feet were numb, but his body throbbed. He did not think of Rubria and Sara. But the diffused image of them remained, like faceless ghosts, heightening his present dazed exhilaration. His limbs sprawled.

Eons passed, quivering with pleasure, with immeasurable thoughts, with conversation. Lucanus came to himself, very briefly, to discover that he was conversing in happy earnestness with a lady near him, and, apparently, had been so conversing for some time. But what he had said to hold her in such black-eyed enthrallment he did not know. He shook his head, as if puzzled, and she murmured to him, "You speak ravishingly. Continue." He shook his head again, and that was another shining hiatus. Yet all his senses were illuminated, heightened; he retired within himself for a while to reflect joyously on this. He was excessively drunk.

The slaves carried out a broad platform of wood and placed it on the grass near the portico. They threw baskets of rose leaves over the guests and sprayed the warm air with perfume. The moon seemed to step closer, until she seemed within a hand's touch, and a brisk breeze rose from the garden and the tops of cypresses crowned themselves with spikes of silver fire. Dancers appeared, wrestlers, singers, actors, but they performed almost unnoticed, for the majority of the guests were either snoring noisily, engaged with a neighbor, or blinking stupidly. But Lucanus watched the athletes, trying to see them through a rosy mist. He said to the lady whom he had enthralled, "They are a poor demonstration." Oris was asleep, but Hyacinth heard Lucanus' words and cried, "They do not use magic! They are honest men." His eye sparkled with rage and jealousy.

Lucanus said with great solemnity, "I could vanquish them all." He drank, nodded, and repeated with heavy emphasis, "I could vanquish them all."

Julia turned to him and kissed his shoulder and murmured, "Yes, so I know, my divine Apollo."

There was a sharp blare of trumpets, and the colored lamps beamed more resplendently on the platform. Slaves threw roses upon it. Five young men, their legs and feet covered to resemble the goatish legs and hoofs of Pan, their loins circled with wreaths of red poppies, sprang upon the platform with high and delirious cries. They held pipes to their lips, and, accompanied by the other music, filled the air with thin and half-mad pipings. Their wild and vivid eyes darted about like dragonflies as they danced, cavorted and bounded into the air. The pipes assaulted the ear, and even those who snored and drowsed heavily awakened and became interested. The dark gardens were a perfect background for these sensually dancing young men; their cloven hoofs rattled and tapped on the platform; sweat streamed from them; they panted; they circled and pranced, their poppy-covered loins heaving. Their gestures were lewd and inviting, their savagely grinning faces excited passions. The music and the pipings became madder, faster, more demanding.

A group of girls dressed like nymphs in floating white transparent dresses, and crowned with lilies, blew upon the platform, their right arms lifted and holding gossamer veils before their pretty faces. Demurely they danced, their glances shy and apparently unaware of the Pans leaping about them. They evaded clutching hands, singing softly to themselves. The Pans became frenzied; their red tongues emerged, licking the air. The pink bodies of the girls glistened through their garments; their young breasts trembled, their thighs daintily swayed. Their eyes shone behind their veils, glimmering black and blue and brown, and their long hair drifted about them. The Pans bounded higher, frantic and lustful, pursuing the nymphs as they circled and floated, singing.

Lucanus did not know at exactly what moment he became coldly sober, in mind if not in body. He looked at the dancers with sudden disgust and revulsion. He wanted to rise and leave, and his temples pounded. It was as if some awful danger threatened him. But his flesh would not obey his command; it half lay, flaccid, on the couch. He was aware of Julia's hot breath on his cheek, her hand stroking his arm, her murmurous voice uttering shameless things. Sickness overpowered him, and a loathing for himself. He wished to leap into cool water and cleanse not only his body but his thick hot mouth, and his mind. He looked at the guests, at their partly opened mouths through which their breath gushed, tainted with wine; he looked at the women with their naked breasts, and a kind of horror came to him, a detestation of them and of himself. His eyes burned dryly, and his stomach retched.

The nymphs were screaming with mingled delight and simulated terror, for the Pans had caught them in their nimble arms. The Pans then, to wilder and more rapid music, tore the veils and the garments from the girls and clasped their nude bodies, winding their hairy legs about them. The guests shouted, maddened, and some half rose, screaming. The Pans lifted the girls in their arms, raised them over their heads like living statues, and bore them into the darkness, with animal whinnyings of triumph and desire.

As if this were a signal, every light in the portico and in the gardens was immediately extinguished, and only the moonlight streamed down on grass and trees and the disordered and reeking tables. The guests sat in the following silence, as if stupefied, silent themselves. Then, couple by couple, clinging together, they staggered to their feet and moved away to the waiting grottoes, and into distant gardens where only the moon filtered. Lucanus watched them go, and the powerful loathing was renewed in him.

Then he was alone with Julia and the two athletes. Oris snored, oblivious, and Hyacinth's face was bloated with lust. When the Empress rose, shimmering in the moonlight, Hyacinth rose with her, but she turned from him. She smiled at Lucanus and took his hand and whispered, "Come," and drew him to his feet.

His body was still numbed and stunned with wine; his knees trembled under him. But the sense of terrible menace came to him more strongly. Now he could think of Tiberius, the mighty Caesar. He regarded Julia with hatred, and his blue eyes flashed in the silver light. She thought this a sign of eagerness and desire, and threw herself upon his breast. He staggered under the impact, for she was not a slight woman, and he was weak.

Hyacinth, drunk and inflamed with wine and jealousy, circled about Lucanus and Julia, and then seized Lucanus by the shoulder, howling obscenities and threats. Lucanus thrust the Empress from him, and strength returned to his body. He grasped Hyacinth, whirled him around, and flung him violently into Julia's arms. They fell in a tangled heap of bodies and legs and arms on the couch.

Then Lucanus ran. He ran down the length of the portico, dodging tables and chairs. He ran into the palace. He rushed down the silent polished floor shining under scattered lamps. He heard someone racing behind him, coming closer, and he swung about, his clenched fists raised. But it was only Plotius.

"Quick!" cried the young Praetorian, seizing his arm. "By all the Furies, be quick!"

He swung Lucanus down a marble passageway, long and narrow, and they flew down it like young Mercuries. "Are you mad!" exclaimed Plotius, panting.

"Did you think I should lie with her?" cried Lucanus, infuriated.

"No, but there are less strenuous ways of rejecting a lady," said Plotius. He groaned. "And I was assigned to you by Caesar as a bodyguard!" He pulled Lucanus to a sudden stop, and his eyes scanned the passageway. Praetorians, yet unaware of their presence, paced with drawn swords at the end. Plotius drew Lucanus behind a huge marble pillar. He whispered now.

"You are in deadly danger. The Augusta will not forget

this. She will have your life if possible, for you have humiliated her beyond endurance." He groaned softly. He took off his helmet and wiped his sweating face with his strong brown arm.

"Listen to me! There is a bronze door eight paces on the left, and officers only have a key, for it leads to our quarters below. I will go on, affect to examine the lock. Then I will engage my men yonder in conversation. At an advantageous moment run to the door I have unlocked, open it swiftly, enter the passageway beyond, and there wait for me." There was a harsh urgency in his voice.

He glanced behind them from the way they had come. Then with a formidable glare at Lucanus, who was feeling violently sick, he left the young physician. He moved in a swift military fashion down the hallway, and stopped at a door and pretended to examine it. Then he marched along and encountered his men, who stopped and saluted him.

Gasping with his nausea, and with sour eructations spilling upwards into his throat, Lucanus peered around the pillar carefully. He waited until Plotius had maneuvered the Praetorians so their backs were to him. He heard their rough young laughter as Plotius jested with them. Then he ran to the bronze door, swung it open as quietly as possible and darted into the cold and gloomy passage behind it, and closed the door on his heels. He leaned against the damp stone wall, folded his arms tightly across his belly, and closed his eyes against the thundering pain in his head.

Chapter Thirty

The passageway was narrow as well as dank; little trickles of water ran between the gloomy stones, and the low arched ceiling pressed down. At the end a lantern, feeble and yellow, swung on a hook, and beyond it was another passage, running at right angles. Here was a deep and heavy silence, broken only by the thin tinkle of the water.

After he could control his nausea Lucanus looked about him and thought. It seemed that he had been waiting a considerable time for Plotius. He frowned. Never in his life before had he been suspicious or wary. He reflected that his life had been too sheltered, too restricted, too scholarly,

bounded by home, family and studies. He had been pre-
cipitated into a scene and an experience tonight which had
left him appalled. He had heard of these orgies; he had
seen one or two smaller versions in Alexandria, which had
not moved him, for he had not been part of them. If I
revolt so violently now, how will it be when I come
fully upon a raw world? Like an infant again?

It disgusted him when he remembered that he had considered Tiberius Caesar only another man, mighty, all-
powerful, but only another man. Now he was a terror, ruler
of the world, husband to a harpy, master of legions, absolute master of all men. Would he avenge Julia? There
was Plotius, devoted to Caesar. Could he be trusted? Had
he lured him, Lucanus, into this narrow passageway in
order to do him to death? Was he even now with Tiberius,
though it was almost dawn, considering these matters? The
son of Diodorus Cyrinus could not be executed publicly,
as a criminal. His death must be seen by no one, witnessed
by no one, and here was the perfect place and the perfect
time. Then his body would be thrown into the Tiber,
and it would be given out that he had died mysteriously
while under the very protection of Caesar.

Lucanus did not want to die. He thought of his mother,
his brothers and his sister. He thought of all the work
he must do. He was prepared to defend himself. Curse all
that wine he had drunk! He lifted himself from against
the wall and tested his muscles. He thought again of Plotius,
armed with the short sword, who would soon be coming
into this passageway. He and Hyacinth alone had seen Lucanus reject Julia with violence. It was possible now that
Plotius was not even with Caesar; his allegiance was also
to Julia, and he might be consulting her as to how best to
dispose of the son of former slaves as quietly as possible.

He is big and strong, thought Lucanus, but I am bigger
and stronger. Deprived of his sword, I could strangle him,
or at least overcome him. However, he has that sword.
Lucanus considered alertly. Someway I will overcome
Plotius, he told himself. Then, someway, I will find my
path out of this abominable place, not to return to my
family, which would endanger them, but to get out of Rome.
He took a step or two towards the lantern. Why wait for
Plotius' return? He would flee now. He heard the grating
of the key in the lock and knew it was too late.

He ran back to the door and pressed himself to the wall

in such a position that the door would open against him
and he would have an opportunity to jump upon Plotius before the captain ... could guard himself. If Plotius entered
with his sw... ...awn, then he must die. Lucanus flinched.
But ...ng. ...h I must protect, the life of my family, and all my
...ph ben Gamliel had told him: "Thou shalt not kill!"
...ut it had not been commanded that a man should not
defend himself.

The door quickly swung open, and Plotius' profile appeared, and Lucanus saw that he had not drawn his sword.
Plotius, not seeing Lucanus behind the door, cursed softly,
and called his name with anxiousness. He stepped into the
... and bolted it, ... understood. He ... saw Lucanus, and his white
...ere prepared, my Hercules," he said. "Ask me no questions. I have talked with Caesar." He was amused.

"What did Caesar say?" demanded Lucanus, not trusting
him.

"Ah, you learn," replied Plotius, wagging his head in
admiration. "I merely told Tiberius that you were inexperienced, and that you had unwittingly offended the Augusta, who is noted for not suffering offense. I have said:
ask me no questions. Your life is still in the deadliest
danger. Follow me."

But Lucanus hesitated. He stepped warily back from
Plotius. "Am I not under Caesar's protection, his guest in
this palace? He has only to say the word and not even the
Augusta would dare lift her hand against me."

Plotius sighed impatiently. "How little you know, my good
innocent. Julia could not, under the circumstances of your
presence here, order your death openly. No, your death
would happen more stealthily, and Caesar could not prevent it. There is poison, you understand, or an accident,
and then your body would be conveyed sorrowfully to your
family, with a scroll in Caesar's hand. Julia has many spies
and devotees on the Palatine, more than Caesar himself.
So you are to be protected. Tomorrow, in disguise, you will
leave the city and a vessel will be waiting for you in the
harbor. In no event are you to return to your home, or
you will bring death there not only to yourself but to
those you love. Once you are safe, Julia will be led skill-

fully to believe that Caesar became angry with you and banished you."

He paused, and stared at Lucanus, who was still watching him. "It was fortunate for myself that Augusta did not know I was lurking at the end of the passage. But it was not fortunate for Hyacinth. He will be dead before sunset, having fallen down a flight of stairs, for instance."

"What a Caesar, what an Augusta, what a city!" exclaimed Lucanus.

Plotius gaped at him, then shook his head. "What an innocent!" he replied.

"I trust no one," said Lucanus.

"Excellent, my dear. I enter and you will follow me. I was compelled to come here for a time in order to ascertain that my fellow officers are either asleep or on duty. But in a few moments the watch will change, and we must hurry."

Still Lucanus hesitated. He knew little of Plotius, after all. Then he said, "I will follow. But first let me remove your sword."

Plotius looked him in the eye, then lifted his arms, smiling, and Lucanus disarmed him. He trotted briskly down the passageway and turned to the right, and Lucanus followed, gripping the sword and glancing cautiously about him. In the farther passageway a long series of oaken doors had been inserted, and faint sounds of snoring came from them. Here it was drier, and there was a scent of grass from an unknown place, and the clean whisper of a wind. Plotius stopped before one door, unlocked it, and entered, silently beckoning to Lucanus. When Lucanus was inside, Plotius swiftly closed the door and bolted it. His voice had dropped when he spoke again. "We must keep our voices low. No one must know you are here, for I, like you, do not trust anyone."

His small bedchamber, lighted solely by a hissing lamp, was stark and austere, containing only a chair, a rough bed and a table on which the lamp stood. Swords and two shields hung on the plastered walls, and in various little niches had been placed crude, toylike heads of various gods. In one niche, by itself, and a little larger, was a skillfully executed small marble head of Diodorus, over which hung a banner of Rome, and it was this that Lucanus saw. Still fumy from wine, he felt his eyes fill with tears. He put Plotius' sword on the table, looked at him straight and said, "I know I can trust you," and he pointed to the bust. "You must have loved my father."

"Yes," said Plotius. He went to the little bust and touched it reverently. "As did my father, and my uncle, the senator, who was done to death by his colleagues because he loved his country and was an honorable man." He paused. "So did Tiberius love him."

Lucanus sat down on the edge of the bed. His headache was becoming more frightful, and he was filled with grief that he would not see his family again, perhaps never. He held his head in his hands, and croaked, "I should like some water, very cold water."

Plotius, laughing softly, lifted a jug from the floor and held it to Lucanus' dry hot mouth, and the young man drank thirstily. Immediately he was nauseated, and Plotius hastily pulled aside a brown wool curtain and thrust him into the latrine beyond. There he retched and vomited the sour wine until he was exhausted. But his headache remained. When he had completed his relieving he re-entered the bedchamber, where Plotius was waiting, still armed and helmeted. He had added a cloak over his uniform, and was yawning as if all this were the most ordinary matter in the world.

"I am not to leave you for a moment," he said. He removed his helmet and laid it on the table. "You will occupy my bed, and I will sleep across the threshold, wrapped in my cloak. Do not protest. Your flesh is more delicate than mine; I am a soldier and accustomed to sleeping on the ground. I have bolted the door, but it may be possible, though not probable, that someone saw us when we fled from Julia's banquet."

"And not even Caesar can protect me!" said Lucanus, with scorn. "Not even from a trumpery woman."

"You did not seem, at one time, to regard her as trumpery," said Plotius, showing all his big white teeth in a happy smile. "I recall occasions when you returned her kisses ardently, and once, I do remember, you removed that Cretan hat of hers and balanced it gravely on your head, to the great admiration of the guests."

"Impossible!" said Lucanus, horrified.

"Indeed, it is so." Plotius was enjoying himself. He lifted his hand in an oath. "So I swear it. You also offered on more than one occasion to give Julia a demonstration of your prowess as an athlete, except that neither Hyacinth nor Oris was willing. You then declared that on the occasion of the Great Games, a week hence, you would challenge any athlete to any demonstration. The guests were much impressed, and Julia was very proud."

Lucanus remembered the shining hot hiatuses during the banquet. While Plotius spoke, he suddenly recalled, with shame, the applause of the guests, and dimly, as in a dream, he saw himself rising and bowing. He groaned, held his temples.

"You bragged," said Plotius, with deeper enjoyment, "of one Bruno, who was like a bear, and who had taught you wrestling in Alexandria, and whom you finally defeated. You also mentioned that you have in your possession a golden cup testifying to the fact that in all athletics you were the best."

Lucanus groaned more loudly. It was true. Plotius could not have known of these things without hearing them from Lucanus himself.

"As for dancing, you declared, you were truly expert. Had not Julia restrained you, you would have given a splendid exhibition at once."

Plotius sighed. "I should have enjoyed that exhibition. It was evident, however, that the Augusta wished to see you perform in private, in that manner and in sundry other ways." He sighed again. "Had you, however, undertaken to show your prowess in that field you would have hurt Caesar immeasurably, not because you had lain with his wife—for she has lain with many—but because he discerned you were a good man." He thrust out his lips, considering. "He understood, when I spoke to him a little while ago."

Lucanus rolled his head in his hands, shuddering. "Why does he not divorce or banish her? Is he a man or a fool?"

"Julia is the daughter of old Augustus, and the people loved him, and they do not love Tiberius."

Lucanus shuddered again. He was still nauseated, and a thousand little devils were knocking on his skull. He was also deeply ashamed. He looked up at Plotius, and then suddenly the two young men were laughing, Plotius leaning against the wall helplessly, and Lucanus sprawled on the bed. Their paroxysms were the more violent because they had to muffle their laughter behind their hands and arms.

When Plotius could control himself he said, hoarse with mirth, "You swore that if Julia would kiss your garland you would eat every rose, including the thorns. But she whispered something in your ear which apparently changed your mind. I should delight in knowing what it was."

"I should not!" Lucanus then saw that at some time he had abandoned his toga and was only in his pale blue tunic. "Let us hope that she considers me impotent, and that I did not wish to give her a demonstration!"

They laughed again. Lucanus cautiously sipped a little more water. Plotius would not permit him to blow out the lamp. He stretched himself out on the stone floor across the threshold, wrapped in his cloak, and was immediately asleep. But Lucanus, now he was alone with himself, could not sleep. He would soon be far from all he loved, in exile. But had he not wished that? He turned on the bed restlessly. It was long past dawn, and he heard the many hurrying feet of the officers in the passageway outside the door before he fell into a feverish doze.

He had a strange and terrible dream. He saw Rome in flames; he heard the thundering of tens of thousands of columns crashing to the ground; he heard the riotous lamentations of a multitude. The black skies reddened overhead, and a vast smell of corruption, as of roasting carrion, blew over the city. He saw bloated Caesars with evil, corrupt or stupid faces, crowned with oak leaves and laurel. Porticoes shot with flame; temples quivered like paper, and were dissolved. Arenas roared with beasts, and lions sprang from their cages upon a fleeing populace. From somewhere came a loud, deep voice: "Woe, woe to Rome!" And the thundering filled the whole universe, and the statues of red-tinged gods exploded into crimson fragments and fell with the columns, and white walls heeled like sails and collapsed, and the Seven Hills fumed like bonfires, and the Tiber ran like bloody water.

When Lucanus awoke he saw that the lamp had been freshly filled and that it was hissing and burning with a yellow light. He had no way to tell the time, but he felt that it was very late. No window opened anywhere in the room. He went into the latrine; high in the thick stone wall he discerned that there were small round piercings for air; he stood on the latrine and peered through the holes and saw a green turfy bank, and a glimpse of cypress trees from which blew a sunny, poignant scent. He calculated that it was past noon. He returned to the sleeping room and for the first time saw that a meal had been placed there for him of soldier's wine, fresh cheese, clean brown bread and a basket of fruit. With surprising appetite he ate and drank. This was the food he knew.

He understood that he would have to wait. His safety depended upon the most unreliable sources, and the most devious. Once he tried the door; it was locked from without. He shot the inner bolt cautiously. He prowled the small chamber restlessly, thinking. If it were not for his family he would have rejoiced at leaving Rome and its environs at once.

At length a key grated in the lock, and Lucanus stood before the door silently. Then he heard Plotius' muffled voice, "It is I." He shot the bolt and stepped back quickly. Plotius entered, with a knowing smile; he carried a large bundle in his arms, which he laid on the bed. "While you were sleeping like a babe, my good Lucanus, I have been busy. First, at the order of Caesar, the Prefect of the Praetorians placed conspicuous notices throughout the palace that you had been banished early this morning. This was to assuage the Augusta's wrath." His face changed. "I was not mistaken. Hyacinth was found dead a few hours ago of poison, in his bed. His friend, Oris, is now in the Mamertine for his murder."

"But he did not murder Hyacinth!"

Plotius pursed up his lips and looked at the ceiling. "I understand he confessed—under torture. If Oris had not been drunk or asleep he would have been poisoned also. Ah, well. All men must die."

"What will happen to Oris?"

"There is nothing you can do, my friend. I have said I have been busy. I have visited your home, and here, in this large bundle, are your medical pouch, some clothing, some keepsakes from your mother and Keptah, and your medical books. What! Are you going to weep? Your mother understands, and Keptah also. There are letters from them."

He added, "Edict of banishment to the contrary, it is very possible that the Augusta has spies about, not only in the palace but at the gates of the city, ready to fall upon you and kill you. Therefore a disguise is necessary."

He opened the bundle and withdrew from it a very coarse brown garment, usually worn by slaves or rural overseers, and a well-executed wig of thick black curls. There was also a pair of wood-soled sandals, and a girdle composed of twined ropes.

"You will go to the Esquiline Gate, beyond which awaits a humble nag. But you will have to walk to the gate. It is a long journey." He fished through the bundle once more and brought out two moneybags. He poured a golden clattering stream on the bed. "The smaller is from your mother. The larger from Caesar, with his compliments. And here is another gift from Tiberius, who must love you indeed." Plotius reverently unwrapped a ring of incredible magnificence. Very huge, it depicted the bow and shield of Artemis in brilliant diamonds, superimposed on a heart of turquoise, and all set in polished gold. "You will observe," said Plotius, dryly, "that it is a virginal ring."

"I am no virgin, though that may astonish you," said Lucanus, with a slight laugh. He put the ring on his finger, then turned it about so that its richness was hidden against his palm. He held out his hand for the letters from his mother and Keptah, and sat down to read them quickly. They were brief, and filled with love and confidence, and, in order not to wound him, they expressed no grief or fear. His mother explained that from time to time she would send him money from the bequest of Diodorus; he had only to write her and she would dispatch the money to any city.

There was another letter in a strange, delicate hand, and Lucanus opened it. It was from Sara bas Elazar, and it too was brief, but ardent and tender.

"I shall love and cherish you always, my dear Lucanus. I should, like Ruth, wish to follow you wherever you go, and be with you eternally. Do not be surprised when you see me, for I shall know where you are. For me there can be no other man, and my prayers are with you. I know that always you will search for my little brother, Arieh, and will find him one day for me, in the name of my father, whom you consoled. God bless you and keep you, and may He watch your comings and your goings and be on your right hand, ever mindful of you, and may His rod and His staff comfort you."

"What!" exclaimed Plotius. "You are weeping. That must be a very touching letter. From a lady, doubtless."

"Quiet!" said Lucanus, and wiped away his tears.

He stood up to examine his physician's pouch, and as he opened it a golden object fell from it, with its chain.

It was Keptah's cross. He hesitated, then clasped it about his neck. Plotius' strenuous brown eyes widened, then narrowed. "A cross!" he said. "And in gold! Why is this?"

"I do not know," said Lucanus. "But Keptah told me it is an old symbol, from Chaldea, called Babylonia by the Jews, that great dead empire. It is a symbol which the Egyptians used also, securing it from the Babylonians; they placed it in their Pyramids. One of their Pharaohs, who declared that only one God existed and so incurred the wrath of the priests, wore such a symbol about his neck and so did his followers. The Pharaoh's name was Aton, I believe, but it was long ago. I wear the symbol, for it was given to me by a girl whom I loved——"

"Well, dry your tears," said the practical Plotius. "At sunset you will leave this room and go into the quarters of the slaves, with a broom which waits you without. You will then be inconspicuous. In the meantime we must disguise that lily complexion of yours with this dark brown oil. Be discreet! Speak to no one; mutter constantly under your breath like a simpleton. Then you will steal from the Palatine, mingle with the crowds of the city, then walk to the Esquiline Gate as fast as possible."

He gave Lucanus a sharp short dagger, which he was to conceal under his clothing. "One never knows," he said. He smeared the brown oil carefully over Lucanus' face and neck, and adjusted the black wig, and helped him dress in the rural garments. "Now," he said with a laugh, standing back to admire his handiwork, "not even Julia would look at you!"

He hesitated, then suddenly embraced Lucanus as a brother, and kissed his cheek awkwardly. "May the gods preserve you," he said. "I do not say farewell, for I believe we shall meet again."

PART THREE

"Life belongs to God; for the activity of
the mind is life, and He is that activity.
Pure self-activity of reason is God's most
blessed and everlasting life. We say that
God is living, eternal and perfect; and
that continuous and everlasting life is
God's, for God is eternal life."

—Aristotle—Essay,
Divine Reason as the Prime Mover

Chapter Thirty-one

"Sara bas Elazar to Lucanus, son of Diodorus Cyrinus:

"Greetings, my dearest friend, my one beloved. The Day of Atonement is over, and I bask in the peace of God, knowing that He has forgiven me and that I am inscribed in the Book of Life. A beautiful tranquillity rests on Jerusalem. From my window I can see the Temple, shining like a golden shield in the light of the full moon, and the city sparkles restlessly like a field of fireflies. The hills are copper, the wind a breath of a winery, and slowly, beneath me, the yellow leaves drop from a tree like small flames. The women are in the courtyard, drawing up water, and their voices are calm, and from the windows and the doorways of the inn there is a pungent smell of roast lamb and bread and spices, and the flicker of lamps. For man has been forgiven of God again, and there is quiet rejoicing, for all know His love and His promise of the ages.

"Ah, if only you were here beside me, holding my hand, and lying in this peace! If only you would come once to Jerusalem! Yet, always when I speak to you of this, you evade my eyes, as if you feared a terror in the city. I do not understand this, but I remember the last words of our dear friend, Joseph ben Gamliel, before he died two years ago in the sight of the Temple: 'One day Lucanus will come here and he will find Him whom he has been seeking all the days of his life.'

"I prayed today for you in your soul, your health and happiness. I pray so each year, all these long seven years since first we met. You have repeatedly implored me to marry, and to forget you; there is not a letter you write to me which does not contain this admonition and plea. But how can a woman who loves forget him whom she loves? How can a spring be filled with water if its source becomes dry? From whence will come the wine if the vine perishes? To ask me to lie in the bed of another man is to ask me to degrade my spirit, to deliver myself up like an infamous woman even though I should first step under the wedding canopy and take the hand of a stranger. My soul is wedded to yours.

"Dearest beloved, we last met in Thebes, and though your words were rejecting and sad I saw the light on your face when you saw me. We conversed quietly in the shade of your garden, but what we spoke in our hearts was not the words of our souls and understanding. Why can you not forget your bitterness against God? I have told you often, as did Joseph ben Gamliel, that God created man perfect and whole, without the threat of sickness and death. But men disobeyed God, and brought these things into the world with their disobedience. It was man who exiled himself from joy, who attracted to himself the spirit of evil, who caused a curse to be delivered upon the earth.

"Wherever I go, through all the cities and the ports, I hear your name as a great physician. I know you care nothing for this; you wish only to alleviate pain, bring comfort, and delay death. Nevertheless, it is a happiness to me to hear you acclaimed by the poor and the abandoned, the slaves and the oppressed. They talk of you in the market places.

"Though I never knew him except in your own words, I grieve with you in the death of your old friend and teacher, the physician, Keptah. I prayed for his soul today, for God has said it is good to pray for the souls of the dead, who sleep in the dust. Their memory is a blessing to us.

"Sometimes, when I am most sad, I remember your stories of Rome and I laugh happily. I understand that there is little in the world of today to excite one's risibilities, for the Pax Romana, in the guise of world peace, has brought oppression, suffering, slavery and exploitation to all the people of the world. Power is corruption; it is in the nature of man to injure what he dominates, and the urge to dominate lives in us all like a dark disease.

"I rejoice with you that no harm has come to you, my dear one, when you have visited Rome once or twice a year during all these years. How I should love to see your beautiful mother, your charming sister, your brothers, and all your friends! I laugh for hours when reading of your old tutor, Cusa, the clever rascal.

"I have had a strange experience, though when I relate it you may find nothing strange in it at all, except the sentimental thoughts of a woman of twenty-four who must fill her lonely life with portents and imaginings and fantasies.

"Jerusalem, as you know, is filled and surrounded by pil-

grims from all over the Land of Israel on the holidays. The
wealthy can find comfortable accommodations in the inns
and the taverns, or at the homes of friends, where they can
celebrate the New Year in pleasant company and at pleasant
tables and in pleasant conversation. But the poor find what
crevices they can in the crowded city, or camp outside the
great walls in tents or in caves. Often I walk among the
huddled thousands of pilgrims outside the gates, observing
their rough clothing, their bare feet, their tangled beards,
their crying children, their herds of goats, and listening to
their voices accented by the dialects of Galilee and Samaria
and Moab and Perea and Decapolis. They make merry on the
New Year, and their browned faces are devout and they
gaze at the Temple with passionate love, and observe the
slightest laws with much gravity. They sleep to the shrill
barking of jackals, and their food is poor and their wine
wretched. Yet they are happy, and the gaiety and prayers
on the dusty hillsides below the walls have a deeper meaning and resonance than those heard in the large houses, surrounded by gardens, within the city. Once you observed bitterly that the poor pray more passionately because they have
no pleasures, but only God. In this truly they are blessed,
for if a man has not God he has nothing, and if he has
God then he has all else besides in his heart.

"At sunset, on the New Year, the pilgrims crowded the
narrow and winding streets of Jerusalem, their children in
their arms or at their heels, and they were a hot and multicolored river, moving under a silver cloud of dust. I alighted
from my litter, on an impulse, and accompanied them beyond the walls, where their poor feasts were set out on cloths
on the ground, and the moon rose over them and brightened their fires. Many were the invitations shouted at me
to join a family for wine or bread or a little meat, for, as I
was dressed humbly, they thought I was a young woman
without a family, or who was lost in the crowded caravans.
I listened to their songs, their laughter, the voices of their
running and hungry children, the cries of their animals,
their prayers. All at once I was oppressed by loneliness,
and my longing. I stood apart near a twisted tree and looked
at the fires spurting on the hillside, and their reflection on
the simple faces. It was then that a young man approached
me in his rough blue robe; his sandaled feet fastened by
harsh ropes.

"This young man could not have been more than eighteen

or nineteen, and he stood near me with tall stateliness and smiled at me, and instantly we appeared alone and infinitely lonely together. It was as if a circle of silence surrounded us, and voices and cries diminished to a dream. There was a deep wisdom and gentleness on his face, and an enormous tenderness, as if he understood that I had no one and pitied me. He had an earthen goblet in his hand, filled with wine, and he offered it to me and I took it and drank of it, as simply as he had given it. All at once my eyes filled with tears and sobs choked me, and I wished to pour out to him all my grief and exile and sadness. He took the emptied goblet from my hand, while I tried to control myself. He waited until I was more composed, and then he said to me in the sweetest and strongest of voices, 'Sara bas Elazar, be of good heart and dry your tears, for God is with you and you are not alone.'

"I was astonished and mute. How had he known my name, and the sorrow in my spirit? He smiled at me deeply, and a near fire flared up and I saw his large blue eyes and they were like infinite stars. In that moment I desired to fall at his feet and embrace them. I felt that he knew everything, not only about me, but about the whole world, and that there was peace beyond imagining in him, and all love and hope.

"The tears blinded me, and when I had wiped them away, and my heart had ceased to shake, the young man was gone. I almost thought I had dreamt this, but the taste of the wine was on my lips. A sudden awful sensation of loss came to me, and I searched for him among the pilgrims, but I did not see him again. I could not sleep that night, but each time that I wept a comfort came to me that was not the comforting of man.

"Enough. Even the memory of him sets me to dreaming and into a sense of joy. Was he an angel, dressed humbly, as were the angels whom Abraham entertained in his tent? I wish to believe it; I almost believe it. I cling to the memory of his face.

"I am addressing this letter to you in Athens, at your home, where you are to remain for a few weeks longer. I salute you now, my dear Lucanus, with all the love in my heart and my spirit, and plan for our next meeting. And one of these days, in your searchings for my brother, Arieh, you will find him. He is nine years old now, and all within me convinces me he is alive, and that one day he will be restored to the arms of his sister and his people. God be with you."

Lucanus had at first reflected that in the land of his people, Greece, he would find his home. But after a while the bitter realization came to him that here too he was a stranger, and that he had, truly, no home anywhere. He had been born in Antioch, and Antioch had not been his home; he had lived near Rome, and had seen it occasionally, but he was a stranger there also. He had visited all of the ports and the cities along the Great Sea, and had small houses in many of them when he left the ships, yet nowhere did he possess a home, or enjoy the company of friends, or have peace. The wretched, the humble, the poor, the abandoned and forgotten, the slaves, the miserable little merchants in the bazaars and shops blessed his name and kissed his hands and his feet. But he was a stranger, forever a stranger in a strange land, and though he knew many tongues it was as if an alien spoke them. His only delight was in comforting and healing, and in the letters he received from his family and from Sara bas Elazar. A terrible restlessness and mournful anxiety and emptiness filled him always, and he was like a man searching for water in a desert.

Three years ago he had bought a little house near the outskirts of Athens. When returning to his home in Athens, as when he returned to his other homes, it was not like one returning to a familiar spot and to familiar voices and gardens, but as a wayfarer, tired and pausing only for a night.

Here was the land of his fathers, but it was not his land, though the aesthete in him rejoiced in its stark and light-filled beauty, its bony plains, it sparkling silver hills, its shining rocks, its fiery blue seas, its rosy or light brown roofs, its marbled history, its white temples, its dusty ilexes, laurels, olive trees and myrtle, its grape terraces under a brilliant sky, its glorious Parthenon nobly rising on the Acropolis like a crown of graceful stone. Here was the land of Helios, the land of demos, of Pericles, of Homer, of Phidias, of Socrates and Plato, of all science and art and grace and poetry, of the very soul of civilized man, of the calm foreheads of the gods, of Olympus. Here law and justice had set their mighty feet on marble, and out of this dry, astringent air had blown the wings of deities, and philosophies, emerging like shadows of brighter light out of light itself. Here the oracles spoke, and the fleets of Jason stood at every port. Here, in this land, heroism had stepped forth, with a shield like the moon and a sword like the lightning, and here the mountains gazed at Marathon, and Thermopylae still vibrated with the memory of those few who had defeated the hordes of the Persian. The glory lay on the brow of Greece for all the ages to see, and would never be quenched.

This modern Greece was not the Greece of Pericles; but she lived as a dream still, eternal and not to be imitated. And here, as always, Lucanus was a stranger, brewing his potions, lonely, nameless except to the poor and lost, cultivating his garden, in which he grew flowers and herbs, drinking his lonely wine, preparing his meager meals with his own hands, reading, meditating, writing his letters, and watching the stars slope down the dark arch of heaven.

Often, at dawn, when the pale sun had hardly thrown its frail rays over Athens, and the city was only beginning to stir slightly, Lucanus would pass the Temple of Theseus and climb the long white stairs to the top of the Acropolis, and to the Parthenon. There alone he would wander through the colonnades where Socrates had taught, and he would gently run his hand over the Doric columns which were silvery in the first light. He would gaze reverently at the winged statues seemingly about to leap into glowing and hollow space, and would stand before the western pediment of the Temple of Zeus, or move through the cella to admire the vast statue of Athena with her high helmet and her great, noble face. He would drift on to the eastern pediment, to marvel at the grouped, reclining Fates with their delicate marble draperies that appeared to move in the dry and luminous wind. As a physician he would wonder at the genius of the sculptor who had carved the recumbent figure of Ilissos on the western pediment, and who had given alabaster the aspect of living flesh. Here wisdom trembled on stone, and beauty set her hand in shining shadows on low reliefs and on argent body and grave face and chaste breast and imperial profile and immaculate limb. Here was silence, but immortal presences could just be detected beyond the bounds of the eye, like a translucent chorus, and all this crowded mighty company carved from marble awaited only a mysterious summons to move into godlike life, to fill the ear with immortal song and sonorous voices. At last the cool turquoise sky stood between the white columns, painted and clear, and the robes of the caryatids turned to gold.

Here Lucanus was less lonely than when among men. Standing among the statues in his white robe, he was one with them. Moving among them, it was as if he were the first to awake. In the midst of beauty and solemn heroism and frozen grandeur he could again hope that, as man had created all this, there was a far possibility that men would become men once more, speaking in majesty and poetry, revealing secrets of eternity. His footsteps would echo among the columns and along the colonnades, and sometimes he would pause, half believing that he heard stronger footsteps behind him made by heroic feet which had stepped down from pediments onto the white and glimmering floor.

The sun would turn a brighter gold and the city below would stir visibly and the pink or light yellow roofs would move into light, and voices, restless and imperative, would rise up to the Acropolis like a flight of quarrelsome birds. Then his loneliness would return, and he would flee from the Parthenon.

Why was it not possible that when men attained the ultimate in glory they could not sustain it, but must fall from heaven? Was it because even at the heights they must commit the follies and the crimes that inexorably led to extinction? Thucydides had written, "The kind of events that once took place will by reason of human nature take place again." Therein was the tragedy.

Lucanus knew, from his growing restlessness, that he must be on his way again very soon. Within two weeks he must accept a berth as a ship's doctor plying between Crete and Alexandria, and he had consented to be employed so for three months. He was much in demand, not only for his healing powers, but because his fee was so low. He always distributed this fee to the crew on his departure.

One morning, descending from the Parthenon, and feeling an aversion to returning to his lonely house at the end of the Panathenaic Way, he merged with the crowds of the Agora and wandered about the Stoa of Attalus, feverish with men and the noise of trade and shops. The little dark Greeks were more active and more effervescent than the Romans and much shrewder, much gayer and more charlatan; they robbed with a debonair manner in their twenty-one little shops at the back of the columned promenades. Their goods were more colorful, and shoddier, for here no stern Roman law of values prevailed; yet their wares had charm. As always, even this early when the shops were

just opening and the merchants were noisily scurrying about
unlocking doors and dusting their stock, a fervid speaker
was already on the platform haranguing the indifferent
crowds. He was an old man with a ragged gray beard, and
with a staff in his hand. Lucanus paused to hear his incoherent words. He was crying, and waving his staff, and rend-
ing his beard: "Repent, repent! The Kingdom of God is
at hand!" The man must be a Jew; they were always exclaiming those words, and no one listened. Lucanus looked
at the impressive public library, and remembered that he
must return some books before his journey; men and wom-
en were beginning to climb the steps to the opened doors.
Young girls, in bright scarlet or yellow or blue robes, had
gathered in the fountain house to fill their pitchers; their
voices were like parrots as they exchanged gossip, and
laughed, and jostled for position in the double line. And
now there was the law court, very dignified, and declaring,
in its broad columns and arches, that the rule of law was the
way of civilized mankind, and not the rule of men. Lucanus smiled cynically. He stared with coldness at the two
Roman legionnaries standing at attention at the bronze
doors. Where naked power existed, there was no law at
all but the law of force. He could hear musicians practicing in the odeum for the day's concerts and plays.
He stopped a moment to look at the round house, where
the bureaucrats squatted and spewed out their onerous regulations, in the immemorial way of all evil and oppressive
men. An enormous procession of the devout was beginning
to march up the Acropolis to do honor to Pallas Athena,
and they carried struggling doves in their arms; Lucanus
stepped aside to let the procession pass, and as he looked
on the troubled faces of the worshipers he felt his old and
chronic sadness again.

Now the city was fully alive and vivaciously deafening,
the hard blue sky polished with sun, and without a cloud.
Heat blew up from the streets and from the crowding columns. What meaning was there to all this activity, this
vehemence, this rapid coming and going, these fast and purposeful feet, this trade, these laughing girls, these vociferous
merchants? A group of lawyers, clothed in white, and with
solemn faces, mounted the steps of the law court, conversing in low voices as if their concerns contained all life
and all death. It was marvelous to believe that one's being
had significance, which it had not. But what would happen

to the world if men ceased to believe that their existence
was of any importance? Are they wiser than I? thought
Lucanus, restlessly. He passed the Temple of Hephaestus,
with its red tiled roof gleaming like huge serrated rubies
in the furious sun. He had walked a long way, and he
was tired and hungry, and longed now for his quiet house,
his little garden with its pool full of pink water lilies, and
the goat's milk and cheese and brown bread and honey
which would form his breakfast. And here was the slave
market, the merchants already arranging their human wares
to the best advantage. Lucanus averted his eyes, sickened
as always; he usually avoided passing this high wooden
platform and looking at the slaves, for he could not endure
the agony.

For some strange reason now he felt a heaviness in his
feet and a great weariness, and he halted directly before
the platform. The merchants were scolding and cracking
whips; a woman was sobbing, a man pleading, a child wailing. Here were exposed for sale those who had fallen into
debt, those who were homeless and had offered themselves
for sale, those who had transgressed some petty law; some
who were criminals. Three beautiful young girls with dusky
faces and large black eyes, and clad very prettily, were being
arranged in a coquettish group on crimson silk cushions.
They were not at all disturbed; they passed a bowl of
sweetmeats among themselves and eyed approaching buyers
archly. So long as their beauty lasted, they could be assured
of good homes and much petting and coddling. They
flung back their long black hair and preened their necks,
and murmured together in a strange tongue, and giggled at
their own lewd remarks. They sat on the platform, demurely
tightening their tunics about them to show to the best
advantage every curve of leg and thigh and breast under
the diaphanous material.

The merchants did not have many to sell as yet, this
early in the morning. A few buxom women, evidently excellent cooks, to judge by the pots arranged at their feet;
a few children in the arms of bewildered and weeping girls;
a few young men of no particular grace or strength; an old
man or two; a group of sullen prisoners. Lucanus began
to move on, but the listlessness remained in him and he
stood there. He attracted the attention of the three beautiful
girls, and their voices rose eagerly, twittering, and a merchant ran to him and seized his arm. "Master!" he ex-

claimed. "Look upon these maidens, virgins from Araby! Sisters! Would they not grace your household? All can play zithers and other instruments to beguile your hours! All can dance like nymphs!"

Lucanus shook off his grasp. The girls gazed at him with rapture and clapped their hands. They were entranced by his appearance. "Apollo!" cried the merchant. "These are your Graces! And the price is ridiculously low, for all of them!"

"I am not interested," said Lucanus.

The merchant bent closer to him and whispered knowingly in his ear, "Master, I have a beautiful plump boy only ten years old, also from Araby, who has been castrated——"

Lucanus half turned to him, filled with a powerful impulse to strike him to the ground. But at that moment he heard the jangling of chains, a shout and a blow, and another merchant was driving a man upon the platform, and Lucanus turned to look, his face already sweating with rage. The slave was literally clothed in chains, which dripped and clattered from his manacled wrists and ended in iron rings about his ankles. No one but a dangerous criminal was ever chained so. The merchant's whip cracked about his body and limbs and shoulders, but he moved with dignity and as though he felt no pain and was not aware of being in this place at all.

There he stood now, his chains glittering in the hot light. He was completely naked; he wore not even a loincloth; he was like a splendid animal, and his skin was a dark brown, shining and shimmering like silk. Kingly, regal, and very tall, with a breast like two plates of joined bronze armor, with rippling muscles and marvelously formed legs and arms, he gazed at the sky with an immutable and aloof expression. His features were Negroid, yet majestic. He wore his black and kinky hair in two short braids twisted together; a golden ring was thrust through the septum of his nose. His black eyes shimmered in the sun like two pools.

Lucanus moved closer to the platform, fascinated. He knew with an instinctive knowledge that, despite the features and the color, this man was no creature from the jungle. He was regnant; he ignored all about him, but his was not the blind ignorance of a beast. The large and shimmering eyes brimmed with grief, but a quiet and resigned grief, and intelligence. Then he saw Lucanus, and the two young men looked silently at each other, one from the height of the platform and the other in the burning dust.

The merchant, seeing this, grasped Lucanus again. "Master! Very cheap! Absurdly cheap! A strong slave, who, if he is kept cautiously chained, will more than earn his keep. Look at those muscles! Look at those hands, those legs! Master, I am ashamed to tell you the price!"

The slave looked down at Lucanus and a mysterious quickening, an eagerness, glowed in his eyes, and he took one step forward. The chains clanked. There was a searching passion on the slave's face now, a pleading, a hope.

"His name," said the merchant, rubbing his Levantine hands, "is Ramus."

"What has he done?" murmured Lucanus, looking up into the slave's passionately searching eyes.

The merchant coughed and scratched his bearded chin. "Why—why nothing, Master." He added, confidentially, "To tell you the truth, Apollo, he is mute. He cannot speak. He came to Athens some time ago, and he walked the streets and stared into the faces of the people; he was found, this heathen, in the Parthenon itself, moving among the statues, invading the temples. The watch saw him at night, walking in the light of the torches, sometimes carrying a lantern. It is said that he had armlets of gold and anklets of gold, but I believe this is a lie, for all he has is the gold ring in his nose. He was taken before a justice, and questioned by interpreters in many languages, and always he shook his head. He was given a stylus and a tablet, to write, but he shook his head. Naturally, he is a barbarian, from some far jungle or desert."

"How do you know his name is Ramus, then?" asked Lucanus. He moved a little closer to the platform; his heart was beating with heavy compassion.

The merchant shrugged. "It is the name the people of Athens gave him, for he was a curiosity on the streets for many months. Crowds of jeering children followed him."

"Then?" said Lucanus, as the merchant abruptly stopped speaking.

"Well, now, Master, you know how superstitious mobs are. It began to be rumored that he possesses the evil eye. You will notice how strange and luminous his eyes are. Women began to claim that his glance caused them to abort; when he passed through a field one night, a peasant saw him, and swore afterwards that all his sheep died and his olive trees withered. The rumors mounted; children fell on the streets writhing after his passage. Girls screamed they were seized by demons in the night, after he had gazed at them." The merchant laughed and winked. "We merchants are more practical men. We know that the only evil is in not possessing money."

"He is not a slave," said Lucanus, bitterly. "Did he have any money at all?"

The merchant pondered, his sly eyes upon the young Greek. He fingered his scraggly beard. "He possessed gold coins with peculiar inscriptions, but of great weight. Scholars examined them; they could not declare the origin. Nevertheless, he bought food with them, though no one knows where he housed himself. The matter became serious when he purchased several loaves of bread and gave them to a gang of chained slaves working on a road. It is true that such slaves are not fed well—— That night the slaves escaped. It is rumored that the evil eye dissolved the iron—— One must remember how superstitious the ignorant are——"

"How was he sold into slavery?" demanded Lucanus in a loud, harsh voice.

"Master, the law court could no longer profess not to know of this creature and the enraged charges against him. As I told you, he was questioned; he cannot speak; he could not defend himself. It was decided he was a dangerous criminal. He was thrown into prison. Certainly the judges are not superstitious, but they are creatures of the people. You will remember Socrates; it was declared that he perverted youth and ridiculed the gods. The judges did not truly believe that, but there was the mob to consider, who have votes. Hence the hemlock cup. We purchased him today from the jailer, and so here he is."

"For no crime at all, but only for a searching!" said Lucanus.

"Yes. For what was he searching, Master?" The merchant peered at Lucanus. "You are a wise man, O Apollo, as well as handsome like the gods! For what was he searching as he wandered the streets day and night and gazed in all faces?"

Lucanus said shortly, "I will buy him. But you must remove the chains." He swung the hooded mantle from his shoulders and held it up to Ramus, who, his wrists jangling, reached down for it with dignity and put it over his naked body. Then, to Lucanus' sorrow, the slave's eyes filled with tears and he smiled a tremulous smile, and a great joy illuminated his dark features.

The merchant leaped upon the platform, licking his lips. He ruminated on the price as he unlocked the chains. Then he frowned down at Lucanus and named a large sum. Lucanus contemptuously tossed a purse on the platform, and the merchant seized it with avarice and began to count the money, his lips slavering. He cried out with delight, "Master, you have obtained a great bargain! You will not regret this!"

"Come," said Lucanus to the slave, who lightly jumped from the platform and stood beside him. A thin chain dangled from his wrist; Lucanus understood that he was to take one end and lead his purchase away with it. He seized the chain and it parted in his strong hands and he threw it from him as though it were a tainted object.

"You are free," said Lucanus. "Follow me to my home. To our home."

Chapter Thirty-two

The little house, painted a pale blue, and with a rosy roof, sat within a small walled court. A pool floating with pink water lilies and broad green leaves, and filled with tiny golden fish, stood in the center of the garden. A large fig tree provided cool dark shade over a stone bench, and a few fruit trees, citrus and apple, and a big date palm, scattered themselves around the walls. Lucanus, besides cultivating his herb patches, also grew some roses, which reminded him of Rubria; jasmine surrounded his austere house. He could see, from his garden, the silvery hills of Greece, spotted, here and there, with the darkness of pointed cypresses and the darker silver of olive trees, and the pure blue of the skies.

The interior of the house, which contained only three rooms, had been plastered white, against which the meager furniture cast sharp black shadows in the blaze of morning sun. Here the curtains at the windows were of some thick heavy blue stuff, and the same cheap material hung over the doorways. The red tiled floor was bare. Lucanus led his new purchase into his house, and Ramus looked about him mutely and indifferently. And always his shimmering eyes returned to Lucanus' face with eagerness and seeking.

Lucanus went to his spring in the garden—the source of the pool—and brought in a large pitcher of goat's milk. He put this, foaming and cool, on the bare wooden table, sliced some dark bread, placed this with inexpensive cheese on the table, and added a wooden bowl of fruit and a dish of honeycomb. Ramus watched him in utter silence, standing in the center of the room. Then Lucanus said, gently, "This is our meal. Sit with me and eat."

Ramus gazed at him dumbly. Lucanus, watching him, repeated his words in Latin, then in some of the Mediterranean dialects. There was no response. Lucanus tried Egyptian, then finally a mixture of Babylonian, Hebrew, Aramaic and African. It finally came to Lucanus that Ramus had understood all these various tongues, and that some terror in him kept him from acknowledging this. So Lucanus shrugged, and said in Greek, "There is some reason why you refuse to admit that you understand me, and if I knew that reason I would comprehend. Until you trust me you may keep your own counsel." He looked at Ramus earnestly, and continued, "In the Greek language the word meaning 'slave' also means 'thing.' To me you are a man, therefore neither a slave nor a thing."

Ramus' majestic Negroid face did not change, but a single tear slipped around his eyelid and his lips trembled. Lucanus looked away an instant, then returned his regard to the colored man. He said, very softly, "I see you hear me. You are not deaf also?"

For a long moment or two Ramus did not respond, then, almost imperceptibly, he shook his head. Lucanus smiled, and motioned him to one of the two benches at the table. But Ramus raised his hands above his head, pressed the palms together, dropped them so to his breast, then fell on his knees and touched the floor with his forehead in silent prayer. Lucanus' face darkened sadly, but he waited with politeness. Ramus rose and seated himself at the table; Lucanus' mantle flowed about his shoulders, and the big golden ring in his nose glittered in the sun. Lucanus broke the bread and gave Ramus half. They began to eat. The light filled the small stark room and lay like a yellow halo about Lucanus' head. And always Ramus watched him as he ate and drank.

"I could take you to the praetor tomorrow and have you given your freedom," said Lucanus, quietly. "But that would do you no service. The authorities would seize you, throw you into prison, and deliver you up to the slavemasters once more. In two weeks' time we leave Greece for a while, for I am a physician, a ship's doctor, with a few homes here and there where I rest. At the first port I will seek out a Roman praetor and you shall have your freedom, and then you may leave for your own country."

He looked at Ramus. Then, to his astonishment, Ramus smiled radiantly and shook his head. He lifted his large dark hand, pointed to himself, then to Lucanus, and bowed.

"I keep no slaves," said Lucanus, sternly. "The owner of slaves is more degraded in my sight than the slaves themselves." He studied the other man. "Ah, I see. You are indicating that where I go you wish to go also?"

Ramus nodded, his smile brighter. "Why?" asked Lucanus.

Ramus made the motions of writing, and Lucanus rose, brought him a tablet and a stylus. Ramus began to write, slowly and carefully, in Greek, then gave the tablet to Lucanus. "Call me Ramus, Master, for such is the name the Greeks have given me, and my own name will mean nothing to you. Let me be your servant, whether you free me or not, for my heart told me, on seeing you this morning, that where you go I should go, for you shall lead me to him."

Ramus had written precisely in Greek, but it was a scholar's Greek, stilted and pompous. Lucanus lifted his fair eyebrows and tapped the stylus against his lips. "I do not understand," he said. "Who is he to whom I shall lead you?" Ramus smiled brilliantly. He reached for the stylus and tablet, and wrote, "He is he who will deliver my people from the curse laid on Ham, my ancient father, and him I seek, and through you I shall find him, and only through you, whom he has touched."

Lucanus looked at the tablet for a long while. Finally he shook his head. "I understand the Jewish religion. It was Noah who upbraided his sons for finding him in his drunken nakedness. He particularly laid the curse on his son, Ham, of the black countenance. It is true that the black man has been truly cursed, but not by any deity, but only by man. If there is God, and I know there is God, He has not cursed any of His children. Nor to any man has He given the commandment to curse other men, but only to do good to them."

He spoke reluctantly; his anger against God made his face flush. He said, half to himself, "I have a quarrel with God, whose existence I cannot deny. I begin to understand that you believe that somewhere in the world there exists a man who can lift the curse of man against the sons of Ham and turn their hatred from them. Do you think only the sons of Ham are afflicted by the rage and hate of men? No. We are all afflicted by each other." He spoke with some impatience. "And how is it possible for me, who am angered against God, to lead you to anyone who can help you and your people?"

Ramus did not answer. After a little he rose with dignity, took Lucanus' hand and pressed it to his forehead. He sat again and studied the Greek piercingly, and a smooth gleam of contentment lay about his large, thick lips, and a tenderness shone in his eyes. Lucanus rose, found his physician's pouch, and said, "Let me examine your throat to see if there is a physical reason for your muteness."

Ramus shook his head, but obediently opened his mouth. Lucanus turned his face to the sun and pressed down his tongue with a silver blade. The throat was remarkably clean and healthy; the larynx showed no injury; the sound box was in perfect order and the cords clear. Lucanus sat down and leaned his chin on his palm. "You can speak," he said, "if you wish. Is it that you do not want to speak?"

Ramus denied this with a vehement motion of his head.

"Have you ever spoken?" Ramus indicated this was so. He lifted ten fingers to indicate years. "What struck you dumb then?"

Ramus reached for the tablet and the stylus, and filled it with tiny, close writing.

"Master, I am king of a small secret nation in Africa, a land which you do not know. It is near one of the ancient mines and treasuries of Solomon, which we have hidden from all men because of their avarice. When I was a youth, my father sent me to Cairo, where I learned the various tongues of mankind, for my father wished to bring his people out of darkness into light. He was a just and noble man. Like my father's, my heart was afflicted by the sufferings of all the dark sons of Ham, who suffered without knowing why they suffered at the hands of others who enslaved and killed them. It was in Cairo that I learned of the curse of Noah. But one night, when I was king only a year, I had a dream, or vision, of a man with a face like light, clothed with light, and with great white wings. He bade me go forth into all the world, seeking him who will deliver us and cause men to despise and enslave us no longer. So I set forth alone, with sufficient gold coins taken from Solomon's treasury, and sought the stranger."

Ramus reached for an empty tablet and continued writing. "And all through the world, where I have wandered, seeking, I have seen only terror and despair and hatred and death and oppression among all men. I have seen every man's hand turned against his brother; I have heard not blessings, but curses. And this afflicted me. When I was drained of tears, but not of sorrow, I discovered I could speak no more. But when I find him whom I seek, not only will the curse against my people be lifted, I shall speak once more in rejoicing."

Lucanus sat for a long time, reading the tablets over and over. He was sick with his compassion. How hopeless is the quest of this poor man! he commented inwardly. He thought of Sara's letter. He hesitated. Then he shrugged, went to a cheap wooden coffer where he kept his letters, and brought out a roll. At least Sara's letter might comfort Ramus, who was superstitious and deluded. As a physician Lucanus understood that faith could frequently help where medicine could not. He put the scroll beside Ramus' hand, and said in a hard and emotionless voice, "This was written to me by a woman I love. She is a Jewess. If it comforts you, then I shall not be sorry I violated her confidence."

Ramus unrolled the scroll and began to read. All at once tears burst from his eyes; he smiled radiantly; he was like one who has received a reprieve from death, and he nodded over and over, his breast heaving with delight. When he had finished reading he pressed his hands over his face and rocked slowly in his chair.

Lucanus said, dryly, "You must understand that this was written by a young woman steeped in her faith, with the promise of a Messias always ringing in her ears. But this I do not believe. I am a doctor and a scientist, and am confronted each day by raw life and death, and there is no meaning in either of them for men. 'What is the son of man, that God should visit him, or man, that God should be mindful of him?' I have studied astronomy also, and there are galaxies and constellations of such magnitude that the mind reels in mere contemplation of them. What is this tiny world to any God? My only quarrel, and it is an insect one, is that His hand should have slipped and made us at all and given us only suffering and death."

He half turned from Ramus, and his face was pale and

stern. "The only hope we can have is to make our way alone, to diminish man's oppression of man, to alleviate his pain. If you think that in the Land of Israel there actually lives one who can help you, go in peace."

Ramus showed him his face, gleaming with tears and joy. He wrote on the tablet, "You will take me to him."

"No," said Lucanus. "I shall never go to Israel, for many reasons. You may leave tomorrow. I will give you money."

Ramus wrote, "No. Where you go I shall go. Do not ask me to leave you. My heart tells me that I must remain with you, and that all will be well."

Lucanus was touched in spite of his severity. He said, "I have long been lonely. So, if you wish, remain with me and be my friend."

He found, in the following days, a great and mysterious consolation in the presence of Ramus, who tended his gardens and cooked his simple meals, and who assisted him in the care of the streams of the miserable who came to his door for healing. It was a strange peace to him, in the evening, when he could sit with Ramus over a humble dinner and tell the mute man of himself, his family, and his friends. "I am not very wise," he said, at one time. "The wisest man I ever knew was my old teacher, Keptah, who is now dead. He had an eloquent tongue; if he were still alive I should send you to him, for I have no real comfort to give you, and no real hope."

He was deeply interested to discover that Ramus could brew herbs in strange ways, and he was grateful for Ramus' understanding of the ill who came to his house, and his deft and gentle ways with them. Though he had known the dark man for only ten days now, it was as if he had been with him always, and he wondered how he had lived without this august and silent presence. They would sit together at sunset, watching the changing hills, listening to the birds, and seeing the long wing of night slowly settling over the earth. They read Lucanus' books together, and Lucanus commented on them and Ramus wrote his own comments on tablets. They sat in contentment, Ramus clothed in the cheap gowns Lucanus had purchased for him, the ring glittering in his nose.

When Lucanus closed his house and left for his ship, Ramus accompanied him. In keeping with his promise, when the ship docked at Antioch, Lucanus took Ramus to the

Roman praetor and freed him, and thereafter paid him a fee.

A year went by, and then another, and Lucanus was over thirty before they returned to the house in the suburbs of Athens, where they would remain for a few months. It was as if they had left but a few days before; the caretaker, a local farmer, had done his work well, and all was clean and in order, the trees bearing fruit and the flowers blooming. The only change was in themselves. The suffering and pain and death which they had encountered weighed heavier on Lucanus than ever. But Ramus had grown in serenity and peace and in skill, and about him there was an air of waiting.

Chapter Thirty-three

Lucanus told Ramus of his search for the boy, Arieh, who, if he was alive, would be twelve years old. "I never see a boy of that age without looking at his little finger," he said, "whether on the street, in the Agora of Athens, in the temples, among my patients, or in every alley and byway of the world I know. But surely he is dead; who stole him was full of wickedness and malice against Elazar ben Solomon, who never harmed a man and who made his fortune justly." He pondered. "Why should man hate other men, out of envy or spite or because they are not of his race or color? That question was asked eons ago; it grows stale and dull with the asking. But it is the tragedy of man."

He talked to Ramus as he had never talked with another man, not even Keptah or Cusa or Joseph ben Gamliel. The first had taught and admonished him, and he had felt rebellion; the second had taught him and, with love, had considered him somewhat a fool; the last had tried to lead him passionately to God when his heart was most bitter. But Ramus smiled at him and folded his hands.

He explained to Ramus that he would not treat the wealthy and the men of position, for they could afford other physicians and could pay them large fees. But time had taught him some shrewdness; he found that quite frequently some prosperous peasants, not wishing to pay fees, came to him for charity. Lucanus said, "When I discover who they are, and I have developed an occult sense which serves me well at times in this discovery, I charge them a fee, though it is small. Why should they take from me my time when they can afford a physician and others need my help? I treat the affluent only when they come to me in despair, having been consigned to hopelessness by their own physicians."

Ramus, when Lucanus had said this, reached for a tablet, and wrote: "But all men suffer, and it is good to help them." Lucanus looked at him with somber marveling; here was one who had endured torments from men and he was compassionate.

One day, as the time drew nearer for Lucanus to board a ship again, a magnificent litter borne by six handsome black slaves stopped at his gate, and the leader, who spoke eloquent Greek, begged him to visit his master, who was at the point of death and had been abandoned by his physicians. Lucanus wished to refuse; he was very weary these days; the streams of the unfortunate began to form before his house at dawn, and then again at sunset.

He said, "If your master's physicians have given him up, I, who treat the harsher diseases on shipboard and in the cities, could not help him." Then his physician's curiosity sharpened in him, and he asked, "What ails your master?"

"He is dying in all his parts, Master. His sons are distracted, and they have heard of you, and they are willing to pay an enormous fee for your help."

Lucanus considered. He had used much of the bequest from Diodorus in charity; he had very little money at this time. He began to shake his head. At least a score of suffering men and women and children were waiting in his garden, some lying on the ground, some fallen on the bench, some prostrate on his doorstep. But Ramus touched his arm, and nodded, smiling beseechingly. Lucanus glanced at his patients; many were ill of chronic diseases; Ramus, who had grown in knowledge and who had a mysterious healing power of his own, and who had learned well from Lucanus, could examine and treat some of these piteous wretches.

"If it will not take more than an hour then," said Lucanus, reluctantly, and got into the litter and was borne away. But still his curiosity was aroused. The litter glided rapidly through the light-filled streets of Athens, then moved away from the crowded section to an area filled with pleasant villas and gardens and white walls spilling with rosy and purple flowers. It stopped at a particularly fine wrought-iron gate, which depicted Apollo and his enigmas, and a slave opened it and admitted Lucanus to the garden, and he saw a lovely house in the near distance.

Lucanus looked at the house admiringly, for it was a veritable miniature of a villa, reduced in scale from magnificence to exquisite small form. The mosaics of the courtyard were rosy, and each tiny flower bed had been outlined in blue tile, like an azure halo. There was only one fountain, a low marble bowl filled with sparkling water and pink lilies, and its central figure was a dolphin standing on its tail; from its open mouth issued an iridescent stream. The house itself shone whitely in the sun, with small but perfect columns in the Ionian fashion.

So impressed was Lucanus with this delightful vision that he did not at first notice three middle-aged men resting together on a curved marble bench on the other side of the fountain, sheltered by a clump of myrtle trees. They were dressed formally in white togas to which they offered a sharp contrast, for, though tall, they had no aristocracy of demeanor and their features were blunt. His physician's eye noted the large, work-twisted hands, the small eyes, the pock-marked and oily dark skins, the rough and graying hair. He also observed that all wore rings of considerable value and that their sandals were of the best possible leather. They were like dull freedmen who had taken on the garments of their master. Their resemblance to each other was remarkable, and he understood at once that they were brothers.

The first one, who was obviously the oldest, said, "Greetings." He added quickly, and in the monotonous and uncertain voice of the lowborn, "Welcome to this house of my father, Phlegon. My name is Turbo, and these are my brothers, Sergius and Meles." Lucanus returned the bows of the three men with a courteous murmur, showing no sign that to him Turbo's voice had none of the elegant accent of the cultured Athenian.

Sergius and Meles were quite content to allow their brother to speak for them. Their passivity was the passivity of those accustomed to obey. Yet, as Turbo went on, Lucanus discerned that all these men had a quality of strength and a crude defensive pride. He began to feel gentle towards them. Turbo said, "It is our father Phlegon who is sick. He has been in his bed for almost a month, and we have had the best physicians. But," and he paused, "he drives them away, declaring them to be fools and rascals."

Lucanus looked about the garden with admiration, and seeing this, the three brothers made themselves taller and bashful smiles appeared on their somewhat grim faces. "One can see that nothing has been spared. What are your father's symptoms?"

The younger brothers looked to Turbo, who said, "He declares he is very weak, and my father has always been a man to speak the truth and not exaggerate. He aches in all his parts. His spine is stiff. There is not a night, he swears, that he sleeps without pain, and he cannot eat."

The symptoms suggested arthritis, Lucanus offered. But Turbo shook his head. "No. All the physicians have told us that there is no arthritis, no swelling or deformity of any joints, no crippling." His small eyes became smaller, as if in bafflement. "One cannot, certainly, believe the words of slaves, and there are five slaves in this house. I have questioned them sternly. They swear that my father eats like a young man, with secret gusto. He will not dine in their presence; they must retire. He says he feeds the food to his large dog, who never leaves him, and that he himself drinks but a little wine for his health's sake. Shall a man believe his old and honored father, or shall he believe the words of slaves?"

Lucanus was silent, but he inclined his head tactfully. He then asked the age of Phlegon, and was told it was seventy-three. "A good age," he commented. "We must remember that the old are often fanciful."

Turbo was offended. "My father's mind is as vigorous as a youth's, Lucanus, and as vital as a young tree. Until a month ago he strode like a man in his early age, and his voice could be heard everywhere, and his hand was heavy." He glanced sideways at his brothers.

"And now," said Lucanus, "his flesh has suddenly withered, he cannot walk without aid, his color has become ashen, and his voice is tremulous and faint."

Turbo scratched his ear and looked down at his feet, and the brothers imitated him so exactly that Lucanus had to struggle to suppress a smile. In the little silence he could hear the singing of the fountain. Finally Turbo, not looking at him directly, said, "No, it is not like that. His color is excellent, his voice louder than ever, and his flesh is full. It is only that he complains and declares he suffers agonizingly. He was always a man of dominance and——"

"And?" said Lucanus, when Turbo paused.

"He is still dominant, which cheers us." The coarse voice had changed, become bewildered. "He lies in his bed, and does not walk, and his temper——"

Lucanus waited, but Turbo was not inclined to discuss his

father's temper. "We are afraid he is about to die," he said, simply. "We have consulted the priests in our despair. He calls the priests imbeciles, and ourselves superstitious fools."

A portrait of a potent and irascible old man was beginning to emerge in Lucanus' mind. He was curious to see his patient, and indicated so. Turbo bent his finger and summoned the slave at the gate. "I wish to see your father alone," said Lucanus.

The slave led him into the house, which was as exquisitely beautiful inside as the exterior, and had been built, designed and furnished by a master. Here were luxury and beauty again on a smaller scale. Lucanus reflected that this might have been the toy villa of some Roman or Pompeian gentleman, and he remembered the grossness of the three brothers and conjectured that it was possible that their mother had been baseborn, wife to a gentleman of Athens. The physician shook his head and looked at the little light-filled halls, the murals on the walls, the whiteness of the ceilings, the fine marble of the pillars, the colors of the floors, the excellence of the furniture.

He was taken to a bedroom streaming with sunlight, the polished floor gleaming with Persian rugs and bountiful with flowers. A big old man lay on a carved ivory bed inlaid with gilt, and with leaves and flowers of enamel. Beside him stood a table with ivory legs on which had been placed a silver bowl of fruit. Seeds of grapes and pits of plums and cores of apples had been tossed on a rug a Caesar would have admired. A large brown dog, very ugly and ferocious, rose growling when Lucanus entered, and the old man sat up suddenly on his bed and glared at the physician.

"Who are you?" he asked, in a furious tone. Lucanus saw immediately that here was no cultured Athenian, no scholar, no aristocrat. All that was on the faces of the sons was on the bearded face of the father, and more. Yet the old man was indeed vital, and his shoulders and his breast muscles and his corded arms resembled those of a strong worker who had known nothing but the most arduous toil all his life, and had not suffered from it.

Lucanus came to the bed and sat down on a chair and put his pouch beside him. He smiled into the impetuous eyes which were brighter than the eyes of the sons, and had no film of age on them. "I am your physician," he said, calmly. "Summoned by your children."

"Another!" roared the old man, and uttered obscenities.

"Will they never have done spending my money? Begone, scoundrel!"

Lucanus folded his hands on his knees placidly. If the old man were ill, it was not evident. Nor could one believe he had a sickness of the mind, for there was no uncertainty about him, and no undirected violence, and no shrillness of voice. He had a fierce temper, but there was calculation about his mouth, an animal strength in the lines of his bulbous nose and mouth, and a profound suspicion of temperament which betrayed the unlettered peasant.

"You must concern yourself with the anxieties of your sons," said Lucanus. "That is why I am here. If I cannot help you, then I shall demand no fee."

The white eyebrows, so ferocious and scowling, tightened over Phlegon's eyes. "Hah!" he exclaimed, and threw himself back on his embroidered pillows. He stretched out his hand for an apple, then bit into it with the whitest, strongest teeth Lucanus had ever seen. Phlegon chewed savagely, then hurled the apple from him. The dog snarled at Lucanus, and began to circle about him like a wolf looking for a moment to attack.

"My sons!" cried Phlegon, in a roaring voice filled with wrath and disgust. "They wait only for me to die, to seize my money! Let me tell you, you smooth white liar of a physician," and he shook a big brown finger in Lucanus' unmoved face, "you will get no fee from me!"

The dog was beginning to make Lucanus nervous, so he frowned at it and murmured a word. The animal stood like a stone. Lucanus murmured again, and the dog suddenly fell on his belly and rested his massive head on his paws and closed his eyes. Seeing this, Phlegon said, "A magician! An utterer of incantations! You have come to poison me!"

"I am no magician," said Lucanus. "It was only something taught me by my first teacher, a physician himself. I thought I detected genuine alarm in your sons, yet you speak of them waiting for you to die, and have almost accused them of asking me to poison you."

The old man lay on his pillows and panted, and stared at his dog. He was frightened. "Release him from your spell," he demanded, "and then I may talk to you."

"Certainly," said Lucanus. "But it distracts me to have him pacing about me and growling threats. Call him to your bedside and bid him lie near you and keep away from me." He snapped his fingers, and the dog sprang to his feet and snarled again, edging his way towards Lucanus. Phlegon called to him in that vicious voice of his, and the dog's ears flattened, he whimpered, then sidled to the bed and lay down beside it. His master eyed Lucanus with cautious respect and continued fear.

"I will talk with you," he said, "but it will do no good. It is very possible that I am being slowly poisoned, on order of my sons. I told this to three other physicians, whose fees could ransom a valuable slave! But they would not believe me. I tell you again, my sons are waiting for my death, and are planning it."

"You have only to forbid them your house," said Lucanus.

"Hah! They have bribed my slaves."

Something slipped over his face like oil, like a secret cunning. He was now, however, willing to talk in his rage, for Lucanus was very attentive. Vigor filled Phlegon again.

"Let me tell you about my sons, my precious sons. Turbo, first, is a thief. He was born a thief, he has lived a thief, and he will die a thief."

He reached for a bunch of grapes and began to eat them with relish, spitting out the stones. He had not offered Lucanus wine, or any fruit. He closed his eyes, enjoying what he was eating and smacking his lips. He said, in a deep and loving tone, "From my own vineyards, in the best of the sun." He opened his eyes and glared at Lucanus.

"Turbo stole from my very coffers, in this house, a most valuable opal, for which I had been offered a fortune. He wears it openly, like the wretch he is, on his finger on his right hand, and you may see it there. Sergius, my second son, has the wit of a sheep, and the soul of one. Yet he is the vilest of plotters against me, and an incurable liar. As for Meles, he is a profligate, with my money. He spends all his nights in the most expensive of the brothels in Athens and lavishes my substance on infamous women."

Lucanus remembered the faces of the sons. He pursed his lips a little. "Are your sons married, Phlegon?"

The old man uttered more blasphemies and obscenities. "Yes! And to loathsome women like themselves, who conceal their villainy under milky faces and soft words. Not one brought a dowry to her husband. I have forbidden them my house, and their offspring also."

He assumed an expression of agonized and defenseless old age, left in loneliness, betrayed and abandoned. A tear slipped down his cheek.

"Yet," said Lucanus, "you have given them homes of their own, I believe?"

Phlegon was wary at once. "They have told you that?"

"No. I merely surmised it. It would have been the act of an affectionate father."

Phlegon sighed deeply, and let Lucanus see the tear he had wiped away from his eye with the tip of his finger. "Yes," he said.

"And you have also given them much of your money, freely."

"Yes. I see, my young physician, that you are a man of understanding." He became excited. "And for all I have done for them, and given them, they have returned nothing but hatred, nothing but thefts, plottings, lies and lewdness. I am left here to die, to fear for my life, to have the company of no one but slaves."

His excitement grew. Lucanus pursued his lips again. There was a deliberate calculation in this excitement. Lucanus reached into his bag and drew out a vial of white pills, and then poured a goblet of wine.

"No," said Phlegon, shrinking back with exaggerated rejection. "I cannot trust you."

"Very well," said Lucanus, and put down the goblet and pill. "You need not take it. I thought only to alleviate the pains of which your sons told me." After a moment he returned the pill to his vial.

Phlegon considered. "What would that medicine do for me?"

"I have said, alleviate your pains."

Phlegon wet his bearded lips with the tip of his tongue. "Give it to me," he said, roughly. Smiling slightly, Lucanus obeyed. The old man drank of the wine greedily. "Now," said Lucanus, "you must tell me of your pains, and I must examine you."

With new and surprising docility, and even with eagerness, Phlegon answered questions and submitted to examination. Lucanus was careful and thorough. It was as he suspected. Phlegon was in the most powerful good health; he had the body and physique of a man at least twenty years younger. His muscles were like iron, his joints supple. Some light came to Lucanus. He sat down and regarded Phlegon gravely.

"Your case is not to be taken lightly," he said, with seriousness.

For a moment Phlegon was gratified. Then he said with fright, "It is not fatal?" and the ruddy color in his cheeks whitened.

Lucanus shook his head, but preserved his gravity. "Not fatal. However, you case should be studied with much thought."

Phlegon was newly gratified. "You are the only physician of intelligence who has visited me, I swear by Mithra! All others dared to inform me that my health was perfect and I was as sound as an apple. What liars! What ignoramuses!"

"They thought only of their fees," said Lucanus, with sympathy.

"Yes, yes!" He put his hand to his chest and rolled up his eyes. "The pain is already leaving my heart! It is quieting, and bounding no longer. I cannot sleep at night for the beating in my throat and my temples."

Lucanus did not doubt that the old man indeed suffered these things. His pulse had been too strong, too quick, his pressure too high, in spite of the good sounds of his heart. Lucanus rose. "I wish to consult with your sons," he said.

Phlegon looked at him craftily. "And what shall you tell them?"

"That your—your illness—deserves every consideration, and must be dealt with at once."

Phlegon smirked, settled himself on his cushions. "Let their hearts be worried then! Let them lie sleepless, knowing what they have done to me in their greed and hatred. Let them fear the wrath of the gods, who have enjoined men to honor their fathers!"

Lucanus left the bedroom and walked slowly through the house, which had taken on more and more the aspect of a precious jewel in his eyes. He went into the garden. The three sons rose in agitation from their bench and came towards him at once.

"What is wrong with my father?" asked Turbo, and his hoarse voice shook.

Lucanus considered all of them. He glanced at Turbo's right hand and saw that a most wonderful opal ring was on his index finger. It shone with rose and blue lightnings and golden sunsets. He looked at Sergius, and his healthy and anxious face, and his ingenuous expression. He looked at Meles, who looked less like a haunter of brothels than Phlegon's dog. Lucanus frowned. Then he pretended to come to himself with a start. "You must pardon me," he said. "But I am an admirer of opals and, Turbo, I notice a beautiful one on your hand."

Turbo was puzzled for a moment; it was evident that his stolid mind did not move with any great agility. Then his small eyes shone with pride and he held out his hand for Lucanus to examine the jewel. "It is very old, and has a great tradition," he said. "My wife is a descendant of a revered line of scholars. Her ancestor received this ring from Pericles himself." He sighed. "I am not a learned man. I can barely read. I honor this ring with all my heart, and I shall give it to my son on my death. I did not wish to accept it from my wife, but we love each other tenderly, and she forced it upon my finger."

Sergius spoke for the first time. His rusty voice testified that he was a man of little speech. He said affectionately to Turbo, "It was on the tenth anniversary of your marriage, when your wife gave the ring to you, my brother. You wear it well, for all you are not a scholar, but your son will bring honor to your name."

Turbo sighed. "Still, my father craves it. I often wonder if I am not a disobedient son in not presenting it to him."

"It is yours, and your son's," said Meles, also speaking for the first time. "It would wound your wife if you gave it to my father. One must consider women."

Lucanus sat down on the bench, deep in thought. Turbo suddenly blushed deeply. He clapped his hands. "You must forgive me, Lucanus," he said. "I should have ordered wine for you, but I was thinking only of my father." A slave appeared, and the order for wine was given.

"My father will be angry," said Meles. "You have ordered the choicest of wines."

Turbo said, and now he had dignity, "His wine cellar may be small, but it is one of the best in Athens, and I keep it well supplied. He can spare a little for Lucanus. But you have not told me, Lucanus, what terrible illness afflicts my father."

Lucanus said, "It is known that a man's illness cannot be detached from what he is, and his environment. I must first ask a few questions, and I wish you to answer me with candor."

"Ask!" said the brothers in a chorus, and he saw their expressions, and he had no doubt that the anxiety on their faces was genuine and their affection for their father deep and unaffected. His face became somewhat sad.

The slave brought a silver tray with four goblets, and Turbo poured the wine and eagerly watched to see if Lucanus approved of it. It was delicious, and Lucanus was frank in his pleasure. The three brothers stood about him and drank with what they apparently hoped was the most aristocratic of gestures and appreciation, and with careful restraint.

"Your father," said Lucanus, after a sincere series of compliments, "must have inherited much wealth," and he indicated the garden and the house.

The brothers glanced at each other, and hesitated. Then Turbo lifted his head. "There are some who scorn humble people," he murmured. "That is their privilege, though it is wrong. We are humble people, and we have done well and have made our fortunes. My father was very poor, though free. He had a little farm, dry and of wretched soil. My brothers and I cannot remember a childhood or early youth when our bellies were satisfied, though we all toiled with our father. Our mother died when we were children."

Turbo blushed and coughed. "You have asked us to be candid. My brothers and I gave this house to our father five years ago. He had never lived in a house that was not humble or stricken with poverty. We engaged the best of architects. We wished to do our father honor in his old age, remembering his earlier sufferings, and the leaking roof of his house, and the dirt floor. We wished him to have the delights and luxuries he deserved."

"There was nothing too good for him," said Meles, his simple face glowing. "We sent for treasures from all over the earth to deck the house. Never in his life had he possessed privacy or the dignity of a home that was not filled with children and animals. He had only to mention what he wished, and we gave it to him at once, for he is our father and has suffered much."

"The furniture," said Sergius, "cost me two years of income. I was proud to give my father this pleasure."

"I see," said Lucanus, with compassion. "Your father would not have preferred to live with one of you?"

"No. He is a proud man, and he does not like children, and we have many. He wished a home of his own." Turbo smiled understandingly.

"And you have made fortunes?" Lucanus was intensely interested.

"And honestly," said Turbo, quickly. "The gods have been very good to us. We sacrifice in their honor regularly. It happened this way. When I was young, and working on the farm, I knew that we were always in danger of constant hunger, and even famine. I had a great admiration for good pottery, which I had seen in the shops. So I apprenticed myself to a potter who is famous for his beautiful vases and plates and statuettes and his cameo work in white on the deepest blue or red. After a few years he expressed his appreciation of me, declaring that I had the surest hand and a feeling for artistry and beauty." He looked defiantly at Lucanus. "You do not believe this?"

Lucanus reached out his hand, took that of Turbo's, and gently examined the fingers. Scarred though they were with endless years of young toil the fingers had the spatulate form of the true artist. "Yes," he said, with reverence, "I believe you."

"Thank you," said Turbo, with a humility that was, in itself, innocent pride. "And there were my brothers. I induced the potter to employ them. Sergius amazingly revealed a power for invariably producing perfect forms, with almost no loss. He still spins the wheel, for he will entrust it to no other. And Meles invented a glaze which is our secret.

"The potter, who had no children, bequeathed his factory to us. And our wares are sought for all over the world, even in Rome itself. We have a fleet of our own ships, and we employ many people, and slaves. If we could produce twice as many we could sell every vase and plate and object of art, but that would entail sacrifice of our best. We prefer to keep our factory as small as possible, in order that no product of ours can evade our own personal inspection, for all bears our name, and no one anywhere must be disappointed."

He stood even taller. "Caesar's palace is filled with our work, and vases bring the price of jewels, and funeral urns are bought by the great patricians in Rome."

"Unfortunately," said Meles, with sadness, "our father scorns our work and will not permit even a head of a god to appear in his house, if made by us."

"But the Egyptians declare that only their ancient artists can compare with us," said Sergius, his little eyes full of light. "They have sent us cherished objects, which we have copied for them. Our Apis figurines and heads of Isis are in the most resplendent of their temples. But it is Turbo who designs, who produces on parchment for me to copy and Meles to glaze."

"Without the glaze, and your mastery of understanding what I design, what I do would be without value," said Turbo.

He sighed. "My father considers us worthless fools," he said, "though the grand ladies in Rome and Egypt and Athens wear our little medallions around their necks on jeweled chains and have them inserted in priceless bracelets. A certain famed senator buys our vases; he swears he prefers them to the most beautiful female slaves. You must forgive me if I appear to boast, Lucanus."

Lucanus did not speak. "Perhaps," said Turbo, timidly, "you would permit me to send you a gift of some of our work."

The young Greek was touched. "I am indebted to you," he said.

Then he raised his head. "I must ask a harsh question, and I pray you will answer. Why do you love your father?"

They gaped at him with unaffected astonishment for some moments. Then Turbo stammered, "Why do we love him? That is a strange question! Did he not give us life, and so make it possible for us to have what we have, and our adorable wives and our loving children? And is it not charged that a man should cherish his parents?"

Lucanus remembered the Commandment of the Jews: "Honor thy father and thy mother . . ." But still, there were parents who deserved no honor.

Turbo spoke with more heat: "Has not my father suffered much also? It is little enough that we can lighten and make brighter his old age, for never could he satisfy his belly when we were young, and never did he wear aught but rags."

Lucanus meditated on the strangeness and innocence of love, and how love can be exploited by the ruthless. He stood up. "I must have a word again with your father. I have given him some medicine. But this I can tell you: when I have consulted with him and given him advice his health will be restored for many years, for he is a strong man."

They called joyous blessings after him when he left the garden. He made his way to Phlegon's bedroom. The old man was considerably relaxed, and lay quietly on his pillows, and when he saw Lucanus he slightly raised his head and gave the physician a smile almost pleasant. "My pain has gone," he said. Then his face changed, became sly and secret once more. "You have talked with my sons?"

Lucanus seated himself with deliberation and helped himself to a handful of grapes and chewed them thoughtfully. And all the time he kept his bright blue eyes fixed on Phlegon. After a few seconds Phlegon's face darkened and became brutish.

"They have lied to you," he said, with a flatness in his loud voice.

"I think not," said Lucanus. "I have been a physician for many years, and physicians learn another sense which enables them to detect lies," and his eyes were full of hard significance. Nevertheless, he also pitied Phlegon, who he knew envied his sons, resented their success and position and fame, for he had been only a poor and illiterate peasant. Moreover, it was quite evident that he knew of the love of his sons, and so tormented them.

"Leave," said Phlegon, abruptly, and turned his head into his pillows, and his powerful shoulders heaved. "I am an old weak man, abandoned, cheated, lonely. Leave me with my gods, for, at the last, they are the only consolers of men."

"True," said Lucanus. "But I doubt that you believe in the gods. I am going to give your sons some sound advice before I leave this house. I am going to tell them what you truly are, and what you honestly think of them. I will also suggest that they return you to your little farm, and never visit you again, for I believe it will be best for them and their peace of mind. There are times when children must abandon parents for their own sake."

Phlegon hurled himself up from his cushions, and his teeth were bared between his bearded lips, and his eyes flashed with the wildest hatred and fear.

"You will destroy me!" he shrieked, and he cursed Lucanus in language so vivid that Lucanus was full of admiration for its gusto and imagination. He waited patiently until Phlegon had exhausted himself, and had burst into genuine tears. Then he said, kindly, "I will not do this, I will not disillusion your sons about you, if you will obey me at once, and continue to obey me."

"Curse you!" bellowed Phlegon. "May the ravens tear out your liver!" He paused when Lucanus appeared unimpressed and somewhat bored. Then he whimpered, "Tell me what I must do. But, good physician, have mercy on an old man! Would you send me back to that wretched patch of land, which is filled with stones and thorns, to live out my days in misery again?"

"I certainly will," said Lucanus. "Unless you obey. The first step is to get out of that bed immediately, and dress yourself in your best, and hang a boss about your neck. And then you will go out into the garden with me and greet your sons like a loving father, embracing them. And you will swear an oath to me, here in secret, that never again will you lie about your sons, nor upbraid them falsely, and never again pretend to an illness in order to tear their hearts." He paused, then added severely, "The oath I will ask of you is a most mysterious oath, for though you do not believe in the gods there is magic in the oath, and if you violate it some monstrous affliction will fall upon you."

Phlegon glared at him in the utmost terror, and Lucanus smiled inwardly, and kept his lips tight in order to suppress a chuckle.

Phlegon tossed aside his rugs and coverlet and sprang out of bed, pale and trembling, naked and big as an elderly Hercules, his brown muscles flowing like silk. With shaking hands he dressed himself in a long tunic of the finest linen, clasped a golden belt about his narrow waist and circlets of gold around his upper arms. He hung a boss about his neck. He combed his long gray curls, and his beard. He was magnificent.

Then Lucanus administered a weird oath which he invented on the spot, calling upon the gods to listen, as Phlegon knelt before him. Lucanus finally sprinkled the old man with a few drops of wine, and admonished him sternly again. He would have helped the old man to rise, but Phlegon leaped to his feet like an athlete, and he pressed his great gnarled fists to his chest. "Am I a weakling?" he roared. "I may be old enough to be your grandfather, you conniving physician, but I could break your back with my own hands."

"That I believe," said Lucanus. "See, henceforth, that you do not break your sons' hearts, for disaster will fall upon you immediately." He gave the vial containing the white pills to Phlegon. "These will calm you for a few nights, during which," said Lucanus, virtuously, "you will be able to reflect on your sins serenely."

Phlegon strode through the house, Lucanus following him. The old man paused here and there to draw the physician's attention proudly to some priceless object, which Lucanus duly admired. "You will observe," said Phlegon, swelling his chest, "that my sons are not to be despised." His broad face glowed, and he was suddenly released from envy and resentment, and Lucanus meditated how happy men can be when freed from baseness and hatred and malice.

They entered the garden, and the sons were amazed and overwhelmed when they saw their vigorous father hurrying towards them, and their eyes filled with tears and they were unable to speak. They fell at his feet, humbly, and he raised them with large gestures, as if forgiving them, but he was in truth forgiving himself, as Lucanus understood, and he embraced each in turn, reveling in their embraces which pardoned him.

"What a physician is this!" exclaimed Phlegon, his arms about his sons. "What gift can we give him for restoring me immediately to health?"

Before Turbo could eagerly reply, Lucanus, with a straight face, said, "It is a blessing when he who has been relieved by his physician gives him a gift himself."

Phlegon, grinning joyously, considered. But he was still a peasant, with a peasant's closeness. Then, as if calling all to be witnesses to an act of supreme sacrifice, he drew a circlet from his arm which was heavily set with gems and thrust it into Lucanus' hands. His eyes blinked with tears.

"May the gods bless you," he said in a husky voice, and in all sincerity.

Chapter Thirty-four

Lucanus was returned home in the litter of Turbo, and he found himself smiling, and pleased. He wondered how many of his stricken patients remained at his home for his ministrations; Ramus would do well; he had the tenderest compassion and the most skillful hands, and was loved in spite of his color, which the Greeks distrusted. Lucanus reflected on the modern Greeks; they lived on the past glory of their country, and exalted it, though they were producing no great men now of any consequence. Why was this? The poet Aeschylus had written: "Gold is never a bulwark. No defense to those who spurn God's great altar of justice!"

He was surprised to hear a silence around his house when he dismissed the litter. The garden gate swung open, creaking in a dry, brisk wind, and it seemed to echo a certain and incomprehensible desolation about the house. The garden was empty, and no patients were waiting there. A voicelessness hung over everything, like an absence. Suddenly Lucanus felt his heart beating very fast, and he ran into the garden, calling for Ramus. He then saw that some evil had blighted his small and pretty garden: the little statue of Eros, which had graced the lily-decked pool, had been overturned in the water and smashed. The flower beds had been trampled ruthlessly; branches had been torn from the trees and the fruit scattered. The jasmine bushes were beaten to the ground, and now he saw a large black stain on the walls of his house as if a fire had been raised against it and then had died down.

He rushed into the house, his head roaring with an inner noise. Here too was destruction. His few chairs, his table, his bed and Ramus', had been flung apart and broken. The pictures which he had painted himself and hung on the white walls had been wrenched down and trampled, the wood dismembered. His vessels and pots had been defiled. The cabinet where he kept his major surgical instruments had been opened, and there were no instruments there; his careful vials were broken, his pouches of herbs thrown open and scattered. And over all hung abandonment and desolation.

Stunned, Lucanus put the palms of his hands to his head and stood, stricken. He looked about him disbelievingly, blinking his eyes. Why this wantonness? And where was Ramus, his friend, his helper? He began to run about the house, crying aloud, his legs unsteady under him. He had a confused thought that the doctors of Athens, who had long been jealous of him, and contemptuous of him, had done this thing; but his thoughts ran apart in a raveling of despair. Ramus was not in the house. Once again he rushed into the garden, then to the walls, so desecrated. It was there, huddled and bleeding, that he finally found Ramus, who was unconscious. He knelt beside Ramus, weeping aloud, for he saw that Ramus had not only been beaten savagely, but that some sharp instrument had been slashed across the upper part of his face, and that blood poured from his eyes, which had been blinded. Unaware and bleeding, they were turned to the blazing sky.

At first Lucanus believed him dying. He raised him against his breast, and feverishly examined him, and felt for his pulse. It was very weak and erratic, but the dark man was still alive. Lucanus, his head spinning like one in a nightmare, gently laid his friend down again and ran into the house for his physician's pouch, and returned with it. He administered restoratives to Ramus, holding a pungent bottle to his nose, forcing a stimulant between his parted lips. He worked feverishly, thinking of nothing but saving his friend. Over and over, he whispered to himself, "This is a dream! This has not happened! No one would injure so kind a soul! No one would do this to my house!"

He did not hear approaching footsteps, and he started violently when a rough and frightened voice spoke beside him. "Master, I ran away when they did this—— I was afraid—they were so furious—— Forgive me—— Oh, what have they done to this poor man . . . ?"

Lucanus looked up, and his blue eyes were wild and distended. He saw that his visitor was a poor peasant whose wife he had been treating successfully. "Siton!" he said, huskily. "What is it? Who did this?"

Siton squatted beside him, the tears running down his sunburned face. But as he answered he kept glancing fearfully over his shoulder. "Master, if they knew I had returned to tell you they would kill me also. They looked for you— they would have murdered you—it was the woman, Gata, who said Ramus had the evil eye—she had heard it long ago in this city—she miscarried, and her husband aroused the people against you. . . ."

Now Lucanus, with gall in his throat, understood. The husband of Gata was a prosperous peasant, with many fine vineyards; an evil, sniveling and lying man, who whined constantly that he was oppressed by the wealthy and powerful of Athens who would not pay him a just price for his grapes. Yet he was the richest of all the peasants for many miles around; his greed was notorious. He and his wife and children lived in quarters which pigs would have disdained, though his gold accounts in the city banks were the envy of lawyers and doctors and lawgivers and scribes. Two weeks ago he had brought his slovenly and swine-eyed wife to Lucanus, pleading absolute poverty and inability to pay a fee for the delivery of his fifth child. He had believed that, living so far from him, the physician would not know of his wealth, but a patient had whispered in Lucanus' ear, and Lucanus had coldly told the man that he would either pay him a very modest fee or go to a regular physician, whose fee would be ten times as much. The two had departed, shrieking threats and shaking fists, and calling Lucanus a robber and oppressor.

"He came here today, in your absence, Master," whimpered Siton, still glancing fearfully over his shoulder. "You know he has the peasants under his thumb; they owe him much money, for only his vineyards, last year, did well, and theirs were poor. He has apparently been watching for a time when you were not here. . . . He came just after you departed, and he declared to the people waiting for you that you were using them for wicked experiments, that you were a sorcerer, that you were a very rich man desiring the death of the poor, for you know that the doctors of Athens have been advocating the control of births among the poverty-stricken. You realize how inflammable is the ignorant and stupid mind, how eager to believe evil and malice, though you have helped them over all these years, and have cured them. The husband of Gata said there was unjust gold in your house, which belonged to the people——"

Siton looked at Ramus, who was beginning to groan with agony. The peasant sniffled, and wiped his nose and eyes with the back of his hand, while Lucanus knelt, stupefied. "I was here, Master, because of my boils, which you are causing to disappear. What could I do in that screaming mob, crying for your death, or your banishment? They attacked Ramus and left him for dead. . . . Master, you must leave here at once; they will return, to kill you."

Lucanus drew a deep breath. "Help me take Ramus within and set up his bed. I must think."

"Master, you must leave at once!"

"Help me. And when I have Ramus in the house, run at once, if you have any mercy or gratitude, to the house of Turbo, the potter, and tell him that Lucanus, the physician, begs him to send a litter for my friend and give us shelter in his house." Behind the roaring turmoil and anguish in his mind, a cold thought emerged. He had no friends among the wretched he had succored; he had not associated with the rich and educated and intelligent in Athens. Turbo was his only hope.

Siton hesitated. He stood up and wrung his hands. He whimpered, "Master, if I help you they will visit vengeance upon me!"

Lucanus rose. He stood over the peasant, and his eyes blazed with wrath and disgust. "I tell you that if you do not help me now, Siton, a great evil will come to you!"

Siton looked at him, half crouched before him, seeing the terrible light on the physician's face, and he did not doubt him for a moment. Sobbing, he helped Lucanus lift Ramus and bear him into the house, then he fled. Lucanus fastened a sharp dagger to his belt, and clenched his fists, and he was full of hatred. He turned his attention to Ramus, sprawled on his bed. The dark man groaned over and over, and feebly threshed. Lucanus examined his eyes, and he wept again. The cornea was torn and bleeding; the pupils distorted and diminished. Ramus would now be blind as well as mute. The heart of Lucanus was wrenched and throbbing, but his cool physician's hands ministered to the ruined eyes and bandaged them. Again he administered stimulants, though he thought, Better that he should die than to awaken to the knowledge that men are animals and deserve only death. The rich and privileged and powerful man is not greater in his evil than the oppressed and the enslaved and the homeless. I have been a child!

He felt deprived and empty and dry as dust. The hatred in him was like a yearning pit, waiting to devour the wickedness which was man and hide it forever. He sat beside Ramus and held his cold hand, and the tears ran down his face. Sara had written him joyously that his name was blessed in every port, and that the poor adored him. Lucanus laughed aloud, bitterly.

Ramus' hand grew warm in his, and the mute lips stirred below the white bandages over the eyes. Lucanus bent over him, and said, gently, "Do you hear me, my dear friend?"

The head moved in answer; the hoarse groaning continued, and Lucanus noticed, for the first time, that Ramus could make some sound after all, if only a groan.

"Help is coming, Ramus. Lie quiet. We will be taken to a place of safety."

He reached for his pouch and brought out a vial of syrup of opium. Ramus must sleep; he must not begin to think of what had happened to him and the people who had afflicted him. He held the vial to Ramus' lips and said, "Take but a mouthful." He wondered why he did not say, "Drink it all." But his physician's training admonished him even while his spirit was embittered beyond imagining. Though death was merciful, he was constrained not to give it. After Ramus had drunk and become drowsy, Lucanus still sat and held his hand, and finally Ramus slept, a faint smile of peace on his large lips.

It seemed to Lucanus that too long a time had passed. Had the cowardly and sniffling Siton been too afraid to obey him? I do not doubt it, thought Lucanus. These are dogs and sheep and ravening jackals by nature. I shall have mercy on them no more, and shall turn from them forever. My life is over. What is left I shall devote to my poor and loving friend, and be eyes and voice to him. He touched his dagger, and he longed to use it as some dagger had been used on Ramus.

The huge and shining silence enveloped the house. Lucanus put his fingers tenderly on the bandaged eyes, and whispered, "I have scorned and hated You because You afflicted men, and had no mercy for them, and left them in darkness. But now I know that You are sternly just, and that we deserve no more than what we have, and even less than that. If You have rejected man, it is because he is not worthy of acceptance. Give me some wisdom. Let my reason know why You created this world, for You are omniscient, and You must have known what the world would be, and how detestable. How can You, who throw the radiant constellations into darkness, forgive me for my blasphemies against You? Enlighten me! And do You have mercy on this good, dear friend, who has been seeking You and weeping for You, until his voice was lost. Have mercy. Mercy!"

His fingers, on the bandaged eyes, began mysteriously to vibrate. He wished to remove them, fearful that the trembling would cause Ramus fresh pain. But he was like one paralyzed; the gently shaking fingers remained on the bandages. Finally, after long moments, he could lift away his hands. There was a strange weakness in them, a numbness, which began to run over his body as if his blood were draining away.

There was a sudden commotion in the court and garden, the tramping of purposeful feet, and Lucanus sprang up and pulled his dagger from its sheath. He felt the longing to kill like a passionate hunger in his bowels. The torn curtain was pushed aside, and it was Turbo who entered, Turbo with a shaken and tear-stained face, and behind him stood armed slaves. At the sight of him Lucanus began to sob, dryly. He held out his arms and staggered to the potter, and Turbo caught him and held him to his breast.

"Do not be distressed, dear Master," said the potter. "I am here to take you to my house, and your servant also. I am honored!"

Chapter Thirty-five

The Roman proconsul in Athens was a young and ambitious and expedient man. He had never been a soldier; his family was great in Rome, and he had committed some considerable indiscretions which had made it necessary for his family to use their money and their influence to remove him from Rome for some time. He had been educated in the law, and was very intelligent.

Lucanus, all this week, had been flinging the name of his adopted father in the proconsul's face when he demanded justice. The proconsul, while admiring Lucanus' appearance, his intellect and his forcefulness, found the Greek becoming tedious. Lucanus was evidently a gentleman, and the proconsul, a gentleman himself, was inclined to be lenient and grave. But the matter was so petty! The proconsul leaned an elegant elbow on his table and regarded Lucanus kindly. Behind him, in his office, the banners of Rome hung in majesty, and the soldiers stood with the fasces surmounted by the imperial eagles.

"My dear Lucanus," said the proconsul, in the most mellifluous accents. "One understands, as I have told you before, your vexation. The rich peasant in question is penitent; he is willing to pay for the repairs to your house. What more can you ask? He is anxious to ask your pardon in public; he admits his wife attempted the miscarriage herself. He will grovel before you. He will weep at your feet. Let us be reasonable."

Lucanus looked at him with all the powerful concentration of his angry blue eyes. "I want him punished. I want him sentenced to a long period in prison. What is his penitence to my friend, Ramus, who is blind? Will the peasant's tears restore his sight and remove his wounds and bruises?"

"You are so remorseless," sighed the proconsul. He offered Lucanus wine, but the Greek repudiated it with a gesture of contempt. "Let us consider, Lucanus. Your servant, a black man, is your slave——"

"I have told you a thousand times that he is not a slave!" cried Lucanus. "It is true he was wrongfully accused of some nonsense and imprisoned, and I bought him, and I have shown you the papers of his freedom, which I gave him!

How can you ask me to accept the peasant's penitence in his behalf? If he had injured my person, I might be brought to forgive him. But I have no right to offer such forgiveness in behalf of my friend, who is not only mute, but now is blind. Where is Roman justice?" he went on, bitterly. "I have heard of Roman law all my life; my adopted father revered it. 'Equal justice for all men!' What a travesty! What a lie!"

The proconsul sighed again. "Your servant is not only a black man, but he is a barbarian. The peasant is a citizen of Greece, though privately I think the Greeks are overrated. I am speaking of the modern Greeks; they eat the reputations of their old great men as bankrupts eat their capital. Let me read you a rule and regulation," and he picked up a scroll and read from it. "'A citizen of Rome, or a citizen of any country under the jurisdiction of the Pax Romana, has certain rights of dignity, recourse to law, and justice by his peers.' But your barbarian servant is a man of no clear origin; he is not even an Egyptian. He has no status. He is a man of color, not a white man. And you ask me to punish a rich citizen of Greece, who sends his taxes to Rome, and who is a friend of Grecian politicians, and send him to prison! One has to look at matters in a frame of reference, without prejudice, and with common sense. Did you consider what the citizens of Athens would think of a prison sentence imposed on this simple peasant, who honestly believed that Ramus had the evil eye?"

"A curse on your rules and regulations!" shouted Lucanus, and slapped his hand hard on the fine table. "What is law, as opposed to justice? Lawyers and judges are nefarious asses, and should be suspect. I demand justice for Ramus. He is a man, and has been injured almost mortally by a man; if I had not come in time he would have died. Has he no rights as a man, whatever his origin? Is his manhood to be despised?"

He drew a loud and furious breath. "What is Athens to me? I shall never return here, where mercy was repaid by hatred."

The proconsul smiled an almost coquettish smile. "That will not displease the Athenian doctors, who are much incensed against you. The doctors say you deprive them of patients who would pay them a fee. They feel that you have injured them by your free ministrations; patients wait for your return."

"I have only helped those who could not pay——"

The proconsul shrugged. "Who cares for such irresponsible

cattle? Besides," and he coughed, "I have reports that you have sometimes accepted rich patients, whose cases were hopeless, and who could pay valuable fees."

"I have cured many of them whose physicians have said they were beyond hope. If I have proved the doctors wrong, and have humiliated them because of their ignorance, it is not my fault." Lucanus clenched his fists on the table, and his color was high and choleric.

The proconsul coughed more extensively. "I have not brought it to your attention before, but the doctors have written me complaints that you practice magic and sorcery, and that is a serious offense."

Lucanus was astounded. "Are you attempting to tell me that the physicians of Greece, these modern physicians! give credence to such barbaric superstitions?"

"Oh, you must know they go to oracles at Delphi, and all men are superstitious, Lucanus! Even physicians. One complaint, in particular, speaks of a wealthy merchant who was afflicted with cancer, and was given but a month to live, and you cured him!"

"I know that merchant. His name is Callias. That was two years ago. I told him his physicians were right, but gave him a potion to help his pain. He is dead; I am certain of that!"

"He is not dead. He is alive and healthy, and has retired to his estates in Cos."

Lucanus was incredulous. "Then his doctors were wrong, and I was wrong. He came to me with all his flesh filled with sores. It is probable he had some skin disease which simulated cancer—we were all mistaken."

The proconsul shook his head. "No. The doctors were correct; you were correct. By some magic you cured him, and magicians are held in deep suspicion, it being believed that they are in league with the darker forces of hell."

"I have heard ridiculous things before, but this is the worst! The doctors merely resent me. What of those who cannot pay their fee? Must they die for lack of help?"

"I honor your compassion, Lucanus, though I deplore it. I must tell you now that the peasant will make amends, but you must forget the injury to your servant. For me to punish the peasant will set all Athens about my ears, and it is the policy of Rome, the explicit policy of Tiberius Caesar, our divine Emperor, to keep peace in the provinces."

"Have you ever thought that an act of Roman justice would inspire respect in Greece, which invented democracy? Have

you heard the people deride Rome, as I have heard them?
It is not that they practice democracy themselves, but like
all hypocrites, they pretend to revere it. Declare to them
that all men have equal recourse to the law——"

"Even a former slave, a black man, a servant, who was
stupidly injured by a Greek? What is your servant?"

Lucanus clenched his teeth. The argument had gone on for
days, and it always ended this way. He glanced down at
his hands vaguely; he always wore the ring of Diodorus,
and the ring which Tiberius had given him. He never gave
thought to them any longer. But now his face flushed, and
he became excited. He removed the ring of Tiberius and sent
it spinning on the table.

"Look upon that ring!" he exclaimed. "I swear to you, by
all the gods, that Tiberius himself, who honored my father
and honored me, gave it to me to wear forever! Do you
doubt it? Write to Plotius, the beloved Captain of the Praetorians, in the Imperial Palace, who is my friend, and ask
him! Tiberius loves him as a son, and trusts him above all
other men, and he is as a brother to me."

The magnificent ring lay on the table, shining and glittering,
and the proconsul, who was a fancier of rings, and knew the
enormous value of this one, was struck dumb. He was frightened. He picked up the ring reverently and examined it with
awe.

"If you do not execute justice on this peasant," said Lucanus, who despised those who used names and influence,
"then I shall send this ring to Caesar and ask him to give
his own justice, for he will not permit me to be humiliated
and my requests contemptuously rejected."

The proconsul held the ring in his hand as one holds a holy
thing, and he said in a shaking voice, "Why did you not
tell me of this before, noble Lucanus?"

"I did not think of it. I did not think that a Roman official
would need the name of Caesar to do his duty!" Lucanus'
face was bright with scorn. "My adopted father was a noble
man and a tribune, and just, but his kind is dead. He would
not have needed a trinket from Caesar to move him!"

The proconsul wet his lips. He rose, still holding the ring,
bowed to Lucanus and, begging his pardon, replaced the
ring on his finger. Then he turned to his soldiers and said
in a raging voice, "Arrest that rascal immediately, and throw
him into prison, to await my pleasure! Shall a Roman cavil
before his duty? Be gone! The noble Lucanus has been un-

pardonably insulted by a mere peasant, and I will avenge him!"

"You shall not go unavenged," said Lucanus to Ramus, as he prepared to remove the bandages from the blind eyes. "I have had the word of the Roman proconsul, yesterday, that he would arrest the husband of Gata and deliver him to justice."

He reached gently for the bandages, but Ramus tore his head from that gentle touch, and his big mouth writhed. Lucanus stood back, and was appalled when he saw a tear drip from below the cloth. "What is it?" he asked, in consternation. Ramus seized his hand, mouthing silently but with despair. "Do not weep," said Lucanus, frightened. "You will injure what remains of your eyes."

The fine chamber which Turbo had assigned to his guests glittered with sunlight. Lucanus, shaking his head at his own thoughtlessness, drew the curtains over the windows. Then he remembered, with a fresh sinking of his heart, that Ramus would never see the sun again. He turned to his servant, and saw the dripping tears. He put his hand to his forehead. "Do not weep," he said, again, and in a muttering voice. Then louder, he said, "Do you think it gives me pleasure to know that even that peasant, who destroyed your eyes, must suffer for what he did? Do you not understand that I wished him only to learn that he cannot do these things to the innocent, that he cannot, with impunity, desecrate a man's home, that he cannot injure those who have not injured him? He will be a better man after a few stripes and a brief time behind bars. Law is law."

He came back to Ramus, who seized his hand once more. Turbo entered the chamber, humbly cheerful. "Ah, the bandages are to be removed today," he said, and patted Ramus' shoulder in passing. He looked significantly at Lucanus, and bowed. He seemed overwhelmed. "Master," he whispered, "the proconsul himself, the Roman proconsul! waits without for a word with you."

"Bring him here," said Lucanus. "I wish him to see for himself what can be done under his jurisdiction, and what can be redressed only upon insistent demand."

His tone of authority made Turbo bow again. "I shall send in my finest wine!" he exclaimed, eagerly. "And wine for his centurions, in the court." He paused. "Do you think the noble proconsul would so honor this house?"

"The Roman proconsul," said Lucanus, wryly, "will appreciate anything of value."

Lucanus almost forgot the proconsul. With a touch as light as a feather he began to remove the thick bandages from the stricken eyes. He tried to ignore the slow slipping of tears from under them. He hoped only that healing had been accomplished, that there was no infection. But he sighed, knowing that the dimmed light would reveal that the eyes had sunken, the lids withered, and the pupils destroyed forever. "Ah," he murmured, "if I could give you one of my eyes, my dear Ramus! Would I not then pluck it from its socket and deliver it to your own! I ask only that you will not suffer any pain from this time on, and that you will be able to resign yourself."

"Resignation, with a fortune, even without eyes, can be a recompense!" said an agreeable voice close to Lucanus, and he turned to see the proconsul, who was smiling pleasantly. "Greetings, noble Lucanus! I bring you excellent news."

"Good," said the physician, frowning, and returning to his work. "You will see that this is most delicate. I am hoping that the eyes of Ramus have been healed, and no inflammation is present."

The proconsul shifted himself to an elegant attitude and pursed his lips as he looked at the black man. All this furor over a miserable, nationless wretch, who was little better than a slave! These Greeks, it was impossible to understand them. Naturally one remembered Thucydides and Xenophon and Aeschylus, who considered all men valuable and God all-merciful and loving all His children. But this was philosophy only. Men had to deal with the raw stuff of life; it was only during relaxation, with such wine as this, that one could utter noble platitudes with virtue and congratulate himself on his sensibility.

"Ah, yes," he said. "I have delivered the peasant to justice, my dear Lucanus. The magistrates have today informed me that when he is brought before them they will order his execution. Moreover, and this will please your servant, his land and money will be confiscated and delivered to the victim in recompense."

Lucanus started violently, and Ramus, lying on his bed, sat upright, wringing his hands. "Execution!" cried Lucanus. "I asked you for justice, not murder!"

The proconsul was not accustomed to anyone speaking

to him like this, and especially not a Greek. He frowned formidably at Lucanus.

"Do not talk to me in that fashion, adopted son of Diodorus Cyrinus," he said, in a cold voice. "You may be a physician, and a citizen of Rome, and the heir to a Roman's fortune—for so I was informed yesterday—but I—I am a Roman!"

"And I am a man!" exclaimed Lucanus, his face darkening. "And what is a Roman, after all, but a man too? Hah! I will have to appear before the magistrates. Then I shall say what I must say, that justice must be tempered by mercy."

The proconsul smiled, and again sipped at his wine. "It was you, dear Lucanus, who haunted me like a shade and demanded punishment for the peasant. Now you withdraw."

Lucanus clenched his hands; he looked into the proconsul's mocking eyes, and he was anguished. "Yes," he said, "I demanded justice, believing it would be only a few stripes, a few weeks in prison. But this is monstrous."

The proconsul lifted his carefully plucked eyebrows under the brim of his elaborate helmet. "Attend to your servant," he said. "Do you not feel him tugging at your arm? Surely one so precious to you should not be ignored."

He leaned against an onyx column, his eyes glinting with mirth. Lucanus stared at him a moment, then gave his attention to Ramus, whom he forced down on the bed. "Be calm," he said, sternly. "You must not struggle. This may be painful, but the pain will be of short duration." He glanced over his shoulder at the proconsul. "I beg of you to wait until I have completed this."

"I have only twenty insistent Greeks waiting for me," said the proconsul. "That is of no matter, of course. A charming house. I have been investigating it. Ah, what a day it is when slaves and peasants and rough-handed men can acquire such delightfulness!"

Lucanus did not answer him. The last bloodstained layer was now under his tender fingers. The proconsul, suddenly interested, craned his neck. Lucanus drew a deep breath, then removed the last cloth. He closed his own eyes so not to see the awful ruin for a moment or two.

Silence surrounded him, and his forehead burst into sweat. No one moved, and then the proconsul said, "Eheu! There is nothing wrong with the slave's eyes! What nonsense is this?"

The physician's eyes flew open. He looked at Ramus, who was smiling radiantly up at him. The large and limpid black eyes were full, shining and without a mar. Lucanus, trembling, bent over the black man and blinked away a dimness. He was incredulous. He could not believe it. He seized Ramus' chin in his sweating fingers and turned his head about. Then he ran to a window and flung aside the draperies. His knees quivered under him. He returned to the bed, and stared, disbelieving, at the eyes raised to him.

Medical skill could not have accomplished this. He had been wrong again! He recalled the plague, the cancer of Callias, the other strange cases he had attended, and now this. He cried to Ramus, "Can you see me? In the name of God, can you see, my friend?"

Ramus nodded. He reached out his hand and touched Lucanus' hand, and a pure light beamed from his face. Then he lifted the hem of Lucanus' robe and kissed it, as one kisses the hem of a god, and laid his head against the physician's hip, like a child.

"I tell you," said Lucanus, through cold lips, "that I saw his eyes! I am a physician. They were diminished, torn, bleeding; the pupil had shrunk to nothingness; the vital fluid had leaked away from it. He was blind!"

The proconsul ceased to smile. He moved a few steps backward and regarded Lucanus with fear. The physician was in a frenzy. "He was blind!" he shouted. "I know blindness when I see it! This cannot have happened!"

"Sorcery," muttered the Roman, backing away a little more. He coughed. He glanced at Tiberius' ring on Lucanus' hand and paused. Then he said, "My dear Lucanus, you know how sensitive the Greeks are to sorcery. I advise you to leave Athens as quietly as possible. I, as a Roman, am above superstitions, but I have to administer this accursed land and I wish no trouble."

Lucanus' head whirled with confused noises and flashes of light. He ran to the proconsul and reached out for his arm, but the Roman, affrighted, stepped back. "The peasant!" said Lucanus. "What of the peasant, after I made so terrible a mistake?"

"I shall counsel his dismissal after a month in prison, for assaulting the person of the servant of Lucanus, and injuring his house, and inciting a riot," said the proconsul, and fled. The sound of his hurrying sandals awakened echoes.

Turbo came in timidly. "Master," he said, "the noble proconsul ran from this house as if the Furies were after him.
Did I offend him in any way?"

"No," said Lucanus, distracted. He pointed to Ramus. "You
see he is not blind, Turbo. I was fearfully mistaken. I am not
truly a physician; I make too many errors. But I am
happy that I was wrong. . . ."

Turbo approached Ramus and looked into his smiling eyes.
Then he stared at Lucanus. Ramus rose from the bed, lifted
his hands above his head, palms together, brought them to
his breast, and prostrated himself at Lucanus' feet.

"My poor friend," said Lucanus, in a shaken tone. "I have
caused you many days of suffering, for I told you you were
blind. I ask your forgiveness."

Ramus nodded. He reached out his hand and touched Lucanus' hand, and a vivid light beamed from his face. Then
he lifted the hem, a fragment robe, and kissed it, as one
kisses the hem of a beloved friend, and laid it against the
breast of the noble physician.

Chapter Thirty-six

In later years Lucanus often thought of the time that followed
that quick flight from Athens—though he returned quietly
many times later—as a period of his "dryness." He moved
through the glowing, murmurous and simmering Empire
listlessly, even if his skill and tenderness as a physician increased. Never voluble, he became even more silent. His personal life narrowed; he was like a seed in its shell, awaiting
spring and the waters of spring, to grow into a great tree.
The seed which was himself in these years did not stir, thrust
out no green tendrils, but lay parched and without much
thought or emotion. He communicated less and less to others.
Only when Sara appeared unexpectedly in some port did his
planed face lighten and his blue eyes shine; but he saw Sara
only once or twice a year. Ramus could not speak to him; they
had devised a code of eloquent signals which conveyed more
than speech. They moved like benevolent but quiet spirits
through the seething ports, and sat in silence in Lucanus'
little houses and gardens, or stood at ships' railings to watch
the stars and the moon, the dawns and the sunsets. Lucanus
preferred to arrive at his houses at night, for fear of a crowd
greeting him, as it had done a few times. When he visited
Athens he had to devise means short of lies to avoid partaking of Turbo's hospitality. Thousands loved him; thousands regarded him as a god. He shrank from them, except

when they came to him in anguish and pain. His listlessness grew; there was a kind of dull abeyance in him. He eagerly awaited letters from home, and especially delighted in those from Priscus and Aurelia, but his few letters in answer were brief. He was like one starving, but who yet has an intense aversion for food. He went home to Rome once a year, and each time he determined that he would remain longer. But invariably, after a few days, a sick restlessness came to him, and he would leave among cries of lamentation, reproach and love.

Once he said to his mother, "Do not ask me what is wrong with me, for I do not know. When I reach into my mind I encounter nothing but dustiness, yet in that dustiness I always feel the movement of pain. I am afraid to penetrate deeper."

Sometimes he reread the vast quantities of writing which Keptah had left to him. There was one which he read over and over, frowning in puzzlement, but feeling that stir of muffled pain. "He who looks to man for his meaning in life looks to a delusion, for men are nothing except in their relation to God. Do not center your heart upon mankind, for it is a chimera, a mirage. There have been those who have glorified man, have elevated humanity as an absolute in itself; they vehemently declare man to be valuable only in his external manifestations. This teaching has reached almost all civilized countries, to their disaster, for law and justice and mercy and kindness are not rooted in men, but in God, and without Him they cannot truly exist, Him who made them. Man is only the receptacle of grace; he is not grace itself."

When Lucanus read this, it was as though old and rusty gates creaked imploringly on their hinges within him, wishing to be opened. But he turned away. There was no passionate anger in him any longer against God, for he thought of God very seldom now. If God intruded into his mind, he recoiled wearily, for God was indeed now a terrible weariness to him, not to be discerned, not to be wondered over, not to be engaged in battle, not to be regarded even as a philosophy or a theorem. Sometimes he contemplated the useless ages behind him, and the shadowed ages before him, and an immense tiredness would overwhelm his senses. He would look at the stars and remember the conjectures of the Egyptian astronomers, who asked if those mighty constellations were not endless planets revolving around the suns, and if new constellations, with new worlds and suns, were not constantly being created. The thought intensified Lucanus' spiritual exhaustion and feeling of futility.

Once, in Corinth, an old priest, very poor, very humble, and very gentle, had told him, "When I lie awake on my pallet at night a great, strange surety comes to me, as if I had received a message. God is never absent from the affairs of men, though we are not conscious of Him very often. But now I know that a tremendous revelation is at hand whose form is not clear to me. God will manifest Himself powerfully again to His children, as He has done in the ages past, and the very earth quivers expectantly. I feel it! I know it! For the whole world has lost the vision of His face, and again He will reveal it, perhaps in anger, but surely also with love."

"Why this faded leaf from an endless forest?" asked Lucanus, cynically. "Why this grain of sand on a beach without borders? Why this mote of dust in a hurricane of dust? This is conceit!"

They were sitting in the old priest's dusty garden, in which chickens scratched hopefully. The priest smiled and pointed to a hen with many little chickens. They followed her, sometimes scuttling under her wings, sometimes wandering a distance. "They know her voice," said the priest. "There are many hens and many chickens here, but they know their own. That poor hen cannot count; her children cannot count, and there are many of them. But if one is lost, the smallest and the dirtiest and the feeblest, she searches for him and finds him. Perhaps that little weak one wonders why his mother should care for him, with his ragged down and his utter worthlessness as a fowl, and his insignificance. How can she, he may ask himself, know where I am, she who has many children, and what is it to her that I must have my share of food, that I must receive her affection and protection? I tell you, my dear Lucanus, that to love nothing is worthless, nothing is too much, too many, too little. Love never abandons. To God this mote of dust on which we stand is as dear to Him as is His vastest crown of stars in space beyond our comprehension."

He added, "You reason with your mind, which is the blind slave of your five uncertain senses. The greatest of the Greek philosophers, who adored reason, finally had to return to the Mysterious, the Unknowable, and always with reluctance, for it is beyond their reason, that tiny little flickering in a dark and unexplored cavern. God can be comprehended only by the spirit."

But always Lucanus was filled with weariness, and he would rise and go away. He wanted no revelation. At times he longed only for death.

When he received letters from his sister, Aurelia, he thought of her as a child. When he returned to Rome on his few visits, he was disturbed to see her growing into womanhood. And now she was to be married, and he must be present at her marriage to Clodius Flamminius, the son of an ancient and aristocratic family. She was nineteen years old, and far beyond the time of normal marrying, which had worried her mother, Iris. Suitors had been in profusion, for the daughter of Diodorus Cyrinus, with her dowry, was to be desired; she was also extremely beautiful. But Aurelia had shown no urge to marry at fourteen, nor at sixteen or even seventeen. She had smiled at her mother's anxieties, and had not been disturbed when Iris had said, "The girls of your age have been wives and mothers for years. Are you contemplating becoming a Vestal Virgin?"

But Lucanus knew that his sister had no particular devotion to the gods, though she accepted them serenely. He also suspected that she was not unusually intelligent, for he had listened to old Cusa's complaints about her pleasant distaste for books. "This is no female companion for a Pericles!" he had grunted once to Lucanus. "Philosophy is beyond her. She is not interested in politics, stocks, law, and banks, as are all the other women of Rome. She does not even know of the existence of the stock markets, business and brokerage houses on the north side of the Forum, as do other Roman women of her age. When her friends, young matrons, sit with her, gabbling of their investments and discussing a sensational case in the courts, or bragging of their own and their husbands' bank accounts, and anticipating social events and winter travels to the south, and the newest fashions, and the games and gladiators, she sits, smiling agreeably, but yawning."

"She appears to want nothing," said Iris, whose wonderful hair was a flowing mass of pure silver now. "But how long can a woman who is no longer young remain contentedly at a fireside, without desire?"

Once Lucanus, persuaded by his anxious mother, talked

with Aurelia when she was eighteen, and an old maiden. He did this reluctantly; he believed that no one should interfere with another's life. But he said, "Why is this, my sister, that you have no concern for your future? Our mother is very old, and has lived long beyond the time of normal life. She is fifty-four; how can it be expected that she will live much longer to protect you? Your brother, Priscus, is a soldier with Drusus, and is the father of a family; our younger brother is immersed in his books, and desires to be a teacher, and will probably never marry. Do you expect to live out your days on this land, the unwanted old sister of Priscus, when our mother dies and Priscus brings his wife and family to this house as the heir?"

But Aurelia had given him her slow deep smile, and had called his attention to a flock of yellow butterflies hovering over the roses. It had been useless. Yet now she was to be married, to Iris' great relief, and the young man was Aurelia's own age. Lucanus must go again to Rome for the wedding.

Now, as Lucanus leaned on the railing of a fast but small Roman galleon which had picked him up from an obscure African port, he gave Aurelia considerable of his thought. Iris, who knew so strongly of love, had not arranged a marriage for her daughter; unlike other women, she believed in the joyous consent of the bride to her wedding. Her friend, the wife of Plotius, though much younger than she, had brought about the meeting between the family of Clodius Flamminius and Iris, and Clodius and Aurelia, at first sight, had apparently fallen into engrossing love, though the young man could reasonably have chosen a more suitable bride of fourteen or fifteen rather than a woman of nineteen. On this point Lucanus had detected a cryptic note in Iris' letters. This puzzled Lucanus, and explained nothing. Iris surely should have shown more happiness and relief in the prospect of a marriage between a member of so distinguished and patrician a family and her daughter. Though Lucanus' restlessness returned whenever it was necessary to think of those who loved him, and their personal affairs, he forced himself to an interest.

Then a whole flood of pictures rose before him of his sister in her childhood and womanhood. He saw her peaceful brown eyes, full of light; he heard her soft laughter. He saw her running to pick up a fallen bird and to hold it against her breast; he saw the dogs of the estate following her with adoring and fatuous eyes; even the bulls gentled when she came to them; horses worshiped her; the servants could not do enough for her. Watching the hot and crowded port, with its vehement mobs milling on the docks, and listening to the endless cries of the East, and smelling its fetid, aromatic odors, Lucanus wondered over this. There was a riddle here which moved his interest.

Ramus stood by his side and watched the loading of the ship. The African's majestic face, as usual, had a look of eager searching upon it, and yet a confident waiting. His black and thickly curling hair had become intertwined with threads of coarse gray, but his body showed no signs of aging, retaining its muscular strength and litheness. His swimming eyes questioned every approaching face. By instinct, over all these years, he knew when Lucanus had turned to him, and had begun to think of him, and he glanced at Lucanus with love, and smiled, then resumed his study of the crowds on the docks.

The ship sailed, and seemed to stand rather than to move over the flat blue silk of the quiet sea. The shore fell back, as if retreating. The sun stared down from a hot white sky, and the sails barely swelled. The next port of call was a port higher up on the continent, where a load of spices waited, and this would be reached in two hours. Lucanus sat down under the red-and-white-striped awning of the deck; there were few passengers, for this was a courier and cargo ship. The Greek began to think of his life; all his temperament heretofore had been objective; he had forced himself to be so, for he feared to be subjective, knowing that to indulge himself in introspection would reduce him to despair. He looked back on his life as one who stands on the highest mountain can look upon the plains of the cities, the far rivers, the distant ocean, the fields and the hamlets. Yet when he looked now at his life it was as if all were obscured, or barren or fruitless or without color. He forgot the countless thousands he had healed and comforted, or whom he had guided, with mercy, to an inevitable but peaceful death. Never had he thought of himself like this, and it disturbed him, for his rootlessness had been of his own choice, and he had made his own life. Now he was confronted by himself, and he saw himself as one who had given nothing and had received nothing, one who would never be missed. His melancholy became a taste of heavy metal in his mouth, a stone on his chest. Ramus looked at him from the railing, and thought in his heart, My Master is sorrowful. He searches, though he does not know for what or whom he searches.

Before sunset the ship docked at the next port, and a centurion with six soldiers came on board. The centurion had his family with him also; he was a dark and eagle man, like most Roman soldiers, but his expression was gentle and patient, and this attracted Lucanus' wandering interest. It was most unusual for a Roman officer to speak so kindly to his soldiers and show such solicitude, in public, for his family, and to wear such an air of tolerant understanding. When he spoke to slaves carrying his household goods—it was apparent that he was returning home to Rome, for he was not a young man—his grating voice had an odd depth and compassion, and he smiled at the slaves and encouraged them. Yet his bearing retained a certain arrogance; his broad, strong body was powerful in spite of his age; his sun-darkened face, somewhat coarse, held its earlier lines of past intolerance. He walked firmly, and he looked about him with the bold scrutiny of the Roman. When his eye fell on Ramus at the railing, Ramus in the rough garb of either a slave or a poor freedman, it did not fall away, though for an instant it hesitated. Then he smiled at Ramus as a man smiles at his brother, and Ramus smiled in return.

Having, with the help of his slaves and servants, consigned his family to a lower deck, he returned to the upper deck alone. He looked at the sea contentedly, and then at the sky, and he smiled. He spread his big brown legs and balanced himself with the slight swell of the ship, his thumbs hooked into his wide leather belt with its short sword. He removed his helmet and wiped his sweating face. His expression became genial as he glanced at Lucanus. It was evident that he wished company, and Lucanus rose and politely asked the soldier to join him in some wine. Ramus went below and brought up the wine and three goblets, and poured the red liquid. Lucanus waited for a look of surprise and affront to come over the Roman's face at the easy presence of the dark man, and his amazement that his participation in the wine was tolerated by Lucanus. But the centurion accepted the wine from Ramus and gave him a kind smile, and then sat beside Lucanus, who had introduced himself while they had been awaiting Ramus' services.

"I left Judea three weeks ago," he said, "to gather up my family where my wife and my two daughters had been enjoying the dryness of the desert air. My family is not very well," and he sighed, but immediately the look of peace returned to his face. "I have now been retired; I have a small estate near Naples, and there I intend to live out my life, with no regrets and no further ambitions." His name was Antonius. He continued, "Once I believed that there could be no life for me except as a soldier and a guardian of Rome. Once I was the proudest of men, and, I am ashamed to confess it, the most impatient."

Lucanus was interested. Pride and impatience were not regarded as reprehensible among Romans, but as part of the national character.

The centurion gave him a shy, hesitating glance, and Lucanus was very much intrigued. The glance had a boyishness in it, and a candor. Ramus, who was standing close by, moved closer.

"But all this must be of no interest to you, Lucanus," said the soldier, in apology. "You must forgive the maunderings of an old man." He sipped his wine and looked dreamily at the sea. "Yet I feel impelled to speak so to any who will listen." He held the goblet to his lips and still gazed at the rising ocean, and a look of exaltation and wonderment shone in his fierce black eyes.

"It is indeed of much interest," said Lucanus, and signaled to Ramus to pour more wine. Antonius thanked Ramus, and Lucanus was freshly astonished.

Antonius withdrew his gaze from the sea and stared into the goblet he held in his brawny hands. He said, "For a long time I lived in Capharnaum. It was there that I was stationed, until at my request I was recalled to Rome. You must understand, Lucanus, that the Jews are much like Romans. They have the same pride and are stiff-necked, and love their country; they are also shrewd, while they are also very religious. They market. And they pray. They are excellent dealers. And they give alms to the poor."

"Yes," said Lucanus, with a fond smile. "I understand. My adopted father was like that. He, too, often mentioned that the Romans and the Jews were much alike."

Antonius nodded. He was very serious, like a youth. "The Jews detested me, as they detest all Romans—and do not brothers detest one another?—and yet over the years we became excellent friends. I learned, not only the vulgate, Aramaic, but the Hebrew of the wise men, and sometimes they would visit me, though not often, and talk to me of many things. I was instrumental, a few years ago, in the building of a synagogue, which, as those in Capharnaum are very poor, was badly needed. I am not a poor man; I poured out my own money for the synagogue. Yes, we were friends, loving one another, the Jews and I. My oldest daughter married a very learned young Jew, and she lives with him in Jerusalem, and they have three little children. They are beautiful," he added, and his eyes misted.

Lucanus listened courteously, but he was becoming somewhat bored. The centurion had a most weighty air, and Lucanus remembered that old soldiers are frequently tiresome, and are given to rambling tales which they find, in retrospect, are very portentous.

"I have left my servant with my daughter and her family," said Antonius, still gazing into his goblet. "I must tell you about that servant, for it is important. He was my childhood companion; he was a slave. We were like brothers. When I went into the army my father gave the slave to me, and I freed him, for I loved him dearly. His name is Creticus; he is fifty years old, two years older than I. He was never a slave to me, Lucanus," and the centurion lifted his eyes as if to challenge the other.

"No men are truly slaves," said Lucanus. The sun was swiftly setting; the sea had turned purple, and the sky was a conflagration.

Antonius fixed his eyes with penetration upon the Greek. "You will remember that the Greeks have a tradition. They pour a libation to the Unknown God before they drink, themselves."

"Yes," said Lucanus, and his heart squeezed and he was filled with an amorphous yet impatient pain. "So my father did."

Antonius held out his goblet to Ramus for more wine. But when it was poured for him he did not touch it to his lips. He looked before him into space, at the wild scarlet of the sky. "I have seen the Unknown God," he said, in a very quiet tone.

Lucanus frowned. The man was becoming tedious. He knew these superstitious Romans, who pretended that they were realists. There was no shrine anywhere in the world, to any obscure or Eastern or Grecian or African god, that they did not visit, affecting to despise them. But they were always there, and they left money at the shrines, and draped themselves with amulets.

"Yes," said Antonius, and his voice trembled, "I have

seen the Unknown God. But now He is not unknown! My eyes have seen Him at a distance, and this was but a few months ago. You must believe me," he said, imploringly, seeing Lucanus' averted face.

"No doubt you believe it," said Lucanus, returning his face to the centurion. His golden hair, now silvered at the temples, haloed his noble head, and the sunset lay in his icy blue eyes.

"I believe it!" cried the centurion, in a voice of powerful exultation. "You must listen; you must not doubt it! It is imperative that you believe, that all men believe!"

Lucanus murmured something in distaste. But the pain was growing in his heart, blossoming like a huge red flower, and he did not know why. He wished to excuse himself; never emotional, except in anger, he was embarrassed before impetuousness, before eager immaturity and insistence. He moved restlessly on his chair. But in decency he could not leave. He looked at Ramus, and the dark face, he saw, was alight as if with rapture. The Greek said, "Tell me about this—this man——"

The centurion stretched out his hand and caught Lucanus' arm; his eyes glowed like dark fire. "This I must say to all men, that I have seen God, and have been in His presence, though I dared not approach Him too near!"

"I understand," said Lucanus, wearily. "I have been in the Court of the Gentiles myself, in the various synagogues. But I have not been admitted to the inner court, where the scrolls are, and the altars. Have your Jewish friends admitted you to that sanctum, though it is forbidden to the Gentiles?"

The hand that clutched his arm tightened strongly, and the centurion leaned closer to him, trembling. The crimson light shone in every crevice of his browned face, in his eye sockets, along the line of his eagle nose. "You must listen!" he cried. "No, I have not been admitted before the altar and before the scrolls. But I have seen God, and that only a few months ago." He lifted his hand in the gesture of a solemn oath. "I swear to you that I have seen Him, with these eyes, and I have heard His voice."

The man is mad, reflected Lucanus.

The centurion touched his eyes with his fingers. "With these eyes!" he exclaimed, and suddenly there was a tear on his cheek. Ramus stood at his shoulder, and the dark man's breath came fast, and his own eyes glittered. "Lucanus," said the centurion, in a voice of the deepest urgency, "you will remember that the Jews have taught for many centuries that a Messias would be born to them, a King. And so He has been born, and He is in the Land of Israel now. I knew of Him before He came to Capharnaum. He is young in the flesh of man, yet perhaps not so young. There were many rumors. He has performed many miracles."

Lucanus' mouth compressed itself until all the color was gone. He was suddenly enlightened. He said, coldly, "I believe I understand. I have a friend, a woman, who has told me of these Jewish miracle-workers, these mystics. Long before the Greek physicians understood that often a sick mind will infect the body the Jews were aware of it. And so the miracle-workers, by freeing and healing the sick mind, can restore the health of the body. It is not new, Antonius. It is not even a miracle, though we do not, naturally, know what the mind is, nor can we explore its mysteries with a scalpel or a probe."

He was, all at once, seized by a strange terror. He wanted to hear no more. But Antonius had clutched his arm again, and the soldier's face was tremulous with some profound emotion.

"Lucanus, I know all about the traditions and the beliefs of the Jews. I have lived in Judea a long while, and my friends have confided in me. This Man is no mere miracle-worker. He is the Messias; He is God. Do you think I believe this alone? No, multitudes of the Jews believe it, since He first appeared among His people to exhort them."

"The Jews are a very excitable people," murmured Lucanus. He could hear the beating of his heart in his ears. Pictures, memories, tried to form before his eyes, and he closed his vision to them. He added, desperately, "When the mind is overcome by hysteria, the body becomes ill. All physicians understand that."

The centurion smiled, and the smile was infinitely sweet. "He is not a physician. His followers call Him rabbi. That is to say, a teacher. I have known many of these rabbis, devout men, who with prayer can heal, and who spend their days teaching the people and comforting them."

The swollen red sun dropped into the sea, and sailors appeared with lanterns and began to hang them about the deck. A cool wind arose, and the sails swelled out and the ship raced over the purple sea.

"But this rabbi is not one of those who went before Him,"

said Antonius, in a shaken voice. "He is the Unknown God of the Greeks, of the Egyptians before them, and of the Babylonians and Chaldeans before the Egyptians. He is the Messias. How do I know? When I heard of Him, through my friends who visited me from Jerusalem and Caesarea, I knew instantly who He was! You must believe me!"

"How did you know?" asked Lucanus, listlessly.

The centurion struck his breast with his clenched fist. "How does any man know the truth, except by knowing it? He knows through his heart."

He dropped his fist to his knee and sighed. "I have told you of Creticus, my friend, my freedman. He fell ill, not of the mind, but of the body. I called in the best physicians for him; I spared no money, no effort. I sat by his bedside through many days, and he did not know me. He vomited blood; he excreted blood; blood embossed his skin. His eyes were suffused with it; his lips were crusted with it. And his flesh whitened day by day until he resembled a shade."

Lucanus started. The white sickness! The murderous, incurable and dreadful sickness for which there was no cure, the sickness which had killed Rubria and had, in her dying, killed his spirit! He stared at the centurion and moistened his mouth, and it was cold and stiff.

"They told me Creticus must die," said the centurion, "that there was no remedy for his malady. At any hour, or day, or week, he must die."

"There is no cure," said Lucanus, in a dull tone.

The centurion nodded, and his eyes brightened as if filled with tears in the light of the swinging lanterns. "But," he said, softly, "Creticus was cured, and instantly."

"Impossible!" cried Lucanus.

"Impossible for man, Lucanus, but not impossible for God. Creticus was cured from one instant to the next, and rose from his bed, his cheeks flushing with life and health, and he embraced me, and said to me, 'He touched my hand in my dream, and He told me to rise and leave my bed!' "

"Who did?" demanded Lucanus. "What is this you are telling me?"

"I have been telling you. It was the Unknown God. Forgive me, I am only a rough soldier; I have no eloquence; I tell my story poorly. I have said that my Jewish friends brought rumors to me of the Messias, and one day He came to Capharnaum. My servants ran in to tell me that a strange Jewish rabbi had come to our city, and that it was said

that He was the Messias. Three of my friends, Jewish elders, were sitting with me, to console me, for Creticus was
dying; he was drawing one slow harsh breath after another, and there was a rattling in his throat and his eyes
were turned up and glazed. The cold shivering of death
was upon him; he groaned deep in his body. The physician had just left, shaking his head."

The memory of those hours made the centurion's voice
quiver. He put his hands over his face. "And I asked my
friends, the Jewish elders, to go to Him and beg Him to
cure my servant, my beloved Creticus. They went to Him,
where He was preaching to the people, and they told
Him that I was worthy that my servant be cured, and implored Him to come to my house. The elders told Him that
I had built the synagogue for them, and that I was their
friend. And so, surrounded by His followers and some of
the people, and accompanied by the elders, He approached
my house."

The lanterns swung in the cool dusk, and a moon flowed
over the high sails like a flood of silvery water. Lucanus
forgot Ramus; he forgot everything but this incredible tale.

"I heard them all coming," said the centurion, and now
his voice was husky and slow. "I knew God was coming to
my house, and I knew I was not worthy that He approach
my threshold. I ran from the bedchamber; I ran from the
house. The sun was high and hot, and there I saw Him!
With these eyes I saw Him!

"Lucanus, you must believe me. The dust was bright yellow over the people and over Him who was in the midst
of them, and He stood tall among them, a young man with
a beautiful face, and the yellow dust was illuminated about
Him. I saw His eyes, like the sky, and I saw His smile, and
I knew again that He was God.

"My legs shook under me; it seemed to me that the earth
and the heavens were incandescent around and about Him.
And I thrust out my arms, to prevent Him from coming
nearer, for I was not worthy. I bent my head, for it was a
sacrilege to stare at Him. And I said, 'Lord, I am a man of
authority, a Roman, having soldiers under me, and if I say
to one, "Go," he goes, and if I say to another, "Come," he
comes. All that I command is done when I command it.
Therefore, Lord, say but the word, and my servant shall be
healed.' "

Lucanus trembled; he clenched his hands together. The evening wind was like ice against his cheek. But he said in himself, No, no! It is impossible!

"And then," the centurion continued, almost in a whisper, "I heard Him speak, and His voice seemed to come from the sky and the earth at one and the same time, and He said to the people around him, 'I have not found such great faith, no, not in Israel!' And, Lucanus, when I opened my eyes He was gone, and the people with Him, and only my friends were there, and we went into the house, and found my servant cured."

Above the sound of the night wind and the thunder of the sails Lucanus heard the faintest of cries, like an echo. He started and looked about him in bemusement, and he saw that Ramus was no longer with him. He got to his feet, then had to clutch his chair, for his knees were weak. He stared down at the centurion speechlessly.

"You must believe it," repeated the centurion. "You look at me, and you know I do not lie. You know I do not lie! He healed my servant and He transformed my soul!" Lucanus turned on his heel and went away.

Chapter Thirty-seven

Lucanus and Ramus ate their ascetic meal together in their cabin. The Greek was more than usually silent. He could eat little. Ramus sat near him, and Lucanus saw that the dark man's face glowed radiantly, and that his thoughts engrossed him. Lucanus spoke with slow carefulness. "Ramus, you must remember that no physician knows all that is to be known; man is very mysterious; philosophers and physicians and priests have attempted vainly to explore his mystery. Magic and necromancy and sorcery are perhaps not what they seem to be; it is possible they operate on natural laws as yet unknown to the majority of us. Once my teacher, Keptah, told me that it was written in the Babylonian holy books that men someday would move across the oceans without the aid of sails; that someday they would fly like birds across the continents. And that someday, in their incontinence, they would destroy the earth on which we live. All the philosophers have known of these prophecies, but they have feared to tell the populace; you will remember Socrates, who was forced to die for his thoughts and ideas.

"Should anyone today, in this modern Roman world of force and might and materialism, proclaim what the Babylonians and Jews have known for centuries he would be called a fool, a madman or a magician, and he would be suppressed. Nevertheless, I believe all these things will come to pass. The story we have heard tonight from the lips of the centurion, Antonius, is doubtless true—from his own viewpoint. Perhaps that Jewish rabbi, the teacher, knows some secrets which seem supernatural to us, but which are part of the natural law we have not yet discovered. And again, and this seems most reasonable to me, the physicians who attended the servant of Antonius made an error. The servant was not mortally ill; he would have recovered in any event."

Lucanus broke a piece of bread, stared at it apathetically, then laid it down. "I have seen that you were much moved by the story of the centurion. You thought that the Jewish rabbi is one whom you have awaited. Do not be deceived."

He looked at Ramus, whose face glowed steadfastly. The Greek sighed. "I have told you that you can speak, that there is nothing organically wrong with your throat and your organs of speech. You are in the grip of hysteria. But one of these days you will speak, and it will be no miracle."

His head ached; little trickles like ice water ran over his flesh; his joints complained. He rose from the table and said, "I am cold. I will go to bed." He drew the screen about his bed, between himself and Ramus, and took out his pouch. He felt his pulse; it was normal. His skin was warm, but only normally so. He performed certain tests on himself, and nothing was wrong. Yet he was overcome with a sense of profound illness. He said to himself, I am not an emotional man, but for some very foolish reason I was disturbed by the centurion.

He went to bed, and he heard Ramus make his preparations for lying on his own couch. When Ramus looked behind the screen, Lucanus pretended to be asleep. Ramus blew out the lantern, and then all was still, except for the murmuring and creaking of the ship, the distant sound of oars lapping water when the wind died, and some far-off voices of the watch. After a while Lucanus slept, but with fitfulness and nightmares ridden by terror.

He stood in a vast hollow room whose walls and ceilings were like cloud, without beginning and end. He was all alone, and he was overwhelmed with a sense of universal emptiness and fear. Then, before him, a great cross arose, white as snow, and rosy shadows ran up and down it, and across it. Its top rose into infinitude; its arms embraced the universe. He stood at the foot of it, and began to weep, and said to himself, I have made myself not remember! And he cried out in a tearing voice, "Lord, come unto me!"

He sank into deep space, black as night, and without a bottom. And then from utter vastness, from the ends of creation, he heard someone call to him tenderly, "I have not forgotten you, O My servant! I have known you from the beginning of time, and you shall hear My voice."

Lucanus awoke in the darkness with a violent start. The ship groaned and muttered to itself. He began to drowse again, trembling at the thought of his dreams. Once he thought he saw a flicker of light, but it died away. He turned restlessly. His flesh felt as hot as fire, and he told himself vaguely that he had a fever. He fell into sleep again, and again desolation pervaded the shifting dreams, and a sense of loss and searching. He was on a glittering and blazing desert, the sand like the huge waves of the sea. He was consumed by thirst. He wandered on and on, looking for an oasis, or a sign of life, or a palm tree, or a line of camels against the burning horizon. He fell on his face into the hot sand, and said to himself, Now I must die, for all about me there is the uselessness of my life, as a desert, and there is nothing to quench my thirst. Instantly cool water flowed against his lips and he drank eagerly, and could not have his fill of it. His eyes were blinded by the light about him, and he heard a voice say gently, "I am He who alone can quench your thirst, O My servant, Lucanus!"

He was staggering on a thin and boulder-strewn road that climbed about a lofty mountain whose summit was blowing with clouds. The mountain had no trees, no grass, no verdure. Its rocks, and its yellowish-white cliffs, appeared to be flowing with fire. Monstrous stony heads, like the heads of a Medusa, or the heads of Furies, thrust themselves from the cliffs, or reared themselves in his path. His

back was bent with an awful burden he could not see; his
shoulders screamed with the pain of its weight. He fell
against the side of a cliff, and panted desperately, telling
himself he could go on no longer. And someone said to
him with a voice that filled all space, "Come unto Me, all
you who are heavy-laden, and I will give you rest!"

Lucanus awakened again, drenched with sweat. The ship
complained, wallowing. The darkness was a suffocation; he
started to rise, to look for water, but fell asleep again.
And now he was hungry beyond all hunger he had ever
known or imagined. It was a roaring pit of anguish and
desire in him. He bit his hands and groaned. Then, in the
mist of pain, he saw two hands and they were breaking
bread, and the hands gave him a piece and he devoured it
and was satisfied. And a voice said, "This is My truth, and
only it can relieve your hunger."

He was in the wreck of cities; he could see the curve of
the world, and it blew with smoke. He walked among the
wrecks, from horizon to horizon, under a murky sky.
There was no moon, no stars, no sun, no hope. The cities
fumed like burning skeletons. Then, far above, Lucanus saw
the star he had remembered as a child, and it moved, and
he began to follow it, running furiously. And as he did so
he heard a chorus of mighty voices, singing from out all
eternity, as if countless multitudes were rejoicing. He called
out, "Wait for me! I am lost!"

The dreams became more confused, more insistent, running into each other, merging, springing apart, spiraling into
nothing, to arise more clamorous, more confused, more
weighted with awfulness and prophecy. He struggled to
awaken, and a shaft of sunlight poured on his wincing face
through the porthole. Someone held a mixture of water
and wine to his lips, and said, "You are ill. Drink, and rest."
He fell into sleep again, but it was as if he lay on a bed
of fire, and he moaned. Hands moved him, and he was
drenched as if in a flood.

He heard concerned voices about him, after what seemed
many ages. He looked, but could see nothing but the lights
of lanterns, blurring like rainbows. Something hot and acrid
was in his mouth, and he swallowed, and his whole throat
became inflamed. A wet coolness swathed him, and he
sighed in gratitude. He felt his head raised, and water poured
between his lips. Lanterns appeared, retreated; the sun
came, and it retreated; a moon shone through the port-

hole, but while he was looking at it the stars were there instead. Dawns wheeled into sunsets, then wheeled again into dawns. He said, aloud, "Am I dead?" No one answered. He felt exhausted; his body had no weight. His head was a globe of flaming glass. He wanted to rest, but nightmares leaped about him.

Then one morning, in a cool and pearly dawn, he awoke and saw a nodding stranger beside him in a white robe. He could not move; he could hear the ship and the whining of the sails. A gray rain hurtled itself against the porthole, and there was a flapping sound made by the curtains. The stranger, in his chair, nodded and dozed. But Ramus was not there.

Then Lucanus, with sudden calm clarity, knew that he had been dangerously ill for a long time. He lay quietly, spent, his flesh moist and clammy, his mind clear. But what was the fever that had assailed him? He had had no premonitions of it, no gathering malaise. He turned on his bed and felt the wetness of the coverlets from his own sweat. He thought of his dreams, and was overpowered at the memory.

The stranger moaned and stirred, shook his head and opened his eyes. Seeing that Lucanus saw him, he bent over the sick man and said, kindly, "You have been ill of a fever for fourteen days, Master, but now you are recovering. I am the ship's physician. For many days I did not believe that you would live. But, thanks to the gods, your life has been returned to you."

Lucanus tried to speak, but his voice was only a whisper. "It was malaria, no doubt."

"No, Master. It was a mysterious illness. I have nursed you since your servant disappeared, and passengers heard you crying through the walls."

Lucanus lay very still, looking at the other man. He moistened his dry lips, and the physician gave him water, yawning, and smiling with contentment that he had brought his patient back to life. Then Lucanus said in that hoarse whisper, "Ramus? He has gone?"

"Yes, Master. But what else can one expect from servants, who are disloyal and selfish and care only for themselves? When the ship docked at midnight, on the first night out, he must have left the ship, abandoning you, for he has not been seen since. Ah. He left you a letter, on this tablet here on the table."

"Read it to me," pleaded Lucanus, and his weakness enveloped him.

The physician, shrugging, lifted the letter and began to read. The pearly light was now suffused with rose and gold, and the ship rocked gently.

Ramus had written, "Forgive me, Master, for I must leave when the ship docks tonight. I must go to find Him whom I have been seeking, and about Whom the centurion told us at twilight. I looked to see if you were awake, but you were sleeping, and then I knew it would be best if I did not wait, for had you pleaded with me I could not have left you. My whole life's searching is in Israel, and when I see Him He will lift the curse of man from the sons of Ham, and I shall speak again, adoring Him. I leave you with prayer and tears, for I loved you more than I loved my father and my brothers, and you have not been master but my friend."

With despair Lucanus thought of that lonely dark man, mute and helpless, going away on foot searching for his hope. He would be a stranger; he could make only gestures. There would be forests to strive through, and deserts, and molten mountains to climb, and hostile cities and hostile villages. There would be, always, hostile men. He would die of thirst, or hunger, or be attacked by wild beasts; he might even be seized and sold again into slavery. Tears came weakly to Lucanus' eyes, and he turned his head on his cushion and did not speak. Finally he slept, and when he awoke at sunset his strength had returned and he could not understand. He had become almost emaciated, but he was strong again.

He sent for the centurion that night and showed him Ramus' letter, saying bitterly, "I do not doubt that you believe that you told me the truth, and that it was, to you, exactly how it all occurred. I myself, as a physician, have my own explanation. But your intemperate tale, Antonius, has sent my friend to his certain death."

The centurion said gravely, "No, I have sent him to his life."

Chapter Thirty-eight

"Is it not time, my son, that you should tell me?" asked Iris, as she sat with Lucanus in the autumn gardens.

"There is nothing to tell," replied Lucanus in a dull tone. His lassitude, which was of the spirit and not of the body, would not leave him. His sister, Aurelia, had been married six months and was already with child, in the home of her husband.

"I should be happy that you did not leave us this time," said Iris, with a meditative sigh. "Perhaps I should not press you for any confidences, for you might become restless again and go away."

He tried to smile at her, but all things were an effort. She sat with him in the cool sunlight, and her eyes were fixed on the deciduous trees, whose baring branches were like fretted gold against the bright blue sky. A fragrance of wine, of apples, of laurel and of ripening dates blew softly through the iridescent air; the distant hills were the color of plums. Lucanus thought that his mother's face hardly changed over the years; its clear translucence was like a girl's; her body was still slender, her eyes still possessed of their vivid hue, her hands fair and chaste.

"When I go, Priscus and his family will remain with you, in this house, and there is also my brother, Gaius Octavius. Are you not happy that your daughter-in-law and the children are with you now? The house sounds with their laughter."

"You forget," said Iris. "You were the child of my youth. I am fifty-five now, and have long outlived the years of expectancy, and so I am old, and my memory goes back to Antioch and I see you as a babe, on a blanket near my feet in the sun, while I spun my thread. Neither Priscus nor Aurelia nor Gaius is so dear to me as you, my strange, my very strange, son."

Lucanus, sitting with her in the outdoor portico, reached out his hand and laid it upon hers, and she smiled at him with tears in her eyes. "If only you had married," she murmured, and held his hand against her cheek for a moment. "If you had married Sara bas Elazar. I have come to love her as my daughter, since she came in the summer

417

and remained with us to recover from her lung fever. She looks at you and loves you as I looked at and loved Diodorus. What greater treasure in the world is there than love? She has followed you into many cities and into many ports. Why have you always rejected her?"

"I have told you, my mother. There was no place in my life for love and a wife and children, and a quiet hearth. Once you told me I was selfish. Perhaps you spoke truly. I know nothing any longer; I am like the shell of a coconut, floating aimlessly on the sea, its living part removed, moving in and out with the tide. Once I had a battle—I have a battle no longer, for my very spirit is weary to death, and nothing seems to me of any importance. I have not left this house because I have lacked the will to leave. I have hurt you; forgive me. But you are one to whom the truth must always be spoken."

He turned his face aside, and she saw his profile, stern and pale, like stone, worn with the years to an ascetic fineness. He said, "Once I knew what I wanted; I was full of fire. There was a time when I rose each morning ready for the struggle. But I am approaching forty now, and it could be that my vital forces are draining, and that the abeyance of age is creeping over me. I remember what Joseph ben Gamliel quoted from his Scriptures to me, though I do not remember the exact words. It was an admonition to young men not to forget their Creator in the days of their youth, before the evil days of satiation and weariness came to them, when they would say, 'I have no pleasure in them.'" Lucanus smiled slightly, and with tiredness. "I never forgot God; He has haunted my life, until a few years ago, when He suddenly departed from me, and left the field where we battled daily. I miss my old Adversary," and for the first time in months Iris heard the old wry humor in his voice.

"But Keptah told me that God never leaves men," said Iris.

Lucanus shrugged. "I tell you, He has left me. There is a great silence where He once was; we contend no longer. Perhaps it is because He knows that He has won, and I am no longer a worthy contender. My vanity is wounded!" and he laughed a little.

But Iris knew that her son was not as flaccid as he believed himself to be. She would hear him at night in

Diodorus' great library; she could hear him pacing. She could feel his seething restlessness, as though he were searching for something. Long after all slept, his lamp burned, sometimes to dawn. A man who was totally without interest or fire relaxed in apathy. But the eyes of Lucanus were strained and tormented.

"What is it that you want, my son?" asked Iris, full of pain and pity.

"I want nothing. I can truly say, I want nothing. And that is the terrible trouble."

Conversation wearied him, and Iris knew this, and they watched the leaves fall and the tips of the cypresses become tinged with light and the hills darken in color. After a prolonged silence Iris said, "I was afraid for you to see Clodius."

"And I was aghast when I did see him, that young man crippled in his childhood with the paralysis, and unable to walk without the support of two strong slaves. What did my sister, who is so beautiful, wish with such a man? But that was before I understood."

He had been appalled when Clodius had come to this house to see him and his betrothed and her family. The young man had a simple and gentle face, with candid dark eyes and delicate features. The eagle profile of the patrician Roman had softened in him; it had a dreaming and accepting expression. Lucanus had anxiously hoped that he at least possessed some intellect, some inner power, some strength of spirit and character. But Clodius was as limpid as Aurelia, and as uncomplex, and yet as unknowable.

And of what did they talk? Lucanus listened without any sense of invasion. He wished to know. Then the very simple truth came to him: they loved all things, without reservation, without malice, without hypocrisy, without fear, whether it was a slave or a leaf, a dog or a horse, the grass or a tree, a man or a little scampering animal. At first Lucanus was aghast. The world would eventually rob them of this absolute love; it was childish and stupid to believe that they lived in a bright and lovely garden where no evil would ever intrude. He thought of the time when death would eventually enter their house and strike down a beloved child or a beloved servant, or one of them themselves. He thought of the sickness which would darken their hearthside, or the natural anxieties of living, or petulance, or irritation, or some long and hopeless disease. What then of the garden and the love?

One day he found his sister alone, playing with some kittens in the garden, and he sat beside her and tried to tell her of these things. He spoke as one speaks to a child, and she listened, smiling, her rosy lips parted, her large brown eyes soft and pellucid. She does not understand me in the least! he said to himself, impatiently. Then Aurelia had said, "I understand you, my brother. Clodius and I have talked about this many times. Certainly we know that the world is full of pain and death and injustice and misery. Have we not eyes? Are we children? We have heard and seen."

She had lifted a white kitten in her hands and had kissed its small head. Lucanus could hear her murmuring affectionately to it. It jumped on her shoulder and put its muzzle against her chin and was content. "But," said Aurelia, "we also know that love is inexhaustible, that there will always be something to love; the world is full of things to love! A lifetime is not long enough for the loving."

Lucanus had thought, wildly, How incredible, and piteous, is this innocence!

Aurelia had smiled at him tenderly. "You think we are children, without reason or comprehension. You think we are vulnerable. I waited for Clodius, though I did not know of his existence until he came to this house with his parents. But I knew him instantly. We are not afraid, Lucanus, of living."

This struck Lucanus dumb. He had searched the shining core of his sister's eyes, not only as a man but as a physician. And a pure light returned to him, gentle and strong. Aurelia, sitting on the grass like a young child near her brother, leaned her head against his knee in utter confidence.

"I am not a scholar, Lucanus, for books are old and the world is young and full of glory. But when I saw Clodius I remembered what Keptah had once told me: Socrates had said that a good man needs fear neither this life nor death."

"The world is full of evil as well as beauty," Lucanus said, with harshness.

"That is because it hates, and does not love," Aurelia answered. A dog raced barking into the garden, and Aurelia called to it and jumped to her feet and went to comfort and play with it, and Lucanus was alone and very still. When he rose to enter the house, musing, he felt as brittle as parchment which has had nothing written upon it.

"They will always be happy," he said to his mother now. "There will never be an end to their happiness and their love. And I confess it is a great mystery to me, and I am not a young man."

Iris smiled at him, and all at once it came to him that his mother was one similar to Aurelia. "I am content," she murmured. "Yes, I am content, for one day, I feel in my heart, you will find such a love and such a happiness."

Sara bas Elazar came into the garden and found Lucanus alone. She walked slowly, for she had been ill for several months, and was a guest in this house where all loved her for her gentleness and charity. She was thirty-five years old now, and no longer young, but her violet eyes were as radiant as when she had been a child, and her sweet and daintily carved face held a wise serenity touched with sadness. Her slight figure was concealed by a woolen garment the color of her eyes, which Iris had made for her to warm and cherish her ailing body, and she wore a white shawl over her shoulders. Her dark hair, streaked with gray, was worn simply in a coronet of braids on the top of her small head, and her beautiful mouth curved in the slightest smile. There was a flush of bright color on her high cheekbones, and this, as she approached Lucanus, and he rose to meet her, was the first thing he inevitably saw about her, especially in the late afternoons. Her hand in his was unusually warm.

He remembered that Hippocrates had warned physicians never to treat those they personally loved, for fear either made them shut their senses against the truth they suspected or they bungled out of frantic anxiety.

"Have you coughed much today, my dear Sara?" he asked, as he conducted her to the chair where Iris had been sitting and as he wrapped her thin shoulders snugly in the shawl against the coolness of the afternoon air. She smiled up at him sweetly. "No. I have coughed very little these last few days, Lucanus."

He said, "You refuse the offices of Rome's best physicians. Sara! You must let me summon some to examine you."

She pressed her cheek against the hand on her shoulder. "I am quite well. Do not alarm yourself. You are physician enough for me." She looked at the hills calmly and with peace. "I shall be sad to leave your home, but I must return to Jerusalem for the holy days. I leave the day after tomorrow."

"But you have not recovered! The travel will be too exhausting. Sara, do you know that I have remained here because of you?"

Again she smiled, for she knew that this was only part of the truth. "Do not be anxious," she murmured. "I long for my people."

He sat beside her, leaning towards her, studying her fragile profile which was as pure as a cameo in the golden afternoon light. If Sara, he told himself, were ill she would not have this calm; flesh, when filled with premonitions of its own calamity, manifested its uneasiness in the twitching of an eye, the distension of a nostril, the constriction of a lip. His physician's penetrating gaze could find none of these on Sara's face. Sara's expression, as always, had a quiet joyousness in it, a fulfilled hope.

He sat beside her in silence, her hand in his; he could feel the frail bones in her fingers, the softness of her silken skin. They looked at the hills and the valley for a long time. Lucanus thought to himself, Why should I not marry her and keep her with me, this dear one I have loved for many years? I have wandered all over the world, for I had no home, and I have always fled away from love. But now I am no longer young; it is possible that my lassitude, my emptiness, my crippling despair are the results of my rootlessness, my sense that I have lost or never attained, the meaning of life. If I marry Sara, then I would have a home, a hearth, a loving companion for the rest of my days. I can buy a small estate, a villa, where we could have our own vineyards and orchards, and, though it is very late now, perhaps a child. I have deprived myself of what men always seek in their lives.

He moved with an access of his old restlessness. He said to Sara, and bent towards her, ignoring the sad stir that had seized him again, "Sara, my beloved, will you marry me, and remain with me in Rome, and build a house with me?"

Her quiet profile remained so still, so unmoved, as she looked at the hills, that he thought she had not heard

him in the midst of her thoughts. "I am filled with emptiness," he said, and put her hand to his lips.

Then Sara said, "You have been made empty in order
that you may be filled with joy and peace beyond your imaginings, Lucanus. Love tells me so, but does not tell
me how. No, Lucanus. I cannot marry you, for in marrying you I will keep you from your destiny. That which
you must find is not in my arms. God calls men from out
the cities, from their own firesides, from their wives and
their children, from all that they love, and His voice cannot
be ignored. He has called you."

"That is nonsense," said Lucanus. "I am empty because
I refused to love, for fear of what love can do to a man.
I have been afraid of living, Sara, and I ask you now to
live with me as my wife."

She shook her head slightly, but firmly. "It cannot be,
Lucanus. Once, when you left Alexandria, I believed it was
possible. But over all these years I have known it was impossible, for you belong to God. You long for Him with a
terrible longing, and it will be satisfied, for you are His."

Sara was gone, and now Lucanus was alone with his family, and the old sick restlessness was upon him again. The
house was filled, but there was no one with whom he
could talk, and he marveled at this. There was his unmarried brother, Gaius Octavius, eternally busy with his books,
a serious young man who lived a secret and engrossing life
of his own. Lucanus knew he had a great intellect, but,
strangely, he was less able to converse with the unsmiling
Gaius than with anyone else in the household. There was
a great formality and courtesy between the brothers, but
Lucanus could not penetrate the reserve of the younger man.
These pedants! he would say to himself. They are narrow
and selfish. They are opinionated and quietly contentious.
They live on a white mountaintop, where they reign alone.

Priscus, the merry and happy soldier, returned home
from his campaigns with Drusus, whom he never criticized
for his manifest follies and lack of organization, but merely
commented on them humorously. Lucanus loved him best
of all the children. He wondered, however, if Diodorus
would have found him so satisfactory, for Priscus accepted
everything with a joke and simple contentment, and was
never very serious about anything. His round brown face

and brown eyes reminded Lucanus piercingly of Rubria; he had her gay manners, her humor, her quick laughter, and her twinkle. He loved war, and he loved peace; he loved his duty, and he loved his family. He was never happier than when guests were in the home; he had many friends, and visited them when he returned. It was evident that he enjoyed life, made no unreasonable demands upon it, loved the games, theaters, dicing, all gladiators, evenings with drinking companions, jests, and good-humored gaiety in general. He adored his children. When Lucanus spoke of politics, he was as bored as Aurelia, and he would relinquish the subject with a broad wink and a smile, and go off to inspect the great farm. Lucanus suspected that Priscus, who loved him, also found him tiresome.

Nevertheless, Priscus was head of his family, and Lucanus felt a pressing need to make the exuberant captain regard the world in which he lived seriously. He had a large fortune; he had military and political influence; he had children, and that was the most important thing of all. So one night Lucanus called Priscus into his rooms, and the soldier swaggered in on his strong brown legs, dressed in a simple tunic. He had been playing with his children before they went to bed, and his rough black hair was tousled and his broad red lips were smiling. He greeted Lucanus affectionately, but his heart sank when he saw the older man's sober expression.

Priscus tried to avoid what he feared would be a weighty conversation by several lusty remarks on the grape harvest, the condition of the orchards, his plans to restock the stream with more fish, his pleasant curses on the limp attitude of freedmen and slaves, his suspicions about his overseers' honesty. His voice was happy, his face unlined, his manner easy.

Lucanus said, "As you know, Priscus, I am leaving soon. You must bear with me; you are the head of this household, and what you think, and what you do, is of the greatest importance not only for your family but for your country."

"Oh, certainly," said Priscus, helping himself to a bunch of purple grapes from the plate on the table. He sighed; he was patient, and he loved Lucanus. "I always do my duty; I find it easy, I must confess." He sat down and ate the grapes with enjoyment, spitting the seeds into his hand and putting them in a little pile on the table, for he was very neat.

"Your real duty," said Lucanus, "would not be easy."

"So you have told me often," said the soldier. He polished an apple on the short sleeve of his tunic. "But I never understand, and you cannot forgive that."

"I suspect you understand only too well," said Lucanus, grimly. Priscus bit into an apple and offered Lucanus the plate, which he impatiently refused. Priscus shrugged. "All too true, perhaps," he said. "But, I am several centuries too late, I believe. What can I do about Rome now, in my generation? Let us be reasonable, Lucanus." His brown eyes were suddenly without laughter, and a little hard, when he stared at the other man.

"Your father died doing what he could," said Lucanus. Priscus' thick eyebrows drew together. He chewed the apple absently. "Yes," he said, "and, as you have said, he died. What profit was his admonition, his death? Did it move one man a jot? Did it make one corrupt senator less corrupt? Did it inspire one Cicero, one Cincinnatus? Did it make Caesar less than what he is? I remember that you told me that Caesars do not seize power; it is thrust upon them by a degenerate people who have lost their virtue and their strength, and who prefer security to manhood, ease without work, and circuses to duty. Did what my father said on the day he died arouse the conscience of one man? Was it ever inscribed for the ages? No. He could not, even in his own lifetime, do one single thing to stop the course of history."

"You misunderstand me, Priscus. I know that it was inevitable that Rome become what she is. Republics decay into democracies, and democracies degenerate into dictatorships. That fact is immutable. When there is equality—and democracies always bring equality—the people become faceless, they lose power and initiative, they lose pride and independence, they lose their splendor. Republics are masculine, and so they beget the sciences and the arts; they are prideful, heroic and virile. They emphasize God, and glorify Him. But Rome has decayed into a confused democracy, and has acquired feminine traits, such as materialism, greed, the lust for power, and expediency. Masculinity in nations and men is demonstrated by law, idealism, justice and poesy, femininity by materialism, dependency on others, gross emotionalism, and absence of genius. Masculinity seeks what is right; femininity seeks what is immediately satisfying. Masculinity is vision; femininity ri-

dicules vision. A masculine nation produces philosophers, and
has a respect for the individual; a feminine nation has an in-
sensate desire to control and dominate. Masculinity is
aristocratic; femininity has no aristocracy, and is happy
only if it finds about it a multitude of faces resembling it
exactly, and a multitude of voices echoing its own tiny
sentiments and desires and fears and follies. Rome has become feminine, Priscus. And feminine nations and feminine
men inevitably die or are destroyed by a masculine people."

Priscus still tried to lighten the subject. He said, jokingly,
"My soldiers, the legions of Rome, are no females, Lucanus!" But he frowned and considered. What was a man to
do? He was absolutely impotent when the people unan-
imously preferred soft slavery to hard freedom.

So Priscus said, "I grant you that you are correct. But I
have told you that my father was born too late. He died
of a broken heart. I was born even later. I do not intend to
die of a broken heart. What price my attempting to call
even a single man to sobriety and heroism? It would accomplish nothing."

"Again you misunderstand me, Priscus. I understand
that you cannot halt history, for decay and death are inevitable in republics. The only society which can endure with
grandeur in the world is an aristocratic society, governed by
chosen wise men, priests, scientists, heroes, artists, poets,
philosophers. Republics breed exigent politicians, and these
politicians always, without end, create democracies, and
death. If men would only watch diligently, so that masculinity would not depart from a nation! But it never hap-
pens.

"Priscus, you as a husband and a father, and most particularly a father, can cultivate the masculinity of free and
noble men in your children; a man must always begin in his
own family, and then reach forth for his neighbors. He
may fail, but at least he has tried. It is not in the failing that
a man is judged, but by the lack of his efforts. At the last,
man is judged singly, and never in the mass."

Priscus was annoyed. "I did not make this world, Lucanus.
I cannot change it. Should I then beat my head against a
wall and crush my skull? I live my life as usefully as
possible, serving my country, closing my eyes to her fatal
defects which I cannot eliminate, enjoying my existence, my
family, my home, my friends. Forgive me, but for all your

philosophy you have never enjoyed life. Who then is the more fortunate?"

"Is that all there is to living, Priscus?" asked Lucanus, sadly, knowing well that his brother had understood. "Merely enjoying life? Surely a man has a greater destiny than that. His life has a greater meaning beyond this world."

Priscus stood up and stretched his arms over his head, and yawned. "You must tell me, Lucanus," and there was a light mockery in his robust voice.

Lucanus was silent. He suddenly thought of Keptah, of Joseph ben Gamliel, of all the philosophers and devout men he had known. He said, hesitatingly, "It is possible that man's destiny is beyond his death, and what he does here decides that destiny."

"You do not believe that!" said Priscus, laughing. "You are the most skeptical of the Skeptics. I have heard you speak many times in this house."

Lucanus was silent again, and he despised himself. He saw the awful responsibility of adults, whether father or brother, that they must forever teach the young that they are more than animals, that their lives have a subtle but greater meaning than what appears superficially. Lucanus put his hand to his head, which suddenly ached. Priscus, looking at him, narrowed his eyes.

"Do not accuse yourself, Lucanus. You spoke always from out of conviction, if bitterly. Could you have made me different from what I am? No."

Yes, thought Lucanus, with gall in his mouth. He said, "And you are satisfied, Priscus? You want nothing else but what you have?"

Was it possible that Priscus was hesitating? Lucanus looked up, in hope. Priscus was now serious; he was scratching his chin, as he absently flexed his muscular arms. Then he spoke, as if to himself.

"I have been hearing rumors on my last campaign. Foolish rumors, perhaps. They came out of Syria, or perhaps it was Armenia, or Egypt, or Israel. I do not remember. But the rumor is to the effect that God is manifesting Himself somewhere, and that He will change the world very soon."

He looked at Lucanus and laughed sheepishly. "Naturally that is a foolish rumor. Our religion is full of the manifestations of deity, as you know; the gods are always cavorting and interfering with men, or quarreling vastly among themselves. Yet," and he paused, "this rumor appears entirely different. A great revelation is at hand, so it says. And the world will be regenerated." He clapped his hand on Lucanus' shoulder. "So be of good cheer, my brother. Perhaps all is not lost."

He went off, humming. Had Lucanus been listening he would have heard that Priscus' footsteps were not as brisk as usual, that they lagged somewhat, as if the soldier were thinking. But Lucanus did not hear. A great terror, a great hunger, a great restlessness, was upon him, and he remembered, though he tried not to remember, his awful dreams when he had been ill of the fever.

Chapter Thirty-nine

"We cannot land at Crete, Master Lucanus," the captain of the ship said.

"Why?" asked Lucanus, with concern. "I have four patients there whom I promised to see at this time, and who have been under my care."

"Master, it is dawn," said the captain, significantly, "and if you will accompany me on board I will show you the reason."

Lucanus accompanied him to the upper deck. The calm blue sea, streaked with the pink and gold of dawn, lay about them, and they stood not far from Crete, green and lighted with the first sun, bordered by a muffled halo of foam. A huge Roman man-o'-war stood close to the port, its tall white sails snapping idly in the dawn breeze, its pennants floating against the sky. About it, like little fish around a mother, was a feverish activity of small boats which appeared to be crowded densely with people about to climb aboard the man-o'-war under a shower of whips. Their wailing voices, frail and far, echoed across the water.

The captain leaned on the railing and meditatively picked his teeth. He was a rascally dark Levantine with black mustaches. "There has been an insurrection," he said, watching with interest. "The people of this town, inspired by the young men, dared to defy Rome and demand their freedom! Is it not ridiculous that so small an island—and the whole island is boiling—should defy the might and power of Rome? What has it gained them? Their streets are heaped with young corpses; men and women and children by the multitude have been seized and enslaved, and are now being taken to Rome for sale. Puny fools! They never had a single hope. But, I have heard, while fighting they called on the Greeks, the Syrians, the Egyptians to join them in their battle for liberty! They received only expressions of sympathy, or silence. I understand they sent couriers with torches racing, for months, over the world, demanding a general uprising against the Roman tyrant. But the others preferred to issue expressions of moral approval in their courts of law—and then went off to dinner. Other countries, I have heard, hastened to assure the Roman proconsuls and the tribunes that they had no intention of joining 'the disorder,' and wished only the opportunity to continue to exist amicably with Rome." He laughed hoarsely.

More small boats were rushing eagerly towards the man-o'-war, loaded with rebels, as if placating. Lucanus now saw plumes of smoke rising from the town, and little darts of scarlet. He thought of the Cretans who had struck one furious blow against the Empire, praying and pleading that the subject nations join them. But they were alone, as all men who fight for freedom are alone, and the pusillanimous peoples, sobbing sentimentally for them, preferred not to be valiant. Men deserve their slavery, their subjection, their suffering, thought Lucanus, with bitterness. They are never really oppressed; they permit oppression.

But perhaps the instinctual love for freedom still lived everywhere, stifled sternly, yet still existing, if so small an island, so small a people, dared lift valorous hands against imperial Rome. Lucanus shook his head. It was always too late. He could not endure the cries and wails and screams of the enslaved men and women and children, and went below. His door opened without a knock and the captain came in and sat down near him in a chair and stared at him. "Death," said the captain, "is always the price a man must be prepared to pay for his dignity."

"When he loses his dignity as man, then he is no longer a man," said Lucanus. "The Cretans, who appear to have been crushed, have had their moment of glory. May God be with them."

"It is evident no one else will be," said the captain, snickering. "But they possibly do not have even the sympathy of the gods, who find men deplorable."

The ship turned about and sailed away. At the next port Lucanus received letters from home, but none, as he had expected, from Sara bas Elazar. Priscus had joined Plotius in Jerusalem. He had written, "I find the Jews very interesting. At the present time all of Judea rings with the name of a Jewish teacher, one Jesus of Nazareth, who prefers to talk with rabble rather than join the wise men in the city. The rumor among the ebullient populace is that he is their Messias, one prophesied from the far ages who will deliver them from Rome! Is that not ridiculous? The priests despise him as a barefoot peasant. He is surrounded by followers as destitute as himself. Naturally no one of consequence takes him seriously. Some of our soldiers declare he performs miracles like a veritable god; one must discount the words of the ignorant, and our soldiers are superstitious. I like Judea; the weather is salubrious, the people of a quick countenance. Moreover, one needs not to fear to eat in their taverns, even the humblest, for everything in the way of food is scrupulously handled and clean. Last night we officers were invited to dine with Herod Antipas, who is a cautious man, and who appears, at this time, to be very troubled. I heard he was almost abstemious in his habits, which is possibly false, for he drank even more than we, and then he burst into tears and talked of one John whom he had had to put to death because of his wild rebellion which stirred the people. This happened almost two years ago, yet Herod still seems disturbed about it. The country seethes."

Lucanus read this letter over and over, and thought of the centurion, Antonius. He shook his head. A miserable, obscure, unlettered Jewish rabbi! He laughed slightly. Was he the Unknown God, as the centurion had declared? God would surely manifest Himself in the person of a great king, a mighty wise man, a noble, a patrician! But this was certainly in accord with the mystical nature of Jews, who saw God everywhere. Then Lucanus thought of Sara, and what she had written him so many years ago about the youth who had accosted her by name, and had consoled her.

He pondered on it. He told himself that in every country there were always rumors of miracle-workers, of the swift appearance of gods clothed with light, of strange happenings. A world reduced to dull and monotonous peace under the Romans turned to myths and superstitions.

Nevertheless, a terrible unease took possession of Lucanus. He felt Judea pulling him like a resistless tide. He began to think of visiting his brother in Jerusalem, and then he recoiled inwardly. He wanted none of the disturbing mysticism of the Jews; he had had enough of men like Joseph ben Gamliel.

At the next port of call he received numerous letters, not only from home but from Sara, and from strangers in Jerusalem. And when he read Sara's letter he became as still and cold as stone and all emotion was numbed in him, for now he knew that Sara was dead. She had written:

"When this reaches your hand, my dear beloved, my most dear Lucanus, I will have been gathered to my fathers, for I am dying. Do not be grieved; do not weep. Rejoice with me that I have had my call from God, who was never absent from me a moment in my life. Pray for me, if you will. When I left Rome I knew that death was upon me, and I was happy. I returned to Jerusalem to die among my people, to die in my home, with no regrets, no longings, no worldly desires. For I was joining my parents and others who loved me. Death is not a calamity to him who dies; it is only a calamity to those he leaves behind, for death is deliverance and joy and eternal peace and bliss. The days of man are short and full of trouble. What is there in the world that can offer consolation? Do not sorrow. I will be with you always, and will pray for you, and our parting is brief. God be with you, and may He bring you His blessed peace. I look upon you from the skies, as you hold this letter in your hand, and I pray that you are not weeping. You will find my brother, Arieh. Before I was finally confined to my bed I saw Him whom you are seeking, and I mingled with the crowds on the street, and touched His garment, and He turned to smile at me compassionately and told me to be of good heart and that my prayers were already answered. Bring my brother home, for now I know beyond all doubt that you will find him. Farewell, but only for a little while, my Lucanus. I kiss your lips and your eyes."

Lucanus was not weeping, as Sara had feared. He felt nothing at all but a great emptiness and silence in him, an abandonment of all sensation. Calmly he read the letters from strangers in Jerusalem, friends of Sara, sonorous letters assuring him that she had died without pain, that her body had been laid in the sepulcher of her fathers, that she had drawn her last breath with a peaceful smile. There were letters from lawyers who were the guardians of the wealth of Sara's family, which they were keeping for the son of Elazar ben Solomon, who was now about twenty years old. They were skeptical men, these lawyers. Nevertheless, Sara had convinced them; they expressed confidence that Lucanus would find the son of Elazar, the brother of Sara, and return him to his people.

Lucanus put aside all the letters and poured himself a little wine. He drank slowly, vaguely wondering why no storm rose in him, why no passion of sorrow, for one he had so dearly loved. Then, as a physician, he knew he was mercifully dulled by shock. He drank more and more, until the walls of his cabin tilted. He drank again, and fell on his bed and did not awaken for twenty-four hours. When he came to himself he was violently sick, and he was grateful for his retching and aching body, for his roaring head, for, concerned with his physical misery, he could not think.

Days later, as the ship went on its way, he felt that he was moving in a hollow world. He went about his work in silence. He smiled not even a little any longer. He feared sleep; he saw the faces of all he had loved and lost in his dreams. He heard their loving voices. And he said to them, "Do not comfort me, for you are dead, and in the grave there is no remembrance."

The dull and colorless months went by, dribbling into each other like clouded puddles. He wrote briefly to his family. A fear came on him when he saw their letters, and a trembling. He was afraid of fresh bereavement, fresh dolorous news. But Aurelia had a fine son, and was again with child. Cusa had two grandchildren. Gaius was actually contemplating marriage with a virtuous maiden of an old sound family, but very poor. "I am pleased with her," Iris had written. "She is very learned. It was inevitable that if Gaius ever married he would marry such a maiden. It has been almost a year since you visited us, my son. I understand that in your grief for Sara you do not wish to look at our happiness, and to hear the voices of your nieces and nephews, or even your mother. But I am growing very old. Return to your home, if even only for a few days, that I may see you again."

But Lucanus could not go home. He shrank at the thought of the living, and their faces; he dreaded their love and comfortings, and their tenderness. He could remember Rubria now without pain. But he could not remember Sara now without agony, an agony that never left him. At each port, when the ship docked, he would look among the crowds for her face. When letters arrived, he looked for one from her. He walked in his desolation; he administered; he sat in the gardens of his little houses; he read, he ate, he slept. He lived like a specter. Once, very calmly, he opened his physician's pouch and looked at a medicine he had brewed, which, given minutely in a goblet of wine, would relieve pain, but which, taken in quantity, would swiftly kill. He held the vial in his hand until it became hot in his fingers. Then he put it away. But always he thought of it in his awful loneliness and cold despair.

He found, at one port, that he had missed his brother, Priscus, by only an hour. Priscus had left him a letter before departing for Rome for a furlough of a few weeks. Priscus had written of his anticipation to see his family, and reproached his brother for neglecting them. He sent Lucanus a message from Plotius, and then went on to write about Jesus of Nazareth, the beggarly Jewish teacher whose influence was growing in Judea. He wrote lightly, but it was apparent that he was deeply serious. "I have talked with many of those who claim he has cured them instantly, by the touch of his hand. In truth, there was a beggar here whom I knew by sight, sitting against the wall of the Temple, who had been blind by birth. At one time I gave him alms, for he had a noble face and considerable learning. Then one day I found him surrounded by many excitable people, and his eyes were open and seeing! I could not believe it, my dear Lucanus! The man was not a fraud; I swear it, yet he looked at me with open and living eyes, and when I spoke to him he ran to me and grasped my hand and cried out, 'The Son of God opened my eyes when I implored Him!'

"Truly, my brother, I have seen this myself, and there is no doubting it. I have been told that this teacher has raised the dead, has cast out madness from men's minds, and that all within the sound of his voice feel ecstasy and joy. He goes from town to town, from village to village, healing, it is said, and when the people speak of him it is as if they are possessed with divine rapture. Is he Apollo, appearing in the guise of a poor Jewish carpenter? Or Mercury? Or Eros? Is there some great revelation at hand? The learned men, and a caste here who call themselves the Pharisees, either laugh loudly or are angered. It outrages them that a man who possesses nothing, who is unlearned, who has no family, no personal power, no recommendations from distinguished men, can draw multitudes to him at the instant of his appearance. They are afraid that he will eventually advocate an uprising against the Romans on the part of the Jews, and here they have a legitimate fear, for his influence is stupendous among the people. In that event, if there is an uprising, there will be general bloodshed, and I dislike the thought, for I have come to admire the Jews and I visit the houses of those who do not think the presence of a Gentile, and worse, a Roman officer, is pollution. But Israel is a very small country, and is of no importance. It is only that when I am there I feel that something portentous is about to happen. Is that not strange? I return there in three months."

Priscus wrote of Pontius Pilate, the procurator. "He is a peaceable man, but vacillating, and prefers his library and the company of his wife to banquets and politics. I like to converse with him. The Jews bore him; he declares they live with one foot in this world and with one in the next, and that their piety is incomprehensible. Herod, he despises, as a womanish fool, at once filled with Greek superstitions and with Jewish prophecy. You told me at one time that Rome had been touched too deeply by the Orient, and that she had been influenced too much by it, and that the Western mind can never comprehend the Eastern. This is true of Herod; the meeting of East and West in him has disordered his spirit and created confusion in him.

"The procurator has not been untouched by the stories of the Jewish teacher. But he is not disturbed by ominous prophecies that Jesus will incite the Jews against Rome. He said that one of his soldiers told him that when the Pharisees, who are stiff-necked merchants and lawyers and physicians and very proud, challenged Jesus to betray his real mission and asked if it were right for the Jews to honor Caesar, Jesus replied to the effect that one honors worldly law, which is Caesar's, and honors the supernatural world, which is God's. Is that not sophistry? But very clever, you must admit. Pontius was much amused by this story. He said this man should be a lawyer, and he would make his fortune."

Then Priscus added some strange words: "I remember our last talk at home, and when I do I think of that miserable, barefooted Jewish teacher. The thoughts come simultaneously. And that is very odd."

Lucanus sat with Priscus' letter in his hands for a long time. Occasionally he shivered. His cool Greek mind reproached him, but he could not refrain from reading the letter over and over. Once or twice sweat broke out on his forehead, accompanied by a passionate yearning. Then he destroyed the letter as one destroys something which throws him into turmoil. "Superstition!" he cried aloud. "Idiotic tales!"

When he was next in Athens, Iris informed him in a letter that Priscus had returned to Jerusalem. The wife of Gaius was about to be delivered of a child. Cusa was ailing and querulous. Lucanus put aside her letter listlessly. There was another for him, in a strange hand, from a country of which he had never heard, in Africa.

"Dear and beloved friend! This letter is from Ramus, who thinks of you constantly, and who prays for you unceasingly."

Lucanus could not believe it. He stared at the letter incredulously, then felt the first joy he had experienced in a long time. Ramus was alive! He had not died, he had not been lost, he had not been sold into slavery. "O God!" cried Lucanus aloud, in delight. He clasped the letter to his heart and tears filled his eyes.

The letter continued: "I have only now returned to my people, with peace and happiness. After I left you—and I still pray for your forgiveness—I made my way for many toilsome months to the Land of Israel. Of my privations I will not speak, for they are as nothing now. I expected hostility, because of what I am, but everywhere, though I could not speak, I encountered kindness such as that extended to pilgrims to a holy place. I was fed and sheltered without question, and so I knew that God was protecting me. No humble home was shut to me anywhere; at each oasis I was given wine and water and food by the lonely caravans. My color was not despised. But that is the least of the marvels, and I shall not speak of them.

"I arrived in Israel, and immediately sought Him for Whom I had been searching. And I found Him in the town of Nain. I dared not approach Him, for the multitude was very great, and I was a man dark of face and homeless and footsore and without money. Can I speak of Him? What words are there a man can use to speak of being in the presence of God? How did He appear to me? Like the sun? Those words do not describe Him. I followed Him, behind the multitude, waiting to approach Him nearer. I could hear His voice, though I was so distant, and it was like muted thunder, and very kind. I understood that He came often to this town, where the people are poor and oppressed by the Romans, and despised by the learned. They are miserable farmers and little merchants, and very humble.

"He approached the gates of Nain, and a dead man was being carried out, the only son of his mother, who is a widow, and a large gathering of her friends were with her. The Lord, seeing her, had compassion upon her, for she was weeping disconsolately, and after looking long and lovingly upon her He went to the stretcher and gazed at the bearers, who became very still. He lifted His hand and said to the dead son, 'Young man, I say to you, arise!'

"Lucanus, you must believe it, for I have seen it, and have I ever lied to you? I declare that he who was dead sat up, and began to speak in a vague and confused voice, like one who has been aroused suddenly from a deep sleep in which he has been dreaming sweet dreams. But the Lord took his hand gently and lifted him from the stretcher and gave his hand to his mother, and she fell upon her son and embraced him, then cast herself down at the feet of Him who had restored her son to her. The people retreated in terror, and then some of them glorified God with mighty shouts, crying, 'A great prophet has risen among us and God had visited His people!'

"Lucanus, I saw it; with these eyes of mine, which you restored to me, I saw it!

"I crept after Him, thinking to myself, If He does not restore my voice, I will not regret, for I have seen Him, and what man needs more? But I wanted to get closer to Him; I wanted to see His eyes shine upon me, though I am a man dark of face. Surely, I thought, He will not despise me, He who made me; surely He will lift the curse of Noah from my people. He was conversing with His followers, young men like Himself, then suddenly He paused and glanced over His shoulder, and His eyes lighted on me. He smiled, and seemed to wait, and then suddenly I felt a stirring in my throat, a trembling on my tongue, and all at once my voice was on my lips and I cried out, 'Blessed am I, who have seen the Lord our God!'

"I must have fallen in the dust in a faint, for when I awakened I was alone in the hot and dusty sunset, and when I rose I knew what I must do. I must return to my people and bring them the message of life and joy, for I had seen God, and I had known Him, and the curse had been lifted from us.

"Peace be with you. May His peace descend upon you, and may He draw you to Him. For He is He whom you have been seeking. Farewell, but we shall meet again where men do not hate each other or despise each other, but understand each other's heart."

Lucanus put aside the letter, and the heavy sickness of heart and depression was on him again, the huge repudiation. He, as a physician, believed he knew what had happened to Ramus. He had seen what he had wished to see; the hysteria which had silenced him had been released, suddenly, and he had spoken again. It was very simple.

But what of the young man who had been raised from the "dead"? That too was simple. The man had been suffering from catalepsy; he had been in a state of suspended animation. Fortunate for him that he had not been locked into a tomb, to awaken to find his mouth stuffed with earth! This Jewish teacher must be a sort of physician, who had known the man was not really dead.

I have many explanations, Lucanus began to think. Then he paused, struck. Must I always rationalize? he thought suddenly. Must I always rush in a frenzy to explain things in the light of reason? What has my reason brought me but sorrow? Yet anything that is not logical to me is disgusting, childish, even profane.

Without knowing why, he began to weep.

Chapter Forty

Lucanus returned to Athens. It was a warm day in the early spring, and even this dry and astringent air had a liveliness in it, a gaiety. The women who sold flowers sat in their stalls with small mountains of laurel, violets, little roses, anemones and poppies before them. They called out in raucous voices. The streets streamed with life; it was never very cold here, yet when the spring came, with blossoms and with a bright blue air, the people became vehement with a kind of joy and pleasure. The little shops rang with bargainers; there was a smell of cooking sausages and garlic everywhere. Children ran and shouted and wrestled in the gutters. Old men smiled at each other, lifted aside their beards and talked in learned voices. The hills had freshened into a pure green. Upon the Acropolis the Parthenon was a crown of frozen light; the

mighty statue of Athena leaned against the sky. Everywhere
there was a quickening, a sense of anticipation. Young girls
and young men strolled hand in hand, smiling. Babies laughed
from their mothers' arms. The Roman soldiers leaned against
the walls of buildings, yawned, grinned, and scratched their
chins as they looked eagerly at the women. The horses drawing chariots pranced. Dogs barked. Lawyers and businessmen
had stopped their bustling; they walked easily, and forgot to
discuss their problems.

Lucanus knew that this was the beginning of the Jewish
Passover. There was a synagogue nearby, but he shunned
it. He had the feeling that he was scuttling, his head bent,
as if fleeing from something. But this was ridiculous. He had
landed at midnight, and had gone to his lonely little house.
He had several old patients to visit, and he would do this
tomorrow. He was not one to walk casually for the pleasure
of it, and he did not know why he had been drawn to walk
the city today. But there was a thirst in him now for the
sight of his fellow men, and he could not have enough of
seeing. I am not young, he thought. I have not been one to
mingle with others or enjoy their company. What ails me?
He smiled at an old flower woman and bought a small
bouquet of little white lilies from her. He walked on, and he
buried his nose in the flowers and the fragrance almost overwhelmed him.

He decided to return to his house and write long-overdue
letters to his family. The garden was quiet and full of sun.
There had been a wind earlier, but now it had fallen. Everything had a patina of light such as he had never seen before.
Each tender leaf was plated with it; each flower was
drowned in it; the fountain sparkled with it; each grain of
earth was illuminated. The walls of the little house shone as
if polished. Lucanus looked at the sky. Never had it been
clearer or more brilliant; not a cloud stood in it.

He ate his small and frugal meal. He drank his wine. He
listened to the silence of his house. It was as if something
had drawn a mighty breath and was holding it. Nothing
stirred. Now everything reflected radiance, even his plain
silver goblet, even his fork and spoon, even the sides of his
hands, even his scrubbed white wooden floor. His eyes began
to sting with such light. He felt an overpowering weariness
and thought, I will lie down and rest.

He lay down and shut his eyes. He hoped to sleep during
the afternoon heat. But there was a glaring, an insistence,

behind his eyelids. He felt himself beginning to sweat. His whole body felt a stretching, an agony. He could not rest. He got to his feet, and he was very weak. Is this the fever again? he asked himself with alarm, thinking of the patients he would have to visit tomorrow and the throngs which would gather at his door. He could not fail them; they waited for him. He stumbled about the house in that awful flood of light until he found his pouch. His groping hand reached to the bottom and closed on something cool and metallic, and he brought out the cross which Keptah had given Rubria and which she had given to him. He looked at it in his palm and it glittered blindingly, as if fired from the sun, and now it burned his flesh.

Blinking, he put the cross down and stared at it, and all his dreams, all that he had heard returned to him in one thunderous clamor. But what had this cross to do with a miserable Jewish teacher in distant Israel, who, it was claimed, raised the dead, performed miracles, and brought multitudes about him? What had this cross of the Chaldeans, the Babylonians, the Egyptians to do with one so far away, and one so humble and unknown to the world of men?

There was no rest in this house; there was no rest anywhere for one so beset and so besieged and so desolate. Lucanus went into the garden, panting for shade. But there was no shade, no protection from the sun. Everything stood in shadowless light, affixed in flaming crystal. Then, all at once, a darkness fell on the face of the earth, swallowing all light, extinguishing it, driving it before it like a tide and banishing it. Ah, thought Lucanus, there will be a storm, a cooling storm! He looked at the sky, the very dark sky.*

Where was the sun? He stared at the black sky, searching.

* An enormous earthquake occurred at this hour in Nicaea. In the fourth year of the two hundred and second Olympiad, Phlegon wrote that "a great darkness" occurred all over Europe which was inexplicable to the astronomers. The records of Rome, according to Tertullian, made note of a complete and universal darkness, which frightened the Senate, then meeting, and threw the city into an anxious turmoil, for there was no storm and no clouds. The records of Grecian and Egyptian astronomers show that this darkness was so intense for a while that even they, skeptical men of science, were alarmed. People streamed in panic through the streets of every city, and birds went to rest and cattle returned to their paddocks. But there is no note of an eclipse; no eclipse was expected. It was as if the sun had retreated through space and had been lost. Mayan and Inca records also show this phenomenon, allowing for the difference in time.

Everything was very still. No cricket lifted its voice; the birds were silent, though they had been murmurous all morning.

Lucanus looked at the city. The Parthenon was a faint outline of pure silver. The city was in darkness. Then he heard a distant and muffled sound as if from a sea, and he knew it was the voice of the city, full of panic and questioning. He ran to his gate; the road that passed it was empty. He looked beyond the road and dimly saw cattle lying down in the grass, as if sleeping.

The air was as clear as water, and as limpid, and as cool. So, thought Lucanus, this is no dust storm. He sat down on a bench, and felt a coldness as of death running over his body. He remembered old myths of the wrath of the gods. There would be a day when the gods, sickened by men, would withdraw the sun and plunge the earth into everlasting darkness and death. He moved his body restlessly. He stood up and walked around and around the garden. A scent of roses and lilies rose on the air, as if they had been crushed under a giant foot. The city began to shine and twinkle with hastily lit lanterns and torches. Lucanus knew that most probably a huge river of humanity would now begin to pour up towards the Parthenon, there to beseech the gods to lift this terrible and inexplicable darkness from the world. As for himself, he was consumed, not with anxiety for himself, but with a passionate questioning.

As one who had been taught by the greatest scientists in the world, he began to conjecture. It was believed that one day the sun would burn itself out, and this planet, earth, would roll through space gathering ice and deathly cold, and all life would die on it. But that, the astronomers had said, would take ages; the sun would slowly die, would redden, would wink out like a cinder. It would occur over eons; it would never occur instantaneously. But this had occurred in a twinkling, between one breath and another. Lucanus searched for the sun, the retreating sun, again. Was it possible that it had hurled itself away from its children to join its radiant brothers?

An enormous sense of excitement suddenly swept over him, and also a terror he had never known before. Where, among those burning constellations, was the sun now? What chaos was it causing among the orderly brotherhood, this intruder from a corner of the universe? What planets was it devouring in its flaming passage?

Then he felt he was not alone. He peered about him in the moonlight and the starlight. Were there pale shadows moving about him in the garden, or only the illusion of his strained eyes? His heart leaped. Shadows paused near him, and he thought he saw the faces of Rubria and Keptah and Sara, smiling dimly. They drifted on like snow, and there, surely! was Diodorus, young and strong and valorous, his hand lifted in greeting. There was Joseph ben Gamliel—oh, this was mad!—with a tender glance. There among many shades of the women he had succored stood Aurelia, animated and smiling. A multitude passed him, paused before him, hailing him in silence and with affection. He shook his head violently, and gasped, and closed his eyes.

Then the earth lifted as if on a wave, shivered, trembled, and slid under his feet. A deep rumble muttered up from its bowels. A wind rose, like a hurricane, then fell as swiftly, then rose again, howling, so that Lucanus' breath was smothered in his throat. Now he was no longer physician, philosopher or scientist. He was a man, and he was overpowered by fear. He stood up and shook, and his teeth rattled.

He walked about the garden, which was ghostly. His flesh quivered as if in an ague. He went to the fountain, and heard its leaping waters. He went into the house. There he forced himself to light a lamp. He stood and stared at it blankly. He picked up a book and put it down. His head throbbed.

In a moment he tried to speak reasonably to himself. He remembered the astronomy he had studied. The sun could not detach itself from the "wanderers," its children, the planets. Where it went, the planets went also. "Certainly, certainly," he said aloud to the heavy silence about him, and nodded his head as if satisfied. But he knew this was an idiot's reflection. The sun was gone; the sky was very dark above. All man's reasons, his most profound reflections, could not alter these facts. For once, he could not attach a name, a theory, to what was impenetrable; he could not adjust what was not known to what he knew. Nevertheless, Lucanus' mind flew out like a distracted bird, feverishly attempting to explain what could not be explained. Again the earth thundered under his feet and a long moaning poured into the cool air.

Had the world tilted behind another planet? A thousand solutions whirled in his mind, and he rejected them at once as absurd. Then for the first time he thought of his family in Rome with a tremor; he thought of Priscus in Jerusalem. If the world was being destroyed inexorably and mysteriously, then all men must die together. Panic, selfishness, fear, terror, anxiety, love—all these could accomplish nothing, could not fling off the cold hand of fate. He lit another lamp, and then another, until his house was full of light. He sat down and stared before him.

He came to himself with a start, conscious that he had fallen into a sick sleep, overwhelmed by the awful thing that had come upon the world. His lamps were flickering low; he got to his feet to refill them. Then he noticed that a gray light stood at his doors and windows like a dawn. He ran into the garden again. The light became stronger, but very slowly. The earth no longer slipped and quivered and rumbled; it was steadfast. Lucanus looked at the sky; a vast rosiness hung there, as if a sunset were spreading from horizon to horizon. The earth lost its ghostliness; color flooded back moment by moment. The birds cheeped or chattered excitedly in the trees. The fountain sang louder, as if relieved. The voice of the city reached Lucanus; it was the sound of rejoicing, but it had a hysterical overtone. Then the rosy hue parted like a curtain and the sun leaped into the sky like a warrior with a golden shield.

Lucanus breathed deeply. Never had the world, no, not even when he had been a child, looked so fair to him, so dear, so precious, now that it had been delivered from death. And from death it had surely been delivered, as a bird is released from an enraged and imminent hand. The foundations of the earth had been shaken; the sun had been lost. But now the terror and the anger had departed, and a sweetness rose from the flowers and the grass, as if the earth had exhaled a breath too long held in fright. Lucanus pressed his fingers over his face and sighed deeply.

Certainly, he thought now, there is a scientific explanation for this. Because I do not know the cause of this phenomenon does not mean that it is beyond explanation. It was late afternoon. He was hungry. He sat down and ate a small meal, and never had wine tasted so delightful, and never had bread and cheese had this flavor before. He wrote letters, and one was to an astronomer in Alexandria, commenting on the darkness, asking if it had been observed there, and what the cause was, and if it was likely to happen again.

When he slept that night it was as if he had been reprieved, and with that reprieve had come not only pardon, but life and a peace and a tranquillity like the first day the world had ever known, and man was born anew.

Chapter Forty-one

Dozens of the patients who came to Lucanus the next day were new to him. They were suffering from shock, were very pale, and some were almost speechless. He reassured them, smilingly, that nothing that could not be explained by learned men had occurred the day before. Very possibly it was an eclipse. Only children were frightened by them. Had not the Egyptian astronomers, long ago, been able to predict eclipses not only for the immediate future, but for ages not yet conceived? One must trust the wise, the men who understood, who could chart the heavens, the phases of the moon, the movement of the stars exactly. Lucanus, while his patients crowded about him, demonstrated an eclipse with an apple and a nut. They were very interested; they followed his demonstration with open mouths and widened eyes, and, as he had done yesterday, they nodded their heads wisely at each other and declared that they had known this all the time. They are no more learned than I, thought Lucanus, with some wryness.

"It is all very well," said an old man, shaking his head and looking shrewdly at the physician. "But you have explained nothing. This is beyond the explanations of man." The others laughed at him merrily and called him graybeard, but Lucanus did not laugh. The old man's strong and piercing eyes transfixed him. He said, "Well, let us look at your rheumatic ankles again, my friend. I have a new salve which I believe will help you." "I hoped, yesterday," said the old man, "that it was the end of the world, for are we not all a wicked people, an insult to heaven?" The others laughed at him even louder, but they glanced at him with some malevolence. Men, meditated Lucanus, did not enjoy being called evil and an affront to the gods, and let the man beware who told them the truth.

There was only one other wealthy family in Athens besides that of Turbo which Lucanus treated. The name of the father was Cleon, and he boasted that he was descended from the leather family famous at the time of Pericles. He and his wife and widowed daughter lived in a splendid villa near the Acropolis, whose gardens were surrounded by high gates and patrolled by slaves armed with swords or scimitars in the Eastern fashion. Lucanus liked none of the family, but Cleon had an obscure disease which interested the physician. Periodically he broke out in enormous hives which became livid, turned slightly pale after a few days, then erupted into hideous boils. Lucanus had seen nothing like this before; he was writing a treatise on it. He had eliminated the usual sources of the hives as a cause. The man's diet had been reduced stringently. As he was a man of evil temper, and his wife no less so, and his reputation foul as a usurer, he was hated by all who knew him, including Lucanus. The physician was beginning to formulate a theory that the man's own temperament was the cause of the outbreakings. His flesh was pitted like old stone, and one eye had been permanently injured. It was not new that vicious humors of the mind could strike somatically, but this was an extraordinary demonstration which intrigued Lucanus.

He went, that afternoon, to the luxurious mansion of Cleon. He invariably charged the old man a large fee, but he invariably gave him some temporary relief. He was admitted at once to the immured rooms in which Cleon spent his tormented days. The hives had arrived a week ago; they were already suppurating. Lucanus dressed the boils, while Cleon complained and winced and cursed. He was a tiny man, with a bloated body, a squint where he had suffered the eye injury, and a little face as riddled and folded as a nut. "After you were last here, my good Lucanus," he whined, "I had surcease for many weeks, and I thought I was cured. Had you not arrived now, I am sure I should have died within a few days." He showed Lucanus a new hive on one of his buttocks, but it was as big as a man's fist, and tumid. Lucanus spread some ointment on it, after bathing it in very cold water.

"You do not come often enough," said the old man, angrily. "I have added a new physician to my household, but he is no better than the others. I have had to have him flogged on numerous occasions, for he has a violent and blasphemous mouth when he is aroused, though for the rest he is a sullen wretch and of a cold, withdrawing temper."

"And what did he say to you?" asked Lucanus, abstractedly.

Within a few days the hive would degenerate into a formidable boil, which would have to be lanced.

The old man sprang up in his bed, and shook his fist. "When these hives occurred this last time I called him in and he examined me, and then he said—he dared to say, the dog!—that it was not my flesh that was ailing, but my spirit! I should have sent him to prison, or flogged him to death, or sold him to the galleys. But I had paid too much money for him."

Lucanus lifted his head alertly. "A physician? A new physician?" The man had considerable astuteness then.

"I bought him in the market place, for a fine sum I can tell you! He is reputed to have been educated at Tarsus, but I will wager that he received what little learning he has from a midwife and a butcher! Do you know what happened yesterday? When the sun disappeared—you will understand I am not an ignorant man—I was aware that it was an eclipse. I heard my wife and daughter wailing; the slaves had fled into the cellars. Then this rascal, this new physician of mine, came into my chamber and looked at me with eyes like fire. And said nothing. He merely stood for a long while and gazed at me until I thought I should go mad. Ah, when I am well again, I shall put him on the block for any use! Preferably, of course, as a miner."

He lay back on his cushions and gave Lucanus his best imitation of an agreeable smile. "The pain is already subsiding, my Lucanus. I am grateful to you."

Lucanus gave the attendant slaves a jar of the ointment and instructed them to use it every two hours, day and night. He then walked into the hall and beckoned to the overseer. "I should like to talk to the new slave," he said, in a low voice. "I think I can give the physician some instructions concerning treatment when I am not here. What is his name?"

"His name is Samos, for it is said he was born there, Master," said the overseer, respectfully. "He is a surly dog. No doubt he was once a thief, for he is branded most unpleasantly." He called for wine for Lucanus, who sat in a comfortable chair in the sun-filled hall and then sent for Samos. The slave returned with a tall, dark young man of a broad but distinguished face, somewhat long black hair and deep blue eyes, strong wide shoulders and the bearing of a king. He walked towards Lucanus silently, and his movements were stately. Then as he stood before Lucanus he raised his hand and lifted the hair from his forehead and contemptuously showed his brand. It was dark purple and knotted, and repellent. Then he dropped his hair over it again and said sullenly, "What will you have with me?"

Pity surged through Lucanus. He asked the overseer to leave, and then he motioned to Samos to sit beside him. But Samos said in his bitter voice, "No. I am only a slave, and have always been a slave. Do not be magnanimous to me. I want no man's friendship, no man's kindness. I am every man's enemy."

"So," said Lucanus, smiling a little though his compassion increased. "Then stand before me like a slave, if that is all you believe you are. As a fellow physician I wished to ask you some questions." He paused, and added in a lower voice, "I believe you are quite correct in your diagnosis of Cleon's hives and boils."

Samos' face changed; his wide and sensitive mouth moved, and his large blue eyes blinked as if suppressing tears. He was not old; Lucanus guessed him to be not more than twenty-two. The young man hesitated; then, with a muttered oath, he jerked a chair forward and sat near Lucanus, and glared at him. "I am correct," he said, and his voice was defiant. "But what can a man do with one such as Cleon, except to call in the priests and have them exorcise his demon? Unless he is a demon himself!"

Lucanus laughed softly. "Who knows?" he murmured. "But tell me. Were you truly educated at Tarsus?"

Samos looked aside; his profile was strong and classical, with fine planings about his cheeks, and with an excellent chin. Lucanus felt a tug in himself: the younger physician reminded him vaguely of someone, and the remembrance was a hurt. Then Samos said, "I was born in a certain household in Samos. They had a fine physician there, and I followed him about, and finally I was his assistant. He was becoming old; he recommended to my master, who was almost as cruel and vicious as this Cleon, and a merchant of the world, that I be sent to Tarsus. And so I was. I spent three years there, and was graduated with laurel leaves, and my teachers were all gentle, good men, and those years were all the happiness I ever knew."

A tear slipped along his eyelids, and he blinked furiously, drew out a kerchief from his belt and blew his nose. Then he stared dully at the polished white floor. "While I was in Tarsus I knew I could no longer be a slave. I must be free or I must die. So I told one of my teachers. But he counseled patience. Physicians did not kill themselves. If I earned enough in gifts from my master I might eventually buy my freedom. But he did not know my master, who was less generous than Midas. I received no gifts, nor expected any. After a year I ran away." He paused and caught his breath. "I was captured and sent back. I expected death, or, at the very best, to be sent to the galleys. But my master had spent much money on me, so he had me branded. Then I became like a wild wolf, he said, and he sold me, and so I came to this household, which is like his."

Lucanus regarded him with a compassion which was as vivid as physical pain. He said, "Would you like to be with me? Would you wish me to purchase you? If I am successful I will free you, asking only that you be my companion, for I am lonely and I have no friends."

Samos started; he swung on his buttocks to Lucanus, with an incredulous expression. He saw the physician's beaming blue eyes, his gentle smile, his graying golden hair, and he knew that Lucanus was not jesting. He uttered a faint, choked cry and fell before the other man and laid his head mutely on his knees. Then he began to weep, not with tears, but with the dry sobbing of a man who, facing death, has been promised life. He wound his arms about Lucanus' waist and clung to him, speechless.

Lucanus put his hand on the head on his knee. The hair of Samos was fine as silk, and very thick, and slightly curling. Lucanus sighed, and let him remain at his feet, clinging to him like a child, until he was more controlled. Then he said with the utmost gentleness, "Remain here while I talk with Cleon. And pray."

He loosened the clutching arms, which were smooth and yet muscular, and went back to the chamber of Cleon. Cleon was half asleep, having been relieved of his suffering, but when he saw Lucanus he raised his head from the cushions. "Ah," he said, "what a treasure you are, my Lucanus. I have not slept for many nights, and now I am as a child in a soft cradle."

"I wished to examine that hive on your buttocks just once more," said Lucanus, and pretended to be freshly interested. "It is subsiding; it is very possible that it will not suppurate. This is a difficult place to have such an affliction; it can extend dangerously."

He sat down and regarded Cleon with an expression he

hoped was kindly. "I have been talking with your slave, Samos. I believe you have been robbed. That is, this young man can never do anything for you, or your family."

Cleon screamed with wrath and beat his clenched fists on his cushions. "I knew it!" he cried. "Cursed be that merchant, that foul vulture! I should never have trusted him. He has a very bad reputation. Hah! I will sell Samos to the galleys." He sucked on his toothless gums and his eyes glittered with pleasure. "It will be happiness to me, thinking of him there. But I have been robbed, plundered! What shall be my vengeance?" He leaned towards Lucanus cunningly. "Can you not give me a letter saying that the wretch has attempted to poison me? Then I can have him executed." A bead of saliva appeared at the corner of his mouth, and he licked it.

Lucanus pretended to consider this judiciously. Then he shook his head. "It comes to me that I need a household slave. Will you sell him to me? He is very proud and arrogant."

Cleon's hard and piercing eyes searched his face. He lay back, grumbling. "Well, now, he cost me a pretty penny."

Lucanus nodded. "One can sympathize with you, Cleon. What did you pay for him?"

The crafty eyes narrowed. Cleon knew all about Lucanus; he knew all the gossip of the city. This fool of a clever physician was a rich man; if he were mad enough to treat the rabble for nothing, and so acquire a godlike reputation, then he should pay for both his madness and his reputation. So Cleon named an outrageous sum, beyond Lucanus' immediate resources. Lucanus was both angry and concerned. "Why, that is the price of the most dexterous physician beyond all price; it is the ransom of a prince!"

Cleon shrugged. He was again sleepy. "Then," he said, "I will keep him and have my pleasure with him, and shall order him flogged every day, in this chamber, so I can delight in the scene."

Lucanus knew his obstinacy. He stood up. "If you do not sell Samos to me, then I shall never return again, and you will surely die. I mean this, Cleon," he added, sternly.

Cleon opened his eyes in fright. "You would not abandon an old man!"

"I surely will. Make up your mind. I have no doubt you paid highly for Samos, but not what you have stated. I offer you now, and for the last time, three hundred gold sesterces, freshly minted. Take it, or find yourself another physician."

"You would condemn me to death!"

"Certainly."

"Why do you want Samos, that dog?"

"I have told you. He has taken my fancy. I have broken wild horses in my youth."

Cleon paused, gasping in fury and spite. He wished Lucanus were a slave; he would have him flogged regularly; he would have him branded with hot irons until his flesh sizzled. He screamed, "Give me the money, and may Hecate haunt your dreams!"

Lucanus smiled. "Withdraw your curse, or I will be unable to return to you tomorrow for further treatment." He tossed a purse on the bed. "And now you will sign a bill of sale to me."

A few minutes later he returned to the hall where Samos was waiting for him. Samos looked at him with wild blue eyes, his lips working desperately. Lucanus took his arm. "Come home with me," he said, as he had said to Ramus long ago.

Lucanus placed all the lamps he had on his table, on which he had laid his sharp and shining instruments. Samos sat in a chair beside the table, rigid and waiting, his eyes fixed with love and devotion on the other man. Lucanus mixed a potion in a goblet of wine and held it out to Samos. "This will relieve your pain," he said. "I do not know how successful I will be in diminishing this terrible brand, but I will do my best."

"You will succeed," said Samos. "Dear Master."

"Do not call me master," said Lucanus. "Call me by my name."

"I will remain with you always, whether you give me my freedom or not—Lucanus."

"I will take you to the Roman praetor tomorrow, and you will have your freedom. You may not like my life. You are young, and in the proud set of your face I see ambition. Swear no oaths, which you may regret." Lucanus smiled, and still extended the goblet.

"How can I regret, ever?" demanded Samos, passionately. "That you have taken me to your house as a friend, the only friend I ever knew! That you have offered to free me, I who prefer to die rather than be a slave! I ask only that I serve you forever."

"Still," said Lucanus, "you are young; you are an excellent physician. The world will be yours. As a free man you will be a citizen of Rome. Fortune could come to your hands. But first, before all this shining future—and I shall not hold you to your promise—the brand must be removed. Drink this at once."

Samos, his hand shaking, took the goblet. He stared into the murky depths. "Opium," he murmured. He looked into Lucanus' eyes, then slowly put the goblet on the table and drew a deep breath. "No," he said.

Lucanus studied his face, then he nodded. "It is painful to become a slave, but is more painful to become free. I understand. You prefer to take your freedom with suffering, for it will cleanse your heart. However, I warn you that this will be agonizing."

Samos gripped the sides of his chair and raised his face. "I am ready," he said.

"Close your eyes so the blood will not drip into them." Lucanus lifted a narrow keen blade. He must work fast. He examined the brand again. Ugly though it was, it was not an old scar; the skin was still tender about it, and flexible, for Samos was young. He would remove the brand carefully, not injuring underlying tissues, and would draw the clean edges together. When the wound healed there would be only a long thin wrinkle from the hairline to the brows, and in a few months it would whiten and be hardly noticed. Lucanus explained what he was about to do, and Samos nodded; his mouth had paled in anticipation, and had become rigid.

Lucanus drew the blade from the top to the bottom with a delicate touch, and the scar opened like a mouth and bled. But there were no large blood vessels underneath. Samos did not wince; he was very still. Lucanus wiped away the dripping blood and carved out the brand. Samos turned as white as death; his knuckles rose on his gripping hands. But he did not move. Lucanus began to sweat in his fast urgency; tears of blood ran from the wound and rolled in red drops down Samos' cheeks; some gathered in little puddles in the corners of his mouth. The lamps flickered and blew in a light wind from the window.

The physician, concerned over the pain he was inflicting, glanced at Samos' taut face for an instant. Again that sensation of familiarity came to him. "You are very brave," he said, and his voice shook. "You are a brave and noble man, Samos."

The brand lay in a little saucer, as evil as a demon's eye, and already shriveling. Lucanus took up his linen thread and needle. Samos had a look of exhaustion about him; Lucanus wished he would faint. But the proud expression about the younger man's mouth did not slacken. Lucanus began to sew deftly, and he talked in a soothing voice of the work he did among the poor, and the odd cases he had encountered. Samos smiled faintly. The young smooth skin had to be stretched to meet together. The scar, oozing little drops of blood, slowly closed. It was done.

"Open your eyes, Samos," said Lucanus, and fell into a chair and wiped away his sweat with the back of his hand. Samos opened his eyes and smiled at him with joy and pride. After a moment Lucanus bandaged the wound, which no longer bled. "Ah," he said, "I am pleased with this. It will be better than I hoped. But now you must drink a goblet of wine with me, for I am undone!"

Laughing in a trembling voice, he poured two glasses of wine. Samos reached for one with his left hand. Lucanus put the goblet into that hand, then stopped abruptly. His heart also seemed to stop, and there was a roaring in is ears. His face became whiter and stiller than the face of Samos.

Samos looked at him, and was startled. "Lucanus!" he exclaimed. "This has been too much for you! You appear ready to collapse."

He got to his feet, wavering, and put his arm about Lucanus' shoulders. Lucanus' mouth opened silently, then he gasped. His eyes swelled with tears. He rose and stood beside Samos, and tried to speak, and he could only croak. Then he looked at Samos and said, in the very quietest voice:

"You are not Samos. That is not your name. Your name is Arieh ben Elazar, and you are a Jew, and I have been searching for you for twenty years!"

He lifted the astounded young man's left hand and raised it to the light. The little finger was very crooked, and bent sharply inwards towards the other fingers. And Lucanus looked into Arieh's eyes and saw the eyes of Sara, and burst into smothered weeping. "God is good," he faltered. "Above all things, God is good!"

Chapter Forty-two

Lucanus wrote at once to Sara bas Elazar's lawyers in Jerusalem. He said to Arieh, "You must leave on the next ship, which will arrive after my letter has reached the lawyers. I would accompany you, for this is a very dear thing to me, but I have a contract for two months on another ship and I cannot break my word. But I will join you in Jerusalem later—perhaps."

But Arieh said to him, "Do not ask me to leave you. I have not had much experience; let me be your assistant for those two months." Lucanus smiled; he knew that Arieh had made this excuse in order not to be separated from him. So Lucanus agreed, and Arieh, walking with the high quick step of released youth, went with him. Then Lucanus, who felt as if some awful abscess had been finally lanced in him, and purified, began to teach Arieh his ancient religion in the watches of the night. Arieh had been indifferently educated in Greco-Roman religion in the home of his first master, and then in Tarsus by his teachers. He listened to Lucanus with the deepest attention, and asked pertinent questions. "It is strange to discover I am a Jew," he said, once, shaking his head. "My masters hated the Jews, and called them avaricious and cunning—and they themselves the most evil and greedy and crafty of men! My first master, in particular, could not sleep for his schemes, and I never saw him rejoice except when he had ruined another man."

When Arieh walked Lucanus remembered what Elazar ben Solomon had said of his son: "He is a young lion!" He questioned Arieh about any memories he possessed.

Arieh frowned, trying to remember. "I was told I was born on Samos, and so was given this name. I was two years old when I was purchased, to be a toy to my first master's children; I was bought from a block. That is all I know." He paused. "I have had a dream which haunted all my childhood, and which I sometimes dream even now. I am in a great and beautiful garden; I see white columns, but no statues such as I saw later in other houses. I see profusions of flowers everywhere, and bright fountains. I have a little white dog, which is my own. It is very lovely, and very peaceful. A young man comes into the garden and tosses me in his arms and kisses me; there is a young girl too, with dark flowing hair, who plays with me."

Arieh brushed his hand over his healing brow. "The dream mingles. Was it the same day or another? I am with two girls in the garden, who romp with me. It is very brilliant and very silent in the sun. My little dog is not there, and I miss him. All at once two dark, almost naked men appear. I look at them without fear, though I do not recognize them as I recognize my guardians. They creep up upon the girls; they raise something in their hands which flashes in the sun. The girls fall upon their faces. I laugh and clap my hands, for I think it is a game. Then I am seized by one of the men, who move like shadows; a hand is put over my mouth, and I begin to suffocate. I cannot breathe. Then something black falls over my eyes. That is all I remember. My next memory is of a strange house and cruelty and blows. How much later that was I do not know."

"It must be a dream," said Arieh, shaking his head.

"No," said Lucanus, "it was not a dream."

Arieh developed an intense hunger to know all about his family, his father, his sister. Lucanus never tired of talking of Sara. Once, while he was speaking, he saw Arieh looking at him with an inscrutable expression. "She was the loveliest of women, and the sweetest and the kindest," he said, in a voice he believed to be dispassionate. Lucanus patted Arieh's shoulder affectionately. "I feel like a father," he said, "and in truth, you could be my son, for I am not young." He was comforted.

He painted a small picture of Sara for Arieh. The fair face and candid eyes and beautiful smile beamed like flesh from the wood, and the white neck was proud. "She is like a divinity," said Arieh. This made Lucanus laugh. "Do not speak like a Greek or a Roman!" he exclaimed. "Your countrymen will look at you with umbrage and detestation if you call any human being a 'divinity.' Let us sit down and study again of Moses and how he delivered his people from the Egyptians. I find the story fascinates you. And, as the son of Elazar ben Solomon, you must do better with your Hebrew lessons."

An attachment grew up between them which was like the deep devotion of a man who has only one son, and whose heart speaks to that son. Lucanus' mysterious sense of comfort and fulfillment increased day by day. It was as if all he had ever loved was embodied in Arieh, whom he taught like a child. They were never weary of conversation. Lucanus, in speaking of his own life, lived it again as he told Arieh of it. When they stopped at one port a messenger came aboard to deliver a large bag of gold to Arieh, and joyful messages from the lawyers in Jerusalem. "We await the arrival of the son of Elazar ben Solomon," they had written. "He will be purified in the Temple and returned to his people. Blessed is God that He has found you."

Arieh distributed the money among the members of the miserable crew. He went into the galleys and gave several of the slaves enough gold to purchase their freedom. For days and nights thereafter the little ship rang with joyous cries and salutes to the gods. Sailors kissed the hands of Arieh when he passed them, and he was embarrassed.

Lucanus could speak fully and with love of God to Arieh now. His spirit was liberated. He was like one who waits for a summons he is sure will come, and waits serenely. He was frank with Arieh, and explained his earlier hatred for God. "Yet all the time I was secretly enraged that He did not manifest Himself to me, but appeared to ignore me! I would defy Him, and there was no answer. That was unpardonable!"

He told Arieh all that he had been told by Keptah and Joseph ben Gamliel, and when Lucanus spoke so it was as if these beloved teachers stood at his elbow, smiling and nodding. He told Arieh of the Jewish, Chaldean, Babylonian and Egyptian prophecies. He told Arieh of the strange Jewish teacher of whom Priscus had written, and whom Ramus had seen. "But we hear no more of Him," said Lucanus. "Once many stories came to me, until two months ago. Since then there has been only silence. I have questioned people in the several ports, but receive only baffled smiles. I have written to my brother, Priscus, several times, asking for more news, but there is none. He has not written to me. Has he returned to Rome? I wrote my mother two days ago."

"We will find the Jewish rabbi in Jerusalem," said Arieh, intensely interested. "He invades my thoughts. Repeat to me again the prophecy of Isaias."

When they found a little Jewish synagogue in the ports Lucanus would take Arieh to it. But they could not penetrate beyond the Court of the Gentiles. "I understand that I cannot approach the Holy of Holies until I am purified," said Arieh, looking about him curiously. "But why are the Gentiles forbidden to enter? God is God of all men. My people must be a proud and obdurate race."

"Had they not been so they could not have survived the ages," said Lucanus. "A man must preserve what is best in him and his people. Still, as you say, God is God of all men. However, I am mindful of the ceremonies in the temples of the Greeks and Romans and Egyptians. Only the priests, the elect, can partake of the mysteries. Only the priests drink the sacrificial wines and eat of the sacrificed animals. There are some things which must be kept from the vulgar and the stupid, for they can only corrupt. The ordained priests bless and perform their offices, but you must remember that they have been ordained."

"My people are a priestly people," said Arieh. "And only they have commanded that men love one another and do justly to each other, not as a matter of philosophy, but as an act of faith. It is a strange commandment." He looked at Lucanus with a stately lift of his head. He touched Lucanus on the shoulder with his hand. "Yes, He has called you."

A great storm arose one night, and the ship was forced to put into a little harbor which was already crowded with ships which had run before the bellowing of the wind and the leaping of the waves. When the day dawned in fire the sea was still tumultuous, and the battered ships swayed at anchor and were fearful of putting out again. Lucanus and Arieh stood on the plunging deck of their vessel, and they saw that their nearest neighbor was a magnificent ship with fine wood; its furled sails lay like heaps of burnished silk on the deck; the sailors were clad in good clothing and walked confidently; the captain was apparently a man of consequence, though he was now pacing up and down with a worried expression and the two friends could see him biting his lip. "It is a private vessel, the toy of some very rich man," said Lucanus. He hailed the captain, who came reluctantly to the railing of his ship, which was inlaid with ebony and pearl and gilt. Lucanus noticed that the ship had no figurehead of a woman or a mermaid.

"Is there something wrong aboard?" asked Lucanus, in Greek. The captain shook his head. Lucanus tried Aramaic, and the captain nodded eagerly. He replied, "Yes, there is something very wrong. My glorious master, the owner of this ship," and he looked about him proudly, "lies ill in his bed. Our physician died last night in the storm; he was thrown against a wall and his head was smashed."

"What ails your master?"

The captain shook his head. "Who knows? He has lain like one stricken by a mortal illness for more than two months. He is from Jerusalem. His physician was very renowned. Two months ago my master took to his bed, weeping violently, and would see neither his wife nor his children, neither his mother nor his father. The physician was bewildered. Then my master said he would sail the seas to forget, but what he is trying to forget no one knows. He has not moved from his bed; he is dying moment by moment, and he wrings his hands and will not speak."

Lucanus said to Arieh in a low voice, "The man is apparently suffering from some illness of the spirit." He looked at the captain and said with hesitation, "I am a physician. I should like to see your master."

The captain's face brightened; it was evident that he loved his master. "Wait, Master! I will arrange to take you aboard, for truly I am afraid that death is approaching."

It was difficult for Lucanus and Arieh to board the other vessel, for the two ships leaped restlessly, but not in tempo with each other. The captain received them like kings. "Oh, God is good!" he exclaimed. "My master will not die now!"

Never had Lucanus seen so wonderful a ship; a Roman Augustale, or even a Caesar, would have been proud to own it. The decks were of teakwood, the walls of ebony inlaid with artistic patterns of flowers and leaves of pearl and gold and silver. They gleamed in the hot sun. Lucanus said to the captain, "You are Jews, I see, for I observe no statues of the gods, no murals of animals. What is your master's name?"

"Hilell ben Hamram," said the captain, and looked at Lucanus and Arieh, expecting their awe. "Surely you know of this family, for not only is it the richest in all Judea, but it is a family famous for its doctors and lawyers and learned men, and my master is a friend of Pontius Pilate himself, and King Herod Antipas is flattered to receive him as a guest."

Lucanus smiled faintly; young Arieh was listening with interest. Lucanus motioned to him. "Let us go to our patient." They were conducted down to other decks, each more lavish than the last, and full of light and precious fabrics and woods and furniture. "You understand that my master owns no slaves," said the captain, with adoration in his voice. "It is against the principles of devout Jews."

Lucanus could not help saying, with a gesture indicating

Arieh, "You are very learned, my captain, about the names of those renowned in Israel. Surely you recognize the son of Elazar ben Solomon, who has been touring the world in order to perfect himself in the arts of medicine?"

Arieh blushed; Lucanus was enjoying himself. The captain's eyes bulged as he looked at Arieh. "The son of Elazar ben Solomon! But his son was stolen from him as a child, and was lost."

"He was lost, but has been found," said Lucanus. "Come. Is this your master's door?"

Speechlessly, and staring at Arieh, the captain opened a door concealed by gold brocade, and the physicians entered a chamber so lavish in its Eastern magnificence that they were dazzled. Curtains of silver brocade swung from the windows; Persian carpets covered the floor; the deck heaved and swayed, but the great gilt bed was bolted firmly. In it, under rich silken coverlets, lay a man of not more than twenty-nine. His face was like worn marble; his eyes were sunken in large circles like bruises. He appeared not to breathe. His black hair lay like a fan on his embroidered cushions; his features were fine and austere. When Lucanus and Arieh approached him he did not stir.

"Hilell ben Hamram," said Lucanus, gently, bending over him, "I am Lucanus, a physician, and I have come to help you."

"And I am Arieh ben Elazar, also a physician, and your countryman," said Arieh, with deep compassion in his voice.

The sick man did not move. It was as if he had already gone beyond hearing. Then Arieh appeared to be listening. He put his hand on Hilell's cold forehead and said, "Hear, O Israel, the Lord our God is One!"

Hilell remained motionless. The two physicians watched him anxiously. Lucanus lifted his slack and icy hand and felt for his pulse. He put his ear to the almost breathless chest. The heart was slow and feeble. When Lucanus looked up again he saw that slow tears were seeping from under the shut eyelids. Arieh sat down beside Hilell and took his hand and held it strongly, and Lucanus was struck by the beauty of the picture of this handsome young man silently comforting his brother. The sun poured through the window and lay on their faces. "Do not weep," said Arieh, tenderly. "For God is with you, and we will help you, with His power."

The tears poured faster from under the eyelids; Arieh believed that the fingers of the sick man tightened on his own.

He said, "I was lost, and He found me. I was a slave, and He delivered me. I was a stranger, and He brought me to my people. Blessed is He, King of Kings! For nothing is beyond His power, and He shall not be silent when His children call unto Him!"

Hilell groaned; it was as if the sound rose not only from his flesh but from his spirit. He did not open his eyes but he whispered, "It is too late. He called to me, and I turned from Him. I did not forget Him, and one day I knew I could not live without Him, though what He asked of me was very arduous. So I went seeking Him again. It was too late. The Romans had killed Him, had nailed Him on a cross like a criminal."

Lucanus stared violently. He caught Hilell's emaciated shoulder in his hand; the soft silk rustled under his fingers. "When was this?" he cried.

Hilell did not reply for several moments; it was as if he had fallen into the sleep of death. Then he said faintly, "It was at the Passover, when the earth darkened."

Lucanus sat down abruptly. His heart was leaping and there was a thundering sound in his ears. He pressed his hands to them to clear them. After a little he reached mechanically for his pouch and brought out a vial which contained a stimulant. His hands trembling, he poured a little into a goblet of wine which stood on a table of lemonwood at the sick man's elbow. He held the goblet to Hilell's lips and cried peremptorily, "Drink this! And then you must tell us, for this story is what we have been seeking!"

Hilell drank without opening his eyes, then Lucanus let his head down on the cushions. The radiant sea threw glancing shadows of light into the chamber; gulls cried near the windows, and the voices of many seamen echoed on the wind. The hot odor of tar and salt and fish was mingled with an aromatic odor like myrrh. Lucanus and Arieh waited for Hilell to speak. A faint color began to creep over his ivory cheeks; his ashen lips quickened to coral, and the sweat dried on his brow. Then he opened tragic eyes, and they were dark and tormented. "You seek Him?" he murmured. "But He is dead. I saw three crosses, tiny and diminished, on the far Place of Skulls, against a turbulent sky of pink and lilac clouds, huge and boiling, and there was an awful light upon the earth. And the people told me, where I stood, that One of those on the crosses was Jesus of Nazareth, and that He had been condemned for flouting the Law and causing insurrection against Rome. And while I stood, a sensation of dying and loss in me, the sun withdrew his radiance and the earth shook, and the people fell on their faces with a sound of great terror and mourning. I was too late, too late forever to tell Him I would follow Him."

"And then?" said Lucanus, as Hilell fell silent, turning his head in anguish.

The sick man made a feeble gesture. "I do not know. I fled that accursed place that night and I went to Caesarea, and remained for a few senseless days, and then I fled to the sea, for nothing was to me worth anything any longer."

"The ancient prophecies say that He will rise again," said Lucanus. He strained towards Hilell, who shook his head. "How is that possible?" he muttered. "Yes, it is true that I heard from my servants that so His followers had declared. At the end He was only a man." He looked at Lucanus imploringly. "He died! You must tell me, for my soul's sake and peace, that He was only a man after all, and that I did not truly betray Him, nor wound Him!"

"Have not men always betrayed Him?" asked Lucanus, sadly. "And will they not always betray Him, world without end? Did I not betray Him myself, though I saw the star of His birth, and I heard of Him from infancy? You repent, and penitence is all that He asks."

Hilell was weeping. "Then I am not lost and He has forgiven me?"

"He will not despise a repentant heart," said Lucanus, and wiped the sick man's cheek with a towel dipped in cool water. "But tell us."

It was some time before Hilell could speak. He twisted his thin fingers together and looked at the shining windows as if seeing something beyond them. "I have been visiting Herod, who is a friend of my family, in his palace at Caesarea. You will understand that was almost a year ago. I, my wife and my children, who were with me also, but as the time of the Day of Atonement approached I could not remain with Herod, who is partly Greek, and a man of caprice who is at one hour a Greek and then the next hour a Jew. I am not a pious man, nor do I observe the strict Law. Nevertheless, I could endure Herod's conversation no longer, nor his moods. He sacrifices in the Roman temples; then he goes to Jerusalem for purification and strews ashes on his head, and cries for forgiveness and heaps gold in the hands of the priests. So I sent my family to Jerusalem quietly, then followed them a day or two later."

He paused, and Lucanus refreshed him again with the wine and the stimulant.

"You must understand that I had been hearing much of that Jewish rabbi who was teaching the people in the dust of the cities and the byways. Herod spoke of Him with uneasy laughter; there were many who accused Him of arousing the Jews to rebellion against the Roman oppressor. But Herod was also uneasy because he had caused the death of John the Baptist, as he was called by the people, for Herod is a learned man in his way and he thought that John was Elias, and had at first spared him. John had denounced him, him the tetrarch, for marrying his brother's wife, Herodias.

"You will understand, Lucanus, that these things are vague in my mind, for what was a poor Jewish rabbi from Galilee to the rich and the powerful? There are always prophets; the Jews breed prophets as locusts breed young. One more or less is unimportant. I should not have listened to any of the stories had not Herod seemed unusually capricious and disturbed, and had he not become unpredictable and savage since he had had that John put to death.

"I understand that Herod might have forgotten John, as one forgets a violently colored dream in time, had not that Jewish rabbi appeared in his footsteps. Herod told me that John had spoken of Him. Then it was rumored that the rabbi was performing great miracles; the palace rang with the news. It was said He was the Messias. It was strange that it was only the slaves and the miserable freedmen who spoke of Him with such inordinate passion and excitement. But rulers listen to slaves, and so the rumors of the Messias came to Herod's ears, and he was beside himself."

Lucanus wiped Hilell's face. Arieh sat in silence, listening, and Hilell did not release his hand.

"It was a hot day when I left Herod, and I drove my own chariot, surrounded by my servants on horseback and on foot. The dust was a white fire, and I wrapped a cloth about my nose and eyes. And then at the roadside we saw a little group of men sitting on stones in the dust, near a small village, and children stood shyly near them.

"Why did I stop? One of my men rode up to my chariot and told me vehemently that yonder there was the humble rabbi with His friends, and I was curious to see the man who

had so ignited Herod, and about whom there were so many
incredible tales. So I drove up near Him and His little band
of followers and the children, and listened with a smile to
One who appeared as poor and humble as a beggar, and I
said to myself, Is this He of Whom they speak?

"He was telling a story, a parable, and the Jews are as full
of stories as a pomegranate is full of seeds. His accent was
gross, for He was a peasant from Galilee, a woodworker as
I was told. He related the story very well, with much eloquence.
I looked at His dusty face and His dusty garments and feet
as He sat on the stone, and I was struck by the story. For He
told of a Pharisee—and the Pharisees are very devout and
rigorous men who defend the Law as the legions defend Rome
—who went up to the Temple to pray, and beside him was a
dull publican of no consequence, who, no doubt, the Pharisee found insupportable. And the Pharisee, fastidiously annoyed at the nearness of the publican, drew his headcloth
over his nose so as not to be offended by the other's presence and his mean occupation."

Hilell's eyes changed, became eager and warm as he
looked at Lucanus. "It was a very interesting story, and I
do not like the Pharisees, who annoy me with their excessive piety which is only the letter and not the spirit
of the Law. I was willing to be amused; it amused me that
this poor and ragged man could speak of the Pharisees who
are a terror in Judea, with their constant accusations to the
priests that the people do not observe all the rituals properly. They are tiresome, and dangerous, these Pharisees,
searching always for heresy."

He panted a little, and once again Lucanus refreshed him.
He lay on his pillows and his eyes became dreaming. "An
excellent story. The rabbi said that the Pharisee prayed to
God, saying 'I thank You, Lord, that I am not as other men,
adulterers, extortioners, unjust and knowing nothing of
Your Law. I am not as this miserable publican, who should
not profane Your Temple by his presence. I fast at all the
fasts; I give scrupulous tithes.' And the Pharisee was very
pleased with himself.

"But the publican struck his breast, weeping, and would
not raise his eyes, and cried out, 'God be merciful to me,
a sinner!' "

Hilell had so far recovered that he could laugh faintly.
"And the rabbi said to His followers, 'I tell you that this publican was more worthy than the Pharisee, and God comforted

him, but did not comfort the Pharisee. For he that raises himself shall be struck down, but he who humbles himself shall be exalted.'

"I must tell you of that rabbi. The sun was vivid but His face was more vivid, for His emotion was more than the emotion of any man. He sat like a prince on a throne, and one forgot that He was only a member of the Amuratzem on a stone, and that His feet were laved in the dust. He smiled like a father; He looked at His followers with blue and tender eyes, and they listened reverently. His beard was golden, His hands rested on His knees. He spoke like one endowed with authority.

"It was then that the children, ragged and barefoot, and standing in the background, approached Him shyly. While I had been listening to the rabbi their mothers had joined them, poor women in rough striped garments, with jars on their shoulders. They pressed their children towards Him, peering about them humbly, as if begging pardon. And His followers said to them, 'Do not disturb the Master, and take your children away from Him, for He is weary and must not be troubled as He speaks His wisdom.' "

Hilell sighed deeply and closed his eyes. "But the rabbi called to the children and held out His arms to them and said to His followers, 'Permit the children to come unto Me, and do not rebuke them. For of such as these little ones are the Kingdom of Heaven.' And the children clambered about Him and sat on His knee and wound their arms about His neck, laughing and embracing Him, and He held them to Him. And I swear to you that I was freshly moved, for I am a father and I know the sweetness of children's kisses and love. The rabbi said to His followers, 'Who does not receive the Kingdom of God as a little child shall not enter within its gates.' "

Hilell opened his eyes, and again they were full of torment. "I understood the rabbi, though never had I understood before. And I stepped down from my chariot and approached Him, and my servants called to the people to open a passage for me. He watched me approach and He smiled at me like one recognizing a brother, and waited. My servants shouted, 'Make way for Hilell ben Hamram, who is a man great in Israel, for he had the rule of a town and his family is renowned and has much gold!' And the rabbi said nothing, and only waited for me, though the people stepped back in fear.

"I stopped before Him, close enough to touch His shoulder, and He gazed up at me in silence. I said to Him, 'Good Master, what shall I do to inherit eternal life?' He smiled at me again, and said, and His voice was sonorous, 'Why do you call me good? None is good, only God. You know the Commandments, that you must not kill, steal, bear false witness or commit adultery. You must honor your father and your mother.' I said to Him, 'I have kept the Commandments from my youth.'

"He was silent for so long that I thought He had dismissed me, He the poor unlearned rabbi with the vulgar accent. Then He raised His eyes to me and said in a thoughtful tone, 'You lack one thing: sell all that you have, for you are rich, and give it to the poor, for then you shall have treasures in heaven.' "

Hilell raised himself on his cushions and looked at Lucanus imploringly. "Physician! You will understand how incredible that was! Why should He have asked me to beggar myself?"

Lucanus looked at the ocean, which he could see through the window, and said, softly, "He asks that each man deliver to Him that which he holds dearest in the world, and it is evident that you held your money above all things."

Hilell groaned, and fell back. "That is true. I understand now. I stepped back from Him, appalled. He saw my agitation and He said to me very gently, and in a low voice, 'Come, follow Me.' "

Hilell passed his hand over his face. "He asked me to follow Him, to be one with His homeless followers! I, Hilell ben Hamram! I told myself this was madness. Then He turned to His followers and said very sorrowfully, 'How difficult shall it be for those who have riches to enter into the Kingdom of God!' And He stood up. He began to speak again to those about Him, and I returned to my chariot and I drove away."

Lucanus and Arieh did not speak. Hilell looked from one to the other, pleadingly. "I was educated in Athens and Rome. I am a man of learning and power and influence and wealth. I am a man of the world. I am Hilell ben Hamram and I was asked to do the impossible."

"I understand. I understand how incredible that must have sounded to you," said Lucanus, sighing. "For did I not myself berate and hate Him when He took from me my heart's darling, and did I not vow to revenge myself upon Him? I did not know, as you did not know, that He takes only to give, bereaves only to extend His comfort, blinds only that a man can see His light. Who am I to reproach you, Hilell ben Hamram?"

He indicated Arieh with his hand. "Who can know the mysteries of God? He surrendered this young man into my hands, after more than twenty years of searching for him, and I know now that when He gave me Arieh it was to deliver me from my hatred and bring me to Him."

Hilell gazed at him. He watched as Arieh leaned his head on Lucanus' shoulder. Arieh said, "Blessed are we that He visited us."

Lucanus stretched out his hand to Hilell. "I can see that you never forgot Him, that He haunted your life and your dreams, and you could not flee from Him. Rest, and be consoled, for you have suffered much and He has forgiven you and asks only that you follow Him and leave Him never. Come with us to Israel, where we will find Him again, for surely He is not dead, but lives."

Chapter Forty-three

Hilell ben Hamram rose from his bed, vital and young again. He would not permit Lucanus and Arieh to leave him. They, on their ship, attending the crew, would be followed by his magnificent vessel, until the time Lucanus' contract was fulfilled. Then Lucanus and Arieh would board his ship and they would go to Israel together. "I was dead, and you called me forth!" he cried to Lucanus, embracing him.

When they stopped briefly at ports, Hilell insisted on sharing Lucanus' houses with him and Arieh. He lay down on a floor pallet, and ate the frugal meals which Lucanus provided, and followed him wherever he and Arieh went to minister to waiting patients. But his bearing, and the bearing of Arieh, awed the humble patients. At night, sitting around the table eating and with lamplight about them, Hilell would tell his companions of what he knew and heard of Jesus of Nazareth. His fine ivory face would glow; his dark eyes flamed, and joy stood in them. "I understand from my servants that the Master's followers scattered after His crucifixion for fear of the Romans, for they had been proscribed for troublemaking. I will bring them to my house in Jerusalem, and we will sit among them and talk of Him!"

Lucanus listened with profound attention to the stories of Hilell. And then when he was alone late at night he began to write down these stories. He wrote with the pellucid strength and precision of the Greek scholar, and with that scholar's calm but compassionate eloquence. It seemed to him that he had witnessed these things with his own eyes; as he wrote he saw the scenes, heard the voices of the people. And so began his Great Gospel, written for all the world and the world of men, for he knew, as Hilell did not, that God had clothed Himself in human flesh not only for Jews but for Gentiles also.

"As you know, Lucanus," said Hilell, "we have had the prophecy of ages that the Messias would be of the house of David, and it is said that Jesus is of that house. I have heard His Mother had been visited by Gabriel, who told her of the birth of the coming Messias. But you must verify these things yourself in Israel."

Lucanus thought of the Mother of the Messias, whose name was unknown to Hilell. One night he remembered what Joseph ben Gamliel had told him of her, when her Son had been a boy and had visited the elders and scholars in the Temple. The sweetest and tenderest of emotions came to Lucanus. She began to embody for him all the dear women he had known, Iris, his mother, Rubria and Sara, and his wise, childlike sister, Aurelia, who loved all things which had been created.

He longed to be in the presence of Mary, though he did not as yet know her name. He wanted to hear from her own lips the story of her Son's birth and childhood and youth and manhood. Surely she could tell him more than any of His followers could tell him. She had guarded Him in her womb; she had fed Him at her breast; she had taught Him to walk; she had washed His garments, had spun them and sewn them. When He had been afflicted with ailments she had nursed Him and had sat by His bed at night, watching. She had heard His first words, had seen His first smile. As Lucanus thought of Mary a passionate thirst for her presence and her voice came to him, and he loved her. She was the great Mystery, and she was a woman, and women always confided in him their deepest secrets. "When we know what she thought, and what she did, then we shall know everything," he said to Arieh and Hilell.

"She was but an instrument of God," said Hilell.

"She was His Mother, and do not mothers know all about their sons?" asked Lucanus. "And why was this child chosen to be His Mother? There was a reason why she of all women was chosen, and she can tell me."

"And do not men love their mothers?" said Arieh. "Did He not love her above all other creatures? Would He not listen to her tenderly as infant, youth and man? Yes."

"Surely she is the blessed of the ages," said Lucanus.

He recorded the story of the centurion, Antonius, and his servant; he recorded the story of Ramus, who had seen the Messias raise a young man from the dead and give him again to his mother. But the first part of his Gospel he left open for the time when he would see Mary. He was disturbed about one thing. He said to Hilell, "When the Messias came for the last time to Jerusalem, you have told me that the Jewish populace lined His way, strewing palm branches before Him and His donkey, and hailed Him as the All High, and crowded about Him to kiss His garments, holding up their children for Him to see and bless. And when He was led to the place of crucifixion, His people crowded the road and wept, and a woman wiped His face when He fell under the Roman whips, and a poor and miserable Jew carried His cross. Why, if they loved Him so, did they permit His death, and denounce Him, and scatter His followers after all He had done in His mercy for them?"

Hilell replied, "It is a precarious relationship between the Jews and the Romans; the high priests and wise men of Israel did their work well. They acted as mediators between their people and Rome, promising that there would be no bloody revolts against Rome, that they would permit no agitators among the people, for they were fearful that if these things happened Israel would be destroyed by Rome, as other nations had been destroyed. And there are the young men called Essenes, who are very devout and spend months in the desert praying for the Messias and for the deliverance of Israel from the power of Rome. And it was said that Jesus was one of their number, though whether or not that is true I do not know.

"Then there are the Pharisees, grim, sour-faced men, who have set themselves up as the guardians of the Law. They are merchants and bankers, lawyers and doctors. They will not live joyously, nor permit others to live so. They despise the poor and humble and homeless, and the Amuratzem, the peasants. They have even suggested that the Amuratzem be forbidden to approach the altars too closely, for they are unlearned and rough-clad!

"And there are the rabble, the market-place rabble, who have no love for their country or their God—the petulant, lightless rabble which afflict all cities and all nations, demanding always, greedy, eager for sport, with lusty animal appetites, quarrelsome, milling restlessly, incapable of learning anything, contentious and dependent. Have you not such a rabble in Rome, and will not Rome die of them, and the taxation they impose on their betters for their idle support?

"Now when the Messias made such a stir throughout all of Judea, speaking to the gentle and the hard-working and humble, promising them that God will never leave them, but loves them, healing them tenderly, and telling them that though they have no money they are not despised of God, as the Pharisees despise them, assuring them that they are as valuable in the sight of the All High as any emperor or king or silk-clothed priest or Pharisee—then this aroused the anger of the Pharisees. Moreover, it seemed to the Pharisees that the Messias was somewhat loose with the Law, interpreting it to His followers and the people as no Pharisee would interpret it. In the eyes of the Pharisees, He was debasing God to the level of the lowest, uttering heresies which would destroy the spiritual strength of Israel. When His followers acclaimed Him as the Messias, the Pharisees were enraged, for did they not believe that the Messias would come to the Jews as the mightiest of kings, clothed in glory and fierceness and power, surrounded by an angelic host, and would He not at once drive out the Romans and put them to flight forever? Yet here was a humble Man, a member of the Amuratzem, of Galilee, unknown to everyone except for three short years, a nameless Man, in rope sandals and in rough garments, speaking in a common tongue like a peasant —and it was said openly that He was the Messias! Was this not a blasphemy against God, against the prophecy? asked the Pharisees. Worse, He did not deny He was the Messias!

"The followers, and the people too, were confused. Here was the Messias, yet He expressed no hatred for Rome; He even condescended to cure some Romans. However, the followers and the people, who had been given joy and surcease by Him, loved Him and knew Him, and accepted Him. They were those who acclaimed Him on the road to Jerusalem, and wept as He bore His cross to Calvary. They hoped, to the very last, that when a Roman would drive a nail through His feet the heavens would open and wrath would descend upon the earth.

"Then there were the priests, many of them members of the Pharisee class, who were honestly horrified at His teachings. They were also fearful that the Romans would use the Messias and His words as an excuse for suppression, bloodshed and oppressive laws—after all the work the priests had done to placate Rome and keep a measure of freedom for their people.

"So you have the priests, frightened for their people and their faith; you have the self-appointed guardians of the Law, the Pharisees, who detest the humble; you have the shrill rabble, always searching for a victim. And you have Rome, ever watchful for signs of rebellion against her power. Considering all these, it is a marvel that He was permitted to live as long as He did! Eventually He was denounced to the Roman officials, and that was the end. Or the beginning," added Hilell.

He sighed. "I was told that long before His death He prophesied it. He said He had been born to die as He died. God had willed it from the beginning of time, to reconcile His people to Him, to show them that He had never abandoned them, that He loved them and was willing to perish for them, in order that they might see the truth, the light and the life, and life everlasting and mercy without bounds. He clothed Himself in their flesh to demonstrate that nothing was impossible with God. The men who killed Him were, at the last, only His ordained instruments. Without His death, as well as His life, there would be no fulfillment of the prophecies of the prophets."

Lucanus was silent for a long time; he nodded over and over as he thought. Then he said, "You do not know what has happened now?"

Hilell hesitated. "No. But His followers said He would rise from the dead on the third day, for so He had told them."

Lucanus smiled. "He has risen," he said. "Be of good heart, my dear friend. He has risen! I know this in my soul."

The joyousness, the clean bright surety, filled his days. He was like a youth, filled with words and regnant with messages. He looked about him, and it was as if he had never seen before, as if for the first time he had been given sight and ears and understanding. The darkness and the grief had departed from him like a storm. When he smiled at his friends or at those he treated, the sun seemed to shine on his face. He would touch the cross he now wore always on his breast. And he wrote his Gospel.

They had intended landing at Joppa, but a storm blew and they were driven off course to Caesarea. Lucanus and Hilell and Arieh stood together at the ship's railing and watched the approaching coast of Judea, and Lucanus thought, There is my home from which I have always fled. The port of Caesarea was a long black spur of rock reaching out into the sea, and Hilell explained that on one side the Roman galleons unloaded or loaded cargo, and on the other side they disembarked passengers or took them on board. He said, smiling, "I have a dear friend, a Roman officer, who was appointed to this region three years ago. You will like him: a wry and pungent man, of no illusions."

Behind the wonderful ship of Hilell a huge black cloud formed like a great tower, outlined with the blazing gold of the descending sun; the sea flowed like liquid rubies. Mars, an amber jewel, stood above the cloudy edifice. The ship glided to the busy spur which was the harbor; several galleons and smaller vessels dipped at anchor, their slack sails stained with scarlet from the sunset. A low ridge of hills lay beyond the harbor, bronze and naked, and the air was poignant with the scent of the East.

Hilell pointed to the hills and said with some bitterness, "The Romans stripped our land of its dark cypresses for their ships." Arieh's blue eyes were sharp and piercing, as he looked at the land of his fathers, and his lips trembled with emotion. Hilell, seeing this, put his hand on the young man's arm and pressed it affectionately. He had a beautiful young sister, Leah, fifteen years old, and ripe for marriage. He began to plan a wedding between her and Arieh, the son of Elazar ben Solomon, a noble name in Israel.

The ship, masterfully handled, slipped within the harbor, all its gay pennants flying, its sails heeling against the awesome sky of sunset. It was hailed by the other ships, and Hilell saluted, his handsome face smiling. His sailors shouted from the masts. The harbors were busily bustling against the night; lanterns began to appear in the swift twilight. A number of Roman soldiers stood idly watching the work, and their officer came running lightly to the dock as Hilell's ship cast anchor. "Hilell!" he called, in a strong and delighted voice. "Greetings!" His helmet glowed like fire from the fast-falling

sun, which shone redly on his strenuous, masculine face. He
began to laugh, standing on the dock, his thumbs in his broad
belt, his bare legs spread, his tunic rippling in the light wind.
Then as the plank came out from the ship he jumped on it
and ran aboard, laughing. Hilell fell into his arms and they
embraced.

"How did you know we were to arrive here?" asked Hilell.
The Roman winked broadly, pretending not to see Lucanus
and Arieh nearby. "How do I know?" he said. "I should like
you to believe, you mystic Jew, that an angel bent and
whispered in my ear, or that an oracle told me, or a priest
mentioned it as he examined the entrails of a sacrificed
animal. But no. It is my affair to know exactly where you have
been sailing these past two months, and whom you have on
board."

He was no longer smiling. He turned abruptly to Lucanus,
who was gazing at him intently. "You do not know me, Lucanus, son of Diodorus Cyrinus?" he asked in a grave and disappointed voice.

Lucanus stared. He removed his elbows from the railing.
"No!" he exclaimed. "It cannot be! Plotius!" And he gripped
the arms of Plotius and could not speak.

Hilell regarded them with astonishment. Plotius said to
him, "These Greeks! They are very emotional, though they
pretend otherwise." He held Lucanus off from him, and his
soldier's eyes were moist. "So. Here you are at last; here we
meet once more. I was at Joppa two days ago, and there heard
the ship would not land there." He paused. "Lucanus," he said,
like one deeply stirred, "we never wrote to each other but I
always knew where you were, for Caesar had you under
his protection."

"I cannot believe it," said Lucanus. "I am very happy! It is
really you, Plotius, my dear friend, after all these years."
He laughed a little to conceal how moved he was; the
blooming lanterns and the crimson torches swam before his
eyes.

"I swear by Castor and Pollux you have not changed!" said
Plotius. His hands were on Lucanus' shoulders; he bent forward to examine his face. "You are still a young man, and
you are old enough to have a gray beard." He looked at
Hilell and said, "This is our dear Hermes, who fled the arms
of Julia, of whom I have told you," and he laughed.

"Nor have you changed," said Lucanus, somewhat men-
daciously, for Plotius was broader and sturdier than he re-

membered, and had the heavy outlines of a man of forty-six, and his eyebrows, below the helmet, were threaded with gray.

"Hah!" said Plotius. "The gods have not given me the secret of eternal youth, as they have given you, my dear Lucanus. Under this helmet I have a bald pate; I rarely remove it, for I am afraid that as with Aeschylus an eagle will mistake my head for a stone and drop a tortoise upon it. I prefer, however, to remember that Pericles too was bald, and retained his helmet for that reason." He laughed again, and his laughter boomed over the water. He embraced Lucanus once more, then slapped him on the back.

Lucanus introduced him to Arieh. "Yes, yes, I understand," said Plotius, heartily. "I have heard of Arieh ben Elazar; the lawyers buzz about him in Jerusalem. I knew he was with you on this ship. Hilell, I am pleased to see that you are not sick, as was reported."

"I am very well," said the other man. "And now you must find us lodgings for the night, Plotius, for I intend to remain here a few days."

Plotius' face changed, became dark and inscrutable. He half turned aside. He did not look at Lucanus when he said, "It is all arranged, since we knew you would arrive here. Pontius Pilate has kindly offered his house for your use, as he will be in Jerusalem for some weeks. I believe he wishes to return to Rome, as his wife has been—disturbed—for some time."

"Your own house will do us equally well," said Hilell. He frowned slightly. "I prefer not to be the guest of Pontius Pilate."

"My house," said Plotius, "was recently sold. I am attached to the household of Pilate now. Now you must not be offensive, my dear Hilell! I know you never liked the procurator——"

"I do not like Herod, who built that fine house for him!" said Hilell in a vehement tone. Plotius studied him craftily. "You mean you no longer like Romans," he said. "Well, then, go to a tavern, you stiff-necked Sadducee! And enjoy the fleas and the dogs."

Hilell hesitated. He looked at Lucanus and Arieh. Then he shrugged. "Very well, if my friends do not object, we will go to the house of Pilate—with no pleasure."

"I prefer to go where you go," said Lucanus.

Plotius looked at him strangely. "I think not, when I tell you that your adopted brother, Priscus, is in Pilate's villa on the hills yonder, and awaits you."

"Priscus! I have not heard from him for a long time! I thought he was in Jerusalem!" Lucanus was freshly delighted.

"So he was, until a few weeks ago." Plotius' tone was very odd and restrained. "He is a friend of Pilate's, and has been visiting him." The soldier paused. "The air here is more salubrious than in Jerusalem, and he has had a slight illness."

Hilell caught the restraint, the avoidance, in Plotius' voice, but Lucanus, overcome with joy at seeing his old friend, and at the news of his brother's presence, did not hear. The three went to Plotius' large chariot, which was drawn by four black horses. A last light lay over the land, and as the chariot was borne off Lucanus looked about him eagerly.

There was little to see in this dusk, except an occasional flickering light on a distant vast fortress, or a lamp in a small house, or a grove of spearlike cypresses beginning to lean against a rising yellow moon. Boys and girls, uttering harsh and guttural sounds, ran ahead of the chariot and its leading riders, herding their kine home, or a flock of goats, or black-faced brown sheep. Lucanus guessed, from the smell of dust, that the land was dry and sandy and crumbling. The city lay below them as they mounted the low hills, its flat roofs shimmering, its narrow streets restless with carried lights, its doorways golden. There was so little to see in this rapid darkness, yet Lucanus was more deeply excited than ever he had been in his life. It was not the deep and intense odors, pungent and hot over the sea breeze, heavy with a memory of incense and spice which the very ground exhaled that stirred him. It was not the peppery smell of trees and parched grass, nor the dust. He knew the East well; the odors here were only more insistent than in Alexandria or Cairo or Thebes or Syria. None of these scents moved Lucanus, but only the thought that here had lived the sages and the prophets, the patriarchs and mighty men, the men of Moses and David and Saul and Elias, the land of Goliath, of Gaza, of kings and warriors, of Samuel and Solomon. Here had sounded the thunder of the ages; here God had walked as an earthquake. Here Sinai had bellowed with thunder and had been stunned by lightnings. Here the Commandments had been given to all men. Here had risen the conception that man could be more than man, and that it was commanded that he be so. Here, in this little land, the giants, the Titans, had truly sprung from the ground and the crash of their voices echoed even in the silence. Here was more wisdom than Greece had conceived, more grandeur than

Rome had struck under the sun. There was not an inch of ground which was not blessed; there was not a tree but which must stand in wonder. Here the spiritual heroes had had their being, and their shades walked on every path. Here a girl child had carried God in her womb, and here He had manifested Himself to man, and here He had lived and here He had died, and here He had chosen to speak as a man.

I am home, thought Lucanus, and there was a profound rapture in him. For God, in this small compass, had made His own home among those He had chosen to hear Him.

The mounted riders before the chariot carried torches like scarlet pennants. They reflected on an occasional tree, on a stone, on the rocky road, on faces, on the backs of the horses. Lucanus saw that they were rising towards two very impressive palaces. Plotius pointed to one. "Pilate," he said. He pointed to the next. "His dear friend, the tetrarch of Jerusalem, Herod Antipas." The white and columned buildings glittered in the moonlight; the palace of Herod was crowned with a golden dome. Roman legions began to line the road, saluting.

The city lay below now, all flat silver-plated roofs, touched with the fire of torches and the paler glimmer of lanterns. From somewhere came the wailing of a woman. "Tomorrow I will show you one of our grandest temples," said Plotius, proudly. "Two vast statues, one of Zeus and one of Apollo, facing each other, Zeus of marble, Apollo of red porphyry. This is a very strange land! The Jews despise our temples everywhere; they avert their faces, and they the most religious of people! I tell you, there is no understanding the Jews. The worst of them spit when we pass. Many of our soldiers have married pretty Jewish maidens, but only after a most painful circumcision, and only after prolonged weeping on the part of mothers and thunderings from fathers. One would think we were savages from blackest Africa." He laughed.

"They wish to keep both themselves and the Law unblemished," said Hilell, somewhat stiffly.

Plotius winked at Lucanus. "I tell you," he repeated, "they are very strange. They detest Herod, even when he stands in the Temple at Jerusalem and pours ashes on his head and sacrifices. They look on his tears with disdain. Ah, but they are stiff-necked!" He flicked the horses with his whip. "But the land has a curious fascination for me. Priscus will have much to tell you. You must make allowances, for he is not himself."

"Why not?" asked Lucanus, with his first alarm, raising his voice over the rumble of the chariot.

Plotius shrugged. "He officiated at the crucifixion of a miserable Jewish rabbi, and it could be that some spell was laid on him. The Jews have incantations of their own, and I have told you they hate Romans. I am happy you are here. You will laugh his superstitions away." Once more his voice was peculiar.

Lucanus glanced at Hilell and Arieh, and they were staring at him mutely in the windy dance of the torches. "As you know," went on Plotius, skillfully guiding his great horses, "Priscus' family is not with him, and until that crucifixion Priscus was the merriest and most robust of men, and my favorite officer. He was also a frequenter of the better and more fastidious harlots, and a roisterer in the taverns. However," he added, "I do remember that he had frequent fits of melancholy and thoughtfulness even before that crucifixion, and he would argue with me about Rome, wishing to be convinced that our nation was not truly depraved and lost and corrupt. Do I not remember my uncle, the senator, who as truly died for his country as any general in battle, and for no reason? But now I must tell you that Priscus has changed."

"In what manner?"

Plotius' soldierly voice became evasive. "Am I a physician? I brought him to Caesarea, for I love him as a son. Do not be alarmed," said Plotius, kindly. "It may be nothing. Both Pilate and Herod have sent their best physicians to care for him, at my request; two of them are with him now, and you may speak with them. They tell me very little. He spends much time in his bed, and appears to have some difficulty in eating. He often bursts into mysterious tears, but the physicians do not permit me to question him. These physicians are very arrogant, and take liberties even with soldiers." He touched Lucanus' arm affectionately with the butt of his whip. "Ah, I have disturbed you! Rest assured Priscus is treated like a satrap from Persia by his friends. As his brother, and a physician, you will cure him at once with logic and reason."

Lucanus was alarmed at the evasion of Plotius. But he knew that Plotius was also obstinate, and did not desire to discuss Priscus any longer. So he said, "On the day of that crucifixion there was a darkness, was there not?"

"Yes. It was also said that many saw the dead in the streets and in the houses. These people are very superstitious! The sun did darken, and was lost for a long time. But it was only a dust storm." He hesitated. "Priscus can tell you, if you can persuade him to speak. He weeps like a woman when I talk to him, on the few occasions when I have access to him."

"And why does he weep?" murmured Lucanus, stubbornly.

Plotius smiled at him with exasperation. "I am embarrassed to tell you, my dear friend, for fear of your laughter. He declares it was God, or perhaps Zeus or Hermes or Osiris or Apollo, who died on that criminal cross! Do not laugh at me, I implore you. I am repeating only what your brother has told me."

Lucanus was silent, and Plotius peered at him with humor. "Do not be distressed," he said, with some concern. "I am certain he is not mad, but only a victim of some spell or his own imagination."

"Why is he here?" asked Lucanus in a low voice.

Again Plotius hesitated. "I suggested it, for he went about in a daze for a long time in Jerusalem, and the soldiers noticed it, and his pallor, and his absent ways, and his sudden bursts of tears. Did I wish this scandal to be reported to Rome, and to Tiberius, who has changed savagely for the worst and now hates everyone? I could not have Priscus disgraced, returned to Rome for punishment for behavior detrimental to his reputation as a soldier of Rome. It is very bad in Jerusalem, I tell you! Since that crucifixion there has been much turbulence there, and many soldiers are part of the foolish hysteria. Pilate was forced to proscribe the followers of that crucified rabbi in order to restore peace, and finally they fled the city. But it is still very ominous there; the rabble clash frequently with those who murmur that indeed the rabbi was of the Jewish God. One knows that the market rabble are everywhere, in the name of Mars! They desire nothing but upheaval and riots, for they have the souls of beasts and love excitement, no matter the cause. Faceless, tumult gives them an opportunity to posture as men and become important even if it is only to the law, which they naturally hate."

Plotius' voice expressed sullen irritation, and so Lucanus did not speak again. He understood that the anger was not directed against him, but against the universal mobs. Plotius muttered furiously, "Ah, if only we soldiers were permitted to quell rabble! Once it was permitted, and it was salutary. But now the rabble everywhere must be cherished, fed, housed and amused, for they are a terror. However, who made them so? Venal statesmen who desire their support, and a curse upon them!"

Lucanus sensed that they were now rising through luxuriant gardens, for sweet scents were pervasive everywhere, and the resinous fragrance of trees. He saw distant fountains luminous in the moonlight, like naiads dancing in loneliness against the night. He heard the monotonous tramping of soldiers, and at each gate helmets shone, and bared swords. The golden dome of Herod's house rivaled the light of the moon. The riders and the chariots turned through the last gate, and Pilate's house stood before them, gleaming like alabaster.

Once in the magnificent lighted hall, filled with statues and flowers and beautiful furniture, Plotius suggested that his guests retire to waiting chambers and rest until the hour of dining. Lucanus guessed that his friend was uneasy and somber with some secret thoughts, and desired to be rid of him for a while. He said, putting his hand on the burly arm, "Plotius, I am not tired. I should like to consult Priscus' physicians, for I am very anxious. Too, I have not seen my brother for a long time."

"Certainly, my dear Lucanus!" said Plotius heartily. "Consider this house, in Pilate's absence, as your own." He smiled at Hilell, and clapped him on the shoulder. "I have missed you," he declared. He stared at Arieh and winked. "There is nothing like a fortune to bring a lost one home! The slaves will take you to your apartments, my dear friends, and later, at dinner, we shall relax and talk of many places." He pushed his thumbs into his belt, and then took off his helmet. He was indeed bald, but the baldness increased his air of virility. He touched Lucanus on the elbow, avoiding the other's eyes. "Come," he said. "The physicians are with Priscus now, and they can tell you much which is unknown to me."

Chapter Forty-four

He did not speak as he led Lucanus through rooms each more charming than the last. Slave girls were singing somewhere to the bewitching sounds of flute and harp. Soft laughter came from behind curtains. Lamplight gleamed on columns of varicolored marble. The muraled walls shimmered with such brilliant paintings that the creatures depicted in them appeared to move in a secret but engrossing life of their own. The marble floors glittered; the whole house was freshly scented. Lucanus reflected that Herod had indeed built a splendid house for his friend, the procurator of Israel. There were glimpses of gold and silver everywhere, and the lamps were of Alexandrian glass. As the two silent friends passed from room to room the sharp and poignant wind from the sea blew about them. Once Lucanus caught a glimpse of the golden dome of Herod's house through smooth columns, and heard the sound of distant voices and the dull challenge of patrolling soldiers. Otherwise a heavy atmosphere of quiet lay over all things.

They reached a tall bronze door, and Plotius rapped on it smartly. It was immediately opened by an armed slave, who bowed. Plotius said, "The noble Lucanus, who is the guest of Pontius Pilate, wishes to consult with the physicians of the captain, Priscus. Bring them to him." He saluted Lucanus lightly, smiled a little, and hurried away as if pursued. Lucanus watched him go, frowning. The slave then conducted him into an antechamber and indicated a chair upholstered in cloth of gold, one of many. The slave brought Lucanus wine on a silver salver; the goblets were encrusted with gems of various colors. Lucanus drank, grateful for the wine; he discovered that it had an odor and taste of honey and roses, delicious on the tongue. The elaborate lamps flickered in the slight wind; Lucanus' feet were sinking into a rich and colorful rug from Persia. Here one could slip into languor, so gracious and so lovely were the surroundings, and so potent the wine. But Lucanus was too anxious. He peered at a door of teakwood, intricately carved, and impatiently awaited the physicians.

They came at last, and bowed to him with dignity, and, as a colleague, he rose and bowed to them also. They were men of stately middle age, and Lucanus perceived that one was a Jew and the other a Greek. They introduced themselves. The Greek said, "I am named Nicias, and this is the physician, Joshua." The Greek had a subtle and somewhat cold countenance which indicated an impersonal nature. The Jewish physician was smaller, and there was a liveliness and unquiet intelligence in his sparkling black eyes. Both were formally robed in blue togas, edged with gold, and both wore physicians' rings set with brilliant jewels. It was evident that they were men of much honor and consequence, and that they were surprised at Lucanus' humble garments.

They sat beside Lucanus, pulling their chairs close to his, in the immemorial gesture of physicians who are about to hold a conference of much importance concerning a valued patient. They drank the wine slaves brought, and stared before them reflectively. Lucanus still waited. Doctors of position were not to be hurried in a vulgar manner. They had a stateliness to maintain, and so they were portentous.

Nicias inquired of Athens, and Lucanus was forced to answer him courteously. Nicias mentioned Isocrates, who was his favorite philosopher, and Lucanus replied learnedly. The Greek was pleased. Joshua leaned forward to listen. "I understand you were educated in Alexandria, noble Lucanus," said Joshua, with a little patronage. "I believe that Alexandria has lost some repute this past one hundred years. I myself was educated in Tarsus. What is your own opinion of the rival merits of both schools?"

Lucanus, devoured by anxiety, nevertheless replied with forced calm. He understood that these men were probing him for any lack of learning and culture before they would confide in him, and before deciding whether or not he was worthy of their full confidence. It was, he thought, with impatience, like a sacred majestic dance into which a stranger had intruded, and during which it would be determined if he should be admitted to the ritual. "I assure you, my noble colleagues," he said at last with considerable exasperation, "that I am capable of understanding our physicians' jargon, and that I have had much experience and know the most modern of treatments! Therefore I beg of you to consider my natural anxiety! Tell me what ails my brother."

Both physicians looked offended for a moment, though the Jew's eyes irrepressibly began to twinkle. Lucanus, startled, thought he saw Joshua's eye wink, but he could not be sure, for Joshua's face remained grave and he retained the physician's attitude, classic through the ages: projected thoughtful head, right elbow on the arm of the chair, right index finger partly obscuring his mobile mouth. Nicias debated ponderously. Then Joshua, after a quick glance at him, apparently decided that there had been enough formality. He dropped his hand, and said at once, "To be sure, you are anxious, Lucanus. Let me put the matter briefly." Nicias gave him a chilly glance, which did not disconcert him. "Your brother has cancer of the stomach; the disease has largely invaded his liver also. You have asked us to speak. I do not believe in vague phrases, and so I have told you. You understand he cannot live in his condition. We have done all we could; he has thickly spiced food for his appetite, which is feeble, and all the wine he wishes, and anodynes for his pain, which is ferocious."

Lucanus sat transfixed, his heart sick with despair. Joshua regarded him with compassion. Nicias locked his white fingers together in his lap. He said, "He may live a month, or perhaps two months, but certainly not for long." It was as if he were politely discussing the weather with two aristocratic friends and that the matter was of no personal importance. Lucanus, struggling with his misery, unreasonably hated him. And so he concentrated on Joshua, in whom he sensed some human concern and kindness.

"How long has my brother been afflicted?" he asked in a trembling voice.

Joshua shrugged eloquently. "He was already very sick when he was brought here. I should judge he has been suffering from this disease at least eight months. That accounts for his moroseness, his listlessness, his loss of flesh, his grayness of visage, his aversion for meat, his infrequent but draining stomach hemorrhages, his unsteady gait, his swollen ankles. He is in the last stages of his affliction. We can do nothing for him but attempt to alleviate his pain, and reassure him. You will also understand that the disease has caused an instability of temper and fits of weeping, for though he does not know how mortally he is ill his body sends his brain signals of distress and premonition of death."

Nicias said in a cold and reproving voice, "That is an unproved theory of yours, Joshua, that the brain receives any messages at all. I am firmly of the conviction that the heart is the seat of emotions and premonitions. I prefer the theories of Aristotle, though in some quarters I am considered oldfashioned." The "quarters" were apparently Joshua himself, and the physicians' eyes locked for a moment in brief combat.

"Oh!" cried Lucanus, almost beside himself. "Must we have a discussion of various theories now? You say, Joshua, that my brother has cancer. Is that certain?"

"Most certain," said Joshua, not offended. His eyes were sympathetic. "Would you wish to examine him yourself?"

The three physicians rose. Nicias' pale eyebrows lifted on

seeing Lucanus' rough and cheap pouch, which rattled with vials in the manner of a rustic doctor. Nicias opened the teakwood door with an air of lofty resignation to the importunities of lesser men. The bedchamber beyond was magnificent, filled with the finest furniture and a gilded bed. Four slaves were in attendance, clothed in white tunics. But Lucanus ran to the bed, crying, "My dear Priscus! I am here at last!"

He snatched up a lamp from a marble table and held it high over the bed. Priscus lay there, and Lucanus was stunned to the heart by his aspect, and almost unable to recognize in this gray and emaciated man his young and beloved brother. The stony lids lay over sunken eyes; the mouth had sunk contracted onto the teeth. For a terrible moment Lucanus thought his brother already dead, for he appeared not to be breathing.

"He sleeps under the influence of our drugs," said Joshua, full of pity. He put his hand on Lucanus' shoulder. "He is, at least, in temporary peace, and for that we must thank the merciful God. He suffers much."

Tears flooded into Lucanus' eyes as he contemplated his brother by the high-held lamp. Here lay one dearer to him than his blood brother and sister, for he had given Priscus life when he was in death. Here was the brother of the beloved Rubria, and dying as she had died. Here was the heart's darling of Iris. Here was the son of Diodorus, that valorous and virtuous warrior, whose name was never forgotten. Here lay the house of Diodorus, the son more fitting and valuable to the name of the dead soldier than the scholarly and fastidious Gaius, who shuddered at the sight of swords and banners. Here was one once merry and brown as a nut, innocently gay yet reflective, one who rejoiced in living and who loved his country and his gods. He remembered Priscus' temperament, affectionate and considerate, kind yet strong, joyously active and eager, loving and thoughtful and full of laughter. Lucanus could not endure it. He put down the lamp slowly and pressed his fingers against his eyes to shut out this most dolorous sight.

"Yes, it is sad," said Joshua, sighing. Nicias approached the bed, moving like one of the statelier gods, and gazed down at Priscus as one would gaze at a theorem.

Priscus stirred. Lucanus, his eyes still covered, heard the faintest voice, thrilling with weak delight. "Lucanus! It is you! I have waited——"

Lucanus dropped to his knees and reached for the gaunt and diminished hand. It was cold and dry to his touch, and the pulse was erratic. He saw Priscus' eyes, filmed with pain and exhaustion, though they had brightened with joy at the sight of him.

"Dear Priscus," Lucanus stammered, struggling to control the agony in him. "Yes, I have come. Are you in pain?"

The shriveled fingers tightened on Lucanus' hand like the fingers of a mummy. Priscus wet his parched lips, then gazed at Lucanus resolutely. "Pain," he said, murmurously, with an effort, "is what all men endure. That you once told me, Lucanus. A soldier understands pain; he is inured to it. But there is a pain of the spirit—— Have you heard recently from home?" He said the word "home" in a tone of desperate longing.

"All is well," said Lucanus, and swallowed the salty bulk in his throat. Priscus would never see his home again; he would never dandle his children on his knees; he would never kiss his wife and lie with her, fondling her long dark curls and brushing his mouth against her dimpled cheeks and breasts. He would never see his orchards and his fields, his cattle and his horses. He would never again swim in the green crystal of his stream, or drink of the wine of his grapes. The loving and simple things of joy and pleasure, which men take so for granted, would never be his again. For he was dying, and Lucanus had understood this at once. The heart of the physician squeezed. Then instantly he smiled, for Priscus was watching him anxiously.

"It is well?" said the young soldier.

"It is well," said Lucanus. Priscus sighed, and closed his eyes for an instant in content.

Lucanus began to examine him, gently, and his last hope for a faulty diagnosis died. There was a huge palpable mass in the right area of the stomach, which could easily be felt through the thin layer of expiring flesh. Lucanus' fingers moved to the liver, and there were masses there also. The peripheral lymphatic glands were grossly swollen, especially the supra-clavicular. The examination cost Priscus the most unendurable pain, gentle though it was, but as a soldier he kept himself rigid and quiet. His eager eyes never left Lucanus' face, not for an expression of relief, but only for the joy of seeing him. He knew, in his soul, that he had not much longer to live.

He said, feebly, "My mother. My wife, my children. You

must tell them," and he could not control a wince when Lucanus found a particularly torturous spot, "that I died in peace——of an accident, perhaps. And quickly. They must not know—— Ah," he sighed, when Lucanus removed his probing hands. "You understand, Lucanus."

"Yes," said Lucanus. "I understand." He put his palm against the feverish cheek like a father, and his breast heaved. He tried to smile. "But all is not lost," he added, in a comforting tone, and in the mechanical fashion of a doctor.

Priscus rolled his head on his cushions. "All is lost," he said quietly.

"One must have hope," said Joshua.

"I no longer desire to live," said Priscus, simply. "You speak of my body, good Joshua. Do I not have a care for my body." He put his hand into that of Lucanus, like an exhausted child. "I must talk with my brother, alone," he said. "There is much to say before I go on my long journey."

"I comprehend," said Joshua, wrung with his own grief, for he had come to love Priscus, as all who knew him did. "But you must not tire yourself."

"Unless I am relieved of my burden I shall not be able to join my father and my mother and my sister in peace," said Priscus. "I have little time."

"Only the gods know that," said Nicias, coldly. He inclined his head and Joshua followed him from the room, and at the last, the slaves. Priscus watched them go, and then with forced strength he said to Lucanus, "Lift me on my cushions, dear brother, so I may speak more easily."

Lucanus lifted him, and he was appalled at the lightness of the soldier's body, the absence of flesh. But he made himself smile comfortingly. Priscus' head fell back on the raised cushions, and he panted weakly for some moments. He closed his eyes. "I must speak," he said, with something of Diodorus' imperiousness. "You must not tell me not to tire myself. I must say all that I must say, Lucanus."

"Yes," said Lucanus. Priscus' hand groped for his, and he smiled faintly. "It is a terrible story," he said, after a moment or two, and his face changed and became ghastly, as though he had just died in torment. And then he began his tale.

The lamps flickered or quickened in the sea breeze which came through the columns outside. The odors of the

East rode on the wind, and the sounds of the tinkling fountains. And Priscus spoke steadily, with an urging of last strength, and Lucanus did not interrupt him once.

Plotius had been stationed in Jerusalem for a considerable time. He had found the city fascinating and full of excitement. The Jews were a strange people, but never were they dull or flaccid. They looked at the Romans coldly, and avoided them, except for the rich merchants and politicians and the owners of cargo vessels. The lesser and humbler people despised them, except for the high priests whose families were engaged in trade and had their fortunes to make. "The people are at once realistic and as materialistic as are we Romans," said Priscus, "and yet are full of piety and mysticism. Even the grossest and most exigent of the tradesmen and merchants and manufacturers will thrust aside worldly concerns on the holy days and become as unworldly as shades, forgetting everything. The Temple is filled with the smoke of sacrifices and the scent of incense, and there is wailing and weeping on some holy days, and rejoicing and dancing on others. The Jews weep eternally, even when they smile. And they speak of a Messias who will deliver them from Rome, and Who will set His foot on the prostrate breast of Rome and never permit her to rise again."

Priscus, youthful and ever full of curiosity, had heard much of the religion of the Jews, for he wished to be friends with those who spurned his friendship. But no one would discuss religion with him, not even his merchant and trader acquaintances. From that subject they would recoil, and their wine-flushed fat faces would darken and turn away. And then he began to hear rumors of a strange, country rabbi, of no learning, from the hills of Galilee, of a people despised by the Jerusalem worldlings and cultured men. He was a man of no family, no wealth. He had nothing but the poor clothing on His back and the rope sandals on His feet. Nor did He possess a horse or a litter, or even the lowliest ass. Yet when He came to Jerusalem He was surrounded by crowds; where He moved, they moved also, listening to Him. It was rumored that He healed the sick and raised the dead. The priests at first laughed, then were angered. It was all nothing to Priscus, who could never understand the Jews, their many quarreling sects, their insistence on certain rituals, their constant vehement arguments about the niceties of the meanings of ancient prophets —even the city rabble would quarrel about these things! They regarded their religion with sternness and devotion, and observed it meticulously. This was true of the meanest man or the highest and most honored. They had no cynical doubts of it, as did the Greeks, nor had they the earthy superstitions of the Romans. That doubtless explained the excitement over the rabbi who was rumored to raise the dead and heal the sick and perform many other miracles. It also explained the wrath of the patrician high priests who detested the common folk and found even their poor sacrifices unworthy. The rabbi was invading their sacred purlieus and was distracting the people from their duties. Almost as bad as this, it was rumored He was inciting the people against Rome, and that was most dangerous.

It was finally rumored, with immense excitement, that He was the Messias. He would rescue His people Israel from the power of Rome, and with throngs of angels would drive the Roman legions from the walls of Jerusalem. For the first time, then, Pontius Pilate, who never interfered with any Jewish affairs, being a discreet man, became concerned. Let the Jews fight among themselves, as they did interminably over some doctrine or other, so long as the fights did not threaten the authority of Rome. The tetrarch, Herod, half Greek, half Jew, was approached by the high priests, who declared that the Jews were in danger because of the teachings of this miserable rabbi, who not only asserted He had come to fulfill the laws of the prophets and that the priests were deceiving the people and oppressing them, but He was causing confusion and diversion inimical to the peaceful relations between the Jews and their masters, the Romans. Herod discussed the matter with Pilate, who visited Jerusalem, which he did not like, and he was annoyed that this visit was forced upon him. He called Plotius and Priscus to him and questioned them. Plotius shrugged and declared that the priests were always in a frenzy and one should not listen to them seriously. Priscus spoke to Pilate of the rumors of miracles, and Plotius laughed. Pilate was more concerned with a possible uprising of the Jews than with the rabbi as a Person.

"I am not certain what happened next," said Priscus, in his feeble but insistent voice, and staring with queer and vivid eyes at his brother. "The affairs of the Jews were nothing to me. I understand, however, that the high priests demanded the death of the wandering, footsore rabbi, and that He was brought before Pilate for a judgment. Pilate found no fault with Him, but the rabble howled for His death, not because they particularly disliked Him but because they wished excitement. It was the Jewish Passover, and I was there, and I was ordered to keep peace. At the Passover the Jews address us as Egyptians, and this is incomprehensible, and insulting. My Jewish friends withdraw from me for the period."

It was the eve of the Passover. The excitement in the city over the rabbi was growing to an unbearable pitch. Groups fought in the streets, and cursed the soldiers who separated them. And then Priscus received his orders to execute the disturbing rabbi with two thieves who had been condemned to death. It was only another disagreeable task, and Priscus followed his orders.

It was customary, under Roman law, that those criminals who had been condemned to the vilest death on the cross be scourged before execution. Priscus had ordered two of his lesser officers to officiate on that occasion; the rabbi was in prison awaiting the final punishment. He himself waited for the hour when he would lead his soldiers and the executioners to the usual place, a mount known as Golgotha, or the Place of Skulls. He sat on his horse, bored to the point of fatigue, for he had spent hours in a favorite tavern the night before, and he was restive that this mean task had been relegated to him. The criminal was only a wretched Jew, stricken with poverty and unworthy of the attention of a high officer such as himself. He did look about at the turbulent, excited throngs with a slightly curious eye. But the Jews were always excited, and quite often over the most insignificant things. He heard muffled curses thrown at him as he sat on his horse among his mounted officers, but the Jews, especially when their holy days approached, frequently cursed the Romans even when on other days they were friendly to them. It was nothing of importance. He even laughed good-naturedly, and jested with his officers, and yawned.

The crowds had gathered all along the narrow road leading from the prison to the Place of Skulls. Priscus was suddenly arrested by the expressions of many of the people. The volatile Jews were unusually, and quickly, silent. Hundreds of women were openly weeping; others held their little children high in the manner of mothers who wish their offspring to catch a glimpse of an approaching prince or high potentate. Many men were wringing their hands and weeping in silence, or beating their breasts. A strange air of doom hung over the city and the people. A mysterious hot light bathed the earth; it was as if the sun, losing his natural golden color, had become fiercely incandescent. And in this light the colors of the garments of the people took on a vivid hue; crimson and blue, striped red and white, yellow and black, rose and emerald—they glowed as if about to burst into flame. The faces became imminent; every line, mold of nose or mouth, color of eye, glimmer of forehead and chin, even most distant, had a wild clarity and vehemence. The odor of sweat pervaded the burning air. There were no priests in that crushing yet oddly quiet throng; they had done their work; they were in the Temple preparing for the Passover. Priscus glanced uneasily at the sky. There, over the bronze mounts, the sky was a most peculiar color. It was as if a cauldron boiled out of sight beyond the Place of Skulls, throwing up its gathering steam of pale red and purple. The steam smoldered and moved. Priscus called the attention of his nearest officer to it. The officer was a young man, and superstitious, and he looked at that malign and colored movement with dismay. "Who is it that we are to execute?" he asked. Priscus had replied, "Only three criminals." The young officer had fingered an amulet and had shaken his head and had muttered, "I do not like this. There are portents here." Priscus had laughed at him, but he had shifted on his horse. He sneezed; the fiery air, so flaming, was filled with hot yellow dust. He sweated under his armor.

Then there was a turbulence before the gates of the prison. A roaring cry assaulted the ears, and a deep groaning and wailing. Priscus and his officers rode nearer the gates. A man was being dragged forth by foot soldiers. He was a tall man, with golden hair and a golden beard. He appeared prostrated. He wore a torn garment of white, and over that a crimson cloak of poor cloth. On His high head a crown of thorns had been thrust and His white face streamed with blood. "What is this?" muttered the young officer to Priscus, but Priscus could not reply.

For he saw the face of the criminal, which, despite the blood and dirt, was noble beyond imagining, and calm and gentle, and appeared to radiate with a light of its own, greater even than the furious light of the sun. His was the countenance of a king, majestic and holy, and removed from any fear. A cold horror, which he could not explain, seized Priscus. This was no criminal; this was a man of the highest blood. His garments took on the majesty of purple; the crown of thorns was a crown of gold. The horror increased in Priscus. Was this the wretched rabbi, in truth? Was this the countryman of no family and no wealth? It was incredible. He had the aspect of an emperor, though the soldiers pushed Him and beat Him, and laughed at Him in the way of all coarse subordinates, and spat in His face.

"Hail, King of the Jews!" shouted the soldiers, and the market rabble howled. But hundreds of sobbing women fell on their knees and stretched forth their arms, and hundreds of men wailed and their faces ran with tears, and hundreds of little children cried. The scene was too chaotic for a single pair of eyes, and the eyes of Priscus became frantic with trying to encompass all things. But finally he could see no one but the condemned, who was staggering under the blows of the soldiers.

Priscus wheeled his horse, and his hands trembled on the reins. He motioned to his officers and they began to canter towards the gates of the city, which were creaking open. Priscus said to himself, Who is this who is about to die? He looked back over his shoulder. A cross had been thrust upon the shoulders of the weakened rabbi, and He was weaving desperately under it, trying to keep to His feet under the weight and the blows of the soldiers. The horror deepened in Priscus. He reached within his armor and clutched his own amulet, a talisman against evil. But the metal burned his fingers, and it was wet with his sweat.

About and around him he heard the most deafening howls and screams and cries and wailings. The light was insufferable; it was as if a dozen suns had joined their incandescent brother. The glare stung the eyelids and inflamed the forehead. The stench of humanity and the acrid taste of rising dust nauseated the young Roman. His head ached fiercely; it was as if his bones within him trembled and quivered. All colors blazed too savagely for him; he half closed his eyelids to escape that fury of hue and fiery light. The near and distant buildings danced wildly before him; heat waves shimmered over all things, giving them the aspect of madness and instability. And beyond Golgotha the red and purple clouds streamed up into the sky like flickering tongues, spreading themselves over the white-hot heavens, leaping from behind the copper of the mount.

A greater cry assaulted the awful air, and again Priscus glanced over his shoulders. The criminal had fallen in the dust; a young woman, her face covered with tears, was wiping his face. A soldier had shouted peremptorily to a bystander, and the man, dark of skin, and huge, came at once and lifted the cross from the shoulders of the condemned. With the assistance of the soldiers he placed the cross over his own shoulders, and he stood up from the crouching position and a deep smile played on his features. He looked at the sky and tears and sweat burst out on his sun-browned flesh. He moved on docilely, like one in an ecstatic dream, and with strength, not faltering. It was as if he bore on his shoulders the litter of a king, proudly. And behind him stumbled the criminal, His lips moving. The populace followed like a varicolored river, shouting or groaning, shaking their fists in the air or weeping. And over it all poured that unearthly and shattering light.

Then Priscus heard a voice, speaking in slurred Aramaic, but pure and sure and strong, like the voice of a ruler: "Daughters of Jerusalem! Weep not for me but for your children. For behold! days are coming in which men will say, 'Blessed are the barren, and the wombs that never bore, and breasts that never nursed!' Then they will begin to say to the mountains, 'Fall on us!' And to the hills, 'Cover us!' "

Priscus was stunned by that voice and the strange words it had uttered. It was as if a thousand oracles had spoken, it was as if Apollo, moved by the agony of men, had wept for them. It was as if Zeus had hurled thunderbolts into the sky. And the people, so clamorous, so beset, so weeping, and so torn with grief, fell silent for a moment.

"Who is He?" cried the young soldier to Priscus, and Priscus could not answer.

The hot and furious climbing road lay before them, rising to Golgotha. And Priscus said to himself in terrible and nameless despair, I must not look behind me again! But he could not shut from his awareness the tremendous lamentation that mingled with the disastrous light, a lamentation that followed the condemned man like the tide of sorrow and despair. And over and above this tide shrilled the shrieks of the market rabble, lusting, as always, in its instinct of hatred and menace and eagerness for a victim.

The yellow battlemented walls of the city fell behind and the narrow way rose sharply to the Mount of Golgotha, whose copper rise appeared to fume with an infernal fire of its own. Stones shifted under the hoofs of Priscus' horse, and dropped back, rumbling. He could hear the clatter of the horses of his followers, and their frightened, muffled curses. Dazed, he looked about the heat-stricken country-side, the terraced hills with their burdens of cypresses and olive trees, its patches of green gardens. But all bore the sinister glare of a nightmare, shifting and without substance. Sweat poured down the face of Priscus, and he removed his helmet to wipe his head and face; his breath came heavily and with enormous effort. I must not think! he cried to himself. I am sick; I see with the eyes of sickness. This is nothing significant; this is only the execution of one who is a criminal before Rome, an inciter of mobs against our authority.

But the terror and the horror grew in him like an explosion, pressing against his heart and his mind and the organs of his flesh. He was appalled at the sky above the mount; the colored flames rose higher, devouring. He could actually feel their palpitation. His superstitious Roman spirit cowered. The lamentations filled the baleful air.

Priscus said to his nearest officer, "Hold back the mob! Let them not cover the top of the mount; they must remain below! Who knows what they will do to us? For we are few, and they are thousands, large with excitement and emotion."

The officers wheeled on their struggling horses and rode down against the mobs, but Priscus would not look back. Panting, he dropped his head on his breast and waited. After a little it seemed to him that the cries and the wailings dimmed slightly, as his officers and their foot soldiers turned back the people to prevent them from ascending to the final height. Then Priscus saw that two crosses were now being lifted against the ominous and streaming sky, leaving a place between them. He could see the naked men clearly, though he was still at a distance, and below. They had dark, contorted faces; their arms stretched in agony on the crosses; one screamed.

Now his officers were about him again, and the youngest one said, "We have kept them back; they will not intrude, for our men have their swords drawn."

Now Priscus was impelled to glance behind him. The people covered the lower stretches of the mount like a turbulent forest of many colors; they moved constantly, shaking and quivering in all their parts. And before them came the little procession of the cross-bearer, a few soldiers and the condemned man. The rabbi climbed with feeble motions, his head bent. Yet all his aspect was royal; he was a captive king awaiting execution. Priscus stared at him with terrible intensity, and at that moment Jesus lifted His countenance and the blue of His eyes glowed in His face. His red robe trailed from His shoulders, and it was a regal garment.

In spite of precautions there was a group waiting on the mount's summit, a few silent women, a young man or two in poor garments, and, to Priscus' nameless anger, a few Pharisees and scribes whom he recognized. Drawing all his strength, Priscus rode up the last difficult stretch, and he said to the Pharisees in a husky voice, "What are you doing here, at a Roman execution of lowly criminals?"

One of them bowed haughtily and replied, "We are here as witnesses, for there is a stupid rumor that this turbulent wretch, Jesus, will not die, but will live and descend from the cross and lead the people into anarchy and uprising against the peace. We will tell the people, later, what we have witnessed, and that will be the end of it."

Priscus did not know why he said in a loud voice, "No, it will not be the end of it! Never will it be the end!" And he struck his fist against his sword and sweat rolled down his face.

The Pharisees frowned, and consulted with one another, and shrugged, and the scribes sneered. But Priscus, his breath loud in the fearful silence at the top of the mount, turned his attention to the women. However, he really saw only one, a silent women of an age not to be determined, for her pale smooth face could have been the face of a girl or a mature woman, serene but rigid with sorrow. He thought to himself, Is she His sister, His wife, His mother? No, it is not possible that she is His Mother, for she has a look of eternal youth upon her, and she is very beautiful, more beautiful even than my adopted mother, Iris, or my sister, Aurelia. The woman gazed at him as if hearing his thoughts, turning the deep blueness of her eyes upon him; a lock or two of her hair, golden as sunlight, had escaped her dark blue headcloth and blew upon her white forehead in a gust of searing wind. Her mouth was sweet and without color, and full of tenderness. But it was her stillness that impressed Priscus, the stillness of her youthful body, the stillness of her remarkable beauty. She was clothed in coarse white linen, and her shoulders flowed with a blue robe of the same material. Priscus wished to speak with her, for she had so noble an attitude and such an atmosphere of quiet grief. He did not know why he dismounted and went to her. She watched him coming, and the mournfulness of her face was turned upon him.

He tried to make his voice rough. "Who are you, and who are these with you?"

She said gently, "I am Mary, His Mother, and these are our friends."

He wanted to order her below. He hesitated. She continued to regard him tranquilly, and her eyes pierced him. Her hands were clasped loosely together; two women stood beside her, like handmaidens of a queen. They wept, but she was not weeping. A profound dignity encompassed her. "You are His Mother," said Priscus, lamely, and he thought of Iris, and the mother he had never known, and he was full of grief for all the mothers of the world.

Mary inclined her head; her blue eyes continued to implore him. He gestured uncertainly. "It will not be a pleasant sight for a woman," he said.

"But I have known of this for a long time," she replied. He stared at her, blinking. And then she smiled a little, and he thought again, incoherently, of the compassionate smile of Iris. How was it possible that this poor woman could feel pity for him, the Roman executioner of her Son? He wanted to speak more with her, but her eyes had left him for her Son, now reaching the summit, and a quiver, as of reflecting water, ran over her face, and she took a single step, her hands outstretched in the eternal attitude of a mother. The women put their arms about her and held her back. The colors of the streaming sky, its rose and purple, flowed upon their faces.

Priscus' officers looked down in wonder at their dismounted officer, who had deigned to approach and to speak to a poor Jewish woman. They saw his miserable expression, his uncertainty, his despair-filled eyes, and wondered more, uneasily. The young officer muttered under his breath, his incantation against frightful events. The Pharisees and scribes stood apart, the Pharisees cold of aspect and unspeaking, the scribes sneering and snickering among themselves.

Then Priscus, looking at the silent prisoner standing near him, and seeing the drops of blood that ran down His speechless face from the thorns of the crown, and His absolute suffering, cried out, "Let us be done with the matter, in the name of the gods!" He turned aside with a disordered gesture and hesitated. "Where is wine and a goblet?" he said to one of his officers, who stared at him blankly for a moment, then reached into his saddle bag and brought forth a vessel of soldiers' wine and a crude goblet. He dismounted to put them into Priscus' trembling hands. "Opium also," muttered Priscus, wishing to give the condemned man some numbness against his pain. Without speaking the officer sprinkled a little opium from a woolen packet onto the surface of the poured wine.

The dreadful and stupendous light increased, like a threatening glare from Olympus. Priscus approached the condemned man, and all on the mount fell silent, and the women ceased their weeping. Now Priscus stood before Jesus and looked fully into His face; his voice could not rise in his throat. The godlike eyes regarded him straightly, as if probing his very soul, and Priscus thought in awful bewilderment, Who is He?

"Drink," he stammered. "It will help You——"

But Jesus shook His head slightly; however, He inclined that head gratefully. And now the look He bent on Priscus was tender beyond all tendernesses he could imagine, and most grand, and most incredibly kind and gentle. Priscus fell back before that look, in greater terror and awe than before, until he stumbled against his horse. "Let it be consummated!" he cried out. "Let us be done with it!" And pressed his face against his horse's neck, which was trembling.

Priscus clung to his horse, his eyes closed. From far below, like the sound of a dolorous sea, came the surge of wailings and lamentations. But above them—and Priscus could not bring himself to look—came the sound of hammering. Why was it so silent here? Why did not the condemned man cry out as the nails were driven into His flesh?

And then He spoke, in a loud voice: "Father, forgive them, for they know not what they are doing!"

Priscus felt a horrible chill rippling over his flesh, and his horse started under his clutch. Is He imploring His God? Priscus asked himself, in the roaring confusion of his mind. Why should the gods forgive, and whom should they forgive? Me? The people? The executioners? What madness is this? Why should any man forgive his enemies, or implore the gods to do so, when he is suffering agonies and death is upon him?

The young soldier wished that darkness would descend upon him, and that he would faint and see nothing further. But the awful light pierced through his eyelids, and he lifted his head away from the horse's neck and was compelled to see. The executioners had finished their work; the condemned man had been stripped naked, except for a loincloth. The men were beginning to raise the cross between the two thieves, against the frightful sky. The cross was larger than the others, and in contrast with the dark rough wood the body of the hanging man was white and smooth as alabaster, and appeared to shine. He seemed unaware of His anguish; His calm eyes surveyed the woman, His Mother, and He smiled lovingly, as if to console and reassure her. Then they left her and looked down at the restless throngs on the lower reaches of the mount, and then they swept over the city far below, its twisted yellowish walls bathed in that eerie light, its roofs and domes illuminated. He heaved a great and gusty sigh, and momentarily closed His eyes.

It was so fearfully silent here. Mary had seated herself upon a great rock, her face in her hands, her women kneeling beside her, comforting her. His friends, as poor as himself, clung together, their gaze never leaving the doomed man. They were young; they were obviously very poor; their small beards moved on their chins in the slightest of winds, and their faces streamed with tears.

The young officer, the centurion, touched Priscus' shoulder apologetically. "The soldiers are awaiting your signal, noble Priscus," he murmured. "As you know, the law permits them to divide the goods of those condemned to death." Priscus looked at him distractedly, for everything was swimming before him. He made an abrupt gesture. The impatient soldiers divided the garments of Jesus, and complained among themselves that they were of such poor stuff, and that there was no money pouch or anything else of value. Discontentedly, and after yawning, they removed a little way and knelt and began to dice. It would be some time before they could leave; those crucified died so slowly; it was tedious. The women sat like statues. Then Priscus saw that over the head of the dying man a script had been nailed, and on it was written in Greek and Roman and Hebrew letters:

"This is the King of the Jews!"

A crash of stunning anger thrust itself against Priscus' heart at this mockery. Clenching his fists, he forced himself to approach the cross and he looked up at the hanging man. His lips shook. He tried to speak. The mysterious eyes gazed down at him with a blue smile that contained both agony and compassion. Priscus put his hand against the lower part of the cross and he was filled with a desire to break down and weep. He turned aside and saw that his hand was blood-stained, and he stared at the shining scarlet, stupefied. Like the loud clicking of dead bones, he could hear the dicing of the soldiers and the excitement of their betting.

A group of the scribes and Pharisees approached the cross also. One of the Pharisees looked up at the dying man, and said sternly, "He saved others! Let Him save Himself if He is the Christ, the Chosen One of God!"

The attention of the betting soldiers was attracted by his voice, and they burst out laughing. One of them, a very young man, came to the cross, a goblet of wine in his hand. His grin was uncertain, not unkind, but rather stupid. He held up the cup to Jesus and said, almost in a friendly manner, "If You are indeed the King of the Jews, save Yourself!"

But the dying man did not speak. A pale glaze had come over His eyes; He appeared to have sunk into some bottomless contemplation.

One of the thieves groaned terribly. He turned his shaggy and tortured head to Jesus, and his clumsy features were distorted. He tried to spit on that heroic face, but his saliva fell into the dust and lay there glimmering.

He cried out, "If You are the Christ, save Yourself and us!" And he fell into a groan of derisive cursing.

Priscus moved convulsively; he wished to raise his sword and batter the lips of the thief. But before he could draw his sword the other thief said in a waning and rebuking voice, "Do not even you fear God, seeing that you are under the same sentence? And we indeed justly, for we are receiving what our deeds deserved. But this man has done nothing wrong!"

Priscus was transfixed; his hand fell from his sword. The second thief turned his head to Jesus, and his coarse features trembled and tears seeped from his tormented eyes. His breast heaved, and his arms writhed on the cross. He sobbed aloud.

Then he said, humbly, "Lord, remember me when You

come into Your kingdom." And he strained towards Jesus as if his miserable soul were impelled by a tremendous force, and as if all his spirit were drawn to his companion.

Jesus did not seem to have heard for some moments. Then He raised His head from the piercing contemplation of the city below, and the weeping throngs, and spoke. His voice was still strong, still clear, and still gentle. He gazed at the second thief with unearthly compassion, and He smiled. "Amen, I say to you, this day you shall be with Me in Paradise!"

Again He looked at His Mother, and again a light ran over His ghastly countenance, on which the blood rolled like rubies. As if she had heard a command, she lifted her fallen head, and Mother and Son regarded each other as if they communed together in speech not to be heard by any man. Priscus watched them, and his heart stammered in fear and with a curious longing.

Uncounted time passed. Priscus had fallen into a dream-like state. He thought that he had always stood like this, his head against the neck of his horse, his sickness always in him. He thought that he had never known anything else in all his life but the glimmer of the light on the soldiers' helmets as they knelt and played, and their flashing hands, and the illumination dancing on their armor. Forever he had seen those boiling colored clouds, like steam, ascending the white-hot sky. And forever his sight had been fixed on those three crosses, and forever he had contemplated that white Figure against the dark wood, the tendons strained and pulsing, the feet white as snow. He was frozen into eternity, and never would he leave this place and never would he know anything else!

The young men, the friends of Jesus, had crept to the cross, and had fallen against it, as if struck by lightning, their postures abandoned in the immobility of grief, their heads leaning against the wood. And the women sat apart; Mary gazed before her, as if looking into the ages, her noble head rising from among her women.

The young centurion approached Priscus again. He was very pale. He muttered, "Priscus, I do not like this! There is something awful here."

Priscus wet his feverish lips. "Give me wine," he said. The centurion gave him wine, pouring carefully. But his eyes stared in affright at the sky. Priscus took the cup from him and drank deeply; it was poor and acrid wine, and it sickened him. He poured the rest of it on the ground, and shivered.

It was the sixth hour. The appalling light pulsed out more blindingly than before, as if gathering itself together for a huge conflagration. Priscus passed his hands over his face; they encountered streams of water. The two thieves, having been crucified earlier, were falling into the unconsciousness of death. But Jesus still regarded the city and the other mounts as if thinking, and as if unaware that He was dying.

Then the light was gone. It was gone as completely as if midnight had settled on the earth. The kneeling and betting soldiers jumped to their feet with a terrified cry. The centurion, with renewed terror, gripped Priscus' shoulder, seeking protection. From the throngs below came a mighty moan. At that instant the ground rose like a ship on a gigantic wave, and shuddered, and a sound like thunder struck the darkness. The earth wallowed and lurched, and from somewhere came a vast groaning, at once from the world and the sky.

"It is true, it is true!" cried Priscus, but he did not know what he meant. He gripped his horse's neck, steadying himself. A dim thought came to him that he should reassure his men, but his legs were swaying under him.

Then all the air was pervaded by a mighty voice, ringing, strong and full of exultation:

"Father, into Your hands I commend My Spirit!"

The darkness deepened; the soldiers stammered incoherently together. The Pharisees and the scribes retreated backwards down the hill, mouthing silently and grasping at each other's arms. But Priscus looked at the middle cross with desolate eyes. The Figure upon it was the only light in the dreadful dusk, and it was like white fire, and appeared to stretch and reach to the very sky far above the mount. The slipping earth, tremulous and heaving, settled, and was still.

Priscus heard his young officer, the centurion, speaking in a dim and shaking voice, "Truly, this was a just man!" And he fell to his knees, then prostrated himself, and the other soldiers, equally stunned, fell also about him, imploring their gods for help and rescue.

An immense nausea overwhelmed Priscus. He pulled himself away from his horse and with weak steps approached the middle cross and its shining Figure. Jesus was dead; His head lay on His breast. The drops of blood dripped blackly on

His flesh in that deep gloom. Priscus looked down at the silent figures of the friends of Jesus; his head ached with a bursting pain. Then again he leaned his hand on the cross, and now he wept.

Lucanus bent closer to his brother, holding his pulsing cold hand. He had not been conscious of time. The lamplight glowed steadily on Priscus' wan face, on which streams of sweat were flowing. A long time had passed. Priscus closed his dim eyes, and there was a silence. Lucanus looked about him like a man dreaming. Neither he nor Priscus had been aware that servants had stolen into the bedchamber to announce dinner. They did not know that finally Plotius had come, in alarm, then seeing the two with their heads together, and then hearing that Priscus was speaking and would not be halted, he had gone away, frowning and pulling at his lips.

Lucanus raised his head. He was full of awe and sorrow, and yet also he was filled with joy and surety. He touched his hand to Priscus' forehead, and Priscus opened his eyes. "There is nothing else," he said, in a dying voice. "There were rumors that on the third day He rose from the dead, but the rumors were suppressed, and His followers proscribed, and they fled from the city in fear. And it was at that time that I became very sick, and wandering, and the pain began in my stomach, and I knew that He had condemned me to death for my part in His execution."

But Lucanus smiled joyfully, and placed his palm against his brother's gray and shriveled cheek. "No!" he exclaimed. "How could God condemn you? It was prophesied from the ages that He would die in that manner, for the salvation of all men, and not only for the Jews. I have known it always. Did He hate you? No, He loved you! You have spoken of His compassionate glance at you, and His understanding. He wishes you to come closer to Him, and rest in His heart, and be one with Him. Listen! I tell you He loves you, and is with you always!"

Priscus' sunken eyes brightened. He leaned his cheek against Lucanus' hand; tears slipped along his eyelids. "Is it true?" he urged. "Is it true?"

"Yes, it is true. And He is risen! Oh, truly He is risen!"

"And He was surely God?"

"He is surely God."

Lucanus bent forward and kissed his brother's forehead. Their eyes were close together, the dark and the blue. Lucanus smiled lovingly, and with strength. Priscus murmured, nestled his withered body closer to his brother, and suddenly slept in utter exhaustion. He appeared not to breathe. An expression of peace and contentment settled over his dying features. He was like one who has come home after a terrible journey which had been filled with threatening monsters. He was like one who had been exiled to the fiery desert, and then been summoned to return.

Lucanus rose and looked down at the sleeping and stricken man. He clasped his hands together and murmured:

"Oh, You who have brought me from the waste spaces, and the darkness, and the barrenness, out of Your love and Your eternal mercy! Oh, You who are compassionate beyond imagining, You who have haunted my life to bring me to You! Oh, You who know the sufferings of men, because You have suffered them! Oh, hallowed are You in my soul, and I implore that You will accept my life that I may serve You! Always have I loved You, even when I contended with You out of my lack of understanding! Be merciful to me, a sinner, a man without importance! Hear my voice that calls to You.

"Be pitiful to my poor brother, who was granted the merit of seeing You in our flesh. He loves You, and knows You. Bring him peace; bring him surcease of pain. If he must die, then grant him a quiet death, without more anguish. Are You not compassionate for Your children? Do they appeal to You in vain? No, never do they appeal to You without Your help and Your consolation! Here is my brother, who loves You. Be You merciful to him, and lead him to You!"

Priscus slept like a weary child. The sweat dried on his face. Lucanus bent and kissed him, his voice murmurous and loving. Then he turned down the lamps and left the room.

He entered the dining hall, where sat Nicias and Joshua, Arieh and Hilell and Plotius. He did not know it, but his countenance shone like the moon, and they started and stared at him. He looked at Arieh and Hilell and cried, "I have heard my brother all this time! And I tell you that he knew God, and saw Him crucified, and he is blessed! And surely, as it was said, God has risen! Surely He has risen, blessed is His Name!"

The others sat like statues, and paling. Then Joshua rose to his feet and held out his hand to Lucanus, and said, "I knew it. From the beginning, I knew it!" Arieh and Hilell rose then and stretched out their hands to Lucanus and smiled, and he saw their tears. But Plotius, disturbed, frowned and pulled at his lips.

Chapter Forty-five

Long after all others were asleep, except the overseers of the hall and guards, Lucanus wrote his Gospel on the Crucifixion. His chamber doors were opened to the sea-voiced wind and the aromatic scents from the gardens. Sometimes, half dreaming, his stylus in his hand, he lifted his golden head to listen to the wild sweet trilling of night birds and to the ceaseless splashing of fountains. All about him burned lamps of gold and silver and glass, and often, not seeing them, he would stare at the murals on the walls.

How much, he thought, had Priscus told him, and how much had he seen spiritually through Priscus' dying eyes? Priscus was not a young man of much descriptive power, yet he had imparted to Lucanus through those hours the grandeur and terror of Golgotha, so that Lucanus might have been an eyewitness himself. It was as if he himself had touched the cross, had seen the Man on it, had received His effulgent and merciful smile, had looked at Mary and had been torn by grief for her, had listened to the howlings and lamentations of the people. What was that cry God had given on the cross, in Hebrew, which Priscus remembered but could not translate? Lucanus paused thoughtfully. As a Greek he was precise; he would put nothing into his Gospel except what Priscus had seen and remembered, and what, through his eyes, mysteriously, he himself had discerned. While Lucanus wrote, his eyes frequently filled with tears and his heart swelled with adoration. Sometimes he could not bear his emotion; he would rise and walk restlessly up and down his chamber. There was no weariness in him. Occasionally he would drink a little of the sweet Judean wine, or eat a date or a piece of bread. Nor was there sorrow for Priscus in him now. The young soldier was safe; he had seen God with his own eyes. The sorrow which Lucanus felt was for Iris, his mother, and those others who loved Priscus and who would mourn him. But I cannot mourn him, thought Lucanus. He has been blessed.

The night birds fell silent, and then suddenly the cool dawn

air rang to the cries of other birds, and the fountains sounded
nearer. The Gospel of the Crucifixion was finished. There
would be other parts to add, after talking with Mary and the
Apostles. A shaft of rosy sunlight, thin and tenuous, struck
through a white column, and Lucanus rose and stepped out
onto the colonnade beyond his door.

He had never seen a more beautiful or peaceful view, high
on this hill. The sea, to the west, was the color of ripe grapes,
flowing in towards the east where the light climbed. The harbor bobbed with tall galleons, their topmost white masts just
touched with a fugitive pink. The western sky arched in purple, and in its lower reaches the stars continued to burn
faintly as they sloped behind the swell of the earth. Like weary
Artemis, the pale moon followed them, sinking down to rest.
Caesarea was hardly awake; the city lay between the sea and
the hill on which Pilate's palace stood, crowding masses of flat
white roofs glimmering like snow. All about this particular
mount rose similar mounts, silvery with olive trees, murmurous with the voices of palms and cypresses, though some
were as bare as brass. But the gardens falling gently away
from the twin palaces of Pilate and Herod were freshly green,
filled with winding paths of crushed red or white stones, delightful with fresh arbors and beds of flowers, fragrant with
resinous trees. The pure air flowed over it all, clarified and
iridescent as the earth brightened, and the white statues scattered through the gardens began to shine faintly.

Lucanus sighed with pleasure and fulfillment. A clean wind
rose from the sea, and the crests of the water sparkled with
delicate rose. Lucanus looked at the eastern sky, wide and
pure, quivering with light scarlet, and above this lake of trembling fire the heavens had taken on themselves a tint of jade,
fathomless and intense. He left the colonnade and went to
the back of the palace, walking softly on the graveled path.
And then he frowned. No windows looked upon this other
side of the hill, and in consequence it was bare and yellow,
filled with sulphurous boulders; even the light that was beginning to emerge here had a citron hue, like the desert, and
the air that rose from it was sluggish and hot. He had instantly
emerged from beauty into ugliness. He was conscious, for the
first time, of being weary, and his eyes smarted. He walked
down the hill a distance, feeling the crumbling of the yellow
dry earth under his sandals, hearing the falling away of small
stones under his tread. It was desolate here, and the desolation
had been created by man.

He sat down on a boulder, sighing and rubbing his eyes. He gazed at the ripple of the surrounding mounts, which were quickening moment by moment. In a few minutes the sun would spring upon the most eastern mount like a warrior in golden armor.

Lucanus heard a pattering and shifting on the stones, and looking down, he saw a yellow dog, the color of the earth itself. The dog, seeing his gaze, halted and gazed up at him. It was a medium-sized animal, and each hair of its prettily curling coat sparkled in the sharp and barren air. It had a curious and sinuous look about it, wild and, shy, and very wary, and its flat head was thrust forward, sniffing, and its eyes glowed like savage rubies. Lucanus felt its suspicion, and he smiled. This was no dog of high breeding, daintily pampered and petted and fed delicacies from patrician tables. It had apparently been abused, for it regarded Lucanus with fierceness, and he could see the quick movement of its ribs as it panted a little.

He loved animals dearly. He whistled softly, held out his hand and snapped his fingers. The dog leaped back a few paces, never taking those savage eyes from him. Then all at once it was very still, its head still thrust forward, its eyes peering at him as if in astonishment. Behind it was a shrubby growth of dusty bushes, dry with yellow powder. Lucanus smiled again to see a litter of four half-grown cubs emerge, whimpering, and they crowded about the larger dog, who was apparently their mother. "Come," murmured Lucanus, holding out his hand and snapping his fingers reassuringly. The dog lifted her ears, and from her throat came a hopeful questioning. Then her mouth opened, showing her teeth in an almost human smile of joy and affection, and she bounded up the slope towards Lucanus and flung herself, evil-smelling and pungent and dusty, onto his breast. Her sharp paws planted themselves on his shoulder; she nuzzled his neck, his face, then lapped his cheeks in frenzied kisses.

He was not revolted by her odor of carrion. He held her in his arms and murmured to her like a father. Poor creature! He remembered that God had blessed the animals of the earth long before He had created man. The wild heart beat against that of Lucanus as if in feverish longing and love. The cubs warily climbed the slope and watched their mother with amazement and examined Lucanus, sniffing about his ankles. Then, sighing, they settled on his feet and laid their small heads against his flesh. He continued to stroke the mother

and to speak to her, and she clung to him as if wishing to
merge herself with him. From her throat came an inexpres-
sibly desolate muttering and imploring.

How comforting were animals! They were never evil; they
lived without hypocrisy according to their natures. They
hunted, not for sport, but for food. They had a wild innocence, and a lovely playfulness, and their loyalties were sure
and without malice. The Greeks declared they had no souls.
But, surely, that was not true. They had the souls of infants,
simple and artless, and even their passions were infantile,
and not corrupt, as were the passions of men. Did they know
God? Who could answer that with surety? Incapable of virtue, they were therefore without true guilt. Even the audacious tiger, the terrible lion, the trumpeting elephant, the varicolored serpents were incapable of real wickedness, as man
was capable. Therefore must not God love them?

The dog suddenly stiffened in Lucanus' arms. She lifted her
head rigidly, then snarled, and she tore herself from him and
leaped upon the ground with a howl that was, all at once,
familiar to him. He had heard it in Syria, in the outskirts
of Alexandria, on the silvery hills of Greece, and he was
astounded. The dog howled to her cubs and they sprang
from Lucanus' feet, surrounded their mother, and fled with
her into the bushes and disappeared instantaneously. They
were jackals, the most hated and most loathed of animals,
the carriers of rabies, the eaters of carrion, the despised of
man and beast! Lucanus had never seen them before, for they
were creatures of the night, the despoilers. He looked at his
hands, which had actually fondled jackals, and at his feet,
on which jackals had lain, and he was filled with a bemused
wonder, for he knew that they both hated and feared man,
and avoided him like death itself.

He looked behind him, and far up on the slope, yellow
and hot and dusty, he saw a group of petrified soldiers, among
them Plotius and Joshua, the physician, and a man he had
never seen before but whom he knew for a Roman. The man
was clothed in a white toga, and had a severe pale face with
an eagle nose, and his head was bald and just fringed, about
the ears, with a rim of black and scanty hair. His bare arms
were circled with gold and rings glittered on his fingers in
the first sunlight. And all of the men were absolutely silent,
and wore aghast expressions. Lucanus rose; he felt slightly
foolish to be found here on this awful slope. He began to
climb. Then Plotius stepped forth with a strange look.

"Those were jackals, Lucanus," he said, in an odd tone, looking deeply into the eyes of the other man.

"Yes, I know," said Lucanus, smiling. "I must wash my hands at once. They carry rabies." Plotius' strange expression intensified. "They sat about you," he said, "and the mother embraced you. Never have I heard of such a thing before." And he shuddered, and still regarded Lucanus with that wondering look.

"I did not know immediately that they were jackals," said Lucanus, as if impelled to apologize. Plotius put his arm about his shoulder and squeezed him. And then Lucanus saw that there were tears in the soldier's eyes. Lucanus started.

"Priscus!" he cried. "Priscus!"

Plotius smiled a most peculiar smile. "No, he is not dead. He—is much better." He seemed abstracted as they climbed together. Then Joshua, detaching himself from the group, came down to meet them. His roguish eyes were misty, and he held down his hand for Lucanus to take it, and helped to draw him up the hill, in silence. The stranger waited, and he looked at Lucanus curiously.

Joshua said a mysterious thing. "I do not wonder at the jackals. I do not wonder that they did not flee from him, but embraced him."

"Nor do I," said Plotius.

Lucanus laughed. "Poor creatures," he said. He wished to go at once to his brother and see if he needed attention. But now he was face to face with the stranger. Plotius addressed him. "Noble Pontius Pilate, this is our dear and beloved physician, Lucanus, son of Diodorus Cyrinus."

Then Pontius Pilate, the haughty procurator of Israel, did an unprecedented thing. He put out his arms and rested them on the shoulders of Lucanus, and he kissed his cheek. The others watched, amazed, for this cold and imperious man, accustomed to adulation, never spoke except impersonally, and with briefness, to anyone, as though no man were worthy of his consideration.

And Lucanus thought, Here is the man who tried to save Jesus, but the market rabble, murderous as always, would not let him. Had he been moved also, as had Priscus? Pilate was smiling at him, the pallid furrows of his face deepening.

"I have heard much of you from Caesar," he said. "Once Caesar said to me, 'I have found one just man, uncorrupted, and good, and without guile or greed, and his name is Lucanus, and he is a physician. I remember him in my darkest moments.' "

Lucanus flushed with embarrassment. "Caesar does me much honor," he said. "But it is not true. I have been the blindest of all men, and the most bitter and the most unreconciled, and without merit."

Pilate took his hand and examined the ring of Tiberius. "You have had this a long time, but never have you sent it to Caesar, and never have you asked anything of him. That alone is a marvel." He examined, then, the ring of Diodorus. "You wear this ring worthily, Lucanus." He sighed. "I have sent my wife to Rome, for she is sick of the spirit." He paused. "But I had a dream two nights ago that I must come back here. I believe in dreams. My wife had the strangest one, much earlier, and I should have listened to her, but did not."

"The dream spoke truly, noble Pilate," said Joshua. He took Lucanus' arm gently. "Come, let us go to your brother, who wishes to talk to you."

Lucanus' anxiety returned, and he forgot to wonder at Pilate's words. "He slept the night? Is he in pain?"

"He slept the night. He is not in pain," said Joshua, in an ambiguous tone. He looked long into Lucanus' eyes, as if seeking.

Lucanus began to walk swiftly, and now only the physician was with him. Joshua said, as they mounted the wide marble steps of the house, "Nicias sits beside your brother, and is speechless, and he weeps."

"Why?" cried Lucanus, with foreboding.

"You will see. I tell you, your brother is much better."

Lucanus began to run, and Joshua puffed after him, exclaiming, "We are not young men, and I am not an athlete like you, my dear Lucanus!" But Lucanus fled like the wind through the brilliant sunlit rooms and came to the apartment of Priscus. When a slave opened the door Lucanus precipitously flung it open faster, and sped into the antechamber and then into the bedroom. He rushed to the bed of Priscus, expecting a corpse, but he saw, to his complete amazement, that Priscus was sitting high on his cushions and enjoying his breakfast. Beside him, sitting in silence, was Nicias, his head bent on his breast as if meditating.

"Welcome, welcome!" said Priscus, putting down a huge goblet of goat's milk. "Dear brother Lucanus! You have helped me; I slept like a babe last night, and awoke without pain, and only hungry."

Lucanus stared at him, stupefied. Priscus' gaunt face was smooth and flushed with the slightest pink. His sunken eyes sparkled youthfully. He flung out his arms. "I could rise from my bed now, for I am well!" he said. "Look at me; do I have the aspect of a sick man? But I must remain here, these foolish doctors say, when health pulses loud and strong in my body!"

Nicias stood up and bowed deeply to Lucanus. "O Aesculapius!" murmured the physician. "You have consummated a miracle." He reached for Lucanus' slack hand and kissed it humbly. His eyes were full of tears.

"I did nothing, except pray for him," stammered Lucanus.

"It was enough," said Nicias. "Do the gods deny their brothers anything?"

"It was enough," said Joshua. "Does God deny His chosen anything?"

Priscus heaved a deep dry sob and leaned his head against Lucanus' arm. "In my dreams it was told me that when my brother came he would free me from pain."

Lucanus put his hand to his forehead and rubbed it dazedly. "I do not understand," he muttered. Then he flung the coverlets from his brother's body and felt over his stomach and liver, and his glands. The ominous tumors had disappeared. The flesh was thin and emaciated, but also firm, and the pulse was strong.

Lucanus straightened. "It is not possible!" he cried. He looked at Nicias and Joshua imploringly. "We made an error."

"No," they said, and smiled at him.

"Through you God wrought His miracle, as a witness to us," said Joshua. "As He cured men by His touch or His word, so He cured your brother at your pleading. Blessed are you, Lucanus, for you are one of His own, and we have seen with our eyes and have heard with our ears, and we magnify His Name."

Lucanus sat down abruptly and stared before him. Then he rose and again examined Priscus minutely. No tumors resisted his fingers. Priscus lifted a bunch of grapes and ate them with heartiness, but his eyes were soft on Lucanus. "I knew you could help me," he repeated. "I knew my illness, and it was mortal. But you cured me."

Lucanus sat down and averted his face, and it streamed

with tears. Oh, that You should have chosen me, I who hated
You! he cried in himself. Oh, that You condescended to me
when I reviled You! Oh, that You walked with me, when I
rejected You, through all the years of my life! Forgive me,
Father, for I knew not what I did!

He turned his face to the physicians, and said, "It was not
I who cured my brother, but only God. It was not I who had
merit, but only God. Praise Him, for He is good and
merciful, and hears His children, and does not afflict them
without a reason."

Joshua dipped his fingers into wine and traced a figure of
a fish upon the marble table. "In Greek what is that," he
asked Lucanus, "if arranged in an anagram?"

"Christos," said Lucanus.

"It is the sign of the Christians," said Joshua. "You will
find them by this sign."

Chapter Forty-six

Though Pontius Pilate, a Roman of Equestrian rank, was
invariably courteous to Hilell ben Hamram and Arieh ben
Elazar, it was evident to the supersensitive Lucanus that he
had no love for Jews. This was very apparent at his expression of relief when both the young Jews left for Jerusalem
to gather news for Lucanus as to the whereabouts of the
scattered Christians. He said to Lucanus, "I am a friend of
Herod, but he is half Greek. But the Jews: I do not understand them. When I built an aqueduct, most needed for
their use, and there was no money in the Treasury, I confiscated Temple funds. The gods, even this Jewish God, must
bow before human needs. One would think, in this confisca-
tion, that I had committed the vilest of crimes. There were
riots, which I was compelled to put down ruthlessly, and many
died. Now we Romans accept our gods with realism, also
with some irony. But smile satirically at an omnipresent God,
and the Jews are at your throat, even your friends! They will
not jest at Him, as we jest at our gods, in a civilized manner.
His Law is above all sensible human law! I have had ten
years of the Jews, and am desperately weary of their fanaticism, their devotion to their God. They talk of Him, and
quarrel about Him; they are full of sects where they preserve
their differences of opinion.

"Let us take the Jewish intellectuals," said Pilate, impatiently. "Do they discuss world philosophies, history, the arts, the sciences? Do they love gossip? No! They are learned. Yet I swear to you, my good Lucanus, that their discussions center almost entirely on what one of their particular commentators meant when he interpreted the most minute Law of their God! They are mad, totally mad. They despise our gods, calling them evil spirits; they denounce us as idol worshipers. I have no particular reverence for our gods, but I feel personally insulted, for it is an affront to Rome. If their God were so powerful would He not deliver them from our hands? I have smilingly brought this to the attention of the priests and they look at me with fiery eyes and are silent."

Lucanus listened and said nothing. Pilate sighed again; he plucked a fold of his toga restlessly. "I have asked Tiberius to recall me, and I have hope. My poor wife, Procula, is in Rome now, almost beside herself. She had a dream about the Man I ordered executed. A Jewish rabbi, or teacher, who was arousing the people against Rome. I found no fault in Him, but Herod was frantic. He and the high priests assured me solemnly that He was inciting the people, and there were many witnesses of another Jewish sect, the Pharisees, who are men of respectability. I myself believe He was only flouting the priests, whom He had offended by some looseness in His own interpretation of the Law. That Law of theirs! They are actually willing to die for their God, and give up all for Him, and that way lies madness."

"Do not disturb yourself," said Lucanus, quietly. "It was prophesied from all the ages that He would die so. You were only His instrument."

Pilate stared at him curiously. Then he shook his head. "My dear Lucanus, you must not listen to these Jews! This is only another of their multitudinous and quarrelsome sects —these men who call themselves Christians. Only two weeks ago I was compelled to order the massacre of some Galileans who, when offering sacrifices, called on their God to destroy Rome and deliver their holy land from her! We have our own law, and it must be upheld."

Lucanus looked at him with horror. "A massacre?"

Pilate shrugged. "I have told you before that the Jews are mad. And they reek with insurrection. And I fully believe that that rabbi of theirs, who I had to have executed, put a spell on my wife, so that she had that dream of hers."

"What of the Christians now?" asked Lucanus in a low voice.

Pilate moved angrily in his carved chair. "I have proscribed them all over Judea. The people look at me sullenly in Jerusalem, because of their new sect and their executed Leader, and they shake fists behind my back, and prophesy evil things for me. I have issued orders that His followers, who now call themselves Christians, they declaring Him the Christus, awaited through the ages, be hunted out, imprisoned and destroyed. They are a danger to Rome."

Lucanus stood up and went to the columns of the colonnade, and he looked through them at Caesarea, glittering in the hot sun, and beyond Caesarea to the purple sea with its blinding crests of light. The harbor was very busy. But here, with the gardens below, it was fresh and cool, and bees hummed over the flowers and the fountains danced.

"It is a relief," said Pontius, drinking a little wine, then rubbing his hands wearily over his pale, lined face, "to talk with a sensible man, and not a Jew. I have heard much of your miracle in behalf of your brother, whom I love dearly. I am sick, Lucanus, and my flesh is a heaviness on my body. My soul is in travail, though for what reason I do not know. Of what use to the gods are men? It is presumptuous to think otherwise. Nevertheless, I feel certain that Apollo has touched you, has given you his mysterious power to cure."

"You wish me to cure you?" asked Lucanus, not turning to him.

Pilate laughed sheepishly. "I tell you, I do not sleep any longer. Do not laugh at me! But I see the face of that rabbi, who appeared to me to be a gentle Man of no particular harm, except for His inciting of the people. Did He put a spell upon me also when I looked into His face?"

Lucanus came back to Pilate and sat down beside him and regarded him with pity. "I will give you a potion, noble Pilate, which will make you sleep tonight. I am glad you are returning to Rome, for something oppresses you here."

"It is so," sighed the procurator. Then he became a little more animated. "But enough of the Jews and their Messias! Let us talk of more important and learned matters. Do you know how long it has been since I have had an intelligent conversation with anyone? I have been studying the Aristotelian theory of the spiritual origin of all things. That theory amuses me, for are not our gods most unspiritual, though immortal? The Romans, who are realists, prefer the theory of the Epicureans, with their mechanistic explanations of the universe. Their theory of Democritus—the atomic theory of the origin of all matter—is most realistic, and appeals to the rational mind. Our Roman virtus is a moral and social quality. You will recall that our Emperor Augustus said, 'Who will venture to compare with these mighty aqueducts the idle pyramids, or the famous but useless works of the Greeks?' I agree with him; as a Roman I prefer our virtus to the incomprehensible aretê of the Greeks, which seeks for and demands an excellence of mind and spirit beyond the capacities of mankind."

Lucanus smiled abstractedly. "I must disagree, for I am a Greek. Man is more than an animal. The Romans are indeed materialistic Epicureans, and so they invented democracy, which carries within itself the seed of destruction."

Pilate's exhausted eyes sparkled with new interest. He roused himself. "But it is said that the Greeks invented democracy, my dear friend!"

Lucanus shook his head. "Not the Roman kind. It was the democracy of the mind—the unlimited meeting together of men of intellect, and not the mere gross meeting together of the physical bodies of the mob for their own interest and the exploitation of their intellectual betters. I do not always agree with Plato, but you will remember his warning that the city will fall when a man of brass guards the gates. The Roman world is guarded by men of brass. Long after Rome has fallen, the aretê of the Greeks will continue to illuminate men's minds. For the things of the spirit are more important to them than the things of the body."

Pilate looked at him incredulously. "You are not serious?"

"I am, most certainly. However, do not fear for Rome." Lucanus smiled wryly. "There will always be materialistic nations following her through time, and her virtus will continue to dominate them: the belief that aqueducts and sanitation departments, and public buildings and bread, science and circuses and highways, can satisfy the cravings of the human soul. The struggle was joined centuries ago, between the men of mind who reverence the human spirit and the gross men who not only declare that there is no spirit but that sewers and conduits and prosperous business and trading are the sole meaning of life."

Pontius reflected. The pale shine of uneasiness was reflected on his face. He drank some more wine. He said, "I am not an obtuse and completely materialistic man. I believe in the human mind, though it perishes with the body. I believe more in the physical welfare of the people."

His uneasiness increased. His thin features tightened as he thought. "I cannot put that Man out of my mind," he said, restively, as though he and Lucanus had not spoken of anything else. "I shall be glad of your potions, Lucanus." He peered at Lucanus sideways. "Your cure of your brother was certainly not in an accepted and orderly manner, in the clever way of physicians. Can you cure me, Lucanus, without potions?"

Lucanus leaned towards him, and there was such a sparkle of vivid light on his face that Pontius shrank superstitiously and felt for the amulet under his tunic.

"Yes!" said Lucanus, feeling a rapturous power in him. He extended the ring of Tiberius to the elegant Roman. "You must remove the proscription against the Christians, and at once!"

"You are insane!" exclaimed Pontius, staring at the magnificent ring. "I tell you, you do not know these God-maddened Jews! Nor do you know what Tiberius has become. He is a savage and terrible man now. He has given me but one command: to maintain order in Judea. I tell you, he is frightful!"

"The rabble have finally corrupted him, as he said they would," said Lucanus, sternly, still extending the ring.

"If I should lift the ban against the Jewish Christians, then there would be disorder again, and rioting, and Tiberius would deal severely with me. What are these people to you, a Greek, the adopted son of a noble Roman?"

"It would take a lifetime for me to answer," said Lucanus. "But I feel something dolorous is upon you. You have said that Jesus haunts your dreams and will not leave you in peace. Do you think you will ever have peace until you abandon your persecution of His people and His followers? I tell you, no!"

He drew the ring from his finger and pressed it into Pilate's palm. "Send this to Caesar. Write him that I have requested that your orders against the Christians be lifted. Tell him I have begged this of you, and that you, presented with his ring, had no right to refuse my request."

Pilate turned the ring in his palm reverently, but with fear. He was in a quandary. He said, "They will riot again, these Jews, and I shall be to blame." He hesitated. "However, this is your request—and it is incomprehensible to me!—and who am I to dare to disobey Caesar's wishes, implicit in this marvelous ring?"

He put the ring in his pouch, and his relief made him relax in his chair as a sick man relaxes after excellent medicine. "Frankly," he said, "I am not happy over my orders against the Christians. I dislike this quarreling about religion, which is a petty thing. The Roman gods laugh; the Jewish God never laughs."

He sat up. "I am already relieved! My depression is lifting, and my melancholy. And, in anticipation, I am enjoying Herod's discomfiture."

He talked of Herod with malicious mirth. "There was a wretched Jew who came to Jerusalem, one who was called John the Baptist, who shouted that he came as a messenger before God. He screamed that he was announcing the Jewish Messias. Herod heard of this, and his Jewish spirit brightened with excitement, though he is anything but a religious man, and is a realist. He questioned John; apparently there was some heated disagreement between them, Herod, the cultured tetrarch of Jerusalem and this wild, unlettered denizen of the desert! Why Herod condescended even to question him is beyond my understanding, except that Herod has Jewish superstitions in his mind. In any event, he prudently had John destroyed. I was in Rome at the time, and Herod to this day, refuses to discuss John, which amuses me. I did comprehend, however, that Herod was disappointed, later, in Jesus, though he questioned Him also. His disappointment reached the point of frantic rage. Do you know what I think? Herod had hoped, in his part Jewish soul, that here indeed was the Jewish Messias, come to deliver Judea out of the hands of Rome and raise His people as kings over the world!"

Pilate was now in good spirits. He felt the returning of health and ease in his body, and a quietness in his mind. He poured a goblet of wine for Lucanus, and toasted him. "It was a good day when you visited us," he said. "And now I know why I had my dream."

"I do also," said Lucanus, with an enigmatic smile.

Hilell ben Hamram wrote to Lucanus from Jerusalem:

"I have found Mary, the Mother of Jesus. She dwells without the wall of Jerusalem, and lives with a young man called

John, who is as a son to her. I have heard that one Peter, the follower of Jesus of Nazareth, is in Joppa, in hiding. Come.

"You will rejoice to know, my dear Lucanus, that Arieh ben Elazar has looked with favor on my beautiful sister, Leah. There is much festivity here, since Arieh came into his father's patrimony. Join us, and be happy with us."

Chapter Forty-seven

Lucanus remained at the house of Pilate until he was assured that his brother was completely recovered. Priscus' health returned swiftly; his emaciated body consumed food at an enormous rate. His face took on its old merry brownness. He was bright with enthusiasm. He and Plotius fenced in the outdoor portico, and the young man could not have enough athletic contests. Lucanus was full of happiness. Priscus would return to his estates and his family; Iris would rejoice. "I do not have much faith in my overseers," said Priscus, darkly. "I will remain for at least a year, if Caesar permits, before venturing on another campaign." He attempted to persuade Lucanus to return with him, but Lucanus shook his head. "I have much to do here," he replied, and would not explain, though Priscus and Plotius stared at him curiously.

When Priscus, one day, insisted that at least Lucanus return to Rome with him for a short while, Lucanus changed the subject. He and Priscus and Plotius were enjoying the bright evening air, cool and fresh on this mountain. Lucanus stood up and said, laughing, "I am weary of watching you clumsy gladiators wrestling." He threw aside his robe and stood in his tunic and flexed his muscles. Though considerable grayness flecked the gold of his hair and there were ascetic lines in his Grecian face, he was like a young man in his body. Priscus hooted at him, took the wrestler's position, while Plotius watched, smiling. Priscus approached Lucanus and stretched out his arm to seize him. Lucanus waited until the fingers clutched his shoulder, then he bent back swiftly and Priscus flew over his shoulder and landed with a hard thump on the grass. Plotius was amazed; he could not even applaud. Priscus lay on the grass, blinking and shaking his head, while Lucanus laughed.

"A thunderbolt hurled me!" cried Priscus, rising. He rushed

at Lucanus again and Lucanus, hardly moving, threw him once more. This excited Plotius, burly and broad. He demanded a contest with Lucanus, and suffered the same flight through the air. Both were now very excited.

"It is very simple," explained Lucanus, apologetically. "I cannot tell you how often this has stood me in good stead when dealing with ruffians and thieves in the cities. It was taught me by my Chinese teacher in Alexandria, on my oath I would keep it secret."

He was willing, however, to reveal his secrets of discus throwing, boxing and fencing, and the broad jump. He even defeated the dexterous Plotius at fencing. "Eheu!" exclaimed Plotius, wiping the sweat from his face with his big arm. "You are like a youth!"

"It is not a matter of strength," said Lucanus, who was enjoying himself. "It is the matter of using your strength skillfully and expending as little as possible."

Priscus and Plotius wished to take him to the circus near Caesarea, but Lucanus had no love for games and the brutality of gladiators. When Pilate announced that he must return to Jerusalem and offered to take Lucanus with him, the physician agreed eagerly. The time had arrived for his departure. He embraced the disconsolate Priscus and gave him loving messages for his family in Rome. Then, accompanying Pilate and Plotius, he took his leave of Caesarea, and Joshua, the physician, whom he had come to love not only as a colleague but as a brother.

Plotius insisted that Lucanus visit the temple of Zeus and Apollo in the city, as the caravan of horses and chariots left the mount. Herod had built the huge and magnificent temple for his friend, Pilate, and the procurator was proud of it. A long double colonnade of gigantic columns led to the temple, alternating in white marble and dark red porphyry, which gave it an exotic appearance. The high roof of the colonnade was frescoed in bas-reliefs of gamboling gods and goddesses, centaurs, nymphs, dryads and naiads, satyrs and Pans, their smooth and voluptuous limbs twining together, their faces laughing and mischievous. The brilliant air gave them a living appearance of movement. The floor was paved in varicolored marble, red and blue circles on white. But the tall temple, wide and square, was oddly austere, and here was revealed the uneasy Grecian spirit of Herod, for there were no frescoes, no bas-reliefs, on the gleaming white walls and ceilings. Two enormous statues faced each other, in a sitting position, three times the size of men, Zeus, with his beard of white marble and Apollo of red. They stared at each other with cold and unearthly faces, their hands on their knees, as if in challenge. Altars stood before them, fuming with incense. And there was a flat altar, on which burned a golden lamp, and on which was inscribed, "To the Unknown God."

Lucanus stood in meditation before the lamplit bare altar. Pilate put his finger reflectively to his lips and stared at the great and simple stone. Plotius dropped a few coins in a bronze box at the feet of Zeus. Sunlight streamed into the temple, and a vast and shining silence filled it. Each breath or movement echoed back from the walls and the ceiling; even the faint hissing of the lamp could be heard. Lucanus turned his head and looked at the mighty figure of Zeus, with his beard, his stern features, his deep eyes. The Greek recalled Moses, and smiled sadly at the thought of Herod, a man torn between two worlds and two religions. Apollo's face, though remote, had a more restless expression: the eye sockets gave an aspect of volatility to his features, as well as defiance. It was as if, in the very carving of his robes, in the lift of his tremendous head, he were about to rise and demand a contest of Zeus for control of mankind. And Zeus, in an attitude of Olympian repose, sat in godlike surety and grandeur. Lucanus was positive, in that radiant and shifting light, that a slight smile played on the bearded lips.

The entourage took the narrow road near the ancient sea, which was of such a cerulean hue that it entranced the eye. Very calm, it lay like a blue floor extending to the horizon, on which ships, their white sails floating, glided majestically. Horses quickened on the road, for it was a long ride to Jerusalem. The air was soft and pure, though yellow dust rose in clouds, for here the land was sandy. To the left of the travelers rose the mountains, low and coiling, some brazen and bare in the incandescent heat, some marked with winding stone terraces enclosing patches of cultivated land, emerald and fertile. Groves of olive trees, like old silver, thrust their crooked branches into the air; sheep browsed or slept under them, leaving their fecund dung to be used by the trees. Clumps of date palms climbed down the slopes; among their dusty fronds could be seen the warm gold of clustered fruit. Vineyards basked in the sun, on the steplike terraces, and fruit trees leaned against the yellow stones, and cypresses stood in sentinel groups, dark and watchful, their spears unshaking. On the lower slopes of the mountains, fresh and lush, cattle were grazing, and little springs rose from the earth, bubbling like quicksilver. Children guarded them idly; a flock of geese ate scattered grain, and quarreled among themselves. Here and there a low house stood in its green patches, surrounded by vines and flowers, and women spun on the doorsteps and lifted their heads to watch the clattering entourage go by. A dog or two barked. It was early morning, but the birds were silent in the hotness.

Lucanus was filled with peace in this peaceful countryside, the sea on his right, the mountains on his left. He sat in Plotius' chariot; mounted men rode before, carrying the fasces and eagles and pennants of Rome, their broadswords at their sides, their helmets glittering in the sun. Plotius began to sing lusty soldiers' songs. Pontius Pilate sat in his own bronze-carved chariot, palely silent, his head bent as if thinking. A slave stood over him with an umbrella of purple silk. Peasants, barefooted, clothed in sweaty black or dark orange or deep blue, walked along the side of the road, carrying baskets of fruit on their heads, or vegetables in baskets on their arms. They silently moved aside to let the important entourage pass, and gazed after them darkly with fierce and resentful eyes. One man was tugging at a refractory donkey, who followed the chariots with a derisive hee-hawing like a string of coarse oaths, and the peasant smiled grimly.

And always, scattered here and there, were the stony fortresses of Rome, on the roofs of which stood soldiers who saluted. Banners hung sleepily in the quiet and blazing air. A sharp scent rose from groves of pine trees, where peasants were bleeding them for their resin. Girls gossiped at occasional wells, where they filled their jugs; they looked at the chariots and the riders with dark and repudiating eyes, the folds of their headcloths filled with iridescent dust, their brown feet bare and supple. So, thought Lucanus, it is not as peaceful as I thought. The people hate the Romans, these simple people of the earth, unlike their more sophisticated brothers in the cities who do business with the enemy and laugh and drink with him. The entourage paused to buy figs and dates from a peasant, who silently dealt them out on broad green leaves, and they stopped to drink from a cold spring and stretch their bodies. Later they sat in a cool grove of pines to eat an excellent meal of cold fowl, beef, olives, pomegranates, pickled lamb tongues, and wine.

"I detest traveling," complained Pontius Pilate, wiping his hands fastidiously on a white linen napkin. "And most especially in this alien land. The wine is loathsome." But it was sweet and honeyed and mellow on Lucanus' lips. Pilate's face was flushed, and he sighed. He said to Lucanus, with an affectionate glance, "I have slept like an infant, thanks to you, my dear Lucanus, and though sometimes my thoughts are heavy I am no longer depressed. I have sent Caesar's ring to him, and he will return it to you by courier."

They went on their way. The mountains seethed with heat. They passed hamlets of houses built of yellow clay, protected by clumps of dark cypresses. The earth danced in heat waves; the sea flashed like blue fire. Here and there the mountains took on a curious square aspect, sulphurous and harsh. White walls along the road poured with purplish or rosy flowers. Once they heard the azure thunder of a narrow cataract on a mountainside. Little vivid green valleys lay like fingers between the mounts.

Here, along this road, going to Jersualem from His home, He must have walked many times, thought Lucanus. He knew this dust, these hamlets where He paused to refresh Himself, these groves, these wells, these cypresses, these flowers, these tiny meadows. Did He sit on yonder stone, speaking to His weary followers? Did He reach for a cluster of dates in that clump there? Did He eat a handful of those small black olives, dripping with brine? Did He smile at these sheep? Did He gaze at that scintillating sea? Did He enjoy a red pomegranate? There is a pond there, like a blue mirror. Did He bathe His tired feet in it? And what did He say, in His gentleness, to those girls at the well? And what did He think of the round or square Roman fortresses on the soil of His country? He must have gazed on their pennants and soldiers and pondered. The air is so silent and luminous here; did He listen to the echoing hoofs of Roman horses and the wheels of Roman chariots as I listen to them now? Lucanus was filled with awe and humility.

They turned around the flank of an encroaching mountain and a flat plain of glowing red poppies lay at their right, mixed with strange yellow flowers, all burning under the sun. And there was a field of grain, pure gold, and bending slightly, and harvesters at work, calling to each other in rough Aramaic. They stopped their toil for a few moments to watch the entourage thunder by, and their silence was ominous. The flaming sky arched over the mountains, and the light was fearful on brazen hills. Pilate would have approved their bare starkness, for did not the Romans need the cypresses for their ships? That they had made the hills desolate was not important.

Then they heard a most dolorous wailing or chanting.

" 'The Lord is my shepherd!' " cried hoarse voices in Hebrew. " 'I shall not want. In verdant pastures He gives me repose. Beside restful waters He leads me . . . !' "

Here the earth was parched and crumbling, and the air swirled with dust, and the barren mountains, slowly darkening, lifted their somber heads at a little distance.

"A Jewish funeral," said Plotius, pointing to the right with his whip.

"Let us watch," pleaded Lucanus, and Plotius halted his chariot at once, for he could deny Lucanus nothing, even this foolishness. The riders went on apace, then pulled up their horses and waited curiously. Pontius Pilate's chariot came alongside that of Plotius, and he said, "What is wrong?"

"A Jewish funeral," repeated Plotius. "Lucanus wished to watch it."

Pilate's brows drew together incredulously.

Weary, bearded men clothed in dusty black were carrying a black coffin, and women, clothed in gray, followed, weeping. One stood apart, chanting the Psalm of David, a black cap on his head, his hands clasped, his eyes raised to the sky. The scene was infinitely dolorous in that dry and dusty place, in that poor cemetery, and in this burning silence. The mourners were unaware that Romans had paused to watch them. They straggled over the blasted earth in a pathetic line.

The chanter cried, " 'He refreshes my soul! He guides me in right paths for His name's sake! Even though I walk in the dark valley I fear no evil, for You are by my side, and with Your rod and Your staff that give me courage!' "

Other men joined in faintly; the bearers bent under the weight of the coffin, for they were old. The women raised loud and desperate voices in grief, and struck their breasts as they followed the men. And then Lucanus saw that still another stood apart, a young man who looked not at the sky but at the ground, fixedly, and who did not join in the echoing chant. His face was terrible and stony. He appeared unaware of all things; the few present did not look at him, except for the chanter, the rabbi, who glanced towards him rebukingly and lifted his voice higher.

" 'Only goodness and kindness follow me all the days of my life!' "

The young man started then, looked about him wildly, and

put his hands over his face. A frightful cry burst from him, sudden and sharp, then he was still again.

Lucanus did not know why he climbed down from the chariot and stood in the dust, and why he began to walk towards the funeral party. "What is wrong with him?" demanded Pilate, with some petulance. The mounted soldiers watched Lucanus, standing in a group, and staring.

The chanting rabbi was now murmuring prayers, and then he saw Lucanus approaching him, Lucanus in his thin white tunic bordered with gold, and with his sternly beautiful face and yellow head. The old rabbi blinked at him confusedly; his red-rimmed eyes were sore with dust and sorrow. Then a look of cold affront passed over his dark face, and he saw the others on the road, the hated arrogant Romans with their eagle-crowned fasces, their rich chariots, their fine horses, their helmets and their swords and banners.

"Must you intrude here?" asked the rabbi of Lucanus. His features worked desperately. He cried, "Let us be, you Romans, you worshipers of evil spirits! You befoul this place where our sacred dead sleep in the dust!"

Lucanus lifted his hand, and said, very gently, in Aramaic, "Peace be unto you, Rabbi."

At this Jewish greeting the rabbi fell silent. He studied Lucanus' face and saw only kindness and love there, and sympathy. Was this man a Jew also, touched to the heart by this little funeral of the poor? The rabbi's eyes filled with tears. He looked at the coffin-bearers, who had paused at a raw grave in the ocher earth.

"Peace be unto you, also," quavered the rabbi. Then he murmured, "It is my daughter, my only child, who is dead. My little one, the ewe-lamb of my old age, and beautiful. She died this morning in childbirth, and yonder is her young husband, who will not be reconciled, and who curses God in his heart."

Lucanus looked at the young husband, so stricken, so silent, with his hands over his face. He stood in the blinding light, clothed in black, tall and slender, and he was alone only as those who suffer the death of love can be alone. "He is desolate, Rabbi," said Lucanus, and thought of Rubria.

The rabbi struck his breast, and tears ran down his furrowed cheeks. "Am I not desolate also, Master, I her father, I a widower, who have no one now but a feeble grandchild? Yet I praise God, and bow to His will, and know that He

gives, and that He takes away. But for Rebecca's husband
there is hope, for he is young and he has his parents, and he
will marry again in spite of his oaths, his cries of hatred for
God, and all his despair."

But Lucanus could not believe this, for in the posture of
the bereaved husband he saw limitless agony. He hesitated,
then slowly approached the young man and put his hand on
his shoulder. The young man did not move, but he murmured
incoherently, "Oh, if only He were here, He who paused to
talk to us and raised the dead! He would call to my wife,
and she would rise and return to my arms!"

Lucanus looked about him in the fierce light. The bearers
had placed the coffin at the edge of the grave, and were waiting. The women stood together, weeping softly. All of them
were now gazing at the rabbi, Lucanus and the husband in
the dazed immobility of grief.

Lucanus said to the young husband, "He is not dead, but
lives. He is not deaf, but hears. He has not gone, but is
amongst us."

His head began to reel in the heat and light, but a slow
rapture was unfolding in his heart. "Let us go to the grave,"
he said, and he took the husband's arm. But the young man
resisted like stone. "I have told you," said the rabbi, "that he
will not be reconciled, will not bow to God's will." And the
old man wept aloud. "Be you reconciled, David!"

"Be of hope, David," said Lucanus, and again drew the arm
of the husband. David dropped his hands; he turned on Lucanus a face as dry as the dust itself, and thin and pale,
and yet handsome. His eyes glowed like fire. "Hope!" he cried,
in an awful voice. "I loved no one but my wife, and we
were children together, and now she is nothing but clay and
her spirit has fled from me!"

Lucanus was trembling, and he did not know why. Everything appeared to expand and contract before him, and all
things had a crystalline aura to his eyes, and there was a command in him, like a great and imperative voice. "Let us go
to the grave," he repeated.

David's bitten lips shook; his eyes fixed themselves emptily
on Lucanus. And now he did not resist; stumbling, he walked
beside the Greek, his head bent. The others watched them
come, followed by the praying rabbi. Then they stood by the
grave and the coffin.

Lucanus was silent. He gazed at the coffin and felt the

mounting tumult in himself, and the louder command, so that his ears heard nothing else. Then he said, "Open the coffin, so that I may see the girl."

The others stood like black and gray statues, absolutely still, and looked at Lucanus with wide, wet eyes.

Lucanus' voice rose strongly. "Open the coffin! I would see the girl."

David's face suddenly ran with tears. He leaned against Lucanus' shoulder. "You have heard him," he said, in a rusty voice. "I am her husband. Open the coffin. I would see her face for the last time."

The bearded men glanced helplessly at the rabbi, whose old lips worked. Then he said, weakly, "He is her husband; I am only her father. Open the coffin, for he would not look on her face before."

They opened the coffin, tugging at its black-shrouded thinness. The nails squeaked in protest. But the lid opened. Lucanus bent over the coffin and saw within its raw-wood depths a young girl, not more than fifteen, lying in her shroud, her hands folded on her breasts. Lucanus lifted the cloth from her face; an odor of herbs and fragrant oils rose in the hot air. David fell on his knees, sobbing aloud, and clutched the side of the coffin and looked at his dead wife.

She was very lovely. Her face was remote and serene, as if she slept. Her flesh was pale and as translucent as alabaster. Her black hair lay about her like a cloak, and her innocent lips faintly smiled. It was impossible to believe she was dead. Lucanus considered. The Jews buried their dead before sundown of the day they died. He bent closer over the coffin; the young bosom was breathless, the lips cold and unmoving, the nostrils motionless. He felt a vast shaking in him. Was it possible that the girl was not dead, but only in catalepsy? His physician's eye eagerly studied the calm features.

He put out his hand and touched the smooth white cheek. It was as chill as alabaster, but not stiff. But then she had died only this morning, and the heat of the day would delay rigor. The imperious voice sounded louder in him and now he heard words: "Take the woman by the hand and raise her!"

"Yes, Lord," he said aloud. He took the girl's hand, and it too was icy in that ferocious heat. Lucanus hesitated again. Then as he held the small flaccid hand he felt a familiar draining and weakness in himself, as if some virtue were flowing away from him. As at an enormous distance he heard the groaning of David and the weeping of the women. For some power was concentrating in him which held off the world and all in it.

He said, "Awake, Rebecca, for you are not dead, but only sleep!"

At these mysterious, these profound words, the others ceased their weeping, and David, kneeling beside the coffin, dropped his hands beside him and looked at Lucanus. And a great radiance shone on his face.

The still hand in that of Lucanus warmed swiftly. The nostrils dilated, the lips stirred. The young breast heaved a deep sigh. Her eyes opened, dark and misty and confused, and gazed at Lucanus. He smiled at her tenderly; drawing on her hand, he raised her in her coffin, and she sat up, throwing back her hair like a dreamer newly awakened.

At this the mourners lifted their voices in a fearful cry and fell back. But the rabbi and David remained beside the coffin, speechless, the old man bending like a black bough over his child. It was David alone who threw himself at Lucanus' feet and pressed his forehead against them, and covered them with tears and kisses.

The rabbi broke out into a rapturous hymn, clasping his hands together and lifting his bearded face to the sky. "She was dead, and You restored her, Oh, King of Kings, Oh, Lord of the Universe! Blessed be the Name of the Lord!"

Lucanus bent and lifted David to his feet, and the young man clung to him. "He sent you to us!" he cried. "Oh, blessed are we that you visited us, in His Name!"

"Praise God, for He did this, and not I," said Lucanus. "For He is the Resurrection and the Life."

He turned away, smiling and rapturous, but weak in all his body. He looked back only once. The women were helping the girl from her coffin; her husband was kissing her hands. The old man was praying. Now all the air rang with rejoicing and confused exclamations.

The men in the entourage had seen everything, and they watched Lucanus approach with terror in their faces. He smiled at them reassuringly. "The girl was not dead. She only slept," he said, and climbed into the chariot again. They clattered on their way in silence.

Then Pilate, leaning from his chariot, said to Lucanus, and there was a shrill tremulousness in his haughty voice, "The Jews bury their dead before sundown. She was not dead then?" It was as if he were pleading.

"She was not dead," said Lucanus. But Plotius gave him a long glance, and his soldier's face was deeply moved, and reverent. Lucanus suddenly fell asleep, like one overpoweringly exhausted.

Lucanus awoke at the changing of the horses. The afternoon air was cool; Plotius had covered him with his own rough soldier's mantle. To the right the sea was one huge and blazing plain of light, too brilliant for the eye to dwell upon it, and without color. The sky had become a hollow arch; the cerulean hue had burned away in the purity of white flame. The country had changed; against the pale and burning heavens reared empty mountains of a blackish hue, fold on fold of heavy stone. High cacti bordered the road, bearing brown and thorny fruit, and dusty tangled thistles like dead hedges wandered over dun fields as lifeless as the fields of death. Even the cypresses were gone; no olive or palm trees redeemed the earth or the mountains. Here and there the bitter mountains showed outcroppings of whitish and broken stone; flat houses, the color of the parched earth, stood in silence and abandonment.

But the roads were filling with noisy people on camels and on asses, on the way to Jerusalem. Echoes rose on all sides. The entourage turned away from the sea and quickened its pace with the fresh horses. Lucanus looked upon the desolation which the Romans had wrought when they had taken the cypresses, and he thought that the very earth was cursed. Even the occasional dull pools of brackish water where goats drank appeared lifeless, and the color of pewter. This was the progress of which Pontius Pilate had spoken, this wild devastation, this loneliness, this encroaching desert. Where man walked, greedy and rapacious, death followed and the ground was blasted.

"A hideous land," said Pontius Pilate. And Lucanus answered, "It was not hideous until man came here. Ugliness walks in his steps; he deforms everything he sees and touches."

Pilate frowned at this sharp answer. Then he said, "You will find Jerusalem without charm, and peculiar. I regret that you will not be with me in my house; you have said you will be the guest of Hilell ben Hamram, who awaits you. My dear Lucanus! The Jews can tell the strangest stories! You will bathe in mysticism."

Lucanus said, "I have wondered why God chose to be born of the Jewish people, and not the Greeks, with their cul-

ture, or the Romans with their power. But now I know." He
shivered under the mantle which Plotius had thrown over
him, and he drowsed again for his exhaustion was very great.
But in his sleep his mind was busy and sad. He thought of
the two thousand Jews in Syria whom the legate Varus had
crucified for preaching rebellion against Rome; he thought of
the execution grounds near Caesarea where Jews were regularly crucified for "inciting against the Empire." He thought
of the myriad and countless crimes man committed against
man, all through the ages, and the groaning which incessantly
reached the ears of God, and he asked himself, in his drowse,
why God did not destroy this human race of devastators,
this horror upon the bright earth, this hater of his brother
and the hater of all innocent things, this pariah from which
all sinless animals fled in dreadful fear and loathing, this
razer of his own cities and civilizations, this looter, war-
maker and vilest criminal, this hypocrite and liar, this murderer and traitor, this restless evil spirit which walked, like
Lucifer, up and down the earth looking for whom and what
he could destroy. But I too am without merit, thought Lucanus, for I had once believed that man was the sinned
against, and not the sinning.

Lucanus opened his eyes. The chariot in which he was riding was climbing up a stony blackish-brown mount. Here it
paused, and Plotius pointed with his whip. "Jerusalem," he
said.

There Jerusalem stood on Mount Sion, to the west, the
shadow of the earth, on this evening, a dusty dim blue
against a pinkish horizon arching over the city. All about
Mount Sion rose other mounts, whitish brown, folded together
in stone or covered with narrow terraces like wandering steps
on which grew cypresses, laurel, olive trees, palms, and grapevines, pomegranates and carob trees, and trees yellow or green
or plum-colored with fruit. High on its own mount, Jerusalem appeared part of it, of a pale brown, seemingly convulsively pushed up from the earth rather than having been
made by man. The winding and battlemented walls, pierced
and forbidding, twisted protectingly around the city, its gates
and towers guarded, the pennants of Rome fluttering on the
topmost heights. Gray-brown steepness rose to the walls, simmering with dust; caravans for the night were already camped
below the walls, fires already lighted and the restless bobbing
of lanterns moving about. No one could enter the city after
sunset; those caught by the evening lifted their tents, seethed

about their temporary little village, tended their horses and their camels, and waited for the morning. The gates were locked, the sharply rising paths and stairways to the walls empty.

Even as Lucanus watched, the swift night began to flow like dull water over the city and its surrounding mountains, and the red flicker of torches sprang up inside the walls and lanterns brightened within them. A copper moon rose over a mount of the selfsame color, and Mars was a topaz jewel near it. Color left the few mountains which were still fertile and planted; the whole scene was stark yellowish brown beneath a sky turning purple above a lake of desolate crimson fire. Lucanus thought he had never seen so barren a sight, so contained, so gloomy, so lifeless except for the campfires and the torches and the lanterns. A cool mountain wind, empty of scent and fragrance, struck his face. Accustomed to cities awakening at night and sounding with laughter and high voices, Lucanus was aware of a heavy silence over this city, as if it had swallowed in itself all echoes and clamoring. From this height he could see over the walls and observe the narrow and twisted streets redly shadowed by torches and filled with voiceless throngs. And there, tall, wide and impressive, stood the Temple, marble yellow and quiet and golden-towered, surrounded by motionless gardens and, beyond the gardens, by crowding multitudes of flat-topped houses all built of the pervading yellow brown of the earth and the mountains themselves. Only occasionally did clumps of black cypresses appear in the city, crowded together as if for protection.

"Compare that with Caesarea, which we have built," said Pontius Pilate in a cold and disgusted voice. But Lucanus understood that the city had withdrawn to itself for protection against the conqueror, and that if many of its hills were dead the Romans had done this greedy and evil thing. The ancient city had repudiated its masters, and its brooding air was the air of desperation.

The entourage swept down the mountain rapidly, the legionnaires riding ahead with their flags and their fasces. The acridness of the dust of the ages was in Lucanus' nostrils. Slits of light brightened in the battlements of the walls which now rose before them. The chariots and the horses drove ruthlessly through the encampments; by the flare of the torches near the tents one caught the sudden glaring whiteness of eyes, sullen and watchful; asses, horses and camels lurched aside for the company, squealing and protesting. Children gathered in groups to watch the passage. Now from the echoing mountains came the sharp howling of jackals, weird and unearthly. The moon was a yellow skull in the dark sky.

The riders and the chariots had some difficulty climbing the steep hill that led to the city; small stones rumbled behind them. A gate was opening, and a Roman trumpet sounded its greeting, awakening shrill and bounding echoes. They entered the city through rows of soldiers who saluted. And then they were in the dusty narrow streets whose shops were closed and whose people were silent. They clattered over black cobblestones. Groups of families appeared on flat roofs; they turned their faces aside from the Romans. Doorways glowed golden in the murky dusk; windows were pale with lamplight. It was a besieged city, silently wrathful, proud in its dust. To Lucanus, accustomed to the colorful East, Jerusalem did not seem Eastern, for it was without gaiety, laughter, music, hurrying footsteps and merry voices. He had the thought that time had settled here like a stony tomb, and could never be moved, and that the torches thrust into sockets diminished rather than heightened the pent life of the city. The red shadows shifted on walls like the shadows of a conflagration burning in the habitations of the dead.

"It is livelier during the day," said Plotius, as if sensing Lucanus' thought. "The Jews do not frolic at night; they are a somber people."

They swung down a wider street, filled with torchlight and citron moonlight, guarded by higher walls. Now Lucanus could smell the fragrance of gardens and the freshness of fountains, and could hear occasional voices, and, once or twice, the sound of a lute or a lyre tinkling timidly against the quiet of the night. Here lived the Roman administrators and the wealthy Jews who collaborated with the Romans and took on themselves something of the Roman customs. The entourage stopped at a gate, and Plotius said, "Hilell ben Hamram's house, your host. We go, on with the noble Pontius Pilate to his own house."

A black iron gate swung open, and Hilell appeared, smiling and handsome in a white robe. "Greetings, my friends," he said. "I expected you earlier."

"Lucanus must stop to attend a Jewish funeral," said Pilate, dryly. "Fortunately he was able to prevent a woman from being buried alive. How eager you Jews are to rid

yourself of your dead before sunset! I often wonder how
many unfortunates awake in the earth, and I reflect on their
terror before they die, smothered in the dark."

Hilell's face changed subtly at this insult, but he remained smiling. He gave Plotius an affectionate glance and
asked the company to join him for wine. But Pilate said he
was tired; he moved restlessly in his chariot. Hilell extended
Lucanus his hand and helped him to descend; his grasp was
warm and full of warning, for he sensed anger in the Greek.
Plotius gave Hilell a flashing grin and saluted, and the
entourage swept on. Still holding Lucanus' hand, Hilell led
him into a large garden full of fountains and the fragrance
of jasmine and night-blooming flowers. The big marble house
in the midst of the garden reflected the moonlight like gold.
Lucanus sighed with pleasure, conscious of weariness. Now
Arieh ben Elazar hurried down shallow marble steps towards them, holding out his hands and crying Lucanus'
name aloud, and with delight, and they embraced.

The two young men led Lucanus into the great hall, and
he gazed about him with interest. Hilell was a cosmopolitan;
the marble walls, of many hues, were hung with the finest
of colorful draperies, brocades and silks and jeweled fabrics,
twinkling and sparkling in the light of many tall lamps and
Corinthian-bronze candelabra set on carved tables of
marble, ebony and lemonwood. Great Persian vases and
vases from Cathay stood about the walls and in the
corners, from which sprayed tall and fragrant lilies and roses
and branches of jasmine and glossy dark green leaves.
Exotic Eastern lattices decorated the windows, inlaid with
gold and silver and ivory; they admitted the cool and
scented breath of the gardens. Chairs covered with brocades and tinted silks stood about on small Persian rugs.
Lucanus had entered many fine homes before, but he
thought this the most restful. He saw no statues, however.
In the center of the vast hall a silvery fountain splashed
into a round bowl and filled the air with perfume. The
three men seated themselves on a soft Roman divan the
color of pomegranates, and a servant brought them Roman
wine and a dish of dates and figs rolled in nuts, and other
delicate sweetmeats.

Lucanus stretched himself wearily, and with pleasure. His
friends regarded him with affection. Arieh said, "My home,
which was my father's, is humbler than this, but in a few
days you must be my guest also." His hand still held that

of Lucanus, like a son. "I am not here to dally," said Lucanus, but he smiled. "You must remember that I am no longer very young and there is much for me to learn and to do." Hilell studied him with concern.

"Once," said Lucanus, "I was without hope. The world was utterly corrupt, and without God. I lived in bitterness and despair. But, as my brother Priscus has said to me, a Revelation has been given to man by God, and never will the world be the same again. Hope and joy have been bestowed upon it; a new age has arisen, full of portent. I am called upon to help it increase, and to bring the good tidings to all I meet."

Hilell hesitated. "I have been to Joppa; I have seen Peter, one of the Christ's Apostles, the foremost among them. He is a man of about thirty-four, impetuous and impatient and somewhat dogmatic. His speech is blunt and forthright. You must remember that he has had little or no contact with the Gentiles; he is a fisherman from Galilee, a countryman; he was a very devout Jew, of small learning about the world. Nevertheless, he is impressive, and full of fire. He is hiding in a small house in Joppa, and spends his time on the roof, gazing at the sea and praying." Hilell hesitated again, then laughed a little. "When I arrived, he did not regard me kindly. For several days he would not see me, for he is suspicious. Then he reproached me in his Galilean tongue; I was a corrupt Jew, he said to my face. I was a familiar of Greeks and Romans and other abominable people. What did I know of the Holy Books? It was evident, he declared, looking at my clothing scornfully, that I lived for pleasure, and that it was very possible that the Commandments were only words to me. I was a man of wealth; how was it possible for me to understand the poor and the humble? The Lord did not come and die for such as I. His message would be incomprehensible to me. Nevertheless, after I had let him have his reproachful and contemptuous say, he listened to my own story, though he kept glancing meaningly at my rings and my silver sandals. He softened, finally; he remembered me as the rich man who spoke to the Lord. Then he began to weep, and said, 'Why should I rebuke you, I who denied Him three times and fled when they took Him and crucified Him?' "

Hilell poured more wine for Lucanus. "Then in halting tones he continued. 'When He returned to us, and abided with us, He told us that we must give the good tidings to all nations. I confess I was horrified. We are few, and we are Jews, and we are without money or friends. We are proscribed by the Roman procurator. What can the Gentiles understand of Him; what can we say to them? We do not know them! To us they have been abominations; the Law has declared we must stay apart and not be corrupted by the Gentiles. The uncircumcised are without the Law; they are unclean; their ways are not our ways. Weak and powerless, we must go among the strangers, with their idols and their vile gods and their unspeakable customs! We must tell them of our Messias, who we believed came only to His people. I came to Joppa not only to hide from the anger of the Romans, who declare us insurrectionists, but to pray and to try to understand. Each night I have stood on this roof and have pondered. And then I had visions. I must do as He has commanded, but still it is a sickness in my heart, and I shrink from the Gentile and all his works, and his cruelty and abominations.' "

Hilell smiled humorously. "Though I have never regarded the Gentiles with the loathing and terror of that humble and emphatic man, I understood. I spoke of you. I told him you had come to talk with him. You are a Greek, a heathen! You have worshiped false gods; you speak an alien tongue; you are not circumcised. Then he fell to weeping again, and reproached himself, confessing that he was again committing the sin of pride and rejection. He has consented to see you. Before I left him, he baptized me. He is not the gentlest of men, and you may find him crude and even insulting, and with the hard tongue of the countryman.

"I have also found two more Apostles, James and John, brothers, sons of one Zebedee, Galileans also. They are called Boanerges, sons of the thunderstorm, and that describes them exactly. They live without the wall; the Mother of Christ abides with them as their mother, for so God commanded. They are very young men, and possess a kind of fierceness and a fanatical dedication. There is even a hint of vengefulness about them. I have heard that they had desired that Christ bring down fire from heaven upon the Samaritan village which showed a disinclination to listen to Him. Even when rebuked by Him, they still breathed flames. They will not regard you kindly, though I have persuaded them to see you."

Hilell sighed. "Even among the holy, even those who walked with Him and ate and slept with Him, and heard His words hourly, there is dissension. Some of them insist vehemently that before a man can become a Christian he must first be admitted to Judaism, and that he must be circumcised. These are the older men who cling ferociously to the Law of the ages. The younger men say it is not necessary; they have their own interpretations. The elder believe that when Christ spoke of the mission to the 'cities of Israel' He meant that literally. The younger firmly believe it means all men. Not only are they kept apart, in hiding, from the ban of Pontius Pilate, but they are kept apart by their opinions. I am very pessimistic."

"I am not," said Lucanus, firmly. "You must remember, my friends, that the Apostles are only men, and men differ. I will go to see Peter as soon as possible."

A young girl glided into the hall, clad in a white palla, with a drift of gauze upon her head. She was about fifteen and extremely comely, with a ripe and graceful figure, fine dark eyes under narrow brows, a skin as white as snow, and a neck like a slender column. Her mouth was a rose; under the gauze on her small head flowed a mass of dark red curls and waves. She had a shy but coquettish expression, and was apparently conscious of her beauty. Hilell rose and took her hand.

"Ah, Leah," said Hilell, fondly. He brought her to Lucanus, and said, "This is my sister, whom I have espoused to Arieh. Is he not fortunate?" He smiled at Leah with pride. Many jeweled bracelets tinkled on the girl's wrists, and a heavy gemmed necklace encircled her throat, and her sandals were of silver. Lucanus was tenderly amused. Leah, though young and cherished, and guarded carefully, wore an air of much worldliness. She answered him softly in Greek, which she spoke with precision. Arieh stood beside her, his dark blue eyes shining with love. She affected to be unaware of him, though a blush was high on her wide cheekbones. She spoke to her brother with the arrogance of the young and pampered. "Why is not our guest in his chambers, resting? You are amiss, Hilell."

"So I am," he agreed. He clapped his hands and the overseer came into the hall at once. "You will conduct the noble Lucanus to his chambers, Simon," he said. He pondered a moment. "You will meet my wife at dinner. The children are in their beds. My parents," and he hesitated, "will not join us, for they are old and have had a fever."

Lucanus understood at once that the parents of Hilell

did not approve of their son entertaining Gentiles and bringing them under this roof. He nodded gravely. "I trust their health is improving," he said. He could not help adding with some mischief, "Would you like me to examine them, and, if necessary, prescribe for them?"

Hilell said with some hastiness, "Thank you, my dear friend! But I would not consider imposing upon you. Besides, they trust only our family physicians. One must humor the aged; they have their peculiarities."

"They are very tiresome," said Leah, pettishly. "They never speak to me without disapproval or reproaches. Do they think we live in the old days, when girls were secluded and kept apart, and dressed in an elderly fashion and hid their hair after they were married?" She tossed her pretty curls. "This is a modern world, and one must have modern ways, which are more agreeable and enlightened."

Hilell laughed, and tugged one of her curls affectionately. "Remember to honor your parents, Leah," he said. She pulled her curl away from him in exasperation. "It is all very well for you, my brother," she said. "You have not had to spend the afternoon listening to admonitions, as I have. I am immodest; I am not versed in the laws of the prophets; I have no regard for the patriarchs; I am ignorant of pious customs; grave doubts have been expressed of me; I will be a wife such as a Roman, and my children will be neglected and will not be taught their holy duties. And as for your wife, Deborah, she is almost as bad, with her hidden hair and her downcast eyes and her silence in the presence of men! If you did not insist, she would not even appear at our table but would eat alone, humbly. To them all I am a Jezebel."

"Run along, child," said Hilell. "You have said enough."

"You do not know how I suffer!" cried Leah, stamping her pretty little foot. "Besides, you are a man, and not a girl!"

"Your manners are deplorable," said Hilell, becoming stern. "One understands that you are much abused, and we sympathize. You weary our guest."

Leah scampered out of the hall, tossing her head. Hilell explained to Lucanus, in apology, "She is the child of my parents' age, and has been coddled excessively. They have only themselves to blame. They delight in her beauty; they are only fearful for her soul. She will become a proper Jewish matron when she is married, and no doubt will reproach her own children and agonize over them."

"She is a joy to my eyes," said Arieh. "She has been instructing me in the Law, and sighs over my ignorance. She is the sweetest of women."

When he was in his assigned chambers Lucanus looked about him with pleasure. He stepped out upon a balcony and looked over Jerusalem, shining with lanterns and torches. He washed his hands in scented water and took white napkins from a servant. Fresh fine clothing, of the whitest linen, had been tactfully prepared for him, and he removed his rough garments, which were dusty and travel-stained. He put his feet into sandals of the finest leather. He glanced at the rich bed longingly. From somewhere in the house he heard a distant harp and suspected that the gay music was evoked by Leah, defiantly. For some reason, hearing that dancing music, his heart lifted. It had an innocence, an affirmation. It believed in life, and embraced it eagerly.

A servant led him through luxurious rooms and then to the dining hall, where Hilell, Arieh, Leah and Deborah, the wife of Hilell, awaited him. Deborah was a young, plump woman, dressed very modestly in a blue robe. A blue cloth covered her hair completely. Her arms and neck were hidden. Her round face reminded Lucanus of Aurelia, and her brown eyes, which rose swiftly once to his face and then were downcast, were lively in spite of her demeanor. A dimple wavered near her prim lips, and spoke of merriment which she doubtless reserved for her husband. She wore no jewelry. She seated herself at the foot of the lavish table near Leah; not once had she spoken. Leah glanced at her impatiently, then ignored her. The girl joined impudently in the conversation, disagreed, laughed, joked, and altogether behaved as a spoiled young beauty in the modern fashion. Deborah exuded disapproval, and Leah sniffed, and tossed her curls, and jangled her bracelets.

"You have an excellent cook," said Lucanus, discovering himself hungry. The fish balls were spicy and succulent, the roast lamb juicy, the vegetables and salad well flavored. There were flaky cakes stuffed with raisins, dried plums and dates covered with poppy seeds. The wine was Roman, and of the finest quality. Candles in silver candelabra shone on a white cloth in which silver threads glistened; the spoons and knives were heavily pierced and engraved, the golden goblets massive and encrusted with gems, the salt dishes also of gold, and encrusted, as were the plates.

"We live like peasants," said Leah, discontentedly. "It is not that I desire that which is unclean. But I would prefer more elegance and variety. My best friend's table is delightful."

"Quiet, child," said Hilell, automatically. "Lucanus, I wish, sometimes, that we still had the old customs and women were excluded from dining with men."

"She is young," said Arieh. He turned to his espoused wife and asked, gravely, "You have said I am ignorant, and it is so. Repeat to me some of Moses' laws regarding temples and sacrifices."

Leah lifted her head proudly, and in a severe voice began to instruct Arieh. Lucanus listened with fond amusement, and Arieh with an aspect of humility. Deborah did not speak, but once or twice Lucanus saw her dimple. The happiness of this young family affected Lucanus deeply. Listening to Leah and seeing her innocence and her pink cheeks and the flash of her eyes and the suppleness of her neck and bare arms, he thought of Rubria and Sara, the dead he loved with such tenderness, and he said to himself that in reality there was no age, no weariness, no pain, no despair, no parting, no death. The world and the planets, the countless suns, rang with immortal youth, and the constellations and the galaxies rejoiced in it. An exhilaration filled him. All he had ever loved was with him forever.

Before he fell asleep that night he heard the howling of the jackals without the gates, and it seemed to him that they were the voices crying in the wilderness and waiting for comfort, and for admittance among the company of the blessed.

Chapter Forty-eight

Lucanus received an invitation to dine with Pontius Pilate, and he was about to refuse it impatiently when Hilell said, "You were a guest in his home at Caesarea. And for some reason you haunt him. He is a very uneasy man since the crucifixion of the Christ. Will it vex you to give him some ease?"

"You, my host, were not invited. That is a great discourtesy."

Hilell smiled. "Let us grant it so. But Romans are careless of courtesy towards those they have conquered. You were about to say that he does not like Jews. We would be intolerant if we were intolerant of intolerance."

"That is a sophistry," said Lucanus, but he accepted the invitation. Hilell decked him out in an elegant fashion. "Romans, so materialistic, are engrossed with rich and proper clothing," said Hilell. "They despise simplicity; they love a show of wealth."

Lucanus wore a blue tunic and over it a toga of the most delicate yet heavy linen, bordered with gold. His sandals were golden, with a tongue of gemmed leather over the instep. Hilell clasped jeweled circlets about his arms. "You are truly magnificent," he said, kindly. "You resemble one of the noblest Grecian statues." He ordered a litter at sunset and Lucanus was borne away to the house of Pontius Pilate, a large house set within high gates and richly blooming gardens, lively with fountains which danced in the red air of the falling sun. But a wind was blowing from the region of the Street of the Cheesemakers which all the fragrance of tree and grass and flower could not overcome. Pilate said, wrinkling his nose, "The stench is abominable." Lucanus, remembering to be polite, refrained from remarking on the stenches of Rome, and especially the odors which drifted from the Trans-Tiber when the wind changed. Pilate wore a preoccupied manner as he led Lucanus into a hall even more lavish than the hall of Hilell. Lucanus was overpowered by the splendor, which appeared too crowded and in bad taste. The central fountain was heavily perfumed, and the scent was cloying. The house seemed full of pretty slave girls, who sat on cushions on the gleaming white floor and played flute and harp and lute, and tossed their long locks.

"We will go to the roof," said Pilate, "where the air is fresh and we have a fine view of the city. I am expecting other guests." His aloof face smiled coldly. "No one less than Herod Antipas himself, and his brother. He wishes to speak with you, and you must understand that that is a condescension! Once we disliked each other; now we are the best of friends. It was a matter of diplomacy."

"You have told Herod of me?" Lucanus was disturbed.

"Yes. By the way, he is vexed over my lifting the proscription against the sect which calls itself the Christians. He is prepared not to like you." Pilate laughed with sudden good humor and led the way up several flights of wide marble steps covered with Persian carpets; Lucanus caught glimpses

of rich apartments during his ascent. Music followed them.
The roof was very wide and long, and guarded by parapets
of high pierced stone in intricate patterns, the floor scattered with rugs, the low chairs and divans sheltered by
striped and silken awnings in many colors, the tables set
with waiting lamps. The slave girls followed them and struck
up music again.

Lucanus was interested in the view of the city at this
height. The crimson blaze of the sunset lay on the stony
or terraced mounts that stood about the city, giving them
an aspect of burning. The twisted and battlemented yellow
walls of Jerusalem had a baleful air about them; a tinge of
dusty scarlet had settled over the narrow and crowded
streets, like the reflection of fire. A dull and murmurous
sound came from the streets, hushed and muttering. Lucanus could see the Roman forum, its white walls and
columns shining like snow in the smoldering light, and the
Roman theater like a serrated cup, and the palaces rearing
high above the endless and broken plain of smaller houses,
the flat roofs illuminated in a wash of red. Dominating all
was the Temple, high set within its own walls, its golden
towers incandescent, its walls rosy. As it faced the east at
this point on Pilate's roof, the sky that stood behind it was
a deep peacock, contrasting with the flaming skies of the
west. In the distance was a vast clump of black cypresses,
huddled together or scattered about a great green garden.
"Gethsemane," said Pilate, noting Lucanus' interest. There was
a peculiar note in his voice. He and Lucanus sat down under
an awning and drank wine. Pilate became silent, as if
thinking. The music rose about them, and a girl sang sweetly.
Lucanus listened; the cadence was unfamiliar to him, mournful and haunting. The song was in Aramaic.

> "How merciful is the Lord our God!
>   His mercy is wider than the sea.
>   His loving kindness embraces earth and heaven,
>   And His words are joyous to my heart.
>   Who can know the Lord and His holy thoughts?
>   Do the hills know Him, or the gray mountains?
>   Or the vast wilderness where no man walks?
>   Or the tiger in his pacing, or a tree alone in majesty?
>   Or the dying lonely in pain? Or the golden rivers
>   Or a woman who sleeps with a babe at her breast,
>   Or the dying lonely in pain? Or the golden rivers

Which run to the oceans, or the gardens at dawn?
In the most secret place is He known!"

Lucanus looked at the girl, and her great dark eyes brooded
under her brows and her face was smooth and pale. He was
surprised at the words of the song, and he glanced at Pilate,
who was apparently not listening. The Roman's elbow rested
on the arm of his chair, and his fingers half obscured his
face. He was engrossed with his thoughts, forgetting
his guest. Then he said, not removing his fingers, and as if
addressing himself only, "It is impossible that He rose from
the dead! His followers took Him away, and healed Him,
for He had been taken too hastily from the cross."

Lucanus waited, not speaking. The music fell to a softer
and less obtrusive note. Pilate said, still in that distant
voice, "I would not be surprised but that that old pious rascal,
Joseph of Arimathea, had a hand in all this. He is a coun-
selor, and it is said that he is good and just. I have met
him, and despite my skepticism, I have not been able to
catch him in a sophistry or in worldliness. It was Joseph
who begged His body of me, and laid it in a tomb. I
had heard enough rumors of that Man, who, I confess, had no
real fault in my eyes! It was the high priest, Caiaphas——
One does not oppose priests except at his own peril—they
can do much mischief. And I was ordered to keep peace in
this country at any cost. Can I be blamed for that?"

Now he looked at Lucanus sharply. "No," said the Greek,
hesitatingly.

Pilate said, "Joseph is a very rich man. It is possible that
bribery enters into this somewhere, and that Jesus was removed from the cross while still alive, and taken to Joseph's
house for care and healing." The Roman moved restlessly.
"Because of the rumors that He would arise from the dead
on the third day, I posted guards at the tomb so that no
chicanery would be employed. The high priest had asked this
of me."

He halted. He averted his head so that Lucanus could not
see his face. Lucanus again waited. Then the procurator sighed.
"Men are very superstitious; they are also hysterical. My
guards later reported to me, and I listened, incredulous. They
were almost incoherent. They had kept fires burning about
the tomb, and drunk wine, and diced and jested. Could their
wine have been drugged by that omnipresent old rascal,
Joseph? He swears to me solemnly that this was not so. Yet

my men declare, with oaths and fearful glances about them, that before dawn on the third day a great light shone about the tomb and they were struck senseless to the ground. When they awoke, the stone, massive and heavy, had been rolled back from the sepulcher and there was nothing within but grave clothes, an empty stone bench, and the scent of spices and ointments!"

He regarded Lucanus pleadingly. "How can a sensible man believe this to be supernatural? This was a grim joke, indeed, intended to deceive and strike awe into the breasts of the simple; a pretense to fulfill the prophecy. Look you, Lucanus, I am an educated man, of a noble family. Do you expect me to believe this nonsense about a miserable unlearned rabbi from Galilee? Who could inspire the gods less?"

"What do you wish me to say?" asked Lucanus, in a low tone.

"Tell me what you believe about this nonsense." Pilate leaned towards him, and Lucanus saw that he was troubled, and angry at his trouble.

Lucanus felt within his garments and showed, by the light of the red sun, the cross which hung about his neck. Pilate stared at it. "Centuries ago," said Lucanus, "this Man was prophesied by the Chaldeans and the Babylonians, and then the Jews. The rumors of Him spread to all the civilized world. The Egyptians decorated their pyramids with this Sign; the Greeks lifted altars to the Unknown God. The Scriptures of the Jews written ages ago tell of Him, of His mission, of His birth, of His life, and of His death."

Pilate was aghast. The crimson light of the last sun lay starkly on his face. He looked at Lucanus piercingly. "You believe all this?" he asked, in an appalled voice.

"Yes. I believe it. I know it."

Pilate was silent for a time. Then he said in a strained voice, "Then what of me, who delivered Him to death?"

"You were only an instrument."

"The gods are vengeful——"

"He is not vengeful. Do not fear."

Pilate meditated. "You cured your brother who was dying——"

"No. God cured him. I too was only an instrument."

"Tell me what I should do!" cried Pilate, suddenly distraught. He regarded Lucanus fearfully. "I have thought much about this. That woman who was being buried—she was not dead?"

"I have told you: she was not dead. There are no dead."

"You speak in riddles, like the Delphic oracles."

"Men make riddles and mysteries of the simplest things, Pontius."

"I am lost," said Pilate, in a despairing tone. The superstitious Roman's heart beat very fast. "Who are you, Lucanus?" he asked.

Lucanus frowned. "I am what you know I am."

"But you have mysterious powers."

"No. I have no power, no merit. Only God has these."

"He, then, has bestowed them on you."

Lucanus shook his head. But at that moment a slave came to announce the arrival of Herod Antipas, the tetrarch of Jerusalem, and his brother, Herod Phillip. The slave girls struck up triumphant music, and other girls ran onto the roof strewing baskets of rose leaves like pink snow onto the floor, and still others sprayed perfume in the air. Pilate went to meet his guests, and, as the lamps on the roof were hastily lighted, Lucanus looked curiously at the two men. Antipas reminded him instantly of a reddish fox; he had a narrow and irritable face, and was jerky and impatient of movement. He wore a short reddish beard, and Lucanus recalled that Antipas grew a beard for approaching Jewish holidays, then had it removed immediately afterwards. But Phillip, the younger man, was taller and had a noble bearing, fine and liquid dark eyes, a classic face like a statue, and a quiet and dignified manner. He appeared to be engrossed in somber thought. Antipas returned Lucanus' greeting and bow with a short word and a glance of hazel-eyed dislike. But Phillip smiled at him and inquired after his health, and asked him courteously how he found Jerusalem.

The men sat down and drank more wine, and night flowed over the city and torches flared below and lanterns glittered. Antipas was most apparently in a bad temper; he confined his desultory conversation to Pilate; they had once been enemies, but now they were friends. Antipas' air towards Pilate was at once arrogant yet almost servile. Phillip glanced at him occasionally, and his black brows drew together. He talked kindly with Lucanus, and told him he had heard much of him. At this Antipas looked over his shoulder threateningly at Lucanus and said in a sharp, foxlike tone, "Yes. We must talk of this!" He jerked a thin shoulder clad in blue brocade and rubbed his beard. Before turning back to Pilate he shot a venomous glance at his brother, who received it imperturbably.

A gong sounded and they all arose to go down to the dining hall, which sparkled with marble and gemmed hangings
and rich lamps. The meal was luxurious. Antipas ate little, and
drank wine abstemiously. He complained of many insignificant matters to the powerful Roman. Nothing pleased him
either in Jerusalem or in his private affairs. His face softened
only when he spoke of his wife, Herodias. At this Phillip
straightened in his chair and regarded his brother with kindling eyes and his mouth took on hard and bitter lines.

"How I should like to live in Rome!" exclaimed Antipas.
"There one meets only the civilized and the realistic. But here
all is God, all is religious observance, all is tedious religious
discussion! Even the high priest can speak only of the
commentaries. To the Jews nothing exists except God."

Lucanus said, "Democritus wrote, over four hundred
years ago, 'If one choose the goods of the soul, he chooses
the diviner portion; if the goods of the body, the merely
mortal.'"

"That is all very well," said Antipas, in a disagreeable tone,
and with a derisive smile. "But man is mortal also, and the
mortal must be nourished." He paused. He said, almost
menacingly, "I have heard strange things of you, Lucanus.
There are rumors you perform miracles!" He laughed, shortly.

"No," said Lucanus, feeling an answering stir of dislike.
"I perform no miracles. Only God does that." His cheeks
colored with affront.

"Hah!" exclaimed Antipas. "That is excellent. We have had
enough miracle-workers in Judea! Or charlatans! I trust
you are not here to excite the people. Or to claim you
have a unique mission from God!"

"I am here only to find the truth and to record it," said
Lucanus, with anger. Pilate began to smile. Phillip listened
with a goblet of wine at his lips and only his alert eyes shining
on Lucanus.

"And I am here to keep the peace among my people, and
order," said Antipas. "I shall be ruthless with troublemakers."
His eyes glistened with threat.

"These Judean olives are delightful, if I may be permitted
to say so at my own table," said Pilate. "What, Lucanus? You
appear to have little appetite. My cook is excellent; this
roast suckling pig is delicious."

"Perhaps our honored visitor does not care for swine,"
said Antipas, with a nasty smile. Lucanus refused to respond

to this goading. He permitted a slave to give him some suckling meat.

He began to wonder why Antipas was so obviously agitated and irritable. The tetrarch put a handful of little salt Jewish olives in his mouth, chewed them gloomily, then spat out the pits.

"So," he said, "you are here to find the truth and record it. Tell me, are you a Christian?"

"I have been a Christian since the day of Christ's birth," said Lucanus. Antipas almost dropped his goblet in amazement; his mouth fell open. "What did you say?" he demanded, incredulously. Phillip leaned forward in his chair, and the subtle smile on Pilate's face vanished.

"Are you mad?" cried Antipas, slapping his hand on the table. "No one heard of the Christians until four years ago! That Galilean first appeared at that time!"

"Nevertheless, I knew Him from the day He was born. It was my own lack of merit which made me forget Him for many years, my own obstinacy and anger." Lucanus looked straight at Antipas, who was stupefied. "Let me explain." He brought forth the cross once more and showed it to Antipas, who suddenly shrank. Lucanus told them of Keptah, of the Chaldeans and Babylonians, of the Egyptians and the Greeks, of their ancient prophecies. He told them of the Magi, and the great cross in their secret temple in Antioch. He told them of the Star he had seen as a young child, and its movement east. Many of the slaves along the walls leaned forward eagerly to hear, and some of their eyes filled with tears.

"I was in Athens on the day of His crucifixion," said Lucanus, in a low and urgent tone. "The sun disappeared; there were the sounds and groanings of earthquakes. I have heard rumors, in my wanderings, that this happened everywhere in the known world. Do you think it coincidence?"

The reddish flush on Antipas' narrow face disappeared; it was replaced by a livid tint. He was silent, but his eyes darted everywhere as if looking for escape. He licked his lips. Pontius brooded; his hand played with his goblet. Phillip smiled, and he lifted his head as if he had come to a profound resolution.

Antipas suddenly began to tremble as if with an inner rage. He said at last, in a pent and furious voice, "All this is nonsense. I talked with Jesus myself. I had hoped He was the Messias. I wished to see His alleged miracles for myself." He shot a furtive glance at Pilate. "I know the prophecies of the Messias. I have heard them all my life." Again he licked his lips and glanced at Pilate. "The Messias was to deliver the Jews from—from the oppressor. You will pardon me, Pontius? This was the real prophecy! But this Jesus declared He was not of this world, that the things of Caesar did not concern Him. I had Him brought to me."

He paused; his trembling grew noticeable. "In spite of the high priest, who accused Him not only of upsetting the Law, but of inciting the people against authority and provoking riots, to the detriment of the safety of the Jewish people, I had Him brought to me for questioning. If He were the Messias he would reveal Himself in glory and miracles to me, and would be transformed before my eyes. But, to my great disappointment, He was only a miserable, rough-clad peasant from Galilee. I questioned Him. I implored Him to reveal Himself if He were truly the Messias. But He stood before me in silence and did not answer. I, the tetrarch of Jerusalem! He only stared at me as if He had not heard me. I had been informed He had called me 'that fox.' I was prepared to forgive Him if He were the Messias in truth, for the gods have no reverence for men, not even for kings."

For the first time, Antipas drank deeply of his wine and held out his goblet for more. He shook his head over and over.

"A wretched Galilean! The impudence of Him, asserting He was the Messias of the ages! There He stood, and only gazed at me, and would not answer. Why did He not answer? He was voluble enough among His followers and before the people! I have come to the only conclusion: faced with the majesty of authority, and full of fear, He could not speak. He had lost His tongue. Therefore I knew this was no Messias, but only an insurrectionist. He was only a poverty-stricken peasant who had deceived the simple-minded and the ignorant. I was deeply angered, both against the blasphemy and the insurrection He had instigated.

"And so I said to Him, 'You are not the Messias. You are a fraud and a liar.' I cannot tell you of my rage and disappointment, and His dull staring at me. So I delivered Him to justice, and to mock His pretensions I threw a gorgeous garment on His shoulders and sent Him away."

Phillip said, "You were also enraged against one called

John the Baptist. He inveighed against you because of your wife, Herodias. You permitted his death, at the bequest of your wife."

The eyes of the brothers clashed visibly, like the coming together of swords.

Then Antipas looked at his brother with hate, and said, "Do not be ambitious. I am the tetrarch of Jerusalem, and the friend of Pontius Pilate."

Phillip shrugged. "You speak of those who are gullible. Yet you hoped that John was Elias, born again."

Antipas turned from him and directed his reddish and malevolent gaze at Lucanus. "And so I must warn you, guest though you are of my dear friend, Pontius Pilate, and a Roman citizen, that I will permit no more disorder among my people and no more inciting. Seek what truth you will, but not among the ignorant and the deceived. I have told you the truth. Let it suffice."

"There is nothing as laudable as frankness," said Pilate, smiling.

"Lucanus, like all Greeks, is superstitious," said Antipas, with another look of hate.

"Nevertheless, I shall seek the truth," said Lucanus, regarding Herod coldly. "Who can stop me?"

Antipas' nostrils distended, and he breathed loudly. "I am a civilized man. I know my duty as a guest of Pontius Pilate. Courtesy is expected of a guest. But I have a quarrel with you, most noble Lucanus." He sneered. "At my request, Pontius proscribed the Christians. He is a just man, an administrator of the Roman law. Now you have influenced him to lift that proscription, in spite of my requests and my arguments. This will set off riots again, and dangerous disorders. I am prepared to deal with them."

Pontius smiled. "I obey Caesar. Tiberius gave Lucanus a magnificent ring. Lucanus asked me to lift the proscription; he put the ring into my hand. Tiberius has great regard for him, and I could not but obey his request." He appeared to be enjoying himself.

Herod Antipas said, "I honor Caesar. But even Caesars can be deceived."

"True," said Pilate, and idly played with the stem of his goblet. Lucanus compressed his lips. He was about to speak with heat when he saw that Pilate and Herod Phillip were exchanging hard and significant glances, and that Phillip's hand had turned into a fist on the silken tablecloth. Then Pilate shook his head slightly, as if denying, and lifted the palm of his hand in a gesture asking patience.

Antipas spoke directly to Lucanus. "I have told you the truth. What you can learn otherwise, except from Pilate and myself, can only be lies. Whom will you question? The contemptible followers of Jesus? You came armed with superstitions. Children imagine many things, and what you have told us was taught you in your childhood may have been fancy on your part, or the vaporings of nameless creatures full of the belief in sorcery and magic. I remember when I was a child also. I had a dream that with my own eyes I would see the Messias!"

"And so you did," said Lucanus.

Antipas struck the table again in complete exasperation. He appealed, with his volatile eyes, to Pilate, as if to say, "What can be done with such a fool?" He said, "I understand you were a learned man, marvelously gifted in the art of healing. You were graduated from the University of Alexandria. You have traveled. Doubtless you have met wise men and scholars. Yet you, who never saw that Galilean, come here with an obstinate belief. Verily, it is too much for an intelligent man to endure!" He turned to Pilate. "I beg of you to reinstate the proscription against those who call themselves Christians, in the name of the peace of the Empire, in the name of Caesar."

"I had no choice," said Pilate, blandly, spreading out his hands in a gesture of surrender. "There was the ring of Tiberius. The meaning of the ring is that the owner may use it in the name of Caesar, as if Caesar was speaking himself. You understand that, my dear Antipas."

Antipas considered that, his small yellowish teeth biting his nether lip. His eyes sparkled, deepened, glowed. Finally he spoke to Lucanus in a changed and pleading tone. "Forgive me that I appeared to threaten you. Try to comprehend. I have heard you have a deep love for the Jewish people. Do you wish to see riots and disorders here again, and the death of the innocent? Do you wish to see the hand of Rome descend in violence on this little land, which has endured so much, and suffered so much? What has Israel to do with you, that you would destroy it?"

"I did not come to destroy," said Lucanus. "I came only as a man seeking the truth."

"Yes, yes," said Antipas, impatiently. "I was not speaking of that. But when you prevailed on Pontius Pilate to lift the proscription against the ignorant and disorderly Christians, who have considerable fierceness and dedication, you opened the gate to desperate trouble again. The Jews are an argumentative people; they will fight each other for an opinion on the Law; they disagree furiously. The proscription has scattered the Christians and has kept them apart and has prevented them from quarreling with their fellow Jews. Now they will appear again, and all will be lost."

"I pray not," said Lucanus, seriously. "Surely He was a man of peace. In time His followers will understand that."

"No," said Antipas. "You do not know the Jews."

Then Phillip spoke. "Nor do you," he said, quietly. "You have not been a friend to your people. You have been an enemy."

A great silence fell about the table. All sat like statues. Antipas looked only at his brother, and Lucanus and Pilate looked only at them. Then, after a long moment or two, Antipas said softly, "Phillip, dare you speak to me so?"

"Yes, I dare," said Phillip in as soft a voice. "You are a little, vicious man. I say this to your face. You have no stature, no honesty, no dignity, no presence. This is the end." He gazed at his half brother with detestation.

Antipas burst into a thin shout of laughter, thrusting his beard up into the air. "Oho!" he cried. "He has not forgiven me for taking his wife, Herodias! You have insulted me in the presence of my friend, but I forgive your lack of manners. You have called me 'little.' If you had been of greater stature I could not have taken your wife from you. Who, then, is the larger man?" His eyes danced malignantly and with mockery on Phillip.

Phillip's lips were white, but he spoke in a low voice. "I bear you no malice for Herodias. Had I loved her, and had she loved me, there would have been no possibility of your seduction of her. I am not debased, for no one can debase another man without his own consent. You speak of manners. It is you who lack them."

Lucanus was embarrassed. He was not accustomed to such raw quarrelings and insults, especially not among kinsmen.

Then Pilate intervened, speaking pleasantly. "You erred, Antipas, when you sought a crown. Never seek a crown from a Caesar. You are in his bad graces. It was only today that

I received a letter from him suggesting that you discreetly remove yourself. Caesars do not often suggest; they command. Will you wait for a command?"

Antipas turned as white as death, and his reddish beard became prominent against the ghastly hue of his flesh. "You are jesting," he whispered.

"No," said Pilate, still pleasantly. "Caesar looks with graciousness on your brother." He sipped some wine, while Antipas clutched the edge of the table and leaned towards him, gasping. "I called you here tonight to tell you, and Phillip. You have your Herodias; you have your enormous wealth. I suggest, however, that you leave Judea. It will be more agreeable for everyone."

Lucanus almost pitied the frantic Antipas, and averted his eyes. The humiliation should not have been before a stranger such as himself.

"I shall call upon Agrippa," said Antipas, in a shrill and choking voice.

"Do not, I advise you. It will not be looked upon with favor."

"I thought you were my friend, Pontius."

"It is as your friend that I give you this message. Were I your enemy I should have sent you a peremptory command and removed you publicly, before the sneering faces of your people."

Antipas swung upon his brother, and his hand leaped to his dagger. Phillip stared at him with haughty disdain. "You have done this!" cried Antipas. "You have betrayed me, you have plotted against me, out of revenge!"

"I suggest," said Pilate, "that no harm come to Phillip. In truth, I have designated my chief officer, Plotius, to guard Phillip's house, in case you are indiscreet enough to violate the wishes of Tiberius and cause Phillip to have an—accident."

Lucanus stood up. He said coldly, "I am weary. I must implore your generosity, Pilate, and ask you to excuse me."

Antipas turned his rage upon him. He pointed a finger at Lucanus, and it shook. "It was you who, using Caesar's ring, not only induced Pilate to lift the proscription against the Christians, but to suggest my exile in order to protect your ragged friends!"

Pilate lifted an admonishing hand. "No one betrayed you, Antipas, neither your brother nor myself. Let us have done with these accusations."

He crooked a finger at a slave and ordered a litter for Lucanus. The Greek bowed to those at the table and left the house.

"I also suggest," said Pilate to Antipas, "that no harm come to Lucanus. He is under Tiberius' protection, and you know what a bloody man he has become."

Chapter Forty-nine

Lucanus told his friends, Hilell and Arieh, of what had taken place in Pilate's house. They listened with profound interest, then Hilell said with joy, "Let us thank God that Herod Antipas is to be removed!"

"Nevertheless, Pilate should not have humiliated him before me."

"He is an inscrutable man, and had his reasons." Hilell then went on to say that Mary, the Mother of Christ, had returned to her people for a visit in Nazareth. There had been a death among her relatives. "I will visit her there," said Lucanus. Hilell remarked it was a considerable journey. "However," he said, "you will be able to see Galilee, where He first taught. It is a beautiful spot! But there is a little town there, called Tiberias, build by Herod in honor of Caesar. The Jews regard it as an abomination, and will not visit it. Nor would the Christ. He spoke on a mount nearby, in the synagogue, which is plain and humble, as are the people. But there is no hurry. Remain with us until Leah and Arieh are married."

"I must be about my business," said Lucanus, regretfully.

"Then we will wait until you return."

When he was alone that night, Lucanus wrote what he had heard from Pontius Pilate and Herod Antipas about Jesus. His Gospel was growing. He put nothing in it of his own opinions, but only the information which had been imparted to him. Sometimes an overwhelming longing came to him. If only he had seen the Christ himself, if only he had been able to speak with Him and look in his marvelous eyes! I should not have deserted Him when His followers forsook him in fear, he thought.

The next morning, early, he went in a litter to the house of James and John without the gates. Hilell had sent a message to the two young brothers, who had agreed, somewhat sul-

lenly, to receive Lucanus. Hilell had written them that but
for Lucanus the proscription against them would have remained. Once beyond the gates, and descending the hill of
Sion, Lucanus looked back through the hot and smarting
dust. Though it was early in the morning, the yellow walls
of Jerusalem glared in a terrible light; a dazzling and bleak
incandescence illuminated the stones of the walls and the
rolling, stony mountains. Even the cultivated hills lay in
darkness, fold on fold of bitter desolation.

The clustered houses outside the walls climbed the mountains, yellowish gray and burning in the light. Most of them
were poor, with little patches of dusty gardens, palms, pines,
olive and fruit trees panting about them. Never had Lucanus
seen so parched a land, so dry, so dusty. The servants who
carried the litter began to gasp when they ascended one of
the hills, and they finally stopped with relief before a little
yellowish house poorer than all the others. A young man stood
on the steps, with a gloomy expression, waiting in silence,
his brow dark. He must have made a remark, for he was
joined by another young man with a very narrow pale face,
fierce black eyebrows, a full but hard mouth, and a mass of
chestnut curls flowing over his high head. The first man was
clothed in a gray garment over which he had thrown a dark
green robe; the second wore a dull yellow robe. Both appeared
to be very poor. They said nothing as Lucanus alighted from
the litter; they merely stood and gazed down at him. "I am
Lucanus, a physician, guest of Hilell ben Hamram," said Lucanus, trying to smile in the face of the combined formidable
stare the others had fixed on him. "You expect me?"

The two looked at each other. The older man's face was
not as narrow as his brother's, but he had a long, thin nose,
a beard, dark hair, and a thinner mouth. He had less of the
younger man's air of indomitable fanaticism and frozen wildness. He said in Aramaic, slurred by the Galilean accent,
"We expect you." They gave Lucanus no other greeting. "I
am James, son of Zebedee of Capharnaum, and this is my
brother, John," and James indicated the younger man with the
intimidating face and large vengeful eyes which had the fixity
of the ecstatic temperament. "Sons of the thunderstorm!"
How well that description fitted them! Lucanus felt their intense hostility, and their reluctance even to speak to him, and
their passionate suspicion.

"I am a Christian," he said, walking towards them, and

hoping to soften them. But they did not answer him. With a movement of his head James indicated that Lucanus was to follow them, and they led him, in silence, to the rear of the little, miserable house, where the walls cast some shade in the violent light. There was no garden here, only yellow dust and stones; two wooden benches stood there near the wall of the house. The brothers sat down on one of the benches and resumed their scrutiny of Lucanus, and he sat on the other bench. He sighed; these men were going to be difficult. He was the stranger, the uncircumcised, the unclean. If they had any wine or bread they were going to offer him none, nor even thank him for rescuing them.

He had thought to tell them of Keptah, of the Chaldeans, of the Babylonians, of Joseph ben Gamliel, of the Greeks and their Unknown God, and all the prophecies which had come down from the ages, not only from Jews but from the others. But he knew at once that not only would they not understand, but they would be incredulous and more resentful than ever. Looking at them gravely, he wondered how these, who had walked with God, could be so inhospitable, so without charity for the stranger, so hard and fierce.

Under their combined and inimical stare Lucanus spoke with hesitation of the Gospel he was writing. He told them that in his travels he had heard much of the Messias. He wished only for them to tell him of what they knew themselves, so he could continue his work. "I never saw Him, but I have loved Him for many years," he said, gently.

John spoke for the first time, in a peremptory voice: "We will tell you what we have seen with our eyes." He drew a deep breath, and the coldly savage ecstasy of his eyes became more concentrated. "But you will not understand. Did you know Him? Did you hear Him? Without that you can know nothing."

Yes, thought Lucanus, you knew Him and heard Him, but His gentleness and love are not in you, nor His charity. You will make good evangelists, but there will be little mercy or tenderness or kindness in what you say or do.

James said in a pent voice, "If only He had struck down this city when it dared to reject Him! Why did He not bring down the fury of heaven upon it?"

Lucanus made no reply. He rested his hands on his knees and waited. The brothers exchanged another glance; they were not twins, but it was apparent that they were inseparable and conversed with each other with eloquent glances and had little need of speech. The terrible heat penetrated even to this dusty shade; Lucanus wiped his forehead and face with his kerchief. The others resumed their staring at him, and now for the first time curiosity appeared on their fervid faces. Lucanus' calm, his gravity, the beauty of his countenance, the serene blue of his eyes, had begun to impress them, and to mitigate some of their natural enmity for the stranger.

It was John, the younger, who started to speak, in short and reluctant sentences. But after a little he was seized with uncontrollable rapture; his eyes took on a vivid and inner light, and he gazed at the fiery sky. His voice became eloquent. "In the beginning was the Word, and the Word was with God, and the Word was God! Blessed is His Name! In Him was life; and the life was the light of men!"

John spoke of Christ's miracles, His teachings, of John the Baptist. When he was speaking of the wild and vehement John the Baptist, his voice took on an emphatic and lyrical quality. Here was one he could truly understand! Here was one who spoke of wrath and the vengeance of God on the unbelievers, of judgment to come, of appalling divulgences. Here was one who warned, who did not speak of mercy! The passionate denizen from the desert, the eater of wild honey and locusts, the half-naked bearded cryer before the Lord, was close to the heart of John. He clenched his thin hands on his knees; he shuddered with delight and joy. "I have had great Revelations!" he cried, beating his knees with his fists. "Of the Day of Judgment, of the frightful things which will take place, of the steaming pits of hell into which evil souls shall fall like snowflakes, of avenging seraphim and cherubim, of the good and the wicked which will be eternally divided, of the anger of God and the forever condemned! I shall write of these things myself!"

"Yes, yes," said Lucanus, soothingly. "But I have come to learn of His words, and His miracles." He did not like the awful gleaming in the eyes of the young John.

John's distended nostrils quivered. He was seeing the most dreadful visions with his inner eye, and he rejoiced in them vengefully. He started at Lucanus' voice, and looked at him blindly. James said, "Our visitor has asked of God's words and miracles among men. We were witnesses. Continue."

So John, whose gestures became more eloquent, more driving, told Lucanus what he wished to know. Time went by, breathless with heat and acrid dust, and Lucanus listened with all his soul. John's voice took on triumphant trumpet notes and jubilation. Whereas others, in speaking of the Christ, talked with love and tender joy, John spoke with rising exaltation and power. Sometimes he could not contain himself: he rose and paced feverishly, his narrow face blazing. He appeared to grow in stature and strength, walking from sharp purple shade to sharper brilliance of light, so his features were alternately darkened and illuminated, his hands at one moment shadowy and the next like hands of flame. In spite of himself Lucanus was fascinated, both by the strangeness of the young evangelist and the stories he related. Sometimes James broke in, when John, weary, stopped for a moment to clarify a parable or a story, and John would stare at him impatiently with a welling eye. During pauses Lucanus wrote rapidly with his stylus, so that all would be accurate. Once or twice he thought, This man would only dismay the thoughtful, the gentle, the compassionate. But he will be like a pillar of fearful fire to the languid, the faded, the selfish, the indifferent, the skeptical, the apathetic, and to those who are capable of excitement by visions and scorn the precise. He will be a terror to the materialistic. He appeals to passions, and can arouse passions even in the most complacent. When John related what he had seen and heard, it was not with the wonder and happiness and sorrow expressed by others to Lucanus. He told his story with a furious air of defiance, as if challenging incredulity and ready to smite it.

He told of the crucifixion, without the grief and fear and sadness of Priscus, but with rage and agony, and his vengeful face became even more vengeful. Sometimes James moved uneasily, not in disagreement with his brother, but at the sight of his glaring eye and the tone of his voice. And sometimes John would regard Lucanus with a fierceness that indicated he almost believed that Lucanus himself had driven the nails into the sacred flesh. I stand condemned as the evil Gentile who destroyed the Body of the Christ, he reflected, and it is apparent that he believes that I am utterly consigned to his simmering hell.

Noon wheeled in intolerable light over the little poor house, and the shade shortened. Now John was exhausted; he fell on the bench and covered his sweating face with his hands and sobbed aloud. He muttered, over and over, "The Day of Eternal Judgment! I have seen it in my soul; my soul trembles with fear and yet is exalted!"

Two goats came around the side of the house, searching for coolness and more thistles and dry grass. James went into the house and brought out a bronze pail and milked the inquisitive animals. He took the pail back into the house and returned outside again with three earthenware cups and a plate of dark bread and a little cheese. He put these beside him on the bench and looked kindly at his brother. "Let us rest, and eat," he said.

"A day is approaching when there will be no more drinking and eating," said John, and his voice shook. Nevertheless, he dropped his hands; his pale face was mottled by the desperate pressure of his fingers. He looked at the three cups foaming with warm goat's milk, and his mouth opened as if to protest. He was not as yet prepared to eat and drink easily with the Gentile, or to accept his presence with equanimity. But James took one of the cups and gave it to Lucanus, and presented the pewter plate of bread and cheese. Lucanus smiled at him gratefully, and James' face took on an uncertain sheepiness. "You will understand that my brother's soul is still unreconciled to events," he said. John frowned implacably. In silence he took a cup also, but refused the food. "It is commanded of us that we must bring the tidings to all the nations of the world," he said, as if in dissent.

"I am one of the 'nations of the world,'" said Lucanus, both with pity and with some vexation for this proud and stricken and ecstatic man. John drank gloomily. His thoughts had already left Lucanus; it was as if he conversed now only with himself, and inwardly prayed with mounting fervor. But James looked at Lucanus with more and more uncertainty, as if his opinion of him was changing and he regretted his former inhospitality. He said, finally, "Do not think we are ungrateful for what you have done for us."

John lifted his head and said, scornfully, "The Lord would not have permitted us long to be persecuted!"

Lucanus made no comment. His litter arrived for him and he rose to go, thanking James for the good milk and the refreshment. James rose and followed him to the front of the house, but John remained on his bench, his head bowed and his breast heaving. When Lucanus entered the rich litter and lifted his hand in farewell James hesitated, then lifted his own hand awkwardly in a salute and turned away quickly. Lucanus felt more pity for the brothers. They had been exhorted to perform a gigantic task among the strangers; their spirits dreaded it, yet they must obey.

When the litter-bearers mounted the hot white stairs leading to the gates of Jerusalem they stopped to rest for a moment, and from this height Lucanus could see the little town of Bethlehem in the distance, all glimmering square yellow houses with flat roofs. There Jesus had been born, in that dusty place, and there, on the mounts nearby, had shone the great Star and the shepherds had heard the voices of angels bringing the message of the ages. A land of portents, a most strange and compelling land!

Hilell awaited him in the gardens, where fountains gave a coolness against the heat. Lucanus looked about him with pleasure. The walls flowed with flowers, spilling in a cloud of purple. Flagged walks wound about square pools of water, in which gold fish swam, and bright yellow bushes were starred with flowers. Blossoming oleanders showed red blossoms in their thick green leaves. Beds of crimson and white roses were surrounded by reddish or brown little paths, carefully raked. Tall thin date palms were rich with fruit, and carob trees cast shade. The chattering and sparkling fountains threw water onto the grass, which gleamed vividly with an almost impossible greenness. Lucanus drank some chilled wine and told Hilell of his visit to James and John. "Such men make life difficult for the peaceful," commented Hilell, shaking his handsome head.

"Tomorrow I leave for Nazareth and Galilee," said Lucanus.

"The lifting of the proscription against the Christians has aroused much excitement in Jerusalem," said Hilell. "By the way, Pontius left suddenly for Rome this morning; he sent me a sprightly message of pleasure; he never cared for Judea. And a group of centurions inportantly delivered a message for you from Tiberius, with your ring." He gave Lucanus the wonderful ring, and Lucanus put it upon his finger, then opened Caesar's letter:

"Greetings to the noble Lucanus, son of Diodorus Cyrinus:

"It was with joy that I received the ring which I had given you, and which I am returning. I am an old man now, and very weary. Long years ago I cynically expected to receive this ring on many occasions. But the years passed, and there was silence. When the ring finally arrived from Pontius Pilate, with the request you had made that some proscription he had placed upon a small Jewish sect be lifted by him, and by inference, by myself, I was surprised. You had asked nothing for yourself. I pondered. I have thought many times of you, my dear Lucanus. I have heard much of you, from the house of Diodorus Cyrinus. You will be happy to know that your family is well. Your brother, Priscus, has been recalled for a long furlough. I have heard that you cured him of a monstrous disease. Will it surprise you to know that I am not skeptical about this? I accepted the story utterly. In my darkest hours I turn my thoughts to you. Sometimes I am tempted to command that you return to Rome, that I may converse with you and look upon your face. Then I know that you would not desire it, though you would obey. I do not command such men as yourself, not even for my own pleasure. I regard them as Romans once regarded their gods; they are not for even Caesars to command.

"You have undoubtedly heard the most frightful stories about my cruelties and oppressions in these latter years. Do not deny them, even to yourself. They are true. I am full of hatred, and my hatred grows with time. I revenge myself on those who corrupted me—the people of Rome, and their creatures, the senators and the tribunes, and the politicians, and all the greedy and lightless vultures who surround me. Once I had a dream of making Rome again Rome, full of virtue, peace, justice and honor, as your father dreamt. What Caesar can prevail against his people? They defile him. They drag his purple down into their gutters. They deafen his ears with their hungry demands. They dishonor his honor with their appetites. They rust his sword with their slavering tongues. I am lost. Think of me with kindness, if you will, for I love you as a father."

Lucanus could not refrain from weeping at this letter, and he gave it to Hilell to read. Hilell, beginning to read coldly, ended by being much moved. "Poor man," he murmured at last. "How embittered and distraught he must be to confide so in anyone."

He said, "In spite of Pilate's advice Herod Antipas has appealed to his brother-in-law, Agrippa, in Rome. Agrippa has much influence. Therefore there will be a delay in Antipas' departure from Jerusalem, until it is decided what power Agrippa has with Caesar. Delays are the formidable arms of princes. There will be no immediate resumption of the persecution of the Christians here; one cannot tell of the future. It depends on their own discretion, which, in fervent men, is lacking. The high priest is in a fury, and sends constant messages to Antipas. Who knows what the future will bring? We can be sure of only one thing: it will bring change, either good or evil.

"I have friends in many places in the world. The Jewish Christians are attempting to proselytize in Damascus, and there is much anger there. So I have heard today. It seems that some of the younger and more fervent disciples of the Christ have arrived in that city, and preach and exhort constantly, bringing their tidings to the very pious Jews there in residence. I have had a letter this morning from my good friend, Saul of Tarsus, a Roman citizen, a member of a noble Jewish house, and a lawyer of much magnitude, and a Roman official. He is going to Damascus to put down the insurrection and disorders in the city. He takes his Roman duties seriously. He had intended to visit me here, but business at the last moment, in the law courts, prevented it. Saul is a man of no meager power, and he is stern. I fear for the Christians in Damascus."

Lucanus considered this with anxiety. Then, as he pondered, he was suddenly exhilarated and mysteriously consoled. "Do not worry," he said, and wondered at his own words. "All will be well."

"I do not like platitudes," said Hilell, smiling, "for I am a logical man with no particular optimism. But when you say 'All will be well,' then I feel that you speak with the tongues of angels, and not with the tongues of men."

Chapter Fifty

Hilell wished to provide Lucanus with an escort to Nazareth and Galilee. But Lucanus refused, with gratitude. He needed only a sturdy, powerful horse, capable of climbing on short legs. He would spend many nights on the road in taverns. Hilell was horrified. Even knowing Lucanus as he did, it seemed incredible of him that a Roman citizen of a noble family, a physician of considerable wealth, a friend of Caesar's, should travel like a common man. "I am not trying to be humble," said Lucanus, smiling. "I wish only to move fast without encumbrances, and to see the country."

The horse Hilell produced was Arabian of a calm disposition and accustomed to long journeys and dust and mountains. Lucanus fastened his physician's pouch to the saddle, a blanket, and his painting materials. Hilell insisted on pro-

viding a basket of fine foods and wines. Lucanus would
wrap his head in cloth against the blasting sun and wear a
heavy mantle to cover his legs. With misgivings Hilell bade
him farewell, shaking his head. Lucanus cantered away, waving his hand to his friend.

It was early morning. He left Jerusalem; the air was already hot. The fresh horse trotted briskly. They crossed the
River Cedron over a stone bridge. The sky possessed a deep
golden color, and this was reflected in streaks and shadows
on the quiet, narrow waters, with its ripples of brighter
gold; the banks were guarded by black pointed cypresses.
Hilell had advised going by way of Bethany and Jericho, so
that Lucanus would approach the River Jordan, following it
to Galilee, which Lucanus would visit first. Lucanus soon
found himself in a wilderness, desolate, reddish brown, tree-
less, the earth tangled with high thistles, all surrounded by
low flat hills the color of brass shimmering with heat. The
rough and narrow road was empty, for it was one little
taken, others preferring the longer way on the Via Mare
near the sea. Sometimes Lucanus passed a lonely Roman
fortress, from the tops of which soldiers peered at him
curiously. Once he was halted and challenged by an of-
ficious officer, who could not understand how a humbly clad
man could be in possession of such a fine horse and on
such a road. When Lucanus revealed his identity the officer
was more puzzled than ever, but respectful. He invited
Lucanus to take wine with him, and as Lucanus was now
thirsty he accepted and entered the cool depths of the
fortress and sat on a stone bench to drink wine with the
young officer. Upon an inquisitive question, Lucanus replied
that he was going to visit Tiberias. The officer noted his
splendid rings and said, "Though no Jew would ever attempt to rob you, not even the barbarian Samaritans, there
will be mean, poor caravans on the road who will not hesi-
tate to cut your throat for those rings." So Lucanus put
them in his pouch.

When he was on his way again he did encounter one or
two small caravans of camels and asses and men with dark
fierce faces who stared at his horse. But Lucanus stared
back at them; he was of high stature and there was a sword
at his belt and his blue eyes were cold and unafraid.

He arrived at Bethany, dancing in wavering heat waves.
The tight little streets were stepped and floating in yellow
dust, and the people moved about noisily chattering and

arguing, their stern faces dark with the sun, their heads protected by headcloths of black, white or brown, with dusty robes of the same color. The tiny shops boiled with people, all of whom appeared irritated, and dogs barked and children played on the steps of the climbing streets, and women with jars on their heads stopped to gossip. A heavy smell of roasting meat, acrid wine, herbs and garlic and offal hung over the little town, and Lucanus was happy to be out of it within a short time. Then he was in the wilderness again. The mountains changed, became dull, terra cotta in color, with outcroppings of clustered villages of a whitish gray upon them. The plains about Lucanus were forsaken, with an infinitely solitary and lonely air, scorched and empty; an occasional sticklike dusty palm battled for its wretched life on the brown and crumbling soil which was scattered with black boulders. Scrub and half-dead bushes, matted with the pervading thistles, and rearing masses of cacti only increased the melancholy of the wild scene. And the sun, like a brazen orb, hurled down its cataracts of unbearable light.

At noon Lucanus suddenly came upon an intensely blue pool of water in the wasteland, fed by an underground spring. To his delight, green-yellow young willows nodded about it and swept their fragile golden branches in the hot air. He tied up his horse, after it had drunk its thirsty fill of the cool water, and gave it a bag of oats. Then he sat down in the shade of the willows and opened his basket of food. He ate a portion of delicious roast fowl, stuffed with breaded herbs and onions, some oaten cakes which he covered with honey, and two rich pastries. He drank Hilell's excellent wine, which he had taken care first to place in the cool water. It was like sitting in the center of a mirage, with the savage and barren land all about him, and the stony hills fuming with heat and dust in the near distance. He saw no living creature anywhere; a huge silence lay on the earth and the hills. He found himself drowsing, shook his head and mounted his horse again.

He took care to keep to the road outside of Jericho, but he could see the town itself, all crowding, two-storied brown houses pierced with clumps of cypresses, sweltering in the heat, and even at this distance clamorous with voices. Now he encountered herds of sheep, browsing on the tawny grass, and shepherds with somber faces, or numerous goats guarded by sweating and noisy children. He urged on his horse towards the River Jordan, for night came swiftly in this land and Hilell had told him of an inn near the river. Almost imperceptibly the land began to grow more fertile; an occasional mount bore terraces upon it, enclosing little patches of green grass or palm or olive trees, and even some fruit. Vineyards threw out their fragrance on the dry hot air. Lucanus climbed a barren mount, stones falling about him loudly in the silence. He reached the top, and there below him lay the narrow and winding Jordan, impossibly green, bordered with willows and tall refreshing trees. Smelling water, the horse bounded down the mount and increased his speed.

Upon reaching the high banks of the river, Lucanus dismounted, and man and horse slipped and clambered down the warm wet earth to the water. The horse drank deeply; Lucanus bathed his head, face and hands. A sweetness of fertility lay on the emerald river, which wound sharply into the distance. Little farms stood near it, the white houses clear in the sun or sheltered by trees and cypresses. From this spot even the pervading mountains had a less stricken and terrible aspect. A child, with a flock of geese, approached Lucanus, staring at him inquisitively with great black eyes. Lucanus greeted the little girl kindly; she hesitated, then replied in Aramaic with the accent of the Samaritans. He beckoned to her, wishing to give her one of the sweetmeats in his basket, but she did not approach nearer. She thought him a Judean, and the Samaritans were always in a quarrel with their fellow Jews, thinking them too cultured, too superior, and playing tricks upon them during the holidays, such as lighting fires on the mountains to confuse the priests. Suddenly she laughed shrilly, stuck her tongue out at him with impudence and ran off with her geese, who hissed and squawked behind her.

Lucanus, mounting again, followed the incredibly winding river, and refreshed his senses with the small farms, the sound of cattle and sheep, the twittering of many bright birds in the dark green trees, the golden fields of barley and oats and wheat in the falling light, and the pleasant white, square farmhouses with their gay gardens. The sides of the mountains were cultivated here; they looked as though colorful Persian rugs, gigantic and many-hued, had been tossed on them. Now the light fell more rapidly. The river changed to running gold between its banks; the sky flushed to scarlet and jade over the mountains. The air became cooler.

Then Lucanus found the inn near the river, with a cobbled courtyard made of gleaming black stone. The inn was small but clean, and the landlord greeted Lucanus with pleasure, noting his horse. Not even Lucanus' unaccented Aramaic annoyed him, or chilled his Samaritan heart. He did not often shelter travelers with such horses, and Lucanus' manner, at least, assured the landlord that here was no poverty-stricken man. He was so pleased at having this visitor that he decided not to charge him more than three times the regular fee for food and shelter. He led Lucanus to a small neat room facing the river, and assured him that he would find the bed comfortable and untroubled by fleas or lice. Lucanus looked at the bare white wood of the floor and nodded.

He sat down wearily on the bed and yawned. The inn was filled with the hoarse voices of men and their loud laughter. Horses stamped in the stable. Feet sounded on the stones of the courtyard; a serving girl or two laughed merrily. Through the rough lattices that covered the one little window a scent of fertile earth and grapes and manure invaded the room, accompanied by the good smell of roasting goat meat and baking bread, and thick spicy soup. A maidservant, without knocking on the door, brought Lucanus a pitcher of hot water, a bowl, and a rough brown linen towel. He gave her a coin, and she was so surprised and delighted that she favored him with an arch giggle and examined him more closely. His appearance pleased her, though his fair skin was hot and red and burned from the sun. She curtsied and left him, and went down to the kitchen to talk of the strange gentleman who had given her such a rich coin.

Lucanus opened the lattices and looked at the blood-red sky over the mountains; he heard the murmurous voice of the river, talking to itself among its trees and willows. He carefully washed his face, wincing, and anointed his burning flesh. He then went down a steep little flight of stone stairs to the common dining room, where at least ten travelers were already seated. A huge stone fireplace crackled with lighted wood, and on a spit meat slowly turned, and a girl basted it with its fat droppings. The floor of the room was flagged, the walls white-plastered. The other travelers fell silent at the sight of Lucanus, their swarthy faces becoming watchful as they tried to place him as a

Judean, a Galilean, a Samaritan. They had put aside their headcloths and their hair had been rudely combed; their eyes glistened in the mingled firelight and lamplight.

He greeted them carefully in Aramaic. At first they did not answer him; they shrugged and exchanged glances. Then they replied, warily. The Galileans were almost as fair as he, and many of the Judeans. But he did not have a Jewish appearance, for all his perfect speech. Now the glistening eyes became suspicious. He smiled at them, but they did not smile in return. He thought anxiously of his pouch upstairs, with his rings. He had locked his door, but thieves were never detained by locks. He remembered old Cusa and his skill, and smiled again. The men did not speak for some time; they felt an alien presence. The men glanced at Lucanus' poor clothing, and were puzzled. He had an air of assurance and calm, in spite of his clothing. They had already heard of his fine horse. He was mysterious, with his princely manner, and they did not like mysteries.

A silence brooded over the once vociferous table. The soup was thick and good, laden with spices and herbs, and filled with bits of boiled flour and meat. The travelers ate in morose quiet, peeping occasionally at Lucanus, who was enjoying his meal. The servants, who had heard of his generosity, served him first and with deference, hoping for more largesse. He received the tenderest pieces of the roast goat and the juiciest share of a boiled fowl. The wine was execrable, but his goblet was kept filled. His plate was constantly replenished with the ripest dates and many little salt olives and boiled vegetables. One of the maids, with a flourish, cut open a cactus fruit and elaborately spooned out the soft interior for him so that he would not be wounded on the thorns of the skin. All this the travelers noted with mingled resentment and heightened hostility and suspicion. Lucanus ate hungrily. At the conclusion of the meal he opened his purse and deposited what was considered an enormous gratuity on the table beside his plate. The travelers stirred and looked at each other.

One of them, an arrogant bearded man with angry eyes, spoke bluntly. "Who are you, Master?"

"I?" said Lucanus, surprised. "I am a physician, Lucanus by name."

"A Roman?" The query was full of contempt.

"No. A Greek." Lucanus smiled.

"You speak Aramaic well, Master."

"I speak many languages." For the first time Lucanus was aware of the hostility.

"You wear a sword. Is it customary for physicians to wear swords?"

"In a peaceful country?" added another.

Lucanus looked at his sword, and then at the threatening faces. "I am an excellent swordsman," he said, quietly. "I was the best athlete in Alexandria."

No one answered him, but all of them glowered. Then one finally spoke, uneasy at the cold blue steadiness of Lucanus' eyes. "We are a peaceable people. We dislike weapons."

Lucanus shrugged. "I sleep with my sword in my hand," he said, and rose.

He had had the thought of wandering about on foot after dining. He abandoned the idea. He went to his room and carefully locked his door and the lattices. He took his sword from its sheath and laid it on the bed. He was suddenly exhausted. He lay down and was instantly asleep. He kept his lamp burning.

He rose just after dawn, and endeared himself to the landlord by not protesting the outrageous bill; the man sent him on his way with loud blessings and the girls gathered in the courtyard to shrill farewell to him. He followed the river as well as he could, but sometimes the road wound away from it and he was in the wilderness again for a short time. Now many of the high hills were broken and bronzed, the color of the earth, against a whitely flaming sky. They echoed back the sound of the trotting horse. Lucanus felt alone in a world of vast desolation; sometimes he saw bleached houses on the hills, with a dusty cypress or two, and he wondered how it was possible for any human being to live in this frightful place. When the road turned back to the brilliantly green river again he rejoiced, and climbed down its banks to bathe his hot arms and legs. At noon he ate of the napkin-wrapped contents of his basket and drank some wine, and panted in the unbearable heat. Patches of the river blazed emerald in partings between trees. But in his hands it was cool and clear and fresh.

He rode through tiny villages, and dogs followed him, barking and snapping at the heels of his horse. He was now in the province of Decapolis, and he noted that the people were becoming fairer and taller, blue or gray of eye and light brown of hair or beard. When he passed a herd of goats on the road the peasant glanced up at him, smiled pleasantly, and saluted with his whip. Riding through a village, he passed the little house of a carpenter; the man was surrounded by his four sons, and they chattered as they worked on the raw yellow wood which had a resinous odor. Lucanus thought of Jesus and His foster father. So he had worked, with hammer and chisel and saw, fashioning the plain furniture of the countryside. So Joseph had admonished Him for striking a nail crookedly. Lucanus felt closer to Christ near the carpenters than he had felt in Jerusalem or with John and James. A woman came out of the house with a pail of milk and some cups, and father and sons stopped to drink deeply. The woman held a distaff in her hands and smiled at Lucanus. Had Christ's Mother appeared so, to refresh her Son and her husband?

That twilight he passed over into the province of Galilee and would have continued to the Sea of Galilee itself, but he found a little inn just as night fell. He was in the country of Jesus, and when he wrapped his blanket about him in that poor place he felt that he had come home.

Chapter Fifty-one

On proceeding the next morning, Lucanus was impressed by the great change in the landscape and the people of Galilee. He passed through a hamlet of little white houses, staring with blinding light under the early sun, surrounded by little fertile gardens and farms and then beyond mountains of a peculiar and gleaming blackness, broken and rough, all against a colorless sky of hot radiance. The clothing of both men and women, whom he passed on the road or saw tending kine and black-faced sheep, was gayer here, and among the dark purple and black robes he saw yellow and red and blue. They were taller than those in Decapolis or Judea, and exceedingly fair, with golden or red hair and bright blue or light gray eyes, and pale or rosy skins. Men were using scythes on the thistles and cacti, preparing the recovered land for wheat and trees, and there was a cheerful air about them, simple and kind and rustic. Children tended small lambs and fowl about rippling little streams that crept from the jade Jordan, and laughing as they splashed in the water or threw stones into it. Women sat on doorsteps, nursing babies or spinning or scolding toddling infants. A deep and quiet peace stood over the countryside, unmarred by the basalt mountains and the heat.

Lucanus left the river to follow the road, which climbed a black and jagged mount covered with boulders the same color. He reached the top to give his horse a breathing space and looked about him at what lay below. He was instantly stunned and awed by the scene. He was like one who had laboriously struggled over a dark and barren mountain from hell and then suddenly was confronted by Paradise, suffused with an ineffable radiance. For, in a cup of folding mountains, pale yellowish heliotrope, lay the Sea of Galilee, shining and absolutely still, celestially blue and brilliant, with darker blue shadows streaking its flat and incandescent plain. Here was not only calm, but an unearthly peace more than a complete silence. Even as he watched, the cup of mountains brightened, and appeared to coil about the Sea like a protecting python, their hollows filled with gilded, dimpled light; the silent purplish shadows on the Sea deepened over the blue expanse.

The River Jordan wound away from the Sea, emerald green and surrounded by rich fertility of willows and trees and shade and warm fecund earth. No voice or movement broke the hushed quiet, though on the blackish slope below Lucanus olive and palm groves had been planted, and vineyards and fruit trees. The foliage of the olives had the aspect of fretted silver; the green palms did not sway in the pure and windless air; the pomegranates bore their red fruit on their branches like jewels. Sheep slept about the olive trees, their wool pale gold. There was no cry of bird here in this aureate effulgence. The peace beyond understanding, the light that never lay on land or sea, was here caught as in glowing crystal, eternal and unchanging.

Lucanus sat on his horse like a statue for a long time, breathing the bright air and basking in the awesome peace. Then he saw Tiberias on the edge of the water, the little city built by Herod Antipas in honor of Tiberius, and accursed and avoided by the Jews, for the city had been raised on the site of an old cemetery which had been called Rakkath. The black basalt of the mountain had been used to build the Roman fortress which guarded the town, and many of the houses, though those in the very center were white and saffron, with gleaming flat roofs.

Lucanus thought, Here was what He had known, and here is where He walked and taught and brought men to Him without question. He knew this turquoise Sea and these amber mountains shadowed with violet.

He began the slow descent to the valley and the Sea, over the little rough road. He had just reached the bottom when he heard the sound of hoofs, and six soldiers and a centurion cantered from the fortress towards him, armored and helmeted, with spears in their hands which caught the light like flame. The centurion rode ahead and saluted him, and grimly smiled. "Greetings to the noble Lucanus, son of Diodorus Cyrinus," he said in Latin, enjoying Lucanus' surprise. He was a squat, middle-aged man with the Roman's eagle face and harsh eyes and a sun-browned skin. "I am Aulus, the commander of the fortress."

"Greetings, Aulus," said Lucanus. "But how did you know I was coming?"

"Your friend, Hilell ben Hamram, wrote me and requested that you be given all honor and comfort."

Lucanus, though reminding himself of Hilell's solicitude, was somewhat chagrined. He had hoped to find a small inn where he could remain for some days, meditating in this holy place and wandering where he would and exploring the territory. But he had no choice except to smile in gratitude at Aulus, who was watching him. Aulus said, and his hard face softened, "I was a young subaltern under the heroic Diodorus and loved him as a father, for he was a great man, full of virtue. It delights me that I now look upon his adopted son."

The soldiers surrounded Lucanus and the centurion, and they trotted towards the little town, and through the gates of the fortress. They led him into the fortress and into a small dining room where refreshments were waiting. Aulus ceremoniously drew out a chair for his guest; here was all blue shade and coolness within the black stony walls. "I cannot offer you ostrich wings or the pointed tongues of flamingos, such as they eat in Rome," said Aulus. "But we have good fish from the Sea, moist dark bread, a goose, fruit and wine of the country." He paused and winked. "Shall we first have a goblet of excellent Syrian whiskey? It is potent and makes a man forget his burdens."

Lucanus thought the day early for whiskey, but he accepted politely. The liquor was amber in the goblet, but acrid and burning on the tongue and in the throat. Nevertheless, after a few sips he felt himself exhilarated, and laughed and jested with the centurion. His sun-flushed face reddened; his blue eyes sparkled; he appeared a youth again. Aulus told him that he had engaged apartments for him in the best inn in Tiberias, on the basalt-strewn shore of the Sea, where he would be comfortable. "You are the guest of Rome," said the centurion. "It is well known that you are under the protection of Caesar." Aulus paused. In his letter Hilell had merely mentioned that Lucanus wished to tour the country, which intrigued him as a traveler and as a physician. He was also interested in Jewish medicine. After his signature Hilell had drawn the minute picture of a fish. The sun wrinkles about the centurion's strenuous eyes deepened. He refilled Lucanus' goblet with more whiskey and pretended to do the same with his. He had observed Lucanus' original reserve; there was nothing like good whiskey to loosen a man's tongue. Lucanus exclaimed over the small fresh fish, which had been broiled over coals of wood; he delighted in the well-cooked goose, which had been stuffed with breaded herbs and onions; the salad, fruit and cheese were simple but fresh and excellent in flavor. The deep blue silence which surrounded them, the whiskey and the food, diminished some of Lucanus' normal taciturnity. He looked at Aulus with affection. "Never have I eaten so splendid a meal," he said, leaning back on the bench to sip his wine and enjoy his sense of well-being.

Aulus smiled; he wondered what the real reason was for Lucanus' visit to this quiet place. Lucanus had been the guest of Pontius Pilate, that ruthless and haughty patrician; he had dined with Herod Antipas. He had been a protégé of Tiberius. He was wealthy, the adopted son of a noble house. Aulus did not believe he was merely touring, and that he would find anything of interest here in medicine. It could be that he was very dangerous, a handsome spy. Aulus scratched his chin and reflected. He had not only himself to protect, but several of his soldiers, who loved him.

Idly Aulus dipped his finger in his goblet, and, as if thinking of something else, he slowly moved his wet finger over the table and drew a crude fish. Then he looked up quickly at Lucanus with his sharp and piercing black eyes. Lucanus saw the wet image drawn in wine. His face changed, became gentle yet amazed. He returned Aulus' regard, then deliberately wet his own finger and drew the same image. Aulus frowned, still suspicious and very surprised. He said,

"Have things become more orderly in Jerusalem since the crucifixion of that Galilean Jew, Jesus? I have heard they were very bad for a time."

Lucanus looked at the wall thoughtfully. He too was suspicious. Then he opened his pouch and drew out his rings and put them on his fingers. They scintillated in the cool dusk of the small dining room, and Aulus looked at them with admiration. "This ring," said Lucanus, "was given to me by Caesar when I was young. I never used it until three months ago, when I gave it to Pontius Pilate, and he sent it to Caesar." He waited a moment. "Pilate had proscribed the Christians, who were innocent men. I asked that the proscription be lifted, and so it was. You have heard of the lifting of that proscription?"

"Yes," said Aulus. He folded his muscular arms on the table and his eyes met those of Lucanus directly. "I did not know you were the cause of it, Lucanus." He looked down at the two drawings of the fish, which had dried red on the white wood. "May I ask why?"

But Lucanus said, "When Jesus was here in Galilee, did you hear Him yourself?"

"I did." The centurion's face was inscrutable.

"I heard of Him when I was a child, on the day He was born." Lucanus then briefly told Aulus of what he had known, and he watched him closely as he spoke. Aulus' face slowly became illuminated, and softened, and a slow look of exaltation dawned in his eyes. When he had finished, Lucanus showed him the cross on the gold chain about his neck. Aulus was silent for a long time, then he whispered, "Peace be unto you, Lucanus."

"And to you, Aulus."

Seeing Lucanus' expression, he knew he need no longer fear. He rose and beckoned to Lucanus, who followed him outside into the dazzling light. Aulus pointed to a mount not far away, on which was a poor synagogue made of basalt, with white painted doors and a flat tiled roof. "There He spoke, often. I could not enter, of course, but I listened at the door. Followed by His disciples, He would stand on the shore and speak to the people. And on a certain day I heard Him preach on the open mount, and I stood among the people, the poor men and women of the region, and listened."

Aulus paused. The sun lay vividly on his changed face. "I tell you, Lucanus, it was impossible to hear Him and not feel your heart move in you! Who is He? I asked myself.

What gods ever spoke like this, our venal, capricious and cruel gods? What hope or peace or joy or promise did they ever bring to men, in their corruption and engrossment with their own godly pleasures? But this Man spoke of God's mercy and love for His children, of His everlasting watchfulness, of eternal life in bliss, of God's pity and desire that men come to Him, not merely to praise Him and prostrate themselves before Him in fear, but to rejoice with Him through eternity, partaking of His own happiness.

"What manner of a man is this? I asked myself, amazed. Why does He speak with such authority, like one who brings a message from a great King? Why did the people regard Him with such joy and love, and silence fill them so that they would not miss a word? Why do they follow Him like a a retinue, and crowd about Him to look upon His face and touch His garments? The children in their mothers' arms laughed with pleasure, and He smiled upon them and His face was like the sun itself. Yet what in His appearance could stir one? He wore the garments of a Galilean peasant, with poor sandals of rope, and He had no money, no servants, and He walked on foot.

"This is a quiet place, Lucanus, but from the hour when He appeared here it took on this peace you observe, this deep and holy peace, and it has never departed.

"One day, my friend, I stood at the edge of the crowd, listening, and He told the people of a prayer they must say. 'Father, hallowed be Your Name. Your Kingdom come! Give us this day our daily bread and forgive us our sins, for we also forgive everyone who is indebted to us. And lead us not into temptation.' His voice ran over the mountains like summer thunder, and the people prayed with Him. And when they had completed their prayer His eyes suddenly found me, wondering and confused, and He smiled upon me over the people's heads. From that moment I was His, and I would have died for Him with joy. But I cannot explain why, for I am a Roman, and He was only a Galilean Jew, and a carpenter.

"Nor did this miracle come to me alone. Several of my men listened to Him also, and He took their hearts in His hand."

Aulus sighed. "I was transformed. The world of Rome was not important to me. My anxieties and troubles vanished. I was at peace. I was filled with exultation. The earth was no longer populated with enemies, but with friends. I had

only one desire: to perfect myself so that I would be worthy
to lie at His feet and look upon Him forever. How can one
explain this? One has to experience it for himself. But I can
say this: I now see all things shedding a light of their own;
the moon never beamed so silvery a light before, nor was
ever the sun so radiant to my eyes. Men, to me, no longer
have a station; one should not be honored for mere position
or wealth, but only for virtue. Moreover, all men to me
now are my brothers, even the lowliest. Sometimes I say to
myself, But you are a Roman, the master of the world! And
it means nothing to me. Again I remind myself, We have
the leadership of all the earth, and a voice in my spirit answers, That nation which seeks leadership of the earth is
doomed to death, for it is an evil nation, no matter its lofty
pretensions; men seek leadership only to dominate and enslave all others."

They looked upon the scene about them. The light had
changed. The coiling mountains were washed with deep purple of various hues. The Sea had taken upon itself the color
of an aquamarine, streaked with cobalt, and the sky was like
blue enamel. Lucanus felt from it all a spiritual emanation,
profound and vast and unchanging, as if unseen celestial
beings hovered over all things, winged with the sun.

"One day," said Aulus, in a low voice, "they brought
ten lepers to Him, weeping women and men and children.
They cried to Him for mercy, and the people moved away
from them in fear. But He touched them and lifted His
hands over them, and they were cured instantly, and the
great crowd rejoiced, and the former afflicted fell at His
feet and kissed them. I saw this with my own eyes! You
must believe me."

"I believe you," said Lucanus, gently.

That evening, Lucanus wrote down all which the centurion
had told him over a period of long hours, all the parables
which Christ had uttered in Galilee, all the glorious things
which He had said. Lucanus remembered the stone which had
been mysteriously removed from the sepulcher where they
had laid Him after His crucifixion. As that stone had been
removed, not by human hands, so the stone which had closed
upon a dead heart can be moved aside only by the love of
God, and the heart made alive again. "Make me worthy to
write of You, and to follow You, and bestow Your grace
upon me, O Father!" he prayed, humbly.

When Herod had built Tiberias in honor of Tiberius, the Jews would not enter the desecrated place. But Herod had had many Galileans seized and impressed into service and houses in the town. They were the wretched ones who had seen and known and loved Jesus, as well as those from Cana and Magdala and Capharnaum, towns near the Sea. What surcease and joy must He have brought to these poor and struggling lives! He had made their lot endurable, those who battled with the black and rusty soil and moved the somber stones of the region, and who were oppressed by the Romans and their own masters.

The inn to which Aulus had taken Lucanus was very large and pleasant, and the innkeeper was a kindly man who was proud of his simple but lavish table and the cleanliness of his chambers. The building stood on the shore of the Sea which was strewn with heavy black basalt stone, tumbling down the slight incline to the azure water. Before it was a flagged terrace, and great willows with whitish trunks spotted with brown leaned over the small and faintly rippling waves. Lucanus sat on the terrace in a comfortable chair, alone, though all about him travelers drank at little tables and ate sweetmeats and conversed with gestures and in eager voices. Many of them were merchants. Lucanus was glad when they rose to enter the inn for the evening meal. Now he could watch the mountains deepen to a deeper purple, and the Sea take on their motionless reflections. Moment by moment the scene became even more silent, vaster, more imminent. The sky darkened to an intense violet, and the water changed with it. The sun left the earth; a crescent moon, fiery white, rose above a mount and looked at her image in the water, and the stars danced not only in the sky but on the Sea. From the small synagogue on the mount to Lucanus' left came the chanting of prayers, intensifying the quiet.

God had seen and heard all this. He had prayed in that little synagogue; He had gazed at this very moon, this hyacinth water shivering with stars, these willows, these black cypresses, these bushes with their yellow, lily-like flowers, these pomegranates near the jade river, these palm and olive trees surrounding Tiberias, this green valley.

Blessed am I that You have given me life to know You, said Lucanus in his heart. I am undeserving; have mercy upon me, a sinner.

Chapter Fifty-two

Lucanus remained in Tiberias only a few days. During that time he wandered over the valley and the mounts; he stood at the door of the synagogue and listened to the prayers of the people therein. He stood where Christ had stood, and looked down at the Sea of Galilee, ever changeful, supernally blue and quiet. Then he left for Nazareth, seeking for Mary. He longed for her, she who had borne God and had nurtured Him and dandled Him on her knee, had brought Him to teachers and to the Temple, had loved Him above all else, and had watched Him die a loathsome felon's death. Thinking of her, Lucanus reverenced her in his heart and the thought of her was a joy. Blessed was she above all women of all generations.

Aulus parted from him with grief. "If we do not meet again on earth, then we shall meet in heaven," he said, embracing Lucanus.

As his horse mounted the stony hill Lucanus looked behind him at the Sea, and he thought that only in Paradise would there be such peace again, such vast blue tranquillity, such smiling calm. Then on the top of the mount he looked towards Nazareth in the distance, on its parched, light brown hills with their white outcroppings of broken stones. The flat-roofed houses were the color of their surroundings, glittering in the sun, and girdled sparsely by thick green trees and pointed cypresses somber against the hot sky. The little town perched there as if struck into eternity and not to be moved again or lost. Beyond it the distant mountains wore fold upon fold of deep brown, like a barrier. Heat waves quivered over the wide scene, giving it an unearthly appearance. Lucanus rode down the mount to a little valley strewn thickly with huge lumps of black basalt, between which there was sparse grass, wan and bleached in the sunlight. Here sheep grazed, guarded by shepherds sitting on boulders. The men looked sharply at Lucanus, their headcloths sheltering their sun-browned faces. He greeted them and they greeted him in return, full of curiosity. He looked at them and thought, They knew Him, and they saw Him and talked with Him; perhaps many of them played with Him in His childhood.

A great sensation of excitement rose in him as he left the valley and climbed the mount to Nazareth. He sweated in the heat and wet drops poured into his eyes. Clouds of white-hot dust followed him, surrounded him, and choked him, forcing him to cough. But he kept his eyes on Nazareth and spurred his horse, longing for shade. The mountains echoed back the clattering and stumbling of the horses, and the crashing of stones in his wake. Then, finally, he was on the outskirts of Nazareth, on a steep narrow little street swirling with dust and boiling with playing children and bordered with tiny open shops selling roast lamb and mutton, sausages and cheap wine, and household equipment, sandals and colored cloths. The clamor here was almost a relief to Lucanus after the silence of the mountains, and as he rode on through more little streets a thick purple shade was occasionally cast by an oak, a carob tree, a tall pine or cypress, an acacia, a myrtle or a group of dusty date palms. In the center of a round cobbled place, made of the prevailing black basalt, there was a well, and girls were filling jars and chattering; the ropes creaked and the buckets dripped bright drops in the sun. The maidens looked at Lucanus, startled, their blue or gray or light brown eyes curious under their colored headcloths. It was a poor place. There were no fine houses, no fountained gardens, no tall walls flowing with red or pink flowers, no litters, no chariots, no well-dressed figures of men and women. Behind some of the houses grew small patches of vegetables, or grapevines hung on stakes. Every street was noisy with dogs and donkeys, the latter patient and heavily burdened with produce for the shops. He stopped at the well and asked the girls if they could direct him to the house of Mary, the Mother of Jesus.

They looked up at the tall fair man on his good black horse, and his bearing made them shy and wary. They tittered and glanced at each other. Then one, speechlessly, pointed up a street leading from the square. Lucanus went on, leaving the girls buzzing excitedly. This street was even poorer than the others, and was at the farther end of the little town, and there were only a few houses upon it. These houses were exceedingly low, with short ladders leading to the flat roofs, where people could gather after sunset for coolness. Through open doors Lucanus could see stone steps descending steeply to cool caves below, where the families lived during the heat of the day and ate their meals.

Lucanus reined in his horse and looked about him hesitatingly. His horse moved impatiently, and twitched his head and tail at the thick flies. In that blinding light of noonday the little steep street had an infinitely desolate air; dust wavered over it. No one was about. Lucanus picked the nearest house and descended and went to the open doorway and looked within, and then looked down the steps leading to the cool cavelike lower room. There were few, and very poor, articles of furniture in the tiny room above the steps, a homemade chair or two, a bench, a table. The walls were plastered, and shimmered with reflections from the sun outside. From the cave below came a pleasant gurgling of water. Lucanus called, and, on receiving no answer, he stepped within the narrow door and glanced down the steps; he could see a tiny well in the floor of the cave, a stone floor, some iron pots, and a black chimney. He called again. There was a rustle of clothing now, and a woman appeared at the bottom, looking up at him silently.

"I am searching for Mary, the Mother of Jesus, lady," he said, "I have come a long way to speak with her."

Without answering she came up the stairs, and he saw, by the reflection of light, that she was young and lithe, dressed in cheap, dark blue clothing with a white headcloth on her head. As she rose up the steps, her face lifted to him, he saw that she was exceedingly beautiful, with a smooth pale face, tapering to a dimpled chin, a delicate nose, pale pink lips and the most charming blue eyes he had ever seen. A lock of golden hair escaped from under her headcloth. She had the figure and slenderness of a young girl; her feet were bare and white.

Then she stood before him in simple dignity, and said, "I am she."

Lucanus was amazed. From all that he had heard, Mary would now be forty-eight years old, yet she had the aspect and youthfulness of a young princess, gently patrician and infinitely sweet. No line marred her flesh; she smiled inquiringly at Lucanus, and her small teeth were like perfect pearls. Yet, as he looked at her, she appeared subtly to change, to become older, to be filled with sorrow and sadness, to be bowed a little. And then again, she was mysteriously young and straight, calm as a statue, with a still white forehead.

Lucanus, without understanding why, began to tremble. He was suffused with reverence and love. He wanted to kneel before her and kiss her work-worn hands. And she gazed at him without curiosity, and her blue eyes seemed to pierce into his soul.

"I am Lucanus, a Greek physician, Lady," he murmured. "I have come a long way to see you, for I love and serve your Son, though I have never seen Him except in my dreams."

She was not astonished. She gave him a tender smile. She spoke and her voice was as murmurous as a softly struck harp. "Let us sit behind the house, in the shade, Lucanus," she said, and led the way behind the house to a bench against the wall. All her movements were full of grace, and as pliant as a willow, and there was a high stateliness about her. They sat down, side by side, and Mary looked into the distance dreamily. All at once Lucanus was certain she knew all about him, but how that was he did not know.

Two or three goats busily cropped low thistles in the bleached grass. A few fowl scraped in the dust. And beyond them grapevines climbed on stakes and filled the hot dry air with perfume. Mary sat, her hands folded on her knees, and her profile was exquisitely quiet and lovely.

Lucanus began to speak. He told her of his life, his teachers. Diodorus, his mother, his studies. He told her of his long bitterness, and then his long searching. He told her the stories he had heard of Jesus, and of his visit to James and John. She did not question him once, or interrupt; her profile was soft with her visions. The short blue shade lengthened; a goat came to nuzzle Mary's knee; little chickens scrambled about her feet. The pale mounts in the distance became golden brown under a golden sky.

Then, having completed his tale, Lucanus fell silent. He looked at Mary's profile, and it appeared to contain in it all the features of the women he had loved, his mother, Iris, Rubria and Sara. Her quietness invaded him; he was filled with peace. He forgot that she was a poor Galilean woman, the widow of a poor carpenter. She held the ages in her still hands; she was a queen among women. And again that mysterious change appeared in her, fluidly moving over her features, giving her at one moment an old and grieving look, and then, at the next, changing her to a girl, a virgin, a pure and untouched one.

"You wish to know about me," she said at last, very softly, "and about my Son. I will tell you. But first you must be refreshed," she added, in a motherly tone. She rose and walked to the grapevines and plucked a cluster of grapes and brought them to Lucanus. They were big and round, amber-streaked on red and purple, glowing like jewels. He took them from her hand and began to eat the grapes. The juice was warm and sweet and his thirst was abated. He looked at Mary gratefully; it was as if she had given him life in this fruit, and she sat and smiled upon him, her face luminous in the shade.

She began to speak, and all the hot hushed air about her was filled with her gentle and musical accents. She spoke of her old cousin, Elizabeth, whose husband, Zachary, a priest. They had no children, which was a sorrowful thing to them. They lived in a small town in Judea, and they were very fond of the young Mary, who was only fourteen years old, and she visited them often on the way to Jerusalem for the holy high holidays, and they would accompany her and her parents the rest of the journey. And always, with her parents, came her espoused husband, Joseph, a carpenter, a good and kindly man.

And one day, while Zachary was officiating as a priest in the temple in his little city, an angel appeared before him near the altar as he was burning incense alone in the priest's office. The people awaited without the office, praying at this hour. Zachary, seeing the angel, was greatly troubled, and full of fear, but the angel said to him, "Do not be afraid, Zachary, for your petition has been heard and your wife, Elizabeth, shall bear you a son and you shall call his name John. You shall have joy and gladness, and many will rejoice at his birth. For he shall be great before the Lord; he shall drink no wine or strong drink, and shall be filled with the Holy Spirit even from his mother's womb, and he shall bring back to the Lord their God many of the children of Israel, and he shall himself go before Him in the spirit and power of Elias to turn the hearts of fathers to their children and the incredulous to the wisdom of the just, to prepare for the Lord a perfect people."

But Zachary cried aloud, "How shall I know this? For I am an old man and my wife is advanced in years!" The great angel answered him, "I am Gabriel, who stands in the presence of God, and I have been sent to speak to you and to bring you this good news." Then Gabriel appeared angered at Zachary's doubt and continued, "You shall be dumb and unable to speak until the day when these things come to pass, because you have not believed my words, which will be fulfilled in their proper time."

The angel stood there a moment, palpitating with light, his mighty wings folded. Then he was gone and Zachary was alone with the smoking altar and a terror and awe in his spirit. When he emerged from the office he could not speak, and tears ran down his old cheeks, and the people knew that he had seen a vision. Visions were no rare things to these simple and pious people; legends of the appearances of angels and portents ran through all their conversation. They questioned Zachary excitedly, but he could only make dumb and bewildered gestures.

Zachary was a poor man, for all he was a priest, and he returned to his little miserable house and looked at his wife, weeping silently. Later, to her great and almost disbelieving joy, she, in her old age, conceived, and she hid herself for five months, saying, "Thus has the Lord dealt with me in the days when He deigned to take away my reproach among men!"

Mary paused and looked at Lucanus, and her blue eyes were bright and smiling with tears. It was as if she were rejoicing again with her cousin, Elizabeth, in this miracle and recalling her words with tenderness and understanding.

The time was approaching for her own wedding to Joseph, whom she loved and to whom she was espoused. She was fourteen, and ripe for marriage, but sometimes she was troubled about whether or not she would make that kindly man an excellent wife. She was the only child of her parents, and she had been pampered dearly by them, and what little they had had been given to her with devotion and love. Her mother had spared her much work; she did not have all the knowledge of wifehood and homekeeping which other girls possessed. She could spin and sew and cook somewhat, and keep a garden in a small way. Her parents had been more concerned with her piety than with humble duties, for they were very devoted to the Lord their God and spoke of Him always and not only at prayers.

Mary's face changed as she spoke, and she gazed at the sky with quiet ecstasy. From the time when she had been a very young child, hardly able to walk, she had loved and known God. He filled her days like the sun; she conversed with Him when she lay on her poor pallet. Her heart rejoiced in Him with passionate faith and joy. She could rarely think of

anything else; her whole life was absorbed in adoration. The
trees and the earth spoke of Him to her; He was in every
spring flower she saw; His presence beamed from the sky
and in the hearts of fruit. She saw His shadow at night, when
the moon was full; she lived and breathed in the thought of
Him. Sometimes rapture filled her unendurably, and she
would steal away from her parents and friends and relatives
to meditate upon Him. Every stone and tree and star possessed
a nimbus of gold, for He was there. Often she would weep
without knowing why, and her heart would shake. Her spirit
would expand and enlarge; she wished only to serve Him,
and spend her life reflecting upon Him.

But of household duties she knew very little; sometimes her
mother reproached her mildly, and then reproached herself
for not being a better teacher of this young girl. And Mary,
finally, was also troubled, thinking of the goodness of Joseph,
and wondering if she would be a good Jewish matron, as he
would expect, blessing the candles, observing every meticulous detail of the sanitary and dietary laws, and being an
honor to his house.

So one evening she climbed the ladder to the roof of this
house, where she had been born, to pray to the Lord her God
and ask for His consolation and guidance. The sky was the
color of a ripe plum; the hotness of the little town had subsided, and there was peace under the stars, and a great
golden moon shivered over all things, casting its yellow light
on wall and tree and making intricate patterns of gilt on the
ground. A cool wind blew from the mountains; there was a
scent of jasmine in the air. Mary wondered at this, for the
weather had been hot and dry and the flowers had withered.
Then the breeze was full of the perfume of lilies and roses,
rising like incense all about her. The moon increased; the
mountains were bathed in copper, and the roofs all about
Mary trembled with gold. She did not know why, but her heart
quivered and she held her breath.

Moment by moment the air grew effulgent under the moon.
Mary stood, her hands clasped, praying innocently. A sense of
portent invaded her. She could have cried aloud in her awed
joy. She turned her head and a mighty angel stood near her,
brighter than the moon; his white garments drifted with flecks
of light; his wings shed silvery sparks; his face was more
beautiful than any mortal visage. Mary's heart failed with mingled fear and veneration, and her lips chilled. She thought
she would collapse there, on the roof. She made a motion to

cover her face with her hands, for the angel flowed in radiance.

Then he said, very gently, folding his light-filled hands reverently together, "Hail, full of Grace! The Lord is with you. Blessed are you among women!"

Mary's hands stood in mid-air, paralyzed at this greeting. Her head swam and her body shook. What was the meaning of his words? Her breath caught in her throat; it emerged, finally, in a loud dry sob. She was very young; she had dreamt of angels, and now that one stood before her she was stricken with terror.

He said, in the kindest of voices, "Do not be afraid, Mary, for you have found grace with God. Behold, you shall conceive in your womb and shall bring forth a Son, and you shall call His name Jesus. He shall be great and be called the Son of the Most High, and the Lord God will give Him the throne of David, His father, and He shall be king over the house of Jacob forever. And of His Kingdom there shall be no end."

Mary, that young girl, could not speak. She looked vaguely and dazedly about her. It came to her that she was dreaming, and that in her meditations she was imagining all this. But the little city lay in its orange light about her, and the fragrance of flowers intoxicated her senses. She could feel the rough surface under her feet; the lightest of winds touched her young face. She was not dreaming; from the corner of her eye she could see that palpitating presence near her, and her heart quaked. She thought of what he had said. She would conceive in her womb, and she would bring forth a Son—— Her head moved slowly and in humble denial.

"How shall this happen, since I do not know man?" she faltered.

The angel smiled, and that smile was like a flash of the sun, and Mary involuntarily stepped back from him and closed her eyes.

"The Holy Spirit shall come upon you and the power of the Most High shall overshadow you, and therefore the Holy One to be born shall be called the Son of God."

Mary moistened her cold lips. She thought of the prophecies of the Messias. She lifted her small hands and gazed at them in bewilderment; she saw the stains of work upon them; she saw the coarseness of her garments; she remembered that she was a girl only fourteen years old, the daughter of Galilean countrymen. How could one such as she be the chosen, and not a princess of Israel surrounded by trumpets and marble columns and perfumed fountains and attendants? Her numbed mind struggled with her reflections. She looked at the angel and dimly wondered why he should regard her, a little unlearned girl of no consequence, with such reverence, and why he should keep his hands folded before her as before a queen. Tears rushed into her eyes.

The angel inclined his head as if in the presence of majesty.

"Behold, Elizabeth, your kinswoman, has conceived a son in her old age, and she who was called barren is now in her sixth month, for nothing shall be impossible with God."

Mary pondered. Then it was as though a large wave of light engulfed her, flooding all her being, and all was made clear to her.

In a loud and joyful voice she exclaimed, "Behold the handmaid of the Lord! Be it done to me according to your word!"

The angel bent his knee before her, and even while she regarded him he disappeared. But where he had stood there remained a light like the reflection of the moon, and it ebbed and swirled, mistlike, for several moments until it died away.

She covered her face with her hands and wept. She did not know if she was weeping with fright or with joy; they mingled in her. Her first thought was of her parents. She crept down the ladder, and then into the tiny house. Joachim and Anna were asleep; she could hear their peaceful breathing in the darkness. She desired to arouse them and tell them of the visitation. Her cheeks flushed hotly. Would they believe? Would they understand? Or would they smile at her with gentleness and tell her again, as they had done so many times before, that she had been dreaming? She thought of Joseph, her espoused husband. She had an impulse to run to his house with her strange revelation. Then her whole spirit recoiled. She leaned against the dark wall and pondered. She must go to Elizabeth, and at once. That old cousin, so strangely pregnant, must be the first to know. On feet that moved no heavier than a breath, Mary passed the room of her parents and went into her own small chamber, and there she wrote to them briefly that she was going immediately to Elizabeth, that they must not fear for her, and that she would return safely.

Alone in the sleeping city, where all slept but she, she left on foot for the long journey, without hesitation, feeling her-

self guarded and treasured. Never had she walked abroad
before at night, unless accompanied. But every little street
glimmered with yellow light, and she could see the clear tips
of the cypresses against the moon and the soft movement of
sheltering shade trees shadowed on the soft and velvety
dust. She was filled with peace and surety. No dogs barked
as she passed lightless houses. She lifted her smiling face to
the illuminated sky and prayed. Once or twice, in her youthfulness, she skipped and ran a little pace. Strength filled
her. How would she, without money or food, find her
distant way to Ain Karim, in Judea? It was a journey of
several days and nights, even when riding on the backs of
donkeys. She only knew that she would arrive, that she was
cherished, that no harm would come to her. With confidence,
she left Nazareth, and the narrow road running south was
before her, its gravelly stones sharp in the moonlight.

She walked a long time, without exhaustion, and met no
one. Sometimes she saw sleeping shepherds on the slopes of
the bleached mountains, resting among their sheep. She
passed through a hamlet or two, where no one stirred. Black
and barren hills pressed against the incandescent sky. She
was suddenly thirsty, and looked about her at the vast and
silent countryside; here the nearer hills were cultivated; she
saw groves of olive trees filigreed in silver under the moon,
and palms fluttering their fronds in the warm midnight air.
Then she heard the tinkling of a little stream, and found it,
running in gilt between black stones. It sang a small song to
itself. She knelt on the bank and drank from her hands,
deeply, and it was as if she drank strengthening wine. She
reached up the trunk of a young palm tree for a bunch of
warm ripe dates and satisfied her new hunger. Then she
resumed her journey, singing softly, her child's feet flashing
from under her poor robe and the dust rising behind her.
At times she could barely control her joy; at other times she
pondered simply in her heart. All doubt was gone. Some pulse
in her body beat strongly and steadily, and it was like a new
and vigorous heart, and she wondered innocently about it.

She decided to rest, though she felt no weariness. She
found a clump of cool oak trees and lay down on the grass
beneath them, and was instantly asleep, curled like a
sheltered child, her cheek on her hand. When she awoke the
sky swam in scarlet and pearl and the ocher mountains
blazed. She found another stream and washed her hands and
face, drank of the water. She stepped off the road to a

grove of pomegranates and eagerly ate of the fruit. She filled
her pouch with two or three for later refreshment. She continued on her way, singing aloud now.

A few hours later, when the sun was high, a caravan came
from behind her, a poor caravan of one or two camels and
donkeys laden with produce for the towns. The men in the
caravan, three of them, had the wild dark features of the
mountains and remote places. Yet one of them, seeing her,
instantly dismounted from an ass and without speech
helped her upon it. It appeared very natural and seemly to
her; once or twice she drowsed. When she awakened she
always found the man's browned hand steadying her. No
one asked her any questions. When the caravan paused to
rest, the taciturn men shared their bread and cheese and
wine with her. They treated her with great courtesy. Their
restless eyes held no inquiry, no wonder that this young
girl, so fair and so smiling, should be alone and unprotected.
They slept on the road that night, and spread a rough blanket on the ground for her. She lay awhile, listening to the
complaints of the kneeling camels, the stamping of the donkeys, the distant howling of jackals. A small fire danced in
the center of the camp. She fell asleep in great content.

And so it went. Sometimes the somber men chanted
prayers, and she, on a donkey's back, joined them shyly.
And sometimes they would stare at her peaceful child's face,
and would smile like fathers. They would bring her gourds
filled with cool fresh water; they would press fruit upon
her. They passed through the savage country and the few
they encountered thought her a daughter with her kinsfolk.

They came at last to Ain Karim, that little village, and,
as if they knew, the men helped her from the donkey and,
hesitating, one of the men touched her warm cheek tenderly
with the back of his hand. She wanted to thank them, but
they waved to her and went on. She found her way to the
home of Zachary and Elizabeth, a poor clay-colored house
perching on a broken hillside among cypresses and other trees.
It was hardly past dawn. Mary knocked on the closed door
of the house, then entered. Old Elizabeth was already
awake, busy at household tasks. She gazed at Mary in absolute amazement, then a great trembling shook her and she
held out her hands to her young cousin and cried aloud in
a strange voice:

"Blessed are you among women and blessed is the fruit
of your womb! How have I deserved that the Mother of my

Lord should come to me? For behold, the moment that the sound of your greeting came to my ears, the babe in my womb leaped for joy! Blessed is she who has believed, because the things promised her by the Lord shall be accomplished!"

Her wrinkled face was transformed, her eyes kindling. She held out her arms to Mary and the two embraced, like mother and child, full of understanding, and without questions. They kissed each other and murmured lovingly against each other's cheek. Delight filled them; rapture misted their eyes. Then Mary leaned back against her cousin's arms and looked joyously into her face.

In her pure and innocent voice ecstasy rose like a song. "My soul magnifies the Lord, and my spirit rejoices in God, my Saviour! Because He has regarded the lowliness of His handmaid. Behold! Henceforth all generations shall call me Blessed, because He who is mighty has done great things for me, and holy is His Name, and His mercy is from generation to generation on those who fear Him. He has shown might with His arm, He has scattered the proud in the conceit of their heart. He has put down the mighty from their thrones, and has exalted the lowly. He has filled the hungry with good things, and the rich He has sent away empty. He has given help to Israel, His servant, mindful of His mercy! Even as He spoke to our fathers, to Abraham and his posterity forever!"

Lucanus listened without moving on the bench. Mary's voice had risen like a pealing of sweet bells as she recalled those days. And, as it had happened between him and his brother, Priscus, he wondered how much he had learned from Mary's words and how much from a mystic insight given to him, through her own eyes and speech.

Mary's face, as she looked at the sky, was vivid with joy, and she lifted her hands so that the palms were gilded with light. Lucanus regarded her with love and awe, this woman who had carried God under her child's breast, and who had delivered Him in a stable. He leaned towards her. She dropped her hands and regarded him, smilingly, and he thought that never had he seen so gracious and noble a countenance, nor one so endowed with a beauty not of earth. He hesitated; then he took one of her hands and kissed it, and said, "Happy am I to have heard these things from your lips, Lady. I do not deserve this happiness."

He gazed at her with reverence, and he thought, Truly,

here is one who is without sin, who was born and who lived without sin, who has endured evil but has never been touched by it. She has known grief, but not guilt. She has wept, but not for transgressions of her own. She has loved, and her love was as pure as moonlight. She has walked among terror and sorrow. But there is no shadow on her spirit, nor uncleanness on her hands. Blessed is she among women.

"Only God can judge whether or not a man deserves happiness," said Mary, gently. "You have suffered much, and He has brought you to Him."

The shadows of the afternoon lengthened quickly; a hot and arid wind stirred the dust. The goats bleated. Mary stood up and said, "I will milk the creatures, and, if you will, drink and eat with me."

"Let me help you," said Lucanus, and both knelt on the crumbling ground and milked the goats, the warm liquid foaming into pails. Then Mary brought out dishes of bread and cheese, little black olives, a few small cakes which she had baked earlier, and a wooden platter of fruit. They sat in silent contentment, eating.

Then Mary began to speak again; she told Lucanus how she had remained with Elizabeth until the birth of little John, who from the moment he was delivered was lusty and full of bellowings, and how at the very instant John emerged from his mother's womb his father's speech was restored.

Zachary had lifted his hands to heaven, while his men friends came to him one by one and kissed his beard, in congratulation, and the old man cried aloud:

"Blessed be the Lord, the God of Israel, because He has visited and wrought redemption for His people and has raised up a horn of salvation for us, in the house of David, His servant, as He promised through the mouth of His holy ones, the prophets from of old: salvation from our enemies and from the hand of all who hate us, to show mercy to our forefathers and to be mindful of His holy covenant, of the oath He swore to Abraham, our father, that He would grant us, and that, delivered from the hand of our enemies, we should serve Him without fear, and in holiness, and justice before Him all our days!"

Exalted, and full of the Holy Spirit, he cried out again while his friends stood about him, gaping and wondering:

"And you, child," and he put his withered old hand on the head of the baby, "shall be called the prophet of the

Most High, for you shall go before the face of the Lord to prepare His ways, to give to His people knowledge of salvation through forgiveness of their sins, because of the loving-kindness of our God, wherewith the Orient from on high has visited us, to shine on those who sit in darkness and in the shadow of death, to guide our feet into the way of peace!"

Mary related how she had returned to her parents and to Joseph, who was greatly troubled. She told of her marriage to Joseph, and then of the decree of Augustus Caesar that all his subjects throughout the world should be counted, and of her journey, with Joseph, to Bethlehem. Faltering now, and speaking in a low and trembling voice, she told of the birth of her Son, of the angels who appeared to the shepherds on the mounts, who were full of fear on seeing the Star, and how they were led to the stable where their Lord was lying in His manger. Much of this Lucanus had heard from others, but he listened with the absorption of one who is hearing the story for the first time. For Mary's sweet and ringing voice was like music to him. The hills about Nazareth turned to the color of ripe lemons and the sky became golden above them, and the clamor of the little city penetrated now even to this poor and wretched street.

Mary was tiring; a pale shadow appeared on her smooth cheeks; her blue eyes darkened with weariness. So, as the sun began to set abruptly, washing all the earth with a sudden fiery light like a conflagration, Lucanus stood up and again kissed Mary's hand.

"Let me return tomorrow for a little while," he pleaded. "I wish to know of the childhood of your Son. In the meanwhile I will find an inn."

"There is but one inn in the town," said Mary, her garments stirred by the evening wind. "And a poor one."

"I care nothing for luxury," said Lucanus. Mary accompanied him to the front of the house, and he was again struck by the dusty desolation of the little street, where goats wandered on the small stones and children cried from within closed houses, and vultures sailed against the burning heavens. Mary directed Lucanus to where he would find the inn. He went down the street and looked back at her. She lifted her hand to him and smiled.

The inn, as Mary had feared, was indeed abominable, a little crude house with an open well in the black-stoned courtyard. Lucanus was the only guest, and the host, an old man with a gray-red beard, greeted him with gratitude and showed him to the best of the four rooms, a tiny chamber with a rush-covered floor, a narrow bed and one chair, and a lamp hanging on the wooden wall. Later Lucanus was alone in the wretched public dining room, but the landlord proudly produced some cold beer as well as wine, a plate of lukewarm and very oily mutton, half a boiled fowl, tough and streaked with yellow fat, some limp turnips, and a bowl of pomegranates, dates and grapes.

"The beer is from Egypt," said the host, standing at Lucanus' elbow. "They make the best beer in the world; the Romans are poor imitators." He coughed apologetically.

"I am not a Roman," said Lucanus, smiling. "Would you join me in a goblet of beer? It has an excellent head."

The host said, with alacrity, putting a finger alongside his nose, "Ah, I have much better even than that!" He winked like a conspirator. "I have some fine whiskey!"

Lucanus gave a dubious thought to the mixture of beer and whiskey. But he was tired; he was also filled with a strange feeling of elation. "If you will join me," he said, politely.

The host was delighted, but, being an honest man and noting Lucanus' simple robe, hesitated. "The price of the whiskey is very high. Perhaps you cannot afford it, good sir. It is three shekels a bottle. That is because of the high tax the Romans put upon it; they, with their infernal taxes! A man cannot live, I tell you! If we export, the Customs is there with outstretched hand and many sheets of papyrus; if we import, and we are a poor people and must import much, there the Customs is again, with more bureaucratic paper and a hand out, and their stamps."

"Bureaucrats are with us always," said Lucanus, with a sympathetic sigh. "But let us have some whiskey and forget governments and their taxes and their officials who devour the substance of the people."

The host reverently brought out a dusty bottle of whiskey. "We must import it from Syria," he said, "for our people do not look kindly on strong drink. But you would be amazed how much is imported, and drunk! Look you at the seal and the stampings upon it. It is a veritable whiskey, and not illicit, made by furtive men in the hills." Lucanus courteously examined the seal and nodded. The host brought two small goblets, and Lucanus filled them, and the host kept shaking his head at the amount but did not utter a word of rebuke or protest. He sat beside Lucanus, and his old eyes gleamed.

He said, "Whiskey is the blood of old age, and I am an old man and need warmth, even in this climate. As we are near Syria, much nearer than Jerusalem——" He coughed again.

Lucanus smiled. "I have told you I am not a Roman. I am a Greek, and, as a Greek, I admire smugglers."

"To cheat an oppressive government is not to cheat at all," said the host, with a wise look. "How can a man live otherwise? Besides, who makes what money we make: the government or ourselves? One should remind governments of one of the great Commandments: Thou shalt not steal! But was there ever anything but a thieving government, in all the history of the world?"

"Never," agreed Lucanus. "Governments, by their natures, are robbers."

He cautiously sipped the whiskey. It was not the best produce, and it had a raw smart and a burning in the stomach. The host drank with pleasure, and said, "Ah!" But he and Lucanus hastily drank a good draught of beer. The old man had a cast in his eye; it gave him a very keen appearance. He said, "If there were no taxes there would be no money for soldiers, and if there were no soldiers there would be no wars and no conquests, and if there were no wars and no conquests men could then learn to live together in peace. But that is not what governments want! They make wars out of greed and in the desire for profits."

He had prudently produced another plate, and helped himself to Lucanus' meal, which the physician did not find particularly appetizing. The old man continued to inveigh against governments and remarked that Samuel had warned the people never to put a king over themselves, for in that way disaster came. The host was not only old, but poor; nevertheless, he had a fine mind and Lucanus listened with interest. The simple, he thought, are often a source of wisdom, and the delicate intellectuals in the cities could listen with profit.

"My name is Isaac," said the host, expanding, and his withered cheeks flushing. "I am also a widower. It is not often I have guests, and sometimes I weary them." He adjusted the black cotton cap on his head.

"You do not weary me," said Lucanus. He drank some more whiskey. This time it did not appear to be so atrocious. His belly warmed; the few lamps in the room seemed brighter. They both quaffed more beer. Lucanus decided that a piece of the fowl, one cake, some olives, and a bunch of dates were enough. After a taste of the fowl he concentrated on the cakes, stuffed with poppy seeds and raisins, the olives and the fruit. He was beginning to feel quite relaxed. The whiskey, now, had a truly intriguing taste. Lucanus believed no longer that it came from Syria; it had been distilled near Nazareth.

Isaac ate the mutton with relish. "You have a delicate stomach, sir?" he inquired.

"Very delicate," replied Lucanus, gravely. "Mutton does not agree with me."

They drank with pleasure. Isaac told a Jewish joke or two, wry and salty, and Lucanus laughed. The physician found himself studying, with fascination, two long cracks in the plaster on the walls. They appeared like winding rivers; blotches on each side took on the aspect of teeming villages. Lucanus abruptly put down his goblet of whiskey. Isaac had become quite garrulous. His jokes now bordered on the obscene, as is the way with old men. "Ah," he said, in apology, "when a man is no longer potent he must amuse himself with naughty words. This deceives the listener that here is a lusty man, indeed. David procured a young wife to keep him warm; I prefer whiskey."

"A goat is very potent," said Lucanus. "But does a goat have a mind in his old age? No, he goes into the pot or on the spit."

Isaac began to love Lucanus. His eyes grew misty, and he put his gnarled hand on Lucanus' arm. "How you understand!" he exclaimed.

Lucanus drank some beer. He leaned his elbows on the rough and splintered table. "I am doing some research," he remarked, idly. "I am interested in one Jesus, who was the Son of Mary, and Joseph, the carpenter. Can you tell me of them?"

Instantly Isaac's face became closed and watchful. He stared at Lucanus, suspiciously. Then he said, indifferently, "Oh, Mary and Joseph. And Jesus."

"I am no spy," said Lucanus. "I am no Roman."

Isaac was not as exhilarated as Lucanus had hoped; neither had his tongue become loose enough. He narrowed his eyes at Lucanus, and said in an astonished tone, "Who spoke of spies? Why should spies come to this small obscure town, and on what errand? A humble Jewish family, Jesus, Mary and Joseph! Of what concern would they be to the world? The father and son—they were carpenters, simple, honest people like all in Nazareth." He rubbed his beard and stared more acutely at Lucanus. He added, "You said Mary sent you to this inn? I must thank her when I see her, for she is a very distant cousin and wishes me well."

He suddenly struck the table hard with his hand, and a handsome dark youth came at once and said, "Yes, Grand-father?"

Isaac spoke in such perfect and cultured Hebrew that Lucanus was surprised. He understood that he was not to understand, he, a traveling Greek physician who could not possibly know the learned language. Isaac said, "Ezekiel, go at once to our cousin Mary and ask her if in truth she sent this stranger to us, this Greek, and if he is to be trusted, and what she wishes us to tell him. He may be lying. Look upon him closely, so you can describe him to her. His name, he declares, is Lucanus, and he is also in possession of a fine Arabian steed, and appears not to be in want of money. We must be very careful; one must remember Pilate and Herod."

Ezekiel studied Lucanus acutely, memorizing his features, and Lucanus drank more beer and ate a handful of grapes, pretending not to comprehend Hebrew. The youth said, "He wears beautiful rings; he has a civilized manner."

Lucanus smiled to himself. The youth left the room and Isaac said, disarmingly, "As I have said, we are a simple people. I spoke to my grandson in one of our dialects, suggesting, as the nights are cool, that he find another blanket for you."

"You are very kind," said Lucanus. "Is my horse bedded down?"

"Ah, yes, Master. I also admonished Ezekiel to take him fresh water."

They drank their beer in a comfortable silence. Isaac abstractedly finished the plate of mutton. Then he said, "I have a room where I sleep and live. I should like to show it to you, Master."

He stood up, his stately garments trailing like a king's robes, for all their poor quality. He led Lucanus into a small room behind the dining quarters, and lighted the lantern on the wall. The room was furnished with simple chairs, a large table, a narrow bed, a chest, and all was shining. Isaac said, "You will observe this furniture. It is not carved nor gilded nor especially fine. But it is excellently worked, smooth and polished. Joseph and Jesus made these things for me; there were no better carpenters in all Galilee. Joseph, alas, is dead, and so is Jesus, unfortunately. Now we must buy furniture done by lesser craftsmen."

Lucanus put his hands on it, and thought, And so He made this, He the Lord of all! He did not disdain to be a carpenter, He who created the galaxies and the constellations and the suns which blaze through eternity. He planed this wood so it gleams like silk; He fashioned this bed, this table. And, no doubt, He took as much pride in it as He did in the creation of the Pleiades!

The physician wished to lay not only his hands but his lips on this calm and simple furniture, which had known the hands of God. His eyes moistened. He sat on a chair. Isaac watched him. He saw Lucanus' emotion. He frowned, baffled.

"There were other men from this place," said Lucanus. "I have talked with James and John; I will soon see Peter."

"Oh, yes," said Isaac, carelessly. "I knew them well." He too sat down. In a few moments Ezekiel returned, his eyes bright with excitement, and he said, "Grandfather, Mary declares you may speak to this man freely, for he loved Our Lord, and is writing of Him, and has come a long way to hear of Him!"

"Mary can never be deceived," said Isaac, sighing with relief, and dismissed his grandson. He turned to Lucanus and said earnestly, "Ask me what you will of Jesus. Mary is a distant cousin of mine, and I have loved her since she was a child. Such a lovely babe, such a lovely girl! She has an eternal innocence and an unworldly wisdom. To know her is to be filled with sweetness, as with honey. Did I not say to my wife when Mary was born, 'She was conceived and born without sin'? One had only to look upon her face to know."

He put his twisted old hands on his knees and dropped his bearded head on his breast. "Mary and Joseph were of the house of David. The prophecies we know of the Messias spoke of that; they also declared that the Redeemer of Israel would be born in Bethlehem, that He would die as He died, in Jerusalem. This was known for centuries. Yet when the prophecies were fulfilled the people refused to accept them, except for the very humble and hopeless."

Isaac talked for a long time. Much that he told, Lucanus also knew, but there was much he did not know. The lamp flickered on the wall; insects, with shrill voices, blew into

the room and blew out again. There was the song of crickets outside, and sometimes the voice of a night bird. Isaac
told Lucanus of the time of Mary's purification after the birth
of her Son, according to the Law of Moses, and how she had
taken Him to Jerusalem to present Him to God. Joseph was
a poor and gentle man, and he had little money for the customary sacrifice, and all he could afford was a pair of turtle-
doves which he carried to Jerusalem in a cage. "He could
not pay the prices of those in the Temple," said Isaac, with
some bitterness. "How is it possible that men can be so
greedy that they will make their money in a matter of holiness?"

He spoke of old Simeon, who had been very devout, and
who, when in the Temple at the time of presentation, looked
upon the infant Redeemer and was instantly filled with the
power of the Holy Spirit. It had been revealed to him that he
would not die until he had seen the Christ of the Lord.
He had taken the Babe into his arms, weeping and praying,
and had cried, "Now You, O God, may dismiss Your servant, according to Your word, in peace, because my eyes have
seen Your salvation, which You have prepared before the
face of all peoples, a Light of revelation to the Gentiles and
a glory for Your people, Israel!"

Simeon had then blessed Mary and Joseph, and he had
then said to the young girl, "Behold, this Child is destined
for the fall and for the rise of many in Israel, and for a sign
that shall be contradicted. And your own soul, Mary, a
sword shall pierce, that the thoughts of many hearts may be
revealed."

"I was there," said Isaac, spreading out his hands. "I heard
those words with my own ears. Was Mary amazed or frightened? No. She appeared to know everything, though her
young face became sorrowful at the words of Simeon."

"And when the three returned from Jerusalem?" asked
Lucanus, gently.

"They became what the people understood. A good mother and housekeeper. That was Mary. A conscientious carpenter; that was Joseph. And a quiet and handsome boy;
that was Jesus. They were one with their neighbors. You have
heard of our Zealots? Yes. They wished only to deliver their
sacred land from the hand of the Roman. There was much
secret talk of insurrection, and of driving the Roman from
our country, the Roman with his arrogance and his taxes.
Galilee was particularly enthusiastic about these matters, for

to the simple all is simple. The Galileans did not seem aware
that Rome was the mistress of the world, that she had a
hundred legions armed and mighty. To the Galileans, who
saw few Romans, it was an uncomplicated matter to dream
of chasing the legions into the sea and delivering the holy
land. One needed only a few sharp knives, stones and a will.
The Jews had been delivered from Babylon and Egypt. They
could, with the power of God, be delivered from Rome.

"All our Zealots were young men. They attempted to
bring Jesus, that young carpenter, into their fold. But He
was not interested. His eyes looked dreamily into the distance. This vexed the patriots. How could a young man not
be concerned with driving the heathen from His country and
purifying the sacred places? Jesus became unpopular. Some
there were who said sneeringly that Mary, who had this only
Son, had ambitions for Him. She had sent Him to the School
of Shammai. Once He had said to the vehement ones who
came to see Him in the house of Mary and his foster father,
Joseph, 'My Kingdom is not of this world.' That was incomprehensible. A kingdom for a Galilean? The youth was mad!
The Zealots were derisive; the old men shook their heads.
Mary was educating this youth beyond His deserts and destiny. He was very strange; He would wander over the countryside and smile at the flowers and the beasts and the birds.
Sometimes He would sit on a boulder, and meditate, under
the sun. I tell you, Lucanus, that no man is more abhorred
than a man who is different from his neighbors. They feel
violated and threatened if one dares to be as they are not.
When he is with his community, then he must conform to
its ideas and customs. Otherwise he is a pariah dog who has
mortally offended the accepted. He must comb his hair and
his beard in the usual manner; he must speak as others
speak. Indifferent to the accepted, he is an enemy. People
are very stupid, are they not, Master?"

"More crimes have been wrought through stupidity than
through armies," said Lucanus. "One could pity the stupid if
they were not so invincible, so vociferous, so positive. But
they are terrible in their universal might."

"But one may pity them, Master?"

Lucanus reflected, then he shook his head. "Unless a man
is born with a defect of the mind, then he cannot be pardoned for being a fool, or faceless, or as completely like his
neighbor as possible."

Isaac wagged his beard. "It was not that Jesus violated any

of the Levitical ceremonial laws, or annoyed His teachers with heretical questions or expressed doubt over the regulations of the Pharisees. Nevertheless, even to the dullest eye He was not as others; hence the vexation of many of the neighbors. He recited the prayers and the Psalms in the synagogue with fervor and devotion, and with tears on His cheeks. Joseph taught Him of His tribe and His house. He taught Him to be a carpenter, for the old-fashioned Jews believe it is not enough to cultivate the mind. One must learn to use his hands also, for it is a goodly thing to know a trade as well as books. In all these Jesus meticulously observed custom. Perhaps it was the far look of His eyes, or His manner, His silences, His smiles, the way in which He walked. As a child He played as a child, and was strong and hearty and had clear boyish laughter. And yet He was not as the others.

"We very few who understood the prophecies, and how He had been born, and for what He was destined, did not find Him strange. But the neighbors were offended by Him. Was He handsomer than young men His own age? That is hard to answer. I only know that to look upon Him was to feel the heart lurch, even among those who did not know who He was. He was disturbing to all who observed Him, and men do not like to be disturbed."

The yellow moon looked into the chamber and some carapaced creature scraped on the stones of the courtyard. Isaac told of the appearance of John the Baptist in the Jordan valley, who cried, "I, indeed, baptize you with water! But one mightier than I is coming, the strap of whose sandals I am not worthy to loose. He will baptize you with the Holy Spirit and with fire." John was a man of furious temperament. Jesus knew he was His kinsman. John wore no robe such as the Pharisees wear, purple gowns with long white fringes, nor was his head covered with the pointed cap of the Levites. He was a wild man from the desert, with a beard of bronze, a dark face, a strong and fear-inspiring voice. Sometimes he roared like a bull, when he was angered, and he was frequently angered. He was dressed in the skins of animals. But he spoke with authority, and the people listened, even the Romans he encountered. His fervor was as compelling as the sun. He spoke constantly of the Redeemer, who was at hand. The people became excited. The day of the Roman was done! The Christ would hurl every Roman into the sea and would deliver His people, Israel, and seat Himself on a golden throne, and the world would gaze at Him and say, "How mighty is the King, and how mighty is Israel!" Sinai would thunder and blaze again, and the Law would again be proclaimed to all the earth, and archangels would stand in the sky above the Temple in Jerusalem. The hearts of the people fluttered with hope and joy when they listened to John, though he said nothing of what they expected. They believed it in their spirits, for how else would they recognize the Holy One? They forgot the prophecies.

"My grandson, Ezekiel, went down to the Jordan to be baptized by John," said Isaac. "There was a great crowd at the river, and above its humming murmur could be heard John's shouting exhortations as he baptized, demanding penance and promising the forgiveness of sins. In the interstices of these pronouncements he inserted his opinion of mankind in general—which was very low and very candid. The least of his cry to the people was, 'Brood of vipers! Who has shown you how to flee from the wrath to come? Bring forth therefore fruits befitting repentance, and do not begin to say "We have Abraham for our father," for I say to you that God is able out of these stones to raise up children to Abraham! For even now the ax is laid at the root of the trees; every tree, therefore, that is not bringing forth fruit is to be cut down and thrown into the fire.'

"The women wept and the men beat their breasts, and the children cried, and all stepped to the bank of the river to be baptized and to confess what miserable sinners they were. I have no doubt that while they felt a thrill of holiness and cleanness they were also unbearably excited at the thought of the coming Saviour, who would make princes of them, in Israel, at His right hand. Some there were from Nazareth, and my grandson among them.

"John was in the midst of another, and louder, condemnation of humanity's crimes—for he was a man who had no patience even with the smallest sin and little compassion in his soul—when suddenly Jesus appeared above him on the bank. What made all the people instantly lift their heads and regard Him in sudden silence? Only a few from Nazareth knew Him, yet they too were silent. He stood on the bank of the deep green river, and a shaft of sunlight brightened His golden hair and beard, and He looked down at John and the sobbing people with His blue and pitying eyes.

"Ezekiel has told me that He had the majesty of a king, the splendor of a great potentate, the glory of a prophet, the authority of a Moses, as He stood there in His peasant's clothing and bare feet. One felt that a Visitation had appeared, and even those who knew Him were awed, for never before had they seen Him clothed in such supernal power.

"On seeing Him, John halted his reproachful speech, and he wept, holding up his hands to his kinsman. And then Jesus, in the midst of that inexplicable quiet, went down the bank and requested that John baptize Him. John was horrified; he folded his arms over his breast, after touching his forehead with his fingers.

"He said, in a faint voice, 'But it is I who ought to be baptized by You!'

"Jesus smiled tenderly, and He looked into the faces of the people, and inclined His head. He stepped into the water and waited calmly. The people crowded the banks. Some of the Nazarenes muttered to their neighbors, 'But this is Jesus, our neighbor, our carpenter, the son of Mary and Joseph, whom we know!' They stared down at the two men in the river, one so savage in appearance, the Other so silent and full of dignity. And so John baptized Him, lifting the green water in his trembling hands, his face marvelously humble, and with tears in his eyes. The thick trees and bushes cast an emerald light on the two, yet the beard and head of Jesus appeared gilded."

It was immediately after the baptism that a strange thing happened, though there had been some dispute as to the details. Jesus was suddenly illuminated as if the trees had parted to admit the sun in all its fiery light, and it was too dazzling to look upon Him. A white bird appeared from nowhere and rested on His shoulder, and a great Voice was heard from the sky: "You are My beloved Son! In You I am well pleased!"

"Ezekiel swears that this happened, my dear Lucanus," said Isaac, and wiped tears from his old eyes on his sleeve, "and Ezekiel has never lied in his life. He returned to Nazareth in much agitation, and told me, and burst into sobs. 'I have heard the voice of God!' he cried over and over, holding his ears as if to retain that sound. He was beside himself with rapture and fear, and he is ordinarily a youth of much composure.

"When our fellow Nazarenes returned home, many of them were in the condition of Ezekiel. They crowded about the humble house of Mary and Jesus, where they had lived alone since Joseph had died. They shouted that Jesus come to them, and finally He emerged through the doorway, and they fell on their faces, prostrating themselves before Him, and He blessed them, smiling His kind and compassionate smile. He knew His people; He knew how poor they were, how despised by the Levites and Pharisees, how oppressed by Roman taxes, how hopeless. He loved them; they were His own.

"But some of the Nazarenes were namelessly angry and derisive. They declared that they had seen nothing of the miracle on the Jordan. What! This carpenter with His airs and graces! This son of Mary, who was even poorer than they were? What presumption! Prophets never came from Nazareth, nor from among such as they. If more gullible neighbors declared that they had seen Him illuminated, and had heard a Voice from heaven, and if a white bird had settled on His shoulder, it was all self-delusion. It was even blasphemy."

Angry disputations came between friends and friends, between fathers and sons, between mothers and daughters, between neighbors and neighbors. It was shortly afterwards that Jesus left Nazareth, and it was said that He had gone into the desert for meditation. "He is a Zealot," said some, darkly. "He will cause us sore trouble with Rome. Is not our life hard enough as it is, without this further affliction? Do you not remember what happened to us when the Romans hunted down the Zealots only a few months ago?"

It was very late now, and Isaac, though exalted, was old and weary. Lucanus could have listened all night, but seeing his host's exhausted face, he rose and bid him good night and went to his room.

Alone, he wrote on his Gospel. The light of the yellow moon lay on his shoulder, and the lamp dimmed. A lonely dog barked, and distant jackals answered in their wild voices. Lucanus wrote rapidly, not pausing until he had inscribed Isaac's story completely. Dawn finally changed the sky to pearl and birds cried out in greeting to the still unrisen sun. Lucanus lay down on his bed, prayed and fell peacefully to sleep. He dreamt that he stood on the bank of the Jordan, and that One in the river, clothed with light, emerged towards him, and he sank to his knees. He felt himself then bathed in radiance and he put his hands over his eyes.

Chapter Fifty-three

In the morning the youth, Ezekiel, knocked on Lucanus' door, and, opening it, Lucanus saw that his face was full of fright and uncertainty. He pushed a package into Lucanus' hands and stammered, "This was brought from Tiberias this morning by a Roman soldier, for you."

"Do not be afraid," said Lucanus, kindly, touching the boy on his shoulder. "They are merely letters for me, sent by my friend in Jerusalem, Hilell ben Hamram."

He sat on the bed and read the letters, which had been delivered at Hilell's home. There was a letter from Iris, another from Aurelia, his sister, one from Priscus, and still another from Plotius. He read them all with love. Sometimes he sighed. Would he ever again see these who had his affection? His mother was old. But for the first time she did not implore him to return to Rome, even for a visit. She wrote: "Dear Son, you must do as your spirit commands you, and I will understand. I have had a dream in which I was told that you no longer belong to your family, and that God has called you and you must obey Him. But remember us with love, for truly you are in our hearts always."

There was much happy news from the family, and Lucanus rejoiced with them. But Tiberius Caesar was failing, and Rome secretly hoped for his death, for he had become most terrible and cruel, totally without pity or compassion. His crimes were legion. It was as if he were taking some awful vengeance on his Empire and people. Lucanus sighed. Let people beware the anger of their rulers, he thought, for they are guilty of his excesses.

He now read Hilell's letter, and with deepening interest and excitement. First of all, Hilell was waiting for Lucanus' return in order to proceed with the wedding of Arieh ben Elazar and Leah.

He had a visitor in his house. "You will remember, my dear Lucanus, that I wrote you of Saul of Tarsus, or Gaius Julius Paulus as he is known in his Roman citizenship. He is a Pharisee, and was formerly of the most narrow religious convictions and a profound observer of the Law in spite of his position among the Romans and his high estate as an administrator and a lawyer. He was also a prideful and arrogant man, of a very supple tongue, like most lawyers, and the most unbending opinions. Partly this is because of his temperament. He is given to strong enthusiasms and dogmatism, and fits of haughtiness. He would never let anyone forget that he was both a Roman citizen and a Jew of a noble and influential family, and insolence, to him, was unbearable and must be punished at once. For a young man he was enor-

mously rigid, and in his pride, most terribly honest. In courts
of law his forensic genius was much feared and admired.

"Above all things, he was always a devout Jew, hating those
who even dared to question the Torah in the slightest detail.
When he heard of Jesus, the humble Nazarene, and the
rumors that He was the Son of God, he was outraged and personally insulted. 'Nothing good ever came out of Nazareth,'
he once wrote to me. 'When God sends up our Messias, He
will arrive like the lightning, among the company of the
archangels, and with the trumpets of the Lord our God, and
all will know Him and the nations of the world will bow
down before Him. How dare this peasant, this carpenter,
this Jesus of Nazareth, be proclaimed the Saviour by the ignorant? This is blasphemy before the face of Jehovah. I am
filled with rage, and just umbrage. The Law has been violated by fools and the unlettered masses. You know how I
have always despised the unlearned, who chant their prayers
by rote and know nothing of the true Law and its implications. If I had my way I would confine them to the outer
courts of the Temple, for their smell and their dull faces
are an affront before the glory of God! And their sacrifices
should be rejected.'

"I fear, Lucanus, that my letters to him only increased his
anger. How could I, Hilell ben Hamram, of a great Jewish
family, a scholar, a man of position, honored in the Temple,
be so deceived by rumors of this Jesus, this Man from the
stark hills and gorges and gullies of Nazareth? A spell had
been cast upon me. It was intolerable! And now the
scattered Christians were causing much trouble in Damascus, quarreling with their neighbors, flouting the Law, declaring that the Messias had been born of a virgin, in a humble
family, had preached throughout Israel, outraging the priests
who were the guardians of the Law, speaking against the
Pharisees who administered the Law and calling them a
generation of vipers and hypocrites. And then He had been
justly crucified for inciting the people against Rome, to their
mortal danger!

"As a Roman administrator he had gone on his lawful
duty to Damascus to put down what the Romans called insurrection, but what he declared was blasphemy. He rode
with his company of fellow lawyers, and with an entourage
of Roman soldiers, full of vengeance and fury. So inflamed
was he that he would not pause at an inn for the night,
but rode on like the whirlwind to Damascus.

"And now, as my friend and a guest in my house, he tells me the most marvelous and the strangest of stories. He is full of passion and excitement as he repeats the story, as if I were a disbeliever and he the evangelist who must convince me!

"He was riding ahead of his entourage on the road to Damascus, his hair and clothes blowing in the wind of his passage. Suddenly his horse screamed out and reared up into the air, and Saul was sore put to it to control the beast. His entourage reared behind him, struggling with their horses and cursing; they milled about on the road, slashing their whips, while the front hoofs of the animals beat the air in frenzy and the harnesses glittered in the moonlight like agitated silver.

"Then before Saul a tremendous light appeared, like a new sun, and in the midst of it he saw a radiant Figure, crowned with thorns and clothed with blinding radiance. And the Figure lifted His wounded hands and said to Saul in a great yet gentle voice, 'Saul, Saul, why do you persecute Me?'

"Saul gazed upon the Figure, half sheltering his eyes from the light. And an awful trembling came to him, and a sense of the most devastating guilt, and a powerful adoration. He did not know what to do, or what to answer. His soul was torn and shattered. This was the Messias, whom he was about to persecute, and whose followers he was about to destroy! He looked on the glorious Face, and his heart leaped for joy, and in humility. Human flesh could not long endure the vision. Saul was stricken with unconsciousness, and he fell from his horse.

"Some there were in his entourage who had seen nothing. Some declared that they had perceived a dazzling light, and had been filled with terror. In any event, Saul returned to Jerusalem, a changed and uplifted man, full of tears, full of mingled joy and anguish and passionate love. He had seen the Resurrected. His whole vehement nature accepted what that same nature had not long ago rejected with contempt and loathing.

"Now he is in my house. He declares that he will go at once to Peter, in Joppa, to be baptized, and to receive instructions. He will then go on his own mission. He has said to me, 'He, Our Lord, came not only to the Jews, but to the Gentiles! I will become a voice to the Gentiles, and lead them to salvation!' Remember this of the haughty Gaius Julius Paulus!

"I have persuaded him to wait until you return from your visit to Mary and to Galilee. He is still a very impatient man, and at first refused. He could not delay a moment in the work he must do. I have told him everything about you, my dear friend. And now he declares that you and he will go together to Peter. I do not know what Peter will make of him, Peter, the poor Galilean, the humble fisherman. Saul is so temperamental a man; he even now cannot forget that he is of a noble Jewish house and a Roman citizen. He is imbued with enthusiasm and adoration. Will he quarrel with Peter, and Peter with him? Saul believes he has received a special dispensation from Our Lord, one, he even hinted, which was much greater than the grace bestowed on the Apostles. Will he be arrogant with Peter? Humility comes with difficulty to him. Peter saw, and believed. Saul did not see the Lord in the flesh, but he now believes with an exultation that is sometimes intimidating. He even lectures me, and admonishes me, I who attempted to convince him long before. It is like having a storm in the house; he paces all night long, muttering to himself and praying.

"Yesterday he said to me, 'I am much interested in this Lucanus, and the stories you have told me of him. But he is a Gentile, and must be convinced by me, for the Gentiles have obdurate hearts, and I am commanded to bring them into the Faith.' I restrained my smiles. Sometimes he almost convinces me I am an ignorant man, unaware of the message of the Messias.

"And now, my dearest Luke, we await you."

This was the first time that Lucanus had been called by the affectionate diminutive. He read and reread Hilell's letter. And his excitement grew. He had an intimation that he and Saul would understand each other, for neither had seen the Messias in the flesh. They had seen with their spirits only, and surely the vision of the spirit was purer than the vision of mortal eyes. He thought of Saul with a sudden affection, which was inexplicable. He smiled as he considered that proud and vehement man, a Roman citizen as he was a Roman citizen. Saul would accomplish great things. He would speak with emphatic authority. He would be a lash to the Apostles, who still suspected the Gentiles, and feared them. He would be a lash to the Gentiles.

Lucanus brought out his paints after he had dined in his

room. He would portray Mary for the ages. He thought of her beautiful and tranquil features, her majesty, her grace, her serene and unworldly aspect. He thought of her piercing but gentle eyes, her heroic smile, her sweet demeanor. He began to work. But Mary eluded him. She was at once old and yet immortally young, simple yet profound. How could mere pigments portray her, the Mother of God?

Chapter Fifty-four

Lucanus went on foot to see Mary for the last time. The barren and silent street on which she lived depressed him; the road was full of holes into which the hot white dust had sifted. The closed windows and doors, shrinking from the sun, glared at him. A few dusty goats and chickens ran from his path. The sepia hills danced in heat waves under a brazen sky. He was thankful that Mary was leaving soon for Jerusalem, to be with the young man, John, into whose care her Son had assigned her. John had spoken of her with tears and profound devotion, his voice breaking, so Lucanus had no fear that she would be neglected by him.

Mary answered his knock, opening her door and smiling gently, and she led him down the steep flight of stone stairs into the cavelike room below, where it was cool. She had prepared a meal for him on the wooden table: honey in a comb, fresh twisted bread, fruit and cheese, goat's milk and wine. A dim blue light suffused the poor room, in which Mary was a bright shadow. While he ate she sat and watched him, her hands folded on her knees, her beautiful face tranquil. He had painted her portrait on wood but, as he gazed at her, he was frustrated. He had thought at the last that he had obtained a fair image of her. But she had changed again; she was a shy maiden, dignified and composed, her eyes far with dreams. She appeared to give out a light from her very flesh, so that there was a glimmering about her.

Lucanus said, "Lady, did your Son always know who He was? From His very childhood?"

Mary pondered, then she inclined her head. "I believe so; I know so. Even in His cradle, which Joseph, my husband, made so lovingly with his hands, He seemed to be always meditating. He was the gentlest of babes; He never cried, even when hungry. He appeared to know us from His very birth. Sometimes at night I would hold a lamp over Him, to be sure that all was well, and that He was sleeping. He would open His dear eyes and smile at me reassuringly.

"He was a strong and vigorous boy, obedient and often silent. He delighted in the toys which Joseph made for Him; He played as other children played. But in the very midst of His play He would become still, as if thinking and reflecting. It was this that annoyed the other children, this, and His sudden wandering away from them so that He could be alone.

"We did not speak to Him of His birth and His mission. There was an understanding between all of us. Once He found me weeping, for I dimly comprehended His ultimate fate, from the prophecies and from what old Simeon had told me in the Temple. I am a mother, Lucanus. My Son was dearer to me than life itself, and sometimes my heart almost broke and I dared to wonder if mankind was worthy of Him. When He saw me weeping, and He was but ten years old then, He came to me and put His arms about me and held me to His boy's breast, quiet and comforting. He asked no questions. He wiped my eyes gently, and I burst into fresh sobs, and finally He said, 'You must not weep, My Mother, for I am with you always.' "

Mary paused, and though she smiled there were tears in her eyes. Her quiet hands began to tremble.

"When He left me, after John baptized Him, and retired into the desert for forty days, it was as if all light had gone out of life for me, for I understood that I had Him no more, that from henceforth He belonged to God and to the world. Joseph was dead; I followed my Son through the country very often, and He was concerned for me, for I was no longer young. Sometimes when the people surrounded Him, listening to Him, I stood on the edge of the crowds, not wishing to trouble Him with my presence. But His eyes always found me, and sometimes they became sad. There was always, between us, the greatest of love and devotion, and comprehension. Often when He was the farthest away He would appear to me in dreams, full of tenderness and consolation. He knew I was a woman, and a mother, and that I suffered for Him, and that always I thought of Him as my flesh and my heart's darling, above all."

She closed her eyes in deep pain, and Lucanus knew she was thinking of the crucifixion, for her face paled and became fixed. After a while she began to speak again, in a low voice.

"There is one strange evening that I remember, when He was but fourteen. He had worked all day in the shop, for He was a marvelous carpenter, and He had many orders. He was weary. But that night, at sunset, He left the house and climbed up the hill behind our home. No one was about, for it was time for the evening meal. I have never seen the sky so red as it was then, as if the heavens were burning. Even the mounts flamed, like glowing rocks. I do not know why I followed Him. I stood below Him, on the little stony path, and looked far up at Him. He wore a white robe which I had spun and sewn for Him, and He stood against all that fiery landscape like a statue. He did not move; it was as if He were waiting. So great and wide and awesome was the scene, so flaming with dull fire, that I closed my eyes for a moment. When I opened them, He was not alone.

"A great dark angel, towering and majestic, stood before Him, and I knew that the angel was all evil, though his face was somberly beautiful. He appeared to be clothed both in flame and in the night, and his mighty wings reflected the sunset like carved basalt.

"He and my Son contemplated each other in silence, and my heart failed with terror as they confronted each other. Did they speak? I do not know. Though it was very quiet I heard no sound. My Son was very young, but He was tall and straight, and He showed no fear of the terrible angel with his handsome face which was sorrowful and yet so proud.

"Then, as I watched, the angel bent and lifted some of the crumbling earth in his hands and showed it to my Son, and now I heard his faint and derisive laughter. How I understood I do not know, but he was displaying to Jesus the worthlessness of the world. He threw away the earth and put his foot upon it, and it was then that I heard a faint pealing of thunder as if it came from the angel himself.

"And then Jesus bent, too, and lifted some earth in His hands, and He held it lovingly, rubbing it between His fingers. It was dry and without verdure, but as He held it it suddenly bloomed into a mass of thick green leaves filled with bending and tiny lilies. I could smell its fragrance; it flowed on the wind.

"The angel looked upon the blooms and he fell back and covered his face with his hand. Then, with a mighty cry, he disappeared, and my Son was alone.

"I fled down the path into my house, and after a while Jesus returned. He looked at me closely, then He put His arm about me and kissed me on the cheek. I clung to Him. We said nothing. We sat down and ate our supper."

Lucanus gazed upon this lovely woman who had seen so much and who had suffered so much. She was smiling faintly, again caught up in dreams. Then he knelt beside her and touched her feet with his lips, and he trembled with reverence and love. She looked down at him, and her face was illumined, and she put her hand on his head, and he thought of his mother, Iris.

Mary refilled his goblet with wine and gave it to him, and still kneeling, he drank of it and was wonderfully refreshed. "My dear child," she said, "do not weep. Am I not the most blessed of women? Rejoice with me that He is my Son."

They went up the stone steps together, out into the incandescent noon, which, however, made the little street appear even more desolate than before.

"I must leave you now, Lady," said Lucanus. "For I have much to do."

She nodded. "That I know. Peace be unto you, Lucanus."

He left her, walking slowly down the narrow street. Then, at the end, he turned about and looked at Mary.

She stood against the background of the hot and brazen mounts, and it seemed to him that she had grown very tall, and that she was clothed in pure light, and that her face beamed like the moon when it is full. Her aspect was incredibly beautiful and full of peace, and intrepid, and the street was desolate no more.

She lifted her hand to him in farewell, and in blessing.

(Continued in the Holy Bible, Gospel of St. Luke, and Acts I and II.)

BIBLIOGRAPHY

(A few selections)

ANCIENT ROME—Chiara Cardona

ARISTOTLE'S POLITICS—Benjamin Jowett, translator

BABYLONIA (or CHALDEA)—The Laws of Babylonia and Laws of the Hebrew Peoples—C. H. W. Johns

CAESAR AND CHRIST—Will Durant

CATILINE, CLODIUS AND TIBERIUS—E. S. Beesly

CATHOLIC ENCYCLOPEDIA, THE

CHRIST AS PROPHET AND KING—John S. Fernan, S.J.

COMPANION TO SCRIPTURE STUDIES, A—Rev. John Steinmueller, S.T.D., Vol. 13

DAILY LIFE IN ANCIENT ROME—Jerome Carcopino

DEATH OF VIRGIL, THE—Herman Broch

DEVILS, DRUGS AND DOCTORS—Howard W. Haggard, M.D.

EMOTION AS BASIS OF CIVILIZATION—J. H. Denison

ENCYCLOPAEDIA BRITANNICA

FROM MEDICINE MAN TO FREUD—Jan Ehrenwald, M.D.

GOLDEN BOUGH, THE—Sir James G. Frazer

GREECE (HISTORY OF NATIONS)—C. W. C. Oman and G. Mercer Adam

GREEK ART—Thomas Craven

GREEK HISTORICAL THOUGHT—Arnold Toynbee

HISTORY OF ROME, THE—Theodor Mommsen

HISTORY OF THE ROMANS UNDER THE EMPIRE—Dean Merivale

HOLY BIBLE, THE

HUMAN DISTINY—Lecomte du Noüy

IDES OF MARCH, THE—Thornton Wilder

IMPORTANCE OF LIVING, THE—Lin Yutang

JESUS, SON OF MAN—Kahlil Gibran

JESUS AND HIS TIMES—Daniel-Rops

LIFE AND TEACHING OF JESUS CHRIST, OUR LORD, THE—Jules Lebreton, S.J.

LIFE OF CHRIST, THE—L. C. Fillion, S.S.

LUKE THE PHYSICIAN—Adolf Harnack

MAN AND GOD—Victor Gollancz

MANSIONS OF PHILOSOPHY, THE—Will Durant

MIND AND BODY—Flanders Dunbar, M.D.

MISHNAH, THE

NEW TESTAMENT, THE—James A. Kleist, S.J., and Joseph L. Lilly,
C.M., translators

PRINCE, THE—Niccolo Machiavelli

REALM OF SPIRIT, THE—George Santayana

ST. LUKE'S LIFE OF CHRIST—Translated into Modern English by
J. B. Phillips

SATYRICON—Petronius Arbiter

SOURCE BOOK IN ANCIENT PHILOSOPHY—Charles M. Bakewell

STORY OF MEDICINE, THE—Kenneth Walker

TIBERIUS THE TYRANT—J. C. Tarver

VOICES OF SILENCE, THE—André Malraux

WORLD'S GREAT RELIGIONS, THE—*Life* magazine